As I dug [...] better to plunge into my mistress – whose dark eyes sparkled with the mutual pleasure of our joy – I suddenly felt a searing pain across my exposed parts, and heard a roar of anger – which emanated, as I found upon turning my head, from the throat of my master, Sir Franklin Franklyn. There was no appeal. Driven from the room by renewed blows from his riding crop on every area of my all too exposed body, and despite my lady's tearful excuses, within an hour I found myself walking through the gates of Alcovary House, a small bundle upon my shoulders containing the one spare suit of clothes I could call my own, and in my pocket three shillings which, wrapped in a piece of paper, were thrown to me from a high window at which the face of Lady Franklyn appeared briefly as I left the back door of the house. If the world lay before me, I speculated, it seemed unlikely to offer, in the immediate future, as comfortable a place as that I had left. Yet I turned a brave face towards it, and set out in the opposite direction from the village, towards the open country . . .

The Eros Collection

Anonymous

HEADLINE

This edition first published in 1991
by HEADLINE BOOK PUBLISHING PLC

10 9 8 7 6 5 4 3 2 1

ISBN 0 7472 3680 1

Printed and bound by
Collins Manufacturing, Glasgow

HEADLINE BOOK PUBLISHING PLC
Headline House
79 Great Titchfield Street
London W1P 7FN

EROS IN THE COUNTRY

The Adventures of a Lady and Gentleman of Leisure

**For the convenience of the reader
we here record a note of
IMPORTANT PERSONS APPEARING IN
THE NARRATIVE
in the order of their appearance**

Master Andrew Archer, our hero.
Master Frank Franklyn, a young gentleman.
Miss Sophia Franklyn, our heroine.
Sir Franklin Franklyn, Bart., of Alcovary.
Lady Patience Franklyn, his wife.
Horace Gutteridge, a flaybottomist.
Spencer Franklyn, Esquire, a young gentleman, later a
Lieutenant in H.M. Navy.
Master Ffloyd, a schoolmaster.
Mrs Tickert, a housekeeper.
Mr Caister, a butler.
Tom, a footman.
The Third Earl of Rawby.
Mr Haddon, an insignificant personage.
Tabby, a maid.
Ellen, another.
Sir Walter Flount, a lecher.
Mr Nelham, a scholar.
The Lady Elizabeth Rawby, a lady.
The Lady Margaret Rawby, another.
Signor Giovanni Cesareo, a musician.
Henry Rust, Esquire, an ancient Beau.
Jack, a lascivious undergraduate.
Coln, another.
George, a third.
Will, a strapping bumpkin.
Rosanna Vanis, a Gypsy.
The Honourable Misses Glaistow, two lascivious sisters.
Derai Bovile, a *dimber damber*

Sam Vanis, a Gypsy.
Anna Soudras, a Gypsy.
Miss Sarah Wheeler, a young lady.
Mrs Hester Muster, her aunt.
Major Willoughby Fawcett, an unworthy officer.
Major Constant Hawtree, his friend.
Captain Dawkin, an inconsequential soldier.
Dean Runciple, a cleric.
A Handsome Fellow of Winchester.
Sergeant Hardy, a pugilist.
Mr Charles Finching, a country gentleman.
Mrs Finching, his wife.
A Highwayman.
Mr Harry Grose, a rich merchant.
Mrs Grose, his wife.
Miss Patience Grose, his daughter.
Bob, their servant.
The Honourable Frederick Mellor, suitor to Miss
Patience.
An enthusiastic Rustic.
Mr Edmund Weatherby, brother to Mrs Finching.
A number of rude sailors.
Mrs Esmerelda Plunkett Cope, an actress.
Miss Cynthia Cope, another.
Samuel Prout Higgens, an actor.
David Ham, another.
Nathaniel Grigson, another.
Miss Jessie Trent, a school mistress.
Dolly, her maid.
Eight young ladies.
Ned Farkin, a jester.
Miss Meg Tamblin, a whore.
Mr Harry Rockwall, a young gentleman.
Thomas Bidwell, a rogue.
Sir Ingle Fitzson, a magistrate.

Chapter One

The Adventures of Andy

'Twould be error to suppose that my sentimental education commenced on that sunny morning in May, 1815, when, sent back from church to fetch my lady's forgotten purse from her bedroom in Alcovary House, I came upon my master's youngest son rogering his sister in their mother's bed.

To be sure, being at that age unversed in the singularities of amorous play, I was somewhat perplexed that Master Frank should have been partially clothed in one of Lady Franklyn's finest Empire dresses, while upon the upper body of his sister I recognised the uniform coat of a lieutenant in one of His Majesty's naval vessels, doubtless the property of Master Spencer, then newly promoted and attending Matins with the remainder of the family.

'Twas not, I say, the start of my education in matters of love. No person whose early years are spent in the same bed with four brothers and three sisters can long remain ignorant, if not by performance then by observation, of the mechanical purposes for which man and women are differently formed. Yet the tangle of pleasure I glimpsed that morning marked a turning-point in my life, as the reader will discover.

I was born the second son and fifth child of one Jonathan Archer, sometime gamekeeper, sometime poacher, of the parish of Bedmoretonham, in the County of Hertfordshire, on the twenty-seventh day of May in the year of Our Lord 1800 and the fortieth of the reign of His Britannic Majesty King George III.

Of my childhood I need say little, for 'twas no different than that of a million other young creatures of our times – spent in a mud cottage of two rooms, one for day use, one for night, where the whole family huddled together in comfortable if fetid warmth. In addition to childish pleasures and play, I was early educated in poaching game, setting snares by the time I was five or six, and learning to break a rabbit's neck almost as soon as I could walk.

It was through my adept capturing of his game that I came to the notice of Sir Franklin Franklyn of Alcovary, a gentleman of independent means and the owner of a large estate which he administered with care, riding out often to see his tenants, interfering regularly in their business, and governing them with more enthusiasm than knowledge of the land. We lived just outside his walls, which I often surmounted in pursuit of apples, pears and medlars as well as more profitable meat.

One summer day when I was seven year old, I had released a rabbit from a snare in a wood not far within his park gates when, emerging from the thicket, I found myself faced by the squire himself, accompanied by two servants and his lady wife. Turning to run, I found behind me a pair of keepers, each smiling broadly – for they knew me as a waster of Sir Franklin's property, and were happy to see me face to face with a painful fate.

Sir Franklin was a portly, red-faced bull of a man, a villain to any thieves who came before him (for he was a local justice, complete in his hatred of any offender who crossed him: he had hanged a man the year before for stealing twelve pence from a man of his).

What took me I know not, for before I could be seized, I fell on my knees before Lady Franklyn and offered the rabbit to her as a parson might offer the host at the altar.

I had chosen the gesture well, as it turned out, for though she was not a woman of uncommon kindness, she was susceptible to flattery.

'What, now,' she said, smiling, 'tribute from so tender a babe?'

'Ay, my lady,' I piped. 'I found this fine fat cony in the wood, and was bringing it to the house for your la'ship's table.'

Out of the corner of my eye I saw Sir Franklin scowl, for not only was I clearly not going towards the house, but the ragged back leg of the beast betrayed the wire of the snare which had been its death. But happily my lady was caught in a snare of another kind; I was a pretty child, and despite my dirty state and ragged clothes – such as they were, for I was shirtless and my breeches, which had covered several arses before mine, were mere threads – she stepped forward and reached out her hand to tousle my hair. Thinking better of the action, which indeed might have resulted in her acquaintance with a number of small animals who had their habitation therein, she drew back at the last moment, but said, 'Franklin, you would not be harsh with so young a culprit?'

Her husband drew in a breath, as I drew mine, for I had heard many tales of the whipping almost to death at the cart's tail of children no older than me. But she continued: 'Something, I think, can be made of him. Pochett, take him up to the house and clean him, and we shall see what we shall see.'

One of her servants seized me by the collar before I could run and marched me off to the hall, where I was wiped all over with a wet cloth, and a shirt and pair of breeches belonging to one of her ladyship's sons were placed upon me before I was taken again to her, when she questioned me at length.

I cannot now remember what she asked, or what I replied, but native wit must have won me favour, for though I was sent packing to my father (who whipped me soundly when he heard my story – not for my capture of the cony, but for allowing myself to be caught) a week later there was a message for him to attend Lady Franklyn, and soon I heard that she had readily persuaded him to allow me to take lessons at the big house with his own children – Sir Franklin's that is – Mr Spencer, the eldest boy, then aged eleven, young Frank, two years my senior, and Miss Sophia, of an age with me. My father was all too pleased that there should be one less hungry mouth to feed in our small cot, and my mother the same. My only elder brother at twelve years of age was already working on the land of a neighbour farmer and had no notion of jealousy of my good fortune, believing that nothing came of book learning, while my sisters, though they looked at me with envy, could do little other than sometimes cuff or scratch me in revenge for having been picked out for favour.

As for me, I was by no means entirely satisfied at being plucked from freedom into the prison of the schoolroom; neither was I pleased when Mr Gutteridge, the schoolmaster (who, as I now know – and as you shall later judge, for he plays some part in this story – was a most ignorant man and most unfit for his position), demonstrated that his chief pleasure in life was in whipping, for I had not been in the schoolroom for more than a day when he tore my second-hand breeches from my body to belabour my bum with a birch he kept for the purpose.

I believed at the time that this was a lesson he reserved for me as an ignorant newcomer to his rule, but on the following day, she not knowing her Collect, he divested Miss Sophia of most of her clothing and, making her brother Spencer hold her arms as she leaned over the back of a chair, raised great welts upon the white cheeks of her backside while she screamed most pitifully. Note that he only ever attacked his pupils in such a manner when sure that his master and mistress were out of hearing, and though the children complained, their parents were reluctant to take to task a tutor they had obtained for a trumpery sum and who was a mark in the neighbourhood of their gentility and superiority, for no other gentleman within many miles employed a tutor for his sons and daughters.

For three years I and my fellow pupils suffered – and without the compensation of knowledge gained, for this master knew almost as little as we; the daily Collect was drubbed into us from the prayer book, and that was all. This cruelty had what was for me an excellent result, drawing us children together in a way which mere propinquity would scarcely have achieved, considering the difference in our rank. I soon picked up their manners, which though not those of the greatest in the land were at least finer than what

I would have learned from my ragged fellows in the village. Frank and I soon became the closest of friends, while little Sophie, who even then seemed to me to possess charms altogether superior to those of my sisters, showed me always the greatest kindness. Master Spencer, perhaps because of his position as the eldest son and heir of Sir Franklin, was cooler towards me – but also towards his brother and sister – though not unkind.

Oppressed in the classroom, I spent many happy hours outside it, Frank and I together exploring the countryside far beyond the borders of Alcovary Park, he eager to learn from me such wiles of country life as the setting of snares and the disabling of man-traps (to which engines Sir Franklin was much addicted), while he taught me how to swim in the nearby river. Our young bodies cleaved the waters between March and September, and being altogether naked turned from white to brown, so that by the by they resembled rather the pelts of wild animals than of human beings. My life became even happier when, on my reaching the age of eight, I was brought to live at the big house. This was the result of the intervention of Lady Franklyn who, seeing how fond her children were of me, approved heartily. She called me 'pretty child' and employed me to fetch and carry for her as a sort of page-boy, when I was not at what she innocently believed were my lessons.

The servants of the house, though at first jealous of the favour her ladyship showed me, soon grew my friends. Sir Franklin kept twenty men and women in his house – clerk of the stables and clerk of the kitchen, baker and bailiff, butler and groom of the chambers, and below them the coachman and footmen, park-keeper and gamekeeper, provision-boy and foot-boy. My lady was served by her chambermaid, and she, with the other maids, was my particular friend.

As we grew in years so my companions and I became more and more discontented with the violent temper of our master; scarce a day passed when one or other of us was not more or less violently beaten, and many an afternoon after lessons we would retire to a private place to comfort each

other as best we might. I found a peculiar pleasure in suc-
couring poor Sophie, whose soft skin broke more readily
than ours under the birch. She found the application of
saliva to her wounds most comforting, and nothing loath I
would often apply my tongue to her backside, cooling the
stripes and affording her much ease. The reader will credit
that, though innocent of any sensual intention, I found this
activity most pleasant – partly because of her expressions
of content and partly because the proximity of her nether
region was peculiarly interesting to me. (My sisters and I
had often explored each others' bodies, as a matter of
course, but the closeness of our rooms at home, together
with a lack of fresh water and the disapproval with which
my mother regarded any application of it to the body – it
was, she believed, especially weakening to the female sex –
rendered their persons noisome in the extreme, and I had,
then as now, a misliking for dirt which made it impossible
for me to enjoy the closeness of those subject to it.)

But to return to my narrative, one day in the summer of
1810, Mr Gutteridge finally achieved his own downfall. It
was a peculiarly hot season and he had ordered us, for the
good of our health, to undress to our shirts, while he himself sat clad only in breeches and a shirt which fell open to
the waist disclosing a chest covered with coarse black hairs
and a bulging, pale stomach which seemed barely confined
by his belt. Upon Frank's failing to complete the recitation
of the day's Collect without prompting, the master reached
– as he had so often done – for his birch, and instructed the
boy to remove his trousers. Bending him over a chair, he
began to lay about him until Frank wailed again.

Finally, seeming to complete the punishment, the master
threw his cane to the floor, but rather than striding from the
room as he usually did, ordered myself, Sophia and Master
Spencer to leave the room for he wished to speak seriously
to the still crying Frank. We went ill-humouredly enough
into the yard which lay outside the schoolroom (once part
of a stable). Soberly waiting there for Frank to join us, we
heard a cry of alarm quite distinct from the sound he had
made when being beaten. Clambering onto a water-butt,

Master Spencer and I looked through the window of the schoolroom, where the sight met our eyes of the naked bottom of our master, who had thrown his breeches from him and was moving with a peculiar violence upon the back of our schoolmate, still bent over the punishment chair. He was holding Frank's shoulders the better to enable him to maintain a position whose significance was then unknown to us, for at that time we were ignorant that one man could dance the goat's jig with another, by use of the windward passage.

Frank's cries of pain and alarm were enough to make us instantly leap from the barrel and rush into the room. Master Spencer was by this time a strong youngster of fifteen, and I was for my age possessed of a certain wiry strength. Together we thrust ourselves upon Gutteridge, sending him reeling back from his attempt at bum-fiddling to fall to the floor, where with amazement I saw that part of him I supposed to be constructed merely for the act of urination was in a state of vast erection – so much larger than I could have imagined by comparison with that of Spencer, which he had been proud to display to Frank and me since it had begun to swell in obedience to his increasing age.

Frank, meanwhile, was sobbing and clutching his backside, still bleeding from the birch. Enraged by Gutteridge's attack, though little we understood it, we soon took our revenge. Seizing the birch, which lay upon the floor nearby, Master Spencer caught his master a whack upon that part of his anatomy which, while it had begun somewhat to shrink, still presented an accessible target. With a cry Gutteridge leaped to his feet and, followed by Master Spencer and me, ran in a state of nature from the room and was pursued across the yard before the astonished eyes of Miss Sophie, and out into the gardens where Mistress Franklyn was showing a spinster neighbour a new strawberry bed. The ladies were more than somewhat disconcerted at the sight of a plumply naked, hairy schoolmaster pursued across the lawns by two boys clad only in their shirts – and those to a large degree torn from them in the excitement of the chase.

While the master hid behind a nearby bush, Master

Spencer explained to his mother the circumstances which had led to the sudden apparition and his mother, pausing only to tell the quaking Gutteridge to go to his room, accompanied us to the schoolroom where she comforted young Frank and the frightened Sophie. Sending them back to the house with Master Spencer, she turned to me and congratulated me on the part I had played in the affair. I never had much conversation with the lady, simply receiving instructions to fetch or carry; now, I found it disconcerting to be standing before her almost without covering while her cool grey eyes seemed to see every part of me, including that part which my hands and the remnants of my torn shirt were attempting to conceal. To my surprise, she placed her hands on my shoulders, drew me towards her, and kissed me, before sending me off to join her children. If, as it seems now to my recollection, her bosom was rising and falling with peculiar interest, it surely could only have been under the pressure of events, although even at eleven my figure was already somewhat manly, brown as it was through exposure to the sun, and muscular through my enjoyment of outdoor exercises.

After the departure of Mr Gutteridge, which followed instantly, there was a period of freedom until a new master made his appearance – Master Ffloyd, a young Welshman of twenty, as kind as he was handsome, whose interest in us and in learning was married to a charm which made him immediately not so much a master as a companion. Besides introducing us to the mysteries of Latin grammar and arithmetic, he spoke to us of Napoleon and Wellesley, of Sir John Moore at Coruna and the taking of Martinique, read to us from the poems of Lord Byron and the novels of Sir Walter Scott, and in general brought us towards the beginning of an understanding of what was civilised life.

As he came to know us more, he grew especially fond of Sophie, and was seen by me to cast many a lascivious glance toward her as, the months and years passing, she grew more a woman. Yet, whether for fear of his master or from natural backwardness I could not tell, he made no open declaration of his feelings – which I approved, for apart from the youth of the object of them, he was altogether too poor a man to be entertained as a lover even by so inexperienced a person as my sister.

Master Spencer, in two years' time, left us to go into the Navy, but Frank, Sophie and I continued our studies for some time, although I was increasingly given duties by my mistress which took me from the schoolroom into the house. I was still more a member of the family than a servant; not only was my mistress almost over-kind to me, but I shared a bed with Frank and we became almost brothers, exchanging confidences and partaking together the pleasures of growing to manhood. This included, of course, much discussion as to the proper employment of those instruments with which nature had provided us for procreation, and which to us at our age soon came to be used for pleasure, and were so used in the manner of young boys throughout the centuries in the way of stroking and playing. We talked much of finding a girl whom we might persuade to inform us of the true nature of the carnal act, but the daughters of the neighbourhood were coarse and unappetising to us both, our tastes being shaped now by higher living than the village provided, while the house itself had little communication with its neighbours except on special occasions which were rare and ceremonial. And for me, Sophie, while infinitely delightful, must clearly be unobtainable.

As we grew increasingly conscious of our needs, so the opportunity to satisfy them seemed to retire. In Sir Franklin's library – of which I had free run – I discovered between the shelves of religion and philosophy a cabinet containing a number of books which at once informed and inflamed me. Some elaborately lascivious etchings showed me what could be done between a man and a maid without indicating how I could acquire the opportunity to perform it, while as I puzzled out the language of M. Chorier's *The Delights of Venus* and Mr Cleland's *Memoirs of a Woman of Pleasure* my impatience to practise knew no bounds, and the relief which could be afforded either in solitary pleasure or in play with Frank grew less and less satisfying. He also, I noted, grew less inclined to play, and after a while seemed to grow entirely uninterested, though I little suspected the reason of it.

But now we come to the accident with which I opened my narrative. I had, as usual, accompanied my master and mistress to church, with Lieutenant Spencer in all his glory, while Frank had pleaded to remain at home to complete a task Mr Ffloyd had given him, and Sophie because she desired to finish a dress she was sewing. I had no reason to suppose that either excuse was anything but the truth – until, that is, I opened the door of my mistress' bedroom, where her reticule – as she told me – lay on the bedside table, and saw before me the spectacle of my two friends in a transport of pleasure. It was Frank who saw me first, for he lay upon his back with his head upon the silk pillows, the green muslin of his mother's dress rumpled about his chest and shoulders, while Sophie sat astride him, the black cloth of Master Spencer's uniform coat making even whiter the skin of her lower back, where it flapped as she moved like a girl on horseback, trotting.

Frank seemed not one whit disturbed at my entry. Indeed, he smiled, and said: 'So, Andy, you find us out at last!' – at which Sophie looked around, and as she did so the coat fell from her shoulders displaying that pair of breasts whose presence I had often noted beneath her thin summer dresses, but had never thought to see unencumbered and as they now presented themselves, swelling gently to roseate buds brushed by the fair hair that swung over her shoulders and halfway to her waist.

Even at that moment I felt some chagrin that Frank should have been enjoying his sister without communicating the fact to me – as I was later to find, they had begun to console each other over a year before the *tableau* now before me, and it was Sophie who, with a modesty which did not preclude her enjoyment of the act, had persuaded my friend to keep their secret. Even now she was more abashed than he at my discovery, though my sudden appearance seemed to have an effect upon her of extraordinary excitement, for as she saw me a strong blush spread to her cheeks and even her upper arms, while her body positively quivered, her buttocks clenched, her eyes rolled, and she was for a moment unable to speak. But then she relaxed and, panting, raised herself to recline at Frank's side, his tool still standing and seeming disproportionately tall, from the slimness of his body.

'Why, don't stand there, Andy, but come and join us!' he cried.

All thought of prayer and purse forgot, I did not hesitate, but threw off my Sunday coat, shirt and small-clothes and mounted the bed at their side. Still shy of the unknown, my first instinct was to lay hold of my friend, who however pushed my hand away and indicated his sister: 'Here's Soph',' he said. 'We've often spoke of you, and though she's shy you'll find her willing!'

Indeed, she lowered her eyes as I gently dared to place my hand upon her breast, for the first time feeling beneath my palm the limber, supple weight of that loveliest part of woman. But soon I felt her own hands stroking my flanks, and then Frank, with a laugh, thrust at my shoulder and sent me tumbling upon my back, with a cry of 'Let the purchaser see the goods!' – and nothing loath, her curiosity stronger than her bashfulness, she bent over me, and I felt her finger tracing my thigh and weighing my cods, while her eyes devoured the part my mother only, among women, had seen – and not to the advantage to which it now showed in its eager readiness for enjoyment.

'Now come, sis!' cries Frank. 'Poor Andy's a dry-tail, and must be allowed to bob!' and drawing his sister upon her back between his legs, his arms about her, reached down to draw her legs apart and display to me a mark to which I was drawn as the arrow to the target. Neglecting in my eagerness more than to glimpse the mark, I immediately let fly at it.

Ah, that in later years we could recall with each new mistress the pleasure of that first encounter! Innocence and freshness endowed my joining with Sophie with a pleasure rarely echoed since then. Though – as will be amply shown – my encounters have been numerous and delightful and my passions often more strangely and generously excited, the sensation as my tool passed without stay into the soul of my young partner was one which still remains in my memory as the most charming. She too, by her expression, enjoyed, and as with that instinct which needs no tutelage I began those movements which excited us towards our goal, her eyes sparkled and her lips parted to meet mine in a rapture communicated by our flickering tongues and the gentle nipping of our teeth. Frank the while clasped my shoulders to draw me more closely to his sister, while the friction of our bodies brought him soon – but not much sooner than ourselves – to the culmination. In youth, haste provokes no reproach, for boy and girl most often race together to the post.

Satisfaction stayed us for a while, and we lay upon the bed in a pool of sunlight from the high windows, our arms about each other, with no constraint nor trouble in the world until Frank, ever eager to renew, leaned to lap at Sophie's breast, while she, stroking with her fingers, tried – and not without success – to rouse me towards a second pleasure. Needing little encouragement, I soon presented Sophie with a renewed proof of my admiration while Frank, jealous of my success, knelt to offer himself to her lips – a meal to which she made no objection.

But in our pleasure and the interest of the situation we had been unconscious of the passage of time. Frank and Sophie had succeeded so far, by ingenious contrivance, in escaping notice of their meetings, whether by me or any other member of the household at Alcovary. But on this occasion in their enjoyment they lost account of passing minutes, until the sound of an opening door followed by a shriek announced the return from church of my mistress. Abashed, we drew apart, and Lady Franklyn ordered Frank and his sister to their rooms, whence they proceeded, white and trembling, clutching their clothes to them. I made to follow, but when my lady ordered me to remain I moved to take possession of my clothes, which lay upon the floor. But Lady Franklyn pushed at them with her foot, sending them to the other side of the room, and made with her hand a gesture which rooted me to the bed.

She was clearly in a passion, though its nature at first deceived me, for I took the flushing of her face and the panting of her bosom (which rose and fell with a peculiar rapidity) to be signals of extreme anger. In my fear, I nevertheless had room for admiration; the fashionable ladies of that time wore excessively little clothing, and through the lawn of her dress I could see the entire shape of her body, more voluptuous than that of her daughter, rather offering the pleasure of a bower in full, dark leaf than a spinney of young green trees.

What was my amazement when I saw her raise her arms and begin to undo her dress! As her bosom fell free of the material that hemmed it in, her breasts swung like ripe pears on the bough, gathered to dark nubs like acorns at their centre. Falling to her feet the folds disclosed a still slim waist, with below it a generous, black bush disguising the entry to love's channel. Yet still so astonished and incapable of response was I that she, now completely naked, had moved towards the bed and thrust me prone upon it before I realised that what I was to suffer was to be far from the chastisement I had anticipated.

My apprehension had naturally brought about my collapse and the speed of events prevented my recovery. But when in silence she lowered her head and applied her lips to that shrunk appurtenance of my manhood which lay fallow upon my thigh, it was not long before the resurrection occurred, and I was ready – so generous is the vitality of extreme youth – for a third bout.

If my education had been started by the daughter, it was continued by the mother, for the attentions she paid me were very different from those I had received from the girl – and, of course, from those I had exchanged with Frank in our mutual explorations of our changing bodies. Youth is centred on self; here, for the first time, in the arms of a woman twice my age, I enjoyed a partner who desired not only to take her pleasure but to enhance my own. Her lips drew upon my body as though parched, while her hands caressed me with a freedom which offered joys of which I was previously unaware.

In truth, under these ministrations it took no long time for me to recover both my confidence and my vigour, and within minutes I was clasped by stronger, more experienced – but no less engrossing – thighs than Sophie's, while half sitting I took between my lips one of those nut-like nipples, my attentions to which were evidently keenly approved by their recipient, who soon began to rise and fall upon me so that my tool was embraced along its full length by lips which, rimmed with dark tresses, were soft as those other lips through which we utter speech. Seeing, no doubt, on my countenance the signal of my imminent decease, she lifted herself from me and placing herself at my side threw up her legs, offering freely that delightful notch into which no man could but hammer a peg – which I swiftly did, setting my plug tail directly between those plump thighs, now lifted so that they embraced my sides, the knees rested beneath my armpits. It was a position I was familiar with from my library studies, but had not thought a woman of my lady's considerable age (for she was certainly thirty years old) capable of; not for the last time was I surprised at the lissom dexterity of passion.

But then as I dug my toes into the bed, raising myself the better to plunge into my mistress – whose dark eyes sparkled with the mutual pleasure of our joy – I suddenly felt a searing pain across my exposed parts, and heard a roar of anger – which emanated, as I found upon turning my head, from the throat of my master, Sir Franklin Franklyn. His unannounced (and as I later learned, unaccustomed) entrance into his wife's bedroom was as a result of the untoward expressions of delight from her lips, loud enough to be heard in the neighbour passage.

To be brief, Sir Franklin's apprehension of my encounter with his dame was not as sanguine as her view of my connection with her children. There was no appeal. Driven from the room by renewed blows from his riding crop on every area of my all too exposed body, and despite my lady's tearful excuses – though what these could have been

I cannot now conceive! – within an hour I found myself walking through the gate of Alcovary House, a small bundle upon my shoulder containing the one spare suite of clothes I could call my own, and in my pocket three shillings which, wrapped in a piece of paper, were thrown to me from a high window at which the face of Lady Franklyn appeared briefly as I left the back door of the house. If the world lay before me, I speculated, it seemed unlikely to offer, in the immediate future, as comfortable a place as that I had left. Yet I turned a brave face towards it, and set out in the opposite direction from the village, towards the open country.

Chapter Two

Sophie's Story

That a lady should set down in print a story as little suited for drawing-room reading as mine might bring a blush to the cheek of modesty, were it not for the fact that I am fixed in my mind that 'twill discourage others of my sex from trusting too much in their emotions rather than their reason – a propensity which has always been my downfall (though as often my delight).

I cannot complain of my birth or upbringing; my father, Sir Franklin Franklyn of Alcovary in the county of Hertfordshire, was a man of independent means who lavished upon his family every luxury save affection; that, he altogether lacked the capacity for – whether for his wife and children or for others. But he in no way hindered us from the pursuit of pleasure, which in a large house in a small neighbourhood was not perhaps so grand a freedom as the reader might at first apprehend. Nor can it be said that he was a willing expender of money, though having no means of discovering the extent of his fortune we had no reason to consider him a miser.

I was the youngest of three children: first, in the earliest year of my parents' marriage, was Spencer, named for my father's father on whom the house's fortune rested, and who showed his gratitude for the compliment by dying three days after the christening. That was in the year of '96, that of the mutiny at Spithead. Two years later, in '98, followed my brother Frank; and in the first year of the new century, myself, christened Sophia Venetia Lavinia after three paternal and maternal relations, none of whom showed the merest attempt at affection or financial endowment.

To my family of brothers was soon added a third – though not of blood – Andrew, or Andy as we called him, the son of one of my father's former gamekeepers, to whom my mother had taken a fancy. This was after my father had engaged a tutor for Spencer and Frank, chiefly to prepare the former, then eleven year old, for his entry into the Navy. On hearing that a boy from the village was to attend lessons, I immediately requested – nay, demanded – that I should also be permitted attendance, for why was I to be excluded from what I innocently believed to be play? I quickly regretted my eagerness, for this tutor was a large and unprepossessing man, a Mr Gutteridge, as lacking in personal graces as in knowledge for, as I was later to discover, he had no Latin and less Greek! And he would not for a moment have deceived any person more learned than my father, or less eager to impress his neighbours at the least possible expense (for Gutteridge was paid a mere pittance, nor even provided with clothing at our cost).

We quickly found our master keener to impress our bodies than our minds, for on the very first day he beat Frank fiercely upon his naked back, and for no good reason, choosing him no doubt because he lacked the conviction that my father would permit him to beat me. However, lack of interference and the realisation that Sir Franklin was interested in nothing so little as our wellbeing, encouraged him, and almost every day after, one or other of us had to strip to the birch, for he was no less ready to beat me than my brothers. They tried as best they might to shield me from pain but since Mr Gutteridge beat us without rhyme or reason, knowing my daily Collect or repeating the Lord's Prayer without error was no protection to me; nor did the boys have the physical means to stop him.

Out of school, Frank and Andy in particular became great friends. Spencer, being the elder, though always courteous considered himself to be more worthy of respect than of friendship and rarely entered our play – indeed, I often felt that he was somewhat jealous of Andy's presence. Nor did Frank at first favour me, but Andy was always pitiful of my cries beneath the whip and many a time I saw him regarding me with tenderness.

After one such day when we had all felt the birch, Andy and Frank, as was their custom, made off across the fields, and Spencer to his rooms. I, limping and sore, took to follow the two younger boys for want of something better to do, and from the sounds of splashing – for it was a summer day – easily found them at an inlet or pool of the river which lay in a hollow below the hill on which our house stood, protected by a fringe of trees. As I approached through these, I saw through the low branches the boys swimming in the dark water, their bodies, though naturally brown from the sun, white against the blackness whence their vigorous strokes struck a sparkle of drops. Soon, as I watched, they climbed the bank. They had so often been stripped of their breeches by Mr Gutteridge in course of his attacks that I was neither dismayed at their nakedness nor specially interested; nor did I consider it strange or unusual that they should display their stripes to each other, though I must admit to some surprise when, as Frank lay upon the grass, I saw Andy approach his face to his friend's fundament and lick the red bands, upon some of which dark spots of blood still appeared. This clearly gave Frank much pleasure, and he wriggled again, till jealous of the attention I burst upon them with a cry of 'Me too, Andy, lick me too!'

At first the boys were no less angry than surprised at my intervention but then had pity. It took me little time to strip and lie down, and soon I felt Andy's tongue cooling the welts on my skin, an activity which appeared to please him no less than it comforted me, though we were quite innocent and childish in the matter for we were not of an age to take any further the pleasure we felt, rooted though it was, as I have no doubt, in that instinct which was at once the pleasure and the curse of our ancestors in Eden.

Our familiarity continued no more and no less intense for some years, until that day when Mr Gutteridge particularly wished to punish brother Frank, for no reason other than whim, and sent Spencer, Andy and me from the classroom. Hearing Frank's cries, my two brothers mounted the water-butt, and what they saw I know not – only that on a particularly piteous exclamation of Frank's they descended with one leap and in a moment were into the room. Then I heard a cry from the master, who in a brief time appeared, naked save his shirt, and rushed into the garden so quickly that my glimpse of a huge, monstrous something below his belly seemed a vision I might have dreamed.

That afternoon I followed the two younger boys again to the river but something held me from announcing my approach, and indeed what I saw was more an education to me than anything I had learned in the tutor's class. My mother had by then impressed upon me the necessity to be less free in the presence of my brothers, for being much together with them, I had taken on somewhat of a tomboyish manner, until being free with a joke upon farting in the presence of Mrs Tenkerton, Parson Tenkerton's wife, she whipped me – though more gently than Mr Gutteridge. And later she told me to mind my ways and become more of a lady, though since she was the only lady I ever saw, 'twas difficult to know her meaning, for she was herself always very free with the servants, joking among them as if she was one of them. Particularly lately, when my breasts had begun to swell and my body become more a woman's, she insisted that I cease to go off with Frank and Andy on their rambles, and introduced me to the pleasures of sewing, which bored me so much I could have yelled.

But after the affair with Gutteridge I followed them to the river, being intent to find why they had suddenly been so violent. As I came upon them, I saw indeed that though they were engaged in the same comforting activity as previously, there was a difference – or more properly, two differences, for between their legs there was now not the small thing which I had seen, but not noted, on previous occasions, but something much more wonderful to me – something like a large extra limb, which I marvelled they could conceal beneath their clothes.

Andy was, as before, applying his tongue to the stripes on Frank's buttocks, the latter kneeling before him. But at the same time one of his hands was playing between Frank's legs, while with his other hand he was caressing himself. As I watched, he withdrew his hands and gently applied them to Frank's fundament, drawing its cheeks apart to reveal, indeed, what seemed to be a bruise or complaint, but as he was about to minister to it, Frank drew himself away with a shudder and a cry and threw himself into the water.

After a brief pause, Andy followed him, and in a short period they were frollicking happily, the dappled sunlight flashing between the leaves onto their bodies as they cleft the dark water. After a while they climbed onto the bank and threw themselves down upon the grass in a patch of sunlight. From my vantage-point I looked down upon them, and a pretty picture they made even to my then innocent eyes, their slender limbs disposed wantonly and carelessly, open to the view, as I had often seen them. Golden drops of water lay upon their skin and trembled as they breathed, before drying in the heat of the day. They lay so still I thought they slept, and was about to leave my place and go down to them to offer my solicitude to my brother, when I saw him reach out and begin to stroke Andy's thigh gently, his hand wandering then down to the spot where his tool – as I had heard them call it – lay quaggy and small below the slight bush of hair that now sprouted at its base.

To my surprise, the flesh almost instantly stirred beneath Frank's hand and began to grow, and as I strained my eyes I saw it become as it had been ten minutes before, long and thick, and at its end what seemed a darkly pink bud appeared within a fold of skin. I had thought Andy asleep and unconscious of the liberty my brother took, but now I saw his eyes were open, and he reached out to pass his hand between Frank's thighs. As the latter took hold of his tool and began to work it vigorously he too pulled at my brother's as though 'twere the teat of a cow he was milking – save that no cow but would have protested at the violence he seemed to offer, but which his friend was amorous of, for he began to buck his arse with pleasure. In an instant I was amazed to see a quantity of undoubted milk spring from both organs – after which the boys laughed and lay back, their parts recumbent on their bellies, still a little oozing.

I withdrew, having much to think of, and forbore to accompany the boys to the river in future, though on occasion they requested it, and I thought they showed an interest in those tender protruberances which now began to swell the bodice of my dress. But they lacked opportunity to explore them, for I was now in the ordinary course of events with them only at lesson time, with a new master, a Welsh man who was kindly disposed and from whom I learned much. I longed to ask him about that strangeness of my brothers' milking each other but some natural caution warned me against such a freedom, which I was later grateful for.

Full four years passed without any incident worthy of recall. They were years of pleasure for me, for I had a natural desire to learning which had been far from satisfied by our former master. Mr Ffloyd, our new teacher, was happy to supply me with all the information I required, for he was a well-educated man, with a knowledge not only of numbers and the fluencies of the English language, but of French, Greek and Italian, book-keeping and drawing, and even of dancing and music. Dark and with a white, smooth skin which marked him out from the brown-skinned house servants, he had a kindness of manner which made him a favourite with us all and as we grew older, he seemed to lose the power of a master, rather becoming an older friend – and not so old, either, for we learned in time that he was still below the age of twenty when he came to us. He roused in me a love of music, of which I had formerly been entirely ignorant, and sounded again the notes of the ancient harpsichord which for many years had lain unused in the drawing-room. He also infected me with his own love of reading, a delight which has lasted my lifetime. Finally, informing me that no educated woman who wished to take her place in society could be ignorant of dancing, he instructed me in some figures, though I had little opportunity of practice for my mother declined to take me even into such slender society as our district offered. Lessons with Mr Ffloyd made the hours fly speedily and these were indeed the last years of my life to pass without the regular tumult of sensual pleasure, which has its rewards but is also exhausting to the senses.

'Twas in the summer of 1814 that I passed my brother's room, and between the crack of the door saw him upon the bed, his shirt thrown up, and at his milking. Andy had gone for a day to see his mother, and after a hesitation which depended more on fear of Frank's disapproval than on want of curiosity on my part, I threw open the door and marched in, whereat Frank hastily drew the sheet over himself and pretended to be reading a book. However, I was not to be shrugged off.

'Tell me, Frank, how 'tis that a boy can give milk as well as a nursing mother?' I enquired.

At first he pretended ignorance, and that I was asking a mere silly conundrum, till I explained that I had seen him and Andy at their work by the river, and confessed that I thought much of asking Mr Ffloyd to unriddle me the matter. At this he hastily said no, he would save me that trouble, and explained that one morning some months before the adventure with Mr Gutteridge he had woken early in the bed he shared with Andy, the clothes thrown off for 'twas hot, and had seen as his brother lay asleep that that part of him wherewith he pissed, and which had been used to be small and pliant, was standing up from his belly and was many times larger than its habit. He had stretched out his hand and touched it to find it was hard as horn, and as he handled it he felt a disturbance between his own thighs and found that his own tool was swelling to match his friend's in dimension.

By this time Andy had woke and they both felt an irresistible itch which they lost no opportunity of assuaging – for rubbing their tools, when in that enlarged state, was, he said, more pleasant than anything they had theretofore experienced. The pleasure mounted (he explained) until he fear'd he had done himself some injury, for there was what seemed more than anything else like the bursting of a vein, whereupon the milk had broken from the head of his tool, and shortly after the same experience was shared by his brother.

They at first feared that they had done themselves damage and for some days watched lest they suffered some calamity as a result, but no such thing showing itself and, recalling the pleasure, they set to their practice again. Soon it was their custom to satisfy the itch whenever it occurred, which was sometimes several times a day, at which, he said, the flow of milk was sometimes lessened in the repetition.

By this time I was most curious to see this phenomenon and invited Frank to shew me the engine which so interested him, which he was loath to do, until I again employed the name of Mr Ffloyd as oracle, whereafter he reluctantly drew aside the sheet and I saw, to my dismay, only the small, limber thing I had so often seen before. At my disappointment, Frank began to fondle it, but 'twas reluctant to stir, whereupon, I put my hand to it and for the first time began with interest to examine it, for modesty had prevented me heretofore from doing so. 'Twas a perfunctory instrument indeed, with a little bag beneath which seemed to contain two small, soft stones, tender to the touch for Frank expressed pain when I pressed one to see how hard it was.

As I continued to press this bag with my hand, I saw his tool begin to swell, and as I drew back the skin at its top to examine the tiny hole there, it grew still more. Then I felt Frank's hand creeping beneath my skirts, and he ask'd whether 'twould not be reasonable that he should examine me in similar fashion. Nothing loath, I threw off my clothes and we lay naked upon the bed, head to tail. By now his tool was of truly surprising size, and bore little resemblance to what it had been before. So large was it, indeed, that the bag beneath was for want of skin drawn up tight at the root which, I felt, ran firmly behind it to the very fundament.

The limb which I now saw was white and smooth, firm to the touch as he had said, though as I passed my hand up its length I could feel the skin move upon it as if 'twere an ivory column clad in velvet. At the top it swelled out, the skin stretched, it seemed, to breaking point – though when I pulled it back it slipped over the rounded edge to lie below it, revealing a bulb brightly pink, the skin caught up at one point to its head, just behind the small aperture which gaped there.

It was clear that Frank derived the utmost enjoyment from this instrument's being caressed and smoothed; at the same time I was conscious of some pleasure derived from his explorations of my lower parts which, at that age, I had scarcely myself explored, but now found not ill-conceived for sensual enjoyment, though as he endeavoured to thrust his thumb within my most intimate part I felt a pang of pain as it encountered some obstruction. But he did not persist, for I was now making with my hands the motion I had seen Andy employ, with a view to producing the flow of milk, and indeed within a short time, as my brother panted, his chest rising and falling as though he was a-running, I felt the instrument leap between my fingers, and a copious flow spurted from the aperture, falling upon both our bodies. Consumed with interest, I took a drop upon my finger and conveyed it to my mouth, but it had by no means the taste even of milk, much less of cream, but merely of a slight saltiness.

This, as the reader may guess, was by no means the last time that Frank and I met to explore our bodies and to begin to tune them to that appreciation of pleasure which became to both of us a great – though secret – satisfaction. At night, he and Andy shared the bed and Frank kept our secret, though, he said, Andy had wondered at his being disinclined so often now for the pleasures they had previously enjoyed. 'Twas because during the day we had entertained ourselves, either in one of the attics of the house or, in summer, in some corner of the woods where there was little chance of discovery, though on one occasion our father passed just behind the bush where we were lying, naked and in a sweat doubled by a pleasurable fear of discovery!

The reader who may exclaim at my shamelessly relating such incestuous pleasures must remember that we had no means of knowing either that such joys were to be condemned, or indeed that it was uncommon for a boy and girl to explore each other without restriction. Indeed, I am told that there are few families in which such pleasure has not formed a part of the childhood of siblings, though the schools have recently taken to discouraging them as dangerous no less to morals than to the health of families where offspring result from early and illicit unions.

But to return to that first scene of delight, 'twas not long before Frank, tiring of simply testing with his fingers that aperture which he found so interesting, suggested that a larger instrument might enjoy exploring it. This was a surprising proposal, for it had never occurred to me that such a thing could be managed, nor, I dare swear, to Frank (though later I found that a book which he had found in our father's library had given him the notion). And so it was that on one afternoon I felt that best part of man make its way, not without pain, into that part made for its reception. Frank was struck with fear at the blood which he drew from my body but after the first fright of it, I was soon able to assure him that the concomitant pleasure was entirely superior to the slight discomfort, and our enjoyment of each other became complete – so naturally so that we completely lacked the clumsiness which I have marked in older lovers whose inhibition inhibits pleasure.

Indeed, so accustomed were we soon to the pleasures of love that 'twas not long ere we aimed to increase them by other play. This included the imitation of adults, Frank dressing up in our father's coats and myself in our mother's clothes, until I expressed the desire to see what sort of girl he would make. At this, without demur, he placed one of our mother's gowns upon him, the brownness of his shoulders looking most strange, but not stranger than the thing which stood out under the gown below his waist, like a barber's pole upon which someone had hanged a drapery! Meanwhile, I tried waistcoats, shirts, top-coats – anything above the waist, for Frank was insistent that my lower parts should always be open to his enjoyment, nor did I demur.

So we were enjoying ourselves in the great bedroom one Sunday morning, I sitting astride him and riding him like a horse – a sufficiently strange occupation for a lieutenant in the Navy (for it was brother Spencer's coat that I wore) – gripping his slender waist between by knees while riding upon his tool as 'twere a broomstick when, hearing a noise from the doorway and looking round, I discovered Andy whom we had thought to be safely at church.

To cut the tails of the story short, Frank invited our brother to enjoy us and he was not slow to do so. Nor was I dismayed, for he was a kindly and dear fellow, and apart from that I was curious to see whether all men were similarly fashioned. As – I should assure my less experienced sisters – is not the case; Andy's tool was thinner and longer than Frank's, with a darker coat and a cluster of almost black hair about its root, while Frank's was almost ginger. Neither colour had much similarity to the hair upon their heads and was, moreover, liker to wires than to flax.

No time was spent in mutual exploration for, throwing me upon my back without ceremony, Frank drew my thighs apart and directed Andy immediately to the seat of pleasure, whereupon he set himself to it like as the end of the world might come before he could experience the joys of love. And it would have had to come quickly, for almost as soon as he entered me, and I felt or seemed to feel the end of his instrument knock truly at the seat of my belly – so long it was – I felt his cheeks quiver beneath my hands and within me distinguished the first flood of his pleasure. Half pleased by the delight, half sorry for the speed of its accomplishment, he lay for a while unsmiling, but I had learned from Frank how to recover the small man to a great one and in a few minutes he was once more able to enter me, and this time our pleasure mounted slowly to its apogee. Frank, meanwhile, knelt at our side, and in a moment offered his staff to my mouth, an offer I accepted, as I always did in later life, with pleasure, its full smoothness lying upon my palate like a fruit.

'Twas as we were at our pleasures that I heard the door open, and a shriek announce the appearance of my mother, who ordered Frank and me immediately from the room. The servants later told me that they saw Andy walk from the house, dismissed, it seems, by my father, to whom my mother no doubt confided her disapprobation of his actions. My brother himself, it was announced, was to be sent to Oxford to continue his education until some occupation could be found for him, for Spencer was the only one of us who could count on an income sufficient for him to live upon, should he not achieve rank at sea. And as for me, my father summoned me to the library that same evening and announced that I was to be married.

Chapter Three

The Adventures of Andy

For some hours I walked through well-loved lanes without determining whither to direct my way. Then I found myself in unfamiliar countryside and before long came upon a main road leading, as far as I could guess, to the north. Growing up in the countryside around my native village I had had no cause to travel further from it than the house and, established there, than the walls of Sir Franklin's estate for on the rare occasions when he or his wife travelled abroad (which was not often) I was never one of the party.

But now the darkness began to close and, already beginning to be hungry, I made for myself a hole in the hedge where I curled up, and nursing my growling innards as best I might, eventually fell into a sleep made the deeper by the excitements and confusions of the day.

It was broad daylight when I awoke – not from the sun striking, as it did, upon my face, but by the sound of the rumbling wheels of a cart, and the noise of a rough song:

> *These London wenches are so stout*
> *They care not what they do;*
> *They will not let you have a bout*
> *Without a crown or two.*
>
> *They double their chops and curl their locks*
> *Their breaths perfume they do;*
> *Their tails are peppered with the pox,*
> *And that you're welcome to.*

Without losing a moment I broke from my warm burrow onto the road, sufficiently startling the plodding horse to bring it momentarily to a halt, its great head nodding, and the song broke off. 'Twas a cart laden high with a great quantity of logs and driven by a great hulk of a man, rough red hair sprouting from his head, his chin covered with several days' growth of beard, and wearing the clothes of a man who paid more attention to the contents of his belly than wherewith he covered it.

'Well, princox!' he cried. 'And what do you do, leaping out upon a fellow like some box-jack on a summer's morning?'

I bade him good day, and begged he would give me a ride to some town where I could buy a crust of bread. I made a more presentable figure than himself, for I had been allowed to dress in those clothes of Master Spencer's which had been passed to me in course, during the past few years, and though these were somewhat threadbare they at least gave me the appearance of worn gentility.

The carter was puzzled. My appearance, and even my speech (for, correcting this, Lady Franklyn and Mr Ffloyd between them had succeeded in giving me an intonation not unlike that of a gentleman) were cultivated. Yet here had I leaped from a hedge in which, from the sticky buds adhering to my clothes and the grasses stuck about me, I had clearly spent the night.

However, 'Ay, and welcome,' he said, whereat I climbed up beside him and, he clipping his horse with a switch, we set off to a new verse of his song:

> Give me the buxom country lass
> Hot piping from the cow,
> She'll take a touch upon the grass,
> Ay, marry, and thank you too!
>
> Her colour's fresh as a rose in June,
> Her temper as kind as a dove,
> She'll please the swain with a wholesome tune,
> And freely give her love.

After which he fell silent, and reaching into a bag at his

side fetched out a crust of bread and some cheese, broke a piece off and offered it to me. It vanished very quickly, for at the very sight of it my belly, which I had managed to quieten by dint of not thinking of it, set up a clamour which was not to be denied.

On the carter's questioning me, I admitted that I was a servant who had left employ.

'And suddenly, I'll warrant!' he cried. 'I thought you were a natty lad and no bumpkin. Your master caught you a-bilking, no doubt!'

When I had got from him the meaning of his words, which might as well have been spoken in French for all I knew, I assured him that I was no thief, nor had I stolen the clothes I had about me (nor the money, though that I did not mention), and on his questioning me further I admitted to him that I had been dismissed for over-familiarity with the daughter of the house, though to what degree I did not confess. On hearing Sir Franklin's name he cursed for, he said, that man had made a friend of his, a walking poulterer, dance at the sheriff's ball – which I learned was to be hanged, and that a walking poulterer was a fellow who stole chickens from one man to sell them to his neighbour. (But I shall give no more examples of his strange language, which was that, I soon learned, of a city man, he having left London a few years before to live in the country, where he made a living by carrying goods, of whatever kind, from place to place.)

In relating my history – or such portions of it as I deemed fit to convey – I had neglected to discover whence my inter-locator was directing his journey, which he volunteered to be the city of Cambridge, where he hoped to gather some trade at the summer fair. He was content to carry me there on condition that I helped him to unload his logs at Rawby Hall, some miles to the south of the city, where he was to deliver them. The Earl of Rawby, he explained, was so proud of his estate that he would have no timber felled within its walls and the fallen branches were insufficient for the use of a huge household.

The size of the estate soon became plain for we followed a

great wall for five or six miles before reaching tall iron gates wrought in fantastic shapes, between two pillars atop which stood carvings of two strange monsters, each belaboured by the club of a naked Hercules. A shrill whistle from the carter brought a liveried gateman to open to us and we turned into a long, straight avenue of elms which ran for what must have been at least a mile towards the Hall. As we drove up, my friend enlightened me about its owner, the third Earl of Rawby, a widower of some half-a-century in age who lived there with his two daughters. Rawby dedicated himself entirely to the life of the Hall – not only to country pursuits (being a great hunter) but to entertaining the nobility and gentry of the country at feasts, routs and balls over which his daughters, though yet young, presided. It was rarely, I learned, that there were less than thirty guests about the house, either in winter or summer, and a great number of servants, both resident and visiting.

It was at that moment, as we came in sight of the house itself, that I decided to try for employment there; I had no taste for poverty, and if my life had recently been pleasant enough, surely so grand a house as this would offer even greater luxury? For it was a fine place indeed; as we took a path leading around the side of the building, I glimpsed through the trees wide smooth lawns before the main entrance, the dew yet on them, and the front of the house itself, perhaps fifty yards across, with tall windows reflecting the slanting, early rays of the sun, and a great double staircase curving up to the front door.

Soon we rattled over cobbles into a yard where – unlike the front of the house, where no-one stirred – all was bustle: maids drawing water, carrying pails, scouring cauldrons and pans, men with baskets of produce, three old women plucking birds in a flurry of feathers in a corner . . .

Without exchanging a word with anyone, my friend backed the cart up to an open shed door and, leaping to the ground, threw down the back flap of the cart.

'Come, young put!' he called. 'And let's see the size of your muscles!'

Meaning to impress, I jumped to it, and we were both

soon at work throwing the logs onto a pile already lying in the shed. In twenty minutes all was done and the carter wiping his brow with the back of a hand, for though the chill was scarcely off the day, we were both in a muck of sweat. He beckoned me to the back door and in the scullery a buxom maid brought us a full tankard of ale, which we made short work of. Through the open door of the kitchen I took an idea of how great the house might be, for it was much larger than the one at Alcovary; here was an enormous fireplace where, though now only a small flame flickered on a bed of ash, there must be a great fire when time came for cooking meats, and before it was what I had never seen: a spit for turning a roast. When first I saw it I doubted its purpose, for at our house meat was cooked simply by placing on a grid near the fire. Then over the fire hung a huge kettle for the provision of hot water, and at the side a great cauldron for boiling meat. From the ovens came a smell of baking bread, the night-fire having been sufficient for that purpose. As we drained, the scullery fell quiet and looking round I saw a tall, bustling woman had entered. Skinny and sharp-faced, and with the manner of one who would brook no nonsense, she was calling for one Ellen.

'She be gone to village, Mrs Tickert, for the redcurrants for the jelly, Mrs Munce having sent only seven pound when ten pound was asked.'

'Right, girl, right! But there's milady's salon not yet cleaned. Find Tabitha and turn her onto that, and – who's this gawping boy?'

Realising that she could only be referring to me, I drew myself up and made my best bow.

'Forgive me, ma'am,' I said, 'I hope not to incommode you,' and gave her a smile, though she looked unlikely to be softened by it. However, she paused for a moment, and then nodded.

'Ah,' she said, 'Mr Caldwell's offering, no doubt. You start this morning?'

She must have seen that I was oblivious to her meaning for 'Is the boy foolish?' she asked anyone who cared to answer. 'Has he no brains in his noddle?'

'I'm sorry, ma'am,' I said, 'but I know not . . .'

At which I was interrupted by a great lubberly fellow who burst in through the door and knocked over a chair upon which someone had set down a bowl of hot water in which some eggs were poaching. The china splintered on the pavings, half-cooked eggs smashed and curdled on the floor, and the boy hopped as some scalding water splashed his legs.

'Hor! Hor!' he cried, and Mrs Tickert threw up her hands in horror.

'Out! Out!' she cried. 'Lummux, silly, nazy, stupid damber!'

'But Missus – Master Caldwell sent me, I was to ask for 'ee . . .'

Standing not on ceremony, Mrs Tickert seized a broom from one of the girls and made to stab him with it, whereon he rapidly ran from the room. Meanwhile, I had taken a wooden trug and was on my knees piling the broken china into it while a giggling maid wiped up the water. As I straightened up Mrs Tickert, panting slightly, handed me the broom.

'So where have you sprung from, if not from Mr Caldwell?' she said. 'No, I've no time to hear endless tales,' (as I opened my mouth to tell her). 'Anyway, he could not think such a lubberly fellow as that could suit! But how did you hear I wanted a man?'

The maid at my side scarcely repressed a giggle, but at a glance from Mrs Tickert ran immediately from the room.

'Well, boy?'

'Ma'am, I am at a disadvantage,' I said, 'I know not . . .'

'You mean you are not come for a footman's place?'

'Ma'am, I was not aware,' I said, 'but the truth is that I have some experience . . .'

'Well, you look pretty enough,' she said, 'and what I can't teach you, Mr Caister will. Fifteen pound a year, and you'd better go and see about your uniform.' Whereat she swept from the room.

My carter friend, who had been making himself insignificant in a corner, came forward and took me by the hand.

'Well, rascal,' he said, 'you've tumbled upon your feet. You'll not get rich here, but there's plenty of food and plenty of ale, and if you've served Lord Rawby you'll be fit to serve any man in the country!' At which he said farewell – without my having so much as learned his name – and left me to myself. The maid who had witnessed the scene was still hanging by the doorway, and still giggling, and I learned from her that I had stepped into a place of footman, one of six in the house, that Mr Caister was the butler, and that it was to him I must apply for my livery.

She conducted me from the scullery through the kitchen and along a passage to a small, dark room where I found Mr Caister, a short, dark man in rusty black, who dismissed the maid.

'Mmmm – where do you – mm – spring from – mm – boy?' he stammered. 'Mm – mm – Mr Caldwell sent you?'

I explained that Mrs Tickert had engaged me upon sight, and said that I had formerly served in the house of Sir Franklin Franklyn ('Mm – never – mm – heard of him!' was the ungracious response), and that I had been sent to be fitted with my livery.

He nodded somewhat grudgingly, and went to a door in the corner of the room, which led into a small room or large cupboard where enough livery hung on rails to dress, as I thought, the whole of Hertfordshire. From one of a number, having eyed me shrewdly, he took a handsome livery comprising breeches of strong, grey cloth and a black coat trimmed with silver braid.

'Throw – mm – this on,' he said, and watched me with what seemed uncommon interest as I removed Mr Spencer's breeches and pulled on the others.

'Ay, not a – mm – whit too tight,' said Mr Caister, and passed his hand over my thigh. 'They do not pinch your – mm – privities?'

Nay, I assured him, they were a perfect fit. The coat too hung well from my shoulders. He then pulled a line, and a distant bell brought a boy of my own age to the door. 'Tom,' he said, 'this is . . .'

'Andrew,' I told him.

'Andrew. Before the house is about, take and show him the ground. And you,' he turned to me, 'you know your duties?'

'I do,' I said with confidence. If I could not copy my fellows closely enough to pass muster, I was less sharp than I thought myself. Mr Caister waved his hand, and Tom led the way from the room and turned to go up the stone steps which led to the main floor of the house.

I cannot swear that I was much the better off after Tom's speedy tour of the Hall than before it, for – as though I stood still and saw a vision – there sped past me a number of great rooms each of which seemed to be the size of the whole of Alcovary House. First, at the top of the stairs and so within easiest reach of the kitchen, was a great dining-room with a long table which appeared to me to stretch to infinity. Beyond it lay a long gallery with paintings and sculptures so prolific that they peopled the empty room in a crowd. Through a door and along a corridor, Tom indicated, were the dressing rooms and sleeping apartments of the two daughters of the house, Lady Elizabeth and Lady Margaret – 'Still abed, I'll warrant, and no knowing in whose company!' he winked.

Turning, he retraced his steps through the gallery and the great hall within the main doors of the house, beyond which a fine circular room rose to a splendid dome. Beyond this again, a saloon gave onto a spacious drawing-room which looked over a pleasant courtyard, covered to my astonishment with glass and decorated with strange plants the like of which I had never seen (brought, Tom told me, from countries over the seas). Across the courtyard he pointed out the windows of My Lord's bedroom. Next the drawing-room was a smaller anteroom (as he called it) and beyond this a range of guest bedrooms and dressing rooms, including a state bedroom only used when royalty stayed at the house ('Prinny came four years ago,' he said; I knew enough to recognise that he meant our Prince Regent, always spoken of at Alcovary with the greatest respect, but here as I was to find regarded by My Lord and his fellows as a creature only fit for jokes and scorn).

Briefly, he showed me the chapel, sombre with dark wood panels, gold gleaming dully from the altar, then led me by another stair down towards the kitchen again, but half-way down, opposite the laundry (from which I heard a splashing and girls' laughter) was a most curious compartment: a door led to four steps which descended into a great stone pit with a contrivance like a four-legged stool hoisted above it and the pit was filled with water. Tom, seeing my amazement, proudly said that it was a bath and that when the men of the house had been a-hunting, and returned muddied, they made their way here to wash themselves, while onto the high legs of the machine a pail was hoist containing hot water which, by use of a string, was released through the bottom of the bucket to shower upon the man standing beneath. This had only been installed for a year, and when it was first placed the mistake had been made of placing boiling water in the pail and badly scalding the inventor, Mr Standing of Cambridge, who personally demonstrated it to My Lord.

By now it was almost ten o'clock and Tom hastened me to the kitchen, for it would be time to serve My Lord and his guests, who were going a-hunting and therefore would be eating large. 'Twas late in the season, I protested; Sir Franklin never allowed hunting over his land after the end of April. At which Tom scoffed, and said My Lord was a law to himself, and let Sir Franklin do what he might, at Rawby when the Earl wished to hunt, he hunted. This year he had started late, having been on envoy to the Low Countries, so he had decreed the season extended until the middle of May. And so food was today required early – usually a draft of ale sufficed to break fast, when nothing was eaten until dinner at three in the afternoon. Today there would be simple food to send them out with their bellies full: twenty rabbits or so, some joints of pork, pigeon pie, and of course ale from My Lord's own cellars.

The kitchen was by now all a-bustle; a fire was blazing and the smell of roasting and boiling flesh rose to us as we entered. The two cooks were contending at the table, the girls preparing platters and setting out meats, and two other footmen whom I had not yet met were bringing the ale from the cellars in great wooden vessels and placing them on trays with tankards ready.

Careful to imitate the others, I served the breakfast easily enough. And if I had wondered whether I would be noticed, I need have had no concern, for My Lord and his fellows had no interest save in their food and drink and their plans for the day – though there was not much talk, and I perceived that several of them suffered from the distemper of too much wine the night before, which was now followed with a great quantity of ale to cure the sickness. My Lord finally rose, a great, fat man with a stomach upon him like a pregnant ewe, and an old-fashioned curled wig which he wore (Tom said) to disguise a bald head upon which there was a great purple disfiguring mark he had had all his days, and was jealously secretive of. Therefore he did not take to the new habit of wearing his own hair, having none to boast of.

'Come ye,' he said, 'we start for Poulton's Brake, and if we don't find there, over towards Baldock. Haddon' (addressing a small, thin man next him at table) 'if ye'r head stay upon ye'r shoulders this morning, it won't be for want of all ye'r efforts last night!'

At which Mr Haddon nodded carefully, as if indeed his noddle might fall into the greasy dish of boiled rabbit he had been cautiously addressing. Then 'Here come the cattle!' said My Lord, and the party all rose and made for the door. Looking out of the window from where I stood against the wall with my five fellows, I had seen a procession of beautiful horses making its way across the grass from a spinney beyond which some gates announced the stables, and in a few minutes the party was mounted, and followed My Lord towards the drive and out of sight.

The rest of the morning was spent clearing the dishes and doing the work of the house which, at midday, included Tom and I carrying two great baskets of bedclothes to the laundry-room, which entering without ceremony we found three girls – one of whom I had seen already in the kitchen – all in steam, pounding at the linen in two great tubs. It being a warm day, the water hot and the effort great, they had stripped to their shifts which consisted of little but loose gowns hanging from their shoulders, and as Tom and I tipped the dry clothes to join the others in the wash, it took but little contrivance for him to slip the thin ties from the shoulders of one of the girls so her shift fell to her waist, disclosing a fine pair of bubs which she made no effort to conceal, but gave Tom a push which sent him reeling backwards into the other two, who laughed with a will.

'Now, Tabby!' cried he. 'Don't show your temper before young Andy – he'll think the worse of you.'

Unblushing, she looked at me, her fine eyes alive with fun.

'And who's Andy when he's at play?'

'Well, now, hasn't he been gifted to us from a great house in the neighbour county, where he got the mistress and her seventeen daughters all with child, and him not yet fourteen!'

The three girls fell anew into giggling, whereupon Tom took his advantage and coming up behind Tabby grasped a breast in one hand while with the other he raised her shift, showing a long white leg which reminded me strongly of the pleasures I had enjoyed with Sophia.

'See, his young eyes are walking up your thigh! Lock your door tonight, little Tabby, 'gainst all save your Tom!'

Tabby leaned back against him and gave him a quick kiss, while he gently tweaked the brown nipple of her breast, and his other hand was at what work I knew not.

Later, while the ladies' maids were caring for their mistresses, upon which I had not yet set my eyes, Tom and I sat with Tabby and Ellen in the sun in the yard enjoying a pot of ale, a crust and some cheese. The other footmen, being older than the two of us – one in his forties, one about thirty, and two I guessed in their middle twenties – were at dice elsewhere. I now learned more about the house. Mrs Tickert's bark was less than her bite; Mr Caister's hand would certainly sooner or later make its way into my breeches (but, said Tom, he was an impotent old man, and what harm? – moreover, he had the provision of ale below stairs); and if I wished to dip my gingambobs, Tabby was the girl for me (at which she fetched Tom a great blow upon the side of his head, wherefore he kissed her soundly).

Meanwhile, Ellen, much quieter than her friend, was silent. She was slimmer and darker, somewhat chicken-breasted. Or so I guessed, for she was modester than Tabby and kept her dress carefully gathered to her neck, while Tabby made no god of decorum and if a titty happened to fall from her bodice, only replaced it when she had first completed what task she was at whether finishing an apple or draining a tankard. While she had laughed with the others at the riot in the laundry-room, I believed Ellen to be less ready than her friend to be a bawd or play at rantum-scantum. Which apprehension was sharpened by the blush which came to her cheeks when Tom rallied her and said that she had surely shared a bed with Tabby long enough to have learned what her madge was for, but he, being a kindly fellow, did not press her but turned again to rallying with Tabby.

Then came the noise of the horses' hooves on the gravel, and we had to run to the bath room with water, for the men would be there directly, Tom said – as indeed was true, for no sooner had we got there and hoisted the first bucket to the top of the stand, than the bath was filled with half a dozen naked fellows of all sizes, pummelling each other, thrusting each other's heads below the water and bellowing for soap (of which there was great quantity, made from goat's tallow boiled with wood ashes in the kitchens). Rushing to and fro, I had no time to think about anything other than minding the stairs while carrying the hot water and had scarcely noticed that not only were Tom and I busy, but that the two girls also were engaged, and in the room with all the naked men were with brushes attending to their backs as they stood beneath the shower.

Finally, when only two men were left, I had time to stand for a while and saw that both Tabby and Ellen were soaked with the water, their shifts sticking to their bodies so they appeared just as though they were naked – a fact which clearly delighted one of the two men, though the other –

who was none other than Mr Haddon, whose head had not
it seemed been much cleared by his gallop – took no more
notice of them than, I suppose, of his horse. But his
companion, a large-boned man in his forties with a great
thrusting of black hairs upon his chest, did not hesitate to
show his admiration of the girls in the standing of his sugar
stick, which rose like a great shaft from below his belly. Far
from wishing to conceal this, he rather brandished it like
some proud marshal's baton.

When he grasped at Tabby and fumbled her, she showed
no distress, though Tom, near me, looked as though he was
face to face with Bonaparte himself, and would be happy to
dispatch him. Then Mr Haddon passing to leave the bath,
the other fellow was forced to let Tabby go while she lifted a
towel and handed it to his companion, and she going with
Haddon to open the door for him, he turned to Ellen. Seeing that she shrank from him, he lifted his hand and with
one stroke tore her shift from her. She coloured, and one
hand went to her small breasts, while the other sheltered her
man trap – at which he took her by the arms and stretched
them wide, so that she was open to his view.

I, who had never seen a man act so with a woman, made
to move towards them but felt Tom's hand on my arm, and
he shook his head. So I stood while the fellow, cursing
because she was not forthcoming, pressed her against the
side of the bath and then placing his hands upon her shoulders, forced her down until he could press his tool to her
face and force it between her unwilling lips, then thrusting
with his great bottom until, in a short time, such was his
excitement, he shouted in pleasure and drew away, while
she scooped water with her hands to wash her face and
mouth.

'Next time, girl, be willing – 'twill be more pleasant!
More water, there!' – turning to us.

We went to fetch more water, Tom explaining as we did
so that the fellow was Sir Walter Flount, a merchant of
immense riches, from whom My Lord had from time to
time borrowed much money, and who therefore was free of
the house though admired by none. Tom was then

summoned by Mrs Tickert, and I was left alone to take the water to the bath room, where Ellen stood silently, with her eyes full of tears, in a corner. I hoisted the water, and she stood to control the flow as Flount lifted his fat self from the water to stand beneath it, the water coursing over his fleshy shoulders and breasts like a woman beneath the veil of hair, then over his belly to where his lobcock now swung heavily.

I left them alone, taking the soap with me (for, I thought, it was a valuable commodity that deserved husbanding). How it came that a piece of it fell to the step outside the bath room is a mystery. However, it cannot be denied that it must have been through my carelessness that one of Sir Walter's bare feet came upon it as he left the bath, when sadly his arms were too wrapped in the towel which Ellen had folded about him for him to be able to save himself from falling down the ten stone steps to the floor of the kitchen passage, where his roars brought most of the servants to his assistance. He was carried cursing to his room and a surgeon sent for, who declared a leg to be broke. The screams as it was laid between two boards and bound reached the ears of Lady Elizabeth and Lady Margaret in their rooms, who sent to enquire the reason for the noise. Mr Caister despatched to explain the happenings and returned to order me to go to their Ladyships' rooms, for they wished to see me.

Chapter Four
Sophie's Story

My father's announcement that I was to be married came upon me with the force of a thunderclap, for I had never heard of such a thing; as with Shakespeare's Juliet, it was an honour that I dreamed not of. But, he said, it was time I was coupled, and when I enquired to whom I was to be shackled, he was mysterious, and said only that I should hear of it soon enough.

I could not console myself with Frank, for he had been locked in a room at the top of the house, the only way to which lay through my father's bedroom, which itself was locked. And I had not seen Spencer since our discovery, nor did I feel he would be sympathetic, for he had latterly seemed to disapprove of Frank's and my closer friendship with Andy. So I went to my bed, and there cried myself to early sleep only to wake in the dark night and lie thinking of my fate. Would my husband be a handsome fellow? That seemed the last thing my father would consider, money above all, and rank next, being the two first. The pleasures I had enjoyed with Frank and brother Andy had given me a taste the flavour of which was still with me, and as I felt my person it still seemed warm with the delightful friction of the afternoon. I began to think I could reconcile myself to any husband possessed of sufficient spirit, and that with one such perhaps after all life would not end within the next month.

But then a strange something stirred in the black air around me, something between a smell, a taste and a sound, and after a while concluding it was the latter, I stole from bed, and opening my door felt my way to the stairway. As I went the sound became clearer, and recognisable: it was the harpsichord in the drawing-room, upon which someone was playing Mr Tomkins' *What if a day*. Its melancholy words fell into my mind as I listened:

> *What if a day, or a month, or a year*
> *Crown thy delights with a thousand sweet contentings?*
> *Cannot a chance of a night or an hour*
> *Cross thy desires with as many sad tormentings?*
> *Wanton pleasures, doting love,*
> *Are but shadows flying.*
> *All our joys*
> *Are but toys . . .'*

It could only be Mr Ffloyd, for no one else in the house save himself and me ever touched the instrument on which I had so often heard him play the same piece. Stumbling in the dark, I made my way to the door, outlined by a dim light, and stole through. At first, he did not see me, sitting at the keyboard with a single candle set upon it illuminating his long face as he played. But as I approached, with a great start he descried my presence and stopped playing. Once near him, I saw that there was a tear upon his cheek and asked the reason, whereupon he said that he had been dismissed that day, since neither I nor Frank would be more in need of a tutor.

'Are you then so sorry to leave us?'

'To leave *you*, Miss Sophie,' he then said, falling upon his knees before me, 'for you must know that of all ladies you are the sweetest!'

Amazed, for I had never suspected these feelings in him, I stepped forward, whereupon he threw his arms about my waist and held his head to my breast. I had not thought to put on my day-dress, and was wearing only my smock of best thin cotton, and his arms being about me, his hands fell upon my lower parts, the warmth of his palms being so pleasant that I could not help responding to it by taking his head in my hands and pressing it to my bosom. The ardent emotion of his whole body, indeed, now communicated itself to me – he seemed to be almost in a fever, and to discover whether his skin was burning to excess I placed my hands inside his shirt, at the back, where it hung loosely from the collar, and felt his shoulders. They were pleasantly warm, but not to my relief morbidly so. Yet my action had a powerful effect upon him, for he immediately rose to his feet, drew me yet closer to him, and placing his lips upon mine made as though to suck my soul out through them.

It was the first real kiss I had experienced, for neither Frank nor Andy had shown any wish to use their lips except upon those other parts where pleasure lies. I was amazed at the pleasure which flowed from Mr Ffloyd's lips and felt a new excitement when his tongue slid, limber and liquid, into my mouth, playing upon my own, running upon my teeth and the inside of my cheeks.

By now we had sunk to the floor, and I felt his hand lift my smock to draw it to my waist. I pushed it away and standing lifted the garment over my head and dropped it at my side. His face was a study of mingled delight and surprise as he looked up at me, then raised himself to place his hands upon my hips and plant a kiss upon my nether lips. Bending, I seized his shirt and lifted it over his head, while he loosened his breeches and drew them off.

He was eager to be at play but I reached and took the candle from the harpsichord and held it so I could see his body – the first of a grown man upon which I had set eyes, my brothers being mere boys. I felt immediately the difference between youth and maturity: the limbs were altogether firmer and stronger, though by no means hardened by toil; upon his breast fine hairs grew in a dark mat, not thick enough to hide the fine shape of that manly platform, but as a garnish upon a delicious dish, and below in fan-shape tapered down his small belly to grow in more profusion where his handsome instrument stood ready to hand, set between two fine thighs, themselves fluffed with hair like the haunches of a brave young animal.

Seeing my admiration, he lay for a moment and let me look, then impatience overcoming him gently took the candle from my quivering hand and set it down at our side, and turning me upon my back began an exploration of my body – not like a squirrel examining a nut (whose curious innocence Frank and Andy had counterfeited) but like a groom attending to a fine steed, trying each part for its excellence. I was soon all liquid with pleasure, and simply content to rest inanimate as his eyes devoured and his fingers played with me, until myself too impatient for further delay I drew him on top of me and felt with indescribable felicity his great part enter into me and move with a reposeful action like that of my maid when brushing my hair, then slowly increasing in speed and pressure until the sparks of delight were struck faster and faster, soon seeming to set light to my whole lower person, then of a sudden bursting into a flame which for a moment seemed to destroy me. My cries would have waked the house had not Mr Ffloyd had the foresight to place his hand over my mouth. He took it away to kiss me again but to my astonishment his movements, though again they had slowed, did not cease.

Now, though there was a certain soreness, the pleasure was of a different kind – a delightful tickling and general glow. I passed my hands over his naked shoulders and arms, down his back, hairless until it swelled to those two charming flexures, covered as it felt with a light down, and moving gently beneath my hands. Grasping these, I pulled them towards me, my hands slipping between, as I did so, to feel a growth of coarser hair. At this he gasped suddenly and began to move again with vigour, until once more I felt the keener pleasure mount and this time as it reached its apogee, I perceived him also to shudder with glee, and within me a warmth that indicated that he had spent that substance which seems to be the liquid core of man.

We lay together for some time, our bodies now so damp with sweat they seemed to be glued together, until lifting himself from me, he took his shirt and wiped my breasts and belly, and with tenderness near to tears kissed me upon the cheek and fixing his great dark eyes all the time upon me drew on his breeches and silently held my smock while I slid into it. Taking my hand then, and the candle, he led me to the door and stood at the bottom of the stairs, still without a word, holding the light high while I made my barefoot way up to my room.

At breakfast next morning I saw him pass the window, carrying his bags, and heard his footsteps upon the gravel path as he left. I opened my lips to speak, but a look from my father – whose single wish it was to keep his eyes upon me the whole of my waking hours – quietened me before I could do so.

I was instructed to ready myself for a journey by two o'clock, and nothing I could ask would elicit the reason, nor the destination. I still had no sight of Frank, nor did my mother appear. Though previously, when she discovered any naughtiness and reported it to our father she had always been ready to pacify me after any punishment he saw fit to inflict, now her absence was marked, and I could not understand it. When I asked my father whether I could not see her, his reply was simply a short 'No, madam, you may not!'

At two, my father led me from the house to where our horses were ready and we set out upon the highroad for some miles to the westward, where in due time we came to a small village on the outskirts of which was a large timbered house, set a little back from the road in the midst of a tangled thicket which had once been a garden. Here we dismounted and knocked upon the door, which was opened by a slatternly maidservant.

My father giving his name, we were ushered into what no doubt was called the parlour, but which was dirtier than any stable at Alcovary. The furnishings were poor and old-fashioned, the hangings threadbare and ancient, and a thick dust was thrown upon everything like a grey snow. I opened my mouth but a glance from my father silenced me before I could speak. Soon a shuffling was heard in the passage outside and, the door opening, a tall, thin man appeared, clad in old-fashioned dress, with thin grey hair atop a sallow face upon the left cheek of which was a great, hairy mole.

I stood and made a curtsy, whereupon he bent his back stiffly, as though it was not a custom with him to bow to anyone.

'Sir Franklin Franklyn?' he asked, and without waiting

for an answer approached and stretched out his hand to me. Reluctantly, I took it; it lay within my palm all bony and limp, as though the flesh had long gone.

'And Miss Sophia,' he said, and bowing pressed dry lips to the back of my hand.

'Mr Nelham,' said my father.

'Delighted, Sir Franklin, delighted,' said the old man – for 'old man' I considered him, yet he may not have been more than forty and five. 'I am most pleased that you should suddenly have acceded to my request. My dear,' (turning to me) 'we have not met, yet I have heard much of your beauty and accomplishments, and I trust our close acquaintance will bring us equal pleasure.'

Close acquaintance! I had clung to the hope that perhaps this man had a son, to whom I was to be married, but clearly he was to be my bridegroom. My senses shrank at the thought, and I turned to my father. He stood implacable and silent, and I knew no mercy was to be sought from him, or if sought was not to be granted.

'And may I ask when . . .?'

'The sooner the better,' said my father. 'Call the banns when you like!'

In short, it was arranged that we should be married three weeks the following Friday and without more ado, we left, the old man's eyes following my every movement with what I now suspected of being a lascivious pleasure. No sooner were we out of hearing than I appealed to my father with all the strength I possessed to free me from my fate, but he simply sat impassive on his horse looking neither to left nor right, and was indifferent to my pleas.

On returning to Alcovary, I lost no time in seeking out Frank, but sought in vain, for in my absence he had been sent from the house, whither, I could not discover, the servants either knowing nothing or having been so frightened they would not disclose it. That evening my mother joined us at the supper table but sat with lowered eyes and said nothing. Next day, I was able to speak with her alone, but all she would report was that my father was outraged at my behaviour with my brothers and had decided upon an immediate marriage as the best solution to the problem, 'for what,' she said, 'if you found yourself with child?'

Here was something which I had not thought of, for no one had explained to me that playing the beast with two backs could bring about the seeding of children; I do believe that somewhere an instinct connected the two events, but not from knowledge. Now, under pressure to explain, my mother revealed that the white substance that came from a man's tool contained the seed of a child, and that when it entered a woman's privy place, a baby sometimes grew from it.

What? I enquired. But surely it could not be that the penalty for a single night's pleasure could be so heavy?

Yes, replied my mother, all too often that was so - though not invariably, which I was glad to hear, for it was plain that either of my brothers or Mr Ffloyd could have seeded a child in me. Asked whether this could not be prevented, my mother (who now the subject was broached, became informative) said that while not every passage of love produced a child, it was possible to make the event less likely by the use of what she called a *cundum*, resembling a little hat or cape made of the gut of a sheep placed over the man's affair, when it was fully extended, to prevent the milk from being spent within her. Asking whether my father made use of such a machine, she replied blushingly that he did not, but that they had now no such connection. I did not enquire further but wondered that my mother at her age could have had a lover to show her such things.

The next three weeks only more firmly sealed my fate, for preparations for the marriage went ahead with or without my assistance. I could find little more about my husband, but that he was a respectable man and a great scholar, reputed also to have a great fortune, though of a miserly disposition. Nothing ill was known of him, though also I could discover nothing good. I caught my mother regarding me with pity, as I thought. My father displayed no emotion, but I soon ceased to appeal to him to release me from a bonding I had not sought nor could delight in.

The marriage was held before breakfast one morning at

the church just outside our gates. The Rev. Fumbling, whose living was in my father's gift, performed the ceremony – not without, I thought, some incredulous glances at the groom, who appeared in a creaking suit of finery which cannot have been less than twenty years of age and had clearly been well-used. Not that my own dress was to be spoken of, for nothing new had been contrived for me, my father setting his face against any public show. Present in the church were only myself and my ancient groom, my father and mother and the parson, together with an aged crone from the village as witness.

After the wedding, and without further ceremony, my husband and I mounted a small coach and made off upon the road to Cambridge, some two hours distant. The road was bad, with many holes, and before long I was sore and shaken. My husband comforted me by producing a packet containing some bread and meat, all dry and tasteless, and a flask of water, and suggesting that I sleep! From time to time we passed through small villages, and once by a pair of splendid park gates through which I caught a glimpse of a long avenue of elms leading to a distant house. But of interesting conversation we had none, let alone endearments one might have thought natural between a new-married couple – for which, however, I was grateful, for the thought of being fumbled by those dry, bony hands was abhorrent to me. My husband throughout the journey buried his head in a book, only raising it as we rattled into Cambridge city – a sight interesting to me, who had never before seen even a large town.

We drew into the yard of the Red Lion Inn, at the very centre (as it seemed) of the city. Galleries ran around its sides, upon which maids were hanging linen to air, boys were rushing hither and thither on errands only they knew the details of, and I was handed out of the coach by a handsome fellow with the air of a host, who also greeted Mr Nelham with respect.

We were shown to the first floor, to a fine sitting-room and bedroom with a great four-poster and furnishings of the first order, my husband taking little notice of me or my

small baggage, but continually warning the servants to take
care of the bundles of books which were unloaded from the
back of the coach. These were placed all anyhow about the
floor, quite spoiling the appearance of the room, but I did not
know how to protest, nor how to ask whether we could not
eat, for after the journey I was sorely in need of sustenance.

Happily Mr Nelham, having assured himself that all his
belongings were now brought up, ordered the servant to bring
'some food', and when asked what he required merely
answered that it mattered not so long as it was palatable!

While waiting for the food I went into the bedroom and,
removing my upper clothing, was wiping my body with some
cool water that stood there when without ceremony the door
opened and Mr Nelham appeared. I clutched the cloth to me,
being unhappy that he should find me unclothed and think it
an invitation to that love-making which I was not eager for.
But he simply walked to the bed and picked up a book which
lay there, returning with scarce a glance at me to the outer
room – which gladdened me, but I was surprised that he
should have shown no interest in the goods he had so recently
acquired.

In some minutes, a boy came with new baked bread, some
cheese and a dish of coffee, to which we sat, Mr Nelham only
complaining at the expense of coffee when a dish of milk (he
said) would have been sufficient. After which, he took his
leave without announcing when he would return, and left me.

Recovered now from the journey I was anxious to see the
town, and shortly set out to walk the streets, which were
crowded with a great variety of people of every class including
high-spirited young men dressed in knee-breeches and white
stockings, whom I took to be students. I walked, and walked,
interested by all the sights and sounds, the traders crying their
wares and the people buying them, the serving women about
their business and the gentle folk simply walking, it seemed,
for pleasure – especially upon the paths by the swan-full river
lying below some of the wonderfully handsome college buildings which I now saw for the first time.

Returning to the inn, I found that dinner was under way and
since there was no sign of Mr Nelham, sat down to boiled and

baked meats, pies, tarts and dishes of fruit and sweetmeats
and a good bottle of Madeira, after which I lay upon the
bed and fell into a sleep from which I awoke only with the
return of my husband, who announced that he had taken
rooms in a house by Trinity College, in whose library he had
much work to do. He then settled once more to his studies,
having called for a servant to remove the remains of my
meal, upon which he seemed to look with disfavour.

It was a wearisome afternoon, for he did not stir and I did
not like to move, not being wishful to fall out upon my first
day as a wife. In due course came supper time, at which Mr
Nelham ordered up merely a dish of soup and a piece of
fish, which he ate in the old-fashioned way with his fingers
(we had had forks at Alcovary, as long as I could remember) and washed down with ale.

Now was come the time I dreaded – bed time – and I
retired first, undressing to my shift and creeping quietly
between the sheets. Before long, Mr Nelham came, drew
off his breeches, and in his shirt and drawers came also to
bed. But he snuffed out the candle and fell immediately into
a snoring sleep, while I lay awake feeling that though I did
not wish for his attentions it was strange for a woman just
that day married not to have knowledge of her husband,
especially since she did not seem so undesirable that other
men kept altogether clear of her.

After an hour of lying wakeful, I slipped from the bed
and went into the next room for a drink of ale, which stood
still in a tankard upon the table next the window. Outside,
the inn yard was now empty and there was only some noise
from a distant room where a party was still at eating and
drinking. As I lifted the ale to my lips, I looked across the
yard where a light stood in a room opposite and there into
view strode a fine, naked fellow bearing a girl, similarly
bare, in his arms, whom setting on her feet he kissed
soundly, as she him, the candle-light flickering over their
bodies in a warm glow and surrounding them with, as it
were, a golden nimbus of light. As I looked, he slowly bent,
or slid as it were down the length of her body, his head
disappearing below the window as it declined to her waist.

She, throwing her head back, showed now all the signs of pleasure, her mouth open and her eyes sparkling while he was at that occupation I could only guess at. But as she threw back her shoulders and her breasts lifted in an ecstasy, the light beneath them bathing their full roundness in a rich aureate lustre, I could not help clutching myself to counterfeit the pleasure, and with the movements of my fingers bringing about a dim shadow of the joy I could see she experienced as she slowly sank towards her lover and out of my sight.

I took another swallow of ale, but it had now lost its savour. Disconsolate, I fumbled my way back to bed, and in time fell into uneasy slumber.

Next morning early we moved to the rooms Mr Nelham had taken and which proved no more handsome than I expected, cramped and dirty and ill-furnished as they were. I begged that at least I could have a maid to clean and serve, and he grudgingly agreed as long as she did not cost more than two shilling a week – to which the daughter of the house, Moll, agreed, being a slovenly creature but better than nothing, and I put her immediately to work to clear the rooms of some dirt, while I attempted to set out to best advantage the few comforts I had brought with me.

The bedroom looked out over the river and the end of the library where Mr Nelham evidently meant to spend most of his honeymoon. By ten o'clock – for we had risen at seven, and were installed by nine, at which time the library opened – a splashing revealed that just below our windows was a place where the students were wont to bathe when the weather was hot. I incautiously put my head out, and was rewarded by a display of naked young manhood in which I must admit to have taken some pleasure. Yet I was somewhat discomfited when I was seen, and far from modestly hiding themselves several of the boys (for they were of age between fifteen and twenty) grasped their persons and, as it were, offered them to me, whereat I was bound to laugh, but withdrew.

Having set the rooms to rights – or lifted them to as bare an elegance as I could command – I found myself each day with nothing to do except walk out and wait for Mr Nelham's return; this soon palled. Then out of curiosity one day I opened a book I noticed he carried always with him, and found it to be Mr William Lilly's *Christian Astrology*, published some one hundred and sixty-five years earlier and of some reputation. I had not previously looked into such matters but now with time at my hand speedily taught myself what was needful to command some scanty part of the subject, and was delighted to recognise its truth. For instance, the pictures of my father (that he was of the nature of the Sun, 'Arrogant and Proud, disdaining all men, cracking his Pedigree, Pur-blind in sight and judgment, troublesome, domineering, a mere vapour . . .') and of my dearest Frank (of Venus' nature, 'very fair Lovely Eyes, and a little black; a round face, and not large, fair Hair, smooth and plenty of it, and of a light brown colour, a lovely mouth and cherry lips, a Body very delightful, lovely and exceeding well shaped . . .') were nothing short of absolute portraits, so that I determined to study the subject fully, though without informing Mr Nelham of it – whom I soon discovered from the book came under dominance of Mercury. His looks were described there, most particularly his 'straight, thin spare body, high forehead and somewhat narrow, long face, long nose, thin lips and long arms', and his manner, 'his tongue and pen against every man' (as I soon discovered), 'wholly bent to fool his estate and time in prating and trying nice conclusions to no purpose.' But the final end, that he was 'given to wicked arts', I did not yet know, but was soon to discover, to my cost.

The discovery of his interest in the black arts came a week after we had set to live in our rooms, where he unexpectedly returned – having forgot a book – to find me looking from the bedroom window at the bathing students and exchanging a word or two with the more familiar of them. At this he first looked displeased, then sitting me down asked me whether I was not surprised that to that date he had not offered me the familiarity of a husband.

I admitted that I had wondered at it, whereupon he said

that it was to his purpose that I should remain virgin for the
time, but that I should soon know why. Indeed he said that
the coming weekend was to see what he described as my
'deflowering', at which I knew not whether to laugh or cry,
not knowing the meaning of half the words he employed,
but only guessing at them. But I maintained a solemn face,
so he called me a good girl and left me. I heard nothing
more until the Sunday following when in the evening, just
as I thought of preparing for bed, he told me to dress, for
we were going out.

In some confusion I put on my outer clothing and we
descended to find a coach waiting, into which we climbed
and rode for half an hour to a hill outside the city, indeed
right into the country, for there was no light to suggest any
human habitation when we got from the coach. In the light
of a full moon which whitened the fields, my husband led
the way across a field and into a wood whence we emerged
eventually into a clearing. There in the moonlight stood
perhaps a dozen men and some women, waiting – and waiting for Mr Nelham, so it seemed. He led me silently into the
centre of the clearing, where was a grassy hummock or
table, and nearby some vessels from which my husband
sprinkled some substances – I knew not what – upon the
ground, muttering beneath his breath as he did so.

At a signal from Mr Nelham, the dim figures gathered in
a circle around the grassy mound, and I saw to my astonishment that they wore upon their heads masks formed like the
faces of animals – foxes, dogs, a lion, a wolf . . . My
husband led me to the hummock and, reaching out, to my
astonishment not only threw my cloak from me, but began
to remove my shift. I held to it but he insisted, and finally
rent it in twain, so that I stood naked before the company,
the cool air raising bumps upon my skin.

In silence, the circle closed. The four people nearest the
altar threw their cloaks to the ground and were disclosed as
handsome naked youths, who then began to embrace each
other lasciviously while Mr Nelham, dropping his cloak,
was revealed in what seemed to be a priest's cope – yet was
strangely embroidered with serpents and with signs and

symbols which were unknown to me. As he turned, I saw that beneath it he wore nothing, his thin body veiled only with sparse grey hairs. He laid me on the grassy mound, upon which I now saw to my horror stood a crooked cross, my face up to the full moon. I lay, shaking in every limb, while from my husband's lips fell a series of strange sentences in which I recognised Latin words, but in an order which seemed entirely without reason even to my small knowledge of the language. The congregation responded with grunts and animal howlings. Reaching behind him, Mr Nelham produced two black candles, one of which he placed in each of my hands, at which there was a positive shriek, and the animal-headed worshippers threw their cloaks to the ground, and nakedly embraced each other. Beside the altar the two pairs of boys were now at the game, two of them bent over with their hands resting near my head and my feet, while their companions, with wild moans of pleasure, held their hips and thrust into them from behind. Meanwhile Mr Nelham continued to recite his gibberish, then bowed himself to kiss between my legs. As he did so the watching figures drew apart and to my astonishment began to piss upon the ground, at the same time chanting Latin words which I recognised to my horror as Our Lord's Prayer, but said backwards. As it ended, my husband called forward a tall blindfold fellow in a cloak, which as he stood above me he threw back to disclose a magnificient figure, a great chest and arms above a slim waist, and a member so large as to make those few with which I was then familiar appear slender indeed (and to be truthful, in my subsequent experience, which has not been small – as the reader will discover – I have never seen a tool so great, being, it seemed, as thick as most men's wrists). Standing behind him, my husband placed his hands upon his shoulders – to which he could scarcely reach – and guided him (for he was still blindfold) to the altar, where by the use of his hands he placed himself between my legs, whereupon he thrust into me with such violence that I shrieked – my cry echoed by the vile congregation, now coupling upon the grass before me.

Mr Nelham – for can I truly describe him as my husband? – placed his hands upon the giant's buttocks as they thrust at me – and despite my terror, which rendered me incapable of movement, I could not but be aware of the pleasure such a lover could convey, nor was it possible altogether to deny that my body responded to his own, for despite myself I felt my loins lifting to meet his as I gripped his shoulders, partly to prevent myself being stifled by his weight, and partly, I confess, in passion. Beneath the fingers of my left hand, I noticed the red scar of a wound which had only recently been inflicted – under, I wondered, a similar circumstance? After a short time, the man raised his head, the black cloth still across his eyes, and shouted 'Now!' as he exploded within me. At which to my amazement my husband thrust his hand between us at the point where our privities were joined and I felt his fingers scrabbling. Withdrawing, he looked at his hand for a moment, then administered a violent smack to the giant's buttocks, who raised himself, whereupon Mr Nelham positively drew his hand across my mound, sore as it was, and again examined his fingers. I saw, even in the moonlight, his face darken with anger. Turning to the congregation, he shouted: 'It is a fault! He will not come!' and without more ado strode from the circle.

My lover, in evident confusion, rose and tore off his blindfold but, without looking at me, groped for his cloak upon the ground; one pair of the youths at my side also broke away, and gesturing at me in distaste made off (though the others were too far gone in pleasure to take notice of the confusion, and continued their congress, as did some of the couples who still lay clasped in each other's arms upon the grass).

I rose and gathering my clothes put them on as best I might in their torn state and found my way back to the road, where Mr Nelham was standing silent by the coach. He handed me into it roughly and without a word; nor did he speak on the way back to our rooms, where he discarded his cloak and the cope beneath it, and threw himself naked into bed.

After a while, I followed him, confused almost to death, and cried to him to let me know in what I had disappointed him.

' 'Twas all flim-flam!' he cried. 'Your father lied – you are no virgin!' – and was silent again.

I was no further informed, for I knew not the true meaning of the word – no one had explained it to me, nor if they had would I have understood that a husband should consider it important that no other man should have lain with their wife before themselves. Did they require, after all, that she should not have kissed another man, or eaten with him, or perhaps even spoken to him? Now, of course, I know better, but then I was innocence itself. Nor did I suspect what I now know, that Mr Nelham had needed a virgin not for himself but for the rite with which, in Black Mass, he hoped to raise the fiend, in concert with his Cambridge friends, many of them students of Dr Dee and readers of his manuscripts on converse with angels and devils which my husband had studied in the library of Trinity College.

So I lay for a while silent, and then perhaps hoping to console him in his disappointment stretched out my hand and laid it between his thighs, but all there was cold and limp, and moreover he struck my hand away with such violence that I let out a cry and thereafter lay quiet and still as he through a long night.

Towards morning I fell into a restless sleep, and woke to find Mr Nelham gone from the bed and in the next room packing his things. I asked if we were leaving, but got no reply, and thinking that this must be so began to pack my own few belongings. But when he had done, he turned and threw a few coins at my feet saying, 'Go, woman, back to your father, or to the D---l for all I care. I divorce you!' and seizing his packets, strode from the room. Desperately, I followed him, pleading to him to stay, for what should I do in a strange town where I knew no one and no one knew me, and did he mean me to starve in the gutter? But he repeated that he cared not, and went from the house only to be speedily lost in the traffic of the street.

I returned to the room and picked up the coins, which amounted to only fifty shilling. Would this be sufficient to hire a coach to return me to Alcovary? And would my father and mother receive me there? Certainly they had been aware of my state before they gave me to Mr Nelham, but this did not mean they were any more happily disposed toward me – indeed, perhaps the reverse.

Below my window the sound of cheerful voices announced that the students were at their morning baths. I looked out to where they were at play, laughing as they ducked and splashed each other, without care or thought.

I wept.

Chapter Five

The Adventures of Andy

It was with some trepidation that I made my way through the dining-room and long gallery towards the rooms occupied by the Ladies Elizabeth and Margaret, upon whom I had never yet set my eye. I feared that Mr Caister must have told them I was responsible for Sir Walter's fall, and as I went it seemed to me that the brow of every pictured Rawby in the many paintings upon the walls was bent upon me in admonition.

I opened the door which Tom had pointed out to me as leading to the ladies' apartments and entered. It had been explained to me that one never knocked at any door in the Hall before entering; servants were considered as furniture, and having one enter even if one of the ladies were upon the close stool was a nothing to them – no more than being observed by a table or a chair.

However, nothing untoward met my eye on this occasion; the two sisters sat side by side upon a couch, facing the door, each fanning herself with an identical fan, and both made the same beckoning gesture to me to come and stand near them. I have never seen two human beings more similar; but that one was dressed in blue silk, the other in pink, one would swear they were matched in a mirror, the one's fair hair dressed in the same way as the other, one's cold blue eyes the counterfeits of the other's, the same slim figure and upright carriage to be seen in each.

'So this is the fellow who is so adept . . .' said one, '. . . at handing the soap,' completed the other.

I bowed.

'A most unfortunate accident,' said the first, 'but one,' went on the second, 'that was after all but accident?'

I bowed again.

'No doubt you were concerned,' said the lady on my right, 'to prevent a misfortune in the bath room . . .'

'. . . by removing such a dangerous commodity from the floor,' completed the lady on my left.

Another bow.

And so, in turn completing each other's sentences, they continued to play with me, but entirely without malice. It was sad that Sir Walter was discommoded, for the women servants would not now have the pleasure of his company abed; such a cause for concern that he was now suffering acute agony and would not walk for several weeks; so tragic that his carriage would have to be sent for to take him to town next day. But they were sure that my care in the matter had been exquisite, and that the fact that a small piece of soap had escaped my hands was no fault of mine. I was not to feel in any way that the family attached blame to me, and I was to be assured that My Lord, though Sir Walter had complained bitterly, had been told by all that I was in no way to blame.

I was of course much comforted, and my bows were now accompanied by a real feeling of pleasure.

'We trust,' said one of the ladies, 'that little Ellen . . .'

'. . . has conveyed her gratitude to her hero?'

'Or that at all events . . .'

'. . . she will shortly do so.'

I made no reply.

'Well, you are a fine fellow . . .'

'. . . but a quiet one. What age are you?'

'Sixteen, my ladies,' I replied.

They nodded in unison, like two toy creatures on a toy couch, and eyed me up and down. I stood feeling like an animal at auction, being measured for my attributes by someone considering a purchase.

They turned to each other, and nodded again. Then one of them picked up her reticule, and fumbled in it, and something dropped from her hand to roll almost to my foot. I bent to pick it up. It was a gold guinea. I made to place it upon a table.

'Ah, what have you found there, young Andy?' she said.

'I think,' said the other, 'it is a piece of soap which fell from his pocket.'

'What a dangerous thing,' said the first, 'you should really . . .'

'. . . keep your possessions more safely about you.'

'That will be all,' the lady in blue said. I bowed again and left, somewhat bewildered but by no means displeased. Later, Mr Caister explained that Sir Walter had – mm – always been viewed as an unpleasant and unwelcome guest by everyone in the house – in particular by the female servants, among whom he took his choice. So did many guests in the house, though often with kindness and always with generous gifts, but Sir Walter had been always boorish in affection and mean in reward. Lady Elizabeth and Lady Margaret had hated him since he had first encountered them, when they were scarcely older than I, and he had rudely assaulted them – something for which My Lord had almost shown him the door, except for the financial hold he had upon him.

'Well, you – mm – you have set your foot well upon the stairs to – mm – advancement,' said the steward. 'Perhaps in – mm – thirty years you may aspire even to my position!' – and placing his arm about my shoulders, he laid a smacking kiss upon my cheek, then patting me on the rump sent me about my business. My delight at the thought of spending fifty years as a servant was limited, for my relative freedom at Alcovary had taught me that the gentle life offered more prospect of pleasure than a lifetime in service, and I had even then, though without conscious planning, laid an ambition to make my way into a class far different to that to which I was born.

I had just time to go to the room I was to share with Tom and hide my golden guinea beneath the mattress of my truckle bed before it was time to prepare the tables for supper, into which trooped My Lord, accompanied by the two ladies and the guests, all of whom were men. When I expressed my surprise at this to Tom, he explained that it was rarely that My Lord's friends brought their wives to the Hall; that some of them had an eye for the maids here, and others sometimes brought doxies, two of whom were even now upstairs, eating their food from trays taken to them from the kitchens, for they were not of a rank to eat with the family.

The meal, though not a remarkable one for the Hall, amazed me by its grandness – or rather by its profligacy, for the manner in which it was taken was far from grand. At Alcovary supper had been consumed in polite silence, with little conversation, Sir Franklin presiding with a noble mien. Here My Lord was deep in conversation with his cronies at one end of the table, while his daughters were equally surrounded by gentlemen whose conversation was no less lewd for their presence. The talk turned particularly on the Prince Regent and his unfortunate wife, every aspect of whose character and person was explored with the utmost frankness, and whose behaviour (if one-tenth of the particulars were reported correctly) reflected the morals of an alley cat.

As to the table, it creaked under beef, venison, geese, turkeys, etc., with Burgundy, champagne (white and rosy), Hermitage, red and white, Constantia, Sauterne, Madeira and punch. Every other breath issued forth a toast, drunk in bumpers, and long before supper was over, which was not until well past midnight, many of My Lord's companions were under the table, though he – not the least assiduous in consumption of drink – remained apparently sober (and Tom told me, in an undertone, that he had never been seen drunk). We had little to do other than bring more supplies of viands and then to stand attentively by – and after the day's activities, I was by then almost asleep, and more than once my shoulders touched the wall and I awoke with a start from a half-slumber. This was despite the most interesting thing to me, which was an orchestra of ten men who played music throughout the meal – to which no one listened. Tom, again my informant, told me that My Lord spent no less than three hundred and fifty pound a year on this band, which he had set up in rivalry to that kept by his distant relative Lord Chandos; it included viols and flute, and an Italian with a guitar, who sometimes played alone (though no one heard him). He, Tom hinted, was a tutor to Lady Elizabeth – 'and not only of music,' said he with a grin.

At last the evening came to an end, the reeking room was cleared, and we were free to go to bed up one of the two stone staircases which led one to the men's rooms, one to the women's. There were doors to each stairway which Mrs Tickert locked with one of the bunch of keys at her waist – a sight which somewhat dismayed me, since it seemed to promise a more monastic life than that which the situation at first had appeared to promise. However, Tom's only reply when I remarked upon it was a wink, and soon we were in the small room beneath the roof which we were to share. We shrugged off our jackets and small-clothes – glad to be free of the constriction – and yawning, I fell upon my bed. But Tom said, 'Not so quick to doze, young Andy!' – and when I looked a question, led me to the window, which he threw open.

There was a half-moon, throwing just enough light for me to see that a parapet or platform ran below the tilt of the roof above the eaves, and what was my surprise when Tom bent to crawl out upon it, beckoning me to follow. A tree-climber since I was a little fellow, I was nothing loath at the height and narrowness of the platform, nor for the cold, though I now wore only my drawers, for the night was balmy and we had been for some hours in a close and smoky atmosphere. But it seemed a strange exercise for a time when I would have been glad to be a friend to my bed.

We crawled for perhaps twenty feet, at one point flattening ourselves to the parapet as we passed below a window inside which I heard men's voices, and supposed they were those of the other footmen. Then we came to a low wall over which Tom skipped and I followed, and in another five or seven feet to a window below which Tom gave a low whistle. It was immediately thrown up, and I followed Tom through it to find myself in a room the exact counterpart of the one we had left, but occupied by Tabby and Ellen who, clad in the lightest of shifts, threw their arms around us and gave us welcoming hugs. From beneath her bed, Tabby produced a bottle, and dry from the evening's fug, we were all quick to imbibe – by which time Tom and Tabby were embraced upon her bed, his hand upon her breast while hers explored beneath the band of his drawers. Sitting by Ellen upon her bed I was uncertain how to proceed, for her natural modesty and the unkind behaviour she had received from Sir Walter Flount made me think that perhaps any offer from me would be unwelcome.

But soon, watching as Tabby drew Tom's drawers from him and threw off her shift, and they fell to play, I grew amorous, and began to kiss Ellen, who replied with an embrace no less pleasant, after which it was little time before we too were in a state of nature. The room was lit only by a single candle in a corner, but even by its low light it was interesting to see the contrast between the bodies of the two girls: Tabby, round and plump, her breasts swinging as she kneeled over Tom's recumbent form, and her ample thighs quivering as he playfully thumped them with his fists, encouraging her to lower herself upon him, and Ellen, her breasts small and round, her waist slim, and her thighs fine and lithe, though strong. As she lay, I bent my head to take her nipples between my lips, gently tweaking them with my tongue and tenderly nibbling with my teeth until I felt them harden and her body began to quiver beneath me. I threw one of my thighs between her legs, and my prick, now standing eagerly, lay upon her belly. Her hands slid over my shoulders and down to my waist, then under, and I lifted myself to let her reach my standing part and caress it gently, then pointed it to the delicious quintain at which I aimed.

As I slipped into heaven her arms tightened about me, and as I began to move the candlelight struck deep yellow sparks from her eyes. A few feet away, Tabby was panting as she rose and fell upon Tom's body. Ellen threw out a hand to take her friend's hand, and we all laughed low and pleasant together as we reached the top of our delight.

After a while, we fell asleep, all tangled together; woke to love, and slept again; and finally I was shook to full wakefulness by Tom to see a dim pink light announcing the dawn, and we barely had time to return to our own room before Fred, the oldest footman, knocked upon our door to call us to work.

The days passed pleasantly enough. They were long, but the work not unduly arduous, and the four of us – Tom and Tabby, myself and Ellen – were together as much as we might be, not only at night, but during the day time. In our free hours we walked in those parts of the grounds which were open to us and plunged often into a little lake in a remote corner of the park – which we were very glad of, for we were forbidden to use the bath room, and the days were hot in that summer.

In the meantime, I had come to know Signor Giovanni Cesareo, the guitar player, who had come originally from Piedmont, whence he had fled because, he said, at the courts there they now favoured only French musicians. So he had travelled to England for employment, and was happy at Rawby, where he taught Lady Elizabeth the guitar and the lute. Seeing that I was interested, he not only gave me some lessons, showing me how to finger the instrument and strike its strings, but, saying I had a natural bent, lent me an old instrument of his own that I could practise upon. Soon I became quite adept, at first fingering without the music but then learning from him how to read the notes – not, to me, more difficult than words upon a page – after which in a short time I was able to play some easy pieces, to the great delight of Tabby and Ellen and, I think, somewhat to the jealousy of Tom.

It was one afternoon at the end of June or the beginning of July – I remember the time because My Lord that day called the whole household together to hear the great news of the victory of Wellington at Waterloo – when the four of us were lying upon the grass after swimming, gently toying with each other, that I saw a white face between the trees, and a dark form. I started to my feet with an oath.

'What's that?' demanded Tom, and when I replied that there was a spy, replied with a laugh, 'Oh, 'tis only Beau Rust!'

This was Henry Rust, the father of the late Lady Rawby, an old man who had passed almost all his life in Bath, was thought once to have been a curate but later gave up Holy Orders for his attachment to the ladies, and was known as Beau Rust for the manner in which by his example in elegance and the care of dress he had been the descendent of his great precursor Beau Brummell, the arbiter of fashion in the town. Now, at an age no one was certain of – but certainly of seventy years, for he talked of travelling in Poland when Poniatowski was elected King in the year of '64 – he lived in rooms above his granddaughters and could be seen like some shadow, always dressed in black, moving silently about the house and gardens.

' 'Tis said,' Tom reported, 'that he spends his time with books, and is upon some great project, but nothing as yet has appeared.'

His meals were taken to him by one of the ladies' maids, and he employed no servant of his own, but lived like a recluse. I had no idea of a closer acquaintance but a week later, as I was passing along the gallery, I was plucked by the arm and found a little old man all in black, an old yellowing wig perched on his head, at my shoulder.

'Boy!' said Beau Rust. 'Boy, come now to my rooms. I have a question to put to you – yet ye shall not minish ought from your bricks or your daily task (Exodus five, nineteen).'

Having spent some time in persuading Mr Caister that I was no twiddlepoop, but one for the girls, I was concerned that Beau Rust had designs on my person, for he being my ladies' grandfather 'twould probably be difficult to excuse myself. But I followed him up a narrow stairway beyond my ladies' rooms, thence into a corridor, and into a room so busy with objects that it dizzied me; it was a litter of books, papers, boxes small and large, pieces of clothing, with not a chair nor a table that was not piled high.

Throwing a small pile of books to the floor, Beau Rust sat himself down and looked up at me.

'Now, boy, I am at work.'

I said nothing, there being nothing to say.

'I am at a great work, and this work goeth fast on and prospereth in my hands (Ezra five, eight). I am to restore the last works of Aretino. Aretino was a great man of three hundred year ago, sent out of Rome for writing indecencies, and in Venice wrote marvellously of the congress of men and women. I have here his sonnets,' patting an old book, 'which I am putting into English, and also the few remaining fragments of the drawings of men and women at pleasure which illustrated them – for the whole were lost and only pieces remain. But we shall gather the pieces thereof, even every good piece, the thigh and the shoulder (Ezekial, twenty-four, four).'

He threw open a large parcel of papers, and there indeed were fragments of drawings – here a leg thrown over a shoulder, there a female arse, there a man's hand clutching at a limb – but nothing full or complete. These drawings were printed, but had been traced onto separate papers, and attempts made – by Beau Rust himself, no doubt – to complete them, but the additions were barely recognisable as human beings, the figures being unkempt and distorted.

Beau Rust coughed.

'Um – hah! – you are a fellow of parts, young what's-yer-name . . .?'

'Andy, sir.'

'Young Andy. Seen you with the girls, out in the woods. Well-muscled princox, and lively at the game. Now for a sovereign or two, would you and your young woman – haven't I seen her about the house?'

'Ellen, sir.'

'If that's her name, Ellen, yes, Ellen then – would you and she care to pose for me? As you see, I haven't a sufficient memory of the human form to be accurate in the matter of limbs . . . I will show the nations thy nakedness (Nahum three, five.)'

'I'll ask her, sir.'

Beau Rust nodded, and coughed again, and shuffled the papers, and waved me away. I found the door, and the passage, and the stairway.

Next day, when we were enjoying an hour's leisure between breakfast and the afternoon meal, I told Tom, Tabby and Ellen. Tom laughed.

'Go on, Ellen, it's all right – an easy sovereign! Only one of the old fogram's quillets. What harm?'

'No', says Ellen, 'no, I couldn't. I'm no quean – what I do, in that line, I do for myself,' and she blushed.

'I'd do it,' said Tabby, 'and no worry! Sovereigns ain't so plentiful that I'd throw 'em away when offered.'

'Well,' said Tom, sharply, 'they wasn't offered to you.'

Tabby lent over and kissed him, and that was that. But later that day she found me alone, when we were setting the supper table and I was to and fro to the kitchen, and she said:

'Andy, make the offer to the Beau. I can slip away – Tom'll never know, and the gold can go to my little clutch. Go on – unless you don't fancy a try with me, of course.'

The difficulty was that I did very much fancy a try with Tabby, but didn't care to display falsehood to Tom – or to Ellen, for the matter of that, for she was a dear, good girl. But the truth was that she now looked upon me as her regular lad and not only followed me everywhere with big eyes, but in our warmish moments was now as lively as a sleeping mole, just lying upon her back and waiting for me to reach my conclusion, so that since I could not help seeing with half an eye the tricks Tabby played upon Tom in the way of lechery, I could scarcely help but be jealous of his happiness.

To be short, I put forward the word to Beau Rust and giving out that she was going to spend the evening with her aunt in Rawby village, Tabby slipped away from Tom and met me at the foot of the stairway to the Beau's apartments. When we entered them we found he had cleared a space in the corner of his room and built a sort of couch (I suppose of books and other rubbish, covered with a cloth), while nearby sat a chair with an attachment upon its arm whereby one could read, or in this case draw, at ease.

First giving us some liquor to warm ourselves, as he said, the Beau sat himself down upon his chair and said, coughing dryly, 'Well – hah! – off with your clothes and settle to it! I have put the bottle to ye, that I may look upon thy nakedness (Habakuk two, fifteen)' and rummaged among the pile of papers at his feet to find one which he had marked.

It being so strange a situation, both Tabby and I found it a cold invitation enough, but hustled out of our things as we were asked, and stood somewhat awkwardly in front of the Beau, protecting our privities with our hands as best we might. He gave a croak.

'Hah! Not as I've seen you many a time up by the lake, my young beauties. Never mind – here, take this –'

And handed me a drawing, which was of the lower parts of a man in congress with a woman, but with her legs at a strange angle to his own.

'My vision – hah! – is that she was lying upon her back, her legs thrown over his shoulders. Kindly adopt the position. When – hah! – you are ready,' he added drily, staring at my gaying stick, which was of no size or movement, and which, because of the oddity of the moment, refused to budge when I handled it. Tabby next turned her attention to it, but not even the warm mumbling of her lips had its effect.

'Hah!' said the Beau, standing up and looking around at a loss. 'I failed to predict such a situation. Hah! The spoiler is fallen (Jeremiah forty-eight, thirty-two). Well, cast your eye upon these,' and handed us a book, which when opened proved to show some lascivious drawings which indeed after a while warmed me to some display, but not sufficient to improve the hour, for by the time Tabby had taken up her position and I mine, Jack had drooped once more.

But then the Beau tripped his way to a corner of the room and, coming back with a box, lifted out what appeared to be a room from a dolls' house – yet furnished with dolls no mother would give her daughter, for they were all beautifully measured wax figures of men and women embracing – upon the couches, the floors, the chairs, the tables. With a grinding sound, and an explosion of dust, the Beau wound a key at its back and pressed a switch – and lo! While from the inside of the box came the tinkling sound of a gavotte, the figures began to move. The chevalier with the flowing black locks pressed his loins against the backside of a large woman who with her lips was ministering to the person of a man in cardinal's robes, which parted at the front to show the distended tool at which she was busy. He in turn grasped in one hand the prick of a young footman, his wig all askew, who had his hand deep in the *décolletage* of a young lady sat with her back to him rising and falling upon the knees of a young man whose hands were raised in astonishment at the size of the prick of the negro servant, upon whose enormous instrument was balanced a cup into which tea was being poured by the mistress of the house, seated proudly at the centre of the picture, turning her head from tableau to tableau in happy approbation.

The lifelike appearance of the figures together with the enthusiasm of Tabby speedily restored my senses, and in a moment I had thrown her once more upon her back, and lifting her legs had dived beneath them to bury myself up to the hilt in her warmth. With a chuckle, Beau Rust seized his drawing paper and set to work. It occurred to me, simply, that perhaps we were expected to prolong our ecstasy so that he could take his time with delineation of our pose, but we were both too far gone in pleasure to attend to his wishes, if so they were, and we spent together in a copious explosion of pleasure. Upon which, panting, I turned to the Beau to find that his drawing had tailed off to an inconclusive scrawl, while he had fished his ancient equipment from his small-clothes and had that moment persuaded it to void up a small dribble of juice, though accompanied with a loud squeal of pleasure.

'Hah! Not had the joy these twenty years!' he said. 'Behold, it cometh, and every heart shall melt (Ezekial twenty-one, seven). My children, thank'ee – and, you see, the drawing – well, the – hah!' Not even the artist himself could pretend that the work of art he had produced was worth the two guineas he handed to us, tucking his clothes back into place the while. Tabby curtsied, all naked as she was, and I placed my gold piece between my teeth while I persuaded my still lively prick into my breeches.

Beau Rust waved us away.

'I shall send for ye again,' he said, 'to complete the next pose.'

We made our way down the staircase and past my ladies' rooms to find Tom at the corner of the long gallery, leaning against the door and looking grim.

'So,' he said, 'how was the Beau? Did he enjoy you both, or did you only enjoy each other?'

Tabby coloured, and saying nothing passed on, but Tom grasped my shoulder and spat: 'I take it unkindly, Master Andy, after the service I've been to you, that you should betray me in such a way. You may look to yourself, for I'm no longer your friend.'

Chapter Six

Sophie's Story

My fit of weeping did not last long – I am not a creature greatly given to self-pity – and soon the ringing of bells all over the city reminded me that 'twas Sunday morning, whereupon I decided to dress myself and walk upon the river bank at the back of the colleges beneath the shade of the willows and consider my position. Indeed it was a less than happy one, my husband of a mere few weeks having left me with only a little money, far from my home and parents, and they unlikely to welcome my return there, even should I wish it.

Half an hour later I left my rooms and turned down the alleyway which led to the river. As I rounded the corner, the noise of laughter greeted me and I realised that the young men were still at their bathing, and in the way in which I was to walk. Nevertheless, I walked on; many times had I seen Andy and my dear Frank bathing in Alcovary park, and they had never shown anything but pleasure that I should witness their sport. I had no distinct knowledge that other young men might disapprove or be ashamed at being seen in a state of nature, besides which these had signalled to me in high-spirited approbation when they saw me at my window. I certainly did not realise that only women of small repute frequented this alley, long claimed as a bathing place for the students, at a time when they were known to use it.

The latter fact perhaps accounted for the ribaldry which in the first instance greeted my appearance as I reached the river and found myself on a sort of platform upon which piles of clothes lay, and below which four youngsters were sporting.

'Come, Moll, dip!' was the cry, followed by 'Ay! Doff

thy bonnet and breeks, and plunge in!' But one of the boys clearly recognised me from my former smilings from the window, and swimming to the piles below the platform, reached up with one brown hand to lift his powerful shoulders above the water while he greeted me politely, waving down the grins and shouts of his comrades.

'Forgive us bathing below your window, ma'am,' he said, 'but it has been a custom here always.'

I assured him that I was not at all disturbed, and that but for the dirt of the river – into which all the latrines of Cambridge poured their waste – I would be tempted to join them.

'Ah!' he laughed. 'I admit 'tis no great pleasure, for we must wash again when we are at home. For real joy, there are other places outside the town where the water is deep and fresh. You are a swimmer, ma'am? For the ladies of Cambridge in general are not greatly given to the sport.'

I told him I had been used to swim every day, in the summer, at my father's house, whereupon he called to his friends to inform them of the fact, and they too came to the bank to talk – and to cut the tale short invited me to go with them that afternoon by punt to Grantchester, there to eat a meal and to swim, if we so chose. Unaffectedly, they pulled themselves up to the platform, and I must confess that while I seemed to avert my eyes from their nakedness, I could not but admire their forms as they shook the shiny drops of water from them and hustled into their clothes, or rather their rags for, as my first friend, whose name he told me was Jack, informed me they wore only old things to the river which would otherwise be soiled by the filth of the water. I wrinkled my nose at this and Jack said that indeed, but for custom, he at least would be disinclined to immerse himself in that part of the river, but custom at the university died hard. Moreover, in the heat of summer it was the easiest way to be cool.

After some bread and cheese and a glass of ale at home, I went at two o'clock to the river bank just above Queen's College – passing the great chapel, whence the sound of singing came sweetly on the summer air – and there met my friend Jack, with two other boys of perhaps eighteen who I had seen at the bathing-place. One, Coln, was a dark-haired Irishman, and the second, George, a slim boy not unlike my Frank. They handed me into one of the wooden boats known as punts which are propelled by poles like Venetian gondolas upon the waters of the Cam, and there we sat waiting, it seemed, for another member of the party. But when I looked a question, Jack explained that we paused for a college servant, Will, from Trinity, who hired himself out as a puntsman for those who did not wish to expend their energy too freely.

'And here he comes, himself!' cried Coln, and in a moment the punt rocked as a large young man of perhaps thirty years leaped in from the bank and pulled a forelock. I felt, as I set eyes on him, that he was familiar to me, and when with a nod of deference he peeled off his shirt to seize the punt pole, I was in no doubt. I had surely seen him before, for he was none other than the giant who had been led to ravish me upon the grassy mount where Mr Nelham had hoped to raise the Devil, the previous night.

My embarrassment the reader will understand! I was forced to lie facing the puntsman, and could do nothing but study those limbs with which I had so lately though briefly been covered! Though a blindfold had veiled his eyes, there was no mistaking the angry, red, recent scar upon his right shoulder which I had clearly seen in the moonlight, nor the shock of brown curly hair which fell to his shoulders and had tumbled over my face, nor – I fancied – the shape of that enormous machine which I now seemed to see bursting at the seams of his small-clothes, and which had come near to bursting me!

Jack and his friends seemed not to notice my preoccupation, for they chattered gaily on about their life at the university, which seemed in the main to be composed of sporting, gambling and wenching – though they complained that too many of the local wenches were poxed, a circumstance they set down to over-willingness on their parts to 'fuck anyone for fourpence' ('begging your pardon, ma'am,' said Coln with a blush).

Soon, in the heat of the afternoon, I simply closed my eyes and surrendered myself to the gliding motion of the punt as it slid over smooth water out of the city and away to the south. The boys, too, fell quiet and seemed to doze (though Jack, nearest to me, fell to gently fondling my foot and lower leg, in an indolent manner). Only the trickle of water from the punt-pole as it was lifted from the water to be plunged in once more disturbed the quiet for a while. Then came a sudden explosion of sound as we rounded a corner and came to a bathing-place at Grantchester Meadows which, George explained to me, was sacred to the dons or teachers of the university and, it seemed, to their catamites. Through lowered lids, for I did not wish to exhibit my curiosity, I saw indeed a cluster of bodies lying upon the bank, some of which seemed to be immodestly entwined, though, Jack explained without my asking, it was in the grove beyond that the more intimate embraces were said to take place. And as I watched a beautiful, fair-haired, naked youth indeed broke from the grove followed by a plump, pale, elderly fellow, white stomach swinging uneasily·as he trotted towards the bank, then, seeing me, turned his back to sit upon the grass scowling over his shoulder while his erstwhile companion plunged into the river only feet from us, causing a wave which rocked us dangerously for a moment.

On we went, between rows of poplars, sometimes passing below the branches of a willow so low that they threatened to sweep our polesman into the water, and which patched us for a moment or two with a shade dappled with round circles of light like the dots on the old rocking horse in the nursery at Alcovary. In an hour or so we passed Grantchester and a little further on tied up where a bank held back a deep, dark pool of water under the grateful green shade of some trees.

This, Jack told me, was known as Byron's Pool, for 'twas here the poet used to come to bathe when he was at Cambridge only ten years before, sometimes bringing with him the handsome boy chorister Eddleston, who was his favourite. We climbed onto the bank – the giant, Will, offering me his hand to steady me. I clasped it, my arm lying along the length of his, and the meeting of our flesh did, I confess, send a thrill through me, for his muscles made it – as I clearly recalled – hard as iron.

The sun beating down upon the punt had warmed us, and without delay we threw off our clothes and plunged into the pool, the sudden shock of the cold water delighting us, though soon it became merely a pleasant coolness as our bodies grew used to the flow of the water around them. Soon the boys were diving to swim between my legs, or vanishing beneath the water some distance away, suddenly to appear behind me. Before long they began to grow familiar, and as they passed beneath me I would feel a hand slide over my thigh. Then Jack, his head emerging from the water at my side, enquired whether I was not cold and applied his palm to my breast in order to discover whether such was the case.

After a while I made for the bank and climbed out, dropping to the grass beneath a tree. I looked around for Will, but he had vanished. Meanwhile Jack, Coln and George were also climbing to the bank, and fell to the ground at my side, George producing from a bag he had been carrying some bottles of ale which he opened and handed us. We drank as the warm breeze played over our limbs and the beads of clear water gradually evaporated upon our cooled bodies.

I lay back in the warm air while the three boys reclined at my side, seeming to admire my form, which I had no thought of covering. I looked, indeed, at their figures with a similiar interest, for my acquaintance with the male figure was still somewhat limited. Coln, as I have said, was not unlike Frank in form, save that I saw to my distress that he seemed to be somewhat deformed, for at the end of his tool the skin, rather than forming a pouting cover, was drawn back in some way, exposing the red tip in what seemed an almost provocatively naked manner. (I later discovered, of course, that this was an appearance some men's instruments had, as the result of an operation more common among the Jewish race, and called circumcision.) Jack and

George were more conventionally formed, George the slimer of the two, with an almost feminine build, Jack more muscular; he was, I learned, a great athlete.

After a while I fell into a doze, and was awakened by a tickling at my right breast, which I soon found was caused by Jack, who was leaning over me and applying the tip of his tongue to my nipple, while the other two boys looked on with interest. I could not fail to notice from the corner of my eye that their tools, while not fully extended, were now considerably larger than they had been under the influence of the cool waters – lying upon their thighs in tumid pride rather than being shrunken between them – while I could feel Jack's nuzzling at my hip like a puppy searching for comfort. I reached down and took it in my hand, which the other two took as a signal of consent, for in a moment George was applying his hand to my other breast, feeling its texture like a market woman examining a pear, while Coln's tongue entered first my navel, then traced a moist path downwards into the hair below, and I felt his fingers part my lower lips so that it could seek out the little bud which is the seat of woman's pleasure.

Soon, they were jockeying each other for position, one no sooner lodged between my thighs than he was nudged away by another, until we all fell into a fit of laughter. At this George rolled over to reach into his breeches for a coin, which they tossed, and they reckoned as a result that Coln should take precedence and George next pride of place, while poor Jack must be content with what he could find.

And so it was that a few moments later George was sitting with his back against a fallen log while I knelt before him, bending to take his tool between my lips. At my back Coln applied his fleshy sword to its proper scabbard, while Jack, with a muttered *sauve qui peut*, sat at George's side, and reaching for my hand placed it upon his tool and the pendant globes beneath, now drawn up into a tight pouch with pleasurable anticipation.

I could not but think of the stricture of that flaybottomist Mr Gutteridge, that 'three into one won't go', for while the sensation of Coln's tool – whose squab vigour was more delightful than his slim body had promised – gave me much pleasure, the hard ground was discomfortable to my knees. And while the saponaceous lubricity of George's gaying-stick slid with exquisite nicety between my lips, seeming to knock sometimes at the very back of my throat, was far from unpleasant to me, it was uncomfortable indeed to rest my entire weight upon one hand in order that the other could occupy itself in Jack's lap, who nevertheless was first to reach full delight, for a fine gush flooded my hand and fell to the grass at George's side. And only a moment later, at almost the same time, I felt rather than tasted the essence of George's own joy, and the warmth of Coln's luxury within my lower belly.

The three boys almost immediately fell into lethargy. George slipped to one side, his head falling into Jack's lap, while Coln drew himself away and fell upon his back. I sat back upon my haunches and at that moment, seeing a movement behind a bush a stone's throw away, recognised rather than his full figure Will's enormous tool, vigourously massaged between his own palms.

Suggesting that I should wash myself, I rose to my feet and strode towards the bush. Thinking perhaps that he was unseen, he remained where he was until I placed my hand upon his shoulder and laying my finger on my lips, seized his arm and drew him to his feet and after me towards the river bank where without further ado I fell to my knees before him and took between my lips his huge piece, reaching around to grasp with my hands his massive buttocks, covered in an animal mat of hair (in contrast to the smooth bums of my three friends, each no downier than a peach).

The truth was that the discomfort of my physical position had been such that even the lively ministrations of young Coln had not brought me to my apogee and I was ready for more vigorous attention. And soon, feeling him move yet quicker, his belly panting against my forehead, I fell upon my back, and in an instant he followed me, and I felt that mingled joy and pain I had felt the night before as that mighty prick – so large and round that an observer would not have thought it possible that it could make its way within the slender portals now distended by it – penetrated into my most secret part. Within six thrusts of those strapping loins his whole body vibrated, while he threw back his head in pleasure, presenting me with a view of the great column of his throat. And at the same time I too spent, with such relish that I would have shrieked aloud had I not buried my open mouth in his shoulder, biting it with sufficient force to make him wince, and, drawing my lips away, I saw a ring of tooth marks on his brown flesh, small dots of blood marking the trace just beside the red mark which had identified him to me.

He would have spoken, but I laid my finger once more upon my lips, rose, and made my way to the river, where I bathed my limbs, now all over sweat, in the black water.

When I returned to my three friends, I found them all asleep as they had fallen: George with his head still on Jack's thigh and Coln with one arm flung over the former's calf, their bodies now relaxed and their formerly eager tools so shrunken and diminished (it seemed) they could not harm the mildest maid. I lay myself down by them, and also fell into a doze.

Later, we woke and dressed, and I was led to a public house nearby, close under Grantchester church and looking over a bend of the river, where in the garden we sat ourselves down to more ale and a cold rabbit pie and salad. The boys showing some interest, I told them the story of my life, which they greeted with no less surprise than sympathy. They had heard, they said, that in reading the manuscripts of Dr Dee some Cambridge scholars had expressed themselves interested in occult matters, and Coln – the only one to have read in the manuscripts themselves – described how the doctor and his familiar Mr Kelley used to converse with a spirit-child, a pretty girl of seven or eight years whom they called Madimi, until the girl ordered the doctor to share his good wife with Mr Kelley for carnal purposes, whereat the said wife had taken exception and the partnership had broken up.

'But,' said Coln, 'then the angelic conversations ceased,

for Madimi herself never more appeared to them.'

'Was not Dr Dee an astrologist?' asked George, and Coln said he was, but that the matter had been put down by Mr Samuel Butler in his poem *Hudibras,* wherein he wrote of William Lilly:

> *Some calculate the hidden fates*
> *Of monkeys, puppy-dogs and cats,*
> *Some running-nags and fighting-cocks;*
> *Some love, trade, law-suits and the pox;*
> *Some take a measure of the lives*
> *Of fathers, mothers, husbands, wives,*
> *Make opposition, trine and quartile*
> *Tell who is barren and who fertile . . .*

But, I interrupted, Mr Lilly was a sensible man who used astrology to its true purpose, as anyone could see who read his *Christian Astrology* . . .

'Aha!' cries Jack. 'We have a white witch among us!'

No, not at all, said I shortly, though witch enough to venture that he had a birthday soon, for 'twas the end of July, and clearly the Sun had been in the sign of Leo at his birth, as could be seen by his great mane of yellow hair, his fine upright carriage, ease of manner and natural leadership.

'But how did you know this?' asked he, whereat I said nothing, but enquiring the day of his birth informed him that he had been born at a quarter of three in the afternoon ('tis a trick easily learned from Mr Lilly's book).

Nothing now would do but that I had to tell the other their birth days, which luckily (for the thing's not infallible) I did correctly, Coln being born under Libra (his charm being no less manifest than his romantic notions, to which he was even then giving bent by tenderly taking my hand), while George's Sun sign was Aries, which I had guessed by his celerity in completing the act of love, Ariens being notorious for their speedy accomplishment of all things, and their motto 'I shall come first!'

It was amusing to see their faces at this, for they doubted

it was anything but black magic until I explained how the matter worked, and how Mr Lilly and those before him had used the science of astrology to help their fellow men, whereat Jack was entirely sceptical, but Coln grew quiet and thoughtful. We finished our meal and strode back to the punt, where Will was lying asleep, having no doubt recovered his small-clothes from the bush where he had dropped them before we took our pleasure. As he woke and sat up there was general laughter, for Jack pointed to where on his shoulder were all too clearly the marks of my teeth.

'Ho! A dark horse, young Will!' he said. 'A girl in every village, old scamp!'

Whereat Will said nothing, but smiled slowly and took up the punt pole, and once, as we slid back down the river towards the city, swans swimming at our side, he caught my eye and moved his hand upon the pole in an unmistakable manner bringing, I must confess, a blush to my cheeks which happily none of my companions noticed.

We parted all good friends. 'Thank 'ee, ma'am,' said Will as he handed me out onto the bank, as warmly as if I had given him a sovereign. The others embraced me, and Coln made an excuse to whisper in my ear that he would come to see me the following day.

And sure enough, just before twelve midday, there was a knock at my door and the girl announced that there was a young gentleman to visit me. It was Coln in black gown and cap, which he threw off to show himself clothed not in the simple shirt of yesterday but as one might expect of a fashionable and wealthy man, with a finely cut coat and nankeen trousers. He greeted me with a little bow, and would have offered no further familiarity had I not given him my cheek to kiss. Sitting, he made small talk until I asked outright why he had come, expecting, I must confess, a profession of love. However, he asked whether I really had command of astrology and could use it to solve a question of his, whereat I replied that I would do what I could, but first, I must know the particulars of his birth – the date, the time, the place. He told me he had been born in Dublin on October the seventh in the year of ninety-seven, at precisely midday, whereupon I sat down with Mr Lilly and completed my calculations to draw up the chart of his birth. Then I asked him what his problem was.

His father, he replied, had a factory in Dublin which made fine china, sent out to all the world, and was anxious that when he had completed a university education he should return there and run the factory in partnership with him, taking particular care of the designing of the china. Coln was not averse to the idea but had doubts whether it was work for a man or whether he could be successful in it for his friends, hearing of it, were inclined to mock at him.

I was able to reassure him that indeed he would do well to follow his father's plan, for not only did his Libran Sun suggest that he had a bent for all things artistic and would thrive in a partnership, but the sign of Sagittarius had been rising over the eastern horizon at the moment of his birth, which gave him a bright and lively intelligence and willingness to study. Moreover, the Moon was in Taurus at his birth, which promised financial success; Venus was in the sign Scorpio, which would give him assurance in business dealings; Mars in Virgo allowed him the capacity to take great trouble over small things and gave a practical ability, while Jupiter in Aries made him practical and forward-looking.

It was, I opined, Mercury in Libra with the Sun that made him doubt his abilities, for that planet within that sign often persuades a person to procrastinate, to look all round a decision seeing all sides of it, and sometimes doubting on which side to come down, while Saturn in Cancer could draw his spirits into a certain timidity, and it was my view that he must be particularly careful in financial dealings with his family. I did not inform him that the fact that Venus had been in Scorpio when he was born gave him all that passion with which he happily pleasured himself on the river bank the day before, nor that Sagittarius, when it rises, offers an inquisitive inventiveness in all matters of loving!

His face, as I told him this, was a picture of agreeable surprise. I had, he said, painted his picture to the life, and much that I had said offered a confirmation of his own feelings. Whereupon he took a guinea from his pocket and placed it upon the table, saying when I remonstrated that it was the least tribute he could pay, and moreover asking whether I had not thought of becoming a professional advisor to people in their difficulties, from which he felt sure I could make a good living.

It was something I had not thought of, but it was certainly something that *might* be thought of! Coln rose to take his leave and embracing me could not but throw his hand into my bosom, at which I was by no means displeased, for I had taken a great liking to this pleasant young Irishman. But he drew back, saying he must go to a lecture, but that if he might he would call upon me again shortly and thanking me once more for my words, he withdrew.

I spent the afternoon working out, then lettering in my best script, a placard offering advice in all matters of the heart, or of finance, or of business, by one well tutored in the movements of the Sun, Moon and Planets, given at a moderate cost at these rooms. And copying it thrice, took it to the Red Lion and two other inns, where for a shilling (which I could have ill afforded except that I now had Coln's guinea) they promised to exhibit them, with the result that within three days I had had five persons call upon me who, satisfied by my words, left me with varying amounts of money. I determined to take from each according to their means rather than charging a general fee, and had from one wealthy shopkeeper (who wished to know was his wife unfaithful, whereto Mr Lilly's formula offered a negative reply, which delighted him) no less than two guineas, and from a poor girl whose lover had left her, five pence to know whether he would return or no.

And so I proceeded for the better part of a month, satisfying myself that I could aspire to a good living if not to absolute wealth, when one morning to my door came a man all in black with an ill visage who asked whether I could tell if he would be promoted to high office or no, and when I concluded no, revealed himself as a local Presbyterian and puritan who threatened to report me for fortune-telling, for which, he said, I could be put in prison. This frightened me, especially when Coln – to whom I went in my trouble – consulted a law student friend who confirmed that the law was indeed an instrument which could be used against me.

I was then at my wits' end, for what else could I do? I walked for a while in the streets, as was my wont when I wished to think, and coming to Midsummer Common found a fair, with a stage and some coarse country play upon it, posing exhibitions, dancing saloons, swinging and riding machines, and a tent in which a pretty woman of not many years more than I was telling fortunes for two pence a time, reading the hands of anyone who cared to pay. Crossing her palm with two pence, I offered her my hand, and to my surprise she said:

'Ah, my dear, but you have the gift – yet you have trouble!'

I could not but agree.

'You are one of us,' she said, 'the far-sighted ones. I can tell you nothing you could not tell yourself, except that your danger could be averted if you came with us.'

'With *us*?'

'Ay, with the Gypsies, for I am one of a band going from place to place and living as we can but living free as the air. I see it here,' she continued, tapping my palm with her finger, 'I see a partnership twixt you and me . . .'

At this, I could not but tell her my position and ask whether the church and the law did not fall upon her as it seemed it would fall upon me.

'No, they but rarely touch us,' she said, 'for fear of our curse, which is still powerful – though not as powerful' (and here she winked) 'as they may think!'

So why did I not pack my things and come with them? I could share her stall and tent, the money was plentiful, the life varied and good, and her brothers and sisters true people of the land, who would be glad to call me one of them.

I gave her a fair answer, and returning home, consulted the book. Mr Lilly said that a journey would be most positive, especially one to the west and south and my new friend having told me that the band was to leave the following morning towards Southampton, I hesitated no longer, but that night packed my few things, wrote a quick note to leave for Coln – the only person I left with regret in the city – and by seven next morning made my way again to the Common. An hour later I was seated upon the front seat of a wagon behind a good strong white mare, my new friend, Rosanna, at my side, making out along the Trumpington Road.

The light was poor, for the sky had darkened for a shower of rain, yet as we left the city a strange vision disturbed me, for I saw three students walking along the pavement towards the city, and one of them who lifted his face to look towards our procession of vans as it passed was the image of my dear brother Frank, so much so that I almost leaped from the seat to run to him. But common sense held me there, for was it possible that he should have been in Cambridge all this while and I not seen him? And so I stayed, and as morning wore on we continued on towards Royston, to camp outside the town upon Therfield Heath where, Rosanna told me, I would have to pledge my allegiance to the band.

Chapter Seven

The Adventures of Andy

'Tis impossible in a servants' hall to be free of one's companions, and so we rubbed along together despite Tom's displeasure, which he took every opportunity of showing not only to me but to Tabby, who from time to time appeared with a bruise upon her arm or (on one occasion) her face which she would not account for. And though I suspected it was inflicted by my former friend, and was eager to visit my disapprobation upon him, she dissuaded me, saying that she had fallen or that Mrs Tickert had taken her too strongly by the arm, or some other excuse. Our pleasant nights were now no more, for Tom threatened if I were to leave our room he would inform upon me to Mr Caister and that would be the end of my situation. So Tabby and I were only able to meet when it was possible for us both to escape the notice of the others – among whom the most vigilant was Tom himself – and go into the park. This was agreeable enough in summer, but what when winter came?

Poor Ellen was at a loss to know what had gone forward; she knew that Tom and I had fallen out, but Tabby did not tell her the reason, and Tom himself held short – no doubt through pride – of explaining the circumstances of our quarrel. Ellen hung about my neck at every opportunity, but I think did not miss our love-making which now was at an end, but merely wished me a friend, which I was glad to be to her. For myself I was somewhat pleased that I need no longer go to bed with her, for after Tabby she was as skimmed milk compared to cream.

It was a fortnight or so after our first summons to Beau Rust's chambers that he again skipped to me one morning as I was cleaning silver, and once more summoned us. Nothing loath, for here was an opportunity of enjoying ourselves in comfort if not in privacy, we made our way to his rooms at three in the afternoon, which allowed us two hours before we must attend to preparing the tables for supper at six. We found the Beau sitting at his table, this time with pen in hand and in front of him a book all in Latin, the title of which I saw was *Sonetti Lussoriosi de Pietro Aretino* first published, the Beau remarked, some two hundred years ago in Italy, but most of the copies were burned by the Holy Inquisition, so that the drawings by one Marcantino Raimondi had all perished, only the verses themselves surviving.

'I have been Englishing them,' said the Beau, 'and intend to publish when I have completed the task, and the drawings with which you are helping. Here –' and he flourished a drawing of a man with a woman's leg thrown over his right shoulder, '– is the one we are to essay today, and it accompanies the following verse . . . Hah!' He cleared his throat, picked up his manuscript, and declaimed the following:

Throw your leg, dearest, on my shoulder here
And take my throbbing piece within your grasp,
And as I gently move it, let your clasp
Tighten and draw me to your bosom dear.
And should I stray from front to hinder side
Call me a rogue and villain, will not you?
Because I know the diff'rence 'twixt the two,
As stallions know how lusty mares to ride.
My hand shall keep my iron dart in place
Lest it may slip and somehow get away,
When a swift frown would darken your fair face.
Your lovely arse delights me, but they say
Only the rider can enjoy that race,
Whilst the front gate gives pleasure every way.
So let us buck and spend, and spend and buck,
For ne'er two lovers more enjoyed a fuck.

He was clearly pleased with his effort, for he thumped the table with his fist as he ended, scattering several papers to the floor, and grinned as though he had been given a hundred guineas. Tabby was blushing, for though always pleased by the game, she was not accustomed to have it spoke of in such open terms, while I knew not what to say, for to tell the truth these seemed to me to be but limping verses. However, I bowed and smiled, and the Beau was too content with his own pleasure to notice any lack of admiration in me.

'And now – hah! – to it!' he cried. 'We ourselves also will serve divers lusts and pleasures (Titus three, three),' and he gestured to us to prepare, whereupon we were not slow to divest ourselves of our clothing, while he swept more papers from the desk and prepared paper for his sketches. But he was in some difficulty, for he kept searching about and finally, as we stood all naked waiting for his direction, he told us that he had left his drawing materials in the library and must fetch them.

'Hah! – warm yourselves – hah! – until I return. But not to excess, not to excess! My lord shall delay his coming (Matthew twenty-four, twenty-eight),' he said, and left us. The library being at the other end of the house, there was some little time before he could return, so we lay upon the pile of cloths he had now provided to make our little platform more comfortable and fell to toying with each other. But as I lowered my head to salute Tabby, my eye caught a curious chink of light in the floor by the edge of the platform, where one of the boards of the floor seemed loose. I bent to examine it and found a knot-hole where a finger could raise one of them and beneath, in the plaster, a neat hole had been made, through which I could see light from a window in a room below. Then a movement caught my sight and I applied my eye to the hole. The first thing I saw was a naked bottom, busily rising and falling in the unmistakable action of love, and looking further I saw my Lady Elizabeth's face turned up to me, her eyes closed in pleasure, and the dark head of her lover buried in her open bosom. I was looking down into a drawing-room occupied by My Lord's daughters, and by the black hair curling at the nape of the neck and the peculiar olive complexion of the skin I recognised the man pleasuring the lady upon her proper couch as Signor Cesareo, her guitar player, one of whose instruments was indeed giving her acute delight, while the other, its strings silent, lay upon a chair nearby.

Tabby, meanwhile, was growing curious and nuzzling at my shoulder. Holding my finger to my lips, I moved aside to allow her to see, whereat she giggled and closed her hand upon my own instrument, which, while it may have lacked the experience of the older man's, was nevertheless ready to play its own tune. Pushing her aside so that she fell upon her back, I thrust into her willing parts, whereupon she gave a little squeal, for no doubt I was somewhat rough in my urgency, being excited by the view beneath. Finding that as I lay upon her I was still able to see through the hole in the ceiling, I found myself without intending it mimicking the movements of the man below as he continued to pleasure My Lady – but as I looked he with a final fillip reached the height of his pleasure and lifting himself fell to his side, his piece still distended, red and throbbing, with a gleam of love's liquid upon it. My Lady Elizabeth was by no means content, for looking aslant, she seized his hand and conveyed it to her lower part, where he continued to rub with his fingers as she wriggled beneath them.

Meanwhile, another figure appeared, the unclothed person of the Lady Margaret who had clearly been observing them from some nearby place and now squatted down at their sides and began mummutting at his slowly diminishing affair. From this I hazarded that her sister had drawn the first chance in the game of love, and she feared that she would lose upon it which, from the expression upon the face of Signor Cesareo, whose instrument was clearly for the moment totally unstrung, was inclined indeed to be so.

Meanwhile Tabby and I kept it up, for the liveliness of the view had entirely taken from me any remembrance of the purpose of our meeting, and our mutual rapture was now incapable of restraint. Before we knew it, we spent together in a happy gusto just as Beau Rust reappeared, for the noise of a bundle of pencils falling to the floor announced his presence just as I fell exhausted onto Tabby's flushed and panting breast.

In brief, the Beau was not pleased at our betrayal, though fortunately, rolling over somewhat painfully upon the floor, I was able to conceal the displaced board and then edge it back into its position before he could guess at its displacement and thus the reason for our excitement. But my shrinking prick he could not fail to see. 'How is the mighty fallen, and the weapon of war perished (Two Samuel, one, twenty-seven),' he remarked pointedly.

'But come, come, at your age it should take but a moment to recover!' he went on. 'Why when I was a young colt at Bath, my mistress had not to wait but five minutes before I could renew the attack. 'Tis all the same with youngsters today, ye're too quick at play and too slow to revive – is that not so, my dear?' he said turning to Tabby, who indeed looked at me with a gleaming eye that showed her ready for another pass. Then leaning over me and lifting my stones with her hand, she gently nibbled with her teeth at the skin between them and my fundament, a delicious play which in a moment caused my nodding head to rise, whereupon the judicious application of her lips rendered it swiftly as sturdy as before.

The Beau this time set Tabby upon her back, and placed her left leg so that the knee fell over my right shoulder while her right leg was stretched out, and when I entered her – as I was now again very ready to do – a clear view was offered to the artist. He approached so closely to observe the play of my piece at its work that at one moment, as my pleasure increased and my movements became less susceptible of control, I actually struck his forehead with my hip, setting his wig all crooked and causing him to cough with such vehemence that our crisis occurred without his observing it, at which he somewhat lost his temper for, he said, it was his belief that the muscles of the male buttock altered their configuration at the moment of relief, which was something he much wished to observe.

'However,' he said, ' 'tis now time that I returned to my studies of the Italian text, and will summon you again,' and patting me on my naked rump, he added, 'Let her breasts satisfy thee at all times, and be thou ravished always with her love (Proverbs five, nineteen),' and once more placed two gold coins in our hands. We made our way from the room having pleasured ourselves, been of assistance to the Beau in his historical studies, and added to our small store of gold, so that we were well pleased.

At the bottom of the stairway we were making our way very quietly past the door of our Ladies' rooms, when suddenly there was a great noise within the door, a sound as of something falling, accompanied by the shrieking of voices, and in a moment the door opened and out came a great cloud of dust, in the midst of which was Signor Cesareo all naked save for a shirt clutched to him. He came up short on seeing us, but then ran away down the corridor. We were in some doubt what to do but hearing continued shrieks from within, entered to see the room covered in white dust as with snow, and at its centre a pile of sticks and plaster with a black figure – or rather one once dressed in black, but now all white with plaster – lying between the two unclothed figures of my Lady Elizabeth and my Lady Margaret, from whose lips were still emerging weaker cries of amazement.

We went forward, and while Tabby was assisting the ladies, I gathered up Beau Rust in my arms and laid him upon the floor, thinking him to be dead. But in a moment his eyes opened and he clapped his hands to his bald head and cried 'Me wig! Me wig! Bring wool and flax to cover my nakedness (Hosea two, nine),' then fainted again.

It was clear that after we had left his room he had raised the boards to watch his granddaughters at play, whereupon the floor had collapsed under him, precipitating him upon them and their paramour who, together with the rugs upon which they were lying, had broken his fall. I fetched some

water from a jug upon the dressing table and applied it,
whereupon once more the Beau's eyes opened and he began
crying for his wig, which I found in the wreckage upon the
bed and placed upon his head. Lifting him in my arms –
for he was of small weight – I carried him up to his rooms
and placed him upon his bed, whereupon he fell into a sleep
or an unconsciousness and I returned below where now the
two ladies were wrapped in loose gowns and were quiet,
having drunk the best part of a bottle of sherry between
them.

The Lady Elizabeth enquired after the Beau, who I said
was resting, and should I send for a doctor? Whereupon
she shortly replied that he was 'tough as boots' and would
doubtless recover by his own efforts, from which I suspected that she realised the cause of his sudden descent. I
must admit that her dishabille made it difficult for me,
looking at her, not to remember the lustful enjoyment
upon her features as she lay below the thrusting body of the
Italian musician. At which, as though she read my
thoughts, she said, stammering somewhat, 'Ah – do you
see – ah – another person in the room?', looking about as
if she expected the musician to emerge from some hiding
place. Her sister was less reticent:

'Signor Cesareo,' she said drily, 'seems to have left his
guitar here – for I suppose he has left?'

I bowed.

'He was not injured?'

'Not in any visible part, my lady,' I could not help but
reply.

Lady Margaret seemed almost to smile.

'Thank you, Andrew, and thank you – ah – ?'

'Tabby, ma'am – my lady,'

Lady Margaret nodded.

'You work in the kitchens here?'

'General maid, my lady.'

'Thank you for your assistance, Tabby. We must see
more of you. You need not, neither you nor Andrew, noise
the accident abroad. Perhaps you, Andrew, would send Mr
Caister to me before supper, and we will arrange for the

ceiling to be mended, without troubling My Lord to hear of it.'

I bowed and we left.

A few days later Mr Caister gathered all the staff together in the great hall – a surprising occasion the like of which the older people among us said had never been seen before – to announce that in a week's time there would be held a great ball and buffet to celebrate the victory at Waterloo. There were to be present many members of the aristocracy and their ladies, and it was My Lord's ambition that his hospitality should equal, if not outshine, anything the county had ever seen.

The following days were so filled with incident from dawn to dusk that we had no time for anything but cleaning and polishing, fetching and carrying, sewing and patching; the kitchens were busy with food to be stored in the icehouse, or in the cellars where ice must be fetched daily to cool and keep it fresh.

In the middle of the week, the footmen were called to Mr Caister's room to be lectured upon the manner in which we were to behave to the guests: how the eldest sons of the dukes of the blood royal were to take precedence over the marquesses; how the marquesses and lay dukes being equal, the dukes' younger sons came before viscounts but after earls; how the Knights of the Garter, if commoners, came before judges of the high court; how the younger sons of viscounts came before the younger sons of barons . . . But as to how we were to recognise them, nothing. We were to address dukes as 'my lord' or 'your grace', marquesses as 'my lord marquess', earls and viscounts and bishops and barons as 'my lord'. We were to stand ready at all times to hand food where requested, to be of assistance when required, but on no account to offer it if not required . . . All this until our heads were bursting.

Then Mr Caister threw open the doors of a large cupboard to disclose rows of splendid liveries, ordered, it was said, for the time of the late King's coronation, the last time when a grand assembly was held at Rawby. Mr Caister took down a pile of beautiful, pale doe-skin breeches and told us all to try them on. I seized a pair that seemed of likely size and, removing my small-clothes, started to pull them on.

'Mm – oh, no!' cries Mr Caister, 'mm – you must remove your undergarments, for they will show beneath the doe-skin, which can on no account be – mm – permitted.'

So I threw off my underclothes, which at the best of times were sparse, and pulled on the breeches, which indeed fit like a second skin, and I had to tuck my privates down between my legs so I resembled a girl. A thick extra layer of skin lay in a flap before the breeches which, pulled up and buttoned, held in place to disguise the male appendage and to prevent the dark hair from showing through to alarm (or excite, as Tom said) the ladies.

Shortly, we were all attired in breeches and in coats bearing My Lord's arms and so much aged and dirty gold braid that my heart failed at the thought of cleaning it all and stood in a row before Mr Caister.

'Mm – turn about!' he cried, and we turned, displaying a row of fine buttocks all tight as drums under the doe-skin. Tom wriggled his bottom in an affected, girlish way, whereupon Mr Caister fetched him a thwack with his stick which made Tom cry out.

'No – mm – nonsense, young Tom!' he cried. 'This is serious business. Turn about!' And we turned again, whereupon he walked along the row, pausing only in front of James, a whacking fellow the front flap of whose breeches was incapable of disguising the organ beneath it.

'Find some way of – mm – disposing of your engine, James!' said Mr Caister.

'But sir!' protested the unfortunate James, 'I know not how . . .'

'Well, either you find some way, or you do not serve,' said Mr Caister, 'for we cannot have you looking as though you are about to ravish the ladies, much though – mm – some of them – mm – well, at all events, draw yourself in, man, or stand behind the door.'

So we stripped again and took our new finery away to be cleaned when we had time to do it, which was little enough, the work continuing day and night.

On the morning of the ball itself the household was awake at dawn and we were out gathering greenery to decorate the saloon and great drawing-room, which had had its carpets lifted and was to act as ballroom, with a platform at one end of it for the orchestra. The musicians were placed for the occasion under the direction of Signor Cesareo, My Lord believing him (and with justice) to have more knowledge of fashionable music than his colleagues. And so they sat, while we decorated the walls, practising dances, with the Signor directing them from the keyboard of a new grand pianoforte especially bought for the occasion at the cost, we heard, of no less than fifty guineas, and brought on a great wagon from Cambridge. Signor Cesareo insisted to My Ladies that no fashionable ballroom in London was without such a thing, the harpsichord being now quite out of date as an instrument for dancing.

By five o'clock a great quiet had fallen upon the house; everyone was in his room preparing. A few of the gentlemen had made use of the bath room and were now decking themselves, while the ladies had not been seen since they broke their fast, so intent were they on their toilette. We, below the stairs, were cleaning ourselves as best we might, every maid in the house readying herself for service, while we footmen wriggled into our breeches and checked each other's coats for perfection.

At seven the first carriages began to appear, and My Lord and My Ladies took up position in the great hall to receive his guests, who soon were coming so thick that Mr Caister had it hard to repeat their names to My Lord as they entered: 'His Grace the – mm – Duke of Hertfordshire; My Lord Marquess of Scrimmage; My Lord Bishop of – mm – Nunquam; My Lady Marchioness of Taciturn; Viscount – mm – Talland and the Hon. Frederick Shake; My Lord the Earl of Readymoney and Fume . . .'

In half an hour the saloon was so crowded it was almost impossible to move; I stood at the door between it and the great dining-room and at a quarter to eight precisely, at a signal from Mr Caister, threw open the doors. The crowd pressed through, as though escaping from a fire, to fall upon the long tables laden with boiled turkeys in celery sauce, pigs' feet and ears in jelly, tongue and *fricandeau*, saddle of mutton, roast woodcocks, sweets and wild-fowl in an oyster sauce, roasted beef and bacon, *raqout à la Française*, and on a side table walnuts, raisins and almonds, apples, cakes, pears and oranges and all manner of other fruit.

Though used to lack of ceremony at table, I had never seen men and women so near to fighting over their food or so intent to fetch the champagne from the bottles, which as soon as they were empty flew across the tables as though they were alive, to break against the wall. Though it seemed we had prepared food for twice the number of guests, in scarcely ten minutes the table was as bare as before we had set it and everyone was making again into the saloon, carrying their glasses with them, where they continued to drink, for each table in the house was laden with bottles which were replaced as speedily as they were emptied, My Lord having ordered cases enough to fill his large cellar.

At half past eight, again at a signal from Mr Caister, the doors to the ballroom were thrown wide and a great gasp went up, for though it was yet light outside a burst of brilliance like sunlight was to be seen in the ballroom, so bright that only the press behind forced the nearest guests against their nervous will through the open doors. The orchestra was in its place and already playing, but above their heads and at intervals around the room stood tall poles on which lights burned with dazzling brightness. My Lord had sent to London and had installed the new gas-making mechanism, and for the first time in England (or so 'twas later said) a private house displayed the new lighting which had only been recently seen for the first time in the streets of the metropolis, and still did not light the provincial cities, for many people regarded it as the work of the D---l. Indeed had I not seen the workmen testing it, and been shown the retorts set up in the cellars, with the condenser, heater and purifier, thus making the whole display less mysterious, I would myself have been apprehensive of the power of so astonishing an approximation to sunlight.

In a while the wonder wore off and the dancing began. We were then able from our posts about the walls to examine the guests and con their persons as they trod the figures of the dances, marked out in chalk upon the boards.

The room made a fine picture; the men were all at the height of fashion and there was scarce a wig to be seen except that of old Beau Rust, who had sufficiently recovered from his fall to attend, nodding his head in a chair next the orchestra. Now the men wore their own hair and since it was known that, despite My Lord's strenuous efforts, no member of the Royal Family was to be present, many were in the new loose or frock coats, and a good number even in pantaloons rather than breeches.

The women made a sight so ravishing that from time to time only the tightness of our borrowed breeches prevented our admiration taking visible, nay tangible form. Their dresses were cut so low that it was impossible that most of their bosoms should not be pressed upon the attention of even the least curious observer, while the high belts of many lifted and displayed their bubs as though offering them to the lips of the beholder. Just as we had been ordered by Mr Caister to eschew any underclothes, it was quite clear that few ladies wore anything of consequence beneath the diaphanous muslin of which most of their dresses were made. And on more than one occasion, as a more vigorous partner swung her about in a quadrille, the swirling of a skirt gave a tempting view of quarters which only a husband should, in strictness, set eyes upon. One or two wore skirts so short that they would only a few years previously have been considered scandalous, and it was clear – so closely did their dresses cling to their bodies – that they had wet them before wriggling into them.

At one moment, one woman – and not of the youngest – threw off the upper part of her clothes altogether and appeared in the ballroom stark naked to the waist, explaining, when My Lord sent one of his daughters to remonstrate, that the Princess of Wales, the year before, had at a ball in Geneva appeared dressed *en Venus* – or rather not dressed, further than the waist. My Lord was not impressed by this explanation and required that the lady's large and unstructured bosom should nevertheless remain covered on this occasion.

Late in the evening when the reels, the minuets, the country dances and the quadrilles were exhausted, Signor Cesareo introduced the new German waltz which (he had told me) Lady Jersey had brought into society at Almack's only this season, and which had generally been condemned (even by Lord Byron) as a dance which no truly modest woman would indulge in. Even in London society the most fashionable of ladies would not perform it unless another lady, or at least a blood relative, were present. Indeed it is a most lascivious measure in which man and partner are forced to embrace as though making love to each other in public. One or two of those present notably turned their backs and left the room, but others were clearly excited by the spectacle and one lady, the daughter of my Lord Bishop of Bellanach, in Ireland, was so overcome that as she stood by me she seemed like to faint, and to help recover herself put out her hand, which fell upon my backside, whereupon she started and passed her palm freely over my haunches before coming to herself.

It was three in the morning and past before the evening ended, and that with more food and yet more wine, so that many of the guests staggered as they met the fresh night air and had to be assisted into their carriages by the only truly sober men in the company, we servants. I will not say that as we did so we did not avail ourselves of the opportunity to support the more beautiful ladies with an enthusiasm more than we showed in pushing their consorts up after them, many stinking of vomit or worse as a result of their excesses. Indeed by the end of the evening, aided by the heated bodies after exertions of the dance and the additional warmth of the gas lamps, the stench which arose in the crowded rooms, composed of sweat, vomit and the farts emitted from bowels overladen with rich food, was such that it was almost impossible to breathe with freedom.

Some of the guests of the house sat around for another hour or more before they made their way to bed. In the meantime the orchestra was almost dead of exhaustion and we footmen were tired enough on our feet, though we had for the most part done nothing but stand about or fetch more bottles up. But Mr Caister was pleased enough with us, as his smiles told when he dismissed us. Tom and I were last to close the doors of the ballroom and the saloon but as we turned to make our way down to the kitchen then to our room – for the clearing up of the mess was to wait until the morrow – a servant approached who had been eating with us and whom we knew to be attached to someone staying in the house.

'My mistresses' compliments,' he said, 'and I am to bring you to them.'

'And who might they be?' asked Tom, who was less disposed than I to take things as they came.

'The Honourable Misses Glaistow of A'Mhoine, in Scotland,' said the man, 'the sisters to My Lord the Earl of A'Mhoine.'

'Hah,' said Tom, 'and what have we to do with them?'

'Ask rather what they have to do with you,' said the man. 'But if you are not geldings, are happy to jock and not averse to a gold piece, you will do well to attend them.'

At which he turned and began to make his way towards the east wing.

Tom and I looked at each other, then followed.

'Look here,' he whispered, 'I'm not your friend, but I'm not for throwing gold away, so it's each for each in the venture, d'ye see?'

I nodded.

In course we came to the door of one of the guest bedrooms, which the fellow opened, standing back for us to enter. Sitting by the bed were the two sisters, perhaps of eighteen and twenty years, one dark and the other brown, and I recognised them from the lowness of their gowns as two of the ladies who had most enjoyed participating in the waltz, and who had shown such attention to their partners that I wondered that they had not lain down in the middle of the floor and gone to it in regular fashion. Their dresses were of the lightest and their rosy nipples peeped above them, at once forward and blushing to be seen.

'Thank you, Edward,' said one, 'and goodnight.'

'My Ladies,' said the fellow, and left.

'Well, now,' said the dark lady, coming towards us, 'what fine fellows My Lord has to serve him, and in what fine uniform. But it interests my sister and me that he should employ eunuchs,' and she stared at our lower parts, where indeed the natural evidence of manhood was disguised by the cut of the breeches.

'Remove your jackets, so that we may examine your figures more closely,' said the brown girl peremptorily. We did so, and they came towards us and turned us about, the dark girl placing her hand below my belly and sliding it down to see what she could feel. By now I was in great pain through the distension of my natural parts beneath the restriction of the breeches, and so by his wincing was Tom, upon whom the brown girl was pressing similar attentions.

The girls looked at each other and laughed.

'I fancy,' said one, 'we have two men in disguise, not eunuchs at all. Shall we see if we can tempt their manhood forth?'

Whereupon they stepped back and at the same time raised their dresses over their heads and dropped them into the bed. Their figures were the most beautiful I had yet seen, fuller than that of Ellen, less full than that of Tabby. Perhaps my dear Sophia, at Alcovary, would have been the nearest in beauty had I ever been at more leisure to view her. I was so roused by their regular, spherical bosoms, their slight waists, jutting hips and firm thighs, that my agony was almost insupportable and it was with relief that I saw Tom, at my side, throw caution away and unbuttoning his breeches thrust them to his knees, his manhood, released, springing up so that all could hear the thwack with which it hit against his belly. The girls showing nothing but pleasure at the sight, I prepared to do the same, but the dark girl came forward, knelt and with her own fingers undid the buttons and drew down the flap at the front of my breeches, then passed her hands down over my hips to draw the doe-skin from my body, reaching to hold my tool and raise it wonderingly to her eyes, laying it on the palm of a small hand so that its head rested above her wrist.

'Look, Annie,' she said, 'what a splendid toy is here to be petted!' and leant forward to kiss its tip with soft lips.

Stepping out of our breeches we were led to the bed, where the two ladies drew our shoes and long stockings from our feet and lifted our shirts over our heads, then laid us on the mattress and began to minister to us with such tender attentions that speaking for myself it was only by thinking desperately of other things – trying to calculate the number of bottles drunk that evening, and the total cost to My Lord's estate – that I was able to maintain myself a man. Indeed, when my lady took my yard between her lips and began to suck upon it with a long, slow motion, the hair falling over her face to conceal my whole middle part, I attempted to draw her head away, fearing that I could no longer contain myself, but she held my hands at my side and, no longer susceptible to control, my whole privities thrust themselves with a life of their own into her face as my life flooded forth. Even then, she continued to suck upon me ever more gently, so that in almost a swoon I lay enchanted, only half aware that a foot away, upon the same bed, Tom was suffering the same glad death.

We both lay still for what seemed an age while the ladies kneeled above us. Then, almost as at a pre-arranged signal, they changed their places and with a gentle but strong motion encouraged us to turn so that we lay upon our fronts, when we felt them begin to stroke our whole bodies, beginning at the neck, their fingers trailing down our backs, over our buttocks, down our thighs to our feet, then up, passing between our legs and the inside of our thighs and up our backs again. After a while this became unbearably delightful and I lifted myself as I once more began to swell with pleasure. When, passing her hand through my legs, my fair partner felt the renewal of life, I was made to turn again and she lifted herself to kneel above me. Taking my staff in one hand, she drew aside her flesh with her other and introduced it to its proper place, sinking upon me so that her dark hair met my lighter hair as snugly as though 'twere woven into a single mat. At my side, Tom and his friend were in the same motion and the sisters twined their arms together, their hands on each other's shoulders as they began slowly to rise and fall, their movements gradually increasing in velocity as their desire mounted and their emotions grew more intense. This time we were more ready to restrain our outpouring and indeed I might have lived longer had it not been that at the moment when her bosom and face flushed with joy, my partner reached down and caught one of my paps between her fingers, pinching it with such fervour that the pain of it joined with the pleasure in my loins to release both emotions in a spasm of delight which almost threw her from her seat. At my side Tom, only a moment later, gave a shout as he too died beneath his tormenter's administrations.

The two women lifted themselves together and without a word descended from the bed, where they threw gowns over their shoulders and, without giving us a moment to resume our clothes, opened the door and ushered us into the corridor, along which we hastily raced clutching our breeches, shirts, shoes, stockings and coats, reaching the stairway to the kitchen with no one seeing us. Indeed, the house was now quiet and, without ensuring that we were upstairs, Mrs Tickert had locked the doors to our room.

Tom's comments upon the ladies could not have been repeated in their presence, but reflected my own feelings towards them.

'Though,' he concluded, ' 'twas as fine a clicket as I've had since you stole Tabby from me,' (he looked unfriendly at that). 'We must hope they've not given us the burner,' and went on to say that he wouldn't mind if I got the burner, as it might quieten me down, for I was far too randy for his liking, especially with other men's wenches.

But I was far too tired to worry about the clap, or to think of Tabby or what Tom thought or believed or would do. I was too tired even to wonder at the freedom with which the two ladies, having entertained us as though we were the dearest of lovers, had dismissed us as the most menial of pimps. Though we must spend the night upon the harsh rush mats before the embers of the kitchen fire, I lay myself upon them as though they were the softest swan's-down and slept a sleep as deep and dark as velvet.

Chapter Eight

Sophie's Story

As we rode out of Cambridge, my companion – whose full name, I learned, was Rosanna Vanis (the name of her husband was well-known among the tribes of Egyptians) – told me how they lived their lives. They were not, she affirmed, the thieves and villains popular legend supposed, but existed for the most part on the proceeds of legitimate buying and selling of horses and donkeys, though they were much harried by the constables, for every theft which took place in a neighbourhood where there was a Gypsy encampment was visited upon them. Indeed very recently a man of their tribe, one Stanley, had been falsely accused of housebreaking, and would have been executed had not all his friends met together and gathered a considerable sum to prove an alibi which had resulted in his gaining his freedom.

She had never, she said, known cases of thieving among them except in the extremity of poverty and despair, which she admitted sometimes occurred. In one case a child who had been scalded to death had had to remain unburied for many days until his father, driven to it, stole some wood from a carpenter to make up a coffin – which was unfortunately discovered but the carpenter, being a humane man, informed the constables that he had given the wood, and so the situation had been saved.

With these sad and some more high-spirited stories the journey was enlivened. Rosanna also assured me that wherever there was a fair there was also an opportunity to make money at fortune-telling and that with my superior manner and dress I would be sure to do well. This I was not sanguine of yet hoped to be the case for to be honest, charming though my companion was, I was not entirely persuaded that the company of the wandering Egyptians was something I cared to prolong further than was necessary, and an accumulation of funds would enable me to free myself, grateful though I must be for this present escape.

As we went, I came to know some of Rosanna's companions. Her horse, though willing, was old and proceeded at only a walking pace, so those who were not mounted – even the children – had no difficulty in keeping up with us upon the way, and from time to time several of them would gather to walk alongside us and exchange banter. The pretty children, with bare feet and almost naked bodies, would jump up to ride upon the shafts of the cart so that I was continually in a fear that they would fall beneath the hooves of the horses or the wheels of our equipage.

The band was indeed scattered over the road like a flock of sheep. Two other wagons with luggage kept within sight, but many women and children and men wandered along the length of the procession to keep their eye upon the whole. One in particular, who could not escape my notice, was a magnificent creature with jet-black hair and a face which, though swarthy, was remarkable for its strong features and piercing black eyes. A ragged shirt did little to conceal the magnificent shoulders from which depended sinewy, strong arms baked in the sun to the colour of mahogany, with which he controlled the reins of a fine nag. Pointing him out to Rosanna, I asked who he was.

'Ah, you've an eye for a *rincana mush*,' she said. ''Tis *Derai* Bovile, and he is our *dimber damber*. You will see much of him, later,' with which she turned taciturn and would say no more.

Here I should say that much of the language in which Rosanna and her family and friends conversed was more foreign to me than Greek, being the language of the Gypsies which, she assured me, was spoken the same throughout the world. In my time with the band I was able to commit to memory only a few words, learning, for instance, that *rincana* was 'handsome', and *mush*, 'man', while they called their leader their *dimber damber*. 'Woman' was *mannishee*, 'boy' *chau* and 'girl' *chi*. Having tied up their *gry*, or horse, they set up their *tanya* or tent, and settled then to a meal, more often than not of roast *hotchawitcha*, or hedgehog. I was able to note, with my little knowledge, that some of the words approximated to those in other languages: for instance their word for 'eye' was *yoc*, which in Latin is *oculus* and in Italian *occhio*; they say *pomya* for 'apple', which in the Latin is *pomus* and in French *pomme*. But I lack the knowledge of more than a few common words in those languages, and cannot make a true comparison. Each person I met, moreover, even the small children, used their own language freely among themselves but was able to speak English to my perfect understanding, if often with a strong accent – though to tell the truth, when they wished to converse without my following them, they would fall into the Gypsy language, to my ill-temper.

On reaching the heath high above the small town of Royston, there we set up camp, Rosanna busying herself with tethering and feeding the horse, then with putting up a tent. She was aided by Sam, a boy whom I took to be her son, but who was introduced to me as her *derai*, or master, which the women call their husbands. He could not, I thought, have been more than twenty, whereas she was perhaps in her middle thirties, but I was to learn that age was not much taken into account among them, the present head of the whole sect of Gypsies in England, said to be into his nineties, having recently taken a wife of sixteen who had already borne him a child.

Their tent was of considerable size, much larger than many cottages I had seen when visiting the poor near our house. In the middle was a space open to the sky which served as kitchen, a fire being built there, and at the two ends were separate sleeping spaces. In this tent lived, I learned, Rosanna and her husband, and his sister who was a girl of about my own age, Anna, whom I now met and with whom I was to share one of the sleeping spaces.

'But you will not need it tonight,' Rosanna said mysteriously, whereat Anna laughed, and set upon the fire a great pot into which she threw various vegetables and herbs, a fine and savoury smell soon mounting from it. And by the end of the afternoon we sat down to a good meal of some meat whose nature was undisclosed, but which was supremely nourishing. Rosanna and her husband then set to discussing how I should be best put to work – something I had thought I might be consulted upon, except that I had no idea how to set about it. Their view was that I should have to myself one of their best tents, and that they should go into the town to tout my presence to anyone who seemed likely to show an interest, and that I could ask half a guinea for a consultation. Sam also believed that it would be best for me to be as divorced as might be from the tribe itself for, he said, I was of appearance no Gypsy and the connection, if known, might result in fewer people approaching me, for though many believed Gypsy women to have 'the eye', many also associated them with the black arts and would not for that reason come near them.

By this time it was evening and the light was beginning to fail, whereupon Rosanna and her sister rose and asked if I would go with them to the stream to bathe. It being a thundersome day with hot air and close, I was glad to do so and must say here that the cleanliness and sweetness of the Gypsy women and the men too would put to shame some of our aristocrats, whose bodies are so often astink with rank sweat and old perfume slapped upon it, while the Gypsies were in the open air for much of their lives and took advantage of the running streams to cleanse themselves. Upon the heath a shallow stream running through a copse or spinney offered an ideal bathing room where we were able to strip and scrub, the water being cold but no colder than I had often been used to in the pool at Alcovary. I was cautious, half expecting some of the Gypsy men to burst in upon us. But they take great care, it seems, to show their women deference and politeness and would no more dream of purposely coming upon them in private moments than some of our men would think of not taking advantage of such a circumstance – another example of the superiority of their manners to our own.

When we had bathed, we returned to the tent and I put on

the only other dress that I had – the white muslin in which I was married. The two other women were dressed too in something approaching finery and they led me out to a clearing between the other tents where most of the band were now met, among them the impressive figure of their leader *Derai* Bovile, around whom the others cleared a space as they saw us approach so that he stood alone, still in the black breeches and torn white shirt in which he had formerly appeared.

With a whispered word to do just what I was ordered, Rosanna and her sister-in-law retired, leaving me standing before his commanding figure.

'What name do you wish to take among us?' he asked.

Bemused, I could think of none but my own and muttered 'Sophia' in an undertone, which I had to repeat, for he had not heard it.

'Then repeat after me,' he said – and I was led in the following oath:

> *I, Sophia, do swear to be a true sister, and that I will in all things obey the commands of the great tawny prince, and keep his counsel, and not divulge the secrets of my brethren.*
>
> *I will never leave nor forsake the company, but observe and keep all the times of appointment, either by day or by night, in every place whatever.*
>
> *I will take my prince's part against all that shall oppose him, or any of us, according to the utmost of my ability; nor will I suffer him, or any one belonging to us, to be abused by any strange abrams, rufflers, hookers, pailliards, swaddlers, Irish toyles, swigmen, whip jacks, jarkmen, bawdy baskets, dommerars, clapper dogeons, patricoes or curtals; but will defend him, or them, as much as I can, against all other outliers whatever. I will not conceal aught I win out of libkins or from the ruffmans, but will preserve it for the use of the company.*

After which Bovile stepped forward, seized me and, kissing me thoroughly, then swung me with little effort under his arm and carried me off, to a rousing cheer from the assembled company.

Before I retail what happened to me next, I must admit that much of my oath was meaningless to me. Rosanna later translated it and it meant, in effect, total loyalty to the band, together with some niceties such as that I must preserve to the common use any money I was able to make, and be prepared to defend as best I might my fellow Gypsies.

It was clear to me as Bovile broke through the entrance of his tent that my first duty was to be to him and, from the manner in which he set me down none too carefully upon a mattress there, then stood to look at me as he stripped the remnants of cloth from his upper body, then put his hands to his belt, that that duty was naught to do with food and drink but more to do with other bodily appetites.

I must confess that I was not ill-pleased, for I had been some days without the comfort of a man's body, having had no connection since the last visit of Coln to my rooms in Cambridge, and that, since he was somewhat the worse for liquor, had been unremarkable. Besides which, Bovile, I now saw, had a figure which would have brought any woman to a state of readiness. It was clear from the brown skin which stretched unshaded from neck to waist that much of his time was spent in the open air and without cover, while I was unable not to fix my eyes upon his essential manly part which, though not yet fully extended, promised to be of admirable proportions, both as to length and thickness. His body was as hairless as those of my brothers, though he was much their senior – indeed, this was the first time I learned that all men did not have hair upon belly and thigh, where all was smooth and white as woman's flesh, a generous, startlingly black thicket at the base of his tool being the only counterpart of that mass of pitchy curls upon his head.

He stepped forward to bestride me, smiling with pride as without the touch of my hand or his own his yard jerkily rose to its full pride.

' 'Tis not only the gentry that have fine tackle!' he said. 'Or that can swive like true Britons.' Whereupon he reached down, with one movement lifted my clothing above my head, and raised me so that my middle section was clasped between his thighs and I lay supported thus as he drew my dress over my head. I was naked as he, and as ready for the fight.

It was evident that this stallion was not interested in the niceties of polite behaviour, for having carried me off like a piece of property, he used me like one, simply dropping me onto the pile of rugs which formed the bed and throwing himself upon me entirely without ceremony so that had I not, knowing what was expected of me, spread my legs widely apart, he would clearly have forced me perhaps to my pain and peril. There was no attempt at tender caress or endearment, but simple fornication such as I had seen the animals perform in the fields – except that it was prolonged far beyond what the goat or horse achieved. His hands were placed upon my shoulders, but though his chest was lifted from my own so that my breasts were free for him to nuzzle, he at no time bent his lips to them but simply and unrelentingly thrust with his hips, ploughing the furrow with force and vigour. He had raised me no less than three times to the ultimate throes of pleasure before he himself spent with a great roar, his body continuing to plunge, though with less and less power, until even he seemed for the moment exhausted, and I, my heart beating as 'twould burst, opened my eyes at last to see his wicked own peering deeply into mine as though he would read my soul – and to my astonishment and no less confusion, behind his head the eyes of four or five men of the tribe whose duty it was (as I later learned) to witness the subjugation of each new female member.

'*Bona kom-kista*!' cried Bovile, waving away these witnesses, who vanished silently into the night. His words meant, literally, 'A good love-ride!' and the meaning was quite clear, if the words were not, and I could not deny him a smile, which in return brought a broad grin to his face which I found irresistibly charming. Though without doubt to have been ravished in such a manner of a sudden, and if one misliked the ravisher, would have been a sorely disturbing experience, his person was so handsome and his power so impressive that few women but would have welcomed his attentions – which now, after the shortest time of relief, began again. Once more, there was no ceremony but the great storm having ceased, 'twas only a minor tempest was aroused in his loins. However, this time he was all eyes, looking deeply into my own, regarding my heaving breasts with what I believed was approbation, and sometimes raising himself so that he could see how his great yard disappeared, appeared and disappeared again within my willing cleft as we rocked like two boats in a swell until once more we came to a happy berth. Upon which, without further ceremony, he simply fell asleep between my legs; after a while his weight became so burdensome that with a great effort I heaved him over upon his back, and myself curled about him, a leg thrown over one of his massive thighs, and fell into a sleep.

I awoke, he still sleeping, to find a woman standing over us with a bowl of water and early morning sunlight showing through the cloth of the tent. With a somewhat surly air (no doubt provoked by jealousy) she set the water down and left us, and I was glad after the exertions of the previous night to lave myself as best I might. As I dried my body in a cloth which she had laid beside the bowl, I felt rather than saw his eyes upon me, and indeed as I turned their twin beacons struck right into my heart – for power and fixative quality I never knew their like. He regarded me kindly and with a smile, then rising picked up the wet cloth and handing it to me represented that I should bathe his limbs with it. I was happy to do so, wiping his broad back and massive shoulders, fine chest and arms, and then, as he stood, the thighs like young tree trunks, finally reaching between them to refresh those parts which had taught me, a few hours before, the height to which animal man could aspire at the top of his bent and which even now were impressive. His instrument, even relaxed, seemed of the same length and thickness it had been when extended so that wonderingly I held it in both hands and bent it this way and that, amazed that while it had such size it was still not hard nor stiff enough to perform a loving function.

It soon became clear from a growing resistance that I was rousing it to its practical state and had not he laughingly struck my hands away and pulled on his breeches, I might once more have felt its power – not that I would have repined at that but he seemed eager to encounter the new day.

Rosanna greeted me with a knowing look, while her sister asked whether I needed any plaisters after the night's activities, to which I was able to reply that I was uninjured, and that indeed had rarely felt in better health, which was received by them with smiles. After we had broken our fast frugally with bread and fresh, clear water, Rosanna and I set out to walk into the town, where at its western end I found to my surprise a small tent already erected, in which Sam was just setting up a small table, and indeed it looked not unattractive and a small group of townspeople had already gathered. Sam had, I learned, on Bovile's instructions employed a small boy to cry me through the town as a master astrologist. I asked whether an advertisement could not be placed in the local sheet but the silence which greeted my words was interpreted by me as meaning that none of the Egyptians could write and I hesitated to show my own superiority by offering to set out a notice for them (or rather, for myself).

However, it was soon clear that no more notice was needed than word passing from mouth to mouth. At Sam's suggestion, I made no charge for the first two people who came to me; one came to know where was a purse of money that had been stolen from him on the day before, whereupon I was able (with Mr Lilly's help) to tell him the thief was a tall, fair man who had hidden the purse under ground in a direction west from the spot where it was stolen – whereat he went off to trace the steps westward from his house, to find what he could find; and another to ask whether her husband should be cut for the stone, and if so, whether he would recover, which I was able to tell her would be successful and that though ill for a time he would soon be a whole man again.

Within an hour after these two, there was a line of people

outside the tent which continued for most of the day as a result, I believe, of the novelty of the situation, for though many almanacs were sold in the town there had not been an astrologer there for many years. The people were of all sorts, both men and women, and of all qualities, some serving maids in poor clothes, some women in what passed for fashionable dress in this small town – kerseymere spencers and white cambric gowns. Many wore straw bonnets, but some neat caps, a few even of Honiton lace, and some younger women had hair curled in ringlets. I was happy that while my dress was now somewhat untidy and badly in need of replacement, it was at least more fashionable than most, which seemed to impress my female visitors.

As to the men, most were still in breeches and wore stocks, but a few wore pantaloons and some the new cravats of muslin. One tradesman, who I learned kept a shop in the town's main street, appeared in a curled wig with a dress coat and vest, knee-breeches and buckles, cotton speckled stockings and square-toed shoes with large, shining buckles – he wished to know whether his business would continue to prosper.

The questions were many and varied, from those concerning stolen goods to whether wives or husbands were unfaithful, whether a woman would consent to be wooed or a man consent to marry his mistress with child. By five o'clock in the evening I was tired almost to sleeping, having paused only for a dish of meat at mid-day, and had gathered no less than seven pounds and fourteen shillings – more money than I had seen together in one place before.

So it was in high satisfaction that I walked back with Sam and Rosanna to the encampment, leaving a man to guard the tent until the following day, for Sam was of the opinion that the tribe should remain for at least another forty and eight hours 'to milk', he said, the remaining enquirers. For there was no need to wait for a *waqqaulus*, or fair, when I on my own could command more than a whole range of fortune-tellers or lucky-card numberers together.

As we came to the tents, Bovile strode out to meet us and held out his hand for my purse, which I handed to him, thinking he wished to see how much money I had taken. But he simply seized it and strode off with it without a word to me – at which I must have looked blank, for Rosanna asked what ailed me. When I asked when the division of my spoils would take place, she reminded me that I had sworn to give all I earned to the tribe – something which I had not taken seriously, but which it was now all too plain was to be the case. I asked whether they did not think the system unfair, but they wondered at that and asked whether I would not be content that we should share everything in common? For those who lacked the capacity to earn money would live in comfort by the aid of those who had it, while those who earned should be pleased to share what they had with those who had it not.

I could not but feel there was somewhere a flaw in this argument but felt it best not to pursue it, especially since I was tired to exhaustion. After a good meal from the cauldron which seemed to be everlastingly on the simmer – and with each hour to become more delicious – and some good ale, I felt much recovered, and in an hour or so was looking forward to the consolation of another term of passion with Bovile whose figure haunted my thoughts to the exclusion even of my memory of the money I had made, and lost, that day.

But there was no sign of him, and when Sam came from the sleeping-tent to the fireside, and bending down to Rosanna and placing his hand on her breast whispered to her that it was time to go to bed, my face must have expressed my disappointment, for she asked why I looked so sour. And when I wondered whether Bovile would not come for me, she replied that it was 'not my night'.

But what did she mean, I enquired?

'Why, you do not think he has the same *com* ever night?' she said. '*Mag* goes to his *tanya* tonight; you are not for his *wuddress* except when your time comes. So you might as well *auriqqu* and to bed.' At which Anna, also by the fire, smiled at my puzzlement and explained that Bovile had his pick of the women of the camp and to avoid the ill-nature which might otherwise arise, took them to his *wuddress* or bed in strict order. I would have some twelve or fourteen nights before it would once more be my turn to wait upon him. This explained the ill-temper of Mag, the woman who had brought us water that morning, whose turn had been delayed for twenty-four hours because of my arrival.

But did not the husbands and lovers of the women complain, I asked, at their leader's making love to their women?

Sam looked as though he might have something to say upon the subject, but Rosanna laughed and asked me whether the complaint of any lover would be likely to prevent me from going to Bovile's bed when my turn next came, at which I was silent, for though indeed he was a man the power of whose loins was mightily attractive, I could imagine myself, if beloved and beloving of some other, not being entirely happy at being at his beck and call whenever the timetable showed it.

But by now Sam had drawn Rosanna to her feet and they had nodded a good night and gone into their sleeping-tent, and Anna too got to her feet and was stretching, then beckoning.

Within our half of the tent I found a single pile of rugs upon which we were both to sleep and was so tired that without further pause I removed my dress and shift and lay down upon them. Anna stood between me and the fire as she lifted her dress over her head, and the flickering light outlined her body to me which was, I must confess, extremely beautiful. I had not, at the bathing place, considered it closely; now, however, in the romantic light and the unaccustomed closeness – for I had never shared a sleeping room with another woman before – I could not but admire her. She was perhaps three or four years older than me, her body more fully formed, slim but firm, the upper curves of her breasts declining to where at the tip they turned slightly upward, the curve below the nipples heavier and more spherical. Then came the small belly – all the women I had seen at the bathing place had been slim and muscular, partly through the hard work they did each day and partly, I guessed, through healthy and unfattening food – above thighs as devoid of fat as a healthy boy's, yet a backside plump and proud.

Naked as she was, she came and stood for a moment before lying at my side, and after a while raised herself on an elbow and whispered to ask whether I was not sad at not being with Bovile instead of her.

I was bound to admit I was, when to my surprise she placed her hand upon my breast and, bending closer, asked whether she could not console me for his absence. Never having received such an offer from someone of my own sex, I replied that I was glad of her friendship.

'Only of my friendship?' she asked, and when I was silent took the lobe of my ear in her mouth and nipped it sharply with her teeth. Then I felt her tongue tracing the curves of my ear and reaching inside it – a sensation new to me, and astonishingly moving.

I was startled by this, but at the same time warmed by it, and was entirely unable to resist as she knelt and drew my sole garment from me – even unconsciously raising myself to make the action easier for her. In the dim light I felt rather than saw her lower herself until she could take one of my toes into her mouth, sucking it like a baby at the teat, while her hand edged up to my knee, then my thigh and, as I opened my legs to accommodate it, between them to my softer part, where she began a stroking which was more tender and comfortable than the action of any man I had yet encountered.

Leaving my feet, I felt her tongue follow her hand up the inside of my leg until she was nibbling at the soft flesh of my thigh and then her tongue followed her fingers and traced the twin lips of my lower mouth, then actually entering me, slowly moving, then quickening to flick lightly at the centre of emotion. A quick shudder ran through my body, at which her action quickened still further, her fingers meanwhile busying themselves about my breasts, teasing them until they seemed about to burst with the pleasure of it, which was no less delicious – though quite different – to that I had experienced even in the arms of Mr Ffloyd, so far by a long way the gentlest of my lovers.

Now, I felt Anna's body shift so that after a while she was lying with her lower parts near my shoulder, then lifting herself so that she was kneeling above me, her lips still pleasuring me, while her knees were on either side of my head. Lifting her hands to her person, she drew her flesh apart with the obvious intention that I should offer to her the attention she was paying me.

And so it was that for the first time I applied my tongue to the lower parts of a woman; to my pleasure, she was sweet and clean, only a slight musky taste falling upon my palate as I found the ultimate seat of her pleasure, hard as a small hazelnut.

Flicking it with my tongue in just the way she was exciting me, I at the same time was able to weigh her charming breasts in my hands, rolling the nipples between my fingers until they were as tight as my own, when at almost the same moment our bodies tensed with ultimate pleasure, and she tightened her thighs upon my head so that I seemed almost buried within her. Then she collapsed upon me before lifting herself to turn so that she could lie with her head in the crook of my arm, our hands between each other's thighs in a comfortable warmth which after a moment or two lulled us into slumber.

I awoke some hours later – for the fire was almost out, only a dull glow indicating the embers – to feel a movement of her fingers and once more, but this time with a slow, casual quiet which produced an equally intense but lazy pleasure, we gave ourselves to each other. And early in the morning, as cold light began to show, for a third time she devoted her tongue to pleasing me, while herself declined the attentions I now felt almost too tired to give but in politeness felt bound to offer.

I was truly astonished at the luxury of the dissipation we had enjoyed. Later, when I had an opportunity to discuss it with her, Anna told me that she had always preferred women to men, and that while she had made love with men on numerous occasions, the experience had never compared in depth with what she had experienced with her own sex. She had always felt, she explained, that men regarded the act of love as a battle which they must win, and the urgency of each occasion much diminished the pleasure she could find in it, while with a woman there was more ease, less haste, less urgency. She had never failed to reach the height of pleasure in such a manner, while with men 'no sooner are they up, than they're down; no sooner hot, than cold; no sooner on, than off,' she said. Moreover, man was too soon exhausted, while with woman there was no reason to conclude activity but the coming of morning!

With what reluctance I rose from our couch, the reader will understand. I was perhaps even more tired than I had been after my encounter with Bovile, for though he had been immeasurably more febrile than my female companion, the centre of my pleasure had not been so roused as by this night's encounter during which Anna had seemed to touch every chord of pleasure within me, so that the ultimate height of my enjoyment had been higher and more intense than on any previous occasion. Perhaps it was true, I considered, that men were always more concerned with their own pleasure than that of their companions.

But I was able to rouse myself, if not until Anna had fetched cold water to splash upon my body, for she seemed instantly to have recovered herself to her normal vigour, while even after I had clothed myself and made my way out to where Rosanna and Sam were breaking their fast, my eyes were still heavy, a fact which brought a blush to my cheek when Rosanna seemed to look questioningly between me and her sister-in-law. However, she may not have guessed what passed between us, while Sam seemed only concerned that I should eat my bread and drink my water and go with him to the tent where, once more, I would make money to be placed in the general coffers of the tribe – an activity about which I was less enthusiastic than he.

As we left the camp, I saw a woman's figure leave the tent I knew to be Bovile's, and as she lifted the canvas I thought I glimpsed for a moment his naked frame behind her. One thing of which I was confident was that if I was not to be summoned to his bed for another two weeks, he would certainly be waiting to receive my purse that same evening.

The day was unremarkable; another procession of the good folk of Royston invited my advice and rewarded me liberally for it, and as I expected, Bovile indeed met me on my return to the camp and seized my purse, nodding in approbation as he weighed it in his hand.

'You do well, *arincana* Sophia,' he said, smiling. I returned his smile only faintly, I fear, and made my way to our tent where Sam and Rosanna had food ready for me.

I retired early to my pile of rugs and was almost asleep when I heard a pitiful moaning outside the tent walls and, rising, put on my dress and took myself out, where I saw Sam and another man supporting a third as he staggered past. His shirt was torn and bloodied and blood streamed from his nose and one ear, while one of his arms dangled uselessly at his side; at each step he grunted and groaned.

Anna was at my side, having come to see, as I had, what was the trouble. She merely nodded grimly, and turned back. As I followed her into the tent, her sister-in-law asked, 'What goes forward?'

'Ah, 'tis only Rafe again,' Anna replied, and when I later asked her what had happened to the man, she replied that he was recently married to a beautiful girl of the tribe, a favourite of Bovile's. The latter had no right to object to the match, since the girl and he were not related, but having shown his disapprobation before the contract, he had insisted ever since on enjoying the girl each time her turn had come round as was his inalienable right under Gypsy custom, which had the force of law.

She had first entreated him then even tried to hide from him when her time came. Once before, Rafe had tried to protect her within their tent and Bovile had beaten him severely before taking her and forcing her to his pleasure. Now, once more, the unfortunate young man had tried to reason with the Gypsy leader not to claim his rights with the *chi* but Bovile had insisted, and when Rafe had once again tried to protect her, had again beaten him and broken his arm, such was his superior strength. The couple's tent stood close by ours and for most of the night I had to suffer his moans of physical injury as much as mental anguish at understanding what pain and humiliation Bovile was at that moment visiting upon his wife. To my surprise, Anna showed no sympathy at all for him and even at one time cried out to him to 'hold his noise' or she would come and break his other arm. I hoped that I would never myself be in need of sympathy from her or the other members of the tribe, for while they evidently took great pleasure in their animal instincts, it seemed that the human emotions of pity and compassion were foreign to them.

Chapter Nine

The Adventures of Andy

The adventure of the night of the Waterloo Ball did not, alas, result in an improvement in relations between Tom and me. On the contrary, for in relating to the other footmen our encounter with the Misses Glaistow, he was quick to magnify his part in the orgy while diminishing mine so that for a time I was known as 'Handy Andy' on the supposition that, my manly part being incapable of maintaining its rigidity until My Lady was content, I had had to bring her to satisfaction by means of the application of my finger – a proposition I was quick to deny, but which afforded the others far too much opportunity for country humour than it was easy for me to sustain.

Tabby only made things worse by stoutly defending me, even to claiming that Tom was not half the man I was. He took this extremely ill and as often as was possible got in my way when I was serving at table, making me appear clumsy and maladroit, so that on one or two occasions I received a stern look from My Lord. Fortunately Mr Caister saw what Tom was about and made allowances for me, though far from knowing the cause. Although he was indifferent to the fact that any guest in the house could summon one of the female staff to his bed without anyone raising an eyebrow, he would by no means have taken it easily had he known that any of the male servants provided a similar service for the female guests, much less for their fellow servants. I cannot guess at the reason for this, unless it was rooted in his own proclivities, but at all events it was the case and Tom dared not reveal to the butler the cause of his ill temper with myself, for he too would have felt the brunt of Mr Caister's undoubted anger.

Tabby and I were able, in our spare time, to continue to provide Beau Rust with the means to illustrate his great work – though I must confess to doubting, from time to time, whether there was not more pleasure taken in the simple sight of our love-making than in the provision of illustrative material for his book, for his powers as an artist were sketchy in the extreme.

During the hours we spent with him, we gradually grew to know more about him, for at the end of our activities he would regale us with memories of his youth, from which we ended with a clear view of how he came to leave the church and become rather a man of fashion than of the cloth. In the suspicion that his account of himself might interest the reader, I take the liberty of appending it here, though with his usual exclamations and quotations from the Scriptures excised, no less for reasons of space than of tedium.

Beau Rust's Account of Himself.

'Twas in the year of 'fifty-nine when half the world was reading M. Voltaire's *Candide* and the other half mourning the death of Wolfe at the victory of Quebec, that I for the first time set foot in the city of Bath. I was then, I must tell you, eighteen years of age, and placed by my father in the hands of the Bishop of Exeter as a curate. My elder brother having entered the Army, and my next elder the Navy, there was nothing left for me but the Church, to which indeed I had no reason to believe I was unsuited for my father was gravely religious, severe upon the Nonconformists and Wesleyans, keeping daily prayers and raising me to be entirely ignorant of such pleasure as music or the stage or the company of women. My mother having died at my birth, I must have had a nurse, I presume, but have no memory of her for at the earliest possible age I was plucked from the breast and offered to the less tender mercies of a tutor who taught me verses from the Psalms before I could with confidence stand upon my feet. My brothers, on their rare visits to the ancestral hall, took great care not to outrage my father's susceptibilities (hoping for his purse strings to remain firmly tied until their succession) and kept to themselves any amorous adventures their travels may have afforded them.

However, in my eighteenth year, by which time my piousness was a legend throughout the cathedral close and my knowledge of the Bible positively encyclopaedic, I developed a troublesome complaint of the skin which declined to repair itself despite applications of the concoctions and decoctions of the Exeter doctors. There was nothing for it but to dispatch me to Bath to take the waters there in the company of an elderly clergyman of impeccable decorum. He, alas, fell ill and died promptly upon our arrival at the Royal Crescent, and I was left to take myself off to the baths as best I might.

My shyness was inordinate and it can be conjectured with how particular a shock I discovered that men and women visited the baths together, and frequently in a state of nature. I, of course, retained my shirt as I paid my threepence and entered the waters of the King's Bath, considered most efficacious for the treatment of troubles of the skin. Indeed, though the water was filthy and the condition of the bodies of some of the other visitors made it difficult for me to contain my disgust, within a day or two my own skin began to clear so that I felt able to go on to one of the other baths where the water was less vigorous in its curative efficacy. The bath I chose was the Cross Bath, simply because an attendant at the King's recommended it as being patronised by all the quality. Again I entered the water in my shirt and again found I was the only being there who was so covered, both men and women flaunting their nakedness. But, as I became soon aware, it was a more attractive nakedness than that of the poor sufferers I had earlier seen, for here were no pustules and putrefication, no scorbutics or lacquered hides; all was rather softness and whiteness, the bodies shapely and appealing, reminiscent more of the Song of Solomon than the Book of Job.

The Cross Bath was indeed a curious sight for one more used to the cloister. The ladies positively displayed their beauties in wanton dalliance, their languishing eyes darting killing glances and before them, often, floated japan bowls in which they kept sometimes fine perfumes, sometimes confectionary. The men, when not hanging by their arms at the sides of the bath viewing the whole, paid court to the ladies of their choice, openly toying with their breasts and sometimes, I suspected, with other parts of their bodies, for often a couple would positively embrace for a length of time, only their heads and shoulders, closely in proximity, to be seen above the somewhat muddied waters.

The great Beau Nash, orderer and king of all Bath, was still living then, though rarely seen, and society was still of the brightest and most colourful, and I spent many hours, in my dark clothes, considering the evil proclivity to pleasure with which the town reeked. The streets, from dawn to dusk, were crowded with sedan chairs for no one ever seemed to walk anywhere, and the place was ruled by the chairmen – stout, brawny fellows, their muscled calves encased in white stockings. Monarchs of the pavement, they gave way to no man, pushing aside anyone unfortunate enough to come in their way. In fair weather smiling and obsequious, when rain fell and they were in demand they became surly and presumptuous, purse-proud and arrogant.

Harrison's and Thayer's ballrooms, to which I took myself on Tuesday and Friday evenings in order to store up for my superiors in Exeter observation of the execrable ungodliness of the city, showed such scenes as I had never imagined. The ladies' dresses were an assault on the senses – black velvet embroidered with chenille, white satin embroidered with gold, green paduasoy embroidered with silver – and the gentlemen were no less handsomely dressed, some in coats lined with ermine, many in velvet, some in silk. The balls began at six o'clock precisely when a single couple led off a minuet, and the same dance continued for two hours, until each couple in the room had for some moments danced alone before the rest.

After the minuet came the country dances, one of the most spirited being 'Hunt the Squirrel' in which the woman fled and the man pursued her – a pursuit which sometimes ended outside the ballroom, and in what activity we were left to conjecture. Young girls were handled, and in public, with much familiarity, and much use was made of a lascivious step called 'setting', which was the very reverse of 'back to back', so that the man's and woman's bosoms brushed in a most wanton fashion. On the very first occasion I was at Thayer's, a young man bid the fiddlers play a dance called Mol Patley, and after capering ungraciously, seized his partner, locked his arms in hers, and whisked her round cleverly above ground in such a manner that I, sitting upon one of the lowest benches, saw further above her shoe than I could ever had believed to be possible.

You may properly conjecture that on more than one occasion I was conscious of a troublesome warmth in my under parts, which previously had visited me only during sleep so that I had awakened with my member erect, and only an application of cold water from my washing bowl would reduce him. At Harrison's and Thayer's however, hot punch was more readily available than cold water, and often I had to remain in the warm waters of the baths for some long time before my body was in a fit state for me to remove myself.

It was at the Cross Bath that I finally met my undoing – or my salvation, depending on how you view it.

I was in the habit, now, of going to the bath as soon as it opened, for thus one took the advantage of clean waters, they being changed each night. Standing one morning immersed to the shoulders in the tepid water with only three or four other people around me, I saw two ladies enter at the far door. Both were wrapped in the large towels which were provided for our covering as we walked from the changing room to the bath; one was a matron of middle years and generous proportions, the other a young girl whose features took me immediately, for she resembled nothing so much as an angel, her fine face framed by yellow curls which seemed to gleam even under the low light of the morning. I watched with peculiar interest as they came to the bath's edge where they would (I trusted) throw off their coverings to enter the water (you see that I was already captive to the flesh, though I still nightly prayed for forgiveness for my concupiscence, which only took the form of imaginings and, when my amorous propensities were particularly stirred, of self-satisfaction). The older woman undraped, revealing a body generously corpulent with pendulous breasts, a belly which rolled as she descended the steps, and thighs which would have provided ample support for a beast of burden. She seemed, however, a pleasant soul, and turning to her companion smiled and beckoned as she entered the water.

The girl looked about her almost in fear, but then allowed the sheet to slip from her shoulders – and ah! It was at that moment that I lost my heart, for she was a ravishing example of her sex, the perfect proportions of her breasts, teasingly sweet, balancing above a frame not one ounce too liberally endowed with flesh, where the fall of her hips and thighs in one sublime line seemed to me as lovely as any in picture or poetry. It was but for a moment that I was allowed a glimpse of her beauty for she slipped into the water like some bird into its aerial element, scarcely seeming to disturb the mirrored surface.

She and her companion remained at the other end of the bath, the older lady laughing and joking, the girl smiling and more thoughtful, but clearly of a pleasing and cheerful disposition. I must confess that I slowly began to make my way towards them for I was eager at least to examine the younger lady more closely, being of too retiring a disposition to hope for an acquaintance.

Slowly, more people arrived at the bath, including among them a young officer whom I had seen at a ball the night before at Harrison's, drunk and importunate with the ladies until he was invited to leave by the attendants there, who were finally disposed to expel him by force. A surly fellow, he clearly believed himself irresistible to female susceptibility and had contrived to offend many of the ladies during the evening by his mock-courtesies, which they properly regarded as insults.

Now, he strode into the bath, barely keeping hold on the towel about his waist, which he threw to the ground almost as soon as he entered, striding to the edge of the water quite naked and with the air of someone who believed his person to be a *sine qua non*. And indeed he was powerfully built, muscular and bronzed, and were it not for the head set awkwardly upon the trunk, with a sardonic look upon its face, he might indeed have been considered an attractive figure.

He descended with a splash into the waters, causing a disturbance in them which made the girl and her companion gasp as for a moment the waters rose to their chins. He saw them at once and was all eyes for the beauty of the yonger creature, and without hesitation he half-strode, half-swam towards them, greeting them with a low salutation which I could not properly hear.

She turned her head modestly aside, at which he reached out and roughly took her chin, turning her face back towards him. Her companion's jaw dropped at the audacity. The girl however retained an astonishing calm, and made a retort which somewhat abashed him, for he released her and bowed shortly. However, he remained at their side, from time to time making some comment, and eventually once more grew rough, bending down and saying something into her ear which brought a blush to her cheek and at the same time, I suspected, placing his hand upon her waist below the water, for she drew back from him. He took a step forward, however, and with the utmost audacity bent to place a kiss upon her shoulder. She gave a little scream – which was enough for me, my temper already roused by what I had seen.

Less than two yards away, I threw myself towards the party and seized the officer by the shoulders from behind, pulling him back so that his head disappeared beneath the waters. He reappeared, spluttering, and with his face red as a turkey cock's took on a sneering expression as he saw the youth who had assaulted him, and raised his hand to deliver a blow which, had it landed, would perhaps have been the death of me. However, with self-preserving instinct, rather than shrinking back I ducked in beneath his guard and reaching out beneath the water, grasped his manhood in one hand and wrenched at it with all my power. His raised arm fell, his face contorted, he let out a bellow which echoed around the walls and he doubled up and disappeared again beneath the waters.

By now, the commotion had brought the attendants, who recognised the source of the trouble and leaping in (as they were always ready to do), rescued him from the bath – for he was entirely unable to stand – and carried him out.

Myself much shaken by the incident, I had almost forgot the ladies, but a voice at my ear reminded me.

'Sir, we are much indebted!' said the older woman. 'Sarah, your thanks to the young gentleman.'

The girl half-curtsied in the water, which had the charming effect that as she rose again the rosy tips of her breasts for a moment broke the surface.

'As my aunt remarks, sir, we are much indebted,' she said. 'That officer has been troublesome before, and I fear followed us here with the intent to be impertinent. I can only offer you all my gratitude.'

'Please, ma'am, say nothing of it,' I protested. 'Perhaps you will allow me to take a dish of tea with you in the Pump Room, when you are ready to retire?'

She looked at her aunt, who nodded, and shyly half-curtsying again turned to mount the steps out of the bath, revealing as she did so a back quite as ravishing as her front, the gentle curve of her shoulders and waist hanging upon her spine with a lovely aspect, and the fall of her posterior below, in two charming globes, resembling a ripe peach. Her aunt, following her, displayed no such beauty as she rolled forth, but since she was clearly well disposed towards me I was prepared entirely to admire her ample proportions, if they did not rouse my passions in the same way. I followed the ladies from the water, turning to the wall as I reached for my sheet, to conceal the fact that my admiration had begun to take corporeal form.

We met a quarter of an hour later in the Pump Room, an imposing setting for the fashionable and beautiful where a woman stood at the pump dispensing King Bladud's water, which aunt and niece were drinking with no enthusiasm together with an old duchess of eighty and a child of four. I took a glass but it was very hot and mineral and it was easy to persuade the ladies to join me, instead, in a dish of tea, while the orchestra played and the company walked up and down, not minding the music, but in a continual buzz of conversation – though at the end of each tune they clapped their hands, not knowing what for.

My seraph was introduced to me as Miss Sarah Wheeler, the daughter of James Wheeler, Esq., a merchant of Bristol, and was in Bath to take the waters under the guidance of her aunt, Mrs Hester Muster, the widow of a major in the Guards. Miss Wheeler was now dressed in a handsome gown, its high waist and *décolletage* provokingly displaying her beautiful breasts, the white roundness of which would have raised passions in a statue. Her aunt wore a voluminous gown of green satin with sufficient material about it to have dressed a positive crowd of younger and slimmer ladies, but her humour was so placid that no one but could have liked her, and my own liking was increased by the suggestion that I should walk her niece back to their lodgings in the Centre House in Pierpont Street. Doubtless her gratitude for my assistance was amplified by the sight of my canonicals in which, my figure being slim and, dare I say, elegant, I must confess I looked handsome enough.

Miss Wheeler – although I could already only think of her as Sarah – had quite overcome her shyness, and as we walked through the streets, crowded with gentlemen in breeches, stockings and cocked hats and ladies in superb pelisses laced with gold cords round them, with great tassels of gold upon their sides and reticules hanging at their waists, she chattered of her enjoyment of the season – how there was a run of balls, parties, concerts and masquerades without end, how Catalini was singing her best songs here, how Kemble was coming to perform at the theatre, how Lady Belmore's masquerade was a great success though three or four others took place the same night, but Sir William James thought Lady Belmore's the most brilliant. And she related how one of her aunt's gentlemen acquaintances had gone to the whole, making a change of dress for each masquerade, and had told her there were better dresses and more lively masks elsewhere and certainly a much better supper.

'But,' she remarked, 'I suppose, sir, that a gentleman of the cloth can have no interest in such affairs.'

On the contrary, I told her, I was most interested by the goings on, of which I had had no previous experience. She was astonished at my innocence and when I asked if I could attend her at Harrison's Rooms for the ball that evening, was pleased to acquiesce, at which, we by now being at Pierpont Street, I kissed her hand (though looking enviously at her lips) and bade farewell.

You can imagine with what a beating heart I waited at Harrison's Rooms at six o'clock that evening, when the minuet began without Sarah's appearance. However, after half an hour, she and her aunt arrived and greeted me with every sign of pleasure. We danced the minuet, after which Mrs Muster, seeing a dew of perspiration on her niece's face, asked if I would not take her into the gardens for some air. I needed no second invitation, nor did Sarah demur at taking my arm and walking out to where a path over a lawn led under some trees. Here the lights shone only fitfully through the still branches and the balmy night air, while it cooled our faces, did nothing to cool my ardour, which had been almost unendurably roused by the proximity of so much fairness during the dance.

At last we came to a seat in a quiet corner of the gardens, and I handed Sarah to it and sat beside her, daring to take her cool hand in mine. You young blades of today would have thrown yourselves upon her, and no doubt the young doxies of today would throw up their skirts to accommodate you, but it was some time before I dared to bend forward and plant a kiss upon her lips – a kiss which was delicately but not unkindly received, so that returning it again I raised my hand and let it fall upon the upper part of one of those alluring breasts, which rose and fell beneath my palm with what seemed like fervour. I dared to slide my palm downwards below the edge of her dress, feeling for the first time the strangely exciting small round bud of womanhood under my hand.

By this time the whole pressure of my eighteen years was ready to discharge and it was at this moment that Sarah unconsciously dropped her hand, which had been resting upon my shoulder, into my lap, so that it fell upon my distended but still imprisoned manhood. No doubt the peculiar swelling in my breeches intrigued her, for she softly grasped and squeezed it, at which with a low moan I felt my manhood flood from me, and almost fainted away at the pleasure of it.

Concerned, she drew away and asked if I was not overcome by the exercise of the dance. I could scarcely explain the true reason for my lassitude but instead fell upon my knee and made an immediate declaration of passion, to which she responded by leaning to kiss my lips and to reply that she, too, felt the power of love – and for the first time in her sixteen years!

Imagine my rapture as once again I clasped and kissed her, my manly vitality almost immediately returning. But I was conscious of extreme discomfort below and thinking quickly explained that I had to return to my lodgings, where I was expecting a communication that evening from my Bishop. But could we not – I implored – meet at some time later in the evening? In short, we agreed to meet in that same place at nine o'clock, which hour, she assured me, she would await with the keenest anticipation.

Sarah then returned to the dance, promising to give my regards and explanation to her aunt, and I slipped out by a side entrance and hailed a sedan chair, in which I returned to my lodging, cleansed myself and exchanged my small-clothes for fresh dress.

Back at Harrison's, I saw with some disquiet Sarah dancing with an elderly man in Army uniform. I went straight into the garden and sat upon the seat to wait and even a little before the appointed time a figure in white flitted silently through the trees to join me and without hesitation sat upon my knee, threw her arms around me, and kissed me. There was no question that Sarah's passion matched my own; later, I was to hear that she, like myself, had been kept from the world, and had never had the slightest communication with a person of the opposite sex. So it was that as her touch inflamed my senses, so mine ignited hers. In a few moments I had unloosed the neck of her gown and was planting my kisses upon her heaving bosom, while she had lifted my shirt from the band of my breeches and was stroking the flesh of my back.

I rose and, lifting her in my arms, carried her deeper into the garden to where bushes provided a more sheltered and private place, where I placed her upon the grass and bent to lie beside her, once more applying my mouth to a swelling breast, and at the same time lifting her skirt to reach upwards – waiting, I must own, for her to cry out or invite me to hold. Far from doing so, she responded as hotly and I felt with increased delight her hands fumbling to undo my breeches, which she found difficult because of the tightness of the buttons. Pausing for a moment in my ministrations, I loosed them myself and drew my clothes from me, while at the same time, to my delight, she slipped her dress from her. In the dim light reflected from the sky, I could see only a blur of white, but what my eye could not discern my hands discovered, and we made a mutual exploration of each other, myself astonished to feel for the first time a mist of hair between her legs (for it had not occurred to me that the ladies could possess such), while she gave a gasp of amazement at the nature of my parts – the size and inextensibility of my prick, the weight and roundness of my cods. Her handling of my parts almost again drew me to the supreme moment so that I removed her hands, and myself began to explore her lower parts, whose sensibility to my touch clearly rendered her equally delirious, for as I kissed the fleshy lips beneath their down I felt her whole body shiver, and she in turn reached down to pull my head by the hair so that I could not reach her.

By now neither of us was prepared to terminate our pleasure without experiencing the final crisis; that instinct with which the Creator provides us all guided me (for I had had no teaching, I need not say) so that parting her thighs I placed myself between them and with little difficulty, its head being slippery with those juices which prepare us for the assault, slipped my instrument into her irresistible person. There I seemed to meet with an obstruction but I was in no mood to temporise, and for a moment losing control of my natural politeness, gave a strong push – at which to my concern Sarah gave a cry of pain, when I made to withdraw, but she threw her arms about me, placed her hands upon my arse and pulled me into her; upon which again with that blessed natural instinct I began to move in the manner of which you know, and after a while felt her body move beneath me as naturally as the waves move to the pressure of a vessel.

It took but a moment for my pleasure to acuminate and as my joy was released, so I felt her arms tighten about me, and she sighed with the same satisfaction.

With a common consent we lay still, close in each other's arms, and such was my youth that my member remained upreared, filling the natural cavity in which it was encased as though constructed for the purpose. Beneath me, I felt Sarah's breathing quieten, and slowly her hands began to stroke my shoulders and back with such tenderness that I felt, for the first time in my existence, that I was the beloved object of another human being rather than a simple thing to be sent hither and thither with nought but impatience and scorn.

In a while, my body again seemed by itself to move and once more, but more slowly, we performed that special act of adoration with which man and woman alone, of all creation, celebrate their union – for I now realised with what completeness my soul was engaged in my body's actions, and with what closeness these united us.

It was without a word that we roused ourselves, put on our clothes, and walked, arm in arm, back towards the light. As we reached it, I noticed traces of red upon her dress, which you will of course know was the sign of her lost maidenhead. Fortunately, she had a shawl which, claiming to be cold, she draped around her, and pleading a sudden sickness, Mrs Muster (who was too occupied with her own pleasure) happily agreed to my escorting her niece back to Pierpont Street.

But as we walked towards the doorway, two figures strode towards me. For a moment, I did not know who it was – merely I saw two officers in dress uniform, one of whom appeared to be for some reason angered. Then I recognised the scowling face of the man whom I had encountered at the baths. He came to attention before me, and without a word brought up his hand, slapped me in the face with his glove and threw it to the ground before me, then turned upon his heel to stride from the rooms.

The second officer clicked his heels, and said: 'Sir, allow me to present myself; I am Major Constant Hawtry. Major Willoughby Fawcett's compliments, and he will be pleased to meet you at Duncan's Fields at dawn tomorrow.' Upon which he clicked his heels again, turned upon them, and left the room. A buzz of conversation broke out, which almost drowned the faint cry which Sarah gave as she fell, unconscious, to the floor.

I was left in no doubt that what was proposed was a duel. Mrs Muster went so far as to congratulate me upon it, as though 'twere some victory, and introduced me to one of her friends, a Captain Dawkin who, she said, would be my 'second'.

'My second what?' I innocently enquired, at which he found it necessary to explain the etiquette of duelling to me while Mrs Muster took her niece, now quite distraught, back to their lodgings.

It can be surmised that I slept not at all that night. Captain Dawkin produced a sword, the property of his father, which he said I was welcome to borrow. He spent most of the hours before dawn explaining Major Fawcett's prowess as a swordsman and saying that he was, however, much disliked and that if I could contrive to wound him before he overcame me, Bath would be delighted – and after all, he might only wound me. He then produced the day's papers and read me the accounts of duels which had took place that week, including one between Ned Goodyear and Beau Fielding at the Play House in Drury Lane, and one between a captain and a young man of fashion in Warwickshire, one of whom now lay in the earth, and the other in Newgate Prison. All this comforted me much.

As dawn broke I waited, cold and shivering, with Captain Dawkin upon Duncan's Fields until out of the morning mist emerged the two Majors, gruff as dragons. Fawcett produced his sword, I drew mine, we crossed, Major Hawtry struck the steel aside, and we began.

While by no means a swordsman, I had at least some knowledge of the art for as a boy an uncle of mine had taught it me with foils, saying that I had a natural ability and could become a great man if I was inclined. Indeed I had some inclination but my father dispatching me at an early age to the care of the clergy, I had never held sword more until that morning. I managed to block two strokes and parry a third. Then, reaching forward in an ambitious pass, the Major's foot fell into a great turd of cow dung which he had not noticed; he slipped forward and positively threw himself upon my sword, which passed through his body without the least resistance, being torn from my hand as he fell to the ground devoid of life.

The result was the best possible for me, for both his second and mine were in agreement that his death was an accident. So that while under severe censure from authority for participating in a duel, I could not be charged with the Major's death but was none the less a hero to Bath, which was thrown into a positive passion of pleasure at the Major's death, he having insulted half the ladies and offended half the men of the town.

Mrs Muster was moved to admiration; Sarah to renewed ardour. I was now in a desperate predicament: I could not think of leaving my love, yet I must now return to Exeter and the cloister, for the time allowed for my treatment was past and messages daily arrived at Bath inviting my return to the jurisdiction of my Bishop. Had I money of my own, I would have known what response to make, but I had none and if I were to resign from the clergy and marry my mistress on what could we subsist?

In the end, after a leave-taking, stolen one evening while Mrs Muster was at bridge with her cronies, when many tears fell from each other's eyes onto our respective bosoms, I left by the mail coach and within a day was once more immured far from the sight of the girl I had come to love. As for her, she was silent, for though I had given her an address to which she could send a loving message, she sent none and after a week's silence, then two, I was reduced to cursing the duplicity of women. My thoughts, rebellious to the command of my mentors, stubbornly declined to soar to heavenly matters, and remained below.

One morning eighteen days after I had left Bath – I marked the days with melancholy thoughts – a fellow student knocked at the door of my room (which indeed was no more luxurious than a monk's cell) and announced to me that 'my boy was come'. This I took to be a joke, for while several of my companions were indeed accompanied by boy servants to care for their bodily comfort, my father made me no allowance for such a luxury, and I looked after my own linen, the cleaning of my room, *et cetera*. But my friend insisted that a boy had come who claimed he was sent to serve me, and wearying of the argument and willing to be fooled if that was the wish of the joker, I told him to send the lad to me. He retired and a few moments later, after a timid knock, a small figure dressed in the black cassock worn by the servants of our house made its way in; he had a close-cropped head of fair hair and blue eyes which somehow reminded me . . .

And yes – you are ahead of me; the boy ran forward to clasp me in his arms, and as he did so I felt the warm pressure of two breasts beneath the black cloth. It was indeed my Sarah. Pausing only to lock the door, I fell with her upon my hard bed and within moments we were joined in that activity which had haunted my every waking moment since we had last parted.

When the storm had sunk, and risen, and sunk again, she told me that she had determined at Bath that we would not be parted and that if I could not stay with her, she would come to me. Making the excuse that she wished to say farewell to a female friend, she had concealed what small store of money she had, eluded the unfortunate Mrs Muster, and taken the Bristol coach. Then she travelled on to Exeter where she had for forty-eight hours watched my comings and goings and those of my friends, and seeing that some of them were served by boys whose bodies were covered by loosely-cut cassocks, had decided that this was the way she should be able to stay with me. First acquiring a cassock by bribing one of the cathedral caretakers, and persuading a friendly barber to crop her hair, she had found no difficulty in passing as a boy to the gateman and then to my friend. The looseness of the cassock was such that she had not even to bind her breasts, which were free beneath it, as I had now discovered.

Though my mind misgave me, for there were sure to be drawbacks to such a crazy scheme, I was too overjoyed at her presence to demur. And for several weeks there was indeed no difficulty. There was in fact only one moment of peril: returning from a day's study during which I had had no opportunity for time with Sarah, I ran up the stairs to my room and threw my nether garments from me, pausing only to lift her cassock (under which she generally wore no clothes, it being still very hot weather, and the rooms stuffy) and throw it over her head, turned her so that she was bending over a table and supporting herself with her hands, and plunged into her from behind (though lawfully) and was bucking with all the enjoyment and vigour of eighteen years when I heard a step behind me. I turned and saw the Dean of the Cathedral – a corpulent and good-humoured man – at the door, which in my hurry I had omitted to close!

'Oh, my dear fellow!' he said. 'Use your pretty lad gently or he will not be able to sit comfortably at table!' and closed the door behind him as he left.

Sarah lifted the cassock from her head and grinned and though I was quite crestfallen from the shock, I laughed too. Mr Runciple was well-known to look with a kindly, nay envious, eye upon the boy servants of the house – most of whom indeed were kept to serve their masters in bed as well as at board – and being used to turning a blind eye had seen no good reason to interfere with my pleasure. Sarah found, however, that he was now given to patting her thoughtfully upon the head, or the rump, whenever he had the opportunity, and took every precaution never to be caught alone by him lest he should attempt her and discover all.

It was a fortnight later that a less sympathetic figure, the prebendary in charge of the house itself and its running, who for that reason possessed keys to all the rooms, let himself into mine in the late evening (for what reason I never discovered, but suspect treachery of some sort). In this case there was no disguise, for we had just concluded a passage of love and were lying side by side as God made us upon the bedclothes, and it would have been a blinder man than the prebendary who did not notice Sarah's pouting and thankful breasts, or the fact that she did not possess the appendage which decorated my own loins.

I was summoned next day to the library of the Dean, where Mr Runcible was prepared to be severe; the long tradition of boy-love within the church was one thing, he explained; to allow women within the sacred precincts was another. But here was news which made condign punishment unnecessary.

What could this be? I wondered. He told me that my uncle had died and left me all his fortune, amounting to no less a sum than four thousand pound a year, which would allow me to live comfortably where I chose and with whom I wished. Pausing only to resign my connection with the church, I ran back to my rooms, where Sarah was sorrowfully preparing for exile, and within the week we were man and wife, with the reluctant permission of her father who, himself having a small fortune, believed he might one day be reliant upon mine.

There is little more to record: we lived together happily for over fifty years and had one daughter, who married My Lord and by him had my two grandchildren with whom – my dear wife and our child, alas, dying within months of each other some five years since – I now live, occupied still, as you know, with those delights I first discovered in Bath so many years ago, though now in recording rather than performing them.

And with that, Beau Rust closed his account, and we left him.

Chapter Ten

Sophie's Story

My disillusion with the Gypsy band had begun with Bovile's calm appropriation of all the money I was able to make, without indication that I would ever see a penny of it. His treatment of everyone under him continued it, for while he was always smiling, and though brusque never outwardly cruel, he acted as though every person and thing connected with the tribe was his personal property and moreover everyone in the tribe accepted this.

As the days passed into weeks and we moved on from Royston through Baldock and Gravely, Dunstable, Wendover and Princes Risborough in the direction of the western coast, and I came to know more of the Gypsy customs – partly through experience and partly through conversation – my discontent grew. The men, certainly, had not such a bad time of it as long as they fell not foul of Bovile who was unregenerate in his treatment of anyone who crossed him. But the women were no more than chattels, and though only Anna complained, they all fell under the same interdicts and were regarded with the same lack of consideration. It was no surprise to me that they bore the brunt of most of the hard work of the train for so it has ever been; that we should be expected to fetch and carry, to cook, to look after the packing and unpacking of the tribe's few possessions, was nothing to me. But in the matter of their family life, I was appalled at the severity of the standard applied to them, and not only by Bovile but by all the men of the tribe.

Except that she was, the moment she became a woman, subject to the desires of the *dimber damber*, every woman was expected to eschew the company of men until she was married, and once married was expected to remain faithful only to her husband until her death – again, with the exception of her ministrations to Bovile. If she was unfaithful, her husband was wont to strip her naked, cut off all her hair and chase her from the camp. This had been done, within the past year, by one of our men who now awaited his wife's return, which could only take place after her hair had grown back to a length of at least five inches.

Men, on the other hand, were never punished for their infidelities (as Anna told me with a laugh) though they feared to make love with the wife of one who was absent or to have dealings with a prostitute, lest they should be subject to the *mokadi*, or taboo.

This was, Anna explained, the only weapon a woman possessed but it could be a strong one, for she was at certain times and under certain conditions capable of contaminating the men of the tribe by a single touch and his falling under *mokadi* would expose him to strong magic and evil. Though the younger girls and the older women lost this power, those who were of years to interest men most strongly had the power also to affect them by magic by simply touching a drinking vessel or a plate in a particular way, by merely walking over a stream of drinking water. In some cases food could be 'poisoned' by being touched by a dress and so a white apron was always worn while food was being prepared.

Anna failed, however, to explain just how this magic could be raised, though she promised to do so if ever I should need to use it. I doubted whether this would be possible, for since I was not of the Gypsy stock, how could I use their magic? None the less, I was interested to hear about it and many hours of otherwise tedious travelling from place to place were enlivened by stories of the strange customs of the people, none of them, after all, stranger than Mr Nelham's idea of raising the Devil.

The more that I saw of the life of the people in the villages and small towns through which we passed, the more I realised the power that could be held over them through playing upon their superstitions. However slender the knowledge I had been able to acquire at Alcovary, at least my father and mother had always been at pains to keep me from the superstitions of the few country people I met, rebuking the maids for talking to me of pixies and elves, and Mr Ffloyd too had been strong against those who believed in what he termed the irrational. But the people we saw as we passed throughout the countryside were almost at our mercy, for they so believed in the capability of the tribe to influence them by means of magic that they were ready to do anything to keep on good terms, from providing food to giving what money they had, on threat of being cursed.

But all was not entirely bad, for Rosanna was one of the women who had a powerful knowledge of medicinal herbs and other cures. Some of these were unpleasant – the drinking of potions made from saliva, urine or excreta, for instance, to expel a devil from a body by inflicting him with nausea. Sometimes small bags were given containing spiders or woodlice which were to be worn until they died, for as they did so, so the affliction would leave the body of the sick man or woman. I once saw her treat a woman for the wheezing of the breath by catching a trout, making her breath three times into its mouth, then throwing it back into the water – and indeed the woman was much relieved. In the same way, a roasted dormouse will cure the whooping cough and a concoction of bacon fat, pepper and vinegar, the croup.

Sometimes a neighbourhood which proved unreceptive could be reduced to hospitality by the simple means of leaving magical charms on doorsteps – elderberry branches and growing bushes to protect evil from entering the house of the kindly, a horse's skull or animal bones to introduce ill into a house. Whether by luck or by magic, the denizens of the house seemed plagued by ill-luck on the introduction of these charms, and would sue for peace.

My own case was a strange one for, far from relying upon strange incantations or charms, my own art was drawn from an ancient study which had for centuries been respectably practised throughout the civilised world, as Mr Lilly explains in his book. Though it was clear that I had con-

nection with the Egyptians, I was in a sense separate from
them, not least in my appearance, for I had declined to
dress myself in the old clothes they begged from any
passers-by or cottagers but had insisted that I should buy
good dresses to wear from some of the money I brought the
tribe. Bovile had at first strenuously argued against this but
in the end had listened to sense, and seeing how I brought
the money in had grudgingly afforded me sufficient funds
to purchase fashionable clothes. As I appeared either in the
best of their tents or, sometimes, in a room of a private
house, or one hired for the purpose, this helped to attract
the better class of enquirer, able to pay more for the privilege of consulting me.

I must confess that I found the celibate life I was expected
to lead between my regulated visits to Bovile's bed
extremely tedious. Having had my passions ignited, as it
were, at so early an age, they needed regular feeding. While
Bovile himself, though I grew increasingly to dislike him,
had a physical power capable of satisfying any desire, few
other men of the tribe attracted me and in any event they
were too terrified of their leader to consider making an
approach to me or responding to any I might make. Anna
remained attentive but, sensitive lover as she was, my tastes
were towards the masculine sex, of whose ministrations I
was now starved.

It was at Winchester that I embarked upon an adventure
which might have cost me dear. We were encamped upon
the outskirts of the town but I had taken a room at the
Coach and Horses Inn, not far from the cathedral, for my
consultations and a steady train of townspeople had come
there to ask me the usual questions. Near the close of the
second day a young man appeared mysteriously wrapped in
a cloak (though the weather was hot) and with a hat pulled
well down, neither of which did he throw off until the door
was closed behind him, when he was revealed as a handsome fellow of twenty years or so, well dressed, with
auburn hair neatly tied.

· His name he declined to give but he was the son of a local
alderman, a tradesman, who wished to marry him to the

daughter of a rich merchant of Canterbury. This was a pleasant but unattractive maid whose company, upon meeting her, he had enjoyed, but who he felt might pall as a wife – 'For,' he said, somewhat stuttering, 'to be honest she is more than somewhat plain, and of a figure less than handsome.' Could I tell him whether their union would be a happy one?

He being able to supply me with the particulars of his own birth and that of the lady, I set to work while he sat nearby to wait. The charts being prepared, I saw immediately that here was an amiable girl enough, ready in conversation and free in pleasantries, but likely to have a small bodily appetite so that, as I told him, while he would not find daily intercourse with her unpleasant, their bed-life would not be likely to be fiery.

Clearly he had not expected to hear a woman talk to him upon such matters and while his face fell as he heard my words, his eyes sparkled more than a little and I felt that they played more than a little around the neck of my dress, which was fashionably low, so that the globes of my breasts were certainly not concealed from view.

My study told me, I went on, that he was a young man of virility and high passions and if not supplied with material for their satisfaction at home, would seek them abroad – was this not the case?

It was, he replied, and had been since he was a schoolboy.

He was now shifting somewhat upon his seat and, bending over in guise of consulting my charts, I stole a look into his lap where I fancied I could see a strong member struggling to be free of its bonds. The sight somewhat roused my passions and I had not been unaffected by proximity to such a handsome fellow who would not, I felt sure, be unwilling to assuage that appetite which had over a week been starved in me. But how was I to broach the subject without being unladylike?

I need not have concerned myself for in leaning over, my dress had fallen away to an inflaming extent and he leapt to his feet, caught me by the shoulders and drew me to him, exclaiming that no woman had previously understood him so well and that had Betty – his proposed wife – been so well-formed, no problem would have arisen. Almost before the last word fell from his lips they were pressed upon my own, while his arms gathered me so closely to him that I could feel his manly part like an iron bar against my thigh.

'Oh, sir!' I cried, as soon as I could free my lips. 'Pray release me – the door is not locked!'

It was the work of but a moment with him to stride to the door – and discover that it had no key, whereupon he simply lifted the table at which I had been working and placed it against the door in such a way that it would at least delay the entry of anyone approaching. He then turned and began to unbutton his shirt as he walked slowly towards me.

I felt a pang of pity for the unfortunate Betty whose sensibilities were so blunted that she could not appreciate such a packet of pleasures. His curled hair fell low over a wide forehead and a quizzical eyebrow, bright eyes and lips which were strong and sweet. His frame, as the shirt slipped from his shoulders, was slim but powerful, the shoulders broad, the chest tapering to a narrow waist from which, as I looked, he slipped the breeches revealing a standing device as stalwart as I had imagined.

'Now, madam,' he cried as he stood before me, 'I have shown you the way; surely you will not deny me an equal view?'

Needing no encouragement, I was out of my gown in a trice and for a long moment we stood regarding each other with a pleasure soon to be keenly enlarged. As he took a step towards me, I fell to my knees before him in wondering delight, taking him in my hands to examine that part to which every woman must sometime, surely, pay the tribute of admiration. In this case, it was not only strong but beautifully shaped, smooth as polished ivory and decorated at its base with a scheme of curls each of which might have been individually fashioned by a hair-dresser, so decorative and well arranged were they. Below, in their dependant pouch, hung twin orbs whose weight decreased as I held them in my palm, for while they swelled in appreciation of my tender attentions, at the same time they drew themselves up in admiration, nestling at the base of their superior companion.

Pausing now only to plant a kiss upon the tip, where a small bead of liquor stood in tribute to the passion to come, I raised myself to be clasped once more in strong arms and laid upon the single couch which stood in the corner of the room, where for a while he was content to graze upon my body, his fingers running lightly as butterflies over my shoulders and breasts, across my belly and thighs, until they came to rest upon my mount of love where, as he bent to kiss me, they insinuated themselves to smooth the way.

My feelings were now near to overflowing but his ardour was wonderfully controlled, so that when I was at what seemed the apogee of my emotion, he raised me still further by the tender moderation of his touch. Parting my thighs he at last slid between them, but palpitating my nether lips with his fingers he placed the very tip of his instrument only between them, moving so that I merely felt it jostling, so to say, at the entrance. Then, still raised upon his arms to afford us the clearest view, he slowly descended so that first the purpled tip, then the lip of skin below, then the fine, strong shaft slid gently in, and my cap of golden hair met his auburn curls in their own embrace.

He then began to move with a peculiarly graceful, slow motion, as though gently riding upon a rocking horse, his hips and buttocks swinging so that his instrument moved into then out of my privities smoothly and without violence, all the time supporting his weight upon his extended arms and regarding my charmed body with the keenest interest and admiration. Then at almost the same moment we were transported with delirium, his teeth fixing upon his bottom lip and nipping it, while a rosy glow flooded over my body, the brown rings about my nipples enlarging so that the engorged tips stood proud within them as witness to my pleasure.

It was at just this moment that the door rattled and the table against it moved and before we could but draw apart, with a hefty blow the entrance was clear and Bovile strode into the room. He stood with his hands upon his hips as I reached for my dress to pull it over me, while my companion coolly drew himself to his feet with a composure unusual in one so young and stood proudly confronting the newcomer, not even troubling to cover his tool, still upstanding and too obviously humid with the juices of our love for us to pretend that we had not been very recently in congress.

'Clothe yourself!' said Bovile shortly, and without a word my cavalier picked up his breeches and drew them on, then buttoned his shirt upon him, all the time facing Bovile without any sign of fear.

'This is your husband?' he asked me, not turning but inclining his head.

'Indeed not!' I replied indignantly.

'Then there is no reason for complaint, sir, and I will bid you goodday,' he said, taking a step towards the door.

'Ah, but there is, *chau*,' said Bovile, 'and I shall take pleasure in splitting your *noc* before you leave this place!' – and tapped his own nose to leave no doubt of the threat he was offering.

I was now in a state of apprehension for the boy, though wiry and strong, could be no match for the brute, and should he be dangerously injured what would be my position in the ensuing trouble?

But now Bovile in turn took a step forward and suddenly swung a punch at the boy's head. The latter, however, with a motion quick as thought, eluded the blow, then seeming to move through the air without the least preparation, caught the underside of Bovile's chin with his head. The Gypsy's own head sprung back with an audible crack, and he fell to the ground like a dead thing to lie unmoving. My lover turned to me and bowed.

'I did not understand that you were one of the Gypsies, ma'am,' he said, 'and I am sorry to have destroyed your – ah – master, but at public school one speedily learns to deal with those stronger than oneself. And now, with your permission, I will take my leave.'

But he must have seen from my expression that I was not at all dismayed by the fate Bovile had suffered, for he came over to me as I still sat, hugging my dress to my middle parts, and bending down planted a kiss upon my raised hand, then upon my lips, and left – turning at the door to say, 'And thank you for your advice. I fear my future wife's beauty will never be a match for your own but if my marriage must be, it must be, and I shall simply be kind in concealing wherever I may have to take my pleasure.'

As he descended the stairs, Bovile groaned and opened his eyes, then sat up, and shook his head, and in a moment was, somewhat shakily, upon his feet.

'Where is he, young puppy?' he cried, and I saw that for a man of his strength a blow which would have put another in bed for a week had only a few moments' effect.

'Gone,' I said, 'and whither, I know not!'

'Then I must satisfy myself with you!' he said, coming towards me with arm raised.

'Whatever you wish!' I cried with a sudden flash of inspiration. 'But I am *mokadi*!'

He paused.

'I have had my menses upon me.'

'I saw no blood,' he said, suspiciously.

'It ceased yesterday,' I said, knowing that after her menses a woman was *mokadi* for at least a week even to the slightest touch. He could not so much as beat me with a shoe without rendering himself unclean and incapable of ruling the tribe until he had purged himself by fasting and travel.

His anger was almost ungovernable, but his superstition greater. He said nothing and left, forced even to leave me the money I had received that day which, since I had touched it, was also *mokadi*. I dressed and, going downstairs, ordered myself a meal and some wine, which I consumed with much pleasure before returning to the camp, where Anna heard my story with great amusement though, she said, she was aware that my menses were not due for at least ten days.

'Be careful,' she warned, 'Bovile never leaves a grudge unpaid.' But she was nevertheless unable to conceal her pleasure that I had outwitted him and I was pleased not only with that, but with the gold I concealed carefully among my few possessions.

The day after, as we were on our first day's march out of Winchester and deep into the country, just as dusk was falling Rosanna clutched my arm as we sat upon the board of the cart. I looked at her questioningly.

'Did you not hear it?' she asked – and held up her finger for silence. In the distance, through the gloom of the falling night, came the call of an owl.

'It is the sign of a death,' she said, shivering, and would say no more. Twice, in the night, I woke to hear the melancholy cry, and though I determined to shrug off such superstitious nonsense, the strange sound could not but affect my spirits. Next morning as we rose, Sam came with the news that an old woman who was familiar to me as a half-deranged creature, muttering on the outskirts of the camp and too infirm to walk, had died in the night and that preparations for her funeral were already in train. Bovile had sent into the nearest village for a *Gorgio*, or non-Gypsy, to prepare the corpse for burial, for all Gypsies have a strong aversion to touching the dead bodies even of their nearest relatives. It was to be washed all over in salt water by the *Gorgio*, and properly dressed for its journey through the next world with particularly strong shoes and a head-scarf over the hair. Since the dead woman had been among the poorest of the band, the other women had come together to give of their best clothes, it being considered an honour to dress the dead.

All her worldly goods were to be packed into the coffin about her, the clothes carefully turned inside out so that she would be too ashamed at being so oddly clothed to return to plague the living.

For two days a vigil took place beside the coffin, the two relatives she had – a son and a daughter – being careful neither to wash, nor eat, nor sleep during that time. Meanwhile outside the tent some members of the tribe were always present, chanting in a low voice some words in their own language, which meant nothing to me. Their purpose was, Rosanna explained, to convince the dead of their sorrow for her departure, so that she would not visit them during the long winter nights.

The funeral itself began with a walk from the camp to the nearest church – a distance of about two miles – behind the coffin which was carried by four of the men of the tribe. The local priest conducted the funeral service, which to my surprise was according to everyday rites, though the Gypsies themselves did not normally attend the church except on this one occasion. Afterwards, the coffin was opened and everyone filed past it to say a parting word and to throw a few coins into the box. As she did so, I heard Rosanna mutter: 'This I throw to thee, so that thou canst pay thy fares and custom duties.' When the final spade of earth had covered the grave, Bovile stepped forward with a jug of beer and poured it down, to provide liquid nourishment for the journey of the dead.

It was to my surprise that everyone at the funeral wore white rather than black, or if they had no white clothes, wore at least a band of white about them. And I was equally surprised to see that only artificial flowers were strewn upon the coffin, carefully made from coloured papers by the women. This was because they wished nothing as quickly perishable as live flowers to be laid on the grave, though the dead woman's son planted a bush upon it before we finally left the area.

Back at the camp, we made preparation to move on. As I asked a question about the dead woman's belongings (which I had seen being piled together upon the ground outside what had been her tent, and which were to be entirely consumed by fire) Rosanna quickly stopped me and warned me never on any circumstance to mention her name, or if I inadvertantly did so, to pray immediately that she forgive me for pronouncing it, for if I did not do so she would think I was summoning her from the grave. I was also told not to wash myself nor comb my hair for one week from the day – an injunction which, I must confess, I disobeyed, not being inclined to consult such superstitions.

During the next ten days the men of the tribe were forced to abstain from any connection with their women and it was on the very day that this injunction terminated that it was my turn to be summoned to Bovile's tent, where the combination of his deprivation together with his desire to revenge himself upon me was sufficiently potent a medicine to persuade him to fall upon me with an even more voracious appetite than usual, and a force so terrible that only my determination not to show him that he had the ascendant over me prevented me from crying out at the pain of his assault. He performed the act no less than four times during the course of the night, but I was wholly excluded from enjoying any pleasure in it. Next morning, upon waking, he pinned me to the ground once more and ravished me with great indignity, forcing me finally to kiss his arse before leaving the tent which, having no alternative, I performed, vowing at the same time to be revenged in my turn.

One thing which perplexed me at the time when I entered the tent was that he was sitting with his hands in a pail of water to which he had added the best part of a pound of salt. I mentioned this to Anna, who nodded sagely and said: 'Ah, then he is preparing for a bout,' and when I asked of what, she replied that from time to time, if the purse offered was sufficient, Bovile would offer a bare-fist fight with some opponent or another. He was, she said, a powerful and skilled opponent, the suggestion being made that he had learned at the hands of none other than the Jew Daniel Mendoza, of whom I had never heard tell, but who Sam, overhearing the conversation, informed me had been the greatest fighter of his time and had a school of fighting at the Lyceum in the Strand, in London.

Sam had heard, he said, that a purse of a hundred guineas had been offered for a combat between Bovile and Sergeant Hardy, a former Army man now working as a butcher in the village of Itchen Abbas, which we would come to next day. Upon my asking how the salted water came in, Sam scornfully asked if I did not know that bare-fist fighters pickled their hands in such manner in order to harden them, both so that they should not be injured by striking, and that they should be capable of inflicting the utmost injury on an opponent.

Two days later the entire tribe together with a number of villagers attended in a field outside the village where a square 'ring' had been marked out by ropes. Bovile was already there, attended by Sam and another man of the tribe. He made, as I must confess, a noble figure, sober and upright, serious and without apprehension. At length, with great noise and cheering, the local champion, Sergeant Hardy, was carried to the ring on the shoulders of his fellows – a big man, of more weight than Bovile, though as he removed his shirt, I believed to be less hardy and more fleshy. Both men prepared by stripping to brief cloths knotted about their loins (Anna whispered that she had attended several fights fought naked, as the ancient Greeks did, but she seemed not specially regretful that this was not now to be so).

The combatants stood at the centre of the ring – Bovile slightly taller, but Hardy more stoutly built – while a man who Sam had said was a local squire recited the rules of the game to them. These were simple: they were to fight until one fell to the ground, when there would be a pause for recovery. The match would be won when one of the two fighters could not come to scratch – that is, stand at the centre of the ring – or by other means admitted defeat. Finally, he summoned into the ring a servant who held a bag from which came the chink of coins – one hundred pounds in gold. The fighters then retreated to opposite corners, and in a moment by means of a stone beat on the side of a metal bucket, the fight began.

Evidently hoping to win the battle before it properly began, Bovile strode to his opponent and delivered a prodigious blow to the side of his head, which staggered him, and then followed with a blow to the breast. But Hardy was made of sterner stuff than one blow could fell and in return smote Bovile mightily below the right eye, where immediately blood poured. Enraged, the Gypsy smashed a fist into his opponent's face, bloodying his nose.

There was little parrying, or what I might call avoiding the blows. I, who had never seen such sport, had nevertheless imagined that half of the skill would be in defence, but in this case it was all attack, the fighters scorning to prevent the opponent's fists landing on their person, but rather determined to show that no amount of punishment could hurt them. All seemed for some time even, until Hardy with two quick blows made Bovile stagger back, and, catching his heel in a turf, fall to the ground. The bucket was immediately smitten by the stone and the men retired to crouch on their heels while their assistants bathed the blood from their faces and shoulders; not only was this evidence of the battle, but bruises were beginning to show upon Hardy's whiter flesh, while upon Bovile's brown breast a cut had laid the flesh open above the left pap.

When the squire had counted to one hundred, the signal was once more heard and they went to it again with no less force. Though I was ill-prepared to mourn for Bovile's hurts, and had been prepared to watch with interest, I was now sickening of the affair – no less for the injuries the two men inflicted upon each other, than for the crowing of the crowd, upon one side or another, at the landing of a blow. It was as though they were cheering not simply for their man, but for the pain he was inflicting upon the other – which, I must remind the reader, they had never seen before that day. The women, I shame to say, of whom there were a number, were not backward in urging on their man, and some with a satisfaction which made me suspect their motives – which I was more conscious of when Anna took my hand and conveyed it to her nether parts, while I felt her wriggling with satisfaction.

There was much I would do for one hundred pounds in gold, but to inflict such pain upon another human being I would not be party to, yet all I could do was close my eyes, for the press was such that I could not escape. In a moment a great roar went up, and opening my eyes I was in time to see Bovile, having evidently received a great blow, stagger back into the path of the squire – also in the ring, to see fair play – so that he fell to the ground. And while he was getting to his feet Bovile sprang forward and with the utmost deliberation punched his fist into the lower part of Hardy's stomach, at which the man collapsed to the ground and lay in agony as the 'round' (which must have lasted ten minutes) ended.

Bovile was perhaps the more tired of the competitors, but the ex-soldier now found it difficult to stand, though the aspect of his face was such that he clearly intended to repay the Gypsy fully for his last blow – which, Rosanna explained, was one not allowed by the rules of pugilism.

At the signal, the fighters rose again to their feet and slowly approached each other. They were both very much bruised, and both with shocking cuts all over their faces and eyes, and bodies too. The battle had lasted in all almost forty minutes. Hardy opened with a blow as low as could be to Bovile's body – at which the squire shouted an admonition. Bovile was rocked upon his feet but, recovering, smote Hardy on the throat, and then before he could recover cuffed him again upon the temple and again upon the ear, and as he almost fell forward, brought his knee up to meet his body, and smashed a fist down with enormous force upon the crown of his head. The larger man fell to the ground as though every bone in his body was broken and remained there while the squire counted off ten seconds, at which he stood forward and raised Bovile's arm in signal that he was the winner. His servant placed in the exhausted man's hand the purse – quickly seized by Sam, who vanished with it amid the tumult which followed as half of the people fell to recovering the loser and half to hoisting Bovile upon their shoulders, where he was carried to the camp, blood all the while streaming from his nose and mouth onto the shoulders of his bearers. Five or six women, of whom I was chosen to be one, attended him in his tent, stripping him and washing his body which was torn and bruised as though he had fought with ten men. The gashes were such that one would have thought them inflicted by some more adamantine instrument than the human fist. Among his injuries we were astonished to find that three teeth had been knocked from his mouth, for we had seen no sign of this at the time, and it subsequently appeared that he had swallowed them rather than reveal to Hardy that he had been hurt.

It was a remarkably short period of time before Bovile was up and about as though he had experienced nothing more serious than a brush with a gamekeeper, though some of his injuries took a time to heal. The gold which he had won had vanished and when I questioned Sam about it he was silent. I gathered that it was an impertinence to question upon any ground what the *dimber damber* did with any money belonging to the tribe for it was considered that all gold was held in common, though I saw no sign of much expenditure on anyone's behalf – even, I must confess, on Bovile's, who appeared always in the same clothes, ate the same food, and was in no way favoured more than the rest of us. We moved on from the place of the fight within a few hours, for though the men of the village had applauded Bovile's courage, it was generally considered that he had not fought fair and there was talk of revenge. Within a day or two we set up camp again, at Walderton, a few miles north of Portsmouth.

Here, after two days during which I had been little able to interest the villagers in my astrological forecasts (for their condition was so low that indeed they had nothing to look forward to other than a quick encounter with some village lad under a hedge, followed by marriage, the bearing of children, and death). At dawn on the third day we were rudely awakened by the sound of shouting and commotion and as we dazedly roused ourselves, men roughly broke into our tent and, barely giving us time to clothe ourselves, we were pushed into the general area of the camp where the whole of the band was gathered, surrounded by constables with weapons drawn. When Bovile was produced as leader of the group, he seemed to me to be a very different man from the one who had won the prize fight, or lorded it over us. He was instead polite and agreeable, even servile, this springing, I am sure, from a fear of authority which had once imprisoned him for some days in the Fleet prison, an experience dreaded by every man but perhaps most of all by a Gypsy, whose natural habitat was the open air.

It seemed that a boy child was missing from a house in the neighbourhood and that hearing there was a camp of

Egyptians in the area, it was the natural and first thing to do to search it, for there was and remains a suspicion that they are prone to child stealing, and indeed I would not like to swear that it never takes place.

As the tents were searched and we were questioned, I noticed a young man standing apart with a sad expression upon his face and, making opportunity to approach him, asked him what he knew of the affair. Surprised at the gentility of my address, he confessed to being the father of the child who, he said, had been playing happily in the garden of his house the previous afternoon, but had then disappeared. And was there any true reason to suspect the band, I asked? No, he replied, except that the constables informed him it was most likely we had something to do with the affair.

Would he accept, I asked, that if the child had been brought to the camp, I would know it, and that since I did not know it, there could be no question that he was here?

Somewhat hesitatingly, he agreed to take my word, and summoning the chief of the constables instructed him to call his men off, which he could do being, as he told me, a magistrate of the area. Enquiring his name and address, I made a careful note of it in my mind, and thanked him respectfully as he left. Bovile was brief in his acknowledgement of my intervention, merely wishing to know why I did not do it earlier. I had expected no more, but invited him to consider whether it would not be worth while to arrange for the band to hunt for the child, for if we succeeded in finding it the neighbourhood, hearing of it, would be sure to be more hospitable to us. He shook his head, saying that we did not need their hospitality, but when I added that I doubted not that Mr Finching, which was his name, would be generous in the matter of financial acknowledgement, he immediately became more enthusiastic and within half an hour had organised four bands of our company, each led by a man who was an acknowledgedly good hunter – or poacher – and who could read the signs of the countryside.

We made our way as quietly as possible to the house Mr Finching had described to me, which lay but a mile distant, and there spread out and began our search, each bush being thoroughy beaten. Meanwhile, I managed to separate myself and entered the gates of the house, intending to look around the grounds, for while its owner might not welcome a band of Gypsies there, he would be less likely to object to my own presence, especially upon such an errand.

The grounds were not extensive but were beautifully modelled; I had not been in such a place since leaving Alcovary, and here was a pool very like that in which Frank and Andy would bathe, which brought tears of recollection to my eyes. At its side was a small hut or barn from which, as I passed it, I seemed to hear a small sound of discontent. The door being shut but not locked, I pushed it open with little effort and the noise became louder, and in a while, upon a search, I discovered it to come from below an upturned boat kept there, and to be the unhappy cries of an infant who, from his appearance, had been there for some time.

It was, as the reader has by now inferred, the missing child and what were the scenes of joy when I walked to the house with it mewling in my arms – joy only interrupted by strictures upon the servants for not having searched with sufficient diligence. One servant indeed claimed to have searched the lakeside hut, and suggested that I had stolen the child and was now, in fright of my offence, returning it, but I am happy to say that Mr Finching disbelieved, or at least discredited it. He offered me a dish of tea and asked my story, for, he said, it seemed I could not have been raised in the company of the rascals who now commanded me.

Affected by this sudden display of sympathy, and alone with Mr Finching and his wife, I broke down into tears and revealed the whole story of my life, omitting, it will be guessed, the more intimate descriptions with which I have favoured the reader.

Both Mr and Mrs Finching were affected in turn by my narrative and were as one in suggesting that I must stay with them until the band had departed the area. If I simply failed to appear Bovile would believe that I had made good my escape, for had I not made it plain that I despised their way of life? This was perhaps not entirely true, for I had been too afraid to speak openly against him or his manner of commanding the troop, but nevertheless I welcomed the opportunity of escape and was taken immediately to an attic room, whence a kindly servant brought hot water with which, for the first time for many weeks, I was able in leisure and privacy to attack the grime which now seemed to engrain my skin.

As I was halfway through this process, I heard footsteps below and looking cautiously out saw on the gravel path Bovile, Sam and Rosanna and some other members of the troop, who for some time talked with Mr Finching at the door. I could not hear what was said but later learned that they had reported that they had learned a rival band of Gypsies had stolen the child and made off with it towards London, and expected reward for the information. Mr Finching greeted this by indicating his wife who stood in a nearby window, the child in her arms, and bidding the band be gone. The discussion then became heated, and Bovile threatening, but Mr Finching was evidently firm, and then summoned two of the house servants with cudgels. At this Bovile called Sam forward, who had been skulking in the background, and something seemed to change hands, whereupon my erstwhile friends retreated, grumbling. Nothing had been said of me and I could only imagine that it was thought I had returned to the camp.

That evening before supper Mr Finching presented me with a purse containing twenty guineas which, he said, he had extracted from Bovile as my due, threatening him otherwise with prosecution on several grounds, from stealing money from me to attempting to extort money from him by giving false information. I could only conclude that, knowing Mr Finching to be a gentleman and magistrate, Bovile thought him cheaply bought off at what seemed to me then to be a small fortune.

So, having thanked my benefactor, I sat once more at a civilised table, eating with knife and with fork, drinking from a crystal glass, and almost overcome by being treated again as a lady. Mrs Finching indeed acted to me as a sister might act, and Mr Finching as a brother, and at last I was returned to my room, with a warning not for the time to set foot outside the grounds. I had no notion to, for here was a bed dressed with clean white sheets which I slid between, finding them as welcome as any lover and much more conducive to slumber. Indeed in no time I fell into a deep sleep, in which all my dreams were of happy past times, and friends so long absent.

Chapter Eleven

The Adventures of Andy

It occurred to me as the Lady Elizabeth was loosing the waistband of my breeches that perhaps I had been at Rawby Hall for quite long enough.

Not only was I weary of a footman's duties, these being extremely repetitive and boring and the hours long, but to the physical weariness inflicted upon me by the work was added that which was the result of my having to make love with Tabby who now expected my attentions not only as a concomitant of the commissions of Beau Rust, but also as that of my supposed adoration. Ellen too from time to time required solace, besides which, Mr Caister was more and more pressing in his attentions, summoning me again and again to his pantry to insist that my breeches needed re-fitting, and making me change and change them in front of him, though offering no affection being, no doubt, afraid of the pillory and the rope, the penalty for backgammon players. And now, it seemed, I was to be pressed into service in My Ladies' rooms. Perhaps it was time to be away, and somewhere else.

During my spare time – though there was little enough of it – I often took myself to Signor Cesareo's rooms, where we played the guitar together. Giovanni was a pleasant enough fellow and though his English was rather poor, he was an excellent player and a no less excellent teacher, so that in time I was a dextrous performer upon the instrument. It happened that the Signor's rooms were close enough to those of Beau Rust for him to overhear our music, and he must have reported our dexterity to the ladies, for I am sure that Giovanni did not do so, being of continental temperament and thus jealous of his intimacy

with our employer's daughters. However, be that how it
may, one afternoon we received a command to attend the
ladies with our instruments and in course made our way to
their rooms, where Lady Elizabeth and Lady Margaret
were at ease, leisuredly fanning themselves in *déshabillé*
upon the twin couches which stood between the two tall
windows of their drawing-room.

'We hear –' said Lady Elizabeth.

'– that Master Andy is now almost as adept upon the
strings as yourself, Signor,' said the Lady Margaret.

'And we wish to hear –'

'– an example of your duetting.'

Setting up our music stands, we played an arrangement
Giovanni had made of some Mozart dances, following this
(in tribute to England) with some music of Mr Handel's.
The ladies expressed themselves delighted and told us to
play on, whereupon we engaged in some earlier pieces. So
intent was I upon acquitting myself well at this, my first
public performance, that I scarcely noticed – or if I noticed,
thought little of – the ladies rising to their feet and moving
about the room, until I felt a soft arm slipped around my
neck and a hand diving into my shirt and falling upon my
bosom.

At this, perhaps unsurprisingly, I ceased to play but
noticed that Govianni continued his part, despite receiving
a similar attention from the Lady Elizabeth.

'Pray continue, Master Andy,' said the Lady Margaret,
and as I did so I felt her lips pressed to the nape of my neck.
I found it increasingly difficult to keep time and the black
notes danced before my eyes as, leaning over me, she unbuttoned my shirt, then slipped it over my shoulders, which she
caressed with her lips, her long hair falling about me like a
shawl. It was not that the lascivious emotions aroused in me
were so new as to preoccupy me entirely, but a mixture of
apprehension, shyness and even modesty was the result of
amorous attentions being pressed upon me by the daughter
of an earl! I had certainly travelled far from the wattle and
daub hut in which I had been born!

Somewhat to my relief, I became conscious that

Giovanni had ceased to play and, glancing aside, I saw that the Lady Elizabeth had now slipped his shirt quite to his waist, trapping his arms to his sides, and that pulling aside the neck of her gown she was offering one breast to the excited Italian's lips, who was gulping at it with no less enthusiasm than he had been paying to the work of M. Lully, upon which we had been engaged.

My own guitar fell with a soft clamour of strings to the floor as the Lady Margaret, whose every action seemed to mirror that of her sister, drew my own shirt to my waist. Following Giovanni's example I did not attempt to free my arms, while an exquisitely white breast fell to my lips, and as I pulled gently at it I felt her hands at my waist, working at the buckle of my breeches.

It was at this time that the thoughts recorded at the beginning of this chapter swiftly flew through my mind, though not, I confess, for long, for by now my waistband was free, the flap of my breeches was opened, and an instrument as tightly strung as the highest string of my guitar was in the loving hands of one who offered to play upon it with no less dexterity than the finest of musical performers.

Acting so in unison that our figures seemed to mirror each other, Giovanni and I were drawn to our feet by our partners who, falling to their knees, released our lower persons from the trammelling clothing and paid us the tribute of a kiss before leading us to the couches and disposing us upon them. Standing back, they then disrobed, revealing bodies as like as two eggs and more beautiful than any upon which I had previously set my eyes.

I have, it must be said, no strong feelings in the matter of society, taking the view that any woman may be as good as any other; nor do I wish to cast aspersions of a derogatory nature upon Tabby or Ellen, or indeed upon my dear Sophie. However it must be said that the figures of the two ladies as they stood before us were of another breed altogether, marking the difference between a sturdy working pony and a handsome racing filly. These ladies were, it is true, more mature, their figures fuller and more generously endowed. Their breasts, heavy with promise, were like rich fruit, peaked with brown tips eager for our mouths; their haunches were portly but firm, enhanced by enchanting dimples; their bellies too, without being gross, were ample, the navels deeply marked, while below delightful sprigs of velvet hair barely masked the dark outlines of their cunnies.

It need scarcely be said that by now any weariness I may have felt at the prospect of connection had vanished and I was all eagerness – eagerness which was deferred, however, for first the ladies must explore our bodies, moving their fingers and palms with an enchantingly careful diligence, playing upon us with every bit as much care as any musician upon his instrument. First, they laid us upon our bellies, and covered every inch of our backs with kisses and caresses, coming at length to our back sides, upon which they lavished attention, smoothing and kneading them with their hands, then drawing the cheeks aside to tickle with a finger the entrance to that aperture in which, I had thought, only a madge cull could be interested. The sentiment this courtesy arose in me was beyond expectation delicious and I was unable not to squirm beneath her hand so that, my prick rubbing against the couch, I was within a moment of the ultimate excitation when she ceased and, first planting a kiss upon my double jug, turned me upon my back. I had noted carefully the responses of the Signor, who had, I knew, been here before, and as he lay still beneath the ranging fingers – save for his tool, which as the Lady Elizabeth played upon it involuntarily vibrated like one of the strings of his guitar – followed his example, taking care not to move despite the exquisite nature of the sensations invoked by the Lady Margaret who, having pleasured every other area of my body, now came between my thighs and began to stroke my almost insanely ravenous piece with her fingers, rousing it if possible to an even greater extension, so that the ring of skin beneath its head bid fair to burst with the pressure upon it. And, as she lowered her head to run her tongue from the base to the very tip, all control left me and with only the presence of mind to throw the lady's head to one side, I died, jet after jet of sap rising high in the air to

fall upon my body. As it did so, I remember that my eye fell
upon a black dot in the recently repaired ceiling, which led
me to suppose that Beau Rust's eye was still able to observe
what went on below; a fine display he had of it, that
afternoon!

I feared My Lady's anger – except that recovering from
the delirium which had resulted in, I believed, too speedy a
resolution, I saw that on the neighbouring couch Signor
Giovanni was in a similar state. I later learned from him
that he had been accompanied in similar orgies by two other
footmen and that the sisters had by some alchemy always
succeeded in rousing the two men to their culmination at
precisely the same moment!

The ladies now handed us fine towels with which to wipe
ourselves and rang the bell; not long after, one of their
maids – a girl whom I had only seen once or twice, for their
ladyships' maids were kept in their own establishment –
entered with a tray of tea, showing not the slightest
sign of surprise at the presence of two naked men in the
room.

For the half of an hour, or perhaps a little less, we drank
tea, all in a state of nature. Giovanni picked up his guitar
and played a little, while the Lady Margaret congratulated
me upon my expertise with the instrument, though asserting
that I had come too quickly upon one of the pieces, which I
took to be a joke, since they both laughed at it. However, I
saw nothing to laugh at since in the last duet (or rather,
quartet) in which we had played a part, Giovanni and I had
reached the end together – a fact at which, when I asserted
it, the ladies also laughed.

In a while, setting down his guitar, Giovanni rose and
took the Lady Elizabeth by the hand, leading her to one of
the couches – whereupon I did the same, and in the manner
they had ministered to us, so we attended to them. I was for
the first time entirely conscious of the beauty of a woman's
back and even ceased to wonder, as I had previously done,
that any man should wish to swive at a tail. However,
Giovanni not making that offer, I thought it best not to
attempt it, contenting myself with insinuating a finger into

the passage, which from the shudder it invoked, gave some pleasure.

Of the joy I took in caressing My Lady's handsome bubs, I need not prolong description; their springy resilience beneath my palm was an irresistible invitation so that I could not but climb upon her, my knees beneath her arms, and place my whorepipe between those delicious spheres whereat, though surprised, she eagerly clasped her breasts with her hands and closed them upon it, moving them in such a manner as to give me great delight. There was a pleased cry from the Lady Elizabeth, and I saw that she encouraged Giovanni similarly to mount her and treated him in the same way. (I was later to learn from him that they had greeted with the same pleasure some new and lascivious tricks which he had learned in Italy and which were not commonly performed in our country.)

It was in no short time that, placing her hands upon my shoulders, the lady persuaded me to lower myself and throwing up her legs invited me to enter her, which I did with no less pleasure. Through the intensity of the delight she had earlier given me, I was able to prolong the ride until she had twice cried out in pleasure before, seizing me about the waist and plunging to meet me with the virility of a girl, brought me off to my own and her satisfaction. I need not say that at the moment when I experienced the apogee, I saw from the corner of my eye an expression of intense pleasure upon the face of my fellow musician, marking the fact that he too had concluded his performance.

We were then bidden to resume our clothes, and picking up our instruments were dismissed with the wish that we should perform again within a few days. Before we left the room we were handed a purse which, examining in the corridor, I found to contain two gold sovereigns, which Giovanni assured me was a usual result of such a connection.

I was none the less still of a mind to leave the Hall and the next day told Giovanni so, who himself having been itinerant in his own country recognised and applauded my instinct for, said he, youth was a time for experience; time enough to settle down when one was twenty. He now assured me that I was of sufficient skill upon the guitar to make a living by playing upon it, in one way or in another, and gave me the name of a merchant in Southampton who had once offered himself a position in his household. He was, Giovanni said, eager to impress his neighbours, and only two months ago had heard him play when My Lord had taken him to Cambridge to perform during dinner at some meeting of mayors and aldermen, and offered him a position.

Back in my room I counted my hidden store of gold which, with the contributions of Beau Rust and the money given me by visiting gentlemen to whom I had been of assistance, now amounted to no less than sixteen pound – almost a year's wages for a labouring man and sufficient to keep me for several months. I went that day to Mr Caister and told him that I had received a message that my mother was ill and should need to go to her. He was suspicious, asking how I had heard. I said, from a passing tradesman by whom word was sent, and took the opportunity to lay my hand as though by accident upon his thigh as I bent to ask him for leave, whereat he could not resist but to take my hand in his and, squeezing it, said he would make all right and I could leave that very day, if I wished to do so. I settled to serve that night at supper and to leave the next morning.

I am sorry now to record that I lacked the courage to inform either Tabby or Ellen of my going, and perhaps fortunately – for though I was at that age resilient, my afternoon's work had sapped my amorous energies – neither requested my presence in their bed that night. I slept soundly, rose before even Tom was awake and, having surreptitiously packed my few possessions the night before, crept from the room and by five o'clock had begged a ride upon a tradesman's cart, to Cambridge.

At Cambridge I learned there was a stage leaving for Southampton at seven o'clock that evening and I determined to use the time to make myself more presentable to any prospective employer. I took myself off to a tailor who by midday had turned me out in a dress both fashionable and hardy: a good broadcloth coat, pantaloons – for I was tired of breeches – hessian boots and a satin waistcoat, plain but elegant. On presenting myself at the Red Lion Inn, a distinctive hostelry from which the coach was to depart, I was welcomed as a gentleman of sorts and ate heartily in preparation for the journey, watching my fellow travellers as they prepared themselves: a squire and his wife and daughter, plain but good-humoured; a parson, blustery and overbearing; a tall, thin woman accompanied by a servant and two small boys at the sight of whom I was glad I had taken an outside place for they were noisy and ill-tempered and the other passengers looked already abashed at the thought of spending a night in their company.

Just before seven, having changed back into my poorer clothing and packed my new dress into a box, I and my fellow travellers boarded the coach, the others crowded to suffocation inside and myself seated beside the driver, divided only by a narrow, low rail from a fall directly onto the road. There was nowhere to place my feet, so that I clung with some attention to the rail as the coach dropped into, then climbed out of innumerable pits and hummocks in the surface as we rattled out of the town.

The first stage ended at Dunstable, in Hertfordshire, where the driver took a tot of liquor. The second was completed at Reading, where he took another and I descended to stretch my legs and ease the soreness in my lower limbs, for I had been incessantly cuffed and bumped by the jolts and jumps of the coach, up hill and down dale. My condition however was nothing to that of those unfortunates travelling inside, for both boys had been sick within and without the coach, and from the door as it opened came a wave of foul and rancid air.

Mounting again, the driver by now inattentive of his charges – which fortunately seemed to know by heart the road to Winchester – we rattled on at a pace which, while not great, due to the badness of the road was sufficiently terrifying. With the greatest care, I climbed from my place into the midst of the luggage piled upon the roof of the coach itself and, inserting myself into a cranny among the parcels and packages, wedged myself into position and disposed myself to a semblance, but little reality, of sleep.

It was nearing dawn and we had just passed (I was later to hear) the hamlet of Popham and were jolting through Micheldever Wood, five miles from Winchester, when I was rudely shaken to my senses by the loud neighing of one of our horses and a sudden jar as the coach came to a halt.

'Down, driver, and all out from the coach!' came a commanding voice, accompanied by a scream from the squire's wife. Cautiously I roused myself as the driver descended and the passengers began to climb from the doorway, to see a couple of feet below me the mounted figure of a masked man, holding in his hand a cocked flintlock, pointed now at the head of the parson, whose bluster had evaporated into a remarkable subservience. Indeed, he was already removing his purse from the pocket of his greatcoat.

With great care to make no noise, I removed myself from the shelter I had contrived and without thought launched myself at the highwayman's head, landing square upon it. As we both fell to the ground I heard an explosion, which at once frighted and heartened me, for if the charge had involuntarily exploded the gun could not now be dangerous. In any event, the situation was safe for, landing on top of the man I had winded him and was now almost winded myself by the driver, the squire and the parson, all of whose bodies landed on top of us.

After some confusion, however, the muddle was resolved and the fellow bound and unmasked. He was revealed as a young man not much older than myself, with a thin starved face, who had not – by his appearance – been too successful in his trade. Though invited to give his name and explain himself, he maintained a desperate silence and was hauled to the top of the coach where, his hands behind him and his feet bound, he was placed between the driver and myself as we made the short remaining journey to Winchester.

Dawn was breaking as we entered the town, and at a crossroads just on the outskirts of the town we passed a gibbet from which swung a cage occupied by fluttering rags

and a miscellany of bones, the skull still imprisoned within
its steel frame. I could not but glance at our captive who
gazed without emotion at his fate (for he was surely for the
morning drop) except that as he lowered his eyes, he
remarked in a low voice, 'I hope you're satisfied, cunning
shaver!' I did not reply, for I could not but pity the man
who no doubt had been reduced to thieving by the distresses
of poverty. I dared not enquire whether he had wife and
family, for my heart would have misgiven me.

There was a delay at Winchester while the constables
were sent for and the man handed over. The parson, as it
turned out, was a native of the place and served at the
cathedral and his evidence was considered in itself sufficient to condemn the thief, so that after hearing my story
and congratulating me, the constables were content to let
me continue my journey. In the meantime we had all taken
grog and eaten, and as we entered Southampton were in a
buoyant mood, increased in my case when I learned that my
fellow travellers had taken a collection among themselves
and now presented me with three guineas in earnest of their
gratitude for my saving them from losing their valuables (no
doubt worth considerably more).

At the Chequers Inn I prayed for a room in which to
refresh myself – a favour granted without charge, for I was
for a moment the hero of the time – and there washed
myself and changed into my good clothes, at which the
landlord was more than a little surprised, now addressing
me as 'sir' rather than 'princox'. And when I asked for the
house of Mr Harry Grose he was yet more impressed and
directed me with courtesy to a handsome building two
streets away.

Mr Grose was a man of great dignity in Southampton;
formerly a yeoman's son, he was now an esquire, having
been not only mayor, but justice of the peace and sheriff of
Hampshire. He was a merchant, collecting tallow from all
over the south of England and selling it throughout the
world. He imported indigo, cochineal, logwood, woad and
other dyes from the Indies and the Middle East; flax,
tow, madder and whale-fins from Rotterdam; alum from

Hamburg; wine, cherry brandy and prunes from Bordeaux; he dealt in tea, sugar, chocolate and tobacco and he sold grindstones. His wealth and influence was such that he had recently obtained a coat of arms and decorated his house in the finest modern style, setting his wife and daughter in the best society of the town, yet remaining himself distinctly rough in manner.

In the style of his house he vied with the first of the nobility, in his table, furniture and equipage; his wife had her tea and her card-parties and he had kept for many years a tutor for the young madam, though now at the age of eighteen she was considered to know everything it was advisable for a young woman to know and all his energies were concentrated upon finding a suitable husband for her – who would have, as I subsequently learned, to be at least of the person and rank of an archangel.

I knocked at his door at an opportune moment, for the day before Mrs and Miss Grose had been to an evening party at the house of a fellow merchant at which a harpsichord player had performed throughout the evening, and were sorely distracted that they had no such attraction to offer when the invitation must be returned. Indeed, Mr Grose had been driven almost to distraction throughout breakfast by their importunings, and no sooner did he hear that I came recommended by Signor Cesareo than I was engaged at a wage of one guinea a week, my keep being provided, which was more than I had dared to hope for. I was also to be provided with a room and, having made my bows to the ladies, asked to be shown to it, for to be frank I was almost dead with fatigue after the joltings and adventures of the journey. A footman led me up four flights to a small attic room, sparsely but reasonably furnished, where I fell upon the bed in my finery and instantly into a deep sleep.

By the time I was awakened in the early evening, news had reached the house of my adventure in the coach and I was somewhat a celebrity; indeed so much so that when, after having enjoyed a good meal, I was summoned to the drawing-room, I was greeted by a polite round of applause from Mr and Mrs Grose, Miss Grose, and five or six of their neighbours (no doubt those they wished most to impress). They smothered me with congratulations upon my bravery in fighting, singlehanded, with so dangerous and vicious a fellow, armed as he was with two pistols and a sword! I am shamed to say it was a picture of which I did not strive to dim the colours and contrived to delight the company by playing a few of the numbers at which Signor Cesareo had said I was most adept.

I was determined to become as skilful at my playing as possible and daily set aside time for practice in my small room, performing exercises Giovanni had shown me for improving the dexterity of the fingers, and learning new pieces – some of which I purchased in sheets from a counter in Bar Street, the fashionable quarter of the town, where I was cordially received, my feat having been noised abroad by Mr Grose in terms which showed me off as a fellow fine as the Iron Duke himself! But fame fades, and within a month or so I was no more regarded than any other household servant.

My work was not arduous; only, of an evening, to play for the family and friends, who gathered almost every night in the drawing-room, where Miss Grose worked at her samplers or made covers for footstools, led her younger friends in spillikins, commerce and cribbage, or propounded riddles and conundrums. Her mother and the older ladies and gentlemen sat at whist or played brag, speculation or *vinqt-et-un*. Mr Grose was rarely present on these occasions, preferring to take himself off to a drinking club whence Bob, the footman, escorted him home at three or four in the morning, often incapable of climbing the stairs to his bed. Nevertheless he was invariably up at seven the following morning, and apparently with a head clear enough to outdo most of his rivals in business.

Mrs Grose was a kindly, middle-aged woman who, conscious of the comfort in which she lived, readily forgave her husband for his absence. Unlike him she had no pretence to grandeur, but being in every way amenable accepted his views in everything and adopted them as her own. Miss

Patience Grose, however, had pretences to even greater things than her father and had so far scorned the young men of the town presented to her by her father as possible spouses. 'She's waiting for royalty,' said Bob, 'but she may wait too long, for she's getting long in the tooth and she's something scare-crow, and one bub's partial, for Rose seen them often and says the left one's higher than the right. If she don't get a man in her mutton sharpish, she'll die an old maid!'

I did not for a week or two feel the lack of female companionship; there was in the house only a cook and a housemaid, the one an old woman of fifty, and the other a girl with a face like a flat-iron, and as demure as an old whore at a christening. However, after a while I began to be proud, and in need of a good strapping. When I enquired of Bob, he said that I was to come with him late that night to Buss Street, near the churchyard, and we would see if we could find a public ledger – by which I understood a common woman or prostitute.

So after the last guest had gone and I had finished my last piece, I made my bow, went to my room and changed my clothes, then meeting Bob (himself out of his livery) we set off through a close and sultry night. We were not two yards inside Buss Street when we were approached by a cockish dell, who enquired whether we would dock with her. Upon Bob expressing that he had no desire to lie with a buttered bun, she went a few steps down the street and gave a low whistle, at which another ladybird appeared. On my asking whether they would take us to their rooms, both they and Bob laughed. 'We'll give 'em green gowns in the churchyard!' he said, for it seemed that that was the place of all, in this as in every town, where the mutton-mongers met to go about their business. Indeed we had to go about for some time between the tombstones before we found a place which was not within touching distance of a grunting pair.

Without more ado the two girls laid themselves down upon the stone slabs of twin tombs – still warm from the day's sun – and throwing up their clothes disclosed that they wore nothing beneath their skirts. Though I had hoped for more comfortable rogering, I was not slower than Bob at dropping my breeches and finding the place, for I was more than ready for the fray. But my entry was accompanied by a loud peal of thunder and scarcely had I made five thrusts than with another peal a bright flash of lightning struck the church tower and heavy rain began to pelt – at which with a wriggle my girl clutched at my cods and manipulated them so exquisitely that, though hoping for a longer passage, my bolt was shot, whereupon she drew herself up and demanded five shillings, which without enthusiasm I paid her, the rain now being so great that all I wished was shelter. Bob at the same time had risen and with a wry grin also paid his term, and we ran for shelter of a tavern, where we consumed several tankards, and he promised me a fuller passage next time. However, I resolved that there should be no next time, or at least not in such conditions, for now that I was spent my mind circled wonderfully on the question whether my girl had been poxed or not and whether I was for the Covent Garden ague, as Bob called the clap. Several days elapsed before, closely regarding my plug tail for signs of the disease, I concluded that I was lucky in avoiding it.

I was very happy, for the space of five or six weeks, to enjoy the relative quiet of my daily life with Mr Grose and his family. My work was so light as to be almost nothing, I had time during the day to wander about the town and familiarise myself with it, and while I lacked the pleasures of female companionship, an occasional bout in the churchyard (for which purpose I availed myself of a cundum or sheath of skin – a notorious protective against the pox – bought at no small cost from a doctor in the next street) satisfied my animal instincts at a very reasonable charge, at the same time teaching me some tricks with which I made no doubt I could impress future conquests.

One day, the household was all agog at the arrival of a gentleman said to be coming from London to court Miss Patience Grose. Bob had this news from the maid, who had it from Miss Patience herself. He was, she said, the son of a lord, whose interest her father had secured by the simple expedient of helping his family from bankruptcy by the promise to purchase at an exorbitant price an interest in a coal mine in the north of the country which, it was generally believed, was exhausted of coal. His eagerness to provide a noble husband for his daughter had been allowed to outweigh his normally sharp business sense.

'But,' said Miss Patience, 'be he a very Adonis, I shall not wed him at my father's behest, for I count myself as particular in the matter, and shall not chain myself to a man at the nod of any head.'

At the first sight the young man seemed extremely pleasant: not of remarkable features, but of some elegance of manner, and a kindly disposition, and on being introduced to Miss Patience he made a low bow which she received without special grace, but not unkindly.

It being quite understood by all what was the purpose of his visit, the conversation at supper was somewhat low and consisted on Miss Patience's part of an almost complete silence, and on her father's part an excess of enquiry about the visitor's family's history, responded to in as short a manner as was concomitant with politeness, so that had I not provided quantities of music by Dowland and Purcell there would have been prolonged periods of complete silence. After dinner, we retired to the drawing-room, where again I played quietly while our visitor – whose name, I must not omit to record, was the Hon. Frederick Mellor – and Miss Patience, left alone in order that they should cultivate each other's acquaintance, sat wrapped in a discouraging hush at the other end of the room.

Finally Mr Mellor, leaning forward, addressed Miss Patience in a low tone, which none the less was audible to me.

'Ma'am,' he said, 'you cannot but be aware that our parents have brought us together in the intention that we should wed. For myself, my brief acquaintance with you has furnished me with ample proof of your delicacy of manner and your exquisite poise and grace, to say nothing of that natural beauty which no man could but regard with approbation. May I now enquire whether you are so good

as to find in me qualities which would not entirely disqualify me as your husband?'

'Sir,' she replied, without a moment's hesitation, 'I have
no intention of putting myself forward to you or to any
other man for the purposes of breeding, much less of sup-
plying my father with noble relatives. It would be best if our
intimacy should proceed no further than an acknowledgement of our relative virtues, in the acquiescence that neither
of us shall look forward to any further familiarity than a
cordial but distant friendship may afford.'

Such a speech could not but dampen the ardour of any
swain, let alone one as lacking in force as Mr Mellor. With a
look of sorry surprise he bowed coldly and shortly afterwards made an excuse and left the room, whereat Miss
Patience rose with something like a sneer and marched after
him, leaving me, if I would, to play on for my own pleasure.

Bob, who was sharing his room with Mr Mellor's servant, confided to me the following day that Mellor was in
despair over his rejection, for if he should not acquire Miss
Patience's consent to their marriage and the arrangement
should fall through, Mr Grose would withdraw from his
business association with his father and the family would be
ruined.

This, needless to say, did not concern me – what had I to
do with the fortunes of a family of which I knew nothing?
But I must confess, in my slight boredom with the sameness
of my daily life – lacking as it did in so many respects the
small excitements of the Hall – I began to toy with the idea
of helping brother Cupid to bring the two together, the
sheer impossibility of the task providing a challenge which,
after a few hours, was almost irresistible to me.

Next day I found myself leaving the house for my usual
morning walks to Bar Street, where I took chocolate and
watched the quality walking and talking, at the same time as
Mr Mellor, who himself seemed in an idle mood. He greeted
me kindly, and invited me to walk with him, and it being a
fine morning we took a turn in the park which lay between
us and the heart of the town. After a while I asked: 'You
prolong your stay in Southampton, sir?'

'Not for more than a day or two,' he replied. 'My business here is, I fear, concluded.'

'You will forgive me if I am impertinent,' I said, greatly daring, 'but it is, I believe, the case that you seek the hand of Miss Patience in marriage?'

He looked for a moment abashed that a mere servant should raise such a topic with a gentleman but, as I had suspected, in his dejection was eager to confide in almost anyone.

'That is so, Master Archer. But I fear the lady has a firm natural aversion.'

'If you will allow me, sir, the problem is I believe one of coolness.'

'Of coolness?'

'Yes, sir. You will not be aware of the fact, which indeed is not generally known, that contrary to her appearance and behaviour Miss Grose is not without passion.'

He raised his eyebrows and I wondered whether my impertinence in speaking of his host's daughter would be too much for him. But I went on.

'You will forgive me, but my interest in what would seem an ideal match persuades me that I should speak out. Miss Patience is of a naturally fiery temperament, warm and affectionate; her maid has often spoke to me of her mistress' desire to be wooed, for she is not one of those ladies who will respond to a cold declaration of interest. She is a great reader of Mr Fielding and Mr Richardson and awaits a hero who will sweep her into his life without a thought that she might refuse him.'

'You mean,' he said, 'that she awaits corporeal evidence of my passion?'

'Indeed, sir.'

We walked for a while in silence.

'Mr Archer, we must speak more frankly. If I understand you, Miss Patience has – ah –'

'Yearns to be clasped to your bosom, sir.'

'To my bosom? To *my* bosom?'

'Indeed sir, for her maid has indicated that she regards you with the utmost admiration. She has spoken, it seems, with approval of your face and figure, and regretted that you have not saluted her with vigour.'

'So it is your belief that were I to –'

'Yes, sir, you should lose no time, but sweep her from her feet. Any tribute a vigorous man may pay to a lovely woman will be greeted with delight, and I am sure that a match will follow.'

He wrung my hand.

'My dear Mr Archer, I am greatly your debtor, greatly your debtor!' he said, at which I found it necessary to excuse myself, on some ground of necessity to call upon a friend, and left him a new and hopeful man. It was now necessary for me to prepare Miss Patience for his assault.

I found her sewing in the drawing-room, and surprised to see me, for we only had the slightest acquaintance and almost never met except when my instrument was needed.

'Forgive my intrusion, ma'am,' I said, 'but if I may have a word with you?'

'Certainly, Andrew,' she said.

'Forgive my impertinence, ma'am, but I feel under the necessity of speaking to you about Mr Mellor.'

'About Mr Mellor?' she said coldly. 'I believe that you can have nothing to say upon that subject which could fall with any degree of propriety from your lips.'

'Ma'am,' I said humbly, 'I speak only as a man who has suffered the despondency of unrecognised love.'

She looked up with some interest at this, partly, no doubt, as one who doubted whether a servant were capable of the emotion.

'Mr Mellor's man, ma'am, has spoken to me of his master's despair . . .'

'Despair?'

'At your rejection of his addresses. If I may so express it, his senses are so overcome by the apprehension of your beauty that they are dizzied by it, and he is made so faint that he has been unable to offer you the tribute he would wish to pay.'

She sat silent but clearly not unimpressed.

'He is known, it seems, as one of the most fiery and

attacking of lovers; his conquests among the London notabilities are legion, and the ladies to whom he has successfully paid his addresses are counted among the most fortunate.'

'Indeed?' she said, with more than a glimmer of curiosity.

'Indeed, ma'am. If you will forgive a certain coarseness, his physical attributes are said to be consumedly impressive, so much so as to be almost unendurable . . .'

'I have not noticed it.'

'But now, for the first time finding himself in love rather than merely wishing to make another conquest, he is tongue-tied and incapable. Knowing this, ma'am, I felt it no less than my duty to make his apologies to you – without, of course, his knowledge or approval. Having myself felt all too keenly the biting cold of a lady's disdain, and knowing the genuineness of his passion, I could not but wish to appraise you of the true situation.'

'Thank you, Andrew,' she said thoughtfully, and more warmly than she had ever previously addressed me. I made my bow and left, and that evening was careful to arrange a screen at the end of the drawing-room, behind which I could play without being seen, but contriving that a gap at the hinge should be so placed that I could observe the rest of the room.

Throughout the meal Mr and Mrs Grose as usual made most of the conversation, but I was aware that the two young people were eyeing each other with a new interest. I noticed that Miss Patience had attired herself in a low-necked dress less modest than any she had previously worn in Mr Mellor's company – one which had previously been reserved for wear when she was with her female friends, when it caused some laughter and giggling should I enter the room. However, since I was but a servant, the generous display of bosom it offered was of no consequence.

I was for a moment dismayed when her father and mother – no doubt assuming that there was nothing else to be hoped for in the affair – seemed about to accompany them to the drawing-room, but I was able to take Mr Grose apart and appraise him that Mr Mellor was to make one more attempt to gain his daughter's hand.

'Fat chance!' he muttered, but led his wife off to another room, and soon Mr Mellor and Miss Patience were in their chairs, while I established myself behind the screen and began upon a carefully selected programme of love-sick lute pieces.

Within a moment, Mr Mellor had fallen to his knees and, taking her hand, declared himself as irremediably attached to Miss Patience – upon which he planted a kiss upon her palm. For the first time in her life, I dare swear, a blush spread across her features.

'Mr Mellor,' she said, 'I fear I have perhaps been mistaken in my view of your virtues . . .'

'Oh, ma'am!' he cried, and bending forward transferred his lips from hand to bosom, at which the flush upon her face deepened – certainly not with displeasure. It may be that my words about her lover's physical attributes came to her mind, for as his lips explored the vale between the twin white peaks, she allowed a hand to fall into his lap, where it seemed to discover something of interest, for they both drew away from each other and their eyes met. Then without pause they clasped each other and in a moment she was unclothed to the waist and his hands were appraising the suppleness of breasts more handsome (I must confess) than I would have imagined Miss Patience to possess.

I may have struck more than one disproportionate chord during the next few minutes, for I confess my own discomfort grew as I was forced to observe the scene of passion before me, while my hands were engaged in continuing the music. Though it was clear to an experienced observer that Mr Mellor in fact had little competence in love, as the speed with which he reached satisfaction showed, Miss Patience's innocence made her unconscious of his inexpertise and her delight first at the sight then at the touch of his not unhandsome body knew no bounds. Before they had done aught but explore each other, handling here, kissing there, and no sooner had he caressed with his fingers her love-bower, than with a cry his soul flew forth – to her great interest, who had clearly no apprehension of the culmination of man's amorous play. Clasping his hand within her own and directing it, in a moment her own joy was accomplished – and without the discomfort of the disposal of her maidenhead; which would now wait for their marriage night. Indeed, with one more kiss they hastily clothed themselves and made off to find Mr Grose and appraise him of their intention to be wed as soon as the banns were approved.

I am happy to say that my contentment that I had achieved the impossible in bringing two such apparantly irreconcilable people together was made the keener by the approbation both of Mr Mellor and Miss Patience, who independently and without reference to each other rewarded me not only with their verbal thanks but with a gift of gold which I was able to add to the store in my room.

Chapter Twelve

Sophie's Story

I note that I have so far given no description of my benefactors, Mr and Mrs Charles Finching, of Gauzy Hall, near Walderton in the county of Hampshire. Mr Finching was a young gentleman of perhaps twenty-five or twenty-six years, but though mature was flexible and open in his attitudes and behaviour, as was his wife, Mrs Lettice Finching, his junior by only two or three years.

The Hall, though a manor house of small proportions with eighteen rooms, was nevertheless perfectly impressive and set in elegant grounds of delightful proportion. Mr Finching had inherited the estate from his father and, both his parents being dead, kept up a style of life which, I learned, had subsisted at the hall for centuries, for the place had been in his family for as long as records could recall. He was tall and slim, and made a handsome figure in the fashionable clothes which he affected even when at home; his face was long but good-humoured, his black hair carefully cropped, his dark eyebrows seeming to comment humorously on the world about him, while his mouth was full and generous.

A magistrate, he sat at the local court whenever required, but otherwise spent his life in his library, or riding abroad to administer the estate (which included farming land of a few hundred acres only); he led a life which might be said to consist of leisuredly but careful preoccupation with duty.

His wife shared his interest in books; most evenings found them in the drawing-room, he reading aloud from the pages of Sir Walter Scott or Miss Austen, or from the poems of Mr Crabbe or Mr Wordsworth, while she tatted or embroidered chairbacks. It had been made clear to me that it would be unwise to leave the house until Bovile and the tribe were thoroughly moved on, something of which Mr Finching constantly expected news, and also that I was welcome to stay with them for as long as I desired. I was also pleased to spend some time in a tranquillity which had been foreign to me since I had left Alcovary.

If tranquillity was the word I at first applied to my stay at Gauzy Hall, the word which I would soon have applied to it, I fear, is 'boredom'. Perhaps because my life had been so crowded with events since I left home, I soon opened my eyes to the day ready to contemplate enormities or face trials, only to find that the most exciting incident I could expect of the coming hours was the taking of tea with the wife of the local rector, a walk with Mrs Finching to the village with a basket of cakes for some poor person, or a reading of chapter seventeen of *Waverley* which, admirable narrative though it no doubt is, scarely brought the blood to my cheeks.

But perhaps that is not entirely true, for soon I found myself waiting with more or less eagerness to hear of the latest adventure of Edward, the excellent hero of Sir Walter's romance, and on hearing of his love for Rose Bradwardine could scarcely forbear from voicing my scorn that he should love such a poor creature; were I to be clasped in those strong arms, I told myself, Miss Rose would have no chance of holding her lover. The fact was, as I gradually recognised, that as the days passed into weeks and still I sat at the Finchings' table (now in the main for want of anywhere else to go), I found myself increasingly in want of that robust male company to which I had been used. Why, lying awake at night, I even thought of Anna and the manner in which she would comfort me in the absence of Bovile, and would on many an occasion have welcomed even her with open arms.

There were few servants at Gauzy Hall, and without exception they were unprepossessing; the single footman, John, was a mean, thin and gawky young man who could never have been a hero to any woman, while the boy who was his general assistant was too young and innocent for me to consider as a possible lover, though no doubt he was only a year or so younger than I!

My loneliness was exacerbated by the marked devotion of Mr and Mrs Finching whose bedroom was just below mine. In the late summer days, when the windows still lay open, I heard from time to time the low, gasping cries of satisfaction and pleasure which suggested that they were enjoying those marital pleasures to which, no doubt, they looked forward during the long evenings. Despite my host's obvious attentions to his wife, I found myself in time regarding him with an admirer's eye and even believing that perhaps he eyed me with approbation. Could any man, after all, be truly content with the attentions of one woman, however handsome? And Mrs Finching, though in all respects a lady, was not particularly beautiful. Nor, if my instincts were correct, was she so addicted to the game of love as to be much capable of lascivious invention, for she seemed rather sentimental than romantic.

In short, I determined to attempt to seduce my host, and to employ to that end the hour before supper when he made use of the room on the top floor of the house which had been set aside for bathing. There, just down the corridor from my bedroom, a large metal hip-bath lay, to which John brought hot water for the use of anyone who wished to bathe themselves. Mrs Finching had led me there in the course of explaining the hall and had made it clear I was to use the room whenever I wished, which I did. Mr Finching occupied the room every day without fail at the hour of seven o'clock and I had glimpsed him, wrapped in a soft towel, making his way from the bedroom on the lower floor, and had heard a splashing from inside.

So one evening, as dusk was falling – for the evenings were now drawing in – I undressed myself to my shift and waited until I heard the soft footsteps and the closing of the door which indicated that Mr Finching was in the bathing room. Slipping out of my shift, I then wrapped a sheet around my person and made my way down the corridor. Hearing the noise of water within, I breathed deeply, took hold of the handle of the door and turning it, strode in. At the sight which greeted me I gave a cry of surprise and, lifting my hands to my glowing cheeks, let go of the sheet, which fell to the floor leaving me naked as I had ever been.

Though of course my action was contrived, I had not too much to equivocate for the sight that met my eyes as I entered was indeed a delightful one. Mr Finching stood in the bath facing the door, soap in one hand and cloth in the other. A film of suds covered his body, their whiteness only something whiter than his flesh, which was pure and unsullied as a girl's, only a sprig or two of dark hair curling upon his breast, where his paps were small, dark and delicately tinctured. The soap between his thighs almost concealed his manly person, which would however be seen nestling, as it were, in a cloud of white.

My acted distress was not mirrored upon his face; he seemed to take in my figure coolly and while clearly not finding it ugly, was not moved by it, for he simply turned his back upon me, with a simple 'I beg your pardon, ma'am.'

I stammered something about not knowing he was there, while at the same time drinking in the sight of his delightful back, broad shoulders and tapered waist, and below, two globes of a handsome, tight plumpness so enticing that almost without knowing it I took a step forward –

But no, 'twas impossible; he simply stood, not so much as glancing at the dish I so clearly offered – for an intelligent man could clearly not but have been aware that my presence was no accident. I bent to pick up the sheet and, wrapping it about me, excused myself and left. No word was said about the incident to me – nor, I think, to Mrs Finching – but it was to my chagrin that later that night I heard from the bedroom below prolonged sounds of amorous congress which suggested that Mr Finching was presenting his wife – unknown to her – with the outward signs of a passion he had concealed from me.

Next morning I woke to unmistakable signs that the summer was indeed waning: I saw from my window a park hung with mist, with here and there the tops of trees appearing above it like the sails of great ships becalmed in a fog. By ten o'clock, however, the mist had lifted and the sun appeared; it was clearly going to be a fine day and I made my excuses to Mrs Finching, saying that I felt sorely in need of exercise and would take a long contemplative walk for, apart from stretching my limbs, I must think of my future – I could not be their guest for ever.

She answered with words so kind that I could not set them down without the tribute of a tear, and I was especially tenderly inclined because of the wrong I should have done with her husband had not he been steadfast in his affection to her. She charged me with a basket for a sick old woman on the outskirts of the village and I took some food for myself wrapped in a kerchief, and set forth.

Having delivered the basket – and without thanks from the cantankerous old party who took it as her right rather than a charity – I left the village and struck into the country, and after perhaps an hour's walk came to a field where a single man was engaged in binding the last products of the harvest, and there sat down upon a loose pile of warm yellow straw, and ate my food. Meanwhile the man continued his work, gradually approaching the corner where I sat. He was shirtless now in the hot sun, and as he grew closer I saw him to be a giant of a man, with shoulders and arms stronger even than those of Bovile. Having no doubt worked in the open all summer, his body was darkened to the colour of mahogany and shone like polished wood as the sweat poured off him.

He seemed to be regarding me with interest, and eventually when his work brought him within a few feet of me touched his forelock and enquired whether I wanted a drink. Surprised by the courtesy, I replied that that would be welcome – which indeed was nothing but the truth – whereupon he dived into the shadow of the hedge and reappeared with a straw-covered bottle, the neck of which he wiped on a piece of rag he took from his breeches pocket before handing it to me. It contained a delicious but strong cider; even after only one pull of it, a delightful warmness seemed to spread over me.

The farmhand had meanwhile sat down beside me, and it

could not escape me that his eyes seemed to be upon my bodice, which since I had loosened it for the heat showed rather more of my breasts than I would have displayed except in ballroom or bedroom. It was not, I admit, unconsciously that I leaned forward to place the bottle at his side, offering him an even more comprehensive view.

I had begun to wonder in what way I could suggest to this man that a bout with him would not be unacceptable, when looking me straight in the eyes he offered the opinion that he saw that my apple dumpling shop was open, and enquired if I wanted a 'buttock ball'. His intention seemed clear if his words were not and my reply was simply to remove my dress; while it was over my head he climbed with equal celerity out of his breeches, revealing haunches solid as those of a horse and, rising from a positive thicket of sweat-soaked hair, a tool which in its size matched his other limbs. I knelt as he came towards me, ready for amorous play, but there were to be no soft words or gestures for he simply pushed at my shoulders as I fell backwards and, lifting my legs upon his shoulders spat upon his hands to anoint his instrument. Then, as I waited for the delicious sensation of his giant limb filling my proper vent, to my horror he presented it at quite another breach and forcefully rammed home. This was the country custom, as I later learned, of those uxorious men who wanted to enjoy carnal congress without the risk of enlarging their families.

The pain was excruciating and did not diminish as he continued to batter me so that his cods slapped audibly against my lower back. I shrieked aloud so that birds rose in clouds from the branches of the trees and horses stirred uneasily in the nearby meadow, but he evidently believed my cries to be of rapture for he continued to swive, despite my attempts to push him away – which were quite fruitless, for his body, now ringing wet with perspiration, was so slippery that I could get no hold and even if I had, he was so strong that I would have failed to move him.

Happily, as is common with the lower orders, he was not long before spending and with a grunt he withdrew and let me fall with relief to the ground. Pausing only to wipe himself with a handful of grass he crammed his parts back into his breeches, took a swig from his bottle and pulling his forelock again thanked me kindly, and made off leaving me lying naked upon the ground – sore, pained, distraught, angry, buggered and still unsatisfied.

Back at the hall, whence I made my way with some discomfort, I found Mrs Finching in a state of great excitement, for the mail had brought news of a visit from her elder brother, who was passing through the county on his way to London and expressed the intention of staying for a week or so with his sister and brother-in-law. Mr Finching seemed for some reason less enthused than his wife, but perhaps I mistook and he was simply preoccupied with some problem of his own.

I had by now determined that I must leave the hall within a week or two but I must confess was eager to see this paragon, as Mrs Finching described her brother; a man, according to her, of all the virtues.

My first view of him as he dismounted outside the hall two days later supported her fervour. Though somewhat stocky, Mr Edmund Weatherby was well-proportioned with handsome, virile features, a fine head of hair and a manner immediately impressive, for having positively lifted his sister from the ground, swinging her off her feet with the joy of their meeting, and having wrung Mr Finching's hands, he turned to me asking for an introduction, upon which he took my hand and bowed low over it. That evening at supper he paid me particular attention, listening to my story (or such a part of it as could be related without impropriety) with the utmost interest and sympathy. He was also kind enough to beg the loan of one of Mrs Finching's horses so that I could ride out with him into the country. We rode sometimes accompanied by Mrs Finching, and sometimes alone, when he acted always with sensitivity and humour so that I grew more and more to admire him, for apart from my host – my relationship with whom, perhaps inevitably, had a flavour of uneasiness about it since my interrupting him at his toilet – he was the first complete gentleman with whom I had spent much time.

One day Mr and Mrs Finching were invited to dine at a neighbouring house and asked whether they should send across a message requesting that Mr Weatherby and I could be of the party. But he declined, on the ground that he would find a visit to these neighbours – whom he had met on a previous occasion – more boring than was concomitant even with the obligations of brotherhood. And he begged that I might remain with him to pass the evening in some agreeable game: 'Perhaps,' he said with a smile, 'you play piquet, Mrs Nelham?'

I replied that I did, and would be delighted to have a game with him.

So my host and hostess made their way, and Mr Weatherby and I sat down to a supper of fowl and salad and some white wine, at the end of which we were in a good humour with ourselves and the world. As we finished eating a peach from Mr Finching's garden, my partner leaned towards me.

'I think we understand each other, ma'am, and need not equivocate. It is my cordial wish to taste the delights of your body and my belief that you would not be dissatisfied with those pleasures I could offer in exchange.'

Though surprised at the directness of his words, I was ready with a response.

'Sir,' I said, 'we *do* understand each other. I shall be delighted to offer you the tribute of which you speak, and to receive what offers in return you are ready to make.'

Whereupon, without delay, he took my hand and led me upstairs, but to my surprise passed the first floor, upon which his bedroom was situated, and went on up the stairs.

'Sir,' I began to protest, 'my room is small and bare, and –'

But he put a finger to his lips, and at the stair-top turned right rather than left to open the door of the bath room, where I found hot water and sheets had already been brought.

'I have become accustomed,' he said, 'to wash myself before a passage of love which, when one can perform the rite in the presence of the loved one, becomes in itself a part of the ritual of pleasure.'

So it was that within a moment or two we were stripped and standing together in the bath, which happily was a large one. Taking a cloth and anointing it with soap, he began to wash my body with the utmost attention and delicacy, passing over my bosom with an expression of delight, reaching around so that as I leaned against his broad breast he could wash my back and buttocks, and then crouching to attend to my nether lips, which he opened with his fingers even to smooth the pink rose within.

Then passing the cloth to me, he stood smiling while I sponged his hard limbs – the chest like the lid of some elegantly carved box, the back like that of a magnificent wild beast, the small, powerful, tapering thighs and finally a male instrument which rose, during my administrations, to a fine power, and seemed as I handled it to be of the imperviousness of polished wood.

By this time I was ready for the battle and even passed one leg about his own, pressing my lower body against his and feeling the expectantcy of his loins against my tenderer parts. But, smiling, he merely wrapped me in a cloth, lifted me in his arms, and strode from the room and down the stairs.

His bedroom, set aside for guests of the house, was of course grandly furnished, with a fine four-poster bed, beautiful furniture and a large mirror upon a stand, which I noticed had been placed next the bed. Dropping me upon the covers, he whisked the sheet from me and, naked himself, allowed his eyes to feast upon me. He stood for what seemed an age, one arm, a cord of muscle running up it, raised as he grasped the curtains of the bed and his body inclining forward so that he seemed to offer it to my view – and indeed my impatience was barely contained, for I too was happy to let my eyes rove over his body, the very sight of which fed my senses almost to repletion.

After a moment I rose to my knees and, taking his sturdy device in my hands, drew back the fleshy veil from its dome and gently slid my lips upon it, delighted to feel by the tremor which ran through his body that he was pleased at the tribute. As I fed upon him, I felt him turn somewhat, and from the corner of my eye caught sight in the mirror of a scene the like of which I had never seen: a fine and handsome man standing quite naked while a beautiful woman, kneeling before him, was ministering to him with her lips, one hand upon the inside of his thigh nuzzling with its fingertips his hanging pouch, and the other clasping with vigour one of the globes of his backside. The reader may find it difficult to credit but for a moment I forgot that that woman was me, and the man the accommodating Mr Weatherby, but the inspiration of the sight warmed me even more so that I redoubled my efforts, my head positively bobbing and butting his stomach in my eagerness, so that after a while he took my head in his hands and drew it away.

'My dear Miss Sophie,' he said, his voice perhaps a little uncertain, 'I must dissuade you for a while from your attentions if my power is not to desert me before I can pay proper tribute to your beauty,' with which he sank upon the bed, taking me with him, and held me close in his arms, his whole delightful length pressed against mine, the bristles of his chin harsh against my cheek. After a while he began to move his hands softly upon my back, stroking me as he might stroke a favourite beast, but with at the same time the most endearing words of praise for my beauty, the softness of my skin, the shapeliness of my limbs.

I was able to reciprocate with the greatest honesty, for he showed a combination of strength and tenderness, of hard and manly comeliness, with an almost feminine concern for my comfort and content that was wholly admirable. I was utterly at ease with him and felt there was nothing I would not do, no action I would not perform, were he to command it. It was a pleasure not only to graze upon his body, but to apprehend his pleasure as my tongue played about his paps or the delicate whorls of his ears, around which his hair curled with a delightful springiness, or as I took a finger into my mouth to suck gently upon it, or transferred my lips to that other, more turbid spur, all eagerness and readiness, which trembled and jumped as I touched it. So much delight did I find indeed in devouring him with my lips that he had again to draw away from me, begging me to lie back so that he could pay me the compliment of his adoration.

He did this with all the courtesy and care I could have hoped, his hands firm and soft about me, preparing the way for his lips until, drawing me to the edge of the bed so that my thighs lay over it, he knelt between them and lifted me to another dimension of pleasure as he proceeded to smooth with his tongue my most intimate parts, first with a very rapid and tickling motion, then with soft gentle kisses followed by long laps up and down the length of the cleft, at the same time gently rubbing with his hand my belly and breasts until I was unable to restrain my joy any longer and with a glad cry curled my legs about his shoulders as I gave up my soul.

Then, conveying his body to the bed, I placed myself astride his hips, lowering myself onto his colossal piece, and with my lower parts milked and milked him, watching, the while, our two bodies moving together in the mirror at the bedside, his hands the meantime busy smoothing my breasts and thighs until both he and I rejoiced in a joyous and simultaneous culmination.

I feared, now, that Mr and Mrs Finching might return but even if they did, he said, there would be no reason for anxiety, for they would simply conclude that we had ended our card game early and retired. So, for two hours or more, we luxuriated in each other's company – and no less in the enchange of confidences than caresses – until finally I fell asleep with my head upon his arm and my leg thrown over his own, to be roused only at dawn, my hand unconsciously curled, in sleep, around his member which, while he slumbered, had grown to a renitent and impressive mass. I cautiously released myself from the grip of his arm about my waist and, leaning, attempted to wake him to a gradual consciousness by running my lips along its length from the coarse hair at its base to the smooth and polished curve of its head. And when after some moments he had still not stirred, looking in the mirror I saw his eyes open and his lips smiling, reluctant to confess to wakefulness lest I should cease my ministrations! At which I laughed, and continued until for the last time that precious night I felt the tremor at the root, and from the tiny slit crept a thin gruel – a tribute to the generous spending of the previous hours, exhausting the reservoirs of his handsome cods.

I crept back to my own room after a final kiss, and we met at breakfast with due ceremony, though I could not but exchange a secret smile with him as I handed him the bowl of chocolate which was his usual pleasure at that hour.

During the next few days we met each night in his room – on one or two occasions almost betraying ourselves to our hosts by my too hasty departure from my own room, so that I almost met Mr or Mrs Finching as they made their way to their own rests. But all too soon came the Saturday before the morning on which he was to ride on to the north. There was, upon that day, a bull-baiting to be held in the village and Weatherby, hearing that I had never seen such sport, invited me to witness it with him. His brother-in-law remonstrated, saying that 'twas a cruel sport and no sight for ladies, but Weatherby replied that Mrs Nelham had not so weak a stomach as to be distressed by a little blood. Though disturbed by his words, I would not be seen to be less adventurous than my lover thought me and so we took our way at three in the afternoon to a field just outside the village, where a large crowd had already gathered around a space by the river bank in which a fine animal was tethered by his nostrils to a rope chain fastened to a post set in the midst of the water. Mr Weatherby explained that this was to add to the amusement, for as he was tormented the bull would often take a new direction in which to try to escape, and the rope then sweep a number of people into the river.

After a while a cart came upon which were three dogs kept in cages and their owners began to take bets upon which would cause the bull most injury, or which might or might not be killed in the adventure. Weatherby, looking about him, found a place for me upon a hummock of ground, and making his excuses went off to place a bet. The press of the people was such that I could no more make my way to him than he to me; nor indeed could I escape from the sight that followed.

The first dog was set on by his owner, and being practised sank his teeth immediately into the bull's nostrils, from which blood immediately began to pour as the wretched, tormented animal raised his head and the dog with it, waving it to and fro until the dog loosed its hold – or perhaps a piece of flesh gave way between his teeth. The dog was thrown several feet into the crowd, which scattered lest its members should be attacked.

The bull, freed for a moment from pain, backed away and, feeling the constraint of the rope, turned in a wide circle towards the water, which indeed as Weatherby had predicted caused two small boys and a woman to be thrown into the river, where the woman and one boy were almost immediately drawn out, being near the bank, but the other child, a smaller boy, was swept away by the current and out of view – a circumstance which was much enjoyed by a quantity of spectators, who made no attempt to ascertain whether the little creature would be saved or not. There was nothing I could do but watch as the second dog was released and immediately gained purchase on one of the bull's ears, the animal letting out a bellow of pain which was echoed by a cheer from the crowd at the sight and sound of more torture.

Sickened by the entertainment, I tried to turn away – and immediately met the eyes of a fellow who was frankly staring at me from only a foot away. I recognised him immediately as my stalwart friend of the straw field. Meeting my eyes, he gave me an enormous wink, and leaning forward, said, 'Tes no sport fur women, ma'm – best come away for another strum!'

At this I leaned forward, and under the shadow of those around, placed my hand upon his thigh and gripping his member, squeezed it affectionately – then saying,

'Certainly, sir – but you must release the bull first.'

His eyebrows were raised almost to invisibility beneath his ancient hat, and he asked, 'What?'

'Release the bull,' I said, 'and I will meet you at the field you know of.'

He stood silent and surprised, then nodded, and turning

forced a way with his great bulk through the crowd in the direction of the space where the bull had just succeeded in dislodging the second dog and was attempting to strike it with a foot, while the smaller animal danced and dodged to the cheering approbation of the crowd. After a moment the dog's owner nipped forward and attempted to recover his animal, receiving in the attempt a blow from one of the bull's feet which seemed from the crack and cry of pain to have broken a limb. For a moment the crowd's attention was on the agonised man, and at that moment I saw my friend dart in, and I glimpsed the flash of a knife as with one blow he severed the rope, eighteen inches from the bull's torn nostrils.

For a moment the animal was not conscious of its freedom; then shaking its head, it lowered its horns and charged straight at the crowd, cutting through it like a scythe through corn. There were cries and shouts, bodies flew through the air, others fell to the ground; a great wave seemed to move through the field as the watchers attempted to escape from the maddened animal's path, and indeed it soon had free ground in front of it and made off through a gap in the hedge, leaving a scene of utter carnage behind.

The crowd had cleared from the river bank, where around one side of the circle where the bull had been tethered lay the bodies of those who had been unable to escape its passage. Some had been trampled, others tossed; all were injured and some perhaps dead, for at least twenty bodies lay upon the grass, some utterly still, others moving, a few climbing uncertainly to their feet. There were shrieks, cries, groans, both from the injured and from those who now returned and sought their companions. I had not thought that such an action might cause so painful a scene, though I could not help reflecting that the injured had brought their pains upon themselves by attending such a horror and inflicting such agony upon a defenceless creature. As I moved towards the injured, however, I came upon a child lying unconscious with an arm dangling at a strange angle from its shoulder, and as a weeping mother watched while a man lifted the small body in his arms, I reflected that perhaps I should have paused to consider the consequences before setting my erstwhile companion on to his sudden action.

Slowly, the field began to clear, one body being carried forth on a hurdle, blood colouring the side of its head, another slung upon a broad back, a brutal and bloodied slash torn in the breeches, no doubt by the horn of the maddened bull, and I began to look about me for Weatherby, whom I had not seen since he left me. Soon, I saw him coming towards me, his arm – I was concerned to see – slipped within the breast of his coat, and he white and dishevelled, his back covered in mud and a graze upon his cheek and the side of his head.

'Ah – you escaped injury!' was his relieved cry. 'I had feared you might have suffered in the outrage. Happily, they have caught the rascal!' – and he gestured behind him, where at the centre of a knot of enraged men I saw the implement of my act, his arms twisted behind him as he was hurried along, while some hurled blows at him with their fists and others attempted to strike at his face with switches plucked from the hedgerows.

'Oh – poor man!' I involuntarily exclaimed, and then felt myself redden as Weatherby looked at me with amazement.

'Poor man' he exclaimed, 'when he has caused such injuries?'

'But no doubt he was moved by pity for the bull,' I said.

'What absurdity is this?' said Weatherby angrily. 'The man is no doubt a revolutionary – he will be whipped and pilloried, and well he will deserve it! But come, Mrs Nelham, you are distraught. We must get you home and to your bed.'

We rode back in silence, which he ascribed no doubt to shock, while in fact I was wondering how I could save the farmhand from his fate, for it had been entirely my own action which had set him on. I could not explain this to my companion, who even if he believed it, rather than ascribing it to ill-conceived pity would certainly have done nothing to gain the man's relief, much less his release. I found myself strangely roused by his anger and disdain at my pity both for bull and for man; his humour and tenderness had been replaced by an implacable sternness which set his jaw and caused his eyes to shoot forth not loving looks but cold reproaches. Yet I could not but be moved by his manly carriage, as women have ever been moved by a strict demeanour and a commanding port.

When we had arrived back at Gauzy Hall, and Weatherby had left me at the door of my room, I rang the bell and sent a message by the maid imploring Mr Finching to come to me. And in a while, hesitating only at the door – I suppose to ensure that I was fully clothed (whereas nothing was further at that moment from my thoughts than seducing him) – he approached. The reader may imagine with what hesitation I explained my predicament, omitting only the carnal scene in the fields, but I finally persuaded him that I had exercised feminine wiles to persuade the man to release the bull from its rope.

He nodded thoughtfully, conceding that he himself had many times attempted to persuade his fellow magistrates that bull-baiting in such a manner was a peculiarly cruel sport, unworthy indeed of the name, and should be forbidden by law.

'I shall see what I can do,' he said, informing me that he would at that moment start for the village. I implored him to allow me to come with him and succeeded, though he attempted to dissuade me.

We heard a noise of shouting and disturbance as we approached, and as we rounded a corner by the one inn the place boasted, and came to the small square by the bridge, saw that we were too late to have prevented my unfortunate admirer from having been hoisted up to the pillory where he now stood, his head and hands through the cross board, while below him stood a rabble of men and women hurling mud, rotten eggs, the entrails of animals (brought in a steaming pail from the butcher's slaughterhouse), dirt from the ground and even stones, so that the man's face was a mat of muck and blood.

With a cry of horror, Mr Finching sprang from his horse

and in a moment had pushed his way through the crowd and mounted the base of the pillory, appearing so suddenly there that an egg meant for the prisoner smashed upon his shoulder and the mess ran down the length of his fine black coat. Equally suddenly, the crowd was stilled.

'Friends,' he cried, 'this man has not been tried – at least allow him to come before the magistrates before punishing him so!'

There was a general outcry at this; 'We seen him!' – 'Ay, and my wife's broke her arm 'cause of he!' – and other similar remarks roused the mob again to full cry, but once more Mr Finching raised his arms and appealed for justice. A young fellow to whom, he later explained, he had done some good, joined him in his appeal, and after a few moments during which the argument could have gone either way the crowd reluctantly began to be still, and Mr Finching was able with the help of two constables to release the man, who was led away supported by the two officers, his head drooping upon his breast, and taken to the lock-up where he would await an appearance before the magistrates. I managed, for shame, to keep my face turned away the while.

As we rode home Mr Finching explained that my man would be tried within the week, and suggested that in exchange for getting him the most lenient sentence, he hoped to persuade him to keep my name out of the affair, and therefore it would be wise of me to leave the neighbourhood within the next day or two. He enquired too as to Weatherby's part in the affair, being outraged that having insisted on taking me to such a show, he should then have left me alone.

Back at the hall, raised men's voices were heard in the drawing-room and when that night – somewhat to my surprise – my door quietly opened to admit Weatherby (to whose room I had not thought of taking myself) it was first that he might inform me coldly that he indeed left next morning at dawn, and second that he might take me voraciously and almost in the style of one inflicting a punishment. Despite the pain in his arm he would allow me no tender caresses but fell upon me as though to teach me subjugation, which at first annoyed and then excited me so that I could not protest, his vigorous and almost painful attack raising flames in me that despite myself excited my utmost ardour. And while he voided himself without any concern for my feelings, I none the less felt a satisfaction difficult to disguise.

I bade him a farewell in which regret was married now to a certain contempt, for his behaviour seemed to me to reveal an entire disregard for any emotion other than the merely animal, and his previous tenderness merely as a means of winning consent and regard for his powers of making love, which indeed were considerable.

Her brother leaving the hall, Mrs Finching was not positively condemnatory but certainly no longer greeted me with special warmth, something I could understand, and could not condemn. Mr Finching came to me at midday that Sunday and presented me with a letter, explaining that it was one of recommendation to a cousin of his, a Miss Jessie Trent, who kept a school for young ladies in Southampton. She was always looking for assistant teachers, he said, and would no doubt be able to offer me at least a temporary employment.

He suggested, though not unkindly, that I should leave the next morning upon the coach which passed through the village at nine o'clock and understanding his predicament – for he adored his wife and I had no wish to be a bone of contention between them – I promised to do so, and would have embraced him but that he took my hand and, bowing, pressed his lips to its back as he took his leave. I went to my room to begin to get my few things together, and to start once more upon my travels.

Chapter Thirteen

The Adventures of Andy

Finding myself in possession of a considerable sum of money, I decided to allow myself some entertainment and, curious as to the pleasures offered by the ladies of a certain establishment in Southampton which, because of the necessary expense, I had not previously visited, determined to pay it a call. I asked Bob whether he would care to be my guest for, though I was beginning to feel my way towards a position in society which would preclude my keeping company with the poorer kind of servant, he was a pleasant fellow enough, good-hearted and a friend to me. He accepted my invitation with enthusiasm.

Our visitations to the mutton-mongers of Buss Street, whom without exception we possessed in the relative discomfort of the graveyard nearby, were short, brutal and to some degree expensive, for Bob himself had on one occasion been accosted by a swaggerer who accused him of seducing his wife, stripped him of his belongings, and beat him before sending him home through the streets without his shirt. However, he had persisted in re-visiting the place, not having the means to visit a bawdy house.

Bob led me to a street not far from the centre of the town and to a fine-looking house with a door guarded by iron spikes. We knocked and a face appeared at a small opening and a raucous voice enquired 'Who goes there?'

'Friend,' replied Bob, whereupon the door was narrowly opened and we were allowed in, one by one. Then the door was slammed shut and an enormous key was turned in a lock, an immense bolt slid across it, and a claim clamped home.

From a room off the corridor inside a great noise came

and when we came to the door, we saw a crowd of men and women, some standing upon chairs or tables, watching a bitter fight between two women, their clothes mostly torn from them, their breasts bare, their faces running with blood. This was a contest such as was mounted once a week, Bob explained, for the pleasure of those who liked such sights. Bets were placed and some trouble was gone to ensure that the competitors were bitter antagonists who would not pull their punches.

Neither Bob nor I were much inclined to watch, and Bob invited the man who had let us in – a massive fellow whose mission it was to protect the house from unwanted visitors and to deal with any trouble which arose within – to give us two tankards of sky-blue and take us to the ladybirds. Two handsome tankards of gin were soon pressed into our hands, and we were led upstairs, where a lady abbess presided over a company of nymphs who lay around the room in various undress. Bob, bowing to the abbess, who was an elderly, plump, kind-faced woman, sedately dressed, made straight for a sofa on which reclined a handsome girl who eyed him with admiration and reached out to take his hand, drawing him into an embrace.

My eye fell elsewhere, for I saw to my interest that one of the girls was black – the first black girl I had ever been in a room with, though I had seen them in the streets of the town, especially those down towards the docks. But this girl was exceptionally handsome with a little, round face, dancing dark eyes and pouting lips, and a figure whose voluptuousness was enhanced by the white dress she wore; one delicious breast was free from all encumbrance and hanging like a ripe pear ready to be gathered, while the skirt was cut to the waist so that one leg from bare foot to fine thigh was completely open to the view.

Bowing in turn to the abbess, I made my way over to the girl and taking her hand kissed it – somewhat to her surprise, I believe, for no doubt she was used to rougher greetings. She lowered her eyes prettily and, rising, asked if I wished to accompany her, to which I gladly assented. She then led me up some stairs to a small but pleasantly furnished room, the furniture consisting merely of a bed, some chairs and several large mirrors, one fastened at a tilt on the wall above the bed. There, she helped me to undress, unbuttoning my shirt and lifting it from my shoulders to fold it carefully and place it upon a chair, then unbuttoning my pantaloons and drawing them from me. Somewhat to my embarrassment and no doubt because of the strangeness of the situation, the originality of the company and – I must confess – my slight nervousness, I was not as yet showing my admiration of her in that part where she might properly have expected to see it. Catching my eye, she smiled shyly and passed her hand gently between my thighs before releasing the shoulder strap of her dress and allowing it to fall to the floor, revealing a body of great beauty, its handsome curves enhanced by the almost purple bloom which lay upon her otherwise jet-black skin.

Taking my hands, she guided me to the bed where, as she drew her length along my own, I saw to my delight our bodies reflected in the mirror – her dark skin making mine seem whiter than it were possible to imagine it. Ah, what transports then ensued! Such indeed, that I can now scarcely record them without putting myself into a passion, for she was in command of every lascivious trick, her fingers playing upon my body, enquiring at every orifice whether pleasure lay within, pleasuring every projection with a smooth and light touch which brought me to the very precipice of delight, her lips sucking my own, drawing upon my tongue like a teat, and conferring upon my now positively resplendent tool such caresses that it seemed likely to burst.

I too took the utmost pleasure in exploring her body as one might a previously unknown land. Her breasts were somewhat longer, or so it seemed to me, than those of our native girls, their extremities coarser and in erection harder and less sensitive so that even a nip from my teeth seemed to give pleasure rather than pain. And below a long undulant belly deeply marked by the dint of an angular navel, the lips of her cunny were large and of a deep crimson, veiled by tightly curled, harsh, black hairs, while between them projected something akin to a little finger, shaped like a tiny counterfeit of a man's instrument, from which, when I stroked it, she evidently received most pleasurable sensations, for a cry of delight seemed to bubble in her throat.

Raising myself I sat upon her thighs, my cods nestling upon the pad between her legs so that I could view the country as 'twere from on high. She wore an expression of friendly pleasure – always the mark of a good whore, for one should always be able to believe that she too is taking pleasure in the encounter, however untrue that may be. She gave me a smile of singular sweetness as I allowed my eyes to relish her delightful body, while her hands, laid gently in my lap, played lightly with my masculine parts. It made an interesting sight, the black fingers of one hand upon the white flesh, running up the length of my instrument, tickling with the most delicate touch its every surface, while she inserted the other beneath, palm uppermost, to pinch with a firmer grip the very base as it projected even below my now tight and almost painful cods.

As I looked, my emotion overflowed and with all the force of a pent stream, I gushed forth the vital liquid, which rose so that it almost struck me upon the chin, then fell glistening upon the dark flesh of her body.

'I's sorry, mister,' she said. 'My fault!'

I assured her that *I* was not at all sorry, except that I had perhaps deprived her of the pleasure – if pleasure it was – of receiving my seed within her. She asked if I would stay longer but, reluctantly thinking of the money I had brought with me, I declined, whereupon she assisted me to rise and with a clean towel wiped my body, lingering especially over those parts which, in the heat of our encounter, were damp with amorous perspiration.

As she was thus ministering to me I was dimly conscious of an uproar below, imagining that it was connected with another fight. But in a moment the girl lifted her head in concern as there was the sound of footsteps on the stair, then in the corridor – and suddenly, as she was still upon her knees before me, the towel in her hand, the door burst open and three men came into the room. They were in the uniform of the navy, one of them an officer, and without so much as a word they dashed forward and took hold of the girl, throwing her upon the bed while they gripped me by the arms. Without allowing me time to seize my clothing and paying no attention to my protests, they hurried me from the room and down the stairs, where a coat – someone's coat, and certainly not my own – was thrown to me to cover my nakedness before I found myself in the street, manacled and marching between two columns of sailors, my bare feet grating upon the stones beneath. Just ahead of me I saw Bob, similarly clothed only in an old coat – but his a short one, so that his sharp buttocks showed beneath it – being hurried along.

I was in no doubt what had happened to me: I was in the hands of the press gang, of which I had heard – nay, been warned. Mr Grose, when the subject was raised, was hot upon the necessity of getting men for the Navy, by force if necessary, though when I had demurred he asserted that no officer would dare touch one of his servants (a fact now contradicted by my present predicament).

Our march to the docks was accompanied by jibes and insults hurled at the officers and men by passers-by, though notably the few men who dared show themselves were chary of joining in the outright condemnation of the women, no doubt for fear that they should find themselves among the captives.

We seemed to march for miles – though perhaps the condition of my feet, by now lacerated and bleeding by the condition of the roads, made the way seem long – before we reached the quayside, and were crowded into two boats. The first man declined to descend the ladder (for it was low tide) and was taken and thrown down some six feet or more, when he landed with a dreadful cry on the bare boards of the craft and fell silent, whereupon the rest of us followed meekly. I found myself next to Bob, who whispered to me to keep my pecker up for he had been pressed before, two years ago, when he had been able to smuggle ashore a note to Mr Grose, who had come to his rescue, and

was now confident he could do so again with the promise of
reward for the fellow who would carry a message to our
master.

Bumping across the waters (to the distress of my stomach, for I was never a good sailor) we came to a craft, the
sides of which seemed to rise sheer, like cliffs, above us – it
being now too dark to see outside the ring of light shone by
the lanterns carried by the ruffians who commanded us. At
a cry from one of them, a rope ladder was thrown down
and we were forced to climb it one by one – much laughter
from our guardians being directed at Bob and me, as,
clumsily climbing it we, having no breeches, revealed our
privities to them.

As I climbed over the rail and onto the deck of the ship
my heart gave a great bound of hope for there, in the light
of a lantern upon the deck, stood the figure of an officer –
and a figure I knew, for above the white starched shirt and
the severe collar was the face of Spencer Franklyn – the
elder son of my old patron, Sir Franklin Franklyn, of
Alcovary!

'Mr Spencer!' I cried, taking a step forward. I am sure I
saw a look of recognition cross his face but almost instantly
I felt a blow upon the side of my head as a seaman nearby, I
suppose believing I was about to attack his officer, struck
me with a stout wooden baton he held in his hand, and I fell
unconscious to the boards.

When I came to my senses, I was in almost complete
darkness, conscious only of the press of many bodies
around me and of a fearful reek of sweat and vomit, gin
and urine. My head was in the lap of my companion, Bob,
who again assured me that we would simply have to live
through that one night and then we would be released, he
was confident of it. After a while, utterly weary, I fell into a
fitful sleep, to wake when the dim light reached us through
the single window and I saw myself to be in a small room,
which Bob told me was a part of the hold of a naval vessel.
As the light strengthened, I saw that we were but two of
about twenty fellows more or less disreputable, who were
also, like us, the subjects of one of the gangs of men sent out

to press men into the service. After a while, a trap opened above us and a bucket of water was lowered, from which we all drank in turn, mutual sympathy lending a certain compassion even to the roughest of us – especially towards one boy, a plump lad of perhaps only fourteen years of age, who cried bitterly at his fate and enquired again and again 'how his mother would do without him', which after some time so preyed upon the nerves of his companions that one man offered to throw him overboard if he did not hold his tongue.

Some hours passed, then the trap opened again, a ladder was lowered, and two seamen descended with a container of rank bread which was to serve us as lunch. One, particularly brutal, took pleasure in kicking and spurning any of us who got into his way and, coming to the youngster, reached out to take his face in a gigantic fist and cry: 'Here's a buxom Miss Molly for us, Jack. Hold up, boy, we'll call on you tonight!' while his companion picked me out, throwing up my coat to display my naked lower parts and crying: 'Here's another – and ready for you, Bill!' reaching down to give me a blow upon the privities which well-nigh took my senses away.

When they had gone Bob looked grave and told me – which I had already guessed – that these were fellows who, deprived of the comfort of their whores by long confinement on board, thought to play at rantum scantum with us. This had happened to him, he said, when he was similarly captured. He, however, had been taught by another fellow how to bear it, which was, he said, not to resist but to loosen the hinder parts so that there was no impediment to the invading tool when, he said, though not pleasant, such a venture at least inflicted no injury, whereas resistance would only increase the invader's passion and bring a resultant anguish.

This, the reader can believe, comforted me but little during the hours that passed. The gentle rocking of the boat confirmed that we were still at anchor and Bob said that this meant we would not be released until the ship (whose size and kind we could not even guess at) had sailed – a fact which concerned him, for on the previous occasion he had been able to get his message ashore only by making a contact with a fellow upon deck as they were allowed to take some air before sailing from harbour. It seemed as though there was to be no such chance upon this occasion.

After a while, I took the opportunity to explore our surroundings, which were plain enough; we were in a simple box, with no furniture but merely the floor. The single window or port was too high to reach and was pretty narrow, though I thought that perhaps I could squeeze through it, unclothed as I was, could I but reach it. But then, how far from shore were we? I could perhaps appeal to Master Spencer but the look I had received from him promised little; then, it seemed I could not reach him until the ship had sailed, when it would be too late for me to be released even should he have the influence to assist me, or care to use it.

I sat in gloom, as did we all, until once more the light faded when, the trap opening, the two fellows we had previously seen appeared once more with a lantern and a bucket from which a smell arose promising food of a kind none of us would have been glad to eat but for our circumstances. The men did not withdraw, however, but placing the bucket upon the ground, came forward and seized the youngest of us and pulled him towards the corner furthest from the glimmer of light which they had placed upon the floor. The boy began to whimper, whereupon there was the sound of a blow, followed by muffled sobbing.

'Remember the toss, Jack!' cried one of the men. 'I'll hold this one for you, then we'll find the other. Come now, boy –' and there was a sound of clothing being rent, and thereafter a violent cry of pain, muffled (no doubt) by a hand being thrown across the mouth of the victim.

I was now desperate to escape my fate. Throwing off the coat which was still my only covering, I made as quietly as possible for the side of the ship below the single port and began to scrabble at the timber walls, but there was no purchase. I looked around; the men in the dark corner were intent upon their business. I glanced appealingly at my fellow prisoners. I believe that my desperation struck a chord in them, and that they realised that I was the only man among them slim enough to make an attempt at the port, for Bob and another came forward, linked hands, and made a step from which I was able to grip the opening, pulling myself up and getting my arms, then my shoulders, through. Wriggling forward, I found myself hanging in the dark, how many feet above the water I could not know. Now my hips had caught, and for a moment I was unable to move. Then, by twisting my body so that my hips were diagonally fitted to two of the corners of the port, I felt them beginning to move again and, throwing my arms forward, and feeling a pain as the wood tore my skin, I was at last free and falling through the dark air for what seemed minutes before I struck the water and sank down, unprepared for a dive (since I had not had the presence of mind to fill my lungs with air before being immersed). Happily, the drop could not have been great, for I quickly felt myself beginning to rise, and was soon able to take a gulp of cool air.

Though the splash I had made must have been a noisy one, there was at present no reaction from the ship, which I could see dimly outlined against the starry sky. There was no moon, which happily would make it difficult to see me were the alarm given, but equally made it impossible for me to see the shore. I struck out towards what seemed to be the nearest light, trusting that it was from land rather than from another vessel. My bathing in the rivers and pools of the land were no real preparation for essaying a sea-swim, but the waters were not rough, nor was the distance too great, for within perhaps twenty minutes I was drawing myself up onto a small beach, cold and shaking. Behind me, at last the alarm had been given, and I could both hear and see (from the lights appearing on deck) that preparations were being made to launch a small boat to attempt to find me.

I had thought myself alone, but as I staggered up upon

the beach a light suddenly came into view along with two figures – a tall, elderly man with a young girl – who, before I could make my presence known to them, began to converse:

'If by my art, my dearest father, you have put the wild waters in this roar, allay them,' said the girl. 'The sky it seems would pour down stinking pitch, but that – but that –'

'But that the sea,' said the man.

'But that the sea, mounting to the welkin's cheek dashes the fire out. Oh, ah – ah –'

'I have suffered,' put in the man.

'Oh, yes – I have suffered,' said the girl, 'with those that I saw suffer . . .'

But at that point she saw me – no doubt a dark and menacing figure – and broke off with a cry.

'What is it now, girl?' asked the man, impatiently; then, when she pointed silently at me, put his hand to his waist and half drew a sword hanging there.

'Oh, sir,' I said, coming forward into their light, and attempting to hide my privities from the young lady with my shivering hands, 'could you perhaps direct me to some hiding-place? The press gang . . .' and I pointed out to sea, where now there was clearly the sound of rowlocks, and a small lantern could be seen bobbing shorewards, carried by a small boat in which, none the less, were several large men.

Happily, the elderly man was quick of apprehension.

'Quick,' he said to the girl, shielding the light sea-ward, 'off with your shift.'

'What?' she enquired in understandable surprise.

'Off with your shift, and into it, young fellow. You, miss, up to the inn.'

Somewhat unwillingly, I guess, the girl shrugged off her only article of clothing, rendering herself bare as I was to the cool night air and, handing it to me, vanished. I drew the article upon my body, and the man looked critically at me. 'Your hair could do with being longer,' he said, 'but if sufficiently ruffled . . .' and reaching up, pulled it forward over my eyes, then reaching out his arm drew me to him – I somewhat unwilling, this time, except that he said, 'Fear not – I am not of *that* persuasion. Remember, you are my daughter . . .' And so saying, he began to walk calmly, leaning upon me, towards the edge of the sea where even now the keel of the rowing-boat was cutting home into the sand, and the men leaping out, led by a rough fellow who came straight to us.

'Who be you, sir, and where be the escaped ruffian . . .?'

My friend drew himself up, though still leaning heavily upon me – which indeed gave me excuse to bow my head somewhat under his weight.

'We have seen no ruffians, sir,' he said, 'except yourselves.'

The sailor looked suspicious.

'What be you doing upon the shore so late in the evening?'

'And who are you, sir, that you have the cheek to enquire?' asked my friend, who was old enough to address even the press gang with impertinence, not being of an age to be of use to them. 'Watch your manners, man, or you'll find yourself arraigned before your betters!'

The man paused for a moment and looked, I thought, suspiciously at me.

'And this girl? She's remarkably silent for one of her sex?'

'Sir!' said my saviour, drawing himself up to his full height. 'Shame upon you that you should refer in such a way to one who has suffered! My daughter has been deaf and dumb from birth; that the heavens should have seen fit to place such a burden upon her and her loved ones is one matter – that some impertinent nazy mort, fresh no doubt from the nanny house, should add to our insupportable sorrow by such rude words . . .'

But by now the fellow was backing away, positively fawning, with 'Ah, sir – no, sir – my regrets, sir, for the inconvenience – he must have put ashore at some other beach . . .' And he made his way back to his mates, where after a short conversation they all leaped once more into the row-boat and pushed off, my benefactor standing staunchly all the while and watching them.

When they were safely out of earshot he turned to me and said: 'Now, sir, your name.'

I gave it him.

'And your condition?'

I told him.

'Then you must come first to our rooms and warm yourself, before we see you returned to your employer's house!' And he strode up the beach, and a hundred yards from the pathway which led down to it we came to a small tavern from the upper window of which issued the noise of singing. This was, as I later learned, the single tavern in the village of Calshot, near the mouth of Southampton Water.

'My companions are so noisy tonight,' said my friend, 'that Cynthia and I took ourselves off to read through Prospero and Miranda on the beach, it being yet early . . .'

And indeed, though I had had no means of telling time, and thought it perhaps to be past midnight, it was barely ten o'clock. But what could these people be? What was Prospero, and what Miranda?

Of course the reader will be before me but must remember that I then knew nothing of the drama, and could not connect those names with Shakespeare's drama of *The Tempest*, nor guessed that the company was one of actors.

However, they soon introduced themselves to me: a company of twelve, including the girl who had so kindly given up her shift and who now stood none too demurely clothed in another garment. At first she was inclined to be short with me, but when I had kissed her hand and begged her pardon, she smiled upon me sweetly – and the more so when my predicament was explained to her. Her friends were equally cordial, though at first they greeted my appearance with many a catcall and ribald joke against Mr Higgens (as my friend was called, and who was the leader of the company) such as 'Turned buttock bouncer, old Sam!' and other niceties, at which he grinned good-humouredly.

'Some gigs from the basket for young Andy' (for I had introduced my name to them) he said, and a young fellow of my own age, introduced to me as David Ham, promised assistance and took me off to the next room, where I was quickly out of my shift, and rubbed myself down roughly before climbing into a pair of breeches and a shirt he produced for me from a trunk.

When we were back in the main room I had to tell to the full my night's adventures, whereupon there were many murmurings against the whole business of the gangs, one elderly member of the company asserting that in one day, in 1802, three hundred men were pressed in Yarmouth – though two hundred and fifty of them were later released by the order of the mayor. Another man said that he had seen a group of fishermen seized in broad daylight while spreading their nets, at South Denes, and David, who came from the extreme west of England, said that he had heard from his father that only twenty years ago at the news that the press gang was coming all the men of Newlyn, in Cornwall, would flock up the hills and away to the country as fast as possible, hiding themselves in all manner of places till the danger was supposed to be over.

They were full of praise for my escape, and shared my anxiety for Bob for, they said, it was now likely, since I would certainly carry the news back to the town that respectable servants were among the drunkards made captive, that the ship would sail before dawn. I felt, too, for the poor boy who was being ill-used as I escaped, but whose predicament I had not fully described in the presence of ladies – for besides the young creature whose dress I had temporarily borrowed, there was also present a lady of more advanced years.

I learned, in my turn, that this was a company of actors who had been appearing in Southampton – 'In,' my friend announced, 'a selection of classical pieces including productions of *King Lear* and *Hamlet*, in which the leading parts are played by myself and my lady wife' – and he introduced himself as Samuel Prout Higgens, and his lady as Esmeralda Plunkett Cope – 'Famous, sir, for her Ophelia!' The young woman was his niece, Cynthia, and I learned the names too of the others, though did not at the time commit them to memory.

The company was interested to hear that I was a musician and thereupon produced a lute, which they invited me to play. Treating it as a guitar, I managed to produced some fair numbers from it, so that we sat and drank and sang for some time, myself carried forward by the excitement of the evening, until a sudden exhaustion came upon me, and I scarcely remember being half-carried to bed, where I awoke next morning to find myself beside young David, sleeping like a babe though the light outside announced broad daylight. I leaped up and ran to the window, which as I thought commanded a view of the Solent clear over to Gosport; but not a single ship lay within a mile. Poor Bob, I feared, together with Lieutenant Spencer Franklyn, was by now in the Channel, heading for God knew where.

I got myself up and awoke Higgens, saying that I must go to Mr Grose's house to let him know what had happened to me.

'One moment, Mr Archer,' said the actor. 'I was most impressed by the tunefulness not only of your fingers upon the instrument, but of your voice last night. Our lutenist left us a se'enight ago, but we must have music for our plays. We start tonight towards Bristol, performing at various hostelries upon the way. I can offer you an emolument commensurate with your skill, together with not unpleasant company. Your work would not be great, and with your musicality, my dear sir, the experience would be invaluable – I can see you upon the London stage, young man, gathering plaudits along with guineas! What do you say?'

Almost before he had ceased to speak I was determined to agree. I had been in one place long enough, for my adventures had endowed me with a wanderlust. I would pause only long enough, I said, to apprise Mr Grose of the facts, fetch my guitar (and my gold, though I said nothing of that), and would meet them just outside the city, on the Salisbury Road, at midday.

It was the work of but a few minutes to rouse David, who

was glad to escape the tasks of packing in order to ride with me on the back of one of the company's horses to Mr Grose's, where fortunately the merchant was at home – though the whole house was at sixes and sevens, for the marriage of Mr Mellor and Miss Patience was to take place in two days' time and great preparations were under way. The merchant was at first disposed to be angry, for he had assumed that Bob and I had simply fallen into drunken company, or decided to leave our employment without notice. But he was outraged to hear of the events which had carried us off – needless to say, I did not say where we had been taken, but that we had been seized in the open street (as so many men were) – and professed that he would take the whole matter up with the Admiralty and that someone's back should burn for it. None of this, however, would be of immediate use to Bob.

Mr Grose acquiesced somewhat unwillingly to my departure, at first being disposed to insist I should stay to play at the wedding, but since Mr Mellor was bringing a small band of musicians from London (for which the merchant was, naturally, paying) he agreed to my leaving, especially when I offered to forego the wages he owed me for the past week. In my room, I recovered my small store of gold and my guitar, which I wrapped in a cloth I had cut for the purpose. I then made my farewells to the family, and was wished well in handsome fashion; I had not informed them in what company I was to leave the town, for they would not, I am sure, have much approved of my becoming part of a band of players.

My few belongings were not a great extra burden for the horse, and before midday David and I were waiting outside the city at the appointed spot, where in due course the procession of my friends approached – four wagons, upon the first of which in state sat Mr and Mrs Higgens, both of whom bowed to me gravely as they rattled past. The wagon immediately behind paused, and I mounted it to sit between Cynthia Cope and a somewhat saturnine young man, Nathaniel Grigson, while David joined the last wagon, behind which he hitched our horse.

The way to Salisbury was enlivened by details of the life of my friends, who comprised a party of theatricals who during the winter played in a part of London known as Fulham Park, while during the summer they toured some part of England; two years before they had been in Wales, last year they had turned north-east to Norwich, and this year they were to end their current expedition in Bristol before returning to London to prepare for the autumn season. They took with them costumes for several plays, but scenery was improvised from whatever they could beg, borrow or contrive in whichever inn or yard they played.

Miss Cope carried, it appeared, the parts of young beauties and heroines: Miss Hardcastle in Goldsmith's comedy of *She Stoops to Conquer*, Maria in *The Citizen*, Bizarre in *The Inconstant*, and was about to essay the part of Miranda in *The Tempest*, in which Mr Higgens was to play once more the part of Prospero with which, I was told, he 'positively paralysed' the audiences at the Theatre Royal in Drury Lane, in the year of '89.

Mr Grigson's parts in general comprised the villains (it being, he said, his fate to be dark, whereas the British public preferred its heroes to have yellow hair and – he added – a stupid expression, which I took to be a gibe at some other member of the company). Mr Grigson was not taken by the parts he was at present assigned by Mr Higgens and longed to surprise the public, he said, by his Sneerwell, his Iago, his Macheath. But Miss Cope asserted, in my ear, that he would never be happy, were he to be offered the part of Hamlet with a supporting cast consisting of John Philip Kemble, George Frederick Cooke and Mrs Elizabeth Farren! None of these were familiar to me, but I took them to be the current kings of the stage. And so we rattled on, my new friends exchanging story upon story of their adventures, most of which consisted of narrowly escaping ruin by some trick played upon an innkeeper or local dignitary, and the four hour journey to Salisbury passed quickly indeed in such pleasant company.

The Bell at Salisbury was almost in the shadow of the great cathedral which though familiar, I make no doubt, to

all my readers, was new to me, so that its majesty and
grandeur made an indelible impression upon my mind,
being so much grander (it seemed) and imposing than any
building I had heretofore seen. The inn itself was an old
one, with a gallery and open yard in which, it was said, we
were to perform; in exchange for the proceeds of which, we
were to be given free accomodation and a division of the
moneys our efforts brought in. Our beasts were quartered
in the stables and we unloaded the seven large baskets
which contained costumes for the plays and placed them
too in the stables, in a disused stall. Then we were shown to
a large barn where sheets had been stretched on lines to
divide the space into a number of small compartments in
which mattresses had been placed, and to which we were
assigned in order of seniority. Once more I was to share a
bed with David, which did not disturb me since he was a
pleasant boy, and much preoccupied at the present time
because he was shortly to be allowed to play his first large
part upon the stage – that of the spirit Ariel in *The Tempest* – and spent much of his time laboriously conning the
pages of the play, and asking someone to interpret the print
for him, for he read but uncertainly.

After we had had supper and a drink or two, we repaired
to our barn, where after a while the noises attendant upon
our preparing for sleep quietened, and David and I began
to fall into a doze. But I was not yet asleep when I seemed to
feel a nudging at my side, and in the pitch dark (for no
lights were left on, the place being dry as tinder and likely
to flame) I felt in a moment a hand upon my shoulder,
which slid down until it held my hand. For a moment, half
asleep, I thought it was David's, either in sleep or in want
of comfort, but soon realised that it was on the other side
of me, and that it must come from someone in the next
compartment, stretching out beneath the sheet which was
all that lay between us. Moreover, I imagined from the lack
of sinew and of hair that it was a female hand, and from its
slightness guessed that it was that of Cynthia.

Not caring to offend her, and by no means without
gratitude for her quick agreement to my rescue the night

before, I turned and passed my own hand up her arm until it encountered a shoulder, then a willing bosom whose alertness seemed to signal a willingness to endure more than mere touch – for she took my hand and first pressed it to her bosom, then conveyed it lower, where a willing moisture suggested compliance with more radical action.

Carefully, so as not to disturb David, I rolled from my bed, and moving cautiously slid beneath the sheet until my body was alongside the softer, willing frame of my accomplice, whereat in a moment she had seized me with a surprising strength and lifted me upon her, throwing open her legs with such willingness that almost before I knew it my ready sword was sheathed to the hilt.

I must confess that at this moment I was inclined to wonder whether Cynthia had not previously entertained a man, for it seemed to me that the manner in which she twisted beneath me, the seeming familiarity with which her hands played about my backside and prised between our bellies to seize my cods, and the assurance with which her tongue plunged between my lips, seemed to hint that she was not entirely unfamiliar with the practices of love.

Our frenzy was conducted in utter silence (though the snores and gurglings proceeding from the next compartment, where Mr and Mrs Higgens lay in complacent slumber, would no doubt have drowned any noise we had made) until the sharp pain of a bite upon my shoulder with a shudder of her body beneath me hinted that she had reached her meridian, whereat my senses, encouraged by her satisfaction, also accomplished their crisis. A quick kiss and she lifted herself so that I rolled off and with the same movement back to my side of the intervening sheet.

With great care not to awake young David, I crept between the blankets; but in a moment his lips were at my ear: 'You've been welcomed into the company in the old way,' he whispered. 'She gives it to everyone on the first night – but now you'll have to fight for it. Me, I'm too young, for she regards me as a baby – which I am not, and could satisfy her more than she might think!' – and to prove it took my hand and thrust it down to where, between his thighs, there was indeed a tool sturdy enough to give any girl occupation. I attempted to remove my hand, but evidently in the throes of an unsatisfied passion he retained it by a gentle force, and in pity I let it remain, moving it in compliance until with a sharp-drawn breath he spent, whereat he whispered, 'Thanks – and I'll do the same for you when she turns you away – as she will!'

So, finally, we slept.

Chapter Fourteen

Sophie's Story

My arrival, clutching my few belongings, at Miss Trent's school for young ladies in Southampton resembled nothing so much, I imagine, as a convict's arrival at her prison; for though I have not, as yet, had experience of such a penitentiary, it could surely be no more securely guarded – by high walls and stout doors and windows – than the former establishment.

Upon ringing the bell, there was after a pause the sound of approaching footsteps, and then a thin voice made its way through a small grille in the door, asking my name and business. On my giving it there followed a great noise of locks and bars being withdrawn, and eventually the door opened for the distance of one inch or so, when I was inspected by an eye applied to the crack and, appearing respectable, and nothing like a maurauding thief, the door swung sufficiently far open to admit me to a stone-flagged corridor, where I was told to wait.

As I stood in the cold, I seemed to hear in the distance the chanting of some kind of choir, which abruptly stopped, and in a moment I was invited to follow the small, sallow maid who had greeted me, and found myself at last in Miss Trent's study, a room furnished chiefly with a large table upon which stood writing implements, some handsomely bound books and a cane. Behind the table stood Miss Trent herself, a tall, severe looking woman dressed in dark blue, her greying hair cut in a masculine style almost to the root – *à la Titus*.

'Yes, ma'am,' she said, 'your business with me?'

Handing her his note, I explained that I came with a recommendation from Mr Finching, and hoped she might have temporary employment for a teacher.

'Ha!' she exclaimed, having read the brief missive. 'My cousin tells me you are adept in music – and indeed we are in need of a lady to give instruction in the harpsichord, the minuet and the country dance. You consider yourself capable?'

I said that I would do my best.

'I am of the opinion that that phrase in general is the mark of the person whose best is rarely of a high standard,' said Miss Trent ominously. 'However, I am prepared to keep you for a week, after which we shall see. You can read, write and figure?'

I began to explain that my reading and writing was of a sufficiently high standard.

'We teach the use of the goose-quill here,' Miss Trent interrupted.

'Arithmetic is not, however, strong with me,' I went on.

Miss Trent shook her head.

'A sad dereliction on the part of your teachers, Mrs Nelham,' she said. 'But I myself impart the usage of numbers, and though an assistant in that area would have been welcome, will clearly have to continue to do so. By the way, what of your husband?'

I said that he had, alas, died within two months of my marriage, and dabbed an imaginary tear.

'Leaving you, I trust, with no child to encumber you?' asked Miss Trent unsympathetically, and when I replied, no, remarked that that would certainly have been a bar to my staying, for squealing children were worse than squealing young women.

'Very well,' she said finally. 'You will not of course expect any payment until we are satisfied with your work, but your meals you will take with us, and we will review the matter in a week or so.' So saying, she rang the bell, and almost simultaneously the little maid appeared, who during her working hours made it her business to follow her mistress around like a pet dog, ready to be useful at any moment.

'Dolly,' said Miss Trent, 'show Mrs Nelham to the dormitory.'

Whereupon I was taken up three flights of stairs to a long room constructed under the roof, containing eight beds, and one at the end about which a curtain could be drawn, and which I was informed was my own. I learned from Dolly – who stood moving uneasily from foot to foot, eager to return downstairs in case her mistress required her – that a former assistant teacher had left a week ago, since when Miss Trent and a visiting emigrant priest, M. de la Cuisse (who taught French and a little Latin) had been the only instructors.

I was prepared to unpack my things and settle into my small space, but Dolly insisted that Miss Trent would require my presence in the schoolroom immediately and so, only pausing to take off my bonnet, I followed her down to the first floor where from a large room, no doubt once a drawing-room, came the sound of chanting:

> *Five ones are five*
> *Five twos are ten,*
> *Five threes are fifteen,*
> *Five fours are twenty,*
> *Five fives twenty-five,*
> *Five sixes thirty . . .*

I opened the door and walked in.

Miss Trent stood in front of a class of eight young ladies, each clad in dresses of neat while muslin with necks cut remarkably high, sitting at desks in two rows of four while Miss Trent conducted them with a cane, which upon seeing me she brought down upon her own desk with a brisk *thwack*, at which the girls instantly broke off.

'Young ladies, stand!' she commanded, and beckoned me to the front of the class.

'This is Mrs Nelham, who will be aiding me in your general education.'

I inclined my head, and the girls bobbed a curtsy.

'We will now have our brief pause for refreshment, after which I shall leave Mrs Nelham to conduct a class in English literature,' Miss Trent said, and swept from the room. Giving the young ladies an uncertain smile, which they greeted with blank stares, I followed her downstairs to her room while a subdued chatter broke out behind me.

'You will find,' said Miss Trent, as we sipped our tea, 'that you must keep a strict watch upon the girls, whose natural propensity to un-Christian behaviour breaks out all too readily.'

She picked up two books and handed them to me.

'We use here Dr Bowdler's editions of Shakespeare and Mrs Trimmer's Bible. As to the first, there are, as you will be aware, many passages in the original which must be kept from tender ears, and which indeed I would be sorry to hear that you have read. Personally, I would be inclined to deny the whole work of that person (who for no good reason has come to be regarded as our national author) to the eyes of all women, but sadly parents seem to expect it. The unbounded licentiousness of this age has made it almost impossible for young ladies to come anything towards years of discretion without such a knowledge of vice as must render them incapable of a proper command over their imaginations. But we can at least attempt, here, to keep the news of the world from them.

'Kindly remember that if any word or expression is of such a nature that the first impression which it excites is an impression of obscenity, that word ought not to be spoken, or written, or printed, and if printed, it ought to be erased.

'As to the Holy Book, Mrs Trimmer advises the use of only some half of the text, omitting those portions which refer to that function which if freely performed leads to the procreation of children. There are many passages in the translation allowed by King James which include terms not now generally made use of in polite society, and in Mrs Trimmer's edition these passages are either omitted or the expressions altered. That prudent woman, while she admired the beauties of the sacred writings, was convinced that, unrestricted, no reading more improper could be permitted to a young woman. Many of the narratives can only tend to excite ideas the worse calculated for a female breast; everything is called plainly and roundly by its name and the annals of a brothel could scarcely furnish a greater choice of indecent expressions. In fact I have this evening to inflict punishment upon Sarah Burtenshaw who not only had in her possession an unexpurgated edition of the Old Testament, but was discovered reading passages from' – she shuddered – 'the Song of Solomon to her unfortunate fellows!'

She pushed the two volumes towards me.

'Here, then, are Dr Bowdler and Mrs Trimmer, from whom you will perhaps now instruct the class in reading, paying particular attention to intonation and clarity.'

Finishing my tea, I took myself upstairs, where the young ladies quieted to an uneasy hush as I entered, and settled to the dullest and most pedestrian readings of the more innocuous portions of the Letter of St Paul to the Thessalonians, which they performed one by one, and very decently, except for one poor, pale girl who stuttered her way through her portion as though she could scarce see it. When I asked her name she announced in an almost inaudible voice that she was Miss Sarah Burtenshaw, at which I assumed she was concerned for the hours of copying out of passages from the Good Book which would no doubt be her punishment for having explored those portions of it considered improper by her mistress.

Excusing her from further participation in the lesson, I told her that she might if she wished go to her bed to rest but, clearly terrified, she said that Miss Trent would not permit it, whereat I announced that I would be answerable to Miss Trent, and after much hesitation and with a wan smile she disappeared. The other girls now seemed disposed to be pleasant to me and we went on splendidly until the end of the lesson, when a bell ringing below took us to the dining-room – a bare, cold place at the back of the house – for a meal of boiled mutton and potatoes, the only one of the day (I was told), apart from some biscuits in the middle of the evening.

As the day went on an unaccountable tension seemed to grow, so that none of the girls could concentrate on their lessons and made a sad showing when I attempted instruction on the harpsichord. Finally I gave up attempting it and passed the time playing some of the pieces I loved best, at which they cheered up somewhat – apart from poor Miss Burtenshaw, who had reappeared for lunch, and now once more sat silent and pale.

The reason for such apprehension over what could surely only be a light penalty was not clear to me until eight o'clock, when, as I sat with the young ladies over the sewing which occupied (they told me) most evenings at the school, a bell rang and we were led by Dolly into a back room on the first floor, which had the appearance of a bedroom. Indeed it was the room in which Miss Trent slept, except that its centre had been cleared and there stood a remarkable erection, the like of which I had never seen before, consisting of three strong pieces of timber fixed together as a sort of pyramid, with cross-pieces to ensure its stability. Completely silent and overawed, the girls trooped into the room and stood in a row by the door, which in a moment opened to admit Miss Trent, bearing in her hand a bunch of birches.

To my horror, I realised that she must be first cousin to that notorious flaybottomist Mr Gutteridge, who had so beaten us at Alcovary.

Miss Trent took up her station facing us.

'Miss Burtenshaw, step forward,' she commanded.

Poor Sarah took a step forward, looking as though she would faint at any moment.

'Miss Burtenshaw, you know your offence?'

'Y-yes, Miss Trent,' she said.

'Recall it to me?'

'I was reading from the Bible, Miss Trent.'

The mistress thwacked her thigh with the birches.

'You were reading from a forbidden portion of the Bible, girl!' she said. 'You know perfectly well that that work is omitted from *our* Bible, lest in the fervour of youth it give too wide a scope to fancy, and interpret to a bad sense the spiritual ideas of Solomon. The purpose of the chapters in question is to exhibit the chaste passions of conjugal life as they existed among the Jews, to whom polygamy was allowed, but their reading cannot be recommended in families, let alone in organisations as chaste as ours. Had I not discovered your impertinence, you had been in the way of corrupting all your companions by admitting them to notions which could only lead in the end to a life of sin which would disqualify you all from participation in decent society. Miss Burtenshaw, prepare yourself.'

The poor girl gave a look of entreaty, which was met only with a cold stare, and reluctantly lifted her dress to her shoulders, revealing her naked back to all. She then stepped forward and, turning to face the wooden structure, leaned against it, clasping her arms around it and bending her belly across the horizontal support so that her fair, plump buttocks were extended.

Miss Trent, as slowly as possible, inspected the bundle of birches and carefully chose one, making it whistle through the air – at which everyone in the room, I believe, shivered.

'Nelly Morrison – apply the mark!' she then said, handing the birch to one of the other girls – one who was, as I learned, Sarah's particular friend. Nelly reluctantly took the birch, went to the fireplace (which contained only a few cold ashes) and taking from it some charcoal, darkened the birch. Then she approached her friend (taking the opportunity, as I saw, being on the right side, of whispering a word of comfort in the poor girl's ear) and laid it tenderly across her buttocks so that a horizontal line was marked upon the backside. She then handed the birch to Miss Trent, who whistled it once more through the air, and took up a stand behind and somewhat to the left-hand side of her victim.

'I have ascertained,' she said, 'by counting them – without of course reading the matter – that there are sixteen verses in the chapter of the work whose indecencies you were so diligently conveying to your friends; you will therefore receive sixteen strokes. Are you ready?'

Sarah's lips moved, but no sound came from them.

'Are you ready?' the schoolmistress repeated.

'Yes, thank you, Miss Trent,' came the weak reply, whereat the mistress raised the cane high above her head and brought it down with a sharp crack upon the bottom of her unfortunate pupil, whose whole body shook.

'One,' she announced.

The birch rose again, and with great accuracy fell upon the dark charcoal mark, now deepened by the red of the former assault.

'Two,' she cried, as great tears began to roll from the eyes of her pupil, now biting her lips in her attempt to remain silent.

'Do feel, Miss Burtenshaw, free to express your emotions aloud; we shall not be distressed – shall we girls?' she asked, turning to the white-faced class.

'No, Miss Trent,' they chorused, meekly.

By the time the birch had descended five times, specks of blood had begun to appear and Sarah had, despite herself, given out a shriek of pain. Seven strokes and blood was running freely, and the girl crying for mercy – which only seemed to rouse her mistress to more vigorous motion. With the tenth stroke the cries suddenly ceased, and releasing her hold Sarah slid unconscious to the floor. Disappointed, Miss Trent threw down her birch.

How I had contained myself, I know not. Perhaps the fact that I knew no one in the town and had no one else from whom I could command shelter, restrained me but now I stepped forward and bent to try to rouse the unconscious victim.

'Mrs Nelham!' cried my employer. 'Pray retire!'

I rose to my feet.

'It is the custom here that the friends of the punished one should minister to her, as a memorial to them of the consequences of disobedience. I ask you, on your honour, to refrain from having anything to do with her!'

She stared straight at me. Looking back, after a moment, I nodded, not trusting my voice to reply, and in any case crossing my fingers firmly behind my back.

'To the dormitory!' commanded Miss Trent, and Sarah, now once more conscious though barely able to stand, was supported by her friends and taken from the room.

'Now, Mrs Nelham, perhaps you would care to join me

for a cup of chocolate?' said Miss Trent. 'Dolly – the birch!' At which Dolly came forward, picked up the bloody instrument, and took it away to clean and replace it in its cupboard for future use.

I made, needless to say, my excuses to Miss Trent, saying that I was tired and wished to retire.

'Of course, my dear Mrs Nelham,' said the mistress, whose dark eyes seemed now to be sparkling with a vigorous and unusual brightness. She placed her arm about my shoulders and walked me to the door.

'Do not allow the young ladies to incommode you; if they prevent you from sleeping, there is always room for you – elsewhere,' and she seemed to nod in the direction of her bed, behind us.

I thanked her with what politeness I could muster, and made my way upstairs, where the body of Sarah, who was now sufficiently recovered to command her weeping, lay face downward upon one of the beds, while her friend Nelly and the others stood around, not knowing what to do to comfort her.

At first I, too, was at a loss, and then remembered how my brother Andy, after Mr Gutteridge's assaults upon me, had salved my wounds; and sitting upon the edge of the bed and bending my head, I applied my tongue to Sarah's cuts – so much more savage than those I had experienced. The salt of blood on my tongue, I felt the poor girl flinch even at so tender a ministration, but after a while, she evidently felt some comfort, for her sobbing ceased, and presently she fell into an exhausted sleep. Making sure the single window was closed so that no cold air should strike upon her, I instructed the others not to lay any bedclothes upon her body, but to allow the air of the room to play upon it, which should seal the wounds and render them less painful.

'She will be excused lessons for three days,' I was told, for this was the custom after a whipping, which took place perhaps once a month, sometimes with far less excuse than poor Sarah had given, and was often more severe. The girls had now learned somewhat to counterfeit pain and eventual collapse, to save themselves from the wilder extremities of discomfort, though they had to do so with great care for if she suspected pretence Miss Trent only laid on the harder, and it was rumoured that she had actually killed one young person, many years ago.

'At least,' said young Nelly, 'now we get some peace,' for after her display of cruel discipline, Miss Trent would then conduct the school strictly but without undue passion for at least a month, before seeking another reason to inflict a birching upon one of her pupils.

My care for Sarah had evidently endeared me to the young ladies, for during the next weeks they showed me great kindness, not only behaving prettily in class but also allowing me every courtesy in the dormitory – especially Sarah, who displayed the utmost gratitude, often creeping into my bed after dark and inviting me to hold her in my arms, which I did with pleasure, she being a dear and charming creature to whom I was happy to be a substitute for her mother. In the meantime several of the girls showed an aptitude for music and, taking the greatest care to conceal it, I was able to acquire a small anthology of poetry in the town from which I read very quietly, after we had retired, some verses from Thomas Campion, Christopher Marlowe, Sir Philip Sidney, Edmund Spenser and even Dr Donne, whose lines considerably roused our spirits.

I was permitted to walk in the town once or twice a week, but as for the girls, they were kept strictly immured. There was a small garden at the back of the house, whose high walls prevented us from seeing anything but the roofs of the neighbouring buildings. There, once a day, the girls and I were allowed to walk and even to throw a ball to each other, but that was their only exercise except on Sundays, when we walked in a column to the cathedral for Matins, led by Miss Trent and concluded by myself. The huge building was almost empty apart from ourselves; a very few townsmen and women could be seen, but the services were otherwise almost unattended. However, the outing was a pleasant one, allowing us at least to see other human beings.

The longer I stayed at the school, the more I felt that it

was unnatural and unreal that young ladies – the oldest of whom was only perhaps eighteen months younger than I – should be kept for so long periods altogether from the world of men. They talked longingly of their brothers and cousins, but of course had no notion of the carnal pleasure of congress with the male sex, and I hesitated to speak to them of it – not because I believed this would harm them, but because I believed that any description I could give, while sufficiently educative, might rouse their emotions to an ungovernable extent.

This led me into some difficulty when, in reading from works of which Miss Trent would no doubt disapprove, we came across terms with which (or so I thought) the young ladies were unfamiliar. Though now sharing confidences with me, they were guarded in their speech, and sometimes I caught them sharing a private joke or giggling in a corner. I thought their jokes to be at normal childish things, until having reluctantly taken chocolate one night with Miss Trent, who treated me now with the utmost courtesy, I came up to the dormitory expecting to find the girls asleep, but heard outside the door little cries and laughs, and on entering was to my surprise confronted with a view of Sarah, quite naked, leaning over the end of her bed, while a figure I thought at first to be a man approached her from behind, his enormous and erect instrument in hand.

The scene held still at my opening the door, whereupon the girls who had been gathered admiringly around the tableau scattered and the man, to my amazement, apparently wrenched his tool from its root and thrust it under a bed where, on my looking, I found it to be nothing more dangerous than a cucumber, no doubt stolen from the kitchen, which Nelly had been about to employ upon her friend in imitation of the act of love!

The girls were clearly terrified but when, unable to control my emotions, I burst into laughter, they too burst into uncontrollable giggling the noise of which was only with great effort repressed so as not to be heard by Miss Trent in the rooms below! It was clear that some, at least, of my companions were more educated in the difference between men and women than I had supposed, and indeed Sarah confessed to me that she had, one day, come upon her brother and one of the village girls in a barn, in the posture which she and her friend had adopted and which she believed to be the only one a man and a woman *could* adopt for such purposes. Nor was she, except instinctively, cognitive of the pleasure such activity provoked, so that I felt I should enlighten them all, and drawing them in a circle about my bed, explained to them the many postures love could adopt, which they begged me to illustrate. So, playing the part of the man, though without the aid of the vegetable, and without the least difficulty persuading Sarah to play the woman, I placed us in the various positions which afforded the most acute sensations of congress.

They were just as amazed as I had been to learn, as I thought fit to warn them, that one such instance of commerce between a man and a woman could lead to procreation, and Sarah was insistent in reproaching the Creator for not arranging things more conveniently (which I was bound to agree with, though I felt it my duty to reprove her for blasphemy). However, I was able to point out that not only the male instrument was capable of giving pleasure to woman, asking whether some at least of them had not found that the exploration of their own bodies gave them some entertainment. Blushingly they confessed it, and Sarah – who was proving herself to be nothing other than a forward hussy, though a most attractive one – confessed to receiving much enjoyment from mutual caresses with her friend Nelly. But had they not also found, I enquired, that the employment of the lips and tongue was equally delicious to our sex? No, they replied with surprise, and invoked my description of those subtle pleasures – which led to their imploring me to teach them how they might best please their future husbands in such a manner.

Once again, Sarah showed herself most forward in wishing to know in the most detailed form how to undertake such adventurings, and after some persuasion I persuaded myself, upon her stretching herself upon her bed, still naked from her experiment with her friend, to apply my lips to her breast, and then my tongue to her most sensitive part – upon which after a moment she gave a shriek so loud that we all took ourselves to our beds and lay trembling for some time, sure that Miss Trent must have heard.

However, it became clear that she had not and after a time we crept from our covers like mice and the girls all decided – driven on by Sarah, who spoke with the utmost relish of the delirium, the transport, the indescribable delight of the emotion she had felt – that they must experiment in the action I had shown them, so that in no time each bed bore two girls, head to tail, busily at work – while I strolled between them to give a hint here, or a suggestion there, which might result in a keener apprehension of passion.

From that time forward, with all the enthusiasm of beginners at joy, the young ladies I fear devoted more attention to the practice of amorous pleasure than to scholastic pursuits, much of the day being spent with yawning lips and half-closed eyes – except during those lessons in which Miss Trent occupied herself, when they contrived to appear more wide awake. I found them willing and grateful pupils, who even drew up a round-list which brought one or other to me every night for such additional tuition as I could contrive, which it was no trouble to me to give, since they were all sweet young things whose bodies were slim and attractive, and which could even – with an effort of imagination – be compared to those of young men; though one thing always was missing, which I must confess I grew increasingly aware of as the weeks passed.

It was on the fourth Sunday of my presence at the school that, as we walked through the cathedral close to service, poor Sarah stumbled and almost fell. Before I could go to her, a young man darted forward and assisted her to her feet, at which she curtsied, blushingly, and walked on. When I turned to thank the young man, he had vanished.

That night in the dormitory it was her turn to visit me, but instead of unclothing herself and climbing immediately into my bed, she sat upon its side and whispered the confidence to me that she had that day received a message from a secret lover!

The sly puss had kept this entirely from me, and indeed from all except Nelly, but hearing us whisper, her companions gathered around and insisted on hearing the story, which Sarah needed no persuasion to tell. It appeared that until three months ago she had been privately educated at her parents' home by a series of female tutors until, the last of these leaving, her father had engaged a young man to come to teach her, believing (most sensibly) that it was time she met some member of the opposite sex other than servants, and that a tutor could be trusted to behave towards her with propriety. As indeed at first he had, but he was (she said) of extraordinary beauty and before long she was drinking in his appearance and actions rather than his words. Desperate for some other attention than the correction of her recital of the conjugation of the verb *asseoir*, she had contrived to stumble while out walking, and to fall against him, forcing him to catch her, whereupon, being human and feeling in his arms this charming morsel of young womanhood, he had clasped her rather longer than the situation truly warranted. The next day Mr Burtenshaw, her father, unexpectedly entering the schoolroom, had seen the tutor pressing the first kiss upon lips which had never previously known such an impropriety.

The tutor left that same afternoon and two days later Sarah found herself at Miss Trent's school, where her spirit had been almost but not entirely subdued by the wicked beatings which that unregenerate mistress had inflicted upon her.

Her Evan (for such was his curious name) had, it seems, discovered by some means her whereabouts; some weeks ago Dolly had brought her a note pledging his love and offering to attempt to release her from the bondage of the school and to marry her. However, the maid was far too terrified to carry further messages so, taking great risk, her lover had that day taken the chance of discovery by passing her another note:

'My love, contrive to send a message to me at Mr Bobbins' lodging house in Fence Street. If you will consent to come away I will somehow engineer your release, and have employment in Wales which will support us both. Your lover, Evan.'

Of course I consented to carry a message – for it was now my solemn belief that no effort to release any pupil from the clutches of Miss Trent could be unjustified – whereupon nothing would content Sarah than that at that moment she should sit down and write a note introducing me to her lover, and confirming that she would agree to any plan for her escape that he and I could construct. After this she slipped into my bed and in her untutored affection amply demonstrated the joy she would eventually give even the least receptive of husbands.

It was not for three days that I was able to excuse myself for an afternoon and took the note from the secret hiding-place in which I had secreted it, finding (for I had not looked at it before) that it was addressed to a Mr Evan Ffloyd. The coincidence seemed too much; surely this must be the tutor who had taught me all I knew, at Alcovary? And indeed, when I had made my way to Fence Street and the appointed lodging-house, I found myself in due course face to face with my old friend, whom I had last seen making his way out of my life through the park at home.

For a moment he did not know me – doubtless the experience of the past months had marked my features with a certain maturity – but then took me in his arms and pressed my lips to his until I pulled myself away and with the uttering of the single word 'Sarah!' not only reminded him of his obligation, but instructed him that I knew of it.

Blushing, as well he might, he escorted me to a room where we could talk and I gave him my friend's note and explained to him the circumstances which had brought me to him. He was able to satisfy me that indeed his intentions were honourable, and within the hour we had made our plans, which that night I explained to Sarah and her friends.

On the following Saturday morning, I made a point of attending the weekly class during which Miss Trent examined the girls in their lessons of the week. After several unexceptional recitations of passages from the expurgated

Bible and an animadversion by the Rev. Anthony Westcott, former Bishop of Salisbury, on the subject of the true dimensions of the Noah's ark, she invited Sarah to recite the verse she had chosen that week to memorise.

Sarah got to her feet, and in the clearest voice began:

> *Come, madam, come, all rest my powers defy,*
> *Until I labour, I in labour lie . . .*

Miss Trent obviously did not recognise Dr Donne's poem but gradually, as the sense came upon her, her complexion became one blush, until Sarah reached the lines:

> *Licence my roving hands, and let them go*
> *Before, behind, between, above, below . . .*

when she gave a loud shriek of outrage and protest.

'Sit down, Miss Burtenshaw! I have never in my life heard such indecencies. Mrs Nelham, what do you know of this?'

Stammering, I lied that I knew nothing.

'Miss Burtenshaw, I have had enough of your impertinence. You will all present yourselves to me at nine this evening in my room!'

Whereupon she swept from the room, and we relieved our tension in an outbreak of stifled laughter.

That evening at nine we filed into Miss Trent's room, where the flogging-frame had been erected in its usual place, and after a while Miss Trent appeared, birches in her hand.

'Miss Burtenshaw, prepare yourself,' she said.

Sarah stepped forward, but rather than stripping herself, drew up to her height and replied, 'No, miss – it is now your turn!'

Shocked and amazed, Miss Trent at first could not reply, then raised her hand to strike her rebellious pupil across the face. But now the other girls crowded round; one seized the birches and the others clutched at their mistress' clothing, and in a little time had removed it, revealing madam's skinny body and then forcing her to the frame. In a passable imitation of Miss Trent's voice, Sarah invited Miss Morrison to 'apply the mark', whereupon Nelly applied the charcoal to a birch, and laid a black mark upon the mistress' lank backside.

The beating which followed was by no means as severe as that the mistress had inflicted upon Sarah, for though the girls applied themselves with enthusiasm, they lacked the power – and indeed the will – to draw blood. However, the indignity their mistress suffered was an additional punishment, as was perhaps the cool stare with which I received her pleas for help. Even Dolly, who had known nothing of our plan, though she cowered in a corner perhaps anticipating the end of the world as she knew it, was not displeased at her employer's fate.

Finally, tiring of their sport, the girls threw down the birch and left the room, locking the door behind us, conscious that Miss Trent, now past the power of speech, could only cry help from a back window and that neighbours were immured to shrieks emanating from this house.

Now we went to our room, where we had packed our belongings, and thence to the ground floor, where the key of the front door was kept in Miss Trent's cupboard. Breaking the lock of this, we discovered not only the key but a large selection of canes and birches of various sizes, together with books entitled *The Whippingham Papers, The Flogging Horse, An Essay upon the Whipping Block*, and several similar volumes, which appeared upon a glance to be of the utmost indecency. Removing these lest they should corrupt anyone into whose hands they might fall, I took the key and unlocked the door, and we all trooped out into the sunlight. From my small store I had given the girls sufficient money to command a chair to their homes for they all, save Sarah, came from the immediate areas of the town, and I accompanied her to Fence Street and her lover.

Mr Ffloyd had taken places in the Oxford coach though he intended, he said, to break the journey at Basingstoke, where next day he would marry his love – news of which delighted her.

Upon reaching the Pestle and Mortar Inn at Basingstoke and enquiring for accommodation, we discovered that only a single room was available, which distressed Mr Ffloyd, who had certainly intended to anticipate the joys of marriage and now feared that his design would be impeded. Upon his suggesting that Sarah and I should share the room while he passed the night in the travellers' room downstairs, Sarah demurred for, she said, I was friend enough to be almost a sister to her (we had not revealed to her that Mr Ffloyd and I had met before).

Upon his somewhat reluctantly agreeing, we were shown to our room, which had a single but large four-poster bed. It was offered to make up a mattress upon the floor, but again Sarah insisted that since she and I had often shared a bed before, there was no reason why we should not do so for one last time. After all, she could sleep between me and Mr Ffloyd to avoid embarrassment and indelicacy. And without more ado she threw off her clothes and got between the sheets. Mr Ffloyd and I carefully turned our backs towards each other while removing our clothing, and climbed into the bed, one upon each side of Sarah.

For a while we all lay still, I suppose somewhat checked by the strangeness of the situation, but Sarah then fell to telling Mr Ffloyd of the rebellion at the school and in the excitement of retailing events sat up in bed, the light of a large moon through the window illuminating the room so that the beauty of her young breasts was clearly visible to the young man at her side, who must have been made of stone had he not given way to it. Indeed in a while he raised himself with a low groan and threw his arms around his love, planting a kiss upon her bosom, in which he buried his head.

Sarah was obviously pleased at the attention, and at another less visible manifestation of his admiration, for she mouthed silently to me over Mr Ffloyd's head the information that he was 'very big', by which she did not, I believe, refer to the stature of his torso merely.

I must admit that his attention to my friend reminded me strongly of the salutes he had given me at our last meeting, and I was unable to resist passing my hand over his neck and shoulders. He may have thought this was a compliment paid by Sarah, for he redoubled his caresses, covering her bosom with kisses and – by her expression – passing his hands over her lower limbs.

Her pleasure obviously increasing, and remembering my teaching, in a while she threw back the covers and persuaded him upon his back. Wriggling downwards and first gasping with a pleasurable admiration of his manly beauty – which indeed was as vigorous and upstanding as I recalled – she applied her lips with such tender condescension that a look of blank amazement passed over her lover's face. This gave way in a moment to a tranquil delight, in the course of which, whether abstractedly or not I could not say, he stretched forth a hand to caress my breast – which welcomed his tickling fingers, for the sight of the couple's mutual pleasure conveyed most vividly to me my recent lack of male company. In a moment I was constrained to join my lips to his in a kiss which lasted so long that when I finally withdrew my lips it was to see that Sarah had raised her head and was regarding us – not with displeasure, but a simple happiness. This encouraged me to join her in making Mr Ffloyd a happy man. First – having that right by her chief place in his affections – she received him within her arms, while I merely contented myself with passing my hands over his back, or reaching to grasp with tender approbation his weighty cods to encourage the ebullient eagerness of his jogging. Then after a while she persuaded me to revive him and to allow him in turn to satisfy me – which, being young and vigorous, he was perfectly able to do.

Finally, in relaxed pleasure, each exhausted of our eager striving, we lay still, our limbs tangled in friendly repose, and fell into a quiet sleep.

Chapter Fifteen

The Adventures of Andy

Waking on the morning after our arrival at Salisbury, I found myself plunged into a day's frantic activity; first, the erection of a rough stage in the courtyard of the Bell Inn, then the sorting of costumes, and – in our barn, so as not too much to disrupt the business of the inn – a rehearsal of that evening's play *Isabella, or The Fatal Marriage*, by Thomas Southern, as altered by Mr Higgens for his small company, with Mr Grigson in the part of Biron, Mr Prout Higgens as Villeroy, and Mrs Plunkett Cope as Isabella, a part played until lately, I was informed, by the great Mrs Siddons herself. Both the latter actors, I soon gathered, were at least forty years too old for their parts, but this was common practice with them.

I was instructed that music would be needed between the acts and was told to play 'something tragic' immediately upon Mrs Plunkett Cope remarking 'Then Heav'n have mercy on me!' and leaving the stage with her child (the three-year-old daughter of the innkeeper, whose pride in seeing her upon the stage resulted in the provision of an excellent midday repast, without charge). Then I must render 'something romantic' upon Villeroy announcing, in heartbreaking tones, 'Next, my Isabella, be near my heart! I am for ever yours.' Finally, I was to play 'a merry jig, or some such nonsense,' at the end of the play, 'to send 'em home happily' – which considering the piece ended in utter disaster for each and every character, seemed to me to be somewhat strange. But 'twas not my responsibility, so I looked out some pieces and practised them quietly in a corner, while everything was in chaos around me.

I was then led off by David to a corner of the barn where

a small, squat woman, addressed by all as 'Wardrobe', was to produce a costume for me to wear 'in the style of the play', as Mr Higgens instructed. Since the players were dressed in clothes from every decade of the past two hundred years, it seemed to me to be immaterial what I wore, but again, it was not for me to protest.

'Wardrobe' was surrounded by a vast quantity of clothes and by several members of the company, ignoring the various degrees of each other's undress as they climbed into or out of breeches and shifts. David pointed out several of the costumes as having belonged to the deceased nobility, for it was still the fashion then for the relicts of noblemen to give or sell their clothes to the actors. So, he said, the suit of scarlet and gold Mr Grigson was trying on had been worn by Lord Northampton upon his entrance as British ambassador into Venice, while a brown suit into which another actor was attempting to squeeze his ample form had been made for the actress Peg Woffington, whose fame and beauty, it appears, is well known, and who had worn it in the breeches part of Sir Harry Wildair, before it had come to this company through a neice of hers. Mrs Plunkett Cope was just divesting herself of a dress which she had worn (so David whispered) in the part of Lucinda in *Love in a Village* forty years since, and which now restrained only with difficulty the generous spread of her bosom.

I was provided with a pair of green pantaloons and a jacket, and without complaint took them away and placed them upon my bed, where I drew the sheet which cut me off, in sight at least, from the general press. I lay down for a rest, being somewhat exhausted by the excitements of the day, following as they did upon those of the previous twenty and four hours.

As I turned over I saw a female arm lying near to me, just falling beneath the lay of the sheet which hung between me and the bed of Miss Cynthia Cope, and thinking to be friendly, I stretched out my hand and laid it upon the wrist, whereat in a moment the sheet flew up and a positive virago attacked me. Miss Cope, though in *negligée* – for she had taken off her day clothes in order to don her costume, but at present had merely laid an excessively thin petticoat upon herself which indifferently concealed her form – threw herself upon me, striking me violently about the face with her fist. Amazed, I at first made no attempt to defend myself, and her nails caught my cheek, laying it open, before I succeeded in taking her by the wrists and restraining her.

'Unhand me, sir!' she cried. 'You think you can assault a defenceless woman! Base upstart crow, keep your dark hands to yourself!'

Whereat I unhanded her, and with a final scornful glance she returned to her mattress, drawing down the sheet with a flounce.

There was a laugh, and I saw that David had appeared just in time to see his fellow player's exit. I must have looked a picture of amazement, dabbing at my torn cheek, quite unable to understand why a young woman who the previous night had welcomed me into her bed with a sharp enthusiasm should have greeted thus what was intended as a simple mark of affection.

Laying himself down at my side so that he could whisper into my ear, David told me that Miss Cope was known not only in the company but abroad for the indelicate profligacy of her passions, which, however, she intended should remain cloaked in night. Never had she been seen to give a sign of warmth to any of her lovers while anyone else was by, but while under cover of night she would, as he put it, share cock alley with anyone near, and was as lively as any Covent Garden nun.

'Fear not!' he said; 'if you bed next her, you'll have another buttock ball before long. But remember' (and his lips tickled my ear as he spoke) 'if you are in need of a strum and she's not by, I can offer you a relish.' Whereupon he stole his hand upon my thigh and pinched it.

Though I had never before been so diligently courted by one of my own sex, I omitted to strike him as some fellows might, for he was a likable rogue, and indeed the whole company had been excessively kind to me, so that I had no wish to offend any of their number. I simply made no sign, whereupon David kissed me upon the cheek and asked me if I would 'hear him' in his small part of Sampson, servant to Count Baldwin. This meant my holding the book of the play (or in fact merely the writing out of his part, with the 'cues' which brought in his speeches) while he recited his part:

'I have no ill-will to the young lady, as a body may say, upon my own account; only that I hear she is poor; and indeed I naturally hate your decayed gentry – they expect as much waiting upon as when they had money in their pockets . . .'

And so on.

The performance that evening went well; my pieces were approved, and indeed when I left my place below the stage at the end of the evening several of those who had seen the play invited me to drink with them, which I did until past midnight, later being told that one could normally expect such hospitalty, for some people liked to boast that they were friendly with the players and their company – surprisingly enough, for it seemed to me we were a raggle-taggle lot. However, I accepted the offered ale with pleasure, in the company of some others of my new friends. Mr Grigson, I saw, left the room accompanied by a young lady dressed in the height of fashion, with a modest high-necked bodice above a dress which fitted her elegant figure so closely that she clearly wore no petticoat beneath it. I must have been looking somewhat jealous, for David – who hovered attentively near by – whispered that Mr Grigson often attracted the attentions of the ladies, and indeed sometimes of the gentlemen – none of which he disliked, it seems, as long as there was financial inducement.

That night, as David had taught me to expect, Miss Cope once more stretched out her arms and welcomed me between her thighs, with no word about the day's rejection, much less apology for the damage to my cheek (which had caused many a knowing glance, and some ribald comment). The ale had had the effect upon me, which sometimes it does, not of making me incapable of standing but difficult of satisfaction, so that the lady twice attempted to throw me off, having gained her own satisfaction. But I continued to pump away, with perhaps unaccustomed diligence which in the end roused her again to a fever, and by the time my own slow fuse had been fully burned out we were both exhausted, and I scarcely had the energy to return to my mattress. There I felt David attempting to fumble below my waist but, without even the vigour to strike his hand away, I fell into a deep sleep.

The following day we played again at the Bell – this time in Shakespeare's *As You Like It*, in which Mr Higgens essayed the part of the Ancient Duke while Mrs Plunkett Cope, crammed into Miss Woffington's well-worn brown suit, played the part of Rosalind, her general appearance being as like that of a boy as the view of an elephant resembles that of a doe. The audience was reduced by this to a regrettable levity which extended not only to the humorous parts of the piece, but the serious, and during the last Act there came from several drunken ruffians a demand for a hornpipe, which was so insistent that Mr Higgens was forced to halt the expounding of the plot while Ned Farkin, the company's comedian, came forward and performed the dance to music I hurriedly improvised.

Unfortunately, Mr and Mrs Higgens in essaying roles which displayed no regard to the reality of their age and size, often reduced audiences to extremes of laughter. The following day we moved on to Wilton and that evening gave the tragedy of *Philomena*. When we came to the part of the final Act, in which the heroine falls tragically dead at the hero's feet, and Mr Higgens struck a pathetic attitude, crying: 'What shall I do? What shall I *do*?' there came a cry from the audience of 'Fuck her while she's warm!'; which remark, though it bitterly tried the sensibilities of Mrs Plunkett Cope, whose dead corpse showed palpable signs of taking deep offence, reduced the rest of the company to an unwonted hilarity which made it difficult for us to complete the performance with any decorum. Happily, however, the people were in receipt of so little entertainment outside the tenor of their everyday lives that they were content with anything that was offered; the success of the evening was assured, and the money received on the next night redoubled.

A few days later, as we were resting in a small village between Amesbury and Warminster, Mr Grigson came to me with a pile of extremely ragged music paper, saying that they had received a message inviting some of the company to perform at a private party at a manor house nearby, the property of a Lord Shaveley. This was something they had done before and it was to consist not of a play, but of an evening of recitations and songs. These, Mr Grigson said, were the songs – perhaps I could con them in order to accompany him, Miss Cope and Ned Farkin in them that evening?

'They are,' he said, somewhat apologetically, 'a little – hah – *warm*, but a young fellow of your experience will not object to that!'

The songs indeed were 'a little warm', and what the recitations were to be I could only imagine. However, since gold was involved, I had no hesitation in setting off with a small party late that night for the manor house, which proved a large establishment in the hall of which we were to perform. It was crowded with ladies and gentlemen who had evidently enjoyed good food and ample wine, and were now ready to be entertained.

We were shown to a small room which I imagine at one time must have been an adjunct to the butler's pantry, and there climbed into our costumes. Miss Cope's, I saw, consisted of an Empire gown of the lightest clinging gauze or fine muslin placed upon her naked body. Mr Grigson wore tight-fitting breeches of stockinette, the flap covering his privities being handsomely decorated with embroidery but nevertheless obviously concealing equipment of impressive dimensions. Mr Farkin had cap and bells, in the old style, and David white silk stockings with brief trunks of black above.

When we were ready, we were announced as 'one of the Regent's most popular bands of entertainers,' and having entered quietly and taken my place at the side of the large but empty fireplace, where there was space for the performers, I struck up a march at which my friends entered and without pause passed into the chorus of the first song:

> *Come, pretty nymph, fain would I know*
> *What thing it is that breeds delight,*
> *That strives to stand, and cannot go,*
> *And feeds the mouth that cannot bite . . .*

This was greeted with a roar of applause, after which Miss Cope stepped forward and with a curtsy rendered the old catch *Have at a Venture*:

> *A country lad and bonny lass*
>   *they did together meet,*
> *And as they did together pass,*
>   *thus he began to greet:*
> *'What I do say I may mind well,*
>   *and thus I do begin:*
> *If you would have your belly swell,*
>   *hold up, and I'll put in.'*

This proved remarkably popular, especially with the verse:

> *She held this youngster to his task*
>   *till he began to blow,*
> *Then at the last he leave did ask*
>   *and so she let him go.*
> *Then down he panting lay awhile,*
>   *and rousing up again*
> *She charmed him with a lovely smile*
>   *again to put it in.*

At this there was a tremendous outcry, with many ribald calls, and one man near the front of the gathering actually interrupted the performance by stepping forward and catching at Miss Cope's dress, for a moment pulling it down to expose a breast, whereupon he was caught a blow upon the ear by one of his friends and restrained.

Mr Grigson and Miss Cope retired after this, and Ned Farkin gave us another prick-song. The couple returned, coverd by the same cloak – and Farkin began the song of *Walking in a Meadow Green*, and when he came to the second verse –

> *They lay so close together*
> *They made me much to wonder;*
> *I know not which was whether*
> *Until I saw her under . . .*

– the cloak was dropped and the actors fell upon it on the floor in a state of nature, Miss Cope beneath and Mr Grigson above, pressed close together as the song described. He began to move upon her with a bucking motion and when Farkin reached the lines –

> *Then off he came and blushed for shame*
> *So soon that he had ended*

– Mr Grigson raised himself, revealing his prick indeed to be small and unimpressive, whereat Miss Cope struck at it with her palm and the company expressed itself most amused.

The song continued:

> *Then in her arms she did him fold,*
> *And oftentimes she kissed him;*
> *And yet his courage still was cold*
> *For all the good she wished him.*
> *Yet with her hand she made it stand*
> *So stiff she could not bend it,*
> *And then anon she cries 'Come on,*
> *Once more, and none can mend it.'*

And suiting the action to the motion, Miss Cope applied her hands and lips to the person of Mr Grigson, whereupon his tool in an astonishingly short time rose to enviable eminence and became capable of its work, whereupon he set to, and the tragedians vigorously presented the beast with two backs to their appreciative audience. Meanwhile David capered about them administering a brisk slap here or an encouraging pinch there, set to it by the cries of the gentleman and ladies watching who themselves (as I observed) were now engaged in sundry amatory experiments, with caresses above and below the clothes and a slapping of lips almost audible above the general lubricious murmuring.

In a moment, Mr Grigson sharply withdrew himself from his position between Miss Cope's thighs, just in time to show the tangible sign of his enjoyment (which Miss Cope took upon her belly) while there was an enormous cheer from the entire company, which then for a while subsided into its own enjoyments. I played on while Miss Cope and Mr Grigson (who off the stage, David later assured me, had no regard whatsoever for each other) lay clasped in each other's arms apparently whispering endearments, in a splendidly effective play of amorous relaxation.

In a while, however, the company began to cry for new amusement. The difficulty was, however, that Mr Grigson, despite the best endeavours of Miss Cope, was unable to recover himself; whatsoever stimulation was offered, his apparatus was incapable of standing. Indeed, as the song put it –

> *At last he thought to venture her*
> *Thinking the fit was on him,*
> *But when he came to enter her*
> *The point turned back upon him*

– whereat a chorus of angry booing broke out, which appeared to me to be unwarranted, for, after all, while a woman may counterfeit amorous play at any time, if a man's body should rebel there is little he can do.

Seeing some of the audience becoming positively angry,

Mr Grigson made his escape, being near to the door, but Miss Cope, all undressed as she was, was restrained by two men, one catching each arm, while two others seized Ned Farkin. However, a lady cried – 'No, he's old meat – who would see him bare? Here's better metal!' and took young David by the arm; he was soon stripped by her and her friends, and pulled to face Miss Cope. He was in no better case than Mr Grigson (and indeed who, in the hands of an angry mob, could be expected to display an outward ardour?). Even when one of the ladies holding Miss Cope let go her grip and to the general applause of her friends fell to her knees before the boy and took his tool, small and shrunken as it was, between her lips, there was evidently no response, whereat Miss Cope remarked, 'You'll get no charge from him – he's a mere Molly, and can only tup another!'

But by then the company was in too coarse a mood to be quietened, and to my horror I felt a hand at my collar.

'Here's the fen for him, then!' cried a man behind me. 'All musicians are notorious madge culls!'

I attempted to assure him that I was in no way interested in making love with my own sex, and turned to appeal to Miss Cope, but seeing her opportunity, she had wrenched free in the confusion and disappeared.

Meanwhile, my clothes were being carelessly wrenched from me, the shirt literally torn from my back, then, my being up-ended, my breeches pulled from my legs. I found myself thrown to the floor beside David, who now looked (as I thought) far less terrified than he had formerly done. Indeed, without prompting, he rolled over to take me in his arms – his prick was stirring, for I felt it against my thigh.

'Take care!' he whispered. 'They've turned ugly, and will not let up without an exhibition. Simply lie still – I will be gentle!' And so saying, he kissed me thoroughly upon the lips, to a cheer from the assembled company and then raised himself upon his hands and knees and leaned to take my reluctant instrument between his lips. I was incapable of making any response. Though shutting my eyes I attempted to imagine that the tongue now playing about me was that of Miss Cope, or even of dear Sophia, who had first wakened me to such pleasure, it was to no effect. Gradually, however, a genial warmth spread through my limbs and I found myself able to relax somewhat, though my tool no more than slightly raised its head. Then my companion raised his own, taking care to cover me with his body, and encouraged me to turn so that I lay face downward upon the cushions which, for Miss Cope and Mr Grigson, had represented a mossy bank.

Now David began to caress and smooth my back, turning so that my head lay between his thighs, his eager prick against my cheek – which, if he or the company expected me to favour with kisses, they were much mistaken. Though it is true that by this time I was not altogether averse to his attentions, as his lips slid down the length of my spine and his hands embraced my backside, kneading the cheeks as a woman kneads bread. Then, to my astonishment, I felt him draw those cheeks apart and his tongue slide between them until it was at the doors of my fundament, when, despite the deep aversion I had always felt to unnatural acts, I could not prevent an extraordinarily reposeful fervidity invading my limbs, so that rather than clenching my buttocks against so intimate an invasion, they became loosened and relaxed, at which David slewed around and placed his hands beneath my hips to raise them slightly, at the same time moistening his tool with spittle. I felt it gently nudging, then beginning to enter the most private of bodily passages.

Fortunately, remembering what Bob had told me when I was likely to have been raped by the press gang, I did not fight against the ingress, and in a moment I felt David begin to move in the unmistakable fashion of a man mounting a woman – a strange sensation indeed for one who had so often played the man's role, but now found himself in the subservient one. I felt no pain, but neither did I feel pleasure; indeed the whole operation was one of excessive boredom – though clearly not to David, whose panting lips now expressed endearments and whose hands, still at my hips, gripped me with what was certainly no counterfeited passion.

After a while, I opened my eyes and saw before me a scene of the utmost dissipation, for inspired by the sight of we twain, the company had thrown all restraint aside. Some of the women had entirely removed their dresses, others had merely thrown their skirts over their heads, while again some of the men were altogether bare while others retained their shirts and even their waistcoats, and one impatient fellow had merely opened the flap of his breeches and, finding no spare woman to hand, was pumping away with his fist, his eyes meantime glued to our display. Right before me lay a handsome young fellow prone upon his back while a woman rode him with as much assiduity as he himself ever rode horse; and at the same time, behind her, a stout fellow rode her in the manner David was mounting me.

The sight, I confess, was a lively one, and I felt my tool striving to arise, though constricted between my body and the cushions. But gradually the familiar transport gripped me, increasing in its intensity until by simple coincidence I gave forth at the very moment at which I felt, or thought I felt, the heat of David's spending within me.

In a short time I felt his instrument relaxing, and he slipped from me, planting a kiss as tender as any woman's upon my shoulder. Throwing his arm about me, he raised me to my feet, whereupon to my amazement there was a round of clapping from the company – even those who were still at their work pausing to shout applause – and in a moment a great rattle of coins as they started throwing money towards us. Picking up my tunic from where it lay nearby, David knelt and began to collect the coins, whereupon I joined him, noting that most of them were of gold. We threw them into the jacket and when we had done folded it, whereon David made a bow and led me to the side room, where Miss Cope sat looking black as thunder and Mr Grigson and Ned looking no better pleased.

'Ah! Here come the twiddle-poops!' cried Miss Cope.

'I'm surprised, Mr Archer, that you should lend yourself to such indecency.'

I could only blush and stammer, but to my surprise David, usually the mildest of boys, strode straight up to her and cried: 'Mind your tongue, Miss Wagtail. You are scarcely free of accusation – what would your admirers at the Theatre Royal think if they knew of your enjoyment of balum rancum all over the countryside? Your chances of playing Desdemona to Mr Kean would scarcely be improved, though doubtless you'd play the biter with him to climb onto any board!'

Whereat Miss Cope fell silent, Ned Farkin laughed, and Mr Grigson enquired after the dibs, which I took to be the money.

'There's plenty of that,' said David, 'and I'll thank you to remember who satisfied the audience most, when it comes to divvying up.'

When we rejoined the rest of the company nothing was asked of our evening's activities, from which I took it that Mr Higgens and the others were entirely aware of the nature of our engagement. My feelings towards the company had somewhat altered now, but I must admit to being pleased when, David and Mr Grigson having counted up the cash and argued long and loud over its division, I was handed no less than seven pounds in gold – an astonishing sum for one evening's work, if work it can be called.

I went to bed that night with a bustle of emotions I could not balance. David made no attempt upon my body, however, either because the evening's enjoyment physically precluded such activity or because he was uncertain of my reaction; he merely kissed me upon the cheek and asked if he had hurt me. I had to reply, which was true, that he had not, but I gave no opinion upon the satisfaction I had or had not received, and he merely suggested that it was at all events an easy way to make a few guineas, to which I was bound to assent. I determined, however, to use my best endeavours to avoid such a situation in future, not only because it gave me no pleasure but because I feared that

Miss Cope, clearly a woman to bear a grudge, might betray us to the authorities, and while I could perhaps overcome my indifference to sodomy for a sufficient fee, I had no love for the gallows, to which such an activity might lead me.

At Warminster I spent a morning placing notices announcing that –

MR SAMUEL PROUT HIGGENS
late of the Theatre Royal, Drury Lane,
will play for one night only
the role of
HAMLET, THE PRINCE OF DENMARK,
in Mr SHAKESPEARE's play
of that name,
assisted by
Mrs PLUNKETT COPE as the Queen
Miss CYNTHIA COPE in the role of Ophelia
Mr Nathaniel Grigson – Laertes
Mr Ned Farkin – 1st Gravedigger
with the acclaimed company
late of London
fully and entirely costumed.
GREAT SWORD FIGHT
THUNDER AND LIGHTNING AFFECTS
FAMOUS GHOSTLY APPARITION.

The performance was greeted with much enthusiasm – though when Mrs Plunkett Cope asserted of Mr Higgens that he was 'fat and scant of breath' a great chorus of agreement went up which much disconcerted the latter – especially during the fight between Laertes and Hamlet at the end of the play, when cries of 'Four to two the fat 'un!' were heard. Upon Mrs Plunkett Cope's seizing the poisoned cup, there were shouts of 'Bring on a barrel!' and 'Free ale for all!' In general, however, all was well and the takings considerable, so that if our chief actors were disappointed in their reception, they were not so at the cash which went into the common chest.

Mr Higgens being now of the opinion that *Hamlet* was above the heads of the public in those rural parts, we gave *Romeo and Juliet* at Westbury, Trowbridge and Bradford-on-Avon, with Mr Higgens himself as Romeo (Mr Grigson becoming very vocal about his elder's inability to climb any balcony over two foot high) and Miss Cope as Juliet, whose virginal innocence was loudly questioned by David in a monologue delivered while she was upon stage but not out of hearing. This made her positively quiver with rage, which seemed to be taken by the audience for an excess of emotion, for they cheered loudly the happy ending when she and Romeo came back to life and were married by the Friar – for Mr Higgens was of the view that Shakespeare had been sadly mistaken in giving the play a tragic conclusion, and preferred to use a new ending written for him for a small fee by some literary person in London.

Eventually, we came to Bristol – my first sight of that bustling port and great city, with its Hot Well, which attracted the gentry of the Westcountry not already drawn to the place by business.

Here my first task, after we had moved into a run-down inn by the waterside, was to spread broadsheets about announcing Mr Higgens' production of *King Lear*, in which Mrs Plunkett Cope would essay the role of Cordelia (to the misgiving of Miss Cope, who considered herself by quite thirty years more suited to the part). David and I spent the better part of nine hours in that business, and were making our way back along the quayside when a hue and cry was suddenly heard behind us and in a moment came shouts of 'Stop, thieves!' and running footsteps. On looking behind me, I found to my amazement that pointing fingers accused us, and while I was for stopping to make our excuses, David shouted: 'Come off – this way!' and in a moment had vanished round a corner, while I, laggard, was in the hands of a mob all accusing us of being pickpockets.

I strongly asserted my innocence, and called on the mob to search my pockets and make themselves aware that I had nothing upon me but my own property – to which they replied merely that of course my accomplice carried the purse we had 'lifted' from the pocket of a merchant further along the quay and, in short, in a brief time I found myself in Bristol gaol.

This was the worst place imaginable – the evil-smelling hold of the press gang's vessel was infinitely preferable. Within one room barely twenty feet long by twelve broad were no less than sixty-three people, no distinction being made between men and women, sick and healthy, guilty and innocent. Eleven were children scarcely old enough to leave the nursery. To my indignation, laughter only greeting my protests, and I was placed in heavy irons, for all charged or convicted of felony were thus bound.

Though I did not consider my dress to be rich – I wore only my everyday clothes – I was an emperor to my companions who were filthy in the extreme and clad only in rags. The uproar of oaths, complaints and obscenities, the desperation of all, the dirt and stench, presented altogether a concentration of the utmost misery – a scene of infernal passions and distress the like of which few of my readers, fortunately, could envisage.

When night fell things became worse, for a scuttling arose, accompanied by oaths and occasional cries of pain which revealed the presence of rats going about to steal crumbs of food and, these being few, nibbling the feet of any unfortunate prisoner who for an instant lay still. A cat was kept in the room to prevent the rats, but no single animal could have dealt with so many. To my astonishment and something to my horror, even their filthy and horrific state, even their ill-health and weakness, could not prevent men and women from sexual congress, so that all around to the moans of pain and hunger were conjoined sounds which, when we are in comfort, are the reflection of pleasure and happiness, but which here were rather signs of a desperation which clutched briefly at forgetfulness through bodily passion.

Happily, with the light came Mr Samuel Prout Higgens in the costume he wore for Malvolio, which he believed would most impress the gaolers. And so it did, for I was released at once to a more roomy cell, and came soon before the magistrates who – the accusing merchant admitting that he did not recognise my face, and that he could not be sure that I was one of the two fellows who had taken his purse – released me in Mr Higgens' company, my having denied knowing anything about my companion.

I denied David because it seemed most appropriate; and indeed it was clear that I was right to do so, for as we walked back to our inn Mr Higgens explained to me that the boy had come to him to relate my difficulty, confessing that he had 'found' a purse which someone had dropped, and that he imagined this to have been the cause of the uproar. This seemed to me to be unlikely and when I taxed him with it, he simply gave me a smacking kiss upon the lips and handed me three gold guineas as my share of the profit, with the words – 'You'll know to be more lively next time!' – which suggested to me that his coming by the purse had been less innocent than he pretended.

Apart from this incident, which taught me to be chary of accompanying David on any excursion he proposed, I enjoyed my first freedom within a large city. Bristol then had something of the order of forty thousand inhabitants, and many amusements which I was able to taste when I could take the time to do so. A fine display of lifesized figures of departed celebrities, made from wood and wax, was to be seen at Colston's Hall; Mr Salmon's toy warehouse and exhibition of waxwork figures was on the first and second floors of a house in the centre of the town; lions and other animals were kept in cages in Parker's Menagerie on the downs; and there was Duborg's exhibition of cork models of Roman antiquities. All these took my attention, as did the astonishing display by Zerah Colburn, the calculating boy from America, able to perform any trick with numbers shouted to him from the audience, bidding fair to distract from our own performances until Mr Higgens hit on the notion of allowing Mr Grigson and Miss Cope to perform Romeo and Juliet for only one night – provided that they divested themselves of all their clothing for the scene in Juliet's bedchamber. The rumour of this built up our takings to an inordinate degree, though upon Mr Higgens and Mrs Plunkett Cope making their entrance as the two lovers on the following nights, there was much libidinous humour at their expense, and some demands for the return of their entrance money from various members of the audience, though others asserted that the additional bulk of the senior actors represented more value for their ha'pennies.

I was, I admit, by now once more eager for female company. Miss Cope had shown no interest whatsoever in my company since the night of our display, and of the three other ladies in the company, Mrs Plunkett Cope was not to my taste (though certain signs seemed to indicate she might have been interested in a passage with me) while the other two had their own lovers, to whom they were entirely faithful.

There were many prostitutes in the city, not only on the quaysides (where they were of the roughest sort) but in almost every street, where they ranged themselves in a file on the footpaths in companies of five or six, most of them dressed very genteelly; there, they accosted passers-by with 'Come and have a drink!', sometimes taking one by the sleeve or tapping one upon the shoulder. Agreeing, one was led into one of the shops where they sell beer, where there was a room behind and a bedroom for any repose.

David, to whom I mentioned my itch (and who was now content to accept that I would not become his intimate friend) persuaded me not to buy such wares for, he said, the French disease or pox was widespread in the city, as in most of the ports of England. But one day he came to me bearing a small book, entitled *The Man of Pleasure's Kalender for the Year*, in which was a list of ladies of the city who, he said, were guaranteed to be clean and wholesome. This indeed named a number of ladies, with their addresses and their costs, such as:

Miss Bearn, 14 Bow Street. This lovely nymph recently attained her eighteenth year, plays upon the pianoforte, sings, and has every accomplishment including the

*amatory. Of slight stature, she has fine yellow hair, and
in bed is everything a man might desire, her every gesture
a delight. Her price, two pounds ten.*

After reading the book through with great attention and
rising interest, I fixed upon Miss Tamblin, of whom the
page spoke glowingly:

*This amorous charmer is but seventeen, and of good
family, agreeable and genteel, full of delightful conversations and a pleasure both in and out of bed. Between the
sheets she reveals a figure plump without grossness, athletic without coarseness. She particularly enjoys the rites
of love in the equestrian manner, in which style she gives
great pleasure, her thighs being powerful, seating her
with a pliancy and balance which make her the satisfaction of every mount. She will converse at any hour of
the day and night, expecting a present of two or three
guineas at least for the pleasure of her company.*

And so it was that, with a purse containing three guineas
(which seemed a large sum, but for which I expected complete satisfaction), I took myself off to the address offered
and hammered upon the door of what seemed a highly
respectable house.

This was opened by a neatly-dressed maid who enquired
my business, then vanished for a moment, and returned to
assert that Miss Meg Tamblin would receive me. She
showed me upstairs to a handsomely furnished drawing-
room, where I was received by the lady herself, who
appeared the very picture of respectability, clad in a
fashionable *robe en calecon* which clearly revealed the
outlines of a fine figure. Upon my taking her hand and
kissing it, she gave a delightful smile and led me to a chaise
longue, where she sat at my side and for a while engaged in
polite conversation, enquiring how long I had been at
Bristol, and how I found the town, without at any time
asking my name or the nature of my employment, which I
found to be most tactful.

After a while, however, she took my hand and said, quite openly:

'I take it, sir, that you wish to purchase my favours?'

'I do, ma'am,' I replied, 'though rest assured that under any conditions I would be happy to pay court to so beautiful a woman.'

She smiled and bowed at this, and said that the custom was that gentlemen should contribute to the expenses of her establishment at the termination of their visit.

'Now perhaps we should prepare a tribute to Venus?' she said, taking my hand and pressing it to her bosom.

The reader can imagine that after some two weeks of abstinence I needed no second invitation, and in a trice we were both as little encumbered with clothing as our forebears in the Garden of Eden, and she was admiring the proportions of that part of me most anxious to be acquainted with her touch.

I must imagine that the tribute she paid to what she termed the magnificent proportions of my manly parts was one she accorded many of her gentlemen acquaintances, for I am not so proud as to believe myself inordinately well equipped. Moreover, I was distressed to find that my need was such that before she had for long been caressing me, I involuntarily gave way to the dictates of nature, in such an explosive mode that the essence flew perhaps two or three feet from my pulsing instrument, at which I feared she would consider our business concluded.

But no, she merely expressed approval of my vigour and the view that I had been too long without female company and, ringing the bell, bade her maid to bring some chocolate, which we drank while she talked of her life, which far from being a sad one she seemed to enjoy, able through good husbandry to live well and to visit London at least once a year, where no one (she said) knew her true occupation, and she was accepted as a lady in all the best circles.

But surely, I said, some of her friends must be coarse fellows whose only attraction was the size of their purse?

No, she said, her maid had strict instructions that she was not at home to any but those who appeared personable, and downstairs there was a stout fellow with a cudgel whose duty it was to protect the house in case of trouble. However, she was kind enough to agree that not all her friends were as handsome as myself – these are her words, and reported rather than repeated in pride – nor, she added with an appropriate gesture, were they all capable of so swift a recovery from collapse to readiness to renew the fight.

She had no need to devote much attention to my prick before it was once more, indeed, fully extended, when to my interest she took from a box nearby a little covering of transparent skin, eight inches long, closed at one end and decorated at the other by a pink ribbon which could be used to tighten it. This she drew over my standing prick – not without my fearing that her gentle touch might again have the unwonted result – and tied the ribbon at the base before laying me upon my back and mounting me to ride with a smooth and rocking motion which gave the utmost delight.

The *cundum*, for such it was, only slightly moderated my pleasure, for while the liquid embrace of an unprotected intimacy must remain the *sine qua non* of delight, the machine had the effect I believe of somewhat prolonging the period of pleasure, and certainly did not detract from the charming culmination. After this she took my friend, while he was still upright, between her fingers and undressed him by untying the ribbon and peeling back the skin, depositing it in a container nearby. She then drew me behind a screen, where was a bath of warm water and towels, and washed me and herself thoroughly, talking all the time in the most charming fashion and with a most delightful and witty air.

It was with nothing but pleasure that I placed three guineas upon the table, upon which she curtsied, and hoped I would call again – which I am determined to do, if I can, for despite the great expense the adventure was much happier than a quick stand against a wall by the harbourside, which most of my companions favoured.

Next day, as usual, I went to buy a broadsheet in which

there was to be an advertisement of our performances, and turning it to see what news might proccupy the city, came upon the following paragraph:

> The brig *Persephone arrived at Bristol yesterday with news from the Meditteranean of the death at Genoa, by the fever, of Sir Spencer Franklyn, the son of the late Sir Franklin Franklyn of Alcovary in Hertfordshire. The baronetcy now falls to the second son, Sir Franklin Franklyn, whose present whereabouts is unknown.*

Chapter Sixteen

Sophie's Story

The morning blushed to find me still abed with the two love-birds, who indeed woke me by their amorous entwinings, which I regarded (the reader may imagine) with all the delight of a fairy godmother who had been instrumental in bringing them together.

In the light of day Mr Ffloyd had the grace to blush as, while he was still embraced by the limber thighs of his bride-to-be, he caught my eye and no doubt recollected the similar compliment he had in time past paid to my own beauty – to say nothing of our play on the previous evening, in which Sarah had been a not unwilling partner.

Rising and making our toilets, Sarah was melancholy at having to dress herself in the one piece of clothing she had with her. So I made our excuses to Mr Ffloyd and appointed to meet him at the parish church at eleven, then took my young friend off into the streets of the town, where we soon found a dressmaker who not only had a delightful piece of frippery which she had made up for a young lady whose wooer had sadly disappointed her at the altar, but was able with very little trouble to contrive that it fitted Sarah as if it were made for her. The latter protested at my insisting upon paying for it from my purse, but it gave me the greatest pleasure to do so, and to equip her – though in that virginal white which was perhaps not an entirely accurate reflection of her moral state – for her marriage. This went forward without hitch, and though the clergyman (notified a mere twenty-four hours in advance by Mr Ffloyd) and I were the only witnesses, it was as stylish and complete a ceremony as can be imagined.

Repairing to the inn to eat, we found all at sixes and

sevens in consequence of the arrival of a company of travelling players, led by an elderly lady and gentleman of enormous dignity and self-importance. There was a clown of a man who immediately began joking familiarly with the maids, a pert young girl with an air of 'touch-me-not' who made her way upstairs with a wiry, dark fellow paying much court to her and a young fellow carrying a guitar, who immediately vanished into a room from which soon came forth the dulcet tones of the instrument, played, I presumed, in practice.

We now considered our position. Mr Ffloyd had reserved places for himself and his wife on the coach westward, but when he and his bride asked whither they should send their news, I was quite unable to supply them with an address – and at that moment realised that I meant to go home to Alcovary. The house, and my mother – to say nothing of Frank – had been much in my mind lately, and I now longed to see them again, and was even able to persuade myself that Sir Franklin's anger might be mitigated by pleading. It is true there was the small matter of my husband, but should he prove troublesome, I had no doubt that a threat from me to reveal his practices in magic would persuade him not to insist on my living with him. In the event that I was not allowed into my parents' house, I had little doubt that my wits, together with the skills I had learned from the writings of Mr Lilly, would enable me to earn my bread.

So I attended the office of the mail and was able to take a seat east to Windsor, whence I could travel north to St Alban's and thence to Alcovary – a distance of some two days' travel only. The coaches arrived at almost the same moment and so it was that, leaning from the window of my vehicle as it began its journey, I received the farewells of Mr and Mrs Ffloyd as they made their way westwards to Cardiff and then to Llandridnod Wells, where a position as schoolmaster awaited my old tutor.

I was fortunate in that my coach contained, as inside travellers, only two people – one a plump gentleman who soon fell into a doze, and the other a young man of a markedly handsome appearance, with clear light blue eyes, an ingratiating smile, and a large brown mole near the corner of his mouth which seemed to emphasise a certain sardonic twist of the lip, rendering him perculiarly interesting. He insisted upon my lying back and placing my heels on the opposite seat, at his side, where he covered them with the tails of his coat against the cool air (though indeed it was remarkably sultry for the time of the year).

I cannot say that I was surprised, after a while, to feel his hand steal upon my ankle to caress my foot, which I had slipped out of its shoe. Nay, it crept up past the ankle, though without a change in both our positions which I had no intention of making, further intimacy was impossible. The expression of his eyes, however, and the motion of his tongue over his lower lip, spoke volumes of his desires – which I met with a steady gaze, though I admit without removing my feet from their comfortable position.

So, with this amusing game of foot and palm, the time passed engagingly enough as we drove on. At the first stage, we descended to take the air, and the young gentleman introduced himself as Mr Harry Rockwall, travelling to Cambridge to college there. When I mentioned that I had lived in that city for a while, and described the house in which I had lodged (or rather, the bathing-place below my windows) he knew it well, and seemed to have something to say on the subject. This, after a while, turned out to be a question whether I did not know 'his friend Jack', who was clearly the young man with whom I had spent such a pleasant afternoon at Byron's Pool, of which my present companion had heard tales which clearly had lost nothing in the telling, as the warmly increased pressure of his palm upon my ankle (when we were re-established in the coach) expressed.

His company was welcome on so tedious a journey and the bottle we shared brought us to a further quiet exchange of confidences, our companion being asleep. He asked whether friend Jack was not 'a pretty dog', to which I was bound to reply that he showed some of that animal's interest in continual congress! I should have met then, he said, a

friend of his who had given up his studies to accompany
him to his house near Basingstoke, where they had spent the
vacation in cutting a swathe through the local female population. Now his friend, declining to return to the university,
for he had but little interest in learning, had remained at his
home as a sort of manager to the estate there, 'for,' my
friend admitted, 'I am deucedly fond of the boy and would
be sorry to lose sight of him – and rejected by his family he
has nowhere else to go.'

The time passed in such interchange and in retailing
accounts of my various adventures. He was amused, for
instance, to hear of my management of the escape of Sarah
and of her alliance with Mr Ffloyd (omitting, however, my
own familiarity with the latter).

We half slumbered on the road to Windsor, where I
awoke to find that he had transferred my foot, under cover
of his coat, into his lap, where I had all unconsciously been
caressing a something with which my sole had not previously been familiar. Our companion, whose snores had
signalled a complete lack of interest in us which had no
doubt contributed to my young friend's forwardness, woke
with a start and jumped down to take, I suppose, some
refreshment, while I leant from the window and looked out
on the busy yard in the half-light of early morning.

The swiftness with which my skirts were drawn up and a
familiar organ was brought into close propinquity with my
lower back precluded all argument, and the enjoyable friction of its introduction into its proper place stopped my
objection before it could find words. Gripping the sides of
the window, I closed my eyes and surrendered myself to the
pleasure of an early morning engagement, which reached its
culmination at the moment when, opening my eyes, I met
those of our plump fellow traveller below me, with a bottle
in one hand and his hat in the other, requiring entrance.

I straightened up, not unblushingly I suspect, and backed
away from the window to allow the man to climb into the
coach, and upon turning I found my young friend seated,
his coat over his lap, and apparently in an innocent sleep.
Only my eyes recognised, in the squirmings and fumblings

which disturbed his covering, the difficulty he had in rearranging his dress, which amused me so much that I had difficulty in not falling into a laugh.

I was only half awake when, many hours later, I looked out of the window to recognise a stretch of road; surely it was that along which I had ridden in such depression with my father when we first went to call upon Mr Nelham – how long ago it seemed! Yes, around the next corner must stand his house! I made ready to retire into the corner of the coach, lest by any chance my husband should be walking nearby. But – what was this? No chimneys were to be seen above the trees around the garden and as we passed the gate, all I could see were the blackened tatters of the outer walls of the house!

As we passed almost immediately into the single street of the village, I put my head out of the window and shouted to the coachman to stop. With a quick adieu to my friend, who was still in a sleepy half-stupor, I leaped down and caught my small bundle, thrown by the coachman, and as the coach moved off I made my way into the nearby inn.

There was no one there I knew, but when I asked the landlord after 'a Mr Nelham' who I understood was a distinguished astrologer, I was told that he had perished some three months ago in a fire, allegedly caused by a furnace which he had established in the cellar for an attempt at the conversion of base metal into gold!

'He left a widow,' said the landlord, 'but no one knows where she is, though Lawyer Cox has advertised in all the local sheets.'

Where did this lawyer reside, I asked, and being told the house, which stood nearby, made my way there with all alacrity and had myself announced as 'Mrs Sophia Nelham', which brought Mr Cox to me at a positive gallop.

I had no difficulty in convincing him of my *bona fides*, though he would need, he said, to see my marriage lines. My father, Sir Franklin Franklyn of Alcovary, had care of those, I said, and would also identify me. At this he informed me that my father had died shortly before Mr

Nelham, of a seizure – and not only him, but brother
Spencer too, of some distemper caught in a foreign port.

I was more disturbed at my brother's death than my
father's, but truthfully not much by either, for I was closer to
my mother and to brother Frank – now, no doubt, reigning
as Sir Franklin! – than the other two.

But there was more news! Frank had no more been heard
of than me, having vanished from Oxford not long after
I had departed from Cambridge, and his present whereabouts no one knew. Again, advertisements had been placed
in all the sheets for, said Lawyer Cox, to everyone's surprise
my father, thought to be improverished, had left a considerable fortune. And more – Mr Nelham, whose miserly
behaviour had been a legend in the country, had in the bank
no less than sixteen thousand pounds in gold, as well as a
house in London, all of which was now mine! Suddenly I
swooned clear away, partly from the news and partly from
the fatigue of the journey, but recovered swiftly thanks to Mr
Cox loosening the neck of my dress and fanning me with a
collection of papers he happened to have by him.

I lost no time now in hiring a hack and making for
Alcovary, riding up the familiar drive at midday to slip in
through the front door and discover my mother, all in black,
sitting in the drawing-room, where also sat a fat, bald, pasty-
faced fellow in a tawdry brown coat, reading at a book.

After we had greeted each other with many tears, and I had
commiserated with my mother on the loss of a husband and a
son at the same time and she had commiserated with me upon
the loss of my husband, which for both of us was a matter of
form rather than of true mourning, the third party, who had
been sitting by, broke in with: 'Patience, my dear, am I not to
be introduced?'

'Mr Thomas Bidwell, my daughter, Mrs Sophia Nelham.'

'Aha! So I had conjectured,' said the fellow, taking my
hand in his large, damp palm and pressing it. 'Welcome
home to Alcovary, ma'am. You have been apprised, I gather,
of the fortune of which you are now happily in command?'

I must have looked surprised at the impertinence, for my
mother broke in:

'Mr Bidwell was your father's man of business in London, Sophia, to whom all our circumstances are well known' and 'we are fortunate that he has consented to stay here for a time to make sure all our business matters are in order,' she went on, without any great enthusiasm. 'There is property in London, as well as a considerable fortune, which he is keeping in trust for Frank' – and a tear sprung now to her eye – 'when he returns.'

'As he will, dear lady, as he will!' said Bidwell. 'Trust me – I shall be happy to remain in this house until my presence is no longer required, and even then would leave with reluctance, especially now that Alcovary is graced with the presence of so handsome a lady as yourself, Mrs Nelham!' – at which he directed at me a look of such plainly lascivious a nature that I almost struck him.

In a while, he made his excuses and left the room, whereat I enquired of my mother whether it was really her wish that he remain in the house? She replied, no, but there were reasons why it was impossible for her to require his departure, and on my pressing her revealed that he had suddenly appeared at the house soon after the news had been printed of my father's death, bringing with him not only information of the astonishingly large fortune of which all details had been kept from his family, but graver news, which only Mr Bidwell and my mother, in the world, knew: for my father had apprised him some time ago that while Spencer and myself were the lawful fruit of his marriage, Frank was my mother's son by a former lover! This, my father said, had been revealed to him during the course of the altercation following upon the scene which he had interrupted at Alcovary just before I had left it, when, it seems, he had discovered my mother and Andrew sharing an amorous congress.

My mother blushed at this, and would have said more of it but I longed to hear the rest of the story, and she revealed that my father had informed Mr Bidwell – at first in a letter in his own hand, which the lawyer still possessed – that he wished to change his will, entirely disinheriting Frank. But upon the very morning when the new document was to be signed, he had been stricken by the sudden flux which had killed him.

Upon hearing news of Spencer's death Mr Bidwell realised that he could now hold over my mother the threat of losing the entire estate, for while she could no doubt count upon being supported by Frank, should he be disinherited the same fate would fall to her, for the entire estate would then pass to a distant cousin of my father's who cordially disliked her, and would have her out of the house with no care for her future. However, as long as she supported Mr Bidwell in comfort, he had promised to keep the document private, and under this threat not only was he living in luxury at Alcovary, but had even insisted upon sharing my mother's bed whenever the mood seized him.

My mother having breached the dam of her confidences went on to reveal the name of Frank's father, whom I dimly remembered as a kindly neighbour who many times took me upon his knee when I was a child, and had shown a peculiar interest in all us children, but perhaps – now that I came to think of it – Frank in particular. He had not seemed to me to be especially handsome, and was certainly not particularly rich, and I must have looked my surprise at hearing his name, whereon my mother blushingly revealed that my father's interest in the fleshly pleasures had been confined to the procreation of children, and Mr Bidwell had hinted that his true proclivities lay elsewhere. Deprived of conjugal joys, my mother had yielded to the advances of her neighbourly admirer who – she confessed – had that one physical characteristic to commend him which was irresistible to all women – 'as you will one day discover,' she said.

I could not help at that moment exclaiming that our adopted brother Andy was also a charming fellow.

'Indeed,' said my mother thoughtfully, 'I remember observing your admiration of him.'

'Not more, ma'am, than you yourself,' was my reply, at which she had the grace to blush, and then to rise and embrace me, saying that we must not quarrel for I was all she had left in the world to comfort me.

Mr Bidwell, returning at that moment to find us in each other's arms, congratulated us on our affection, and himself on being so fortunate as to be living in a house graced by the presence of two such charming women.

Going to my room to change for supper, I was eager to find a clean gown, for the dresses I had were all now travel-stained and over familiar. I had grown considerably in stature since I left Alcovary, with the result that the gowns I used to wear were tight about me (my mother was of a larger frame altogether, and I would have looked ridiculous in one of her dresses). However, I managed to climb into one which at least did not constrict my movements too much, though it was I must confess like a second skin to me and Mr Bidwell's eyes, on my presenting myself at table, almost fell from their sockets, only the intensity with which he fixed them upon my bosom seeming to keep them in place.

My mother took the end of the table, myself sitting opposite Mr Bidwell, who poured much of his soup over his person, so eager was he to observe me at every point. While consuming the bird which followed, I felt his foot making a progress up the inside of my leg which, waiting until it reached my thigh, I greeted by dropping my fork, and bending to recover it plunging it with what energy I could into his ankle, so that he almost choked upon the drumstick over which he was slavering at the time. This did not disconcert him, however; he was clearly a man to whom resistence was the greatest aphrodisiac, and from the glances which my mother exchanged with him, and the disappearance of his left hand beneath the table, he was obviously paying her some attention while at the same time stroking my lower limbs with his foot.

We cut the meal as short as we decently could and then retired to the drawing-room, where my mother requested me to play the harpsichord, thus releasing me from the necessity of fending off Mr Bidwell's attentions, so that he merely sat ogling us both and booming out ridiculous compliments whenever the music ceased.

At length my repertoire was exhausted, and I rose from the keyboard.

'If you will pardon me, ma'am,' I said, 'I will retire. The day has been a long one, and I am fatigued.'

'My dear Mrs Nelham,' said Bidwell rising, 'you must indeed pay to Morpheus that tribute all beautiful young women owe if their loveliness is to be preserved. Would that my arms could receive the compliment you will shortly pay to his!' And he took my hand, raising it to his lips and kissing it with a loose-lipped motion that even included the insertion of his tongue between my fingers, so that it was only with a great endeavour that once more I commanded myself sufficiently to refrain from striking him.

'My dear Patience,' he said, turning to my mother, 'shall we also retire?' At which, coldly and it seemed to me with a despairing air, she rose, embraced me, and we all walked together into the hall and mounted the staircase to the passage where my mother's and my bedroom lay and where, to my astonishment (though I might indeed have expected it) Mr Bidwell disappeared through the door of what had been my father's chamber!

I had no sooner stripped off my clothes and fallen into bed then I fell also into a deep and dreamless sleep – but not, I imagine, for long, for I awoke at the opening of my door (which had never had means of barring it) and the glow of a candle which showed me the face and figure of Mr Bidwell. His arrival was a shock, but not a surprise to me; I had merely hoped that his attentions would be pressed that evening upon my mother rather than myself, nor did I think he would have the impertinence to appear in my bedroom without devoting at least a little more time to the seduction he hoped to accomplish.

I feigned sleep as he approached, but could not continue to do so as he sat down upon the side of the bed, which was thrown upon one side by his weight, so that despite myself I rolled somewhat and fell towards my night visitor, and in putting out my hand to save myself placed it – entirely, I need not say, without the intention of doing so – upon the hairy, plump and naked thigh beneath his shirt.

'Ah! Miss Sophie!' he sighed, and gripping my hand with his own raised it so that it was truly between his legs, where in a thicket of wiry hair I felt what I had expected to feel, though happily it was somewhat less massive than I might have expected in a man of his size.

How I resisted the temptation to grasp and twist with all my might, I can never explain, but I feared to rouse his temper, for so large a man would have been impossible to resist should he attack with all his force, and I still hoped to find a way of declining his advances.

'Make me, my dear Miss Sophia, the happiest of men!' he breathed, leaning over me and slobbering kisses over my face and bosom, while attempting to plunge his hand between my own thighs.

'Ah, sir!' I said. 'I did not believe in my wildest dreams that I could hope . . .' – at which he ceased his slobbering, perhaps in astonishment, for it must have been many years since a lady paid him an unforced compliment.

'I would have come to you, sir, but that I feared rejection!' I cried, and persuaded myself to reach for his cods and caress them, at which he shook like one about to have a seizure.

'But sir,' I went on, 'let us go to your chamber, for my bed is narrow and I fear that upon it it would be impossible for me to give you that full joy which so handsome a man merits. Nor, I think, could it support the vigorous activity of one so virile!'

He was much complimented at this and rose to his feet, taking the candle in one hand and my arm in the other, and whispered: 'Most amiable of young ladies come, then, come,' and led me forth.

Outside my door, we turned to the right towards my father's room, myself careful to take the inside path next the wall. As we passed the top of the stairs, on our left, I suddenly wrenched my arm away from his grip and, bracing the other against the wall, gave him a push with all my force. Not in the least expecting it, he did not even give a cry but staggered, missed his footing, and plunged down the dark stairway. The candle almost immediately went out but in the pitch dark I heard the continual rumble of his descent, a final crash as he reached the stone floor of the hall, and then a silence which was only broken, after a while, by the opening of my mother's bedroom door.

In the light of the candle which she carried, we could only see a dark shape at the bottom of the stairs.

'Alas, Mama,' I said, 'Mr Bidwell has had an accident.'

She said nothing but descended the stairs where, on lowering the candle, we saw our guest's head lying in a pool of blood, his face ashen white, his breast still. I was reaching for his hand, to feel for a pulse, when there was a sudden loud knocking at the front door, only a few feet away.

I looked, terrified, at my mother, and she at me. We stood in silence for a moment, when the knocking redoubled and we had no recourse but to open. Two men stood outside, one holding the reins of two horses, the other with a lantern held on high.

The man with the lantern stepped forward to take my mother in his arms. It was young Sir Franklin Franklyn of Alcovary and behind him, smiling broadly, was Andrew Archer. Frank and Andy were returned! My head buzzing, I looked into my brother's eyes for a long moment, then fell at his feet in a swoon.

Chapter Seventeen

The Adventures of Andy

We left Bristol after some five weeks, having made a very considerable sum which, when shared out between us, would amount to sufficient to keep me in comfort while I decided whether to join the company on a permanent basis. I was a little in doubt of this, for while there were many things about our life which I enjoyed, I must confess that I found many of the actors tiresome and over-full of their own importance.

Our first pause after Bristol was at Chippenham, where Mr Higgens and Mrs Plunkett Cope gave their Romeo and Juliet once more. Then, after two nights, we proceeded to Devizes, which was delighted by a performance of *Hamlet* in which Ned Farkin, who had partaken rather too enthusiastically of small beer in the company of some fellows in the taproom, was so well received in the gravedigger's scene that he declined to leave the stage, appearing in several subsequent scenes by default. When Osric came to issue Laertes' challenge to Hamlet, Ned suddenly appeared from behind the scenes and danced a jig of his own devising which much disconcerted Mr Higgens (especially since, being somewhat hard of hearing, he was not aware of Ned's cavorting behind him, mistaking the roars of laughter for roars of applause, and taking several 'calls' before the truth of the situation was conveyed to him).

From Devizes we travelled a little to the south, performing at Everleigh and Weyhill, Andover and Overton, and then received a command to attend upon Mr Harry Rockwall at his house on the outskirts of Basingstoke, to entertain at a party of some kind. I agreed to accompany the usual small group but made it clear that I was to provide music only for the occasion, and not take part in any exhibition which might be expected, my taste being, on the whole, for privacy in matters of love.

The house proved a small but capacious one, with a fine hall above which, at a height of only perhaps eight or nine feet, hung a little minstrels' gallery where I installed myself with my guitar. The party was in the way of a farewell to Mr Rockwall, a handsome young man whose beauty was if anything enhanced by a large, brown mole at the corner of his mouth. He was clearly the owner of the property, but young enough still to be at Cambridge University, whither he was bound next morning. Some twenty of his friends, men and women, had dined and drunk well and were ready for some boisterous entertainment, which began with Ned capering in an obscene dance of his own devising based, he said, upon that of an Italian jester of two centuries previously, and in which he wore a conterfeit cock and balls of gigantic proportions, with which he belaboured the ladies about the buttocks, to their great amusement.

Next, Mr Grigson delivered himself of *Love's Physiognomy*, a song he always performed before an intellectual audience, for there were many classical allusions which, he explained, enabled young ladies and gentlemen of education to derive additional pleasure –

> *If her hair be yellow, she'll tempt each fellow*
> *In the Emmanuel College;*
> *For she that doth follow the colour of Apollo*
> *May be like him in zeal of knowledge.*

> *If she be pale and a virgin stale,*
> *Inclined to the sickness green,*
> *Some raw fruit give her to open her liver*
> *Her stomach and the thing between.*

– while Miss Cope appeared cleverly disguised to counterfeit the different kinds of woman sung of. This item indeed gave much pleasure, though it was followed by a cry of: 'Now, something hotter, for 'tis almost fairy time!' So Ned gave them *Riding Paces*, pretending to be a description of a horse-ride, but in reality quite other:

> *When for air*
> * I take my mare*
> *And mount her, first*
> * She walks just thus:*
> *Her head held low*
> * And motion slow,*
> *With nodding, plodding,*
> * Wagging, jogging,*
> *Dashing, plashing,*
> * Snorting, starting*
> *Whimsically she goes,*
> *Then whip stirs up,*
> * Trot, trot, trot,*
> *Ambling then with easy flight*
> *She wriggles like a bird at night . . .*

Miss Cope, now devoid of cover, meanwhile mounted Mr Grigson, bare as she, and rode him to a climax which ended with the song:

> *Mane seized,*
> * Bum squeezed,*
> *I gallop, I gallop, I gallop,*
> * And trot, trot, trot,*
> *Straight again up and down,*
> *Up and down, up and down,*
> *Till the last jerk, with a trot,*
> *Ends our love chase.*

I must confess to admiring the remarkable control which enabled Mr Grigson to lift Miss Cope from her seat just as the last words echoed out, to show himself spilling over with pleasure at the expertise of his rider, and the applause and shouts of encouragement from the audience showed that many among them shared my surprise and admiration. The scene was by this time, as I expected, one of a bacchanalian orgy, most of the young ladies and gentlemen now divested of their dress and lying upon the rugs generously spread upon the floor, some warming their partners with caresses, others already engaged in the act. Mr Grigson and Miss Cope retired, while Ned seized a bottle and sat himself in a corner to look on – being himself, for one reason or another, unconcerned with matters of love – while David, as usual, had divested himself of his clothing and was darting among the company, stopping to twitch a lady's buttock here or a breast there, but contriving all the time to bring his loins into close contact with some part of the anatomy of their partners. Some knocked him away with an oath, while others accorded him a pat, and one or two (for, as I have heard, the universities are full of young gentlemen whose tastes are for whichever sex comes most readily to hand) offered a more intimate caress.

I suddenly became aware of a young fellow who, I guessed, had been seated directly below the small gallery in which I was perched, for I had not seen him until now, stretched out upon the body of a handsome young woman who he was enjoying with some zest. There seemed to be something familiar about the turn of his back, so that I could not help but stare (the lady beneath him believing me to be staring at her, and giving me a broad grin as he worked away upon her). After a while, having reached his goal, he lifted himself and, turning, lay upon his back at her side, whereat I found myself staring right into the astonished eyes of my old friend Frank – now Sir Franklin Franklyn of Alcovary!

In a moment I had dropped my instrument, was out of the gallery, down the narrow staircase, and had clasped him to me – seeing to my amusement as I embraced him, an extremely jealous look from David at the sight of me with a naked man in my arms! So great was our pleasure and surprise that it was some moments before either of us could speak, but then Frank covered himself with a cloak from the floor and led me up to a bedroom on the first floor where we could talk.

This is not the place in which to relate all his adventures, though he told of his short time at Oxford University, whence his father had sent him, of his meeting there with Harry Rockwall ('my companion,' he said, 'in many a jape which will amuse you when we are at leisure'), how Rockwall had invited him to pass the vacation with him at his home (where he was lord of all he surveyed, his family being dead) and how . . .

But here I stopped him, for it was clear to me that there was certain information he had not heard, and I broke to him the news not only of his father's death, but of his brother's and that he was now a baronet, in possession of whatever small fortune his father had commanded.

Though shocked at the news, his pleasure was perhaps more than his pain; though he felt for his Spencer, somehow (he said) it was not with that keenness with which a man might be expected to mourn his brother. 'But we were never close,' he said. 'Poor chap.'

He had not intended ever to return to Alcovary, believing his father entirely turned against him, and since his sister Sophia had been sent away and married to some elderly clown (which was the first I had heard of it, and was sad to hear). But now, surely, he must return to comfort his mother and to discover what estate he had inherited.

What pleasure I now felt, sitting before a fire with my old friend, upon whose familiar limbs, as he sat half-covered with the cloak, red light flickered, and whose face was relaxed into the old companionable smile I remembered! We remained talking long into the night, until we heard the noise of my companions leaving the house (doubtless perplexed at my disappearance) and with a knock at the door Harry Rockwall appeared, to be introduced to me and welcome me to the house to stay as long as I wished – 'For,' he said, 'young Frank stays here to care for my estate while I am in Oxford!'

Then, bidding farewell to Frank – for he left for Oxford the next morning – he left us and we retired to bed, still talking for a while, and then fell asleep, Frank throwing his arm about my shoulders in a gesture of friendship for old times.

My friend evidently lay awake for much of the night, for next morning he announced to me that we must leave that instant for Alcovary, not being able to bear longer to be unsatisfied as to the knowledge of his fate. Would I return with him, he asked, for now fate had thrown us once more together he would not be deprived of my friendship.

'Nothing,' I said, 'would give me more pleasure,' and while he settled to write a letter to Mr Rockwall explaining the change in his plans, I went into Basingstoke, where the latter had taken the early morning coach, and found my companions at the Mail Coach Inn. They were sad at my decision to leave them but it was not a disaster, since they were almost at the end of their tour, and Mr Higgens pleasantly handed me a small but welcome bag of gold pieces, the reward of my time with them.

'If you have need of employment, my dear Mr Archer,' he said, 'pray seek us out. We present in the new season the play of *Timon of Athens*, and need some pleasant music to lighten it; you will be always welcome upon any stage where Mrs Plunkett Cope and I take our stand.' With great condescension that lady bade me farewell, and I went off to take my leave of the others; whereas Miss Cope merely allowed me to kiss her hand, David threw his arms about me and whispered that it would be some time before he had another so pleasant a bedfellow, and seemed almost to have tears in his eyes at our farewell.

By the time I returned to Mr Rockwall's house, Frank had two horses waiting, and bade me prepare for an arduous journey for he did not intend to stop except for food and sleep and to change horses until we reached home.

And indeed so it was; with little pause, it seemed no time before we were within reach of Alcovary and though the night had fallen, Frank demanded that we should press on. By the light of a lantern we made our way forward, coming in time to the gates of the house, and passing up the drive to the front door.

All was in darkness. Lifting the lantern and handing me the reins, Frank went forward and knocked. There was no answer. He knocked again and there was a shuffling from

within, the door opened and who should stand there but
Sophie, who looked for a moment into her brother's eyes,
then fell at his feet in a swoon.

Tying the horses, I rushed forward, and together we
raised Sophie from the floor and placed her in a chair. Lady
Franklyn now came forward and greeted her son, and soon
Sophie was stirring, and we were at leisure to consider the
fifth figure in the hall – the body of a large man clad only in
a shirt, who had lain all this while upon the floor (for my
part I had thought he was drunk) and whose head, now we
came to examine it, was broken and bloodied.

Sophie, now quickly recovered and having greeted us
both with a kiss, explained briefly that the dead man was a
villain who had fallen to his death as a consequence of an
attack upon her virtue and that there was much more to tell
us, but first the servants must be roused, a magistrate sent
for, and all done in order.

When I had roused a man and sent him for Sir Ingle
Fitzson, a magistrate and a neighbour and a good friend of
Lady Franklyn's, we went into the drawing-room and took
some brandy while Sophie and Lady Franklyn between
them explained not only the circumstance of Mr Bidwell's
death (whom Sophie said quite frankly she had pushed
downstairs, and would be happy to do so again) but the fact
that Frank was heir not only to the house but to a fortune
the size of which was not precisely known, but which certainly comprised an income of not less than seven thousand
a year, and property in London which included a house in
Brook Street.

'So,' said Sophie, 'we are both landowners now, Frank!'
And when we expressed amazement, she told us of the
death of Mr Nelham and the unexpected fortune he had
left. Frank immediately embraced her, and an air almost of
gaiety supported us until Sir Ingle arrived, who had met Mr
Bidwell and liked him as little as Sophie and Lady Franklyn. It was clear to him, he said, after looking at the body,
that Mr Bidwell had risen from his bed in the dark for some
purpose of his own, that his candle had gone out, that he
had lost his footing in the gallery and fallen downstairs to

his death. He failed to congratulate the family upon the incident, but pressed affectionate greetings upon Frank and Sophie, complimented Lady Franklyn upon their return, and took his leave.

The servants now lifted Mr Bidwell's body and took it off to an outhouse, remaining to clean the flagstones while we all went upstairs, Lady Franklyn to her own room, and we three to Sophie's, where in a counterfeit of our childish days we crept into the same bed and fell almost immediately into a sleep.

Waking, it was with great joy that I saw upon the pillow at my side the faces of my two best friends in all the world – Frank, his manly visage framed by close-cropped hair, resting in the arms of his sister, who was now one of the most beautiful women my eyes had ever fixed upon. I had paid the day the tribute, as was so often the case, of waking to it in a state of readiness for amorous combat, and it was with great difficulty that I refrained from waking Sophie with a caress, but knew not how she would take it and so contented myself by laying up against her warm body until she and Frank also stirred, and we three regarded each other in the light of morning with the affection we had shared before our last meeting. Sophie lifted her head to kiss my lips, and then Frank's – but he drew away, and when she asked what was the trouble, replied that childish affection between brother and sister was well enough, but they were now grown and should have regard for decency.

Sophie was for a moment quiet at this and then, lifting herself upon her elbow, informed us that there was something she had still to tell us, and thereupon told of the circumstance of which Mr Bidwell had been aware – that Frank, while his mother's son, was no relative at all of Sir Franklyn's.

'So I am disinherited!' cried Frank.

'Far from that!' said Sophie. 'If you are disinherited, so is our mother, and everything she has will go to cousin Bartley in Staffordshire, a greater nincompoop and swaggerer than whom I have never met, apart from the fact that he is already in possession of a fortune entirely sufficient for so considerable a ninny as himself.'

Frank was thoughtful for a moment, and then expressed himself of the opinion that it would be a pity that his mother should become a pauper on his account, and that it was clear he would have to put up with wealth in her interest. Upon which we all burst into laughter, and on its subsiding Sophie pointed out that being only his half-sister perhaps he would now allow her a kiss, for (she said) if Lord Byron could father a child upon his sister (as was put about) she had no objection to a certain degree of familiarity from her half-brother. He needed no encouragement but kissed her soundly, a kiss upon her lips leading naturally to a kiss upon her bosom, and a gradual descent until neither were in a condition to delay further from the ultimate embrace.

I lay all this time merely laying a hand, from time to time, upon one limb or another, and as they concluded their endearments was (I must confess) in the way of affording myself what comfort I could by manual application, whereupon Sophie cried out that while I might not command the blood tie of a half-brother, I was an honorary brother nonetheless, and laughingly pushing Frank aside welcomed me to her body. I was able to show that I had gained in experience since we had last been so joined and, I believe, afforded her something of the same satisfaction as I, certainly, received. Frank too (I must in modesty report) was complimentary about my amatory skills, whereupon I promised to import to him some secrets, when we were in private.

We rose in great good humour to join Lady Franklyn at breakfast, and later that day rode with Sophie to Sir Ingle's house where he sat in inquest on Mr Bidwell's body, returning a verdict of his being accidentally killed.

Back at Alcovary, in what had been old Sir Franklyn's room, was Mr Bidwell's box of papers in which we found what must be the only record of his discovery about Frank's parentage, which we had the pleasure to burn, and we also found notes of the investments and property in London which now made Frank a gentleman of property.

We set about putting the late Sir Franklin's will in order

and satisfying the lawyers, too, of Sophie's claim on her late husband's property, which resulted before long in the whole business being settled to the satisfaction of the men of law.

For seven months we all lived together very pleasantly, but when spring came the three of us – but perhaps Sophie and I in particular – began to feel restless, and I believed that I could at any event no longer batten upon the hospitality of my friends. So one evening, just when the small green buds were beginning to show, I announced that I would take myself off once more into the world.

'But where will you go, dear Andy?' asked Sophie.

'To London,' I said, 'to seek my fortune, for alone of the three of us I have nothing of my own and can no longer press upon you for my keep.'

Both Sophie and Frank were kind enough to find the statement ridiculous and when we began to argue, Frank at last cried:

'But we both have property, sister, in London, which we have not seen. We have an income sufficient to keep us in comfort. Why do we not *all* go?'

Sophie was loud in her approval but I demurred, saying that I could not live on my friends.

'Then you shall come as my steward – companion – tutor – what you will!' said Frank. 'But can you not see, dear Andy, that we will not under any circumstance be parted from you?' and they both embraced me and warmly enjoined me not to leave them.

And so it was, reader, that our life in the provinces was over and that we three bumpkins, with only the experience of life we had gathered during our rambles in the country, were now headed for the city – and the greatest of them all, London town.

EROS IN TOWN

The Adventures of a Lady and Gentleman of Leisure

For the convenience of the reader
we here record a note of
**IMPORTANT PERSONS APPEARING IN
THE NARRATIVE**
in the order of their appearance

Master Andrew Archer, our hero.
Sir Franklin Franklyn, Bart., of Alcovary, Herts, and
Brook St, London.
Primp, a servant.
Blatchford, a coachman.
Mrs Saunter, a madam.
Six nymphs.
Mr Chafer, an agent.
Mrs Sophia Nelham, sister to Sir Franklin.
Mrs Polly Playwright, a servant.
The Viscount Chichley.
Miss Moll Riggs, a lady of the town.
Mrs Aspasia Woodvine, sister to Mrs Playwright.
Sam Rummidge, a coffee-house keeper.
Mrs Jopling Rowe, a madam.
Miss Xanthe Holden, a lady of the town.
Miss Rose Stibbs, another.
Miss Constance Moran, another.
Miss Sally Reed, another.
Miss Cissie Minards, another.
Miss Ginevra Briere, another.
Sir Philip Jocelind, an impoverished gentleman.
Lady Frances Brivet, a lady.
Bob Tippett, a Cockney.
Will Pounce, a countryman.
Harry Riggs, a young man.
William Langrish, another.
George Float, a third.
Ben and Tom Maidment, brothers.
Spencer Middlemas, a mature gentleman.

An Uncle to Xanthe.
His wife.
Robin, a servant.
A tailor.
His wife.
Gossage, an apprentice.
Mordan, another.
An Uncle to Sir Philip Jocelind.
Robert, his footman.
Mary, sister to Robert.
John Riggs, brother to Moll.
Mr Ambrose Forfeit, a man of law.
Six mermaids.
Sergeant Gross, a watchman.
Five young ladies of quality.
David Ham, a young person.
Miss Jenny Portland, a *coryphée*.
Miss Pussy Markham, another.
Mademoiselle Louisa Veron, a dancer.
Monsieur Jean Fiorentino, another.
Mr Sam Berensi, a merchant.
Miss Elizabeth Fawcett, a lady.
Miss Penelope Gayley, another.
Miss Rhoda Gosse, a third.
Three ruffians.
Carlo Gaskill, chief of pimps.
Bill, a workman.
Two young postulants.
Mrs Damerel, a county lady.
Lady Curd, a dowager.
The Misses Priscilla and Louise Minuet, young ladies.
Miss Mary Yately, an heiress.
Albert, a footman.
The Honourable Mathilda Yately, aunt to Miss Yately.

Chapter One

The Adventures of Andy

While we had been used to hearing tales of the lecheries of London, it was nevertheless something of a surprise to Sir Franklin Franklyn (of Alcovary in the county of Hertfordshire) and myself to discover that his house in that city was one of the best-known brothels the town could boast.

After a long but not unpleasant journey in the fresh airs of spring, our coach rattled at last down the road from Edge Ware at about eight o'clock of a fine evening, past Tyburn, and finally up to the door of a tall town house in Brook Street, near the elegant new Grosvenor Square. It was a finely proportioned house, the walls of which however were peeling, and the entrance to which indeed seemed a little shabby. But this was not surprising since Frank's father and mother had not, to our knowledge, visited it for the past twenty years, nor as far as we knew had it been inhabited but for a caretaker. Its handsome proportions, however, promised well despite the fact that shutters stood closed at every window and the dust lay white upon the glass, advertising the fact that the casements had not been opened for some time.

We were glad to leap down and stretch our limbs upon the pavement before my friend (for so I called him, we having been intimate since childhood) impatiently rattled out a fusillade upon the door with his cane. After a moment it opened, though only to the extent of five or six inches. In the dark gap thus offered appeared a cadaverous face which regarded us in silence.

'Yes, gentlemen?' enquired the face.

'Well, open up, man!' said my friend peremptorily.

'Certainly, sir; in a moment. But first, who sent you?'

'Nobody sent me, blockhead,' said my friend, over whose shoulder I was now peering.

It did not surprise me that the face showed no intelligence of Sir Franklin's person or rank, for to the best of my knowledge there had been no communication between my friend and the caretaker, and our decision to start for town had been taken of a sudden only the day before, and there had been no time to send instructions to open up the house or apprise its caretaker of our arrival. 'If the beds are damp, a night on bare boards will do us no harm,' Frank had said.

'Ah, well now, gentlemen,' said the face.

'Will you open this door?' demanded Frank, and in an access of impatience (for he was not a man to wait for long upon the convenience of others) he applied his shoulder to the oak, and it only being held by the foot of the doorman there was an oath and a clatter as the man fell to the floor, and we were past him and into the hall.

The house was evidently a most capacious one – more so than its narrow frontage promised, for it ran back for some distance, and thus there was room for a fine, tall hallway, with a handsome stone staircase mounting from it, and doors to left and to right. It was somewhat a surprise to us that candles were lit in the candelabra which hung above, for this seemed a signal of expectation of our presence – which could not have been the case. Even more surprising was the appearance upon the stairway of an astonishing apparition – a large, blowsy woman upholstered, rather than dressed, in a fine collection of satins and plushes, and upon whose head was hair of such astonishing redness that one could only infer a wig.

'Well, Primp, what's all this noise?'

Primp, for that was evidently the name of the door-keeper, was still picking himself up from the flagstones upon which he had landed, and as he did so muttered something about gentlemen and impatience and violence and only trying to protect the house . . .

'Well, gentlemen,' said the apparition, continuing down the stairway towards us, 'Mrs Saunter at your service, and if your impatience is so precipitate I have no doubt we can find something to quiet it!'

She had now reached the floor, and though the light from the candles was dim it was possible to confirm our first impression that this was no housekeeper – or if so, a strange one. Beneath the surprising wig her face was so thick with paste and powder that it cracked, here and there, into thin lines, three curiously shaped black patches giving the impression of holding the whole together, while bright spots of red upon her cheeks matched the scarlet of her lips.

It seemed time to set her to rights.

'Madam,' I said, 'you cannot know who this gentleman is . . .' but a violent dig in the stomach from Frank's elbow took the breath from my lungs, and I was unable to complete my sentence.

'Glad to hear it, ma'am!' he said, with a bow. 'Perhaps we can inspect the house?'

'No refreshment first, gentlemen? Not so much as a dish of tea? But no, I can see that your spirits are too high to be satisfied with tea. Perhaps a bottle of claret while you are at work. Please to follow me.'

She waved a hand, and sailed off up the stairs, which were nobly proportioned though, like the rest of the house, distinctly grubby. Pictures – no doubt of earlier Franklyns – hung askew upon its walls, some uprights were missing, like vacant teeth, from the balustrade, the stairs themselves were chipped and in need of sweeping. At the top, on the first floor, was a roomy landing, and right ahead of us double doors which, I had no doubt, led into the chief drawing-room.

It was a fine room, and the furnishings had once been handsome enough, though of a former age. The shutters were closed despite the bright daylight and the room was lit by candlelight. As far as I saw, the usual sofas and chairs stood about, and had been joined by piles of cushions upon the floor, but my attention to the furniture was incomplete, for my eyes fixed upon the half a dozen young women dressed – or, rather, undressed – in a most lascivious manner, who were using the room as though it was their own. It was a scene such as Mr Rowlandson might have been pleased to draw: wherever the eye fell, a naked limb engaged it – a long thigh scarcely veiled by thin lawn, an arm negligently thrown over the arm of a chair, a bosom the rosy tips of which were palpably exposed, the flesh lit by the mellow, warm light of naked flames. One girl, a charming bosom visible through the drapery which made only a gesture towards concealment, had a drawing board upon her knee, and was working at a portrait of another who, entirely naked, lay face downward upon a pile of cushions, the sublime contours of whose arse stabbed me with their beauty. The other ladies were employed in various negligences – one painting her face, one with a book, one at darning.

I glanced at my friend, whose interest was no less palpable than my own, for we were lusty fellows still not twenty years of age and had not been in the company of ladies for some weeks – except that of Frank's sister Sophie who, being like him my friend, was not for common use in the way of love-making (though when a mood of familial tenderness turned to sensuality, such was not unknown to happen, to our mutual satisfaction and the tying of the firmest knots of friendship between we three).

I half expected a protest from Frank for the scene, however pleasing for a whorehouse, was not one that a man might expect to find in his own drawing-room, though the ladies were of a beauty not always to be found in such places – at least not in my experience, which however – as readers of an earlier chronicle will be aware – had been confined to the provinces of England and had not encompassed the capital, to which I was entirely new. But to my surprise, my friend simply threw his cane to the floor, and in a moment had thrown off his shirt and was turning his attention to his breeches.

'Come, Andy!' he said. 'Lose no time! Was it not worth the journey to be presented with such delights?'

I did not long hesitate in following his example. As I stripped, the blowsy commander of this company of trollopes was remonstrating: 'Sir, if you would care to choose one of these nymphs, I will conduct you to a chamber. Besides, we have not discussed terms.'

But before she was able to complete her sentence, Frank, now being in a state of nature, and his enthusiasm advertised by his rampant manhood, had thrown himself upon the equally naked object of the artist's attention and, pausing only to turn her upon her back and to spit upon his hand and anoint his tool with saliva, thrust into her with an intemperance which if at first surprising and even painful was soon giving her obvious pleasure, for after an initial squeak of apprehensive protest she soon began to buck to his thrusts, her hands asplay upon his buttocks the better to pull him towards her, so that their bellies slapped together in applause at the enthusiasm of their congress (a sound at which her friends could not suppress some envious laughter).

'We can discuss terms later,' said he, pausing for a moment in his ministrations. 'Meanwhile, ma'am, no interruption, I pray!' – whereupon he grasped his lady's breasts, pinching her nipples between his fingers and thumbs so that she squealed from the enjoyable pain.

I was by now divested of covering and hesitated only through a surfeit of choice, until two girls advanced upon me, one fixing her lips to mine, gripping the lower one gently between small, sharp teeth while the other fell to her knees before me, and I felt the softness of her tongue flickering about the tops of my thighs.

Presently, while Frank single-mindedly ploughed his way towards a final pleasurable leap, I found myself at the centre of the five remaining young women, each eager to obtain some satisfaction, for they had obviously been dull without company. One offered to my lips the most delicious nether mouth, to my surprise entirely divested of hair and thus smooth as can be to my delighted mouth. 'Twas my first experience of so smooth a target, and was inexpressibly exciting to me, so that I was scarcely sensible that two more girls were clasping my naked feet between their upper thighs and encouraging me to tickle them with my toes and that two others were guiding my hands over their bodies, a hardened nipple one moment beneath my palm, a smooth posterior the next. From time to time one would bend to kiss my almost painfully distended staff, to take my cods in her hands and roll them enticingly, or to tickle my nipples with their tongues – until, mad with delight, I seized about the waist the girl whose quim I had been pleasuring with my tongue and lifted her bodily upon me, lowering her so that she slid down to embrace my essential manhood like a soft, smooth glove, laughing with pleasure as the plentiful hair which embellished its root came into contact with her own unusual smoothness.

Almost immediately I came off with an excited spasm, regretting only – as the nymphs, I believe, did – my inability to pleasure each one in turn.

I had naturally been for some time unconscious of Frank's doings, he being still preoccupied with his single girl, but now I heard a cry and lifted my head just in time to see his delighted expression as he plunged finally into her from behind, she bending over the back of a chair above us. They must have at some time, unnoticed by me, altered their posture so that they could observe my pleasure and the pleasures of my companions, while still gratifying their own senses.

Exhausted with delight, we disposed ourselves to lethargy while our ladies, with warm towels fetched from another room, ministered to our hot and sweaty bodies, wiping the moisture from our chests and buttocks, and with a gentle delicacy cleansing those parts which a few moments before had been so actively engaged.

After a while, the manageress of the tribe appeared with a tray of wine and we enjoyed a glass while the girls completed their favours. They had not paused to cover themselves, and their postures as they bent and rose were so pleasant that I began to be ready for another bout. My favourite houri noticed, and laid her hand upon me in a manner which would have proved fatal had not Frank shot me a meaningful glance, and rising to his feet drawn on his shirt. In what was for me too short a while, we were dressed and, bidding the nymphs farewell, left the room. At the top of the stairs, our hostess waited.

'You will forgive me, sir,' she said, 'but I must now suggest a gift of twenty guineas for our girls. They were clearly delighted to serve you, but I have the expenses of the house to pay . . .'

'Ah, madam,' said Frank; 'I see the time has come to introduce myself. I am Sir Franklin Franklyn, of Alcovary. I think my name is not unfamiliar to you?'

Speechless, the woman drew back, her mouth falling open. At last, 'Sir,' she said, 'forgive me – I was not aware . . .'

'Clearly,' said Frank, 'but perhaps we could repair to your room of business, where you might enlighten me as to the conduct of this place?'

To cut the tale short, Mrs Saunter told us that the house to her knowledge had been a brothel for the past ten years. She had been approached by Mr Thomas Bidwell, representing himself as the man of business of Sir Franklin, Frank's father, and informing her that he wished to let the house on advantageous terms.

'I was then,' she said, 'running the house in Frith Street of which you must have heard . . . No? Well, you are young gentlemen, but 'twas a famous house, though small – so that I was glad to come here, where there was more room and I could enlarge my stable of fillies. And here we have been since then.'

It appeared that each month no less than two hundred golden guineas was handed in person either to Mr Bidwell or to his representative, and had no doubt made its way into the late Sir Franklin's coffers – which went some way to explain the large sum which the miserly baronet had left, so unexpectedly, at his sudden death. It was also clear that she had heard neither of the old man's end, nor of Mr Bidwell's sudden death, for she had been paying his agent, Mr Higgens, regularly until that very week – something about which, as Frank remarked, we should have words with him.

'Well, Mrs Saunter,' said Frank, 'I mean to live here, so you must vacate the place – and soon.'

Mrs Saunter was not in the least discomfited.

'Well, sir,' she said, 'as it happens I have been contemplating a move to Hammersmith – 'tis all the rage to the fashionable, and I have obtained a lease upon a large house there which I am almost finished fitting out. It will be possible there to offer hospitality not for a mere hour or two, but for an entire weekend. Some gentlemen find that one evening in the company of such girls as I commonly supply is all too short a time, and will welcome the opportunity for a dalliance which will last for some days. You two gentlemen, if I may say so' – and she eyed us with a significant smile – 'seem yourselves to be of such sort, and I shall always be glad to see you there. In the meantime, there is on the upper floor a room which was always kept in readiness for Mr Bidwell when he occasionally spent a night with us. Though, to tell truth his appearance was always less than welcome, for he insisted on three of the girls attending upon him at one time, which on a busy night seriously depleted my profits. Not,' she concluded, 'that you would not be welcome to such comfort tonight, should you desire it, for the evening is uncommon quiet.'

Frank bowed his acknowledgement, and Mrs Saunter led us upstairs to a small but comfortable room with a single, large bed, and in a short time Primp, not in the best of tempers, had struggled up with our luggage, and we had ordered a chop from the establishment nearby whence Mrs Saunter secured food for her clients. This proved excellent, as did the second bottle of claret which she sent up 'with her compliments', and when we had dealt with both, the journey and the events which followed it having proved sufficiently exhausting, we threw off our clothes and were a-bed and asleep without more ado.

I was woken next morning by a soft hand upon my shoulder, and opening my eyes for a moment thought it was still night, for the branch of candles which had lit us to our bed, and which we had extinguished at last, was once more lit and shone upon the face of my nymph of the night before, who was bending over and softly shaking me. But then behind her I saw a streak of white light outlining the shutters of the window, and realised that 'twas day.

Beside me I felt Frank stirring, and glancing toward him saw his own partner of the previous night's pleasantries at his side, and that upon the tables at the bed's side were trays bearing pots of chocolate, cups, and . . . But as I was about to examine the trays more closely, I was made aware that a hand, not my own, was closing upon my prick, piss-proud as often when I awake. Nor did I protest when, throwing back the covers, my lady bent to slip it between her lips, permitting myself the liberty to place my own hand beneath the single garment she wore, to trace the line of her spine down to where it fell into the divide of her delightful nether region.

Though we had not noted it, having been so tired that we could have slept upon a plank's breadth, Frank and I had shared a bed scarce three feet wide, and when the girls, having thrown off their light frocks, attempted together to climb upon it to mount us, side by side, like twin horses in a stable, it was clear 'twould not accommodate them. So with a glance at each other and a wink, as though it had been planned, we rose from our places and, taking each a girl by the hips, threw them across the bed, one from each side, so that as we went about our work my head was next to Frank's busy bottom, while after a moment I felt his girl's hand slipping between my thigh and my accomplice's, rising until it could seize my stones and fumble them, adding a delightful titillation to my increasing pleasure.

Reaching his goal somewhat before me, Frank raised himself and took to slapping my buttocks as they rose and fell beside him, this, together with the continuing ministrations of his lady and the delicious smoothness and liquidity of which my girl was mistress, before long encouraged me to throw out a tribute to the occasion, when as one man we rose and handed the girls to their feet – upon which, without even pausing to cover themselves, they poured us out chocolate and lifted the cups to our lips.

We lay for a short while, until the swift gallop of our hearts engendered by our recent race steadied to a mere trot; then with an oath Frank jumped from his bed.

'Enough of this damned candlelight,' he protested. 'Let us let in some of God's good sunlight!' – and striding to the window, he swiftly threw off the bars and turned back the shutter. For a moment my eyes were dazzled, and then, as they grew accustomed to the light, what a sight met them! The room, which in the dim and friendly light of the candles had seemed pleasant enough, was revealed as dingy and dirty, scarce fit for a beggar to inhabit, with the filthy hangings tattered, the carpets threadbare, and the bed linen, now that it could be seen, grubby and unclean. Thick cobwebs hung from the curtain rail and clustered in corners, while all manner of stains and excrescences disfigured the walls.

The girls had hastily donned their single garments, but even had they not, our disillusion would have been plentifully fuelled, for what could be seen of their flesh was grubby and unwashed, their dresses – if that word can be applied to the shapeless, greying material which now hung about them – equally shabby, and their faces, which had seemed pretty enough by candlelight, betrayed that they were of a certain age, and that the amorous experience of which they were undoubtedly queens had been long and hard in the winning.

They were clearly conscious of our surprise and dismay, for they turned away with a shamed look, and made towards the door.

'Nay, please remain!' said Frank in as kind a manner as he was capable of – and he was always a fellow of the greatest charm. 'Please, ladies, join us in a cup –' and gesturing them back, passed them his own cup of chocolate, a gesture I was happy to imitate, since it could now be seen that the china was cracked and stained, and the liquid within it a purplish grey.

The girls – or, rather, women – sat upright upon the bed as we pulled on our breeches and shirts, and our being clad seemed in some way a comfort to them, for they were soon more relaxed, and Frank began to question them about their accommodation. Yes, they lived at the house, as did their four companions – all in a single room above the drawing-room, which had once, they supposed, been the main bedroom. Mrs Saunter looked after them well – which turned out to mean that they were properly fed, given a small proportion of the money they earned, and allowed a certain freedom which placed them far above the other whores they knew who worked in similar houses, for (they said) 'twas often the case that a girl might be taken in only for a night or two, then thrown upon the streets once more to make her way as best she could.

Both had earned their living from their childhood up by pleasing men, there being no other career open to them except the lowest kind of domestic service; at least whoring allowed them to save a little money for their old age, and to be fairly comfortable the while.

And what of the men who frequented the house, asked my friend? It became clear that whatever Mrs Saunter might pretend, those were of the lowest sort, for some were violent, others escaped without payment, some few were diseased – and seeing our alarm, the girls were quick to assert their own freedom from the pox, though Mally, one girl, had been turned off last week as Frenchified, having been tipped a burner by some seaman from the docks, which she was known to frequent.

Perhaps too hastily for politeness Frank thanked the girls for their attentions and showed them the door, whereupon with a wordless glance at each other we divested ourselves of our breeches and seized the soap, ignoring the coldness and, I fear, pollution of the water provided in jugs for our toilets, and scrubbed our cocks diligently until they were more sore from our attentions than from the first rogering they had done for several days.

Still far from confident we had escaped disease, we then dressed and tidied ourselves as best we might, and were just preparing to leave our room when a knock at the door announced Primp, who begged that we would attend Mrs Saunter and Mr Chafer downstairs.

From the way Chafer made his obsequious bow, Madam had obviously revealed Frank's identity. He was a thin little man all in black, with a continual nervous giggle which he disguised by thrusting a fist into his mouth. It became clear that he, too, had been unconscious of Bidwell's death. He had heard that his master was visiting Frank's father at Alcovary, but since he had done so often before, frequently staying for some time, had thought nothing of his absence and had heard neither of the baronet's death, nor of Bidwell's. Fortunately for us, Bidwell had been sufficiently a tyrant to prevent his agent from attempting any fraud; the rent for the house had been paid into account as usual and, yes, he would in course be happy to accompany Sir Franklin to Coutts's bank, where he could check upon the account and the veracity of his statements.

He was clearly much impressed by being in the presence of a member of the nobility, however young, and backed his way bowing and scraping to the door, leaving us alone with Mrs Saunter. Frank, as he had done upstairs, walked to the window and despite her protests – 'No, pray, Sir Franklin, pray, I have not yet made my *toilette* . . .' – threw back the shutters. If the wreck of what had once been a pleasant room was immediately notable, 'twas nothing to the wreck of Mrs Saunter, who looked desperately around for something to shield her face but found nothing larger than a notebook, which did little to conceal her white-washed visage, heavily rouged cheeks and blackened eyes.

Frank was unfailingly polite – as he was to all whose offence to him was impersonal.

'Will it be convenient for you to leave within the week, ma'am?' he asked.

'In course, Sir Franklin, in course,' she said. 'You must please believe yourself master here.'

'I do, I assure you,' said Frank firmly, with half a wink in my direction.

'And you will remain in your room here?'

'Well, no, I think not,' said Frank. 'We will perhaps take rooms nearby for the while, for there are certain refurbishments . . .'

'But of course,' said Mrs Saunter, 'a gentleman of your quality . . . I am of course all too aware that the place has been let go, but 'twas not my place to speak to Mr Bidwell about it, and as you know your late father never did us the honour to visit us . . .'

No, the income had contented him – and for over ten years, we learned. But we were not inclined to stay any longer than we must, and Primp was soon in the hall with our cases, and opening the door onto the street, where we stood for a moment in the spring sunshine, breathing deeply. Frank's coachman was leaning against the railings nearby.

'Ah, Blatchford,' said Frank, 'you found somewhere to stay, I trust?'

'Very good coffee house nearby, sir,' said the man, who knew enough of his master to engage pleasant accommodation for himself, whether told to do so or no. 'The horses bedded down at the back, sir, all tight and snug. The rest of your luggage to be brought round, sir?'

'No, Blatchford, thank'ee,' said Frank. 'We shan't stay here.'

From his look even at the outside of the building, the man entirely understood.

'Thought not, sir, and emboldened to enquire at the coffee house for rooms. A fine set in Hanover Square to be had for fifty guineas a week, sir. A Mr Plant, at number 14, with the lease. If you would care to inspect?'

Bowing to Mrs Saunter ('Yes, Sir Franklin, honoured, Sir Franklin, will leave within these five days, Sir Franklin, and pleased to see you at any time . . .') we made our way down Brook Street – a noble and wide thoroughfare in which, Frank confided, he was ashamed to see that his was the least cared for of houses – and were led by Blatchford to a handsome square somewhat to the east. Within an hour we had been introduced to a gracious set of rooms on the first and second floors of one of the houses there – drawing-room, dressing room, dining-room and two bedrooms – ('Cooked food available from the Blenheim coffee house, gentlemen, in Bond Street, not two minutes' distant,' advised Mr Plant) – and had taken them for a month.

Ordering up hot water to the dressing room, we stripped and cleansed ourselves thoroughly, then dressed and, feeling more ourselves, strolled out and made a breakfast at the Blenheim, a house catering for single gentlemen, then took a turn westward and into Hyde Park, the new young trees of which were just beginning to green with the spring. We strolled slowly down to the Serpentine and along its brim to the beautiful enclosure bordered on one side by the small gardens of the keeper's lodge, on another by the noble grounds of Kensington Gardens, and on the third by the park wall. There sat a woman with a table and chairs, and glasses for the accommodation of visitors who wished to drink from the mineral spring which filled a marble basin. Children were drinking directly from this bowl, while servants, sent from their mistress's carriages out upon the main road, waited with jugs for their turn to fill with the liquid, a vast quantity of which was cast up into the reservoir.

We turned into the footpath which ran from this enclosure back towards town. I was not the first to remark upon the circumstance of Frank's father proving a brothel-keeper. Frank himself was, he said, not surprised; he was not aware of any family riches, nor that his father had ever worked to acquire a fortune, so the extent of that left him at Sir Franklin's death had astonished him, and he had felt that it must have been acquired clandestinely. He was sure that his mother knew nothing of it and that Bidwell, in making an attempt on her virtue, had thought not so much of marriage for affection as of acquiring in some way a share of the capital.

'Well, Andy,' he said, 'now I have it, and will you be surprised to hear what I shall do with it?'

I could not think.

'What most struck you about last night's adventure?' he asked.

The fact that his father's house should be a brothel, I replied.

'Certainly, but about that house itself?'

'Well,' I replied, hesitantly.

'Were you not surprised by its shabbiness, and certainly when we let in the daylight, this morning, was not your impression one of disgust and horror?'

I was forced to acquiesce.

'And our companions?' he said. 'I was as ready for a fuck as yourself, and will not say that I was not pleased by our reception. But was the sight of our ladies in the light of day not less pleasing than you would have wished? To say nothing of the suggestion that they might be poxed?'

I raised my eyebrow.

'Well,' he said, as we passed the enclosure where cows and deer were already turned out and grazing, 'we shall see what has been earned in such filth and disorder, and then we shall see what *can* be earned.'

My lower jaw must have dropped, for he laughed and slapped me on the back.

'Yes, Andy,' he cried, 'I shall see what a little care and money, a little organisation and thought, can make of the house in Brook Street. I can just imagine the kind of man who has been attending there. If we smarten the place up, engage some girls of the better sort, allow for comfort and guarantee cleanliness – why, whatever my father's scale of charges, we can charge five times as much. I've always believed there was a fortune in fucking, my lad, and now we shall try the question!'

At which he laughed so infectiously that I could not but join him, and in a moment we were leaning against a tree helpless with laughter, to the astonishment of the passers-by.

When we had recovered somewhat, we walked on in silence for a while. The sun was low in the spring sky, small buds were appearing on the branches, the city was beginning to stir – though here, in the park, we could have been in the country. Surreptitiously, I put my hand under my coat-tails and pinched myself. Was I, Andrew Archer, sometime footman, lute-player, childhood friend and now companion of Sir Franklin Franklyn of Alcovary, now to be an associate in a brothel? It seemed so. I glanced towards Frank, and caught him watching me a trifle anxiously, I thought. I grinned at him, and he threw his arm across my shoulder.

'Let us see what Coutts's bank has to say about our funds!' he said, and we turned on our heels and strode off towards the city.

Chapter Two

Sophie's Story

I set off alone on my journey to London, taking not even a maid, and catching the stage coach from Alcovary village – for my half-brother Frank and our friend Andy had driven off a week earlier in the family equipage, taking with them our coachmen. I had remained behind to close up the house, leaving only one servant in residence to care for it during an absence of I knew not how long.

My friends will know from my previous narrative that, despite my relatively slender years, my experience of life had already been sufficiently wide to render such a journey as I was upon – a mere eight hours consumed the fifty miles or so between my home and destination – entirely free of anxiety. And I knew that in the town my own house awaited me – or rather the house which had been the property of my late husband, Mr Nelham, a gentleman whose lack of humanity and affection was balanced by an extraordinary degree of miserliness. Upon his death I found myself heiress not only to a considerable fortune in coin, but to a house in the district of London called Soho, which, it seems, he kept to avoid having to pay the expense of hiring rooms when he was engaged on dry-as-dust research at the British Museum or some similar receptacle of musty documents. While my brother had been unable to discover anything about the property our late father possessed in London, my enquiries had revealed that my own house was small and compact, and in the charge of a Mrs Polly Playwright, whose letters to me had been written by some public scribe, and were signed by a simple mark, but who seemed, for aught I could tell, honest enough.

And indeed it was a cheerful, round, good-humoured face which greeted me when I knocked upon the door of the narrow house in Frith Street at about four in the afternoon;

the face almost of a good country maid, except that it was rather paler, as most city faces are. She made a curtsy and stood back for me to enter, then ordering the carrier who had borne my luggage behind my chair from the White Hart in Piccadilly, where the coach had ended its journey, to set it down in the hall and be quick about it, handed him his one-and-sixpence fare together with an emolument smaller than I would have dared to offer, and berated him for ingratitude when he protested.

It did not take long for me to see over the house, which indeed consisted simply of a set of rooms one upon the other; a kitchen in the cellar; a drawing-room upon the ground floor; a bedroom over the top of this; and a small upper room in which Polly had her residence. She had informed me that the house was barely furnished, and only with old and discomfortable things, so I had sent her money with which she had bought modest but comfortable new furnishings – chosen, I should say, with a taste far superior to that which I might have expected. A bright fire burned in the hearth against the slight chill of the spring afternoon, while food was set upon the table in the drawing-room, for which I was more than ready, and which she served with cheerful application.

I was eager to see my brother and our friend, and the house which had belonged to our father. A brief note had informed me only that 'twas unfit for habitation for the time, and gave a nearby address where Frank and Andy were living. I lost no time in setting out, with Polly accompanying me, and a decent linksman from a neighbouring hostelry to marshal us, for though Polly was perfectly aware of the way to Hanover Square, she let me know that it was best we should be escorted by a man – not in fear of theft or violence, though such sometimes occurred, but lest I should be affronted by some gentleman taking me for 'a common woman,' as Polly put it. By this I took her to mean a whore, but neglected to inform her that I was entirely capable of defending myself if such an incident should occur, for I did not yet know her so well as to realise that no such barrier against complete confidence need exist between us.

Having been seated all day, I was ready to stretch my limbs, and a thirty minute walk was no hardship to me –

first north to Oxford Street and then along it to the westward to a point at which we could march into Hanover Square, where we were soon knocking at the door of Frank's rooms.

The affectionate claspings and kissings with which I was greeted might suggest to the uninformed witness that we had been parted for a year rather than a mere week, but the degree of affection between us was such, and a long parting – as I have previously recounted – so relatively recent, that we were ever reluctant to be parted and pleased to be reunited. In no time the claret was flowing and we were telling each other our news and I learnt, to my astonishment, that they had found my father's house a brothel, only that week vacated by its whores and now awaiting redecoration – 'And to what purpose?' enquired Frank, with what seemed a sly grin.

'Why, I suppose you mean to live there,' I said.

'Indeed, you might suppose so,' said Frank, 'but how are we to fill such a large house, and to profit?'

I thought I saw a wink pass between Andy and Polly, who had indeed been eyeing each other with mutual friendliness.

'May I guess, gentlemen?' she said unexpectedly. 'Begging your pardon, ma'am' – (with a bob in my direction) – 'do you not think of continuing in the same business?'

Frank's jaw dropped before he burst out laughing, 'Indeed you have it, Mistress Playwright!' he said.

'A brothel?' I enquired.

'What's good enough for my father is good enough for me,' said Frank, 'and I have the notion that a really superior establishment would be an ornament to the town, and would be much frequented.'

'Right you are, sir!' said Polly, then blushed and fell silent, feeling that she had stepped out of her place. But I am the last person to take a snobbish view, and encouraged her to speak out.

'You have experience in that area?' I said.

'No, ma'am, not directly,' she said, 'but I know that many of the gentlemen of the town have a dislike to the dirt and disrepute of the profession. Many of the girls are well-meaning enough, but are much taken advantage of by the pimps, and a respectable place . . .'

We could not but burst out laughing at the idea of a respectable whorehouse – 'Though,' said Frank, ' 'tis what I intend, and can see that Mrs Playwright will be of the greatest assistance to us.'

He poured another libation, and we drank to Polly, who blushed with pleasure and responded by lifting her glass and emptying it in one swallow. Enquiring her history, we found that she had been engaged by Mr Nelham four years previously, when she was sixteen. He had found her weeping on a doorstep down by the river and offered her a position – an uncharacteristic act of charity, as I thought, but more likely inspired by the knowledge that a distressed young female could be engaged at less expense than another.

'And your title is an honorary one, Mrs Playwright?' asked Frank.

'No, indeed, sir,' she responded, explaining that four years previously she had been married by a young sailor of uncertain birth, who had given her his name before a magistrate then 'had me twice in the yard at the back of Newgate, left me, and was never heard of since.' The magistrate seemed to us a problematical fiction, though we did not say so, yet at the memory (and no doubt under the influence of the claret) poor Polly became somewhat tearful, whereupon Andy, whose eyes were more and more attracted to the fullness of her bosom, slipped an arm around her and filled her glass again. And while Frank and I spoke a little more about his plans, which indeed were not yet far advanced, his familiarity grew, so that in a while I turned to see that one of his hands had slipped within her dress to fondle a breast, and his other palm lay upon a knee whence it had crept beneath her skirt while he pressed kisses upon her neck.

I had been sitting with my back to the couple, but Frank, while speaking to me, was affected by the view of their increasing familiarity, for I could now see beneath his breeches a swelling which – as I had discovered when we were still but innocent children – denoted a rising passion.

' 'Tis all very well, Andy!' he said. 'You and Polly leave brother and sister without the means of satisfaction, while you take your pleasure!' – and so saying, passed between the two of them, and began gently to undo the ribbons at the neck of the girl's dress. Her eyes opened wide and turned towards me – but I gave her a smile of approval, for I guessed what was the truth – that she was not displeased by the attention of two such handsome young men, for both Frank and Andy were in that bloom of youth in which every part of them was attractive to the female senses, though one part more than the rest.

It was not long before the girl was entirely naked – a pleasing sight, for though of a generous figure her heavy breasts, sturdy thighs and broad hips were all of a proportion, so that the fullness of her bosom (which on a slighter figure would have been too ample) was entirely apposite. That she was as attractive to the male as to my female eyes was attested by the fact that my brother and his friend had in no time thrown off their clothes, giving her, as myself, ample evidence of their readiness to embody their admiration.

I must confess that the sight arose a certain warmth within me, and leaning forward I laid my hand upon the firm globe of Andy's arse, slipping a finger below in a manner which I knew to be an irresistible signal to him. And indeed, leaving Polly to the ministrations of my brother, he turned to me and, raising me to my feet, clasped me in his arms, and began immediately to unlace me.

I should say here that we had been familiar, in this way, since we were children – and indeed that the adventurous period of my life had begun when our mother had discovered us both a-bed with Frank, in a state of nature, when we were scarcely old enough to perform those acts which we were essaying. However, since our re-union six months ago, after many vicissitudes, Andy had been somewhat withdrawn from me, and while we had made love upon occasion, it was (it seemed to me) only because no one else offered, for he seemed to regard me more as a sister than as a lover – something I regretted, but understood, for Frank and I had ever treated Andy as one of our family.

Even now, it appeared to me that he turned from Polly only because I desired it, and not especially because he preferred to do so, and could not suppress a pang of regret. However, as he slid my clothes to my feet, following their descent with his lips, first paddling at my neck, then brushing the tips of my breasts, then tracing with his tongue the line of my belly until I felt it approaching my most sensitive part – as I felt all this, I say, pleasure entirely overwhelmed me, and soon we two were upon the floor before the flickering firelight, our limbs bathed in a rosy glow, engaged in pleasuring each other to the utmost.

There is something most comforting in the love-making of a partner with whose ways one is familiar, and though our amorous passages were now somewhat infrequent, I knew well those turns of lip or finger which could give Andy most joy, just as he knew how to arouse me to the utmost – his tonguing of my nether part accompanied by a light pinching of my tits with finger and thumb; the caressing of my neck with his right hand followed by its passage along shoulder and arm until it lay over the small of my back, pressing me towards him. And I remembered the delight my biting of the skin of his thigh could bring, the pleasure I gave in stroking the fur of his arse until my fingers slid down to flick at his cods, and finally the joy – almost to culmination – that my lips gave as they slid over the knob of his standing instrument, and then with a gentle motion rose and fell upon it.

Meanwhile, a disparate pleasure was experienced by Polly and Frank, who being strangers could only by experiment discover what pleased each other. A cry of surprise and pain came from Frank, for instance, when the girl applied her teeth rather too firmly to a nipple, and she gave a vigorous shaking of the head as he thrust several fingers into her secret parts – which, it was clear, she preferred to be otherwise occupied, for before long she had forced him upon his back, and was mounted upon him – not yet indeed taking his instrument within her, but rocking to and fro upon it, causing him (evidently) a mixture of pleasure and pain which was at least as gratifying as it was uncomfortable.

Finally, implored by his eyes and hands alike – which latter gripped her about the waist and positively lifted her so that she sank upon him to the hilt – she joined me in being engorged by that delicious flesh which makes us truly women, and we begged our lovers to steady themselves so that we could enjoy some minutes of delight before that moment, alas almost always premature, which signals man's keenest pleasure and (too often) woman's keenest disappointment.

Soon, however, we were urging them to more vigorous movement, our mood changed by the warm caress of sword in scabbard, and we both cried alike, and almost simultaneously, with pleasure as we mounted to our apogee, our lovers proving their devotion by the release within us of their vital juices. And at the moment when we collapsed into a lethargy, what was my surprise to find that I had reached out to take Polly's hand – whereat she leaned over to where I lay, my head now lying upon my brother's flank, and kissed me upon the cheek. In a moment, she realised what she had done, and coloured, but I reassured her with a gesture and we were, from that moment, not only mistress and maid, but sworn companions, however much circumstances might keep us within our stations.

Now Andy, having kissed me upon the lips, drew himself from me and, taking a napkin, wiped me tenderly between the thighs before cleansing himself. Polly, evidently reluctant to move, sat for a while still impaled, until my brother's tool, having done its duty, shrank from her, whereupon she knelt to kiss it before ministering to herself, and we sat together in a state of nature before the warmth of the fire, hand in hand and flank to flank. Then, without asking, Polly wrapped herself in her clothes and called from the window to the linksman that we would need him no more that night, throwing him a coin, and we repaired to a bedroom where one large bed shared our tired limbs, and we spent a welcome quiet night.

We woke next morning all four cramped together in a tangle of limbs – a sensation pleasantly warm and friendly to one who otherwise might have felt alone in a strange city – and I could not but congratulate myself that my first night in London had not been spent in a necessarily lonely bed in Frith Street. Though I certainly did not foresee waking to first daylight to see my brother Frank in the arms of my servant, when she awoke, stretched, and paddled across the floor in bare feet to draw the curtains, her gentle smile towards me, accompanied by an acknowledgement as friendly as it was respectful, showed that she was entirely conscious of our relationship and ready to honour it.

By turns, we cleansed ourselves – in the most luxurious manner, too, for as with most of the houses in the area (I was informed), lead pipes brought water three times a week to a grand cistern in the roof, and while it must still be heated by fires, it was plentiful and fresh, and large vats brought to the bedrooms by a man employed to do so made it much easier to be continually cleanly and sweet-smelling than even our best endeavours had formerly attained.

We broke our fast modestly upon fresh, warm bread from a nearby bakery, and a pot of chocolate (for at that time I much preferred it to coffee, then more fashionable, while the modern infusion of tea was still regarded as vastly unhealthy). Polly returned to Frith Street, where she said she had much to do, and I accompanied Frank and Andy to my father's house in Brook Street, and found it as they had said. Its interior was empty and almost ruined; the furniture had been carted away, exposing tired and cracked plaster, woodwork badly in need of repair and painting, and floor-boards often almost split through. After I had been conducted over the house, a knocking upon the door announced the arrival of some workmen whom Frank instructed to repair everything that needed repairing, and to paint all the woodwork white (except that in the large room on the first floor, where there was fine panelling). 'Then,' he said to the chief man, 'I will have further instructions, for my plans will have been fully made.' These he promised to reveal to me when he had properly worked them out; they were to prove, he said, something remarkable.

While the men set to work we strode out that I might see the town – which was a revelation to me for richness and sophistication far in excess of that I had seen in such provincial towns as Southampton or Bristol.

We walked through Bond Street, Albemarle Street, Berkeley Square, Piccadilly, St James's Street and Park, Pall Mall, St James's Square, the Strand, and several other fine thoroughfares. Well-dressed men and women thronged all the streets – many dressed in black (Frank explained that this proceeded from the general mourning for Princess Charlotte, who died some weeks ago). Nevertheless, the show of fashion was remarkable, as was the press of traffic

in all directions, for the roll of chariots and carriages of all
kinds was incessant. Coachmen with triangular hats and
tassels, footmen with cockades and canes added a dignity
and even a gaiety to the show – yet Andy informed me that
'twas nothing to the display to be seen in Hyde Park upon
a weekend.

Here and there in the streets were lines of hacks, poor
worn horses eating out of nose-bags. Sometimes enormous
wagons filled with coals, and drawn by great, shaggy horses
would lumber by. And on market day, it seems, cattle are
often driven through even the most fashionable streets to
that part of town where they are sold and all too publicly
slaughtered.

It was soon clear that the quarter where Frank and Andy
were dwelling, known as Mayfair, was the best and most
fashionable, for houses elsewhere were often a muddle of
ancient and modern, too frequently huddled together without form, space or proportion. But the shops – the haber-
dashers, poulterers, fishmongers and butchers. The open
squares and gardens, the parks with spacious walks, the
palisades of iron or enclosures of solid walls wherever
enclosures were requisite. The countless number of
equipages and fine horses; the gigantic draft horses. What
industry, what luxury, what infinite particulars, what an
aggregate!

The men were taller and straighter than the peasantry in
the country where I had spent most of my life, and dressed
(where they were gentlemen) in the height of style. Altogether, it was a remarkable taste of a city which I hoped
soon to call my own.

I said farewell to my brother and our friend in Piccadilly,
for, I said, I wished to stroll in the new Burlington Arcade,
among the pretty shops with their show of millinery, hats,
silks and shoes, tambours and furs, all displayed with the
greatest taste and delicacy. The number of unescorted
ladies strolling there was somewhat of a surprise to me, my
brother having (unless he was unaware of the truth, which I
cannot believe) mischievously failed to explain to me that
the Arcade, while certainly a showplace for pretty things,
was equally one for those ladies whose interest was in
acquiring the money with which to purchase them. Nor had

he mentioned that most of the shopkeepers there had rooms behind or above their shops which could be hired by the hour for a matter of a shilling or two.

I was soon educated, however, for halfway up the arcade I paused to admire a window of engravings, some of mythical scenes, some of foreign views, and out of idle curiosity, entered and asked if I could look through some of them. The middle-aged woman curtsied, handed me a folder, and showed me into an interior room where there was a comfortable sofa and a table, at which I sat and opened my folder. You may imagine my surprise when I saw that it indeed contained views of antique scenes, in which the gods and godesses were nobly shown, but that rather than being semi-nude, their figures politely disguised by a fold of drapery or a leaf, they were on the contrary depicted not only completely naked, but in eager congress. Here was a Judgement of Paris in which the handsome young god, his manhood joyfully extended, toyed voluptuously with the three candidates for his approval; here were satyrs thrusting their hairy staffs gleefully into the persons of soft maidens or nymphs; here was Vulcan at work while on a bed behind him Mars, clad only in a gleaming helmet, lay between the legs of Venus, one thigh thrown artfully upwards so that his tool could be seen enfolded by her pleasant, eager parts; here was Lotis lying on the ground, viewing with amazement the cloak of Priapus, held aloft by the proportions of a vast Something beneath it, the quality of which she was clearly frightened to try . . .

I had seen nothing of this sort before, and was engrossed in the pictures when a soft voice at my back enquired whether I was at liberty. I looked up to see a young man – younger perhaps even than Frank – dressed in clothes superlatively cut, which fitted him like a glove. His blue coat was single-breasted and set off by a buff waistcoat; his nether garments leather pantaloons, and he wore hessian boots. Round his throat was a huge, brilliantly-white neckcloth of many folds, out of which his chin must struggle to emerge. The picture was completed by a finely brushed beaver. His visage was sensitive and open, and from it sparkled a pair of eyes of intense brightness, vivacity and humour.

'I beg your pardon, sir?'

'I asked, ma'am, if you were at liberty?'

'For what?' I naively enquired.

The boy paused, as if wondering (as he might well have done) whether I was a mere tease, then replied: 'For such pleasures as you witness in those pages.'

While in my life I had many times been approached by men for carnal purposes, the enquiry had never been so forthright, and despite the boy's tender years I rose to my feet with the sternest of rebukes: 'I am amazed, sir, that you should address such remarks to a woman with whose name, even, you are unfamiliar, and whose person surely requires greater respect from one so young!'

This was something of a quirk from me, who could not have been but a year or two older than he – for I doubted that he was more than sixteen or seventeen years old, despite his outward assurance and manner – and he coloured immediately, stepped back a pace, and said: 'Madam, if I have offended you, of course I apologise. It was finding you unescorted in these premises, where . . .' and his eyes moved to a curtain at the end of the room, which, I now saw, was drawn slightly aside to reveal a bed.

At once, of course, I realised the true circumstance, and why the boy had approached me so confidently. Still blushing, he was backing away from me; I owed it to him to elucidate my mistake.

'Sir,' I said, 'I regret my curtness; the truth is that being from the country I was unaware of the reputation of this place, and quite innocently entered it to view some engravings, the nature of which – and I ask you to believe me – were as great a surprise to me as my reaction to your approach was to you.'

The boy removed his hat, revealing a tumble of fair hair.

'Ma'am,' he said, 'please forgive me. I understand now the nature of your response. This place is, I fear, not one for respectable persons such as yourself. Gentlemen, liable, I regret, to appetites foreign to ladies, frequent it in order that such as yourself should not be troubled by our importunities. I beg you, once more, to forgive . . .'

But this was too much! 'Appetites foreign to ladies', indeed! The lad must be taught a lesson.

'Ah, sir,' I said, 'it may be that the ladies of polite London society lack that eagerness of which you speak. In the country, however, it is otherwise . . .' And striding forward, I reached for his lips with my own, and slipped my tongue between them, while at the same time pressing my form firmly against his.

After a moment's surprise, his dark eyes twinkled again, and – whether under the misapprehension that I was indeed a professional lady or believing my words (which were of course entirely true) – he threw his hat to the floor, swept me up in his arms with an ease which betrayed greater strength than might have been supposed, and carried me to the bed, pausing only to close the curtains before undressing first me and then himself.

It soon became clear to me that, while forward in speech, the child was not only inexperienced but entirely without understanding of the fine art of making love. Not for the first time, I pitied the wife whose husband came untried from altar to bed. His was so beautiful a person that my first tribute was to slip from beneath his slim, white body and, falling upon my knees beside the bed, to salute the long, pale wand with the purple tip which stood from a cloud of blond hair below his belly. No sooner had my lips embraced it however, than a deep shudder ran through his body, and I drew back hastily – but too late, for a paroxysm overwhelmed him, the muscles of his slender thighs tightened, and a moan escaped his lips as from his instrument an eruption of liquid signalled the premature extinction of my hopes of pleasure.

He had the grace to blush, and indeed even covered his eyes in shame, but I drew his hands away and kissed him upon the lips; in one so young the juices run almost continually, and in no time he would be recovered. With his handkerchief I mopped at his chest, whence the power of the spasm had thrown the nectar, and, laying myself at his side, gently stroked his body with my hands, then very gradually with my fingers, and finally with my fingernails, flicking at his nipples, which swiftly tightened and were as erect as my own. Against my thigh I felt a stirring, marking the beginning of his recovery, but meanwhile he lay supine, not making so much as a gesture towards my own body, which was crying out for satisfaction. So, throwing my leg across him, I knelt astride his chest and applied my forefinger to that part which most eagerly cried out for friction.

His eyes grew wide, for though he must have played with other boys and been entirely aware of the manner in which they could excite themselves (or each other, as I had observed Andy and my brother at play when together we began to feel the stirrings of warmth in our bodies), it had clearly never occurred to him that women had the same propensity for self-pleasuring. After a while, and with a look at me that seemed to ask my permission, he reached out with his hand and allowed me to guide it so that soon he was giving me a more febrile delight than any touch of my own could raise. After a while I was positively panting with delight, and to my added pleasure felt his hands under my arse, lifting me so that he could reach out with his tongue to touch me where, I would swear, he had previously touched no woman.

Meanwhile I was reaching behind me and gently frigging his own most tender part, which became hard as ivory, so that in a while I could no longer resist and, pushing his shoulders back to the pillow, slid down until I could raise myself gently (for fear of once more depriving myself of the ultimate joy) and slide his staff within me, watching as first the tip, then the perfectly shaped length, slipped into me, and finally my dark hair knit with his own fair. Then, still gently, I began to rise and fall, his flesh appearing, pulling my lower lips to follow its movement, then disappearing again. His eyes caught at mine, and sparks seemed to fly between them as gradually my movement quickened, and I felt him thrusting up towards me, and finally, this time with exquisite slowness, the waves of his pleasure broke within me just as I – roused by the luxury of pleasing him as much as by my own physical delight – also reached the final mark.

We kissed gently, and dressed in silence. He began to fumble with his purse, and then refrained.

'Ma'am,' he said, 'I know not . . .'

I laid a finger on his lips.

'I took great pleasure,' I said. 'You must know that I do not throw myself into the arms of every man I meet; but I am pleased to have given you joy.'

'May I call upon you?'

'Certainly,' I said. 'I have yet no card, being freshly arrived from the country, but –'

He produced a tablet, and at my dictation wrote my name and address.

'And perhaps you have a card?' I said.

He reached into his pocket and handed me a slip of card, bowed, smiled, and was gone. In the shop, I heard from the woman an expression of delight that could only be commensurate with a very considerable emolument. I looked at the card:

THE VISCOUNT CHICHLEY

7 Charles Street, W.

Wenscombe, Buckinghamshire

That, I thought, might be a useful acquaintance, and stored the card safely away in my reticule, bowing with what I hoped was a sufficiently distant politeness to the woman in the shop, who was talking in a delaying manner to a florid man and an equally florid, not very young woman, as – I saw – behind me a girl was hurriedly remaking the bed.

Chapter Three

The Adventures of Andy

Two days after the anticipated but no less keenly pleasurable arrival in town of dear Sophie – and my enjoyable encounter with her admirable servant Mrs Playwright – Frank returned from Brook Street to our rooms in Hanover Square with the news that work was going forward well there. Slapping me on the back, he said, 'Well, my boy, the serious work now begins – we must do a little research into the stock-in-trade of the business into which we are to adventure.'

I had wondered how he was to find the women to employ in Brook Street, both of us being entirely ignorant of the city and of what went on there. I had no doubt that a sufficient number of bobtails existed here as elsewhere and had heard of those parts of the town where they were most readily to be met with. But as to the manner of recruitment, I suspected that Frank must take pot luck, unless we should be fortunate enough to meet someone who could inform us fully on the matter.

'We shall need half a dozen girls only at first,' Frank said, 'and of various shapes and sizes, and I've no doubt our good taste and varying ideas of what's fine in a woman will lead us to success if we follow our noses.'

'Follow our sugar-sticks, more like,' I said, at which we grinned. He advised me to put on my second-best clothing – 'For,' he said, 'we want to appear neither wealthy nor poor, and thus we shall find the girls whose chief regard is for the game rather than the gold.'

I had extreme doubt whether such existed, but followed his example and, dressed in decent but not remarkable clothing, we set forth at half-past six in the evening and made our way first to the Haymarket, which already was thronged, not least by women evidently of the class we sought. The whole street – and Regent Street to the north of it – was brilliant with lights, the shops, cafés, Turkish divans, assembly halls and concert rooms all advertising themselves with a degree of opulence not seen anywhere, I would guess, outside a great European capital. One glance showed the troops of elegant girls rustling in silks and satins and laces, walking in the fashionable crowd. Some were tall, elegant, worldly, with pale cheeks and a haughty mien; others were clearly not long from the country, their cheeks rosy from working in the open air, but now determined to seek what employment they could find indoors.

There were too, it must be said, blowsy old women still occupied long after a lifetime of vice and lack of care had reduced them to wrecks; these offered themselves with a whine for a few pence, and were sometimes to be seen led off by some young punk to a narrow alley away from the main streets.

But it was on the elegant that we fixed our gaze, some of them finely dressed and clearly accomplished in manner, many with the style of a lady, and plainly of education – reduced perhaps by ill fortune to their present straits. Some of these latter, I later learned, were at one time milliners or sewing girls in genteel houses in the city, and perhaps ruined in character by their mistress's husbands, or having quarrelled with their relatives, were reduced to a life of prostitution. Others had been waiting-maids, similarly destroyed either by fellow servants or by gentlemen, and now devoted themselves to a wild life of pleasure.

'Well,' says Frank, 'we can't hunt in couples. I'll leave you now; it's – what – seven o'clock. Let us meet at Fenton's in St James's Street at nine, and compare notes. If you find a likely girl, note her name and address and tell her we shall be in touch – you can hint for what purpose, but give no promise and no address.'

And he made off down the street, where I saw him first eye then approach a girl in a brilliant yellow dress, and after exchanging a word or two, they vanished into a side street.

To survey the crowd at my ease, I entered the Royal Coffee House and found myself a seat near a window whence I inspected the passing crowd. It was not long before I caught the eye of a pretty young girl in a willow bonnet and a green dress which I glimpsed beneath the black cloak she held about her. Walking down the bustling pavement towards the window she held my eye, then paused – it seemed to study the bill of fare – while passing her tongue slowly over her lower lip and glancing sideways at me, for whom her appetite seemed as keen as for the food upon offer on the bill. She had a fine if sallow face, framed by jet-black hair, her eyebrows beautifully arched and the eyes deep and inviting. I rose, threw money upon the table, and left, whereupon she came straight up to me and said in a low voice, 'I believe, sir, that we are to be acquainted?'

'I think so, positively,' I replied.

'You wish me to come to your rooms?'

Ah – I had not thought of that. 'Perhaps, ma'am, you know of somewhere . . .?'

'Certainly,' she said; 'please to accompany me.'

She walked up the Haymarket, catching prettily at my arm, and though at first I felt inclined to shyness, a glance about me told me that almost every man in the street had a similar girl on his arm. We turned into Orange Street, then into some other, and stopped at a small coffee-house the lower room of which was deserted save for a few elderly men at one table, playing at dice.

My siren saluted the owner, who stood behind a table in a white apron idly polishing some glasses.

'Mr Rummidge,' she said, 'may we have the use of a room?'

'Certainly, Moll,' came the reply. And then to me: 'That'll be two shilling, and in advance, sir.'

I fished in my pocket and found the coins, he handed the girl a key and a lighted lamp, and we mounted a narrow staircase for two flights. My friend then unlocked a door and ushered us into a small but decent room whose furnishings simply consisted of a small table with a basin of water and a dish of soap, and a bed the linen of which was passably clean, as far as I could see, though clearly rumpled by previous occupants. Setting the lamp down upon the table, Moll turned to lock the door, and without more ado began to undress – at which there was nothing for me to do but follow her example.

When we were both naked, she approached me and

without ceremony put out her small hand to my cods (how cold but how inspiriting it was!) and said, 'Perhaps you would like to give me some money, ducks?' Her accent, I could not but remark, had suffered deterioration since we climbed the stairs.

Enquiring how much would be her fee I learned that she expected half a guinea, and fetching it from my pocket handed it to her, whereupon she tested the gold with her teeth, smiled, and placed it in her reticule.

'Now, ducks, what's your fancy? A simple buttock ball, a screw up, a throw in my diddeys, or something strange? If 'tis too strange, there may be a few shillings to speak for it . . .'

No, no, I assured her, ordinary congress was sufficient for me – though truth to tell I had no notion what the strange phrases she spoke could mean.

And indeed such was the case, for having wiped me thoroughly she bent her head to my lap and I soon felt the soft warmth of her lips upon me, accompanied by the run of her hands upon my hips and flanks.

Not to weary the reader – for it is ever my wish to avoid the mere repetition of lubricious detail – I need only say that she was indeed mistress of her art, with all that appearance of enthusiasm and pleasure which is a true aphrodisiac (for I have often confirmed that those women who appear to perform the act solely for the gratification of their partners fail to arouse acute delight, and dealing with them is little more satisfaction than dealing with the palm of one's hand). It may of course be that the writhing of her body under my embrace was counterfeited, that the small whinnies of pleasure (like those of a young colt) were mimicked, and that her final explosion of delight, when she clung to me so fiercely I thought my ribs would crack, was a calculated display of acting – but I believed not.

As we lay afterwards upon the bed, she stroked my body with what seemed a loving care, kissing me gently as with the cloth she wiped down my heated limbs.

'Thank you, sir,' she said. ' 'Tis some time since I danced the jig so pleasantly.'

'Nay, Moll,' I said, 'surely 'tis I should thank you,' though indeed I suppose that not every one of her visitors would have shown the consideration with which I was careful to nurse her to an excitement which clearly pleased her. There was a pause, for I could not think of the sort of conversation proper to the occasion.

'You are in a good way of business?' I finally asked.

' 'Tis always spring in this town,' she replied with a smile, 'though 'tis rare the evening brings me a friend so charming as yourself,' bending her head to nip the lobe of my ear. 'I trust we shall meet again.'

'I trust so,' I said. 'Where may I find you?'

'You can enquire here,' she said, 'Rummidge's Coffee House in Whitcombe Street – Moll Riggs. I'm never far away, after six, and Sam Rummidge downstairs will take a message.'

I reached for my note book and jotted down the details. 'Then we shall meet again,' I said, 'I'm sure of it.'

'No doubt,' she said. 'A lad so riggish as yourself cannot go long without strapping.'

Still naked herself, she helped me dress, handing me my clothes piece by piece, drawing up my nether garments, buttoning my shirt – and only then drawing on her own clothing, which consisted, now that I looked, merely of a single garment with a cloak thrown over it.

'Well,' she said, seeing my glance, 'a swift unveiling is sometimes a necessity, and fortunately the winter is now over and the evenings in this town positively sultry.'

To my astonishment, it already wanted only fifteen minutes to nine o'clock – in my passion I had lost count of the time, though my partner had not, for as she made to unlock the door she said, with a pretty hesitation, 'I remark, sir, that we have been occupied for some hundred minutes, which is forty longer than would normally . . .' breaking off with a little cough. Whereupon I dipped into my pocket for an extra half-a-crown, with which she expressed herself delighted.

Having bade her farewell I made my way back to the Haymarket, and thence to St James's Street and Fenton's Coffee House, where I found Frank, who greeted me with: 'I have arranged a brine bath for us both.' Seeing me look a question, he explained that this was a house in which warm sea water baths could be had for seven shillings and sixpence – which seemed to me to be an exorbitant price, but since my friend was paying I acquiesced. He explained that sea water bathing was all the rage in town, the water, it was said, being brought in pipes from Brighthelmstone, a resort much favoured by the Prince Regent. Meanwhile, artificial sea water was provided.

'There are,' Frank said, 'several large public establishments – one indeed in St James's Street itself – but I wished to see a smaller one.'

Directed towards the back of the house, we found ourselves in a middle-sized room in which were four large wooden tubs in which water steamed, and climbing each into one of them found ourselves indeed immersed in warm salt water. It appeared the recipe for such a bath was to fill the tank with water and to add to it about as much common sea salt as there is water. Such a bath will keep good any number of years and may be employed in the midst of frost and snow without danger of the bather catching cold. Spluttering from his immersion, Frank asked whether I had not indulged in sea bathing – which indeed I had not, apart from the dip I had had when escaping from the press gang at Portsmouth the previous year.

'Ah,' he said, 'our Prince Regent has made it popular at Brighthelmstone, and now 'tis spread to London, and is said to be mighty healthy.'

'Mostly nonsense!' remarked a voice, and the head of an elderly man, the face much decorated by whiskers, appeared over the brim of one of the neighbouring tubs.

This proved to be the visage, so he informed us, of Major Trumball, of the medical corps of one of our great regiments, and recently returned from a tour of duty in Turkey – where, he said, they ordered their baths better, aided by the heat of the climate and the ready supply of those he described as 'the most amiable bum-boys east of Cyprus, as amorous as a sackful of whores, and in the dark quite as capable of entertainment.'

As to the health-giving qualities of salt water, he exclaimed, 'twas mostly flim-flam, and a fashion spread by 'that fat fool' (for so he alluded to our gracious Regent) in order that he might have excuse to escape to Brighthelmstone with his doxy, one Mrs Fitzherbert – a lady whose name I now heard for the first, but not for the last, time.

'The one purpose 'tis good for is to relax the muscles,' said our new acquaintance, 'and for that purpose 'tis to be commended, but for no other – why, 'tis useless even for cleansing the body, for soap has a great antipathy to salt.'

Somewhat to my surprise, for to be honest the man seemed to me to be a tedious bore, Frank cultivated conversation, asking whether regular bathing in hot, fresh water – even daily immersion – was in his view not a fine thing, and received the answer that 'twas.

'Bodily cleanliness is now much under discussion by our masters at the War Office,' said the major. 'Though 'tis impossible to maintain under conditions of battle, we are experimenting with the installation of machines for dispensing hot, or at least warm, water in barracks, and engaging the men to bath each day in it, and the information we have so far gathered shows that an increase in health runs with cleanliness of body.'

'The pox, I suppose, must concern you greatly when men are stationed in a great city?' asked Frank.

'Indeed, sir, but again, there is much to be done by care. The Spanish gout is punishment enough, and if by example we show ways of avoiding it, we find even the roughest of men in time take care.'

'But how do you do this?'

'The cundum, sir,' said the major. 'I have sometimes wished we could tie each man into one before letting him from barracks, but what persuasion can do, that we essay. And now many of the women of the town, themselves a-feared, use these preventatives, which prove to be a salvation.'

He heaved himself over the edge of the tub, preceded by a large paunch.

'Pleasure to be acquainted with you, gentlemen,' he said, and made off.

No sooner had the major left than the door opened and three women entered bearing large pails of steaming water. Without ceremony they tipped it into our tubs, highly amused when we cried out with the shock of it – for it was almost boiling!

When they had retired, Frank asked how my evening had been spent.

'You mean you found only one girl?' he asked. 'Why, at this rate 'twill be 1850 before we have a crew together!'

So how many had he found, I asked, at which he laughed, and said about twenty – but this merely meant, I found, that he had approached some likely women in the street and engaged addresses at which they could be found. And when I asked how he knew their performances would come up to their appearance, he was at a loss to answer except to say that they would be well tried before their engagement. We begged to differ, then, about our relative activities (though I pointed out that ten or twelve days at the most would, by my method, result in our engaging a full stable of known and tested mistresses of amorous play). But what, I asked, was his notion – the building of a set of baths in St James's?

No, he replied, but in the cellars at Brook Street!

Noting the rage for baths, he said, he recalled what he had heard at university about those of the ancient Romans, and also from travellers of those still in existence in Turkey, and that though some were of gigantic size, others were small and capable perhaps of establishment even in a private, modern house.

' 'Twould have been impossible,' he said, 'even a few years ago, when water was delivered in pails only twice a week or so, but now with the advantage of water piped to the house, it should not be impossible to put it to the use which we are now making of it . . .'

But it would be enormously expensive, I objected.

'Ay – but think of the advertisement!' Frank said. 'The curious would be immediately attracted, and moreover, as I suspected and as the major has confirmed, there would be a great advantage in that both the girls and the visiting gentlemen would be clean, for it is my intention not only that the men shall be protected from dirt, but the women also. My understanding is that there is increasing fear of the French disease, and that a reputation for avoiding it would do us the most good. But,' he went on, 'I have discovered one obstacle to our plans.'

And what was that?

The fact, he explained, that while the law did not prohibit a lady selling her body for gain, nor did it prohibit another woman from organising such sales, it was adamant against any man who made profit from such a business.

'So,' he said, 'we must have a woman to manage the trade.'

We were silent for a moment, both, I suppose, with the same thought, and both hesitant to express it.

'Sophie,' Frank began, 'though I would not hesitate to consult her in the matter . . .'

'I do not care for the notion of her as brothel-keeper,' I said.

'Though,' Frank agreed, 'we know her to be enthusiastic for the game it is somehow a position that I would not care to offer her. But at least we could discuss it, and invite her opinion.'

The water was now beginning to grow cool, so we hauled ourselves from our tubs – I must say with a glow on our skin and very agreeable sensations – dried ourselves, dressed, and made for Frith Street, where we found Sophie absent, but Polly Playwright sitting before a good fire, happy to entertain us to a cup of chocolate. After a while, she enquired of Frank how his plans were progressing, and he opened with her the problem of the law's inhibitions.

'You must clearly put in a Madam,' she said.

'Ay, but who?'

Polly was silent for a moment, then said: 'I was reluctant to let you know of it, for many gentlemen would regard it as a matter of shame, but I think I can introduce you to the right person – someone of considerable experience, who herself was kept for some years by some distinguished men of the town.'

Polly went on to explain that apart from the women of the street, and those who worked in houses such as that run by Mrs Saunter, there were others – usually the more beautiful and intelligent – who became the kept mistresses of individual men – a nobleman, perhaps, an officer in the Guards, or someone of wealth in the City or on the Stock Exchange. These women had an income often of twenty or thirty pounds a week – some, much more – while their sisters who plied the Haymarket or appeared at the theatres and gin palaces rarely earned more than ten or twelve pounds in seven days.

Polly's sister Aspasia (not, it seems, her real name – which was Nan – but one she had adopted as soon as she went to work) had been from the age of seventeen under the protection of Mr Peregrine King, the well-known man of finance, who had become enamoured of her at first sight and proposed within a fortnight that she should keep company with him. She had accepted without hesitation, for he was then a man of distinguished appearance, though considerable age, and he had taken a house for her in one of the terraces overlooking the Regent's Park, allowed her two thousand pound a year, and came as frequently as he could to pass his time in her society.

'She brought me to London from Ipswich, where we both grew up, to be her maid,' said Polly, 'for she lived in great style, setting up a carriage, and taking a box at the opera on the pit tier. Her friend, far from finding her beauties cloying, grew the more addicted to her company as the months passed, and he was unhappy except when within her sight.

'Unfortunately,' she continued, 'Mr King's amorous performance was scarcely on a level with his generosity, and after eighteen months or so she found herself incapable of resisting the attempts upon her person of a young but impecunious Guards officer who, one evening, Mr King discovered in her box at Covent Garden. She introduced him as her cousin, but the incident aroused her protector's suspicions and he determined to watch her more closely. For a time, more by accident than anything else, she escaped discovery, but the betrayal of a footman, who we both treated too kindly, led to Mr King's appearing unexpectedly one evening to find her and the Guardsman in a state of nature enjoying each other and a bottle of champagne in the bed for which he was so generously paying. The next day, with a few sarcastic remarks, her protector gave her her *congé* and five hundred pounds.'

With this, however, Aspasia had set herself up in rooms in Curzon Street, and took her position among those who, in rank beneath the single kept woman, take several lovers who call upon them at different times. This life must be conducted with considerable skill and she was adept at it. She had no hesitation in admitting to her favours any man to whom she took a fancy, and when approached, perhaps at a fashionable ball, or at Vauxhall or some other public place, she would produce her diary and appoint a time when he could call at her rooms. She had led this life for the past five years, and was now in a comfortable way of life, with some half a dozen lovers who were happy to support her.

'She would certainly advise you,' said Polly, 'and might indeed consent, were the terms agreeable, to manage the whole affair.'

Much excited by this news, Frank asked whether we could not instantly call upon this paragon, and though it was now late, Polly happily consented, with the proviso that were she occupied, we must return on another occasion.

Hailing a coach, we were in Curzon Street within half an hour, and upon Polly's announcing herself and finding her sister at leisure, we were within a few moments ushered into a handsome sitting room.

Few men would, I imagine, be proof against such a beauty as Aspasia. Slimmer, though some years older, than Polly, her carriage was more graceful and her beauty altogether finer – though whether her passion matched that of her sister remained for us to discover. In addition she had – no doubt through her continually keeping company with the fashionable rich – an assurance of manner which was however matched by a lightness of wit, a humour and a delightful ease which at once commended her to me and, as I immediately saw, to Frank.

Having introduced us, Polly put, in a few words, the intention Frank had of opening – as she put it – 'the handsomest of private houses' in Brook Street.

'That,' her sister remarked, 'will be an expensive business.'

'Expense is not a bar,' Frank assured her – and indeed our visit to Coutts's bank a week before had assured us that the coffers were even fuller than we had had cause to hope.

'Then you cannot fail,' said Aspasia, and prompted by Frank went on to explain that although there were perhaps as many as twenty thousand prostitutes in London, most of these were what she called 'rank amateurs', mere harlots, and if one were to ignore those at both ends of the spectrum of love – those kept by the rich or living in private apartments and those frequented by the poor – only a minority lived together in houses, many in the neighbourhood of Langham Place but some as far afield as Pimlico or Brompton. These are what are known as 'board lodgers', for they give a portion of what they receive to the mistress of the brothel. Many are disreputable places, regularly raided by the police, the men who run them continually engaged in criminal proceedings – though these, it seems, are so tedious and expensive that the magistrates prefer that they are dealt with 'unofficially'. The few which are decently run are left alone, though with an occasional 'sweetener' to the local watch.

But was it not true, Frank asked, that only women who ran such houses were free of prosecution?

Indeed, said Aspasia, but if the house were properly run the law's eye winked upon it, provided some lady was at least prepared to lend her name to the house as its nominal president.

And were these houses popular, asked Frank.

Indeed, Aspasia replied. Men frequented them often because they were private – for many who were in a certain position desired secrecy above all things – and because they believed the women to be free from disease (which was often, though not always, the case). A house which was pleasant without being so luxurious as to be frightening, where the fees were substantial enough to command respect while not of a degree to be punishing, could not in her view but succeed, and the guarantee of a regular income of, say, fifteen guineas a week would enable us to engage girls of the first quality, and ensure their constancy.

And would Aspasia perhaps be interested in advising us?

'With pleasure, Sir Frank. I am at the moment somewhat at leisure, having only two gentlemen upon my books. Perhaps I could look over the house at some convenient time, and approve the plans?'

Indeed, said Frank, that would be of value, for he had no notion what was the done thing in the way of decoration.

Upon hearing this, Aspasia (as I intend to call her, for her surname was never used, even among friends, though 'twas

I believe known to tradespeople) kindly showed us the extent of her own rooms. That in which we had been sitting was delightfully set up, a double candelabrum shedding generous light upon handsome furniture, carpets and hangings. Next to it was a dressing room, divided into two. One part, which was Aspasia's own, contained all those articles which are most precious to the sex in the way of perfumes and pommades and a large closet in which her clothes were hung, while the second had only a mirror, chair and small hanging closet, together with razors and soap. And both had large tubs for bathing, though in light metal rather than wood, a new notion to us, but, Aspasia explained, easier for her maid to empty, for they could be tipped and the water thrown into pails, rather than disposed of by tedious baling.

'From what you have said,' she remarked, 'you will agree with me on the notions of cleanliness, and I find that even those gentlemen – usually the more elderly – who object to regular bathing can be persuaded to it if I offer my help, while the warm water often communicates to the most withdrawn or nervous of them an ease of intimacy conducive to amorous pleasure.'

Next, we were shown into her bedroom, which was simply furnished with a great bed capable of holding at least four persons, and surrounded by several adjustable mirrors.

'The tools of this trade are few, and the only prerequisites comfort and space,' Aspasia remarked. 'Cramped conditions, I do not enjoy, nor indeed do they permit of that freedom of movement which, if a mere immediate convulsion is not all that is required, is concomitant with real pleasure.'

As she bent to straighten a line of the bed's hanging, Frank caught my eye and with a nod and a wink indicated that Polly and I should withdraw. As we did so, I saw him lay his hand upon Aspasia's shoulder in a gesture the warmth of which was undoubted. Heated, no doubt, by the evening's research, and clearly admiring the person of our new friend, he was now ready for more corporeal congress.

I looked at Polly, who smiled back as we seated ourselves upon a comfortable sofa. I hoped, I said, that her sister would not regard an approach from Frank as impertinent.

That day, she replied, upon which her sister was not ready to entertain an amorous passage with a young man as personable as my friend would be one upon which pigs would fly. And by laying her hand upon my arm, seemed to say that where she too was concerned those animals need not expect too immediate a translation to the skies.

My difficulty was, of course, that I had not long since shot my bolt with my friend of the Haymarket, and as is often the case when a partner is new to me, my spirits had been considerably fanned, so that I was now exhausted to a degree which seemed unlikely to promise a quick recovery.

But I reckoned without Polly's determination, for she was not to be denied her pleasure, and leaning against me placed my arm about her neck so that my left hand was prettily close to those heaving breasts incompletely disguised by her dress. In a moment or two, indeed, almost of its own volition my palm found itself testing the softness of that globe nearest it, while she laid a hand upon that part of my person where normally a signal of approval of beauty might be expected to reveal itself. However, such was not the case, for I was still lobcocked, and it was impossible that she should not discover it.

Far from taking offence, however, she smiled and, placing a kiss upon my lips and fixing my eye with a kindly but mocking look, began at the greatest leisure to divest herself of her clothing – first bending to remove her shoes, then reaching up beneath her skirt to roll down her stockings, not neglecting to permit me such a bewitching glimpse of marble white thigh that 'twould have been a colder man than I who would not have felt a tremor at it. Finally, she bent and took hold of the hem of her dress, raising it as 'twere the curtain of a theatre to reveal the pleasures beneath – the line of her calves, then of her full thighs (a smudge of dark hair between them – for she was scornful of the filthy modern habit of wearing drawers), the deep dint of her navel, a narrow waist above the generous breadth of her hips, and finally, as she drew the dress over her head, those two splendid bubbies which were – or so it seemed to me – her most admirable part.

Slowly, she revolved before me, showing her figure to the finest effect, now her front, now her back, the full globes of her generous arse tempting my to run my hands over them. But on my starting forward she moved away, keeping me in my seat until I was once more entirely conscious that I was a man, my tool starting up from my lap until my breeches seemed ready to burst, so that when, drawing me to my feet, she divested me of my own clothing, I was proud to display an instrument whose vigour I do not hesitate to say she could scarcely have expected to encounter within the whole of Mayfair. Embracing me, she lowered herself, my standing the while, until her breasts, pressing like pliant cushions about my member, completely surrounded it with the most delicious tissue – whereupon she revolved them, as it were, in a movement conferring an astonishing pleasure, and despite my previous exhaustion I felt myself capable of anything, and bent to lift her with such vigour that, my arms under hers, and her legs now thrown about my waist, she was able to embrace my sturdy lower limb with her nether parts. Soon, however, the natural necessity for freer movement encouraged me to lower us both to the carpet, where I did justice to her beauty with the utmost pleasure, she being so ready for the combat that the smoothness and liquidity of the motion prolonged our ecstasy and it was only as we heard the door open, and our brother and sister appeared to smile down at us, that we finally reached a conclusion as charming as it was lethargic.

After a final embrace we climbed somewhat sheepishly to our feet, and were encouraged to follow the example of our peers and refresh our now satisfied parts in the dressing rooms before Frank and I took our leave and made our way back to Hanover Square – he having arranged for the fair Aspasia to view the house in Brook Street as soon as it was finished.

Chapter Four

Sophie's Story

The morning after my encounter with Viscount Chichley, Polly woke me at nine o'clock, bringing up a note which had been sent round by a one-horse chaise from Charles Street. 'My dear Mrs Nelham,' it ran, 'I trust you are in health, and that when I give myself the pleasure of calling upon you at noon, you will be ready to accompany me to see some of the sights of the town, and later to take supper at Ranelagh. Yrs affctly, Chichley.'

The reader will imagine with what alacrity I arose, what a fussing and fuming then took place as Polly was set to making neat my finest gown. I much regretted that I had not as yet had an opportunity to replenish my wardrobe, but I had with me a couple of gowns of the first quality which I had purchased at Cambridge at the end of the previous season. One of these I trusted would be sufficiently elegant; it was of gauze, in *eau-de-nil*, with long sleeves, and I prevailed upon Polly (who had great dexterity with her needle) to lower the bosom, especially at the corners, and to plait a dark blue ribbon round the top. Over it, I wore a dark blue velvet cloak and of course my pretty cap with a peak and a large full bow over the right temple. I believe that I presented myself in my full beauty, such as it was, and indeed when Chichley made his bow prompt at twelve I think I read in his visage an approbation as full as I could desire.

He escorted me immediately to a handsome private coach – which, I later learned, was leased to him at a guinea a week while he was in London – and proposed at first a drive, which indeed was what followed: to Piccadilly, down St James's Street and past the Palace and handsome park which mark the western extremity of the town; then to Whitehall Palace, which stretched along the northern bank

of the River Thames from Privy Gardens to Scotland Yard.
Here, next the Banqueting House, several of the nobility
have houses, among them the Earl of Fife and the Duke of
Buccleugh.

'I hope,' said Chichley, 'to have the honour of showing
you to them, at no distant date.'

I should have said that the noble boy – for I could think
of him only as that, his face being as open and ingenuous as
that of a virgin – presented himself as a figure of great
elegance which would have made my brother and his friend
(had they been present) seem shabby. His tight pantaloons
were of pale yellow, cut to show his narrow waist and
shapely rear parts to advantage. With them he wore a fine
pair of soft black boots which rose to a point, within a few
inches of the knee, from which a yellow tassel was hanging.
At the waist, the pantaloons were gathered into the waistband giving almost the impression of a petticoat under the
waistcoat, and a high-collared coat of a slightly darker
yellow set off his usual brilliant-white muslin neckcloth,
superlatively arranged in no less than five folds.

As we drove eastwards through the city it was my amusement to watch the street activities. The closer we got to
Saint Paul's church the less fashionable the crowd, and the
more merchants and men of business were to be seen. And
there were urchins of every age between five and ten, bowling
hoops among the people, dropping corks into the gutters to
race them in the rancid waters, vaulting over the wooden
posts, fighting with fists and stones – one of which striking
the glass of our coach and causing me to start, gave my friend
the excuse to grasp my hand and press it.

In due time we reached the Tower of London, that massy
dark structure to which some apprehension must always be
attached. I had not thought of it as a centre of amusement,
but to my happy surprise found there the most delightful
menagerie, to which for one shilling we were admitted,
seeing at close quarters lions, leopards, tigers, racoons, and
a curious mild beast known as an ant bear, from the country
of Canada. These, exhibited in dens behind bars, for the
perfect safety of the visitors, were of great interest and
considerable beauty.

By now it was almost three o'clock, and Chichley swept

me off to Tom's Coffee House in Cornhill, where many Italian, French and other foreign merchants were already at dinner. Our food was dressed and presented to us in a handsome mahogany chamber which Chichley had bespoken and where a table was laid with good white linen and silver. But behind it hung a curtain which failed to disguise a bed – seeing my apprehension of which, Chichley stuttered a little and murmured something about believing that I would not wish to dine in the general press downstairs. I was in as little doubt of the dessert I would be offered as of my readiness for it, many of my night thoughts having revolved around the previous afternoon's encounter. But my eagerness to match it was balanced by my readiness for the viands brought to us, which had been chosen with the care Chichley always showed in each social department of life: a little steamed fish dressed with some oyster sauce, a roast fowl accompanied by spinach and potatoes, then a *ragoût à la Française*, macaroni and pastry, and finally walnuts, raisins and almonds. The whole was accompanied by champagne, of which we consumed two pints.

While we ate I learned something about Chichley: that his father had died a year ago and he had succeeded to the title and estate in Buckinghamshire, a fine house set in a great number of acres near Aylesbury, together with – it seemed – sufficient funds. His employment, he told me, consisted chiefly of keeping a watch on his stewards. This, since he was an intelligent youth, was a source of disappointment to him, and he had in mind a political career – 'For', he said, 'there is much to be done to wipe away abuses and to confirm our freedoms.' He was a splendid guide to London and its society, for his youth encouraged him to explore it and his natural intelligence to examine its quiddities and to know its quirks.

When we had eaten all we could and drunk all we wished there was a brief pause, which I did not allow to grow so long as to be embarrassing for it was clear that it was for me to provide a final *bonne-bouche*. So I rose to my feet and, to spare my friend's blushes, affected to discover with great surprise that a bed lay in the corner of the room.

'My lord –' I said.

'Mrs Nelham – Sophie –' he said, 'will you not call me Robert?'

'With all the pleasure in life, Robert,' was my reply. Then I continued, 'I wonder if you will forgive my proposing a period of rest? The exertions of the morning have been happy and rewarding, but in order that I shall be fit to enjoy the time before us, which will no doubt be equally so, I would like to recline for a while.'

He bowed slightly, but looked, I thought, uncertain what his action should be – which I found enchanting, for after a passage such as ours of the afternoon before most men of experience would by now have thrown themselves upon me without ceremony.

'I beg,' I said, 'that you will not think of withdrawing.'

My hat and cloak already lying upon a chair, it was the work only of a few seconds to lift my sole remaining garment over my head and to lay myself upon the soft mattress. In his haste the previous day young Robert had perhaps not sufficiently regarded me, for now, not moving to undress himself, he simply advanced to the bed's side and looked down at me, his eyes full of tender feeling. At last, and looking a question to which I returned the warmest of approving glances, he divested himself of his clothing (folding each item, I was amused to see, with care before placing it upon another chair) and was about to lie by me, but thinking again turned and went to the door to lock it, affording me my first full view of his figure, which was that of a boy, certainly, but with all the appurtances too of manhood: a slight figure, but one the firm muscles of whose calves and buttocks advertised him to be a horseman. The narrow waist of a youth swelled to the broad shoulders of someone given to regular exercise – as I learned later, that of rowing upon the Cam during his period at Cambridge University. It intrigued me to think that I might have known him during my largely unhappy sojourn in that town only twenty months or so earlier.

As he turned, with some diffidence he held his hand to guard his manhood from my invading gaze, but when he reached the bed and laid himself beside me, I raised myself to enjoy the closer sight of a breast almost devoid of hair (the lightest shading only of it around his paps), and to see more clearly the springy, fair bush which lay about the base of an enquiring tool which was by now ready for another acquaintance with my person. As I laid my cheek against the springy brake, to nuzzle that most delicate of triggers, the flesh between the cods and the under parts, it seemed as though some great tower hung above me, where a parapet swelled at the top, surmounted by a handsome dome of deep red, even to purple.

By now he had turned so that he could direct his close gaze to my intimate parts – the first occasion, he later confessed, on which he had examined how a female was made, for apart from our single previous meeting his encounters had only been with women of the town whose persons had not been sufficiently attractive for more than a penny fuck (as it might be vulgarly be expressed). Now, the gentle probing of his fingers gave place to the delicious acquaintance of his tongue, grazing, as it were, upon my lower lips then stroking in so loving a manner that I could not prevent a violent tremor from exciting my limbs – at which he immediately raised his head to enquire whether he had hurt me! I gave no other answer than the most contented of sighs, and he returned to his ministrations.

He was ever quick of apprehension, and from our previous bout had learned that leisure was the best approach to final ecstasy. From time to time he would gently persuade my head from between his thighs, in order that too swift a culmination should not prematurely conclude our passions. When, in course of time, slow waves began to enfold my body as I rose towards the summit of the ecstasy, I ignored his signals and applied my lips more fully to his body, and as the wave broke within me felt that salty evidence of his delight at the back of my throat.

After only a moment, his concerned enquiry revealed that he believed I was offended by his spending in such a way, but placing a kiss upon his lips, I reassured him, pointing out that in a passage of genuine love nothing could be indecent nor improper – at which I felt his body relax, and within a short time we were asleep in each other's arms.

A rattling of the door and the voice of a serving-man awoke us some time later, whereat Robert gave out a roar louder than I would have thought him capable of uttering, commanding silence and departure with a picturesque eloquence. (What he actually cried was, 'Off, Jack Whore, or I'll cut off your whirlygigs with your own snaggs!')

His first action was to kiss me again and to ask if I was rested, and when I returned that I was, to enquire whether we might enjoy ourselves once more before continuing our more public explorations. My answer was to fall upon my back and pull him on top of me, where he soon found a more conventional home for his instrument than hitherto, and began with a slow and graceful motion to raise me once more towards the heights. His beauty was such, and his care and love so clearly honest, that I responded with an equal warmth, gently stroking the small of his back and the fine roundels of his arse as his bucking grew gradually the more urgent and I was unable to resist a smile as he let out a cry of satisfaction and pleasure and relaxed – only immediately to ask whether I had not reached his own degree of pleasure.

It was another lesson I was able to teach: that while most men need to achieve the expulsion of their pleasure in real form, with us the simple enjoyment of a caress may often satisfy.

'Then your natural enjoyment is at a lower level?' he asked.

No, I replied, and indeed at some times it was possible we could enjoy three or four eruptions of joy within as many minutes, something surely to be envied by men, who after their first enjoyment must wait some time before they can attain a second. But our satisfaction was perhaps more variously achieved, and more subtly, than that of men.

I could see he remained puzzled, but reflecting that he was as yet a child, I placed my hands beneath his hips and bodily lifted him from me – something he greeted with a surprised laugh, for he had not apprehended my strength. Kneeling beside me, he bent to kiss first my lips, then my breasts, and finally that part which had given him most recent pleasure, and we set to dress ourselves, a glance at his watch revealing that it was now no earlier than half past six o'clock.

As we drove westwards in his coach, Chichley told me about the two great pleasure gardens of the city – Vauxhall and Ranelagh. Vauxhall, he explained, was near Lambeth, to the south of London, and ten years ago had been simply a tea-garden enlivened with a little music, to which a shilling admittance was not too much. However, when other similar gardens opened in the neighbourhood, the proprietor engaged himself to make Vauxhall the best, and it now costs two shillings to enter – or more on occasions when there are particularly splendid illuminations among the variety of walks, where variegated coloured lamps and transparent paintings are disposed with the utmost taste.

An orchestra plays each evening under Mr Brookes, and Robert mentioned the names of several singers – Mrs Bland, Mrs Franklin, Miss Tyrrell, Miss Daniels, Mr Dignum, Mr Gibbon, and so on.

'Tonight is a quiet night there,' he said, 'and so I proposed Ranelagh, but I shall take you to Vauxhall on the night of a great display, for fireworks of the most ingenious kind have lately been introduced to heighten the attractions of that charming place, and can bring upon occasion as many as fifteen thousand people there, always well-dressed and politely behaved.'

The time passed in such description, together with an account of other distractions of London, including the British Museum, where there are now some wonderful marbles to be seen, recently fetched by Lord Elgin from Athens (that same Lord Elgin whose wife conducted so spirited an affair with Mr Ferguson, MP, that it resulted in the peer's divorce). Meanwhile we drove for some two miles to the village of Chelsea, notable only for the Ranelagh gardens and splendid rotunda. There, the place was just opening, and Robert having paid half-a-crown for our tickets we walked through some of the gardens to the rotunda, where a fine promenade accommodated the fashionable, and a neat orchestra played. We were shown to a small box where supper was laid, and though we seemed but recently to have eaten, we toyed with some more wine and with a chop or two, while a delightful concert took place, the most charming airs being performed. Then came a pleasant masquerade, and a mime during which a handsome young couple made polite but no less spirited love (though fully clothed) while Mrs Mackenzie performed Burns's ballad:

Come rede me, dame, come tell me dame,
   My dame come tell me truly,
What length of gear, when well drove home,
   Will serve a woman duly?'
The old dame scratched her wanton tail,
   Her wanton tail so ready –
'I learned a song in Annandale,
   Nine inch will please a lady.'

My friend became, as the evening proceeded, more and more affectionate and more and more thoughtful, and finally after some preliminary stammerings, enquired whether he might not install me in a small house he owned at Chiswick, allowing me a thousand pound a year to be his companion?

'I must marry,' he said quite frankly, 'it is expected of me, but the young woman my family has always destined for me is not someone to whom I have a great admiration, and to be frank with you I could only tolerate wedlock were it possible to have at the same time a friend like yourself who could solace me.'

It would no doubt have been possible for some women to take offence at the implication that I was good enough for his lordship's bed but not for his table. But while society demands such pretence, it is fruitless to pretend that one in Chichley's situation will not seek to solve the problem in the time-honoured way.

'My dear Robert,' I replied, 'I shall always be pleased to call you friend, and I hope that we shall have many more pleasant encounters, but I have never seen myself as one content to be devoted to a life of complete leisure, and have every intention of finding some useful employment, though to what I shall apply myself, I have not at this moment made decision. Please forgive me if I decline your handsome offer, and believe me when I say that if any man could persuade me to such a course it would be yourself.' Which speech I concluded with the warmest of kisses.

His disappointment was manifest, but he was too much a gentleman to press the point and once more, when he had poured me another glass of wine, we settled to enjoy the entertainment, after which he drove me to Frith Street and took his leave. Somewhat to my surprise Polly was absent, but I went to bed and settled to sleep.

Next morning I heard from Polly, with some amusement, of the activities of Frank and Andy on the previous evening. Her revelations about her sister were no great shock to me and, indeed, I longed to meet her.

As I had said to Chichley, it was my firm intention to turn my attention to some activity or other, for the wasting of time seemed to me to be a sin. But for at least a week or so, I would explore the town and come to know it as thoroughly as possible. At the time of which I speak this was not so great a task as it would be now, for it was then only some two miles in breadth (as it were), and while it extended for perhaps seven miles in length, the eastern extremities were given over to docklands, and much of the rest to that part of the city concerned with finance and business, which interested me little.

With no other object, I set out to walk to the British Museum, where one of the hours of admission, I learned, was twelve midday, and where I hoped to see the carvings of which Chichley had spoken, and which were everywhere described as extraordinary.

That great national depository of antiquities, books and natural curiosities I found in the noble house formerly belonging to the Duke of Montague, in Great Russell Street, Bloomsbury – a mere ten minutes' walk from Frith Street. I found it necessary from the manner in which the place was organised to pass through many other rooms before attaining those where the marbles are displayed, but such was my interest in what there was to see that this was no punishment. Two rooms, for instance, contained Egyptian monuments taken from the French at Alexandria during the last war; then came more Egyptian ornaments, including two great monuments of black marble from the mausoleum of Cleopatra, that most splendid of queens, and many things from Greece and Rome, one or two (because of their supposed indelicacy) awkwardly placed so that the erect members of fauns or – on one pot – of an athlete balancing a vase on the end of his tool, should not offend.

Finally I reached the room in which those marble relics

are which Lord Elgin has recovered from Greece. They are, it seems, fragments from the frieze of the Parthenon, designed by the great sculptor Phidias, and other buildings on the Athenian Acropolis, and are a marvel of the sculptor's art. Indeed I could not but take the opportunity, with some other ladies present, of passing my hand over the limbs of the warriors depicted there, for these are so true to life that it is impossible to praise the figures too highly, and it is a positive shock to feel cold marble beneath one's palm rather than warm flesh.

In a neighbouring room refreshment could be taken, and while I was sitting for a while to allow the impression of the carvings to form themselves in my mind, I was amused to hear two ladies at the next table discussing the figures as though they were alive, and how they would like to entertain them. This one would do for an afternoon, that for a season, the other, however, they would happily marry – except that as a husband he would immediately lose his attraction!

'Is it not strange, Maria,' said the younger of the two, 'that no sooner are we married than our husbands lose all their vigour, all their wish to persuade and to love, and thus all their fascination?'

'My dear,' said the second, ' 'tis a fact of nature. What is unfair is that they can enjoy their' – she lowered her voice – 'their whores and kept women, while we are left alone to whistle, or if we take a lover are held up to contempt. Why cannot there be convenient houses which we can visit in secret for our own satisfaction? 'Twould be an unparalleled convenience!'

The other agreed, and after a short regretful silence they turned once more to a discussion of the various points of the warriors they had seen figured in stone.

As I walked home, my mind began to revolve around what they had said.

Indeed, it was true that for a lady whose husband had lost his taste for her, unless she was unregenerate and out of society, there was no recourse other than complete retirement from the life of the senses. Certainly some notorious women, if they were rich enough, could have their lovers and keep their place in society – sometimes even with the connivance of their husbands – but for most no such relief was possible.

Back at home, I invited Polly to take chocolate with me and asked her after a while whether there had never been an attempt at keeping a brothel for ladies.

She had never heard of a successful one, she said, but then paused and left the room for a moment, returning with an old piece of newspaper.

'I took this from a paper called *The Voluptuarian Cabinet* three years ago,' she said, 'thinking it interesting,' and handed it to me. 'The Mrs Wilson who placed it was known to my sister as the madam of a well appointed brothel for gentlemen in Jermyn Street.'

It was a short advertisement for 'promoting Adultery on the part of Married Women and Fornication on the part of Single Women and Widows', merely announcing a plan to set up a house in which gentlemen of robust and handsome vigour would attend on ladies prepared to set down a few guineas in return.

'I never heard that the plan went into operation,' Polly said, 'and believe that for some reason it never did so. But Aspasia may know more.'

More than ever curious to meet that paragon, I asked whether Polly might introduce us, and nothing loath she escorted me at about seven o'clock to Curzon Street, where I found both the house and the lady fully as attractive as Frank had done (for Polly had recounted to me the speed with which he had been captivated).

Polly made her excuses and left, and Aspasia entertained me at first with perhaps somewhat less warmth than my brother and his friend – this I believe due to a simple preference for the male over the female sex. But she was pleasant enough, and on my opening the question on which I had come, confirmed that her acquaintance Mrs Wilson, though eager to experiment, had never indeed completed her plans to offer to the ladies of the town a convenience equal to that enjoyed by the men. She was quick to see what I was thinking of, and admitted that she had herself considered the idea.

'But,' she said, 'some considerable capital is required, for while most men will put up with a little dirt in this connection – and even prefer it – ladies will always require comfort and cleanliness, distinction and elegance, and such a house must involve the expenditure of several thousand pound! This was the reason Mrs Wilson finally abandoned the notion.'

'I think I can say . . .' I began, but the ringing of the bell interrupted me, and shortly afterwards the maid announced two gentlemen who immediately entered – Mr Winslow, a plump, hearty man of perhaps fifty, and his friend Mr Mulville, of much the same age, but thin and of a mournful mien.

Aspasia rose to greet them.

'You will forgive my bringing George,' said the first of the two, 'and I see now that indeed it is convenient, for your friend,' and he bowed in my direction, 'will no doubt be happy to entertain him.'

Aspasia bowed slightly, and seeing me about to speak, laid a finger to her lips behind their backs, then asked if they would excuse us for a moment.

In her dressing room she confessed that it was much in her interest to keep in with Mr Winslow, for he was a client whose payments were generous and regular.

'I have heard something from Polly of your life,' she said, 'and you will forgive me if I suggest that while of course never performing the rites of love for money, you are not averse to . . .'

I was about to dismiss the idea with contumely (in particular, since Mr Mulville's person almost repelled me) yet, considering the use Aspasia could be to me were I to go further with my idea, thought it best to concur.

'Excellent, my dear!' said Aspasia. 'Now do make use of my bed; I will accommodate Tom in the other room.' Whereupon she showed me into her bedroom and left me to undress, which I did without more ado, so that when Mr Mulville entered he found me sitting up in bed, a sheet clutched to my bosom – yet not altogether concealing my charms.

He strode at once to the bed and taking the sheet, tore it from me in silence. He seized me by both my arms, pulled me to my feet and into his rough embrace, the metal buttons of his jacket bruising my flesh as his teeth (which, surrounded by a rough beard and moustache, felt like some strange apparatus of torture) bruised my lips.

He did not even bother to remove his clothes, but merely unbuttoned the front of his breeches revealing a long, thin instrument – seemingly fleshless as his body must be, could one have seen it – which, throwing me onto the bed, he plunged into me without ceremony. I was greatly annoyed at this, yet was reluctant to deal as I would otherwise have done with the impertinent fellow – that is, in a manner which would in no short time have rendered him incapable of continuing the action in which he was now engaged. But as things stood I decided merely to remember the favour I required of my new friend, lie back, and contemplate Tom Thumb.

My difficulty was that the man seemed set to continue his performance for some hours. His action was strange – far from the generous, rocking motion of the best lovers, his was a short, sharp jig, almost a twanging, even a vibration, which became after some minutes distinctly arousing, despite my repulsion to his person and the discomfort of the roughness of his clothes. In short I found myself in a state of excitement which culminated in my reaching an apogee of pleasure as keen as it was unexpected. Ignoring my inadvertent cry, however, he grimly continued his action, until a second and even a third time my body responded with a climactic shudder. Over his shoulder I saw, after what seemed half an hour, the door open, and the curious face of Aspasia appear. I made a helpless and pleading face at her, but she vanished and I had to lie for some time yet, exhausted physically and emotionally, until without apparently having achieved satisfaction, the man simply and suddenly pulled himself from me and without comment or thanks merely stuffed his still rampant limb back into his breeches. He strode from the room and by the time I had recovered myself, both men had gone.

However, after Aspasia, not unashamed, had revived me with a cup of coffee, she said, 'My dear, I am sorry for that; I fear that neither gentleman is to be recommended as a lover, and I took Mr Winslow myself because his predilection is, from time to time, for the whip, and that is something many women are averse to. I feared that you would receive little politeness from his friend, but at least –' she raised an eyebrow.

'True,' I was forced to admit, 'there was a kind of satisfaction. But surely it must be unpleasant, in your line of employment, to have to face such importunity upon a regular basis?'

'Indeed,' replied my friend, 'but as with everything in life, 'tis a matter of checks and balances, and a comfortable living has much to commend it. Indeed, it is also true that from time to time business may be combined with pleasure . . .'

Thinking of Chichley, I could not but agree with her.

But to return to business: 'You think it possible,' I enquired, 'that such a house as I propose might be set up with success?'

'Certainly,' Aspasia replied, 'but with some care. For instance, it should be out of town – yet not so far out as to be inaccessible by, say, an hour's drive. Your brother's house, for instance, will be ideal for the gentlemen, for it is expected that they should visit such a house, and none of them would be shy of being seen to enter it. Ladies, however, demand a more modest facility: a place at Hammersmith, say, or Chiswick, would be better. It should be large enough to accommodate five or six rooms each with its own dressing room, and it should be comfortably furnished.

'Then there must be added facilities not necessary in a male house of assignation. You will have, I would say, no difficulty in recruiting a stable – there are many young men whose appetite for women is not to be confined to a single friend – though they will have to be most carefully chosen and tried, for of course none of them will be gentlemen. The ladies will talk among themselves – indeed, you can rely upon it to spread the news of your establishment – so however discreet, none of your stallions will remain unknown for long, and will be disallowed by polite society. However, this has the advantage that you may establish a legend for the best of them, who should become a positive hero, and an attraction on his own account.

'These men must also be well displayed, and discreetly. Once more, there is a difference – no man is shy of striding into a roomful of whores and chosing the one which he would most like to bed, but we women on the whole take a more modest view, and there is the necessity of a room where the men may be seen from behind a screen, or some such contrivance.

'All this will be expensive, as I have suggested, but if you have the means (and I do not wish to be impertinent) it seems to me that the investment would be a most satisfactory one – though we must always remember that investments can be ruinous as well as rewarding.'

I agreed with all she said, which indeed accorded strongly with my own feelings. I thanked her for her advice, and hoped that while she was working with my brother we would meet again, and that she would give me the benefit of further comment – adding that of course I would be happy to make a financial consideration in return, for clearly, Miss Aspasia was of the strong opinion that nothing should be given for nothing.

She made me a curtsy. 'Certainly, madam,' she said. 'I hope I may call you Sophie, for the future? Clearly you are a lady of business much as myself, and I shall look forward with pleasure to our future acquaintance.'

Once more she apologised for my experience with Mr Mulville whom, not entirely to my surprise, she revealed as a well-known preacher at an arcane but popular nonconformist church, which taught that illicit connections outside marriage could be sanctioned as long as there was no expulsion of the vital liquor – something which explained much. She then showed me to the door and I returned in a thoughtful mood to Frith Street, where in the evening I took Polly into my confidence; she greeted my plan with enthusiasm and with laughter.

'Why, what fun we shall have!' she exclaimed.

I had not thought of it. But of course, the wench was right.

Chapter Five

The Adventures of Andy

The next fortnight was concerned with alterations to the house in Brook Street. The cellars – or rather, the kitchen and single cellar – were to be made, as Frank intended, into a baths, and for that purpose a large charcoal-burning stove had been installed into the former, 'For,' said Frank, 'we can send out for what food we want, and there is room for wine to be stored elsewhere'. Meanwhile the latter was completely stripped of its storage compartments, its wine racks and its coal containers, and channels dug in the floor in which half-pipes were laid, then grills set atop them, so that hot water could circulate, its steam rising into the room above. Blatchford, it appeared, was to be engaged as stoker and general handyman, though he had not indeed been consulted in the matter, and I wondered what his reaction might be to a sudden transportation from the driving seat of a fine equipage to the fumes of a stoke-hole. However, that we should discover in time, and no doubt Frank would make it so considerably worth his while that any scruples he had would be balanced against the additional remuneration and would prove negligible.

At one end of the large cellar two sunken baths were dug, and excellent imported marble used to line them and to construct small steps at one end. These baths were large enough to take two persons, and deep enough for them to submerge themselves without difficulty – provided, I suppose, all our clients were not six-footers. A small room was constructed near the foot of the stairs, which was to be a warm room where rest could be taken before visitors repaired to the upper chambers. This was all on the Roman model, Frank explained, showing me drawings of men's baths uncovered in the town of Pompeii, near Naples. The steam room was known, in those ancient times, as the *sudatorium*, the warm room as the *tepidarium*. There should be, classically, a *friqidarium* or cold room, with a cold bath, but as Frank said, no one would come to Brook Street to be cooled down. There should also be a gymnasium for exercise, but this would be taken in sufficient vigour, we concluded, upstairs.

The ground floor was now one great sitting room in which the girls could take their ease, and where our visitors would be introduced to them. Frank had ordered the finest furniture from a Bond Street emporium, and had had the walls hung with a most delightful dark green silk to which were matched rich window-hangings. For lighting he had rejected the modern gas lights or 'mantles', as they were called, which an ambitious manufacturer had offered, for, Frank said, nothing could be more charming than the kindly light of candles. And so he had bought great candelabra from a house in Grosvenor Square which itself was being turned over to gas.

Upstairs – and the cold stone of the stairs had now been clad in fine, warm carpets of the deepest red – the single large room had been divided into four smaller compartments. To tell the truth, each was a handsome room of its own, for with Aspasia's advice Frank had scaled the contents to the space available, only the beds being of a full and generous size. The single chair and dressing table, which contained washing bowls and cloths, were the only furniture in the room and were of mahogany and rosewood with bronzed ornaments and inlay. All was handsomely done – but it was in the decoration of these rooms that Frank had excelled himself. He had noticed in *The New Monthly Magazine* an account by a Mr Francis Marsock, an artist, of some of the paintings recently discovered during excavations at Herculaneum, an ancient Roman town near Pompeii. Although the language of the account was somewhat veiled, Frank had concluded that the paintings were of an erotic nature, and indeed Mr Marsock, upon Frank's contacting him, confirmed that they had been discovered on the walls of a brothel. Frank immediately commissioned him to reproduce some of them in the form of frescoes on the walls at Brook Street – which he did, in splendid warm brown colours which recalled the hot southern sun. Here were handsome women climbing upon the laps of readily aroused Roman gentlemen, satyrs and nymphs in every attitude of copulation, young men and young women disporting themselves in every ingenious way.

What all this cost him, I cannot imagine, nor did I ask. But when I did show some surprise at the largeness of his plans, he simply replied that if a thing was worth doing, it was worth doing well.

A message came from Aspasia while he and I were discussing with the workmen the organisation of the space on the second and third floors, where the bedrooms for our girls would be. Frank was determined that they should live in the house – though not as prisoners, for they would have one day's leisure a week, and one half-day during which they would also be at liberty. Meanwhile Aspasia invited us to wait upon her the following morning with our carriage, and to bring with us everything we required for a night away from home – which indeed consisted merely of razor and a change of shirt.

When we appeared in Curzon Street we found that interesting lady dressed for a journey and provided with a small portmanteau, which Blatchford placed on the roof with ours. She then climbed in, sitting opposite us.

'Where to, madam?' enquired the coachman.

'Brighthelmstone,' answered the lady, and we set off to the south across Westminster Bridge, that most handsome of edifices, in warm sunshine which quite soon made it necessary to lower a window a little lest the interior of the carriage should grow oppressive. Blatchford, being a fellow of independent accomplishments, needed no instruction, for he had been spending some time studying the city and the land around it from various maps he had acquired at Hatchard's in Piccadilly, and was equal to driving us anywhere between Cambridge on the north, Windsor on the west, and any part of the coast between the mouth of the Thames and the city of Portsmouth!

Aspasia meanwhile explained that through the agency of a friend she had heard of a small house of some reputation along the coast at Worthing, not far from Brighthelmstone, which was closing due to the retirement of that friend, its madam. The girls, who were of some refinement and beauty, would now be available. This would be a considerable advantage to us, for not only would they be unknown in London, and thus a curiosity, but they would be familiar each to the others and problems of jealousy should therefore be avoided, for, she said, this was a great difficulty when setting up a house. If, for some reason or other, one girl was considerably more popular than the others, and in greater demand, an unpleasant atmosphere could result, fuelled on the one side by envy and on the other by pride.

'Besides which,' she said, 'I have enough confidence in my old friend to know that her girls will be in command of every refinement of polite society and every variety of comforting concupiscence.'

The warmth in the carriage was now considerable, and lowering the blinds we became somnambulent as we rattled south through the villages of Thornton Heath and Croydon, Sanderstead and Warlingham and Limpsfield. In a while, despite the atrocious state of the road, with pot-holes which every moment rattled every bone in my body (though the Brighthelmstone road was better than most, due to the royal paymaster who regularly used it to transport him from London to his mistress's arms) I fell into a doze, and was half-awakened some time later by what I fancied was a small cry from the lady opposite. Half-opening my eyes I saw a distinct tumble of movement in her lap, and realised in a moment that my friend had wriggled out of his shoe (which stood empty upon the floor) and had run his foot beneath her skirt to that point at which, no doubt, his enquiring toes could encounter a sensitive target the palpitation of which caused Aspasia some pleasure – for surely it had provoked the little cry which I had heard?

As for my friend, I could see from the corner of my eye that his breeches betrayed the presence of an unmistakable enthusiasm for the lady – an enthusiasm which soon became acute, for he made a pleading gesture to Aspasia, who looked to see if I was awake. But I continued to counterfeit a slumber, for who was I to interrupt their pleasure? Aspasia then leaned forward and opened the flap of his breeches, whereupon there was revealed something patently in need of diminution if it were ever again to be comfortable beneath a set of small-clothes. Taking it in her

hand, she lowered her head, and my friend settled back in
his seat with a sigh, inserting a hand beneath the front of her
dress to take in its palm one of her generous breasts as she
returned his compliment, bobbing her head as his breath
came quicker, then was finally released in a gasp which
advertised the culmination of his enjoyment.

It can be imagined to what a state the sight reduced me; I
was determined to maintain my posture of sleep, and
trusted that the bold evidence of my arousal, which an
inspection of my lap would have revealed, would be put
down to a dream – and indeed when I had allowed Frank
and Aspasia time to recover and re-settle themselves I acted
my awakening with a sigh and a stretch, to enquire where
we were – at the very moment when Blatchford slowed the
horses and asked whether we wished to stop for food.

We lunched simply but well at an inn at Horsham on
shellfish and a dish of potatoes, with buttermilk and some
ale, then made on for Brighthelmstone, where at the sea
side we turned to the west and drove along the coast road,
the ocean flat and calm and gleaming, to the town of
Worthing – little more than a rural village only a decade
ago but now, in addition to the miserable fishing huts which
still stood upon the beach, it offered accommodation for
the first families in the kingdom and began to vie with
Brighthelmstone as the residence – in the season – of noble
families and country gentlemen.

From the town itself we drove along the coastal road (on
Aspasia's instructions) to where a fine pair of gates stood
giving upon a drive; this in turn led to the front door of a
remarkably handsome house of perhaps eighty years of
age, and on knocking at the door we were shown by a rough
but agreeable manservant into a parlour where we were
greeted by a delightful old lady, I would guess only a few
years younger than the house, who embraced Aspasia with
great pleasure.

After we had been introduced and offered tea, which we
declined, we were shown into a large sitting room at the back
of the house where we found the girls we had travelled to see
gathered demurely together and looking as though they were
expecting a visit from the local Society for Giving Effect to
His Majesty's Proclamation against Vice and Immorality.

'Shy' would not perhaps be the word to apply to them, for no doubt had we arrived in the evening as conventional customers they would have received us with enthusiasm. But they were now demure as tabby cats and, to be frank, I had doubts whether any of them had ever retired to bed even with a friend, let alone with some gentleman who had paid for the privilege – and wondered, even, whether Aspasia had not been the subject of some joke by her friend who, herself, seemed not the kind to run a house of pleasure.

Frank, however, had his own idea for getting to know the girls.

'Ladies,' he said, 'don your cloaks, for we are driving into Brighthelmstone for the evening!'

There was an immediate stir and flutter, and in no time we were all packed into carriages hurriedly summoned from a nearby stable, and in half an hour were set down in the neighbouring town, which as the world knows combines charm and elegance to a fine degree. Leaving the carriages, we walked by the Pavilion – upon which the Prince is said to have spent no less than fifty thousand pound – and then through some of the fine streets, which were lively with movement and cheerfulness even though the season was not yet started. Mrs Jopling Rowe, as I learned was the name of our elderly friend, informed me of the changes that had taken place in the town since the Heir Apparent had shown an interest in it:

'Every year 'tis more and more crowded,' she exclaimed, 'and where the people are to bestow themselves who are announced as coming here this summer, I cannot conceive, as the place was already so full last season that not a good house was unlet. The only ones that still waited for tenants were asking twelve and fourteen guineas a week, even until Christmas. But,' she continued as we strolled after Frank and the girls, who were now clustered around him delighting in his small talk, 'to my taste the society is not of the pleasantest. Of course there are exceptions: the most prominent among them being Lady Charlotte Howard, wife of the major general of that name now serving in the Peninsula and a daughter of Lord Rosebery. Another conspicuous character here is one of your Bath set – Lady Aldborough. She has one of the best houses in Brighton, and gives us,

very often, little merry parties and dances where you can
enjoy yourself immensely, and get a good supper.'

By now we were turned into a fine house of entertainment
in sight of the sea, where we ate and drank well at Frank's
expense, the ladies under the influence of wine becoming
yet more friendly and free, though still extremely ladylike – something I expressed my pleasure in to Mrs Jopling
Rowe, next to whom I found myself seated.

'My dear Mr Archer,' she said, 'I have always insisted on
their behaviour being such as would attract only admiration
even in the best society, telling them that their carriage
when they are alone with, eh . . .' (she looked around to
make sure that we could not be overheard) ' . . . with their
gentlemen is a matter for them, but that in public they
should be entire ladies. I trust I have succeeded.'

'You have indeed, madam. But where, if I may ask, did
you acquire them?'

'In a variety of ways which would be tedious to recount,'
was her reply, 'but I may say that had I not employed them
they would all have vanished into domestic service, having
to live on a few pence a week, and probably in the most
fearful conditions. Perhaps Aspasia has told you that for
some years I ran a very successful milliner's shop in Bond
Street with a small room behind, and then two more above,
where gentlemen could be accommodated, and I think I can
claim to have entertained some of the cream of Europe as
well as of our own aristocracy.

'But seeking a more healthy air, I came to Brighton some
eight years ago, where in course of time I made the acquaintance of these delightful children. For five years I have
educated them as best I might, with the help of local mistresses to teach them music, deportment, French and other
niceties. I then explained to them that if they wished to leave
me, they might do so, finding if they could positions as
governesses in the neighbourhood. Or they could become
part of the establishment which I meant to set up, upon
which they would receive a proper proportion of the income
from the business, together with their accommodation.

'I am glad to say that each, independently, decided to
stay, and has remained with me ever since. But now I feel
that the time has come to retire entirely, and when I heard

from Aspasia of your friend's scheme – substantially similar to my own – which would also give the girls an opportunity to experience the pleasures of the city, I explained the position to them, with the result that you now see.'

Indeed, the girls were entranced by my friend and by Aspasia, who was describing the delights of London, and when we had returned to Worthing and Mrs Jopling Rowe's house they gathered around him to hear his proposal without a trace of shyness or distance. Indeed, by this time two of them had attached themselves to me, and seated one on each side of me upon a sofa were tenderly embracing and kissing me. But they ceased upon Frank demanding their attention.

'Ladies,' he said, 'allow me for a moment to address you seriously. You have heard I think from your delightful guardian that it is my intention to set up in London an establishment very like her own. You will be provided with accommodation and with necessary food. You will be protected from any unpleasantness by the presence, always, of Mr Archer, myself, or some other male guardian. You will have one and one-half days at leisure each week, and will receive one third of the sum derived from each visitor – and since I mean to charge the sum of five guineas for each encounter, you will receive the sum of one pound seven shillings and sixpence each. I would not expect each of you to entertain fewer than five gentlemen in a week, and indeed there may be considerably more.'

From their expressions, I could see they were working out the total, aware that this was a great deal more than they could ever have dreamed of!

'You need not answer me now,' said Frank, 'but I should wish you to come to Brook Street in two weeks' time – that is, on Monday May the fifth, for I wish to open my doors three days after that.'

The girls looked at each other, then one of them said, 'Sir Franklin, I speak for all when I say that we need not have time for consideration, but would be delighted to close with your kind offer this instant!' The rest nodded agreement, and all came to kiss him and then myself; and one thing leading to the next, we began to toy and play, and soon I noticed that Mrs Jopling Rowe and Aspasia had left the room – presumably to entertain themselves with talk and reminiscence – leaving us to ourselves. Frank was soon upon the floor, laughing with pleasure as two girls undressed him, while upon the sofa I had a girl upon each side undoing a button here or slipping a hand beneath my clothing elsewhere, while a third, standing behind me, had drawn my head back and, leaning forward, was allowing me to sip the honey of her tongue between parted lips.

There are moments when pleasure becomes so keen that it almost ceases to be pleasure, and to find myself part – as soon I was – of a band consisting of my friend and of six delightful girls, all of us as naked as the day we were born and each engaged in an attempt to convey the utmost zest to the other, was such delight that I almost found my senses slipping from me and was forced for a moment to withdraw from combat and observe.

The six girls were each entirely different in body and, as we were to discover, in temperament. Their persons were of delightful proportions, ranging from the extremely slim to the generously endowed, the long-legged to the almost plump.

The most slender, Xanthe, at this moment contenting herself with leaning over Frank to apply her kisses to his cheeks, was as one might expect from that name, a blonde. As I saw her, from behind, she might almost have been a boy, so narrow were her hips, so lean her thighs, except for that roundness of the haunches which can never be mistaken for those of a man. Those delightful thighs, with their velvet, white skin, were thrown apart to disclose a charming nest marked by tiny blonde locks which might have been curled by a hot iron, so tight and shapely were they. Her breasts were small, and as she bent over hung down like small lemons, and Frank was happy now and then to turn, gather one and convey it to his lips, as the strands of her long hair, now loosed, fell to brush his cheek.

Rose was almost a twin of Xanthe's, quite as slender, but very dark, with tumbles of hair which fell over her shoulders as she rose and fell upon Frank's lower parts, his tool (so large it might have appeared dangerous to insert it within so small a sheath) appearing and disappearing within her body, its length upon appearing to the view showing it to be bathed in a delightful dew, as much a sign of her ecstasy as his own. Upon the upper part of her right breast, a dark mole or beauty spot appeared, making its whiteness more apparent. Xanthe and Rose were inclined to solemnity, and so devoted to each other that each almost seemed to prefer the company of the other to that of a male companion.

Behind Rose knelt Constance, so dark as almost to be a Negress, her flesh in violent contrast to Rose's creamy skin as from time to time she laid it against her friend's back. The centres of her breasts were gathered to nipples which seemed almost the colour of chocolate, and erect with excitement as she reached around the body of Xanthe now to toy with a breast, now to lower her hand to explore the adamant hardness of my friend's busy vital part, and to discover the tightness of his cods beneath. Constance, I was to learn, was not only naturally dark-skinned but became more so by reason of her delighting to lie naked in the open air not only in summer but even in winter, were there the slightest trace of warmth in the sun. I was not surprised to learn that this display had attracted the attention of Will, the boy – or rather young man – who acted as general handyman about the house, and there was now what almost amounted to a marriage between them, except that he understood that she wished to continue to provide the service to male visitors which had been her common practice. She was saving her money in order to enlarge Will's savings so they could eventually purchase an inn when the time came for her retirement.

Two more of the girls, Sally and Cissie, could never have been mistaken for boys, for their figures were generously full, mirroring each other in the tremulous shivering of parts as they moved. Their temperaments were generous and happy; they were tomboys now very obviously delighted to be giving pleasure, which they did partly by caressing Frank's upper limbs, tweaking his paps and running their fingers over his chest and belly, and partly by encouraging him to apply his hands to their most delicate parts, even taking his fingers into their mouths and sucking them (something which, from the way in which he turned his head to left and to right, was entrancing to him).

There remained Ginevra, a brunette, and though with little trace of an accent, evidently of French extraction. She had been contenting herself by toying with the limbs of her friends – Frank's being unavailable to her – but now turned to me, remarking that I must not be left out of the feast and enquiring whether I was not inclined to be part of it? Her body was muscular and hard to the touch, for she was greatly given to exercise, and rode daily upon the downs behind the town. Like many European women (as I was to discover during those adventures on the continent which it is my intention to describe in a future narrative) she left her limbs untouched by the razor which British women now increasingly use as an essential part of their *toilette*, and beneath her arms sprouted little locks of hair, while her thighs too were covered not so much by that light down which most women's limbs bear, but almost by pelt.

My answer to her question was to draw her towards me, where I buried my face between two of the most delightful, flexible yet firm bubbies, licking from each a slight salt savour, and bringing their tips to small peaks of satisfaction. Delighted at this, she laid her hand between my legs and laughed aloud at what she found there – for, she said, she thought that I had come off early in the proceedings and was not yet recovered, yet here was a key ready for any lock!

I smiled, and explained that it was because I had not wished too speedy a consummation that I had retired from the play. 'But now,' I said, 'if you will allow . . .' – and pushing her gently back upon the couch, laid myself between her generous thighs and glided into a well-prepared refuge.

Not far away, Frank (whose stamina was ever greater than my own) was now upon his knees, with Xanthe on all fours receiving his still unsatisfied instrument. At her side stood Rose, one thigh thrown over Frank's shoulders so that his tongue could apply itself to satisfying her, while Sally and Cissie, one upon each side, encouraged his fingers to prompt them to the ultimate pleasure.

The sight of all this, together with the succulent, spongy embrace with which Ginevra was pleasuring me (in an embrace so typically female as to belie the slight moustache which I now saw decorated her lower lip) did my business, and with a delight which almost made me faint, I succumbed way to pleasure.

In a while, Frank having been made happy too, we sat and talked, the girls being curious about London, whence they had never ventured, and wishing to make comparison between it and Brighthelmstone. But the day had been a long one, and we soon retired to a room which had been made ready for us. The girls invited us to choose who should accompany us, or whether we would not prefer to share their company in the large room they all occupied, but I was entirely satisfied and ready for sleep – as indeed was Frank who, remember, had been pleasured twice that day!

Next morning, we awoke – rather as on our first morning in Brook Street – to find two ministering figures bending over us – but how great was the contrast! The curtains had been drawn, and the golden rays of the early morning sun struck through the window upon the spotless smocks of the girls – Xanthe and Rose – and set sparkling the white cups and saucers and the pot of chocolate which they had set upon the bedside table.

We sat ourselves up against the pillows which they pummelled and made comfortable for us, and they joined us in a breakfast of still warm, fresh bread and jam, prattling happily about their anticipated future – whether the clothes they had would be sufficient, whether the London men would require more heavily painted faces than their present sweet ones – just as though they were girls about to set out for a new school, and once more I marvelled at the education, both in deportment and pleasant manners, that they had been given by the remarkable lady under whose care they had been.

I enquired whether they had been completely happy in the employment she had offered them.

'Indeed so,' said Xanthe. 'Our practical instruction came from two gentlemen of our mistress's acquaintance to whom she brought us at the proper time, and whom she invited to demonstrate to us the duties which she hoped would be both enjoyable and profitable to us. Our masters were of middle age, kind and thoughtful, and with considerate caresses brought us to the full understanding of womanhood, and were so assiduous in proving to us the pleasure we could

enjoy that from the first we were always looking forward to
the next encounter.'

'But do you not sometimes have to entertain those who
are less than courteous and considerate?' I asked.

Of course that was sometimes true, replied Rose, but
most men, she found, were kind if properly wooed, and
Mrs Jopling Rowe had employed Will, from the village, not
only to act as groom, gardener, footman and general help
but always to be present in the house when there were visitors, and to be ready at all times to protect them from any
unpleasantness.

By this time we had finished breaking our fast and the
two girls had slipped off their simple garments and were
reclining for comfort upon the beds at our sides, not one
whit discomfited by the informal nakedness of the group.
And though I could not speak for my friend, my equanimity
was beginning to be affected by the comfortable way in
which Xanthe, at my side, was stroking my chest and belly
with a delightfully soft hand. Then, as the bedclothes slipped
to reveal another limb which seemed more in need of attention, she immediately transferred her courtesies, first
wetting her finger and thumb at her lips and then turning
them round and about the tip of that limb until my entire
middle parts seemed to be one delicious knot of pleasure.

In the meantime, as I in turn caressed her neck, shoulders
and back, I could see that Frank was exploring the rich
contours of Rose's body, who herself was lying now upon
her back with a welcoming and inviting flush enhancing
every limb.

I leaned upon my elbow and attempted to persuade
Xanthe, too, upon her back, but to my surprise she slid
sideways to lie upon her belly, looking with keen invitation
to me – and indeed her backside was a delicious sight, those
narrow hips and that delightful bottom, in downiness and
soft, full colour like a small peach ready for biting, needing
no commendation. Without hesitation I placed my body on
top of hers, nestling those delicious twin spheres against my
belly, then reached beneath to raise her, when she herself
took hold of me and guided me so that I slid into her,
finding the aperture tighter than I expected. She showed
such delight, however, moving with so free and enjoyable a

motion, the gasps of pleasure so freely expressed, that it was with astonishment that I realised only after some minutes – when she took my hand and brought it between her thighs – that I had been persuaded to enter a foreign port, and not that into whose harbour I had intended passage.

Surprising though this was, it now seemed too late for protest, and indeed a final wriggle of that entirely delightful bottom brought me off, while she at almost the same time sighed with pleasure and collapsed upon the pillows!

I glanced over at Frank: he and Rose had evidently been regarding us with interest for some time, and he raised an eyebrow with a quizzical look as he took my eye!

We rose, after a while, and took an early walk upon the cliffs, where Frank expressed himself delighted with the result of our expedition. And when we left, having bade farewell to Mrs Jopling Rowe ('How large the house will seem and how empty, when they have all gone!' she said, sadly), the girls all waved to us with their handkerchiefs, looking forward to a reunion in a short time. It did indeed seem to have been a worthwhile endeavour.

Our talk on our return journey was all of the detail of our plans, and I argued for the inclusion in our band – for it had been Frank's notion that six girls should be the complement – of Miss Riggs, whom I had met in the Haymarket. The other six, while delightful, and quite sufficiently riggish and high-spirited, were all of that polite and genteel mould which might delight most men but could deter others, and we needed one rough diamond among them.

So that evening, when we had bade our farewells to Aspasia and dined, we set out for Whitcombe Street, where Sam Rummidge's coffee-house was as deserted as previously – it seemed he undertook precious little business other than the provision of the upstairs rooms.

Moll, he said, had gone upstairs a few minutes before, but would no doubt be down directly, if we would care to take some coffee. Cups of somewhat unappetising liquid having been set before us, we settled down to wait until Moll and her friend had completed their arrangements. But in ten minutes we were disturbed by the unmistakable sounds of an argument upstairs, which in a moment or two were replaced by screams and the noise of what seemed a fight. We rose and made for the stairs, and without pausing to consider whether we might be breaking in upon some stranger (for we knew not whether Moll was the only woman in the place) we soon attained the room from which the noises were issuing, now more compelling than ever. Charging the door with his shoulder, Frank immediately broke the lock, revealing Moll lying unclothed in a corner of the room and, standing over her, a great ox of a man who, though naked, appeared to be clothed, so thick was the growth of black hair upon his enormous haunches and back, and in whose raised hand was what seemed the leg of a chair. He looked around at the noise of our entry, and in a moment was charging us like a bull. Our minds worked as one: at the last minute we stepped one to each side, then as he passed us took each a hold of a shoulder and administered a shove in the small of his back, whereat he vanished through the doorway and the entire house seemed to shake as he descended the staircase (without, I would guess, touching many of the stairs). Complete silence then fell.

Fearing that perhaps he had been killed, I went to the top of the stairs. Sam Rummidge was standing over the body, and looked up at me:

'Chuck 'is clothes down,' he said, ' 'e's only stunned. I know 'im – from Maiden Lane. Gets like this when 'e's 'ad a few.'

I gathered together an armful of evil-smelling clothes and threw them down the stairs, then shut the door behind me. Frank, meantime, was seeing to Moll, across whose back a darkening weal revealed that one blow at least had found its mark.

Through tears, she apologised for giving us trouble. 'I've just had a bad week, gentlemen,' she said, 'or I'd never have taken him – him always being bad luck. But . . .'

Frank laid a finger on her lips, and together we took her to the bed and wrapped her in the sheet and blanket there, when I went and fetched a dram of brandy, which soon encouraged her to realise that her ordeal was over.

After a while, Frank, with a look in my direction, explained that we had come to ask whether she would care to join a house of pleasure we were setting up in Brook Street, and described the same conditions as had been offered to the girls at Worthing.

She was immediately eager to acquiesce: 'If you two gents are running it,' she said, 'I shall be pleased.'

And could she, Frank asked, live for the next fortnight? But before giving her time to answer, he pressed ten guineas upon her in earnest of our intentions, which she viewed as though he was some prince from a fairy tale, and kissed him full upon the lips with the greatest enthusiasm.

We then left her, on our way out passing Mr Rummidge who was leaning over the great pile of our assailant, now groaning in a corner. He would not, we asked, return to an assault upon Moll, when we were gone?

'No, gen'lmen,' said Sam, 'he's for a drunkard's bed.'

Poor Moll had obviously caught him just at the wrong moment between rage and stupefaction.

Upon leaving Whitcombe Street we walked for a while and then, it coming to rain just as we were passing the Drury Lane Theatre, we slipped in and, finding a couple of seats, saw the final act of Edmund Kean's performance as Richard III. I had myself (as I have recounted elsewhere) some experience of the provincial stage, but never had I been in the presence of such transcendent genius: his vigour was astonishing, his appearance at once handsome, in his carriage, and malevolent, in his character, and the charge of his emotion could be clearly felt throughout that huge theatre, where the flushed faces of the women betrayed a keen interest, and the admiration of the men was not stinted.

After the performance was over and the plaudits had faded, I was hot to pay court to this amazing actor, and persuaded Frank to accompany me to the stage door, where upon slipping the door-keeper half a guinea we joined those who crowded at the door of his dressing room.

There sat that remarkable man, the upper part of his body bare, cleaning the make-up from his face, and attended by what I describe as a blowsy trollope whose person we would not for a moment think of engaging for our house. While she pretended to help him by disposing of the cloths with which he was cleaning his face, her hand could clearly be seen fondling his thigh and more, a fact which roused all the keener spirits in the ladies who were with us, and from whose bodies I could actually feel a glow rising, as though they were animals in heat.

On my expressing astonishment to Frank at the actor's freedom in allowing such attentions in a public place, a man standing next to me remarked that 'twas common with Kean, and that it was a known fact that he always consumed a half-bottle of brandy and a whore, at the side of the stage, between each act. I was inclined at the time to think this a fiction, but have many times since heard it repeated as true.

Having joined with the people in shouting our plaudits – which Mr Kean accepted as though they were his due (which indeed was nothing but the truth) we made our way down the stairs and passed across the stage, where a motley collection of actors and musicians were bidding each other goodnight – the latter bringing me a little shiver of pleasure, for I felt myself to be in a sense one of them, though I had not touched my guitar for many weeks, and I determined to do some practice, for who knew when my adeptness at it might not prove useful?

Frank was all eyes for the actresses, and I had much ado to persuade him against making an approach to one of them, assuring him that for the most part they were respectable girls – unlike those who appeared at some of the unlicensed theatres in town, which he expressed a desire to visit. But that must be for another time.

Chapter Six

Sophie's Story

My task now was first to find a house, and then to equip it to my purpose. I determined when I had discovered a property which suited to sell the house in Frith Street; I could then live in a part of the new property, the better to supervise it, while the funds I would raise from the sale – which should be considerable, the present house being in the heart of the town – added to those I already commanded would enable me to furnish with real luxury.

I was conscious of course of the gamble involved, but determined to try it, and as certain as might be of my success.

So I turned my attention to the newspapers, sending Polly out each morning for *The Daily Advertiser, The Times, The True Briton, The Morning Herald, The Morning Chronicle, The Morning Post* and *The Press*, and again in the evening for *The Star, The Sun, The Courier, The Traveller* and *The Globe*; then, at weekends, came in addition *The General Evening Post, The London Chronicle, The Observer* and *The Weekly Dispatch*. And with all these my time was fully occupied in the evenings, while the days were spent travelling around the outskirts of the city visiting some of the houses advertised for sale and – quite as important – examining each neighbourhood, for it was clear that this should be respectable if I was to attract to the house ladies of discernment, wealth and position – those, in short, not only willing to spend money but capable of finding it.

I had not till now apprehended the varying atmospheres of the suburbs of London, or villages as they still were in the time of which I speak. My first journey was to Hampstead, upon a hill to the north of London. Here, having first lunched at the Spaniard Inn near Caen Wood, the favourite retreat of the Lord Chief Justice Mansfield, Polly and I strode among the delightful villas and elegant mansions which comprise that pleasant district, the variety of whose local situations recommends it to the inhabitants of London as a place of retreat during the summer months and of retirement at the close of life. A great number of houses were to let here as temporary lodgings at prices varying from twenty guineas to two or three a month, and charming they were, often with a view to Windsor Castle, Leith Hill, Boxhill and other places within twenty or thirty miles.

We looked, there, at one spacious villa next to Caen Wood, but it was rather too large for my purposes, and I apprehended at any event that Hampstead was too far from the centre of town for ladies to travel for a few hours' pleasure.

We walked in the sunshine, after our inspection, down to a series of large ponds situated below Caen Wood, which supply Kentish Town, Camden Town and the Tottenham Court Road with water, and there we sat upon a seat for a few moments' rest – when suddenly, out of a green thicket, burst the unclothed bodies of perhaps a dozen youths. It seems they are used to bathing here all year round, and were now enjoying the uncommon warmth of this spring of 1818 and making the most of it. Upon seeing us they were not one whit abashed, though they were of all ages from perhaps ten to twenty, but hurled themselves straight into the water and began to besport themselves. For perhaps five minutes we watched, delighted, the play of golden sunlight upon their young bodies, some swimming upon their faces, the water eddying around their alluring haunches, others paddling upon their backs, when it parted momentarily to show a white, pliant something decorated with weed-like dark hair; then while some continued to play, others climbed onto the bank and lay upon the grass while the sun dried them.

The reader need not imagine that Polly and I turned aside, but took our full opportunity to gaze – 'For', as Polly said, 'a pastoral view is always pleasant to the female eye.'

'What a place for our recruitment!' says Polly. And indeed this was true – but how to approach these boys? Looking down to where not six feet away an entrancing, hard-muscled artisan was half-asleep, beads of moisture sparkling on his broad chest and sturdy thighs (though the skin was made rough by goose pimples) it seemed an ideal opportunity to open with him the topic of his being employed to please ladies (and here were two ready to be pleased!). But at that moment we were startled by the light, warm voice in our ear of another young man who leaned over the back of the seat between us to wish us good day – not a whit embarrassed by the fact that while we were fully dressed, he was completely unclothed, though a bar of the seat did conceal that essential part to which a lady's eyes might otherwise fly.

'You will forgive me, ladies, for remarking that you have come upon an area of the heath normally reserved only for gentlemen,' he said – but with a smile which voided his words of even slight offence.

I opened my lips to apologise, but he raised a hand: 'Please, ma'am, think nothing of it; it is a pleasure to address you.'

I asked whether he and his fellows were usually to be found here.

'Yes, ma'am, some of us throughout the whole year, some only when the spring comes, and on through the summer. It is one of the most agreeable bathing places north of London.'

And what was the employment of the gentlemen, that they could afford to sport themselves during the afternoon?

Some, he said, were local workmen who happened for the moment to be out of employment; some few were gentlemen of no occupation; some youngsters not yet employed.

'But you will excuse me, ladies,' he said. 'I see that my friend has finished his swimming, and we must dress and be away. You will forgive me for not being able to raise my hat to you!'

And giving us a sort of salute by raising a hand to his damp locks, he straightened up and walked off, proudly displaying a body that I – and from her looks, Polly – would have been happy to pay amorous attention to. But he then greeted another young man, similarly in a state of nature, and they walked off towards the brake, arms about each other's waists, and with a lethargic affection in the resting of the fingers of each upon the flesh of the other from which Polly and I assumed that he was not 'pricked out for woman's pleasure', as Shakespeare puts it.

So we rose and made our way back into the city, but determined to make a mental note that the Hampstead Ponds might contain material worth engaging.

Two days later, we travelled similarly to the smaller village of Highgate, at about the same distance from London, but that place does not possess the same variety of prospects, though its views are perhaps superior. A principal road to the north passes through it, which would have been perhaps to our advantage, but it is full of places of entertainment which lower its tone, and though the house we saw there was convenient, we decided against it.

Kew, though enchanting, was too far to the west; Richmond even further – eight miles from Hyde Park Corner, and though the royal gardens attract many visitors, the village itself seemed to be beyond the area we would regard as satisfactory – though one villa there, on the north bank of the Thames just by the elegant bridge, was most attractive.

It was on our way back from Richmond that we paused at Hammersmith to visit Brandenburgh House, once belonging to Prince Rupert and modernised with magnificent additions before being purchased for no less than eighty-five thousand pound by the Margrave of Anspach, who married Lady Craven. On application, we obtained admission to view the house, whose state drawing-room, gallery, hall and library all exhibit marks of princely taste and grandeur. On the west side, near the river, and connected to the house by a conservatory of one hundred and thirty feet in length, is an elegant little theatre where the Margravine occasionally entertains the public with dramatic entertainments, and sometimes gratifies them by exerting her talents both as writer and performer.

It was from one of the windows of Brandenburgh House that I saw a delightful little white villa standing in its own grounds, the garden abutting the Thames, and asked the housekeeper escorting us whose house it was.

The reply came that it had belonged to Sir Nicholas Jocelind, an ancient city merchant long retired but who had died six weeks ago, leaving a family so impoverished that the villa was about to be placed upon the market.

It can be imagined with what speed Polly and I made our apologies to the kindly matron and found our way beyond the theatre to the small iron gates which opened onto a path winding through shrubbery to an enchanting small house, fronted by a handsome entrance flanked by pillars. We knocked at the door, but there was no reply, so we turned the corner of the house and, entering a door in the tall wall which lay on that side the garden, found ourselves in a smaller, private garden entirely sheltered from public view by tall walls, and evidently running down to the river. We knocked at another entrance to the house which advertised itself, but still no reply.

Then as we were turning away, a cry greeted us, from the lips of a sturdy youth across whose shoulder lay a shovel and whose whole body, almost bare, was covered in what seemed black mud. I prepared myself for a brush with a rustic, but when he spoke it was with a fine accent, and in a voice peculiarly vibrant and attractive.

'Ladies,' he said, 'I am sorry not to have been at the door to greet you. I apprehend that Mr Barlow sent you to see the house? I must apologise for my appearance, but I have been working down at the boathouse, which has become clogged with mud during the winter,' and he gestured towards the river. 'However, allow me to admit you, and if you care to explore the building while I make my toilet, I shall be ready to answer any questions.'

His sparkling brown eyes met mine for a moment, for by now he had determined that I was the mistress, Polly merely accompanying me. An open and catching smile flitted across his full lips. Reaching down to overturn a stone by the back door, he revealed a key and, opening the door, stood back to let us enter.

'Please allow yourselves the liberty to explore the house as you wish,' he said. 'I will see you in, let us say, half an hour?' And with this he ushered us through the door, motioning us into the kitchen, and then disappearing along a stone-flagged passage.

The entire house was beautifully furnished, though in a slightly old-fashioned style. In the kitchen pots and pans gleamed as though just now placed upon their shelves; a pantry and capacious cellars were nearby. Along the passage lay a door communicating with the main portion of the villa, through a fine dining-room. From this we passed through a second door which led to a retiring-room which I imagined from the collection of pipes lying in a glass case upon the table the late Sir Nicholas had used as a smoking-room. Returning to the dining-room, we discovered that a third door gave onto the hall just inside the front door – and a similar door opposite led into a capacious sitting room behind which was a music-room with a remarkably finely decorated harpsichord – beautifully in tune, I found as I ran my fingers over its keys – and cabinets of music. Finally, at the back of the villa a library ran the whole width of the building, disclosing a collection of books I longed to examine.

Polly and I looked at each other and smiled.

Turning up the staircase, we examined the five bedrooms which lay there, each happily appointed, with furniture which would entirely fill our needs with the addition of some more comfortable bed-furniture. One door only remained to us, at the back of the house, and opening it we were presented with a view of the young man who had let us in standing in a tub of water, his body streaked like some strange forest beast with black and white stripes and a fine froth of white soap-suds covering his manhood. On seeing us, he hastily turned to present to us a prospect of a back scarcely less interesting, for while he had cleaned the lower part of himself streaks of mud from the upper part had run down covering his arse and the backs of his legs with stripes of black!

'I beg your pardon, sir,' I said – at which he smiled over his shoulder.

'Please,' he said, 'I did invite you to make a complete exploration of the house. This, as you see, was my uncle's bathing room.'

So, he was presumably the master of the house?

'Sir,' I said, 'you are very good. But perhaps I can be of assistance?' – and, turning, I immediately closed the door firmly in Polly's disappointed face. Well, there are certain times when the mistress must take precedence over the maid.

'I am afraid,' the young man said as I advanced, 'that your clothing will be in danger of fouling, for this river mud is very contagious . . .'

The answer to that was patent, and in a moment I had stepped out of my dress, at which he smiled and offered me the cloth with which he had been washing himself, and I took pleasure in passing it over his shoulders and back, then his lower back and legs. As it was removed the mud revealed a body perfectly white, not at all the leathery, brown body of someone used to working in the open air; he then turned, revealing an equally pearly breast, relieved only by twin pinkish nipples almost like those of a young girl – but below, a machine not at all resembling anything appropriate to the female sex, but being reared and ready was most fetching. And when I laid my hand upon it – merely to remove the soap which still surrounded it with a snowy cloud – it proved utterly rigid, like some warm marble – and yet, from the sigh which escaped his lips, still capable of transmitting sensation.

He reached to take me in his arms, but I dodged aside and, lifting the towel from a chair nearby, enveloped him in it and dried each part of him with a gentle but firm pressure which, as my hands passed to and fro over his body, clearly did nothing to assuage the fever which was increasingly gripping him. At last he took the towel from me and, hurling it across the room, enveloped me in a passionate embrace, his lips fixed upon mine and his tongue exploring my mouth as his handsome equipage below found its way between my thighs, where I could feel it a-twitching, eager to explore my lower lips.

In a moment, he picked me up in his arms with a strength his slender frame might not have been thought capable of and, releasing the door, strode into the passage and straight across it into a bedroom – where, we had noticed, a bed lay partially made. Clearly this was his own room, and now he made it mine, showing to its ceiling the most intimate parts of my anatomy as, like a monkey with a nut, he turned me to view every aspect, then to test it with lips and fingers in such a tender display of love-making that it was clear he was no novice. In the end he knelt upon the bed and I sat astride his thighs, my arms about his neck while, with his hands clasping my arse, he raised and lowered me upon his still impervious tool, and we reached a mutual apprehension of pleasure before collapsing exhausted to lie with our heads together on the pillow.

After a while he raised his head and kissed me tenderly upon the lips.

'I need not express in words the pleasure you have afforded me,' he said, and by my smile I let it be known that an equal delight had been mine.

'Perhaps I could ask your name?'

I gave it, then demanded his.

'Philip Jocelind,' he said. 'In fact, Sir Philip, for upon my uncle's recent death I have succeeded both to the title and alas to his debts, for as I think you know – the family fortune, or lack of it, compels me to sell this villa.'

In a few words he gave me his history. Orphaned at an early age he had been brought up by his uncle, his only blood relative; had left university, travelled to Italy, and returned to England only in time to be present at his uncle's death-bed, and to learn that the old man had died leaving no funds whatsoever, but only the family's house, which now he was forced to place upon the market.

'I am reluctant to do so,' he said, 'but I have no money, and while I discover how to earn some, must live!'

'Perhaps,' I said, 'we could come to some arrangement, for this house would be ideal for a business purpose I have . . .'

'Which was why you obtained an order to view from Barlow?' he asked.

I explained that I knew nothing of the agent, but had simply happened upon the villa, and asked whether he would consider a scheme whereby I would either rent or buy the house, but perhaps – if he approved my scheme – he could remain in it in some capacity.

He was of course agog, and taking perhaps some slight risk of his disapproval – but doing so in the confidence that the events of the past hour had denoted him a young man of spirit – I explained my plan.

As I had hoped, he was interested, amused and finally enthusiastic, and offered that we might dine together to discuss the matter further – whereupon we recovered our clothes and found Polly amusing herself in the library with a number of books on marriage customs among the Indian tribes of North America. She raised an eyebrow as we entered, and was clearly understanding of the situation, but when I explained that Sir Philip might be of help to us was all too happy. And after I had introduced her and she had been greeted by the young man (I was glad to see) with a warmth completely free of condescension, we made off for town and the Royal Hotel and Tavern in Pall Mall, which Sir Philip said the nobility and gentry found the finest of its kind, with the choicest viands and every luxury in season. There we bespoke a table and settled down to discussion.

Our new friend proved entirely sympathetic to our scheme and intensely interested in the practicalities of it; he had no doubt, he said, of its success, and would be delighted to engage himself to help us. When I expressed some surprise that a gentleman of title should be prepared to turn his talents in such a direction, he laughed and said that he saw no difference between Sir Franklin Franklyn running a brothel in Brook Street for the entertainment of men (for I had told him of Frank's enterprise) and Sir Philip Jocelind running one in Hammersmith for that of women – with which we were forced to concur.

Seizing a napkin and producing a pencil, he immediately began sketching a number of possible alterations to Riverside Lodge (as his villa was called): his uncle's retiring-room, he said, could be made into a sitting room for the lads, and between it and the dining-room might be broken a sort of window in which a screen could be inserted – 'Not unlike,' he said, 'those screens which the Moors have in their palaces to protect their women from the view'. It would be of pierced wood, so that with one room kept dark, anyone standing in it could look into the other and contemplate those inhabiting it without themselves being seen!

I had obviously found someone with much my own notions and very much my own enthusiasm. But what about our stable of stallions, as I put it to him, which much amused him.

'Well,' he said, 'of course it would be possible to find temporary staff of that kind; there are young men in uniform who will be pleased to take an evening in Hammersmith once or twice a week, when their duties allow, and who at the moment are reduced to working the Parks . . .'

And what, I asked, did that mean?

He explained that St James's Park in particular was a known place where any Miss Molly could pick up a lad who would permit him a fondle, or even for a sufficiently large consideration, offer the double jugg . . .

At this I had to invite a translation, to Polly's amusement, and she explained in a low voice that Sir Philip was talking of those men who enjoyed carnal amusement with their own sex, and whose particular pleasure was intercourse with the only male aperture capable of receiving them – something I had heard of and, had I been quicker, might have apprehended. However:

'Most of these boys simply lie down for the money,' said Sir Philip, 'playing a part while thinking of their female friends; they would, I am certain, be happier in your establishment.'

'But,' I said, 'would it not be better to build a more regular stable, so that ladies who wished to return could be sure of finding their favourites?'

He took my point, but wondered how it could be achieved, though he was sure some way could be found if only (he suggested) by my own and Polly's efforts at exploration, something to which he guessed we would not be entirely averse.

At this point we were interrupted by a voice at my shoulder – it was that of Chichley, who had just entered with an extremely beautiful, dark young lady, splendidly dressed, on his arm.

'My dear,' he said to her, 'may I present Mrs Sophia Nelham and Mrs Playwright – Mrs Nelham, this is Lady Frances Brivet.'

We rose, and I introduced Sir Philip.

'Lady Frances and I have just announced our engagement in marriage,' Chichley said, with a look whose meaning I alone could apprehend – a mixture of public pride and silent rebuke. I wished them joy, not perhaps without some hint of melancholy, and they were conducted to a table not far from us.

Sir Philip was curious; he had heard something of Chichley at Cambridge, who it seems had a reputation as something of a mother's boy, and had never joined in that exploration of the connections between the sexes which has ever been an essential part of a university education. I refrained from informing him that the young man's education was now in a fair way to being completed, and both Polly and I listened with amusement to the sympathies Sir Philip expressed towards Lady Frances in her engagement to a eunuch. Only an exchange of glances between us conveyed our mutual suspicion that if that lady was marrying Chichley in the belief that she would be spared the task of sharing his bed, she would be disappointed – though her appearance being decidedly cool and haughty, I wondered to what extent he would be satisfied.

But we returned then to our plans, and continued our discussion of the best way to use the space which would be available to us at Riverside Lodge. Sir Philip was of the opinion that some of the upstairs rooms should be made into luxurious accommodation for those ladies who might wish a prolonged stay, while the library might be divided into four or five small closets to accommodate those who merely wished an evening's entertainment.

'I do not see,' he said, 'why you should not offer weekend parties, in the summer. The gardens are most attractive, there is a corner of the river which runs through the private grounds and where bathing can take place, and it may be that some ladies whose husbands are perhaps a-travelling or otherwise engaged, would be pleased to spend two or three days from home in the company of agreeable men.'

This seemed to me to be an excellent idea, though it introduced some new notions – as of providing meals, and so on – which I had not previously considered.

Sir Philip declined to discuss the terms on which I might purchase or hire his villa. That, he said, was a matter for his agent, for his uncle had died leaving many debts which he was under some obligation to pay – 'otherwise I would of course be happy should you wish it to come in with you upon equal terms'.

Then what part did he think of playing in our affair? I asked.

'That is largely a matter for yourself,' he said. 'My own

susceptibility to the ladies is well-known to my familiars, yet I am not sure I would wish to sell my charms, such as they are, upon the open market.'

'It seems to me that we will need no protector,' said Polly, 'as a female house might do – at least, not in the usual sense. Yet it might be that we will need a peacemaker among the young men themselves, for it is not always the case that the male sex, any more than the female, is able to resist argument and even quarrelling when in a close confinement.'

'Then may I not be your major-domo, so to speak?' asked Sir Philip. 'To see to the general running of the house, as well as supervising the young men? If it were convenient, I could continue to occupy my room and another could be reserved for yourself. This would still leave three for the use of long-stayers, while in the attic (which I believe you did not see) the former servants' quarters are remarkably comfortable and capacious, and I am sure that Mrs Playwright would be happy there. It is even the case that, were the demand great, you and I could occupy other rooms there – it might at all events be well to have them made ready.'

Our conversation was broken off from time to time as the waiters appeared with dish after dish, for Sir Philip was clearly determined that he should show us the greatest hospitality: cod's head and shoulders was followed by boiled turkey and celery sauce, then by roast woodcock, and finally by a large selection of fruit, while he plied us first with champagne and then with Constantia, and now with Sauterne and port. As the cloth was withdrawn, he asked for paper to be brought.

'And now,' he said, 'we must plan our advertisement.'

Polly and I glanced at each other: he now clearly saw himself as part of our company, but we said nothing – we would discuss it later.

He sat writing silently for some time, which I spent watching the ladies and gentlemen around us – including Chichley and Lady Frances, who seemed completely preoccupied with each other. Yet from time to time her eyes fell elsewhere and I caught a glance or two from him which spoke still of some regret . . .

Finally, Sir Philip threw down his pencil and handed me the paper; in fine, clear handwriting I read the following:

AN ANNOUNCEMENT TO ALL LADIES FATIGUED BY THE INDOLENCE OF THEIR HUSBANDS

I have purchased extensive and luxurious premises situate within a few miles of the centre of town, entered discreetly by a private way near a place often frequented by ladies of complete respectability.

Within a handsome villa has been contrived a large saloon contiguous with boudoirs most elegantly and commodiously fitted up. In this saloon are to be seen the finest men of their species I can procure, occupied in whatever amusements are adapted to their taste, and all kept in a high state of excitement by good living and idleness. Some fine, elegantly dressed young men play at cards, music, &c, while others, more athletic, wrestle or otherwise sport themselves, in a state of perfect nudity. In short, there is such a variety of the animal that no lady can fall short of suiting her inclinations.

A lady need never enter the saloon, but views the inmates from behind a darkened screen. Having fixed on the man she would like to enjoy, she has only to ring for the chambermaid, call her to the screened window, point out the object, and he is immediately brought to the boudoir in which she is installed. She can enjoy him in the dark, or have a light; masks are provided for those who wish to preserve a complete anonymity.

A lady may stay for an hour or a night, and have one or a dozen men as she pleases, without being known to any of them. A lady of seventy or eighty years of age can enjoy at pleasure a fine, robust youth of twenty, and to elevate the mind to the sublimest raptures of love, every boudoir is surrounded with the most superb paintings of Aretino's Postures after Julio Romano and Ludovico Carracci, interspersed with large mirrors; also a sideboard covered with the most delicious viands and richest wines.

The greatest possible pains have been taken to preserve order and regularity, and it is impossible that any discovery can take place by the intrusion of the watch or enraged cuckolds. No male creature other than those occupied in the business is admitted into any part of the temple (other than the trusted, tried and appointed functionaries who are well paid for their services, and not let in to gratify curiosity).

The expense of this Institution, which has been notable, is defrayed by a subscription from each lady of one hundred guineas per annum, with the exception of refreshments, which are to be paid for at the time.

Having thus made it my study to serve my own sex in a most essential point, I trust to their liberality for encouragement in my arduous undertaking and am, Ladies, your most obedient servant.

Sophia Nelham

It must be admitted that I was most impressed by this document – though upon reading it my first thought was that the preparation of the place would strain my finances to the utmost. Sir Philip clearly saw this, for he hastened to point out that the terms of no advertisement coincided entirely with the thing advertised, and that there were ways of making the most luxurious impression without too great a cost with low lighting and other similar devices.

And the sum asked as a subscription? Would this not be too great? Here, I found Polly and our friend at one: the former confirmed that, on the evidence of her sister, there were many ladies to whom a hundred guineas was a slender sum, and the latter insisted that the charge suggested was moderate, and the lowest possible upon which the place could be properly run.

Clearly, Polly and I should now discuss the matter of Sir Philip's involvement in our project; that he was a prime gallant, a considerate and inspiriting lover, and a knowledgeable gentleman, were not in question, but did we wish to employ him? Clearly, someone whom we had first seen grubbing out a river was not a man to stand on ceremony, nor to be afraid of work, and provided he showed no inclination to take over the entire organisation of Riverside Lodge, all would be well.

I nodded to Polly, and rose to my feet. But she was blushing, and was slow in following my example – from which I believed that my foot was not the only one to have felt the pressure of his, beneath the covers.

A man came hastening with the bill for the evening's entertainment which he offered to Sir Philip, who took it with some embarrassment, and I realised that he was incapable of paying it – as indeed I might have realised had I given the matter any thought. The freedom with which he had pressed us to eat, and with which he himself had enjoyed food and wine, now took on a slightly different complexion. But I was not angry and, having settled up, we found ourselves in the street and I bade him farewell with a good spirit.

He shifted uneasily upon his feet, however. 'It is somewhat late to make my way back to Hammersmith,' he said softly, 'and to a cold and lonely house . . .'

I was still comfortably reminiscent of the entertainment he had offered only a few hours ago, but could see that Polly would be gratified by any offer he might make, and so said that if he wished to walk with us to Frith Street he could perhaps find a chair in which to spend the night.

And so we walked back in the evening air, one of us on each side of him, and our arms through his. And when we had reached the house and he had admired it sufficiently, a silence fell, which I broke: 'I am now for my bed, sir, if you will excuse me. Polly, perhaps I may leave you to find Sir Philip a corner in which to sleep?' – and took my leave.

As I settled into my bed, I heard not one but two sets of footsteps making a quiet way up to Polly's room, above my own, and as I sank into an undisturbed slumber, could not but hear, though quietly expressed, those sounds which escape from a man and woman engaged in that comfortable activity to which we are all delighted to address ourselves with an agreeable companion.

Chapter Seven

The Adventures of Andy

Over the next few weeks, Frank was much engaged at the house supervising the workmen in interpreting his plans and revealing, I must confess, an application and talent for detail which I had not suspected in him. Meanwhile, Aspasia had obtained from Mrs Jopling Rowe the measurements of the five young ladies of her Worthing establishment, and had commissioned a number of dresses for them (at Frank's expense) which were intended for a surprise which would both gratify them and please their eventual partners.

I was invited to obtain the measurements of Moll Riggs, and went off to Sam Rummidge's to find that she had not been seen since our last encounter, and indeed had announced her retirement from business on account of coming into a large fortune (by which I assumed she referred to the present we had made her). After some persuasion, and since I was her particular friend, he directed me to her address, which was in the neighbourhood of St Giles, close by Seven Dials, of which I had no previous knowledge.

I reached it from the Strand by walking up the narrow street of St Martin's Lane – and there to my surprise encountered none other than Blatchford, our coachman, in company with another young fellow whose face was not known to me, and who was introduced as Bob Tippett, a Cockney who worked (as I gathered) on the edges of criminality, never quite descending to rob, but not shy of a little sharp practice, and whose acquaintance Blatchford had cultivated for the sake of getting to know London and its ways better. They were spending the morning, he said, in just this way of exploration, for Tippett was pointing out to him some of the notorious sharks and thieves of the area.

Asked if I would care to join them for an hour, I acquiesced, for my own education in the ways of the city was sadly lacking. First, we were taken into a beer shop, and there over a pot of ale several gentry were pointed out to us, among them a quiet, intelligent looking man who was a distinguished coiner just released from ten years' penal servitude for coining and passing base coin. With him was his friend and assistant, who watched out that no officers of justice were near while the coining was performed, and carried the bag of base money when they went out to sell it at low prices – five shillings worth being usually sold for tenpence.

Tippett explained that apart from selling base coin, it was easily 'passed' by one man offering a shopkeeper a good sovereign to be changed, which would be 'rung' upon the counter and found true. The coiner would then discover he had change after all and did not need it, pocketing the true coin. But then, he would find that in fact he had not sufficient small coins, and would produce a false sovereign which the shopkeeper would generally change without testing it.

Leaving the beer shop, we walked to Bow Street, where Tippett pointed out three young pickpockets, who looked like well-dressed costermongers, in dark cloth frock coats and caps. Then we saw a fashionably-dressed man arm-in-arm with a companion, dressed out with watch-chains and rings; they seemed pleasant and friendly, and as I caught the eye of one of them he paused to ask if we would accompany them to a gin-palace nearby. But Tippett shook his head, and we passed along – he then explained that they were well-known card-sharpers looking out for rooks. A young man of the most engaging appearance and tasteful in dress, he pointed out as a burglar; then came two more pickpockets dressed in suits of superfine black cloth cut in fashionable style, who were entering an elegant dining-room. And nearby, another expert burglar of about twenty-four years of age, standing at the corner of the street – his friend, Tippett explained, had been taken from his side about a fortnight ago on a charge of burglary.

Moll's address was at a house in Church Lane, a narrow street which at first seemed decked out for carnival. But we soon saw that the wooden rods suspended across the street from windows on the second and third floors bore nothing more festive than clothes set out to dry – cotton gowns, sheets, trousers, drawers and vests, some ragged and patched, others old and faded. The street itself was crowded, groups of the lower orders sometimes drinking and laughing, sometimes merely standing and watching each other with what seemed an air of suspicion – though all seemed reasonably clean and orderly.

Here were several lodging-houses – out of some of which landlords made an unconscionable profit. Tippett pointed out one house, number twenty, which had been let for twenty-one pound a year, then re-let in separate rooms for ninety, and finally again let by parties who made a total of over one hundred and fifty pound – the demand for rooms was such that this could easily be done despite the general poverty of the area, which forced many young women into prostitution of the most desperate kind.

The house at which I was told Moll had her rooms was evidently a lodging-house, and, having bade farewell with thanks to my friends, I entered through a basement kitchen (for the front door had evidently been unused for many years, and looked as though no force could open it) where several people were gathered around a group of tables, so that it resembled almost an eating house; some were reading, others pipe-smoking, yet others supping on potatoes, bread and fish. Others lay asleep, perhaps drunken.

Upon asking for Miss Riggs, I was directed to the second floor, and climbed three sets of narrow stairs, finding myself on a dark landing with a choice of three doors. I tapped upon one, which was opened by a young woman at whose breast a large child was assiduously sucking; she pointed to one of the other doors, at which I knocked, and hearing what I took for an invitation to enter I walked into a small room crowded with furniture, but mainly occupied by a large bed upon the pillows of which two heads lay, one of them Moll's.

Muttering an apology, I made to leave, but Moll, sitting up with a fine disregard for decency (she being unclothed), welcomed me by name, then dealt her companion a dig in the ribs with an elbow, whereupon a surprised youth of perhaps sixteen sat up beside her.

'Why Mr Archer,' says Moll, 'what a pleasure to see you! May I present –' then she giggled, aware no doubt that neither the time nor the place required formality, and went on – ' 'Tis my brother George, sir. George, get along out of it!' Whereon the youth threw back the covers, jumped from bed, thrust a tattered pair of trousers over his nakedness and, taking up a shirt, pushed past me to the door, muttering something under his breath which I did not catch.

'George works nights, sir,' said Moll. I thought it best not to enquire what at. 'Well, now, am I to rise, or will you join me?' she asked – a question which I answered by sitting upon the bed and informing her that I had come merely to ask her for her measurements – a request which seemed to nonplus her, and indeed which seemed at first incapable of answering, since she had no idea of a tape measure, nor any notion of her girth or height.

We solved the problem by my discovering a number of pieces of string lying upon the floor. Throwing back the covers, she passed one first around her waist, knotting it to indicate length; then another about her breasts; a third from shoulder to ankle; a fourth from shoulder to wrist. Upon her asking whether any other dimension was required, I was unable to answer, but in play she then undertook to examine my dimensions, which required the removal of my clothing and culminated in the measurement of my proper male parts, which I demur from recording for fear of being accused of pride – and which she then requested should be put to a proper use. I had some reservations about her cleanliness, and half thought I should wait until I could ensure it, but at that moment a tremendous noise arose in the street and, curious, Moll rose from her bed and went to the window, throwing it up and leaning out, displaying as she did so that entrancing open triangle between thighs and cunny which so distinguishes the fair sex – and which was so inviting that I could not resist coming behind her to close the void, an action which from the delicious wriggling of her body, she did not at all resent.

So busy did I become at pleasuring us both, that I failed

to recollect that we were displaying ourselves quite clearly
to anyone who wished to see, and was reminded only by a
cheer from below, whereupon I saw that the crowd which
had previously been giving its attention to a street brawl
had had its notice directed to us by one sharp-eyed boy, and
was now entirely aware of what was going on, encouraging
us by ribaldries the nature of which I would not wish to
offend any lady readers by recording. Moll was nothing
loath, not even troubling to conceal her breasts with her
hands, but waved to her friends, then lowered her head so
that my own action could be the more readily observed,
which attracted a renewed cheer.

This, alas, had the opposite effect upon me than Moll
might have expected, for instantly my courage and my
prick failed, the one leading me to withdraw to the interior
of the room, and the latter reducing itself to the proportions of a peascod. Moll, I regret to say, was ill-tempered at
this, though no less ill-tempered than I, who blamed her for
the disruption of our passion. She tried to make amends by
falling to her knees and attempting to rouse me again to
enthusiasm, but failed, whereupon I gathered up my pieces
of string and bade her a cool farewell – sent on my way by
waggish remarks from some still gathered in the street as I
left the house, which put me in no more pleasant a temper.
Ere I reached Hanover Square, I regretted the frigidity of
my farewell, and could not resist chuckling at the memory
of the situation in which I had, after all, placed myself;
finding Blatchford in the street outside our rooms, I sent
him back to Moll with half a guinea and a cheering word. I
learned much later that she had taken the money for his
own, and encouraged him to finish the job I had started.
But his honesty in the end led him to admit my message,
which comforted her considerably, for she had feared that
my ill-temper signalled perhaps the intention not to employ
her in Brook Street. It occurred also to me that Bob Tippett
might make an admirable addition to our household, for it
would be too much to expect Blatchford to be the only man
concerned with the work of stoking the stove, keeping an
eye on any visitors who might be difficult, and having also
to continue his duties as coachman and general factotum to
Frank and myself.

In time the day came when our young ladies were to join us. Frank and I made our way around to Brook Street after breakfast, to find Blatchford in the hallway. He had already admitted Moll, who had arrived, he said, at nine o'clock by hackney coach, with nothing but what seemed like an old tablecloth stuffed with soft goods. Upon Frank's enquiry, it proved to contain what clothes the girl possessed, and he persuaded her to place them in the corner of an upstairs room, to be inspected by Aspasia when she arrived, for he suspected that the new wardrobe to be provided would supply her entire needs.

Bob Tippett, who had also arrived, had been entertaining Moll with some ribaldry in the hall. But now she was much overcome by the splendour of the sitting room in its full glory, and even in the cold morning light (for the windows were now curtained and admitted the sun, the candles only to be lit when darkness fell) it looked sufficiently imposing. Frank and I were in the hallway, where he was showing me the small but comfortable cubicle constructed there for Aspasia's use, when an incoherent cry from the sitting room brought us back, and we found Moll looking with a mixture of respect, fear and admiration from the window. When we joined her, we saw Aspasia climbing from the chair she had hired, for she enjoyed that rather old-fashioned mode of transport during the daytime, it being capable through using the pavements of avoiding the press of traffic in the public street.

Having admitted our friend, we introduced Moll with feelings perhaps as tentative as her own, for although Aspasia had agreed with us that in theory at least one girl of rather rougher origins would be an excellent addition to the house, we wondered whether she and Moll would hit it off. But had reckoned without the fact that Aspasia, while a made rather than a born lady, entirely lacked those false airs and attitudes which the imitation aristocrat too often assumes, and soon they were chattering away comfortably, and on Moll's part with an enthusiasm she had not revealed even to us.

It was in late afternoon that at the Swan, Charing Cross, we greeted the stage from Brighthelmstone. Our party of young ladies comprised most of the passengers, some inside, some out. The girls outside were accompanied by Will Pounce, their servant and chaperone (and Constance's favourite) who, quite frankly, I had completely forgot. One bemused merchant who had spent the ride inside crushed between Rose and Cissie emerged with the look upon his face of one who has seen visions. The girls' excitement was such that it was almost impossible to control them, and it was all Blatchford and I could do to keep them from rushing off instantly into the streets. Finally, however, we persuaded them into three hackneys, together with their luggage, and conveyed them (hanging half out of the windows in order to see as much of the city as possible) to Brook Street, where the house silenced them immediately with its grandeur – not, indeed, that their home in Worthing had not been sufficiently capacious, but Mrs Jopling Rowe's taste had been that of a previous era, and the furnishings here almost appalled her pupils by their sophistication.

Frank and I stepped aside to discuss Will Pounce, whom he too had forgot. We could scarcely turn him away, we agreed, for not only had we in a sense promised employment, but there would be difficulties with Constance, his friend, and probably with the other girls, for they were used to his company and protection. And after all Bob Tippett was still rather an unknown quantity to us. So we instructed Blatchford to obtain accommodation for him in the house where he himself lodged, and decided to use him as a general handyman.

Leaving the girls in Aspasia's care, Frank and I made off for dinner at Dolly's Beef-Steak House in King's Head Court, and then spent the evening walking around to some other eating places frequented by gentlemen of a certain tone – the Marlborough Head at Bishopsgate (where the gentlemen of South Sea House are accustomed to dine), Guidon's French eating house in Poland Street, the Constitution in Bedford Street, et cetera. And by dint of dropping half a guinea here and there we were able to persuade the waiters to take a supply of the cards which Frank had had printed, and which simply gave the Brook Street address, the words 'Sympathetic female company assured', and, in one corner, 'Under the supervision of Madam Aspasia', which we were decided would be advertisement enough. Across several of these had been stamped the words 'Premier opening', followed by the date and the promise of free wine and eatables.

A few days later – twenty-four hours before the official opening of the doors – I dined at the Royal Hotel and Tavern with Sir Philip Jocelind, a young acquaintance of Sophia's; we were to act the parts of visitors to Brook Street, to be received as strangers (which indeed he was) in order to test the girls' behaviour no less than the conveniences of the stablishment.

After two bottles of claret and a few glasses of port – for strangely enough, I found myself a little nervous at the coming experience – we arrived at the house at nine o'clock and knocked upon the door, which was opened to us by Pounce, looking somewhat uncomfortable in a handsome footman's dress, though with hair unpowdered in order to establish a certain informality. Bidden to enter, we were received by Aspasia, handsomely dressed completely in black, relieved only by the glitter of her personal jewellery.

'Welcome, gentlemen,' she said. 'May I outline to you the rules of the house? A fee of five guineas will introduce you to the lady of your choice, comprehend accommodation for no more than three hours, and include also the use of our heated rooms, unique to this city, and as introduced by the establishment in imitation of the hot baths of Turkey, much admired by visitors to that place.'

Having counterfeited to hand over our guineas, we were shown by Aspasia to the sitting room, lit now by candles, in which seven of the most charming ladies imaginable sat. I scarcely recognised my former friends, so altered were they; the simple clothes they had worn before had been put aside in favour of charmingly modern dress, enhancing their beauty so that one could not but admire Aspasia's taste, who had chosen it.

None was altered so much, it may be imagined, as Moll, whose fresh, forthright charms were now emphasised by the low neck of a rich crimson gown which cleverly lay between the reserved and the forward, close-cut to emphasise the charms of her body while at the same time artfully concealing what it most seemed to promise.

Ginevra's rosy, delicate skin was set off to great advantage by a pale pink *crêpe* dress, her dimpled arms quite uncovered and encircled with elegant but simple bracelets composed of plaited hair. There was a voluptuous and purely effeminate languor about her character which made her infinitely graceful – as indeed was Rose, darker than Ginevra, whose skin was of quite as delicate a texture, but without its vermilion tinge, and the blue veins less defined; she wore a dress of white silvered *lamé*, on gauze, with a Turkish turban of bright blue, fringed with gold. The large, straight, gauze sleeve did not at all conceal the symmetry of her graceful arms. Xanthe wore a yellow satin dress, fastened round the waist with a gold band. Her profuse yellow locks were entirely unadorned, and her neck, arms and fingers were devoid of decoration, relying entirely on the loveliness of their shape to impress. Constance's dress was of figured white French gauze over white satin, making her dark skin seem even more voluptuously strange and attractive, and she wore a delightful pair of earrings which emphasised the perfect oval of her face.

But I cannot give over more space to description of the appearance of our nymphs; without having met any of the young women, Aspasia had cleverly provided a dress for each which not only suited her character but was a comment upon it. And I could imagine no spirited young man who would not stand – as Sir Philip and I did – undecided who he would be most delighted to entertain, for it was a constituent of the ladies' elegant appearance that one felt instantly that we were to distinguish them by our favours, rather than the other way about.

After a moment or two, Aspasia took us by the arms and withdrew us into the hall.

'Gentleman, have you made your choice?' she asked.

Sir Philip announced for Sally while I chose Xanthe. Aspasia nodded.

'Pounce will show you downstairs, and they will join you,' she said.

Downstairs, we were invited to divest ourselves of our clothing, Pounce showing himself sufficiently polite and helpful, though indifferently perfect in folding our clothes, which he threw over his arm and disappeared with as, wrapped in two large sheets of towel, we were directed to the hot room. Blatchford had evidently been at work all day, for the place was full of steam and of a pleasant, determined heat, so that in a moment we had thrown our towels aside, made our way over the floor to the baths, and lowered ourselves into them – one to each.

'I did not know that your friend had travelled in the east,' said Sir Philip.

He had not, I explained, but had constructed the baths in counterfeit of those he had seen illustrated from Pompeii. My new friend offered his congratulations, and lay back with a sigh of pleasure – for which he had additional cause in a moment, when the two girls stepped into the room, themselves also divested of their clothing and wrapped in towelling, which fell gracefully to the floor as they joined us in the baths.

The heat had already created a certain lethargy, and the sight of the two beauties in rosy nakedness added to the delight of our pleased senses, so that our immediate desire was to rise and take them to the place where we might embrace them. This they were not averse to and, indeed, we were to learn that one of the advantages of the hot room was that even gentlemen chilled from the night air, or who for some other reason were not in an amorous mood, were speedily raised to a state of passion requiring immediate slaking, which resulted in a speedier turnover of custom than might otherwise have been the case.

So, we rose to our feet and I saw that Sir Philip was as disposed to *amour* as myself, and were led to the warm room, and to benches covered in more loose towelling and forms of cushions. Here, we were invited to lie while Xanthe and Sally took bowls of warm water and soap, and with them washed our lower parts, not without certain gestures and caresses which raised our expectations of delight even further – so much so in my case, I must admit, that I was forced to dissuade Xanthe from her work and complete my toilet with my own hands, lest I should in a moment betray her and myself. Sir Philip, I saw from the corner of my eye, had no such inhibitions, and lying upon Sally's bosom was massaging her body with his own, his prick pleasuring itself upon her belly while he nibbled the lower parts of her ears so that she already gasped with pleasure.

Now, wiped dry with more towels, for a while we lay with our ladies while still the heat was upon us, our skins slippery with perspiration which had almost the effect of oil, and offered a delightful pinguidity to the palms of the hands.

After a while, they rose to their feet, wrapped their towels about them, and led us upstairs, where now hangings tactfully hid us from the gaze of anyone entering from the street, to the suite of retiring-rooms upstairs, where we parted, Sir Philip and Sally going into one, myself and Xanthe into another. Here was a fine painting upon one wall of a handsome girl lying upon her back, her legs thrown over the shoulders of a bearded warrior who was about to penetrate her with a vigorous instrument to which she showed no aversion.

Handing me to the bed and taking my towel from me, Xanthe enquired whether I found the room cold. On the contrary, heated as I was, the cold air playing upon my body was charming, and I felt a new vigour upon me as she removed her own towel and asked me, now, whether there was any particular game I wished to play? None, I replied, but that which would give her equal pleasure with myself – upon which she lay down at my side and began to stroke my body with her pliant hands, gradually moving closer and closer to the centre of my being, until, reaching it at last, she joined lips to fingers in raising my emotions once more to a pitch.

After a while, wishing to delight her – for it has ever been part of my pleasure in making love that the object of my desire should also experience some luxury – I raised myself, turned until my head was towards her feet and, kneeling with my knees each side of her body, bent so that my tongue could play about her belly and thighs before making its way to that delightful aperture where sensuality is concentrated. Meanwhile, she was able by raising her head only slightly to take me into her mouth, while her hands remained free to rove over my body, stimulating my breast and sides, then sliding over my back and reaching my loins, to play within the crack of my arse, producing a sensation which made me stretch my thighs wide to welcome her exploring fingers.

By now, she was panting delightedly, and finally almost threw me off before placing herself in a position mimicking that of the woman in the fresco, whereat it was the work of a moment for me to raise myself and become part of her body. And so happy were we both at the union that it was after only three or four motions of my loins that we collapsed upon the bed with a mutual expression of bliss.

We lay for a while in a state of pleasant lethargy, when I became consumed with curiosity to see what was happening elsewhere in the house and looked about for my clothes. Xanthe explained that I could ring for them, but produced from a small cupboard two charming robes of silk which, she said, were provided for those who wished merely to lie for a while and relax, perhaps with some food and drink, which also a ring of the bell would bring. But that evening, it being a purely private one, there would be food downstairs – upon which she led me down to the sitting room, where Frank and Aspasia had joined the girls, and the company greeted us with a cheer, at which I fear a blush rose to my cheeks.

A table had now been set up on which was a selection of cold dishes, together with red, white and rosy wine, glasses of which were pressed upon us. After a while, Constance approached Frank, and asked whether her friend Will might not be sent a glass.

'I had quite forgot!' said Frank. 'Please fetch him, and Blatchford and Tippett. They can let the fire out, and may certainly join us.'

While we ate and drank, he and Aspasia questioned me closely upon my experience of the house, the appointments of which I had no criticism to offer. Certainly Pounce's manner had been a little rough, but time and experience would cure that, and the hot rooms had been a notable success.

'Yes, I count on them to become a talking point,' said Frank. And when Sir Philip and Rose joined us, clad also in silk gowns, he, similarly, had nothing but praise to offer, of the appointments and conduct of the house.

Pounce, Blatchford and Tippett now joined us – a curious looking trio, for Pounce was in full footman's uniform, Tippett in ordinary day dress, and Blatchford was merely clad in a shirt undone to the waist and thin pantaloons (for he had been attending the fire all evening).

We attacked the food with enthusiasm, washing it down with generous draughts, and then Frank invited me to provide a little music. I slipped out and fetched in my guitar, which I had not played for some weeks, but I was soon able to produce a tune or two, to the delight of the ladies.

By this time Tippett had removed his coat and Pounce, his footman's jacket discarded and his wig hung upon the corner of a chair, had Constance upon his knee, his hand in her bosom.

'Pounce,' said Frank with imitated severity, 'your friend's gown was extremely expensive, and I shall be severely displeased if it is made dirty.'

Pounce looked suitably discouraged.

'Yes, sir,' he said, removing his hand, at which Constance pouted.

'Would it not be best if Miss Constance removed it?'

Both parties brightened at this, and standing for a moment, Constance stepped out of her gown before replacing herself upon Pounce's knee, but soon began to wriggle upon it in a strange manner, as though something was making her uncomfortable – or perhaps was instilling some pleasure . . .

Frank had clearly determined that everyone in the house should feel at ease, for he now, without false modesty, simply removed his own clothing and, inviting Aspasia to do the same, took her in his arms and began a waltz. Within a very short time a ballum-rancum had begun – as Tippett called it – the Cockney name for a dance at which the dancers were altogether unclothed. Frank danced with Aspasia, Pounce with Constance, Tippett had taken Sally in his arms while Sir Philip was embracing Cissie; Xanthe and Rose were in each other's embrace, breast to breast, while Moll and Ginevra were seated one on each side of me, Ginevra admiring my fingering while her arm was about my neck and her lips fumbling my ear, and Moll showing her own adept fingering at quite another instrument.

In due course the lascivious movement of the waltz had brought Tippett and Sally to a point at which they simply sank to the floor in each other's arms, whereupon Frank announced that for this occasion everyone was free to make use of the rooms provided – and though Tippett and his friend were now in too close an embrace to be capable of rising without discomfort, the party broke up. Despite the ministrations of my two angels I was not yet myself ready for a second bout, so excusing myself I simply wandered from basement to attics, bringing the sound of my guitar within earshot of the lubricious couples, who in their eagerness to embrace had neglected to close their doors. Within the finest of the upstairs rooms, Frank was deeply engaged with Aspasia – the older woman's embraces proving, it seemed, ever more attractive to him despite the younger flesh which had been all about him. Indeed, as she half-lay, half-sat upon the bed, his head between her thighs, her wonderfully prominent breasts rising and falling in her passion, she was a noble sight. Passing on to the next chamber, I saw – nay, heard – Cissie at the height of pleasure, yelping as Sir Philip, once more in full vigour, which I envied him, bucked between her legs like a young and untamed colt.

Pounce and Constance lay in a quieter embrace in the third chamber, his body almost as brown as hers – though a white band appeared about his loins, for unlike her he, working in the open rather than merely lying in the sun, had been used to be covered in case of prying eyes. Aroused by these country sights, I beckoned with my head to Ginevra, who was with me, to come to the fourth room – which I had occupied with Xanthe – only to find on reaching the door that it was already taken by Xanthe who, still warm from my embrace, was now locked in delighted combat with her friend Rose, lying head to toe, each with her free-flowing hair enveloping the loins of the other, their hands tightly clasped about each other's buttocks, which themselves were moving in unmistakable rhythm.

Reaching around me, Ginevra pulled the door quietly shut, and without a word she and Moll took me each by an arm and led me downstairs, past the sitting room – where

Tippett and Sally were still in vigorous play – to the warm
room, where I lay between them upon piled towels, my
hindquarters pressed into the belly of Moll, whose hands
lay upon my hips governing the movements with which I
was now able to satisfy Ginevra, who lay facing me, one
thigh thrown over my hip to lie across both our bodies.

We woke next morning, all three of us, chilled by the
cool air which had replaced that of the night before, and to
the sound of Blatchford raking out the ashes of the fire to
replace them with fresh charcoal for the evening, for this
was to be our official opening.

The day was spent first in repairing the ravages of the
previous evening – cleaning, removing the soiled linen and
replacing it (Frank had obtained what seemed a bottomless
store of sheets and towels – 'For,' he said, 'I am determined that everything about the place shall be fresh as
paint') and in making sure that every smallest detail was in
place.

Sophie and Polly appeared at the middle of the day, and
without describing with exactitude the events of the night
before – for my regard for Sophie is such that I am shy to
reveal any commerce I may have with any other woman,
though I am sure sure she must realise that I do not live as
a eunuch – I was able to assure her that our 'rehearsal'
had come off smoothly. Walking around the house, she
expressed herself pleased. Her own plans, it seems, go
forward smoothly, with the help of Sir Philip. I have not
yet myself established what might be termed a friendship
with that gentleman, who must himself feel on less than
intimate terms with myself, but it appears that he is making
himself useful to Sophie, and perhaps in more than one
sense, for when they met (he having spent the night here) I
felt that she hung upon his hand with rather more warmth
than she might have been expected to betray to an
employee – for such I am to believe he is or is to be. I must
confess that I gave myself the pleasure of enquiring pointedly after Cissie's well-being, but my thrust did not land,
for he merely announced that he believed he had given her
every satisfaction, at which Sophia laughed, bade me farewell, and left.

I need not perhaps describe the success of our first night. Though the earliest guest did not arrive until seven o'clock, and in the meantime we had wondered whether anyone would appear at all, a steady trickle of gentlemen then knocked at the door, so that all our four rooms were continuously occupied, the girls once out of their dresses never having the opportunity to replace them, and Frank forced to tell them to do their best to satisfy their partners in the lower parts of the house. This they had no difficulty in doing, the warm room becoming an additional bedroom as it had for Ginevra, Moll and myself, and one gentleman being satisfied in the hot bath itself, which Moll described later as having the property of complete freedom from weight, 'a floating fuck,' as she described it, being for her a most pleasurable sensation she commended to us all.

The last visitor did not leave the house until three in the morning, by which time we were all tired, the girls through an obvious cause, Blatchford through his attendance to the stove, Frank and Aspasia through attendance upon the clients, Pounce through looking after the carriages to and fro, and myself with fingers aching from playing the guitar. The girls, delighted by the sound on the previous night, had decided that it added to the pleasure of the atmosphere – something which may be so, but it is too much like hard work for me to wish to make it a common pleasure!

Before we retired to bed, Frank called the girls together and announced that the house had taken exactly a hundred guineas.

'I have given some thought to this,' he said, 'and have decided that rather than each of you receiving a proportion of the fee a gentleman might pay for being entertained by her, it is fairer that you should each receive a proportion of the complete profit. I therefore intend to pay each of you a seventh share of one-third of the takings for each evening. You will receive this invariably – that is to say, should one of you be ill, or on a regular leave of absence, she will still receive her share. Should one of you be remarkably more or less popular with our visitors, then some adjustment may in future have to be made, but I do not at present envisage it.'

He then handed each girl six guineas – considerably

more than a proper share for the first night, but a generous gesture at which their faces lit up. I wondered whether he might be being a little over-generous, for he had also to pay salaries to the three young men, and then had the expenses of the house and its renovation to recoup, but I must trust his instincts and superior sense of business to my own, and wait to see what the future holds.

Chapter Eight

Sophie's Story

The eagerness with which Frank and Andy set about their plans resulted in the opening of their establishment in so short a time that it was impossible for me to believe that all could run smoothly. Yet I must confess that the furnishing of the house at Brook Street exceeded in comfort and beauty anything I had imagined possible. Polly and I looked over it on the day before its opening, and were as pleased as my brother with its effect. And from what I subsequently heard from Philip – for we now, as partners, refer to each other simply by our forenames – the house is as well-managed as it has been well-designed.

About the ladies Frank has employed, I am not sure; briefly introduced to them, I was pleased with the modesty of their demeanour – apart from one Cockney woman who is clearly from the streets and betrays it in every word she utters and many of the actions she performs. Yet she too seems well-intentioned and cheerful, and is a great favourite with Andy (he betraying in this a taste for coarseness perhaps originating with his own birth, which was not gentle).

But to return to my own plans, I had soon made arrangements through my late husband's solicitor, an honest man who has continued to serve me as he did that miser Mr Nelham (and I believe with considerably more pleasure) to buy the Lodge from my friend's estate, and without difficulty sold the house in Frith Street to a merchant from York who is setting up in business in the city, and at an excellent price, so that it was my pleasure to sign a draft to Sir Philip Jocelind for a sum considerable enough to keep him out of financial difficulty for some time to come.

He had the best of all worlds, indeed, for he continued to live at what had been his home since childhood, and had the additional pleasure of improving it in line with plans he had had for some time for its modernisation: the piping in of water, at no small expense, from the source which also supplied Brandenburgh House next door, and the renewal of certain furnishings – though many we retained, as we wished to preserve the atmosphere of a pleasant, private house at which our guests were to be guests, no matter how much they paid for the privilege.

For two or three weeks we worked at this – or rather Polly and I worked, while Philip appeared, disappeared, and reappeared, for I had handed over to him responsibility for stocking our stable with young men. Though I was to make an inspection of them before they were finally engaged here, it was not proper for me to roam about London on such a mission, however much the task might appeal in my more riggish moods. I did, however, suggest to Philip that he might make an excursion to the pools at Hampstead, for the scene we had witnessed there frequently returned to my mind.

One afternoon, Polly and I were taking tea when Philip appeared to announce that preparations were complete, and that six young men to whom he had spoken would appear before us on the following day! Since we had just been congratulating ourselves that our task was completed, we could now fix the date for the opening of our establishment – which we did for a week's time, Philip promising that the bills (on the lines he had sketched some time ago) should be distributed to a number of shops in town whose owners would, for a small consideration, ensure that they came into the hands of a likely clientele.

'And this evening,' he said, 'we should enjoy some entertainment; I have taken the liberty of obtaining tickets for the Contrary Ball.'

This I had never heard of, but Polly assured me that while it was not precisely fashionable, it was attended by many ladies and gentlemen of note. 'Besides', she said, 'it is invariably the source of great amusement.' She would not reveal more, but busied herself readying clothes for us to wear, and in the early evening had me in a chair while she arranged my hair with a care and wit that I had not suspected in her.

The ball was held in a large house somewhere south of the river – where, precisely, I do not know to this day, for it was after dark when we set out. Our carriage set us down at a fine entrance where we were received by a footman who directed us to rooms where we left our cloaks, and then up a grand staircase at the head of which stood a fine, tall woman who (Philip told me in a low voice) organised the Ball each year. I curtsied to her, and was raised to my feet by a steady hand, and greeted most kindly in an enchantingly husky voice.

The sound of the German waltz greeted us, and a picture of great gaiety, colour and movement, a swirl of masked dancers – for each wore a mask, some of plain black, others in beautifully embroidered silks of various colours, some of painted canvas.

We stood for a moment and watched, and gradually the meaning of the occasion came upon me, for while many of the guests were entirely conventional, a number were far from what they seemed. The first I saw who was an obvious pretence, was a large, fat woman who stood nearby, drinking wine at such a rate that she could surely not for long remain upright? There was something too square, too solid about the great haunches which could be seen under the silk of her gown, while the skin of her shoulders – though pale and hairless – seemed somehow over-coarse, as did her face, in profile, the heavily rouged lips and cheeks underhung by enormous jowls. But then she dropped her reticule in reaching out to take yet another glass of wine from the tray of a passing footman, and as the front of her dress fell away from her large and pendulous breasts, I saw not flesh but what seemed to be padded bags within the bodice.

I looked with amazement to Polly, who grinned.

'Bean-bags, madam!' she said. And immediately, upon looking about me, I saw that many of the ladies in the room were in fact gentlemen in masquerade – some acting the part with such enthusiasm that they were caricatures, others so neat and graceful in their behaviour that only the large size of their hands and ankles betrayed them.

I had never been before in the presence of so many gentlemen whose preference was to imitate those of the opposite sex, nor did I feel that they especially held any interest to

me, and was surprised to see Philip, from time to time,
dancing with one of them, talking and joking in an animated manner, and later, when he asked me to join him,
asked him what satisfaction such a proximity could give
him. To which he replied that he found it 'amusing', and
had nothing more to say on the subject.

Happily, there was a sufficient number of ladies and
gentlemen present in their own character, though most of
them seemed to be in attendance to laugh at the others,
which I found to be disconcerting. I saw Polly from time to
time in conversation with other ladies present – I mean,
real ladies – and myself spent my time observing the scene
from a corner of a room, uneasily occupying myself with
inspecting the furniture if anyone came too close to me.

But in time, I found myself addressed, happily by a
young man in the clothes of a gentleman and with a polite
demeanour.

'Ma'am, I find you alone. May I hand you a glass of
wine?' – and with a bow, offered me a libation, which I was
pleased to accept.

'You seem somewhat uncomfortable, if I may remark,'
he observed.

I admitted that that was the case.

'It is your first attendance at the Contrary Ball?'

It was, I said, nor had I any notion of how it was composed until an hour ago.

'It was somewhat unkind of your escort not to have
informed you,' said the young man, in a grave tone, and
with a head sympathetically inclined.

I made no reply, simply inclining my head in turn.

'You are new to town?' he asked, and after my reply,
went on to speak of other similar occasions, which had
begun – he said – as a meeting for those gentlemen who
found a satisfaction in dressing in women's clothing, and
even pretending to be women – though it was by no means
the case that all such were eunuchs, either in fact or in
imagination, for many found great satisfaction in making
love to the opposite sex, and simply took pleasure in silks
and satins, cottons and gauzes.

'However, there are some who are interested to regard
such people as one might look at the animals at the Tower,'

he said. 'And others who – to put it plainly – are only stirred by the embrace of their own sex, and hope to find such partners here. So, the ball has become a popular affair. You will forgive my speaking of such things, ma'am,' he said, 'but it is as well to be informed.'

'I am grateful to you, sir,' I said; and indeed was, not only for his exposition of the situation but for his company. He was of slight build, and I supposed very young, for his voice still seemed to have the tone of a boy's. His manners were gentle, and his address impeccable.

'Perhaps,' he said after a while, 'you would like to retire from the noise for a few minutes? There are some retiring rooms where we could sit for a while, and I could inform you further.' At which he laid his hand upon my bare arm, with a tender and melting touch, and I felt a slight pressure of his fingers which was a patent invitation to dalliance.

And why not, I thought to myself, looking around? Everyone was enjoying himself; Polly I could see talking animatedly to an elderly gentleman whose whiskers seemed unequivocally to confirm his sex, while Philip was for the time nowhere to be seen. I looked at my companion, and thought I glimpsed, behind the mask, a pair of invitingly sparkling, dark eyes. I inclined my head again, at which he took my arm and walked me from the room and along a corridor, then another, with many doors, behind some of which I seemed to hear sounds of pleasure. Finally, we came to a door which stood ajar and, first knocking gently to ensure that the room was empty, my companion stood aside and allowed me to enter.

I found myself in a small withdrawing- or perhaps dressing-room, simply furnished with a couple of chairs and a *chaise longue*. But before I had time to see more, I felt myself clasped in my new friend's arms, and his lips upon my own, a tender tongue playing about my mouth and finding my own tongue, while his hands fumbled at my back attempting to discover the laces which held my dress in place. His attentions were sudden but, after all, neither unexpected nor repugnant to me, whose preoccupation with business had now for some time restrained me from amorous activity.

He released the bands of my dress, loosed it gently from

my shoulders, and for a moment withdrew so that it fell to my waist, freeing my breasts – which have ever been, though I myself say it, a major adornment of my person. I heard him catch his breath, and he bent his head to kiss for a moment each peak, while I in turn slipped his coat from his shoulders, and began to unbutton his ruffled shirt. He stood, smiling, while I did so – a smile which broadened at the sight of the expression upon my face when I discovered beneath that shirt not the broad, manly platform I expected, but a pair of small, perfectly formed, inexpressibly feminine breasts. Despite myself, I drew back. The smile vanished instantly from his – her – face.

'Why ma'am,' she said, 'surely I cannot be mistaken? Surely you were aware . . .?'

But it was clear from my face that I was not, and instantly, though with a certain coldness, the girl turned and drew her shirt about her, beginning once more to button it.

'I apologise, ma'am,' she said. 'Had I realised . . .'

But almost despite myself, I stepped forward, placed my hands upon her shoulders, and planted a kiss upon the back of her neck, beneath the short, curly black hair. She turned at this, and clasped me in her arms, our bosoms meeting, then in a moment leading me to the *chaise longue*, upon which we collapsed, still embracing.

The truth was that I had certainly expected the embrace of a gentleman, and that a certain disappointment was unavoidable. Yet I was also too warm for my fire to be extinguished instantly, and my past experience had taught me that the embraces of my own sex were by no means invariably repugnant.

My new friend's body was soon fully revealed by my first removing her boots, then pulling the breeches from her, and it was slim and muscular as a boy's. Indeed, but for her breasts (which, when she was lying upon her back almost ceased to have any prominence) and the silky shrub between her legs from which no attentive engine arose, it could have been that of a young man of fifteen or sixteen. My own figure is much fuller, but evidently offered the greatest gratification to my partner who, having already paid tribute to my upper body, now watched me step out of my skirt and paid my hips and thighs the compliment of admiring them, turning me so that she could possess every plane with her eyes. And finally she lay me upon my back and knelt between my legs (one of her knees pressed tightly against my sex) to cover my face, neck, bosom and arms with kisses so vehement and rejoicing that even were I not already committed to enjoying her attentions I would surely have been persuaded – for what is more aphrodisiac than admiration, which here was to the point of adoration?

No one has a keener apprehension than myself of the hard, firm body of a man, even of the discomfort of his rough face pressed against the softness of an intimate part. But it must be confessed that even this firm and somewhat unwomanly body possessed a smooth and supple sympathy which was as inspiriting, in its own way, as the male embrace. One thing, of course, was lacking, but as the most sympathetic of men understand, the male part is not always that which provides ecstasy, and the attentions first of the girl's tender fingers, then of her sinuous tongue, brought me over the cliff of my desire once, then again. More than once I attempted to persuade her to turn her body so that I could similarly compliment her, but she firmly declined, remaining half-kneeling before me, her head buried in my lap, her slim backside in the air, far from my reach so that all I could do was to grasp her shoulders and perhaps reach round to her small breasts – now almost rigid with pleasure – before delight swallowed me again, so acutely that I almost fainted.

When I recovered, I found her turned and lying so that her head was upon my belly. I half sat, and again attempted to take her in my arms, but she rose, and slim as a wand stood for a moment, then said: 'Please ma'am, do not put yourself out. I am entirely satisfied by having given you pleasure, and would not wish to incommode you.'

By this time I was in fact desperate to show her my admiration of her own delightful form, but before I could find words in which to express this, she had drawn the male breeches once more over her loins, and was buttoning her shirt, and it was once more the young man who stood before me.

Making her bow, she withdrew immediately, leaving me

curiously unsatisfied, and also wondering who she might be. I dressed myself in thoughtful mood, and found my way eventually back to the ballroom, where the scene was now one of strange lassitude, for many people had withdrawn, either to other rooms in the house, or altogether, while over those that remained a sort of weariness had descended. Philip was still nowhere to be seen, but Polly made her way to me across the floor. She told me in a low voice, and with obvious irritation, that she had been courted by an extremely good-looking young man who, the moment they were alone, had plunged his hand into her bosom, and discovering that it consisted of flesh rather than padding, had in a moment angrily withdrawn. 'To have been mistaken for a Miss Molly,' said she, 'is a compliment I could well do without!' – but upon my laughing, could not but herself smile, and we took ourselves off home, leaving Philip to return as best he might. I could not but feel (though not opening the matter to Polly) that it was a curious event to which to have brought us. And then, where was he? I had last seen him dancing with a young person who might have been female, but could equally have been male. The impression I had received on the first occasion we had met – indeed, his behaviour when I had approached him – was not that of someone whose devotion was directed at members of his own sex; moreover, Andy had informed me that he had much enjoyed himself at their establishment.

But I was now too tired to speculate further, and retired to bed, falling asleep long before any sound could have announced his return to his room, next door to my own, if, indeed, he did return before morning.

At what time Philip did return I know not, but he certainly appeared at midday the next day – the time at which we usually met to survey the work which was being done about the house, and to discuss what was to be done, over a glass of wine. Today, it seemed that there was nothing left to do except approve the young gentlemen he had engaged, which was planned for the afternoon. In the meantime, we walked back to what had been his uncle's library, and was now divided into a series of small but comfortable retiring-rooms, each decorated in a different colour but with the same furnishings. Fine, full curtains hung at the windows and, where there were no windows, covered a space where such might have been – in the former case to ensure privacy and in the latter to avoid a feeling of closeness or stuffiness in the atmosphere. Then there was a low couch in each room, expressly made for the house by a furniture-maker at Chiswick Philip had recommended, sufficiently wide to allow space for two, or even three, bodies and carefully sprung so as to be comfortable without being too soft, for nothing is so inimical to love-making as an over-soft bed, on the surface of which no purchase is to be had.

Apart from this and a small closet, together with a table with bowl and jug, to be kept continually supplied with warm water and fresh, clean cloths, that was all. I was well pleased, as indeed was Philip, who insisted on bouncing in turn upon each couch, to ensure its pliability and resistance to his form. I had half a feeling he wished me to join him in the test, but for several reasons I refrained.

At three o'clock in the afternoon, Polly and I were joined by Aspasia, who had been invited to inspect the premises and to look over the livestock. The three of us went into what had been the dining-room, but was now a pleasant sitting room. A screen stood in front of the window which had been broken into the next-door room, hiding it from view, while a table and chair stood by the outside window, where business could be done, and a contract drawn up between the visitor and the house, to ensure the payment of the annual subscription. This could be paid at once, or in the sum of twenty pound a month – an additional forty pound per annum being in recognition of the delay in receipt of the total sum.

Drawing the curtains and plunging the room into darkness, I led the way behind the screen, where three chairs had been set before the pierced wooden barrier laid across the window. I explained to Aspasia that of course there would normally be only one chair, though if two or three friends wished to share the pleasure of choosing their partners together, there would be no objection.

So finely cut was the barrier – again, Philip had discovered a craftsman who had counterfeited a genuine Moorish screen in the collection at the British Museum – that it afforded me a clear view of the room beyond. I had that morning tried it from the other side, and found that though Philip called to me that he could see every detail of my dress, I was entirely unable to discern that anyone was watching me.

The room which was to be devoted to the young men, for their recreation and also their display, had again been comfortably and elegantly furnished. About the walls were several couches on which they could sit or recline; by the window (hung only by the lightest curtains, for it gave onto the private garden, and there was little if any chance of anyone looking in at it) was a table and chairs at which card games could be played. Another table was to bear daily and weekly newspapers; just within the window was a small billiard table, ready for play.

I had scarcely looked about and made myself comfortable when the door opened and Philip showed the first of the young men in.

'This is the room where you will spend your time when unoccupied by guests,' I heard him say – for there was no barrier to sound passing from one room to the other.

'Please divest yourself of your clothing, which can be placed in the closet next the door. Your colleagues will be joining you shortly.'

This first young man was of perhaps twenty years of age. He was dark, and well-built – indeed, as he removed his clothing he revealed a body not only extremely muscular but, even so early in the year, dark with exposure to the sun. I guessed – rightly as it turned out – that he was one of the bathers from the Hampstead ponds. The breadth and strength of his shoulders seemed to confirm this, for they were well-developed, as were his thighs, seeming to speak of the exercise of swimming as well as of whatever occupation he had formerly been engaged in.

'Excellent,' whispered Aspasia. 'Such an animal is essential – one with which almost every female would enjoy a ride.'

But our eyes had not long enjoyed the pleasure of examining a body which embodied every elegance concomitant with strength and virility, when Philip ushered in a second – as dark, but slimmer than the first – with the same words.

'This is a rum go,' said the first.

'It is,' said the second. 'I'm William. And you?'

'Harry,' said the first, holding out his hand, which the second gripped briefly. Then he began to undress himself, while Harry threw himself upon a *banquette*, his hands behind his head.

William was, by appearance as well as by his speech (which was softer and more educated than that of Harry) evidently more of a gentleman. His limbs were less developed and whiter, his body almost completely hairless, and more slender but as shapely, if in a less athletic mould. His arms were almost like those of a girl, his breast less muscular, but his belly flat and without a trace of fat. He folded his clothes very carefully as he took them off, and placed them neatly upon a shelf, then sat upon a chair, somewhat uneasily, at a distance from his new friend.

'What d'you make of this?' said the latter.

'No more or less than you, I suppose,' replied William. 'I am told that we are expected to – er – minister to a number of ladies.'

'Fucking's the name of the game,' said Harry, 'and I've waited all my life to be paid for it!'

'Not to my taste,' said Aspasia in a low voice, 'but there are those who look for a young man of somewhat delicate nature, in order to offer a more motherly affection.'

But the conversation was broken off by the unexpected appearance of the third stallion of our stable – who to my surprise as well as that of the two others, was a black man, whose brilliant white teeth flashed as he threw the two others a broad smile.

'This,' said Philip, 'is George – I'll leave you to instruct him.'

Harry looked at George with what seemed to me to be a great deal of suspicion, but to my surprise William, who had seemed to be the more withdrawn, was quick to rise, step forward and greet him, giving their names. George's voice, when he spoke, though it was low and as dark as his face, proved mellifluous and cultivated, and he was clearly of a pleasant disposition. I watched with curiosity as he divested himself of his clothing – which was of a decent quality, though not fashionable – for I had scarcely seen a

man of colour before, and never undressed. The colour of
the skin of his shoulders, back and buttocks (for he had his
back to me) was the same as that of his face – deep and rich,
and with a bloom almost of purple. His backside was
delightfully firm and well-shaped, positively demanding a
caress, and his body beautifully proportioned and shaped,
so that I believed him likely to be one of Philip's most
successful discoveries. As he removed his trousers, I
thought I saw a shock pass over the faces of both other men.
Was he in some way deformed, I wondered? That would be
sad indeed. But as he turned to put away his clothes, I saw
what had caught their eye – a member so large that I was
forced to rub my eyes and lean forward for a clearer view,
not believing it possible. Though clearly unaroused, it was
as formidable as most male instruments when they stood
ready for the fray. Of what monstrous dimensions, I
thought, could it be when persuaded to stand? Would not
the thought of being split by it frighten most ladies? It
certainly frightened me yet my curiosity was such that I
could wish it possible to see such a display. As he sat, it lay
across one thigh, seeming as thick as his wrist, for his limbs,
apart from this essential one, were rather delicate and
small.

In her excitement Polly had gripped my arm with her
fingers, and was clutching it so that I felt sure my flesh
would be bruised – yet in my surprise I had scarcely at the
time noticed her grip.

'Well,' said Aspasia drily, 'you certainly have an original
member of the household there! I have never myself seen a
black man unclothed, but I have been told of their inordinate size, and now see the rumours confirmed. You either
have a great success, or –'

She was clearly much of my own opinion.

The three men sat in silence until, in a moment, Philip
appeared again with two others.

'Ben and Tom,' he said, 'here are Harry, William and
George. They will show you where to put your things.'

Like Harry and William, the newcomers were transfixed
by the sight of George's remarkable weapon, turned to each
other, and giggled.

'What chance have we got against that?' asked Tom,

whereupon all the boys broke into laughter, including George, who had begun by looking embarrassed, never perhaps having occasion to be seen unclothed by other men.

Ben and Tom turned out to be brothers. Both fair, their bodies rather short and squat, everything about them seemed to have much the same plumpness – buttocks, muscles of the calves and thighs, little pot-bellies (though not what one could call fat), and chests upon which there seemed under-developed breasts. Yet there was nothing in the least feminine about them, though their chief male attributes seemed so small as to be almost altogether absent.

'Well,' said Harry, who seemed to be the one among them least given to equivocation, 'there's a contrast. That's the biggest one I ever set eyes on. All you darkies that size?'

'I believe I am particularly blessed,' said George, modestly.

'I should think so,' said Harry, 'but' – turning to Ben and Tom – 'if George has too much, you've scarcely enough, between you.'

'Never had any complaints,' remarked Ben.

'Get along!' said Harry.

'No, really,' said Tom seriously – and both he and his brother had a rather endearing, somewhat childish, solemnity about them – 'you've no idea how we grow . . .'

But now the door opened once more, and Philip introduced the last member of the party, who turned out to be by far the elder – a man of perhaps forty years of age, with tinges of grey hair at his temples. He carried himself well, and when introduced – as Spencer – nodded his head in an almost military manner and, turning his back, unclothed himself deliberately and without either ostentation or undue modesty. He had kept in good shape, for though the hair upon his chest was similarly greying, there was only a slight thickening about the waist to show him any less fit than the others.

'Now that is an excellent notion,' said Aspasia. 'Time and again you will find that a lady desires a man older than herself, and though the world knows that they are easy enough to find, they are usually either ugly or faithful to their wives!'

Spencer's arrival, and his faintly military bearing,

seemed to have dampened the spirits of the others, and they sat in silence for a while.

'Congratulations,' said Aspasia quietly. 'You are more adept than I took you for – where did you find these gentlemen?'

I had to admit that they had all been found by Philip, who of course Aspasia had met for a short time in Brook Street.

'Ah,' she said, 'Sir Philip has hidden depths. It is not every man who has such a fine eye for what will please a lady.'

But now the door opened once more, and Philip reappeared and, taking up a position with his back to us, addressed the company.

'Gentlemen,' he said, 'I have put the same proposition to all of you, and you have all agreed to its terms – that is, that you shall be paid the sum of five pound a week each as a retainer, and that upon each occasion when you lie with a guest, you shall receive an additional three pound. Food and wine will be provided, but accommodation only if you are required to stay overnight with a lady. That is understood?'

They all nodded.

'Now just a word as to procedure. You will be here each day at eleven o'clock in the morning, unless you have stayed overnight or have been specially summoned at an earlier time. As soon as you arrive, you will bathe yourselves and then make your way to this room. You will be expected to remain within call until midnight, or later if required. If the weather is fine you may of course walk in the grounds, but must always be within hearing of the bell which will be rung when a visitor is due, or arrives. We expect as time goes on that more and more ladies will come by appointment, which may allow some slight relaxation of the rules, but this will depend on circumstances.

'As to dress, in order that the ladies may make their choice, we would prefer that you remain unclothed while you are in this room, though if you wish to devise some covering which seems to you likely to attract the opposite sex, we have no objection – except that clearly should it have the result that you are not in fact chosen fairly regularly, it will be to your advantage to reconsider.

'As you see, a billiard table is provided; also cards, for play, and newspapers. If you wish to bring anything else with you to occupy the time, please do not hesitate to consult me.'

He glanced at some notes he had in his hand.

'When you hear the bell ring, you will know that a lady or ladies have arrived, and from that time on you must behave in the supposition that you are being observed. Behind this screen' – and he seemed to point straight at us – 'is a room from which the ladies will be able to see you without being seen. Someone there will point you out by your Christian names, and the ladies will make their choice and be escorted to a room; you will then be informed who is to attend her. Allowing perhaps five minutes in order that she may prepare herself, you will then put on one of the gowns which you will find hanging in the cupboard there' (he pointed to a corner) 'and will go to her. You will be expected to behave satisfactorily in her presence. That is to say,' he went on sternly, silently rebuking a laugh from Harry, 'you will endeavour to satisfy her physically but you will also behave as a gentleman is expected to behave. The manner in which you make love is entirely a matter for you, but you are expected to match it with what the lady requests or seems to expect, and not to force upon her any attentions she does not request, remembering always that here the more normal state of things is reversed – the lady does not exist to slake your passion, you exist in order to make her happy. Is that understood?'

Again there was silent approbation.

'Very well. Only two more points. Firstly, remember that the ladies behind the screen can clearly hear what is said in this room, for there is no glass behind the screen, so be careful in your language. Secondly, you are not to make appointments to meet any lady away from this house, and anyone discovered doing so will be instantly dismissed.'

He paused.

'Are there any questions? No?

'Well, you may have wondered why I asked you to divest yourself of your clothing on this occasion. In fact, three ladies are at this moment behind the screen and have been observing you.' At this there was a general stirring, each man reacting in a different way – Ben crossed his legs, while Harry threw one leg from the *banquette* to the ground, displaying his male parts with ostentation. Spencer drew himself up even more erectly in his chair, while George lay his hand along the length of his instrument, attempting – but failing – to conceal it.

'They will now make their choice, and three of you will be asked to go to them. Of course this will not suggest that those of you who are not chosen are in any sense inferior, and indeed, you must not feel this upon any occasion.'

Whereupon he left the room, and the boys looked extremely uneasy, glancing out of the corner of their eyes. Only Harry, with what seemed perfect equanimity, smiled towards the screen with a sort of easy insolence, at the same time reaching down between his thighs to lift the trappings there as though for our inspection, at which I felt Polly positively shiver at my side.

We rose to our feet and made our way back to the other side of the room, where by now Philip was waiting, and had pulled the curtains. Blinking in the light, Aspasia said: 'Sir Philip, I congratulate you.'

'They'll do?'

'Admirably.'

He looked at me, and I nodded my approbation.

'You have done splendidly,' I said.

'And you wish now to try the goods?'

I looked at Aspasia.

'I have the first choice? Then I choose the older man – what was his name? – Spencer,' she said.

I was slightly surprised; I would have thought that most of her gentlemen friends were of a certain age, but it was not for me to criticise or show any emotion. I turned to Polly.

'Well, if it's all the same to you,' she said, 'I'd like the first one, with the wicked eye.'

'Harry,' said Philip. 'And Sophia?'

'George,' I said.

Polly giggled.

'And the best of luck,' she said. 'Shall we send for the surgeon now, or later?'

'Mmm,' I said with mock solemnity, 'I feel merely that I have a duty to the cause of research!'

We made our way each to one of the small rooms, where for myself I was not long in attaining a state of nature. A soft knock at the door was followed by its opening, and the appearance of the splendid figure of the young negro, clad in a brilliantly white gown, which no doubt seemed more pristine than upon the bodies of any other of the young men.

From my position upon the couch, I smiled, and beckoned.

He was – as I suppose was to be expected – somewhat nervous, but walked over and stood uncertainly at the couch's side. Again I smiled, and this time had a glimpse of those white teeth as his lips also parted. I reached up to the single tie which caught the robe together at the waist, and pulling, undid it. The edges parted, and at first it looked as if there was no body beneath, so dark was it, but then he shrugged it from his shoulders, and stood before me in all his beauty. My eyes fixed, whether I would or no, on that one feature which must startle any beholder. And seeing my gaze, he could not but smile again, and stepped forward so that reaching upward I could hold in my hand that amazing limb – it was as though I caught at a forearm, except that it was utterly pliant.

I drew him down to me, and he laid his body along mine, warm and smooth, the skin feeling almost oily, and that remarkable limb lying up the whole length of my belly, the tight, hard, wiry hairs below tickling as he pressed against me. Throwing at once my arms about his shoulders and my legs about his waist, I felt a certain stirring, and stroking the length of his back, lightly tickling the curve of his buttocks, all the time taking between my lips his own thicker lips, I endeavoured to rouse him, and then rolled over and raised myself to inspect the effects of my labours.

What was my surprise to see no change at all – or, rather, a change only in angle, for his tool remained of the same size, though it was now utterly firm. Seeing the expression on my face, he said softly: 'I hope I don't disappoint you?'

In answer, I bent and kissed the now unyielding flesh.

'We are different from your men,' he said. 'We do not grow – we are already big!'

I did not care; the unusual sight of that shining, blue-black skin had captivated me, and placing the tip of his prick within me, I slowly pressed down until it disappeared within my fluid lips, then gently moving, while he lifted his head. With an expression that suggested that the experience was somewhat new to him, he paid my breasts the compliment of kneading them with his marvellously soft, thick lips, at the same time gripping my waist to encourage my movements.

If he was young, he was – unlike, for instance, Chichley – either practised in love-making, or somewhat insensitive, for I twice rose to ecstasy, and still he lay, his instrument perfectly firm. Finally, worn out, I was forced to lift myself from him and lie at his side, panting.

'I am sorry,' I said, 'you do not find me sufficiently attractive?' – for I hate to leave a man unsatisfied.

'Not at all, ma'am,' he said, 'it is simply . . .' and he looked embarrassed.

'If there is any way in which I can help?'

In answer, he raised himself, and throwing one leg over my body, sat astride me, and while his left hand played about my body, with his right he rubbed his instrument with a positively angry vigour, while to make the sensation perhaps more effective I caressed his cods at the root. Within a minute, his action being so violent that I feared he would do himself a damage, he gave a sigh and one or two drops of white liquid fell upon my belly.

'You see, ma'am,' he said, 'I must employ such vigour that I might injure a lady . . .'

I was sure that some ladies would welcome so remarkable a motion, though given the size of the instrument I doubted whether my body could have sustained it. But he was looking embarrassed and guilty, so I reached up and kissed him upon the cheek.

'That is of no concern, George. Thank you.'

We lay for a moment in comfort before he rose, and taking a cloth wiped my body and then handed me my clothes before bidding me farewell and leaving me to complete my *toilette*.

Polly and Aspasia were curious, when we met a little later, as to my experience, but I told them they would have to try for themselves, thinking it would do no harm that they should think me capable of accommodating a thing so large as they thought George's tool to be, *in extenso*! They themselves had been well pleased; Spencer was, Aspasia assured me, a gentleman of experience and sympathy, while Polly's choice, the athletic Harry, proved sufficiently active and courteous, though 'a rough stone' as she said, comparing him to the girl Moll, at Brook Street – as indeed in my mind I had done.

Leaving them to take tea, I made my way to the boys' room, where I found them all dressed, and announced myself as the mistress of the establishment (which George took with some surprise, and the rest, I thought, with some envy of him). We would open the business, I said, in five days' time, with an evening party by invitation only. They seemed entirely satisfied – especially when I handed them a guinea each for their trouble in coming this day – and so they made off, already it seemed on friendly terms each with each.

Chapter Nine

The Adventures of Andy

Affairs in Brook Street went on with remarkable quietness, the girls settling to their work with all the professional zeal for which one might have wished, and with what seemed an almost remarkable degree of mutual friendliness. This merely underlined the wisdom of Frank's decision to employ them as a group rather than hunting the streets of London for a random collection of women, most of whose time might well have been occupied in distressful rivalry and internecine jostling. Even Moll, previously unknown to the others, was popular, enjoying the opportunity of 'setting the girls right' about London low life – as she put it – while she in turn was ready to learn from them that degree of discreet but affable behaviour which she was all too ready to agree she lacked.

Business was brisk from the first, then as time went on and the reputation of the house was noised abroad it became almost too much for our seven ladies to cope with, so that from time to time Aspasia herself was forced to attend to the requirements of superfluous guests – though 'forced' is probably the wrong word, since she was in general more than happy to celebrate the rites of love with any personable visitor who showed her polite attention.

There came a day, however, on which we found ourselves in the early part of the afternoon, almost for the first time, without a clientele – a result, we supposed, of its being blustery and unpleasant weather, for normally there was a knocking at the door not much after one o'clock, the earliest time at which we admitted friends. We sat for a while in idleness, then Frank took himself off with Aspasia to Bond Street, where he was to search for some cloth with which to furbish a fine summer room which he was building into the garden at the back of the house, to give us some additional capacity. The girls and I, in relaxed mood, began to talk. First I told them of my capture by the press gang (which I have recounted in an earlier volume) which they heard with some excitement though without surprise, for living for the past few years near the coast they were not unfamiliar with those villains who plunder the streets of our towns to conscript our able men for the naval service.

Having exhausted my tale, I asked whether one of them would not in turn regale me with the story of her life, and after some hesitation, Xanthe agreed.

'I was born,' she said, 'the daughter of a county family near Brighthelmstone, my father a merchant in a good way of business, and my mother with a charm which made her the belle of the neighbourhood. However, when I was no more than seven years of age my father's business suffered a blow so serious – through the late wars – that in no short a time he was declared bankrupt, and we found ourselves thrown upon the streets. Even those who had seemed our greatest friends – for such is man's inhumanity – now deserted us. My father survived only a few nights of inability to afford my mother the comfort to which she had been used all her life and, though the poor woman made no moan, in a fit of awful remorse he strangled her and then threw himself from the cliffs, leaving me to wander in the cold night until found by a neighbour, who for a while gave me shelter, then sent me to the care of my paternal aunt in a small village not a hundred miles from the town.

'My aunt's husband was a mere journeyman, making his living by whatever came to hand – throwing up a partition at a small charge, mending a roof here, laying a floor there. He was not an unpleasant man, and though he seemed to me to be old, had in fact perhaps about forty years. His wife, my aunt, was friendly enough to me, but immensely scornful of him, perhaps due to the financial expectations raised upon her marriage, which had never been fulfilled. One of the results of this was her refusal of all those rights a man might properly expect of a wife, as I now realise, though at the time, without the slightest knowledge of commerce between the sexes, I was not aware of this. I knew not the reason for his fidgets, nor for his fondness to have me play upon his lap when his wife was without doors in various games, which I now suppose were all designed so that my body should come as closely as possible into contact with that part of his own most sensitive of his lady's neglect. He was, however, careful not to display his naked self to me – perhaps more for fear that I should in childish prattle tell of him than because he did not wish to do so – and I reached the age of thirteen years without knowing more of man than was apparent from his street-appearance. Nor, though my own body was beginning to take on the appurtenances of womanhood, did I know anything more of that than I could discover by the examination of it in a mirror, or through the enquiry of my own fingers.

'When I was sixteen, another person had joined the household, a pleasant young boy named Robin who had come to help my uncle in general by carrying his tools and making himself useful about the house. He was older than myself by two years or so, and considerably more knowing, so that he was continually looking for excuses to come upon me unclothed or to brush against me in the passages of the house or make jokes which I did not understand. This was far from disconcerting to me, for starved of the company of young people of my own age I welcomed his presence, and we got on well enough, though without my understanding why he should find my company preferable to that of boys of his own age.

'However, I soon discovered the reason, for on a day when he had been given the afternoon off, my aunt was visiting her cousin four miles away and my uncle had driven into Brighthelmstone on some errand or another, I took myself into the garden at the back of the house and in the balmy summer's air stripped off my clothes and bathed in the sun – something to which I was then much given.

'I must have dozed in the warmth, for the next thing I knew I suddenly awaked (perhaps through the sound of a breaking twig) to see Robin standing over me, his eyes wide and his mouth thrown open, obviously enjoying a sight such as in eighteen years he had never been offered before. I too found a sight to interest me, for Robin's breeches, at second hand, were not only worn but positively in holes, revealing firm flesh, and at the front a strange bulge where the cloth was lifted away from his body in an odd fashion; perhaps by a stick which he had in his pocket? Yet some instinct – together with his thrusting his hands into his pockets in an attempt to conceal it – told me that was not the explanation.

'I had no idea of covering myself – and indeed in raising myself had even thrown my legs somewhat apart, which peculiarly captured Robin's attention and seemed to move him curiously, for a groan escaped his lips, and in a moment he dropped to his knees before me and appeared to be pleading for something, but in words so incoherent that I could not understand him. However, clearly I could not have seemed unsympathetic, for in a moment he reached out his hand and I felt it very gently but firmly placed next to my body in a place to which no human hand but my own had ever adventured.

'It will come as no surprise that after a first pleasant shock from the unfamiliarity and unexpectedness of the movement, I was not inclined to consider his attentions impertinent. I wondered whether perhaps he wished me to reciprocate the motion, so placed my own hand as high up upon his thigh as I could reach from my recumbent position, whereupon he fell to his knees the better to enable me to explore the strange elongated shape I discerned there. It was more pliant than I had expected, and at the end nearest the body seemed to be decorated with two ball-shaped appendages whose purpose I could not guess at, but which were certainly attached to his body, and seemed by nature to be somewhat tender, though upon my weighing and trying them, pleasure seemed to be conveyed.

'My curiosity was at once enlarged and, reaching for his hand, which was still familiarising itself with my body, I prevented it from further progress and informed Master Robin that should he wish to continue his explorations, he should strip as bare as myself. This was not a notion repugnant to him, for almost before I had concluded, his shirt and trousers were thrown to the ground, and I saw before me my first manly machine, no less intimidating than beautiful, no less frightening than exciting, for even in one so young it was of considerable proportions, not only in length but girth, and in its proud standing assertion of boyish masculinity displayed an admirable elegance and firmness.

'For some time we were content simply to explore each other's persons, but then became more adventurous. With that instinct with which the Creator has endowed humanity, we were soon attempting to place ourselves in such a position that those parts of our bodies in which we already felt uncommon pleasure should be more delightfully engaged, rather than provoked merely through the agency of our digits. It can be imagined that we had no idea of applying our lips to such a task, they being as yet untutored even in kissing let alone any more adventurous activities.

'Such is the ingeniousness of youth that we soon discovered how it is that a key unlocks a door, and within a few minutes had made each other happy. After a short pause, we were once more at the game, and so occupied in it that we did not hear my uncle return, so that coming into the garden he saw two bare young animals cavorting freely upon the grass, limb entwined in limb with a fine lascivious freedom, enjoying an activity which he himself had been denied for some years – for I suppose he was of far too nervous a disposition to engage with any other woman than his wife.

'To cut a long story short – for I fear I grow tedious – Robin found himself, from lying between my thighs, flying through the air, while his master, pausing only to open his clothes, took his place with such an enthusiasm that he came off even more quickly than the boy had done, and was as quick to recover and offer another bout. Despite the fact that, plundered so thoroughly upon a first engagement, I was more than a little sore, I cannot deny that I thoroughly enjoyed the occasion and continued to relish a two-fold engagement – for though my uncle now crept to my bed at every chance that offered, and was madly jealous of the boy, he could not turn Robin away for fear the lad would inform my aunt. So almost every night for sixteen months I was enjoyed by one or the other, and between them learned as much as any girl of my age needed to know about the pleasure that can be obtained from congress. One contrast between them was that my uncle (for the reason of preventing my being with child, though I knew it not) introduced me to congress from behind, which far from abominating I actually came to enjoy, especially when it was accompanied by other manual dexterities, and I still occasionally persuade my gentlemen to take me so, sometimes to their displeasure but often to their surprised delight.

'Our eventual discovery by my aunt – which was of course inevitable when we were all living in the same house – put a stop to our enjoyment with an argument loud enough to apprise the whole of the village of the circumstances. Indeed it made an end of my living with my relatives, for unable to countenance life without even the few comforts my uncle's house provided her, and so unwilling to leave him, my aunt turned me away. Driven to Brighthelmstone and left there to sink or swim, I found myself upon the streets, and but for the happy circumstance of my encountering that very evening our dear friend Mrs Jopling Rowe, must have come to a far worse pass than that in which I now find myself.'

Applause greeted Xanthe as she finished her narrative, and – not, I thought, without a sly glance which promised some secret about to be revealed – she persuaded her friend Rose tell her own story.

'Mine,' Rose said, 'is a simpler tale, and one known to everyone present except you, sir. But it might, perhaps, amuse you in its somewhat unexpected conclusion.

'An orphan, I was chosen by Mrs Jopling Rowe from a house on the outskirts of Brighthelmstone, and taken straight to the place where you found me. I discovered more friendship there than I had encountered during the relatively short course of my previous life, and was so grateful to Mrs Jopling Rowe that I would have been happy to reward her by my aquiescence in a fate far more unpleasant than that for which she designed me. Though to tell the truth I was far less pleased than my friends by the attentions both of the kindly gentlemen who made me a woman, and those others who later were eager enough to pay me the compliment of making me their bedfellow.

'I felt myself, indeed, to be entirely unsuited for the profession for which I was chosen. And not only that, but inferred that something was missing from my life, for my friends were always recapitulating, almost boastfully, the pleasure they took in the embraces of certain of their gentlemen friends, while in the arms of the most handsome of those who courted me I felt nothing but impatience that the affair should be over. Their beards chafed my skin, the hairiness of their bodies was unpleasant to me, and the forceful bucking of their ridiculous bums encouraged me rather to laughter than to passion.

'So dispirited was I – considering it a sad lack in my nature – that after a while I found it impossible not to dissolve into tears after each such encounter, until one day Xanthe, coming into our room, found me in such a state and enquired if someone had insulted me or been more than usually rough, reminding me that Will was always within call should I require assistance. But continuing to sob, I was able after a while to confess what I was bitterly ashamed of – that I was completely lacking in that proper feeling which the others possessed, that clearly I was unnatural, and that I was bitterly jealous of the pleasure that was felt by the others in an occupation which at best bored and at worst nauseated me.

'But had I never felt such pleasure? Xanthe enquired. Even (and she excused herself for asking an indelicate question) when I had employed my own fingers, as all girls did in their youth? Yes, I admitted, there had been such pleasure, but a lonely pleasure of that kind was not what I sought, and was I never to experience it in the arms of another?

'Her reply was to lift her dress over her head and to take me in her arms, naked as I was from my recent encounter with Mr Miners, a Brighthelmstone fishmonger. I had of course many times seen my friend unclothed, for no modesty of that sort existed between us. We had even embraced each other innocently, but I had never so eagerly clasped anyone as I now clasped my dear friend, and with a passion new to me, which she clearly reciprocated, for as my breasts pressed against hers, and her thighs parted so that mine could insinuate between them, our bodies shook with an emotion we scarcely knew how to contain. So complete was my surrender to that embrace that it was without the least surprise that I found myself lowering my head to take between my lips those delightful buds that broke from my friend's charming breasts. Nor, on feeling her body respond to my embraces, was I amazed to find my own way to that grove where sweetness resides and there graze upon those soft brakes, so much silkier and kinder than the rough pasture (if you will forgive me, sir) that surrounds the base of that great oak with which men love to batter us.

'The pleasure of that afternoon taught me how to love and continues to comfort me to this day, for though I have learned, I trust, to comport myself so that the gentlemen I entertain believe me to enjoy their embraces, yet I must still counterfeit the ecstasy that I genuinely find in the arms of my dearest friend' – with which she leaned forward to plant a kiss upon Xanthe's cheek, who received it blushingly and looked about to protest. Rose put a finger to her lips, and went on: 'I must tell you, lest you reach a wrong conclusion, that my friend's pleasure in her engagements with men is unfeigned; but she is kind enough also to delight in my company, and you will I think in neither case find us wanting in our duties to this house. But you wished to hear our stories, and there is little point in telling them unless honesty is a requisite.'

There was, I thought, a slightly uneasy silence as Rose's story ended, and I soon realised that the ladies waited with interest my reaction – upon which I took Rose's hand and kissed it, saying that I was honoured by her confidence and would respect it, and that I had every faith in her loyalty and professional deportment. Whereat the atmosphere immediately lightened, and we all laughed.

'And who will be next?' I enquired. 'Constance, will you not give us your narrative?'

'I too,' said Constance, 'was an orphan, and at an early age was taken in by a tailor and his wife of Brighthelmstone, less as a daughter than as a maid of all work, for from my earliest years I remember nothing other than what was virtual slavery. Up at five o'clock in the morning cleaning out the grates, and to bed at ten at night after waiting upon my master and mistress, who liked to feel they had a much larger establishment than was indeed the case, for they were of no class or consideration in the town, and their neighbours laughed at their pretensions.

'Unlike Xanthe, I did not even have the pleasure of being introduced to love by some vigorous lad, and at the age of sixteen had known nothing more gratifying than housework – for even in summer I was kept indoors, with no time of my own in which to take the air and no garden to the house in which I could snatch so much as five minutes' breathing.

'Where I found the courage to run away even from so unpleasant a life, I know not, but finally I did so, leaving one afternoon when my master and mistress were both from home, and happily was discovered by our friend Mrs Jopling Rowe as I wandered along the edge of the sea positively intoxicated by the fresh air, the sunshine, and the bright blue of sky and water. Had it not been for that beneficent lady, Lord knows where I would have found rest. But discovered I was, and she took me in, looked after and educated me with the same assiduous care she devoted to my friends.

'There was some difficulty when I discovered for what occupation she intended me, for my former master had been notoriously religious, given to reading the Bible at all hours, and had convinced me that to have any commerce with men (not that I understood his words) was to be forever damned. Mrs Jopling Rowe was not of that opinion, and persuaded me to accede to her wish that one of her two friends should introduce me to the pleasures of the bed. I did not find these as lacking in interest as did Rose, yet was far from welcoming them as did Xanthe, and determined merely to put up with them in deference to my good mistress, and to make the best of things.

'I was by no means discontented with my fate – indeed happy that provided I was prepared to tolerate the fumblings of those gentlemen who from time to time visited me, I was to enjoy a life of comparative leisure and considerable comfort. No woman could fail, after a time, to be cognisant of those little attentions which best please a man, and I found that a little pretence at enjoyment – for the gentlemen like to be flattered that their bodies are irresistibly attractive to the female sex' – and here she glanced at me –

'resulted in my being popular enough to pay my way.

'My other great pleasure was the open air, for after so many years of being starved of it, it was delightful to me to bathe and run upon the beach in a state of nature, for, except at the height of the season, the beaches near to us are devoid of people, and what people use them for bathing will have no truck with the modern conceit of bathing clothes. And I loved to take my ease in our secluded garden. By this, my body became after a while completely brown, which I found an advantage, many gentlemen deeming it an interesting contrast to the milk-white flesh of ladies of fashion.

'It so happened that on one occasion a visitor, a former seaman in a somewhat drunken condition, attempted to force Cissie to a kind of commerce she was averse to, and it had taken three of us all our strength to subdue him – indeed, it was only the shrewd employment of a full bottle of wine applied to the back of the head, by Xanthe, that finally concluded the altercation.

'Mrs Jopling Rowe decided that it was time that there was a man about the house, and going off to Brighthelmstone returned not with a man, but with a youth of some twenty years, strong and intelligent, whom she employed as a general handyman, and who should give her ladies any help they required.

'I dare say that Will (which was his name) thought that he had died, proceeding straight to the Elysian fields. And upon seeing him, for he was comely enough, one or two of my companions may have felt that some entertainment was at hand rather more attractive than that offered by the somewhat elderly gentlemen who usually came to the house for the purposes you know of.

'However, as it happened, I did not hear of Will's engagement, nor did I know upon what day he was to come,' here there was general laughter and expressions of disbelief, upon which, she insisted, 'Nay, but 'tis true! So it was that in the heat of an afternoon I was asleep in the costume of Eve upon a grassy hillock in a corner of the garden – that very corner to which Mrs Jopling Rowe dispatched Will in order that he should tidy up a brake of bushes.

'It was there I first saw him. He had taken off his shirt

against the heat of the sun, and was wearing only an old pair
of pantaloons rather too big for him, so that the piece of
string with which they were secured having loosened, they
hung about his hips, revealing a slim waist and an
entrancing swelling towards the twin spheres of his back
side, which was towards me. Indeed, in the very failure of
his clothes completely to conceal the figure they veiled, he
was unconsciously accomplishing what we women purposely design – the advertising of our charms by a discreet
and apparently negligent revelation.

'Will was of course unaware of the picture he presented
as he stood at work, the muscles beneath the light brown
skin of shoulder and back reacting to the pressure upon the
handle of the rake he wielded, a fur of brown hair running
across those shoulders, then down his spine to that very
point where I clearly saw the beginning of that cleft dividing
a posterior which promised to be so charmingly round, so
enchantingly limber, that my eyes almost pierced the cloth
in their attempts to uncover it. How I wished that that string
would break, and the covering slip from those lower limbs!
Or that some circumstance should permit me to loosen it!

'But now I speedily closed my eyes, for turning to spy out
more ground for raking, he suddenly saw me – lying, as I
have said, clothed as Eve was when Adam first saw her in
that other Eden. I almost felt his eyes devour me, afraid to
re-open my own for fear that he should take fright, for I
may admit that for the first time I was conscious of a positive desire to be clasped by a pair of male arms!

'Happily, I need have had no fears, for Will, unlike
myself, had been raised in a large family in which the
presence of four sisters and four elder brothers had resulted
in that easy familiarity which had made him aware at a very
early age of what woman expects from man. My eyes still
closed, I heard soft footsteps approach, and then a rustling
of clothing, at which I could no longer pretend but opened
my eyes to that view which can never fail to impress a
woman – that of a splendidly formed cock in full anticipation of pleasure, springing from a dark cloud to stand
against the furry background of a firm, small belly. Seeing
me open my eyes, Will stood for a moment, hands upon his
hips, his trousers kicked from his legs, and far from

attempting to conceal his eagerness for congress, he positively advertised it. He was waiting, as now I suppose, for a word of protest from me, or some sign that I found the prospect unattractive. No such hint escaped me, which he properly took for acquiescence, and kneeling between my legs bent to press a tender kiss upon my willing lips while his hands, rough with work but tender with an eager mildness, clasped my bosom, then moved down to my waist, and finally drew my thighs even more widely apart while he lowered himself. As I looked wonderingly down, struck dumb with surprise that the approach of a male appendage so obviously ravenous should fill me rather with delight than with apprehension, he placed its pouting point at the entrance to my cunny, already swamped with the eager juices which stood ready to render its passage the more easy. Slowly, its long length slid within me – so slowly, so gently, yet with such determination that the sensation of that gliding motion made me almost faint with pleasure – until our fleeces met, and with gradually increased pace he began to swive, my hands the while embracing what felt to me like the soft pelt of a satyr, so completely were his limbs covered with enchanting and velvet fur.

'Need I express the pleasure our encounter brought? The sun shone down charmingly upon his body and mine as they acted and reacted in delightful unison, and I cried out again and again with pleasure – until fetched by the sounds Xanthe and Rose came running to see whether I had injured myself! Then, seeing the quality of the injury and the instrument which was inflicting it, they paused to applaud, whereupon a shudder ran through Will's body as joy erupted from him, before lifting himself from me he reached for his small-clothes and attempted to cover himself.

'Myself, I was much beyond shame, and simply lay upon the warm ground, legs apart, the dew still falling from my most satisfied part. And in a fit of laughter my friends tussled with my lover, trying to drag his breeks from him, and eventually forcing him upon his back where, in no ill humour, he suffered them to examine his fallen staff, and – such was their expertness – revive it to a full stand, whereupon Xanthe in no time had removed her meagre clothing and was ready for him.

'But with a blush, he protested, "Lady, forgive me, but I have ever been of opinion that man should cleave to one woman at a time – and this is she!" – pointing at me.

'If I was astonished, it was no more than they, for in the nature of things we had grown to regard men as always craving some other creature than the one with which they were yoked. Well, I thought, that time might come, but until then . . . And reaching up, I captured my friend again, so that in a moment we were once more enjoying each other, while my two friends consoled themselves as best they might.

'From that time to this, Will has remained my lover; I cannot say my only lover, perhaps, since my profession precludes that declaration, but he is the man to whom my love, rather than simply my body, is given, and I have grown adept at pretence where other men are concerned. Will, I think, will be happy enough when we have saved sufficient money for me to retire from my present occupation, but until then, he tolerates my way of life.' At which Constance looked for a moment I thought sadly, but then smiled again: 'And that is my story,' she said.

Now Sally and Cissie looked at each other, and encouraged by Xanthe offered their narrative – first one then the other contributing a word or two, for they were so inseparable and so alike that it had often occurred to me to wonder whether they were not sisters. But no, they said, they were merely cousins, and the latest to attend Mrs Jopling Rowe's academy, having come there only at the beginning of the previous season from the city of Bristol.

There, they had grown up in two houses, side by side, belonging to their fathers – brothers who were successful merchants in the town. They had been raised to the age of fifteen with every advantage of polite society – for which, Sally asserted, they were not especially grateful, for the activities of society were ineffably boring to them, they having no enthusiasm to learn music, or set dances, or the art of conversation. Indeed, most of their time had been spent playing in and around the docks, and wishing that they had been born boys so that they could sail upon the tide for the Indies or for China.

'However,' said Cissie, 'we were soon to discover another occupation to please us even more than playing shadows to the cabin-boys upon the Bristol quays.'

In answer to their incessant pleas – they had been continually in each other's company from the very time they could stand and walk – their fathers had broken down the wall between the attics of the two houses and there had constructed one room which the cousins shared. It contained their beds, their clothes and all they had, and was sufficiently large (running as it did over the tops of both houses) to provide a quarterdeck for any nautical games of exploration they devised.

One warm day in summer, not long after their fifteenth birthdays (both celebrated in the early weeks of August) two young men appeared. They had been engaged by the brothers as apprentices to learn the trade of chandling, and were given a room upon the second floor of one of the houses, lying immediately below the girls' room.

'These were the first young men with whom we came into daily contact,' said Sally, 'for Cissie and I could not be familiar with ship-boys, and our families kept us apart from other young men expressly because they had it in mind to marry us to two particular gentlemen, with an eye to empire-building on their own account. And so, meeting Mr Gossage and Mr Mordan – if only at breakfast (at which we now became more punctual than before) and supper – we discussed them thoroughly between ourselves when we had retired to bed. They were reasonably handsome specimens of young manhood, being perhaps seventeen years old, upright in carriage, well-built, and with that happy elasticity of limbs which in youth gives each movement such interest and charm.'

It was Cissie who suggested a means of studying these two young animals more intimately, and borrowing a carpenter's auger from a quayside store, bored two holes with it in the floor of their room, above that of the two young men.

That evening, retiring early upon the excuse of a headache, they waited until they heard the shutting of the door of the room beneath their own, and then applied an eye to their peep-holes – to find themselves immediately

rewarded with the sight of Mr Gossage and Mr Mordan
entirely unclothed, lying face downwards upon their beds in
the heat of the evening, each studying a book of mathematic
problems upon which they were to be examined upon the
morrow.

'Our pleasure was only equalled by our inquisitiveness,'
said Sally, 'for it was the first time our eyes had fallen upon
any naked creature other than the small boys who daily
bathed from the quaysides, and whose childish bodies had
quite failed to raise in us the emotion we felt upon studying
the long backs of the two young men below us, so pleasantly
relaxed, the swelling of their backsides so differently
shaped to our own.'

'And here,' said Cissie, 'we stripped ourselves, the better
to examine the difference in contours between our own
arses and those of the gentlemen which consisted in
theirs being rounder and higher, as it were, while ours were
fuller and more oval. We could not but agree that their
bodies were far more interesting than our own and longed
for a further exposure, for between the legs of Mr
Gossage, which were thrown open, a shadow seemed to
conceal something which might we believed be of unusual
interest.

'After a while we thought of withdrawing, for though we
lay upon pillows, the posture of applying an eye to a hole in
a floorboard is without charm. Then Mr Mordan threw
down his book, and said (for with the keen ear of youth we
could hear, though dimly, their conversation), "There's
enough of study, Bob. A little exercise before we sleep?"
To which his friend in reply placed his own book more
carefully upon the floor, and to our surprise rose, walked
over to his friend's bed, and sat down, resting one hand
upon the other's bum and sliding it between the cheeks until
it rested upon that something which lay there, and which
now seemed to stir.'

Thereupon, Mr Gossage turned over and rose to sit at his
friend's side, enquiring what was the record, whereupon his
friend replied that it stood at three foot ten. And without
further exchange they reached into each other's laps and
began to make there with their fingers motions which
clearly gave each other pleasure, and which soon offered

their onlookers equal joy in presenting to them their first view not of one but of two male instruments in their full glory. When these erections had been achieved, each took hold of his own tool and manipulated it with increasing enthusiasm until from the end of each sprang a positive jet of liquid, which flew through the air to some distance before falling upon the bare boards of the room. Thereupon Mr Mordan produced from his wallet a tape, and measured the distance between the bed and the point at which the furthest jet had fallen, then announcing that his friend had 'broke the record', which now stood at three foot ten and a half. At this they laughed and, having wiped the floor – and themselves – with their handkerchieves, fell into bed, leaving the girls to withdraw from their spy-holes and retire together to satisfy their own excitement with manual dexterity, after which they discussed for no short time what they had seen.

They continued to repair, each evening, to their spy-holes, despite the redness of their eyes due to a draught, which caused some concern to their mothers, and were regularly regaled with the sight of those two handsome young men in a state of nature, who seemed almost to pose for them, so completely did they exhibit their every limb to such advantage. The cousins were regularly reduced to near an hysteria of desire to come at them – until, one evening, they overheard Mr Mordan and Mr Gossage, lying together upon one bed and toying with each other in an idle manner, discussing *themselves*. How Mr Gossage would like to teach Miss Cissie 'what it was for' (whereupon he caressed his tool in strangely meaningful manner), while Mr Mordan longed, he said, to set eyes upon Miss Sally's Thing. At this Sally rose from the spy-hole and, beckoning to her friend, left the room quietly and repaired down the staircase, opening the door of the young gentlemen's room without knocking. To the girls' pleasure the admired ones showed no sign of reticence, but rose to welcome them as though they were expected guests, striding towards them preceded by that limb in which the cousins were most keenly interested.

Motioning to her cousin to shut the door behind them, Sally at once lifted her smock over her head, providing Mr Mordan with a clear view of what he had so eagerly wished to see, and which, falling upon his knees, he saluted with a kiss.

To the girls' surprise, Mr Gossage burst out laughing, joined by his friend, and the two young men embraced them closely. 'We thought that would bring you!' they exclaimed, and confessed that from two small piles of sawdust upon the floor of their room they had discovered the holes in the ceiling at the first, and from that time onward had been putting on a display each night for the girls – even speaking somewhat above their normal tone of voice in order to enchant them further.

The boys and girls then took immediately to bed, where Cissie and Sally learned at first hand the game of love. But alas, after two weeks of such pleasure their parents became suspicious. One evening, engaged in a game at fours in which no part of a single body was sacred to any participant, they heard loud cries from the girls' room above, where, finding their children absent and noticing the holes in the floor, their mothers had applied their eyes. They had been rewarded by the sight of Sally drawing the cheeks of Mr Gossage's fundament apart in order more closely to caress with her tongue what lay between, while the latter's face was buried between her thighs. And Cissie stood leaning, her hands upon the bed, while Mr Mordan caressed her ready bubbies, enjoying her from behind with a fine bucking motion like nothing so much as the ready randiness of an enthusiastic ram.

The long and short of the discovery was that the two mothers had the vapours, breaking off to fetch the fathers. The fathers dismissed the apprentices and, seeing in the local newspaper an advertisement by a Mrs Jopling Rowe for young ladies prepared to offer themselves to a life of sacrificial devotion to the care of the elderly and lonely, dispatched Sally and Cissie immediately to her care with the desire not to see them again until they had repented – which, their being inclined rather to enjoyment than repentance, had not yet occurred.

The story was told with such enjoyment and zest that I could not but relish it, and indeed we all broke into applause. Shortly afterwards, two guests made their appearance, and the business of the day began. I took myself thoughtfully from the room, and spent some time conversing with Aspasia, now returned. I had always inferred that for young ladies of our sort the ordinary commerce of love must be undertaken as a duty, but that it should be so often so little pleasurable dismayed me somewhat; when performing the act, was their smiling, were their cries, always a matter of deceit?

Yes, said Aspasia, that was more often than not the case, for they felt not infrequently that the men who used them were not doing so in real admiration – 'but to be plain, Mr Archer,' said Aspasia, 'as a mere substitute for their own palms, rather than in genuine compliment to their beauty.' Often, having made love to them, their partners would be contemptuous, even rebuking them for their way of life; complimenting them on their beauty before the act, they would go out of their way to criticise, after it.

'Leaping between our thighs,' she said, 'men feel they have won, and that letting them win we have in some way insulted them. The performance over, they feel sullied and disgusted, and they show that disgust to us. It is, of course, themselves that should examine their own actions. All we wish, in the situation in which we find ourselves, is that the gentlemen who visit us should be reasonably friendly and pleasant – which many of them are, and in my position I can afford to turn the others away. It is more difficult in a house, but I shall attempt to build here a clientele of agreeable visitors, for women need affection more than men, and I see no reason why our girls should be altogether deprived of it.'

I returned to my room in a thoughtful mood, for everything that Aspasia said was true, and though the girls were charming, there had been in the career of each more than a touch of neglect. I determined to do my part to see that their lives with us were as pleasant as possible given the circumstances of their occupation – to which, I must say in our defence, none had voiced objection.

Chapter Ten

Sophie's Story

What an agreeable time we had of it during the first months
or our experiment! I would not have desired things to fall
out better. The boys all got on well together, there was no
sign of jealousy or envy, no quarrelling. Our custom built
from the first moment to a regular trickle, then to a stream
of visitors – not so broad nor so fast that we could not cope
with it, but not in any way diminishing, so that we were all
kept busy and in profit.

Polly, Philip and I also lived in perfect amity. Though
Philip spent perhaps more time abroad than I had anticipated, he carried out his duties to perfection, watching the
boys with particular care, correcting any faults, making a
suggestion here or a comment there which might result in
an easier or more pleasant running of things. Polly
continued to please me with a perfect combination of service and friendship. The only thing that cast a slight
shadow upon the weeks was my being deprived of male
companionship.

How, you may ask, could this be, when I was surrounded
by the male animal, whose sole employment was to please
ladies? But the truth is I felt disinclined to lie with my boys
(as Andy and my half-brother did, I believed, with the girls
in their establishment at Brook Street). While as for
Philip – the truth is that the original interest he had shown
in me seemed now to have declined until our association
had become purely a matter of business.

I realised this on the very occasion of our first opening
our doors, when I had spent the evening showing off our
lads to some fourteen ladies. The conceit of escorting them
to the window where they could see, while remaining
unseen, was a perfect success. All the boys had determined
– the room being quite sufficiently warm for it – to appear

entirely unclothed, and the contrast between them, and their carefully contrived 'careless' poses invited admiration. Harry, as usual, seemed to flaunt his maleness, William generally lay face downwards upon a *chaise longue* so that his neat buttocks positively invited a caress, Spencer's lean and hard body was displayed to advantage as he played billiards with Tom and Ben, while George – why, the mere appearance of his splendid instrument attracted attention in whatever attitude he stood, sat or lay!

Our choice – or rather Philip's choice – was proved immediately to be an excellent one, for the ladies who visited us by no means showed any disposition particularly to favour one boy above another, though a certain type could not resist George for his uncommon and individual appearance, black men being very rare in London at this time. And it was interesting that William was similarly always attractive – ladies showing, as I have noticed, a peculiar delight in the rear *façade* of a gentleman's body, even those who would have preferred a more muscular figure often finding the prospect of connexion with William an irresistible temptation.

At the end of our first evening, then, I was in a state much enlivened from the continual spectacle which I could observe but not taste (and you will remember that at this time the bodies of the boys were still unfamiliar, and thus the more attractive to me) and the general excitement of the evening – not least the satisfaction of our guests, each of whom was enthusiastic in praise of the entire operation.

It was past midnight when all were gone; some few of the boys had accepted our invitation to sleep in the house, and Polly had taken herself to bed in exhaustion, while Philip and I sat over a bottle of wine discussing the arrangements, and any changes which might profitably be made – which were few. He had thrown off his coat and sat in his shirt, while I had still the low-cut single muslin dress I had worn all evening, and – as was the fashion – nothing beneath it. I could not but believe he was entirely conscious that my body invited his attention, yet he sat at my side without offering any caress, nor even responding to my placing my hand upon his thigh as I leaned to refill his glass with claret.

At last, my need being considerable, I bent to offer him a

kiss, lifting his hand at the same time in my own and placing it upon my breast, but to my surprise he returned my kiss in what can only be described as a fraternal manner, looking extremely uneasy, and after a while was forced to admit that he was not ready to embrace me. My look must have spoken volumes, for he immediately laid a hand upon my shoulder and assured me that he had the utmost regard for me, 'but,' said he hesitantly, 'sadly 'tis the case with me that after one passage of love with a lady I am usually unable to repeat that pleasure . . .'

Why should this be, I enquired? To which he said he did not know, but volunteered the following story of his life, which went some way to suggesting an answer.

'I was brought up, as you know,' he said, 'by my uncle, in this very house from the age of three years, at first with a nursemaid, but then from my sixth year by a series of male servants who all treated me extremely well and kindly, so that I have no complaints upon that score. My uncle was something of a recluse, but having had the responsibility of caring for me placed upon his shoulders had determined to do the best he could for me, and gave me a great deal of his company during those hours when I was not engaged upon lessons given me by a series of excellent tutors.

'This did not mean, however, that I swiftly became educated in the ways of the world, for my uncle's main interest was in literature, and he spent almost his entire time with his books, so that my experience of a social life was to sit at the other end of a long table, opposite him, giving my attention to some volume of prints while he merely looked up from his work from time to time long enough to throw me a word. After a while I begged to be excused such daily attendance, but was still confined to the house and, in summer, the gardens.

'I thus reached the age of puberty without any sensible knowledge of the corporeal world, and it was something of a surprise to me when my uncle – certain stains upon the bedclothes having I suppose been reported to him as evidence of my young manhood – summoned me one day to the library.

' "My dear Philip," he said, "you are now, I understand,

a man. That is to say, hmmm, you are ready to perform that manly act which our creator devised for the propagation of the species. You will be aware that humanity consists of two sexes, the male and the female.''

'Here I interposed to say that while I was indeed cognisant of that fact, it was a theory short of demonstration, for the entire household was male – even to the cook, a Frenchman, and those who cleaned the place. I might have gathered from this my uncle's taste in the matter, had it been a subject I ever considered, but as it was, since the world outside these walls was unknown to me, I had no means of knowing what was normal and what unusual. However, to return to my narrative, my uncle continued thus –

' ''I have always found the female sex to afford me little pleasure – neither that of conversation, nor that of companionship – though I believe that I am perhaps relatively unusual in this. I have no wish of course to dictate to you, my dear boy, the slightest course of action, but I have suggested to Robert that he may place himself at your disposal, and that if you find yourself unsatisfied he should enable you to continue your education – um – elsewhere.''

'At which he dismissed me to leave the room knowing little more, I must confess, than when I had entered it. I was entirely unaware of the kind of pleasure to be offered me by women, whose pictures in the prints, even naked, had stirred nothing in me. Nor did I take in the fact that my uncle was, as I now realise, confessing to me his inveterate addiction to his own sex (if only infrequently) as bedfellows, and suggesting that I should follow his example. This, however, was soon to be made clear, for outside the door of the library I found Robert waiting for me – a charming young footman whom I had of course seen about the house, and who had always been affable. I had understood his main employment to be as body-servant to my uncle, but without fully understanding that the term, in this case, meant more than it might have done in another establishment.

'Robert greeted me kindly – he was perhaps five years older than myself – and said, ''Now, young Philip, I believe I have something to teach you?''

' "I believe so," I said, not knowing how else to respond. To my surprise he placed an arm about my shoulders, and walked me upstairs to the guest bedroom next my uncle's (only used, to my knowledge, once or twice in the past five or six years, when he had legal or literary advisers to stay in the house). Entering the room, Robert turned and locked the door, and then to my surprise clasped me in his arms and planted a smacking kiss upon my lips.

'I did not, I confess, find this unpleasant, nor did I demur when, first removing his own clothing, he stripped me bare, admiring my person as he did so – for my young prick automatically rose at the caresses he conferred upon it, not in the least to my amazement as those four or five months past I had been delighting myself by manually persuading it to such a stand.

'The pleasures we then enjoyed, however, were surprising, for it had not occurred to me that what I had assumed to be a private matter could be so charmingly enhanced by sharing, nor that it would give me pleasure (as, after a while, it did) to imitate the actions of my lover.

'Not to prolong a description which must surely be somewhat uncomfortable to your ears' – which was far from the truth, for indeed his account fascinated me – 'I took much pleasure from Robert's attentions, and Robert, I believe, found his additional duties not at all unpleasant, for my uncle was an old man and though generous and undemanding, was no great ornament to a counterpane.

'One afternoon as Robert and I lay bathed in a delicious perspiration after a passage of love, he asked whether I never felt it a lack that I had never lain with a woman.

'No, I did not, I said, for what could they offer that someone of my own sex could not?

'Well, said Robert, there were attractions, as he himself knew who was as attached to them as to any other, though at present circumstances confined him to the embraces of myself or my uncle. It seemed a shame that I should not be permitted familiarity with a female, for, he said, why should I live my entire life with one hand tied behind my back? And apart from enjoyment, what if I wished to procreate? This was something no male lover could aid in. And in short, he persuaded me to try, and to that end introduced me to his sister, who lived with her mother not far from our gates. She was a fine young woman of some twenty years or so, sufficiently spirited to welcome the opportunity of congress with a handsome young boy (as I confess I was) some years her junior – any more than she had been, it seemed, to reject the embraces of her natural brother, for they had grown up in a small Kentish village far from the city, and in those days incest flourished where the roads were bad.

'I had not been prepared for my first passage with Robert himself, my uncle having given me no hint of what was to come. However, I set about preparing myself to meet Mary (for such was her name) much in the manner of a schoolboy preparing to meet his master at examination time. I pored over those books of prints in my uncle's library which depicted unclothed young women – and such there were, for my uncle was a genuine student of art, and if his preference was for such prints as those of the paintings of Master Caravaggio, or the sculptures of Michelangelo or Donatello (and he had a fine miniature copy of the latter's charming portrait of David upon his desk) he also had portfolios of other great paintings. Among these I paid especial attention to Mabuse's *Hercules and Deianeira,* where the entanglement of the couple's lower limbs speak an enchantment not to be contradicted by the intent gaze with which they fix each other, to Corregio's *Io,* in which a young woman positively swoons in the embrace of a cloudy monster, and to the numerous paintings of mythical scenes in which gods and goddesses pay less attention to ruling the mortals in their care than to affording each other carnal pleasure.

'I also asked Robert his advice on my approach to his sister, upon which he asserted that the things I did with him, with the addition of one other which he explained as best he could, and which sounded no less exciting than curious, would equally delight her. But would she permit the liberty? I asked. He responded that he was in no doubt of it, insisting that nothing we had done together would render his sister uncomfortable.

'We met one late afternoon in the boathouse which still stands upon the bank of the river. The sun was low and striking warmly across the lawns. My new friend, Mary, was awaiting me when Robert ushered me through the door and stood guard outside – for my uncle might not, he said, be happy at my choosing to sample the company of a young woman. My first sight of his sister struck me instantly as the counterpart of a scene from a painted Elysium, for she lay quite naked and face downward upon a rug on the floor, her legs slightly parted, and a cushion beneath her throwing her fine posteriors into a prominence highlighted by the golden rays of the sun striking upon them.

'Divesting myself of my clothes, I advanced at her beckoning gesture, and sat at her side, laying a hand upon the warmth of her back, and without considering it, I found myself stroking the length of it in a languorous gesture which clearly did not displease her.

'Somewhat to my shame, I was not at first able to display any enthusiasm for the congress to come, for my nervousness took from me the power of standing. However after a moment or two the purring of contentment which greeted my caresses conveyed to me a warmth which soon resulted in a display of vigour. This led Mary to place her hand admiringly upon my firing-piece, then to bend her head to examine it more closely, and finally to take it between her lips with a liquid embrace which sent a shiver of pleasure through my limbs. In a moment, I persuaded her to turn, and saw before me the first vision it had been my privilege to encounter of an unclothed female.

'My delight at the sight of her ravishing breasts (and indeed at their tender weight as I hesitantly put my hand to them) was unfeigned. But I could not restrain a start of astonishment as my eyes passed from them down over a gently undulating belly, carrying in its centre the deep dent of a bewitching navel, to her most secret place – for there, in violent contrast to the smooth surface I had observed in paintings or sculptures, I saw a nest as plentifully endowed with hair as that which lay between my own thighs!

'Mary could not but observe my amazement and, opening her legs, took my hand and placed it between them, where I found a resilience and softness far from repulsive. You can imagine that soon I knelt to examine the phenomenon more closely – and what was my surprise, as I watched, caressed and kissed, to see certain changes there which seemed to mirror those others I had observed in my own and Robert's bodies: the swelling and opening of the lips even as I touched them, the alteration in the colour from pale pink to a deeper, purplish-red, and the appearance of what seemed a miniature replica of my own swiving instrument which, when I touched it with the tip of my tongue, I conceived from her movements and pantings gave Mary not inconsiderable pleasure. Indeed, as I continued to apply my tongue and lips to the purpose, fascinated by the effect I was producing, her response became more hectic until at the last her body bent like a bow and a thin wail escaped her lips.

'As I lifted my head, I saw Robert as he still stood in the doorway give me an unmistakable signal of approval, then by moving his forefinger within a circle made by the finger and thumb of his other hand, he indicated that I should mount his sister in the manner which, in a drawing remarkable more for its explicatory than its artistic effect, he had demonstrated to me.

'Rising, then, from my position at her side, I knelt between Mary's still open legs, and lowered myself so that my prick was at the entrance to the portals and paused, afraid that the action would prove painful – for without boasting I must repeat that my instrument was of uncommon size for a boy of my age. But she impatiently raised herself so that already its tip slipped between her lower lips, lubricated to a fine mucosity by a combination of my own saliva and those natural juices which we extrude in moments of passion, so that it was almost without effort that I found its entire length sheathed in that welcoming scabbard, while sinking upon her body, breast to breast, I felt her hands upon my shoulders and back, stroking and caressing, then slipping between us, toying with my cods in much the same way as her brother was used to do.

'It would take a more adept tongue than mine to define the difference between lying with her and lying with her brother. He and I had never played the beast with two backs in the manner of the sodomites, for though he had offered, I had a natural objection which he could not overrule. But in lying together face to face, the natural friction afforded by a rapid motion of our bodies naturally brought about the completion of our pleasure in much the same manner as it did, now, with his sister – except, of course, that in the latter case the culmination was reached in a manner rehearsed by man and woman for a thousand years. The smoothness of Robert's body counterfeited that of his sister; the roughness of a hairy man is of course most different – but I need not say this to you, my dear Sophie, who must be sensitive of it.'

Philip paused for a while, and looked at me as if to discover whether I was offended. But I was indeed more interested than affronted, and begged him to continue.

'My story is nearly over,' he said, 'but now comes the sad part, for though I was delighted by my experience, and grateful both to Robert and his sister, I found that the next time I met with the latter, my piece remained unfired, and despite her most ardent caresses, failed to stand. And indeed I found I could not be enthusiastic to repeat our mutual pleasure, though she much wished it, and was I fear offended. And ever afterwards, though I delight in the company of women, I find that once I have been granted familiarity, I am unable to repeat my tribute to their beauty – which explains my failure to pay you the compliment you richly deserve, and will no doubt receive again and again from happier men.'

I could find no reply, except to wonder at it.

'I wonder, myself,' said Philip, 'and sometimes believe myself cured, for I have no difficulty in accommodating ladies who are strange to me – as your brother will testify, my visit to Brook Street being a test of my manhood which I did not fail. However, though that young lady was the most energetic and handsome of partners, I fear that were we to meet again I would disappoint her.'

It would be fruitless to pretend that I was not myself disappointed, and though I attempted to smile sympathetically, and kissed him upon the lips as I left, I was not comforted. If I had been warm before, Philip's description of his passage with Miss Mary had heated my blood yet further, and I went into the hallway intending at the very least to make for my room and find what comfort I could in solitary caresses. But who should be standing ready to leave the house, but Harry. He looked at me and smiled, and almost before I was conscious that my good resolutions had crumbled, I found myself looking deep into his eyes with what meaning I could convey – and that, I fear, as open an invitation as any of the ladies in Brook Street could offer.

He was not slow to react, for in a moment he had lifted me in his arms and turned back into the room, now deserted, where my boys were usually seen at home. Placing me upon the couch, he took my dress at the throat and with one movement tore the slender material from me, almost in the same moment releasing his trousers and falling upon me. Dewed as I was by the liquor which had fallen in my excited state, his sturdy prick, strong as an iron bar, seemed to mount to the top of my stomach, and beneath my hands his brown body seemed carved from wood, so firm and hard was it. In my pleasure, I tore the shirt from his shoulders and sank my teeth into his flesh, which persuaded him to a violence of motion which sprung both from that and, I would guess, from a kind of desperation, he having already given service to three women during the course of the evening, a scant hour separating the last from the present time.

Concomitant with his ardour was the slowness of his body to respond – a delight to me, for no less than three times was I roused to the utmost rapture, draining my body of its gathered tensions, before with a shudder he ceased, and lay upon me as if dead, his body and mine in a lather of perspiration which as we drew apart smothered our lower parts in a foam.

I wriggled from beneath his weight and, reaching for a towel, wiped his limbs, then with a push turned him onto his belly and dried his back and buttocks – noticing as I did so a strange, triangular mark upon one, a birthmark almost hidden by dark hair.

He should sleep there, I told him, for I was sure he was now too exhausted to leave, and should he do so, so heated that the night air even of a mild evening might do him harm. Covering him with another towel, and bending to kiss his cheek, I left him already asleep and went to my own bed, conscious that I might have been foolish in favouring

one of my boys rather than another, yet also that the
occasion was a remarkable one.

As I walked to the door, I am almost sure that I heard a
rustling movement behind the screen below which we had
been exerting ourselves. The only person who could have
been there, watching us, was Philip. Should I have been
angry, or pitiful, or scornful? I could not, at the time,
decide, but I did not allow the episode to create difficulties
between Philip and myself – we were too much friends,
and indeed were making too much money, to permit anything to place a barrier between us. I felt more sorry for
him than anything else and, conscious of his comings and
goings, wondered how he satisfied those itches which must
surely be in the blood of so young and virile a man. Was he
a secret but confirmed twiddlepoop? But this was clearly
not my concern.

Two weeks or so after the episode I have just related, I
received an invitation to the marriage of Viscount Chichley
with the Lady Frances Brivet, which was to take place at St
George's Church in Hanover Square (where I recalled Sir
William Hamilton married that lady who subsequently
became the mistress of the Lord Nelson). Then to supper at
a house in the Portland Place, Mary-le-Bone, which
Chichley had built upon the edge of the great field where a
thousand cows grazed, providing much of the town with
milk. It was the only house north of Devonshire Place,
between which and Hampstead no other dwelling was to be
seen.

It can be supposed that much time and some expense was
spent upon my preparing a costume for the occasion which
would distinguish me among the horde, yet would not be so
distinctive as to mark me out as more a cynosure than the
bride, who wore a magnificent white gown from France.
Chichley was splendid in a simple and plain cut-away coat
in dark blue with a crimson waistcoat – not a wrinkle to be
seen either in these or in the breeches which clad his fine
lower limbs.

The ceremony was conducted with great solemnity by a
bishop carried from the provinces for the occasion, who
seemed amiable enough but was clearly unused to such a

great occasion, and whose voice in consequence was scarcely heard beyond the immediate vicinity of the altar. Afterwards, we were taken by a fleet of coaches to Chichley's mansion, which proved as handsome and sufficient as one might have imagined, furnished according to the latest taste.

There, a splendid feast was set out to which the large company gave full attention. This banquet quite exceeded in profusion anything I had previously seen: a first course of oyster sauce, fowls, fish, soup, roasted and boiled beef, boiled turkeys and celery sauce, pigs' feet and ears, tongue, *fricandeau,* saddle of mutton, roast woodcocks, wildfowl, spinach, bacon and vegetables, followed by creams, pastry, cauliflowers, *ragoût à la Française*, cream, game, celery, macaroni and pastry, and finally by walnuts, raisins and almonds, apple cakes, pears and oranges. The wines comprised champagne (white and rosy), burgundy, claret, sherry, Hermitage (red and white), Constantia, Sauterne, Madeira and port, with small-beer for those who wished it. Toasts were made, first to the bride and groom, then between guests, until for the most part those at table were virtually incapable of remaining upright or making themselves understood. Coarse jests and erotic undertones became common and, by nine o'clock, half the company did not know whether they were on their heads or their heels. The reverend and learned orientalist of the British Museum (having taken glasses of brandy at intervals between his port wine) at length fell helpless and insensible beneath the table, from which position he was lifted by the servants, at Chichley's direction, and placed in a hackney coach to be driven to his lodgings.

My friend had remained, I noted, remarkably sober, as did his bride. The latter had received me coolly, her husband with a warm pressure of the hand, yet no other sign of familiarity, which indeed I would not have expected of him. And I could not but recognise, regarding them as they sat at the head of the table, that they did not behave as a newly married couple might have been expected to behave – there was no exchange of smiles, no catching of hand in hand, let alone the placing of lips to palm or cheek to cheek, but a solemn politeness as formal to each other as to the least known of their guests.

Finally, though neither of them seemed eager for it, the moment came when the bride must prepare for bed. Her bridesmaids rose and, taking her by the arms, wafted her from the room. Chichley immediately caught my eye, and with an appealing look excused himself from the table (no difficult task, since those around him were to a large extent insensible) and went from the room – again looking at me as though to invite me to follow him, which after a moment's pause, and looking about me to make sure I was not particularly observed, I did. I found myself in a small ante-chamber where my young friend stood moodily, one arm stretched along the mantelshelf, staring in melancholy fashion into the dying embers of a fire.

'Well, my lord,' said I, 'this is no mood for a groom upon his wedding night!' – whereupon he took me by the elbows, and tears started to his eyes.

' 'Tis like marrying a sister,' he said. 'She is no warmer now than when we were eight; she is insensible to all approaches, cold and distant, with no notion of what could please a man – and here am I shackled to her for life!'

I did not enquire what had led him to this pass; it must, I supposed, have been a family requirement. Nor, I confess, did I resist when he clasped me to his bosom and pressed kisses upon my lips, for he was clearly in search more of sentiment than of carnal comfort, contenting himself with my lips and making no motion to improve the occasion.

I said nothing, and he said no more, but in a while and with a deep sigh released me – just as a group of his drunken friends broke through the door with incoherent cries. Taking him by the shoulders they bustled him off, myself following, into the hall, up the stairs, and through a door into what must surely be the bridal chamber. So indeed it proved, for once through the door I saw the bride, sitting upright in the large four-posted bed, now clad in a simple shift cut sufficiently low to show a breast which no man would be ashamed to covet, but which she was protecting by a modest inflexion of her hand, her looks betraying neither fear nor lust, but simple indifference and a desire that the charade should be immediately terminated.

Meanwhile, not content with snatches of bawdy song which they were in no position to render either melodiously or even coherently, Chichley's friends had undone him at the waist, encouraged by the women who now resembled harridans rather than wedding guests, and were engaged in stripping him bare. Off came his coat, his shirt, finally his breeches and stockings, and naked as he was born he displayed (as they mockingly drew attention to) a manly part shrunken to the size of a hazelnut. One of the brides-maids (though 'maid' was indeed no word for her) sank to her knees before him and, encouraged by his friends, tried to rouse him to a show of enthusiasm, but signally failed, at which there was more ribaldry which I knew to be falsely founded, having the keenest recollection of the sensitivity and feeling of which his male instrument was capable when aroused by the propinquity of a woman to whom he was genuinely attracted. Finally, tiring of their sport – with a 'one, two and three!' – his friends simply threw Chichley upon the bed, drawing the curtains about it (how grateful he must have been for the relief) and with a final fusillade of bawdy cries, swept from the room.

I paused for a moment. From the bed came only a faint rustling; no other sound, either of pleasure or resistance, and I could not but conclude that it would be a cold night of it – and very possibly, a cold life – for the newly-wedded couple. It was not a fate I would have wished upon Chichley, a boy capable, as I knew, of as much ardour as humour, as much tenderness as high spirits. Damnation, say I, to all made marriages.

Determining to leave the house immediately, I made my way from the room and prepared to descend the staircase – but passing an open door, my eye could not escape falling upon the orgy taking place within the room upon which it gave. On the bed, but also on the rugs of the floor, lay in a variety of lascivious attitudes perhaps eight or twelve persons of both sexes engaged in the performance of every variation of the act of love – not only man and woman in natural congress, but man with man and woman with woman. It was a scene which, painted for the pleasure of exciting lust, or even presenting itself to the senses under different circumstances, would no doubt have excited my susceptibilities. But in this case the persons engaging were so voided, by liquor, of sensibility that their actions were those of animals rather than of men and women – a fact reflected in a certain vicious carnality which divested their actions of consideration, taste or subtlety. This circumstance was underlined when two of the ruffian men, looking up from the women they were swiving and seeing my passing glance, leapt to their feet naked as they were and reeking from their congress, and came towards me with a cry of 'Here's a fine bushel bubby! Come and blow the grounsils, wench!' – which I understood only by their obvious intention, which was to force me to their pleasure.

Inclined though I usually am for pleasure, there were several reasons for my disinclination at that time: the first being my melancholy from observing Chichley's unhappiness; the second my reluctance to throw myself into such a tangle of strangers' bodies as lay before me; the third that the two men who now stood before me were to the last degree unattractive. One was vastly plump, his great belly hanging so low it seemed to be supported only by his pouting instrument (though that, indeed, was not of such dimensions as to bear even a lesser weight), while the second, though hung to a punishing degree, and evidently of such corporeal power as under other circumstances might be promising, was so drunk as scarcely to be able to stand. Even did I not suspect that this would damage the prospects of his continued phallic erection, I was not ready to bear closer acquaintance with that stinking breath which assaulted my nostrils even as I stood some feet away.

However, there was a difference between my reluctance and their insistence, and before I could move, they were upon me, and one, taking my delicate and costly dress at the throat had with one lunge split it to the waist, releasing my breasts, upon which he placed his horny hands. The second got himself somehow behind me and pushed me into the room, where in a moment I stumbled and fell to the floor among the mess of unclad bodies – each of which was too engaged in incoherent pleasure to take notice of my sudden appearance. I steeled myself for the assault to come.

Happily, however, my two assailants now fell out, one

with the other, about which should take me first, and soon came to drunken brawling, the one planting a fist in the pendulous belly of the other, who immediately vomited copiously over several of the lovers nearest to him. This caused a considerable confusion, during which I was able to make my escape, flee down the stairs and, clutching the remnants of my clothing about me, summon my carriage and return home. Too shaken by the experience even to speak to Polly, I took myself to a bed more solitary than Chichley's and, I suspect, as quiet if more content.

Chapter Eleven

The Adventures of Andy

It is a strange fact that even the most unusual circumstances, if prolonged, become common, and that the most remarkable incidents, if repeated, appear unremarkable. If only a few months before coming to London I had been told that I should be occupied in the administration of a house of pleasure, and that during the course of each day I should be continually in the presence of a number of delightful women in all forms of dress and undress, I should have considered myself fortunate. And that such a situation should be anything less than exciting would have seemed strange.

However, as the weeks became months, both Frank and I had to confess to a certain tedium; each day was like the last, and the hours became – to tell the truth – more than a little long, for as was not the case with Sophie, we felt that we should attend at the house while any guests were on the premises, in order to guard the women from possible unpleasantness. Blatchford, Will Pounce and Bob Tippett were of course men enough to outface any physical force with which they were likely to be confronted, but being of no education were easily confounded by a display of superior carriage, whereas I, though humbly born, had by now had considerable experience of putting the unruly of whatever rank in their place, while Frank had a natural haughtiness which gave him authority.

In time, however, we worked out an arrangement whereby one or other of us absented himself and found what entertainment he could about the town, though generally making sure that the other knew where to contact him in case of emergency. I took to practising my guitar once more, which pleased the ladies and gave me also some pleasure, while Frank began to establish himself at a political club nearby, for he had an eye to enter politics perhaps as a member for the constituency in which Alcovary was situate.

I continued to learn a little more about the characters and histories of our friends, though indeed once the bare bones of their stories had been told there was little to add. Moll was the last to tell me her secret, and that in private conversation, for with her somewhat rougher manners she felt partly ill at ease with her companions, friendly and kind though she agreed they were, for indeed never an unpleasant word was exchanged between them.

A knock upon the door one evening was answered by Will and, hearing raised voices and believing that there might be trouble, I went to his aid. I found him denying entrance to a youngster who seemed a little familiar, and who indeed soon revealed himself as Moll's brother, whom I had seen fleetingly as he left her bed upon my visit to her room in Church Lane. I immediately afforded him entrance and summoned Moll, and having thrown her arms about him they went to a private room, whence eventually he departed and I found Moll in tears. Pouring her some wine and putting my arm about her, I did my best to comfort her and asked what was amiss.

It was nothing, she said, but simply a disappointment. John had come to tell her (and here she whimpered a little) that some hope he had had of finding their lost brother had failed.

Had she two brothers, I asked, and one lost?

Ay, she answered. It was her elder brother, with whom she had grown up. He was some five years older than she, and her companion from as distant a time as she could remember, for they had shared a bed from her being five or six years old. This, she said, had made her familiar with the sight of the male body before she had seen that of any stranger – though it was all in innocence, 'for Harry never touched me in the way of carnality, and whenever I in teasing mood attempted play – as when in the morning I discovered his prick at stand, and came to toy with it as with a doll or other plaything – he would dissuade me. And he only once hit me, which was when I took hold of it while he was asleep, and toyed until, as he awoke, it involuntarily gave forth its juices, whereupon he said 'twas wicked for brother and sister to play so.'

Later she was to follow this rule with John, the young one, and though they were often naked a-bed together there was no familiarity except that of sisterly and brotherly comfort, and though they lived in the closest propinquity they were as moral as any preacher's family.

'But when my mother died,' she proceeded, 'my father having long since left us and she raising us by simple work, the landlord of our small room threatened to throw us out upon the street – whereupon Harry, then only fifteen, assured me that he would support us. But his work as a labourer in a brickyard fell away, and we came into debt. He would go further and further abroad to find employment and so was out when the landlord came and claimed our room, throwing me and John, then only five, into the street.

'I asked to remain at least until Harry returned, but was driven away, so that when he came we missed each other, and despite all my efforts I have not seen him since for eight clear years; though returning again and again to the street in which we once lived, in the hopes of seeing him.

'It was to support myself and my brother, who without me would be forced into chimney-sweeping or some other dreadful trade, that after some precarious years begging for crusts in the streets, and surviving only by the kindness of a few friends, I turned to the work of which you know, though my mother had always spoken much against it. And once I had taken the first step, I found myself quickly too used to the comforts I could purchase by only a moderate effort to forgo them either for me or for John.

'But,' she said, 'I have never lost hope of once more finding Harry, and John had recently heard that someone like him had been seen at work ditch-digging in Southwark. But now he tells me enquiries have led nowhere.'

But how could she describe her brother, I asked, one young man being much like another, and it being so long since she had seen him – for a young man of fifteen may be much changed in ten years.

Indeed Harry had been unremarkable, she said, and it would be difficult to give a description which would not apply to any young man of his age, save that he had a small three-sided red birthmark upon the right cheek of his buttocks – a thing which would come to the notice of others only in intimate circumstances, and which would be difficult to noise abroad without indelicacy.

The wine, of which we had now drunk an entire bottle, had considerably enlivened Moll, and expressing her gratitude to me for having lent her my ears, she began those familiarities which through long acquaintance she had learned provide pleasure to the male sex. And since I was, as ever, susceptible we soon arrived at a mutual warmth, and with my breeches loosened she sat astride my lap with my prick happily housed in that warm and moist habiliment where it was most at home. So, comfortably embraced, we began a second bottle, but before we could turn our attention fully to carnal pleasures, Will Pounce broke into the room without knocking – something which had never happened before.

'Master Archer! Master Archer!' he cried. 'The watch is below and demanding to see the mistress of the house.'

Here was a pretty pass, for Aspasia, pleading a proposed visit by an old friend, had begged absence and been accorded it. And now the very purpose of her presence here was foiled, for she had told us it was entirely illegal for a man to run such an establishment as we had at Brook Street, and there was no woman here capable of impersonating an experienced madam.

In my consternation I had leaped to my feet, tipping Moll inconsequentially to the floor, and now stood there anxiously, my essential part shrunken already to a poor thing.

But Moll leaped to her feet and cried, ' 'Tis no use, Andy, 'twill have to be you!'

While I stared uncomprehending, she sent Will below to equivocate until his mistress came.

'How many is it?' she asked.

'But one,' Will replied.

'Bring him upstairs and give him a glass with the girls, and tell them to make themselves pleasant.'

Will looked at me, but all I could do was nod. As he left the room, Moll already had me by the arm and was leading me – hanging on to my drooping breeches with one hand – into the room across the passage where was a cupboard in which Aspasia kept some of her clothing. Opening it, Moll seized a gown of purple velvet.

'Throw this on!' she said, and when I hesitated, almost tore the shirt from my back, so that willy nilly I stripped and obeyed her. She looked at me critically, and bundling up two dusters thrust them into my bosom to fill the empty space beneath the bodice.

'I have always envied you your complexion,' she said, 'and now, with a little help . . .' And taking a dish of powder which lay nearby she began to redden my cheeks and, spitting upon a finger, to apply some colour to my lips.

'A bonnet next –' and she reached down one which, being of an antique style, had side-pieces and when fastened disguised my head completely. 'Speak in a low voice,' Moll said, 'do not attempt to raise it. You will know the answers to the questions he will ask. He may simply be after a bribe.'

This was true, for the constables and watchmen of London at that time depended for their wages mainly on fees and perquisites, and were almost invariably extortioners, connivers at every form of wrong doing, pensioners of tavern and brothel keepers (frequently of the lowest order) and receivers of stolen property. It should not indeed be too difficult to deal with one of them. But still I hesitated.

' 'Tis no crime you commit,' Moll said, 'and if you do not make a try, the entire venture must fall!'

Perhaps happily there was no glass in which I could see myself, so I simply obeyed, making my way – almost tripping over my unaccustomed skirts – downstairs and to the door of the sitting room, in which I could hear a male voice among those in conversation. Drawing a deep breath, I entered to be faced by the girls, whose countenances were blank with surprise at they saw me, and the back of a man in dark clothes who, turning, disclosed a face covered with a bristling beard.

I strode in, trying to restrict my pace to a womanly tripping.

'Who have I the honour of meeting, sir?' I asked in what I hoped was a matronly voice (though a hysterical titter from Cissie suggested I was not entirely successful).

'Watchman Muffin,' said a thick voice. 'You are the mistress of this establishment?'

'I am.'

'May I congratulate you upon these admirable young ladies?' said the watch. 'They show a spirit only equalled by the delightful aspect of their persons.'

'To what, sir, do we owe the honour of this visit?'

'It is a happy part of my duties to visit all similar establishments in order to ensure that they are properly organised. You are . . .'

'Mrs Aspasia Woodvine,' I said (another titter from Cissie).

'May I ask where you attained the experience to govern such an establishment?'

I coughed.

'Ah – in the university of life, watchman,' I finally replied, provoking a laugh this time from Xanthe. 'You wish to inspect the house?'

'No, no, madam, I am quite sure simply from a view of this room that the appointments are excellent, while I need make no comment on the admirable qualities of the young ladies I have already had the pleasure of meeting. Perhaps, however, it might be possible . . .' and he raised his eyebrow in a gesture I thought I understood.

'Perhaps, sergeant, we might offer you the hospitality of the house?'

'My dear madam, it would give me the greatest pleasure.'

Mightily relieved, I asked whether he would care to indicate which of our ladies he would like to show him the hot baths which were the signal distinguishing attribute of the house? But he demurred.

'I had hoped, madam . . .' he said, and stepping forward stretched out a hand as though to place it on my bosom. I felt the blood drain from my face as I apprehended his meaning. But what was this? To my horror, Moll, who had been standing beside me, stepped forward and plunged her hand into the sergeant's beard. I opened my mouth to remonstrate, when with a tug – and to my amazement – the beard came away in her hand, revealing the face of none other than Frank, who a moment later sank almost helpless with laughter into a chair!

I was too relieved to be either angry or amused.

'Forgive me, my dear old fellow!' said Frank, when he had recovered himself, 'but boredom got the better of me, and besides, I was curious to see what solution you would offer were a watchman actually to call. I must congratulate myself on my disguise, which so thoroughly deceived all save one!'

I turned to look at Moll – had she been a part of this plot? But she assured me she had not, and indeed it turned out that Frank had conceived it entirely of himself, and had gone unrecognised both by Will and by the girls.

'I think a revenge should be taken!' cried Xanthe. 'Seize him, girls!' – which they did, and in no small time had stripped him and laying him upon a couch bound his hands and legs to the arms so that he could not move. With the utmost deliberation they then slowly removed their clothing and stood before him in their naked beauty – and though, as I have already said, I was accustomed to seeing each of them in every stage of undress, I must admit that it made a delightful picutre. Xanthe, her fair hair about her shoulders, her arm about her friend Rose's shoulders, their slim bodies, small breasts and slender thighs one a counterpart of the other; then Constance, her skin almost as nut-brown as it had been in the country (for she slipped into the garden at every possibility to lie in the sun, to the pleasure of Will, who would sit admiringly at her side); Sally and Cissie, as like as Xanthe and Rose, but rounder-limbed, their breasts plumper and their hips broader; and finally Ginevra and Moll, each with her peculiarly entrancing points of admiration. I felt my own manhood stir, despite my ridiculous attire, and Frank, bound as he was, had no way of disguising the interest that this display of beauty had for him – a fact to which Xanthe drew attention, saying, 'Look, friends, scarcely yet a display to frighten a lady. But we must see what we can do.' And she immediately took Rose in her arms and, the latter nothing loath, led her to the very foot of Frank's couch and began to kiss and clip her, passing her hands over her person to display its every delight, and compliment it by a touch of finger or tongue. The sight was delightful enough to raise the dead, and Frank's tool soon swelled to its full proportion and, empurpled, stood in approbation of the view offered him. His smile had by now faded, and he was gripping his lower lip with his teeth, determined to be silent.

But how long could he do so? Determined to have my part in the revenge, I threw off Aspasia's dress and, myself prepared for pleasure, took my place between Sally and Cissie, throwing an arm around each pair of shoulders and bending to kiss their pouting titties while their hands found their way, as water does to a vacant channel, over my belly and thighs to stroke and make much of that part of me which longed to compliment them upon their beauty.

By now Frank could not resist imploring his release, but no one took more notice of him than to concentrate even more upon their own pleasure, Xanthe and Rose falling to the floor at one side of his couch, and my kneeling at the other so that Sally could straddle my knees and, as I entered her, I could pleasure her cousin with my lips, while Cissie's hands employed themselves where they might about our occupied bodies.

'But do not forget our master!' cried Xanthe at last, raising her head from her friend's breast; 'Constance, Ginevra, Moll!'

And to Frank's delight, the three girls came towards him – but rather than releasing him, merely sat upon the edge of the couch and made much of him, one kissing his mouth, then flicking his nipples with her tongue, kissing his breast, his neck, his shoulders, catching with her lips at the hair which sprouted from his armpits, his hands the while desperately attempting to catch at the breasts which brushed his lower arms, but always failing to reach them. Meanwhile her friend was running her tongue between his toes, then sucking each in turn as she stroked his calves and thighs. And the third – Ginevra, whose lips were peculiarly adept at it – was bringing his now throbbing tool time and time again to the point of eruption by the most gentle, feathery touch, now upon the tip, now at the base, first running full, liquid lips over its whole length, then merely covering the tip like a cap. When he could release his lips he cried for relief, but Ginevra, whenever she felt by the tautness of his instrument that release was near, would fall to nibbling his cods, or that muscle which runs beneath their base like a second, concealed cock.

Finally, Frank found release, imagination no less than caresses overrunning his body. With a great shout he bent himself into a bow, and like a fountain erupted to a height I would have thought impossible – whereat I, too, for some time in the same critical state, also voided myself into Sally's friendly embrace.

Frank, when he was recovered and had been released, explained that while the whole exercise of his disguise had been, certainly, amusing, it had also been something of an experiment for, he said, the possibility of a real visit from the watch was not something we should entirely discount, and must indeed be prepared for. And though my impersonation of Aspasia had been a brave attempt, he was not entirely sure that it would have deceived the dullest officer for long (nor was I!) and we must persuade Aspasia to train one of the girls to take her place should she be away, though she should always be referred to as the proprietor of the place, while myself or Frank should pretend to be clients rather than having anything to do with the running of the house.

'Will, Blatchford and Tippett we can leave alone,' he said, 'for the place must have its men about both for service and protection. But it would be a pity if the operation should come to a premature end' – as indeed it would, for we, and the girls, were making more money from it than we had ever imagined possible. The girls were indeed delighted, for our visitors, having paid their fees, were only too pleased to leave them more money in recognition of their kindness. We at no time enquired about this, but there was no pretence that it did not take place, and everyone was content that it should.

It was shortly after this that Frank received a letter bearing news that Mrs Jopling Rowe had suddenly died, just after placing the house in which we had visited her upon the market, and that her man of business wished to see him upon an urgent matter. Since it had been some time since we had been out of town, it was decided that we should both travel down to the coast, the weather being now extremely warm, and spend a night or so there not only to deal with whatever business was in hand, but also recreate ourselves. Blatchford was left in charge of the house, though we gave

Tippett and Will to understand that the three were to work together – for indeed we trusted all of them equally – while we hired two good mounts and set out on horseback for Brighthelmstone, which we reached after two days' pleasant riding, sleeping one night at an inn on the way.

We rode out to Worthing, and past Mrs Jopling Rowe's house, the windows of which were all shuttered, on our way to the office of her man of business, a plump and agreeable person who greeted us pleasantly, and immediately asked after all the girls, but particularly Constance (who, it seemed, had been his special favourite). In short, he revealed that just before preparing to sell up the house Mrs Jopling Rowe had made a will leaving all she had to the girls, in equal portions, which would amount to a sum enabling them to retire immediately from business should they wish to. 'But,' said the lawyer, 'they all seem to me to find their life so enjoyable that they will not desire it.' I was not quite so sanguine but of course we delighted in their good fortune and agreed to convey the news to them, while Mr Forfeit (as was his name) would complete the formalities.

'I hope,' he said, 'I have not dragged you this distance without cause, but I felt the matter to be of sufficient import to deliver the news personally, and I travel, these days, as little as possible.'

Not at all, returned Frank, we were glad of the excursion, for we had been busy of late . . .

Mr Forfeit had heard from Mrs Jopling Rowe of our venture, and was now full of questions on the subject, which we answered as completely as we could. Then we asked of him the address of an inn in the neighbourhood where we could stay.

'I can do better than that!' he cried. 'I have a small cottage which is let by the week, in the season, and which happens just now to be vacant; you are welcome to it. I shall send straight away for the girl to go in and open it up for you, and by the time we have enjoyed a glass of claret and a chop – for I hope you will join me? – it will be ready to receive you.'

The message having been sent, we indeed sat down with him, and he entertained us with highly indiscreet anecdotes about the people of the town while we ate and drank. Then he sent us off with his man to the cottage, with the invitation that we should make use of it for as long as we wished.

This little house lay at the top of a small cliff or incline a few feet above a beach. The windows opened to the view of a sparkling ocean, and we were greeted by a buxom young maid who dropped us a curtsy and showed us the place – which did not take long, since it comprised simply one small sitting room with a bedroom over (Worthing becoming so popular that even the smallest cupboard could command a considerable rent in the season).

The girl then departed, with the indication that there were cold meats in the tiny kitchen, together with milk, but that the centre of the town lay only five minutes' walk to the east should we wish to take a meal there later.

It was now one o'clock in the afternoon, and the sun beating down out of a cloudless sky, and sitting in the small garden, separated only by a low hedge from a path which descended to the sea side, we soon became drowsy and, stripping to our trousers, fell asleep in the sun, lying upon the grass.

I woke, some time later, to the sound of whispering and giggling, and half opening my eyes saw against the sky the outline of a row of heads looking over the hedge. It was half a dozen girls, of what age I could not guess, but I supposed not of many years. And glancing to my side I could understand their interest, for before falling asleep Frank, thinking us safe from prying eyes, had thrown off the rest of his clothes, and now lay quite naked to the view, a handsome enough figure to engage the interest of any female.

The girls had seen my movement, however, and now withdrew, so I nudged Frank and, when he woke, informed him of the entertainment he had afforded, whereupon he did not demur, but asked why I did not invite the young persons in!

Soon, cries and the sounds of splashing were heard from below, and looking cautiously over the hedge we saw that the girls had thrown off their clothing and were bathing in the sea – a delightful sight for, as in those days was the custom, they had not crammed their limbs into swimming dresses but were as free as fish, and their flesh so shining in the sun that indeed they resembled strange aqueous creatures, and had they proved tailed we would not have been surprised!

'What do you say,' Frank enquired, 'to our allowing ourselves the pleasure I gave them?' And he began to stride from the garden and when I followed, persuaded me to remove my clothing altogther for, he said, it was our beach, and our right to descend to it and use it in what manner we might. It was they were the trespassers and must bear the consequences.

It can be believed that a considerable furore was consequent upon our appearance on the sands; Frank was utterly assured, and walked down to the water's edge without the slightest diffidence, the sun flooding every inch of his body with light. I was less inclined to display, and hung back, but turning, he beckoned me forward – and after all, why should I be less proud than he? – for I did not suppose myself to be less well built.

The girls for a while pretended not to see us, giggling, screaming and playing in the water, though we could see them casting their eyes towards us as we strode to and fro, when they thought we were not looking.

'Shall we join them?' I asked, but Frank said no, the moment we were in the water they would make good their escape, and he was not inclined to let them off so easily. Whereupon he lay down at ease in the very centre of the small beach, and I lowered myself to his side, the sand warm to my flesh. There, we enjoyed the sight of the girls, now clustered together and wondering what to do, for the sides of the beach gave onto steeper cliffs which were unscalable.

After a short period, they reached a decision, and simply turned and walked towards us, emerging slowly from the sea as Aphrodite did at Petra tou Romiou, the water falling first below their shoulders, then revealing twelve handsome breasts (a feast so ample my eyes did not know which way to glance), and finally hips, thighs and what lay between – only two of them being sufficiently shy to attempt to shield their most intimate parts with their hands.

Their leader was a fine young creature with red-brown hair, who coolly strode up and stood over us, so that water drops fell from her body upon our legs, and the tiny bumps upon her skin brought out by the cold were clear to view.

'Perhaps, gentlemen,' she said, 'you would not object to sharing the sunlight with us? Unless, of course, this part of the coast is your private property?'

Frank smiled, and patted the sand at his side – where without mock modesty the girl lowered herself and sat, and after a pause the others too lay near us, looking like nothing so much as a group of mermaids suddenly endowed with human limbs, and none the less handsome for that.

'I had heard,' said Frank, 'of the beauties of Worthing, but had not thought to encounter so many of them so readily.'

'And we have heard of sea-monsters,' the girl replied, 'and had not thought to encounter *them*, for we come here regularly by permission of Mr Forfeit, and have always previously been private.'

Inclining his head, Frank admitted that he had believed them to be making use of the beach without leave, but now (he said) it was his duty to apologise – though, he reminded her, it was their looking over the hedge that had led to the degree of openness which we were now enjoying.

'Not at all,' said the red-headed one, and reaching out drew her finger down the side of Frank's shoulder, along the lower side of his breast to his hip, and along the line where the leg joined the trunk to the very point at which, in a cluster of hair, lay a limb now betraying some enthusiasm for the propinquity of so many delightful creatures. And, indeed, I felt a similar stir of interest, and was conscious that the ladies were also cognisant of this.

'You will forgive me for suggesting,' said Frank, 'that young as you undoubtedly are, none of you seem to be entirely unfamiliar with the male form?'

'Not,' said the young lady, 'so familiar that we decline any opportunity enabling us to examine it further – which I trust explains our perhaps overweening curiosity of half an hour ago, and may even excuse a further familiarity which the present situation suggests.' And she placed two fingers upon that part of my friend's anatomy which (I guessed) was all too happy to welcome their caress. At the same time there fell upon my own shoulders a pair of hands which then slipped down until they embraced my breast, while against my back I felt the gentle pressure of two cool breasts, the nipples of which – whether by cold or desire I could not say – were hard as pebbles.

In a moment we were submerged by a tide of flesh, at first cool from the recent embrace of the sea, but soon, from the warmth of increasing lust no less than of the sun, torrid as in any bed-couplings.

To what extent those embraces were the product of genuine curiosity it was impossible to discover, but certainly the nymphs seemed intent upon exploring every secret we had to offer, their fingers prying into each corner, their eyes devouring each surface. I was too much the object of the attentions of three of them, myself, to observe the activities of the others, but could imagine that these were the counterfeit of those I was welcoming. One was intent upon kissing every part of my face, her tongue probing the whorls of my ears, the corners of my eyes, my nostrils, passing under the corners of my chin, inserting itself between my lips. At the same time I could feel another turning my hands, sucking each finger in turn, exploring the dint of my elbow and the pit of my arm, tiny nips – delicious as 'twas painful – of the flesh announcing her progress from shoulder down across the platform of my breast. And the third – ah, most adventurous! – was examining my middle parts, exploring the dint of my navel and pulling with gentle lips the hairs of my belly before proceeding to the tops of my thighs, biting the skin there with appreciative pleasure before thrusting my knees apart with her hands so that she could feast her eyes upon those parts normally more modestly possessed. I felt, after a while, her fingers weighing my cods, then the soft gesture of lips enclosing each in turn before proceeding to that instrument which (I need hardly say) was by now almost aburst with appreciation of such tender attentions, measuring its length, and with gentle fingers pulling the skin away so that its lambent tip could be annointed with tender kisses.

But now, the other two, bored with the more frequently displayed parts of my body, joined with the third, and I had the unaccustomed view of three female heads – two blonde, one black – pressed close together as their owners concentrated attention upon my essential maleness; a sight balanced by that a few feet away, where Frank was in the same circumstance. We caught each other's eyes, but our situation was so grave that we could not even raise a smile, simply observing each other's state, now approaching a remarkable fulfilment. I began to draw short breaths as my pleasure rose, placed my hands upon the nearest shoulders I could reach, felt the lips move softly, gently. . . . Then, I apprehended a shadow fall across my face. With a rude shock, just as the curve of pleasure was about to reach its height, all sensation had ceased, and opening my eyes I saw my three tormenters standing looking down at me – as the other three stood regarding Frank, who half sat with the same dumbfounded expression as myself, and the same distended and unsatisfied limb between his thighs.

'Gentlemen,' said the leader of the band, 'we now bid you good afternoon.'

And without looking back, they strode to the spot a few yards away where their clothes lay, and in a moment – women's dress still being scant – had drawn them on, and were climbing the path away from the beach.

Uncomfortable though we were, we could not but laugh at their revenge and rising, thrust ourselves immediately into the sea to cool our ardour – looking up as we did so to see several arms raised in farewell from the line of girls walking back around the cliff towards the town.

We enquired of good Forfeit who the young ladies might be, and were informed – to our amusement, for we had thought they were perhaps the denizens of a girls' school in the area – that they were in fact employed at a place of entertainment in Brighthelmstone which was the equivalent there of our house in Brook Street. 'I frequented it when younger,' said the lawyer, 'but I find the exertion now too much for me, and give myself only the pleasure of allowing them to use my beach for their summer entertainment, when they drive over. For them to bathe at Brighthelmstone would be impossible, since they are so well known about the town.'

We did not tell him of our adventure, but could not but be amused at our being so taken in. We shared a lonely bed that night, but the next afternoon repaired to Brighthelmstone, and for a modest fee – considerably less than that we charged in Brook Street – gave ourselves the pleasure of a renewed acquaintance with our tormenters, enjoying the joke at our expense, but this time reaching a conclusion which left us – and at least two of the girls – replete. We then returned to London to give our girls the happy news of their enrichment – which however would not be real for some weeks, until the estate had been gathered, the house sold, and an official determination made of the property. Whether they would then wish to remain in our employment was a question with which we would have to deal when the time came.

Chapter Twelve

Sophie's Story

I heard with some amusement of the prank brother Frank had played upon Andy and the girls in Brook Street, but was warned by Philip that nevertheless I might expect a visit from the local watch – partly because my uncommon arrangements would arouse their curiosity – 'but also,' he said, 'because I am in no doubt they will wish to take a proportion of the profits which they will have heard accrue to us here.'

When I asked about the degree of payment I would have to make, he could not say, for it would depend, he said, upon the cupidity of the officer concerned.

I had not long to wait for this information, however, for one evening Polly answered the door to a ring and found not a lady eager to inspect our wares but a man from the local watch-box, who demanded to speak either to Philip or myself – asking for us by name, so that it was clear he had some knowledge of our proceedings.

As luck would have it, Philip was out on one of his private excursions. I received the man in the front room, which he entered unceremoniously and without more of a greeting than a simple nod in my direction. He was a large, sturdy man, with close-cropped hair and a bullying manner, carrying his enormous rattle as if it were a lethal weapon. He minced no words.

'You will have expected a call, no doubt, ma'am,' he said. 'Such a house as this may be tolerated – if only for its originality – but since we are not paid by the public to protect organisations of this nature, you will agree that it is proper you should make a contribution to our expenses.'

I did not ask what expenses could have been incurred when he had to the best of my knowledge never set foot within a half-mile of the house, but merely enquired how much he wanted. To my amazement, he answered that ten pound a week would suffice – which indeed was a ridiculous sum, as I told him.

'Whether you pay it or not is a matter for you,' he said absently, 'but your friend will be aware that his own association with the place will be enough for us, should we wish it, to close the house down – much though we would regret the inconvenience to the wives of West London.'

All this time he had been wandering about the room, casting an eye on the decorations; then he came to the screen and went behind it.

'Ah,' he said, 'I have heard of this convenience, and indeed 'tis a remarkable one.'

It was a quiet evening, and all but William were occupied; he, as was his wont, and no doubt hearing voices and believing that a visitor was approaching, was lying face downwards upon the *chaise longue*.

'Very handsome,' said the sergeant. 'You will not object if I sample your wares?'

I must have looked uncomprehending, for 'Come, come, madam!' he said. 'It is a pity for such a delicate rump to be unoccupied.'

'This house is not for such purposes, sir,' I said. 'Moreover, William would not permit it, and at all events I have no room – they are all occupied!'

'I doubt that, ma'am, but in any case the boy need not move from his present position, which is admirable for my purpose! Nor will he, my strength being superior. His consent is not necessary – indeed, resistance adds a spice. You will prepare my little – *pourboire*? I shall be only a few moments; this display has quite engaged my fancy!' With which he strode from the room.

Amazed, I called to William through the screen. He rose and came towards me, but in a moment, the door opened and the sergeant burst into the room, unclasping his belt as he came.

'Come, ma'am, watch if you please, but do not intervene!' he cried in my direction, seizing the astonished William and throwing him once more upon the couch, then without pause lowering his breeches to reveal an enormous instrument – one which might have been welcome to some ladies, but from which a male person could only have shrunk, as William did, who alas was far too light of build to think of opposition!

Pausing only to spit on his hand and anoint his instrument, the watchman leapt upon William and thrust at him, whereupon the unfortunate young man gave out a howl of pain which might have been heard clear across the house – and indeed was, for in a short period the door opened and in strode Spencer, who had just said farewell to the lady he had been entertaining, and crossing the hall had heard the disturbance. In a moment he apprehended the situation, strode to the couch and, seizing the watchman by the arm with surprising strength, hurled him off William's body and clear across the room.

'Out!' he said to William, indicating the door. The latter rose and without argument left the room while the watchman, with a roar of anger, climbed to his feet. But in the face of this man, much larger and more powerful than himself, Spencer maintained a silent dignity which halted him in his tracks – and then, the watchman seemed to recognise him, for he looked curiously at his face.

'Why, Sergeant Gross,' said Spencer.

Despite himself, it seemed, the watchman came to a sort of attention – ludicrously so, with one leg still entangled in his breeches, and his shirt tails barely concealing his now much diminished person.

'How interesting that we should meet again.'

The man was silent.

'I had heard that you were attached to the watch hereabout,' said Spencer. 'It is fortunate that you have called upon us, for I am sure you will wish to use your influence to ensure that we are not troubled by the attentions of your colleagues?'

To my astonishment, the man – though looking unhappy – nodded.

'Sir!' he said.

'I trust not to see you here again,' said Spencer, 'and you will kindly refrain from paying your attentions to any of my colleagues. No doubt many unfortunate lads in the neighbourhood will be as used to your depravities as some were in the field – here, we enjoy more conventional pleasures. In short, should we see you here again I may be forced to mention the circumstances of La Haye Sainte, and even perhaps to communicate to the Duke himself some facts about that unfortunate affair.'

The watchman seemed to shiver. 'No, sir, of course, sir, I shall – we will – you shall not be troubled.'

'Well, sergeant, I suggest you cover yourself and leave,' said Spencer, seating himself negligently on the corner of the billiard table. Scrambling into his trousers, while still somehow comically giving the impression of remaining at attention, the sergeant saluted and left the room almost at a run – so speedily indeed that by the time I reached the hall, the front door had already closed behind him.

I entered the back room, where Spencer was now reading a newspaper.

'Ah, good evening, Mrs Nelham,' he said as though nothing had happened.

'My dear Mr Middlemas,' I said, feeling that a little formality was the least I could afford him, 'how on earth did you do it?'

He raised an eyebrow.

'Ah, ma'am,' he said, 'I had not realised you were an observer. Oh, 'twas nothing – I happened to have met the man before.'

'Evidently,' I said. 'But how did you subdue him? What is La Haye Sainte?'

He showed a marked disinclination to explain – but on my pressing him, admitted that he had served as an officer under the Duke of Wellington at the late great battle of Waterloo, and had been with the King's German Legion at La Haye Sainte, just towards the centre of the Duke's main force. The French forces had mounted a severe attack on this stronghold, and one English sergeant's nerve breaking, he had cried defeat. Whereupon the Dutch-Belgian brigade which was assisting had broken and run, and the position had only with the greatest difficulty been held, only a last-minute charge of the cavalry – Royals, Scots Greys and Inniskillings – saving the situation.

'I see,' said I, 'and the cowardly sergeant . . .'

'Exactly, ma'am,' said Spencer. 'I happened to know the man, and recognised him. I said nothing at the time; we

were all frightened enough, and no man can be fully responsible for his actions under such pressure. The Duke himself
made attempts to find the culprit, but none but I could
identify him, and I refrained – and for that reason sadly
was forced to leave the service. But I see nothing wrong in
using such knowledge to protect this enterprise.'

'Indeed, I am most grateful – we all must be.'

'I pray, ma'am, that you will not inform the others,' said
Spencer. And indeed was determined that I should not do
so – nor, especially, make known the fact that (as was
clearly the case) he had held an officer's rank upon the
occasion of the battle. It seemed sad that circumstances
should have rendered it necessary for him to seek his present appointment. At all events, the particulars of his rescue
of William were never known – though the latter told his
story, and the others ever afterwards regarded Spencer with
additional reverence – though, indeed, he had always been
regarded as a sort of father to them, being older by some
years than they.

I reported this incident to brother Frank only in case the
same man should trouble him, though the distance between
us made it unlikely, and thereafter life resumed its even
tenor, disturbed only by an unexpected message from
Brandenburgh House, summoning me to call upon a
Madame Fouquet, who was at present renting it from its
owner. I found her a spirited lady of perhaps forty years.

'Mrs Nelham,' she said, 'we have not met, but I have
heard of course of your establishment, as who has not?'

I inclined my head, wondering whether perhaps she was
about to rebuke me for conducting my business under the
shadow of her walls. But not at all.

'I have three daughters,' she said, 'twin girls of eighteen,
and another of sixteen, who have been raised (because of
their father's feelings upon the matter) only with the barest
notion of the connection between the sexes. There are also
staying here two English girl cousins equally innocent. It
has now come time however when they should be educated,
for I am cognisant as you are, ma'am, of the troubles which
may arise later in life as the result of ignorance in that
important area.'

She paused. Was I to be asked to propose some of my

stable to entertain the girls? There would be no difficulty in that. But no.

Indeed it was the case; but more – in order that such intimate business, suddenly proposed, should not be too shocking, 'What I wish to do,' she said, 'is to demonstrate, as it were, the mechanics of the business, and to that end engage your help. We have in France a book written a century and a half ago by a M. Michel Millot and a M. Jean L'Ange.'

'You mean *L'École des Filles*, or as we know it here, *The School of Venus*?' I asked.

The lady bowed.

'I beg your pardon, ma'am,' she said, 'I had not realised you were a scholar.'

'To no great degree,' I said, 'but that book I have been familiar with since the subject has been a preoccupation with me.'

'Sadly,' she said, 'none of my girls is of a scholarly disposition, and I could not hope to persuade them to read it, despite the warmth of its contents. So I wish to present it in dramatic form, with your help.'

The little theatre attached to the house sat only a dozen people, she explained; she hoped that I could persuade one of my gentlemen to appear upon its small stage with some lady, and there to act out some readings which she had prepared from the book.

In short, I saw the benefit of the plan – not only to the young ladies, but to the actors, to whom she was prepared to pay fifteen guineas each. I was sure that there would be no difficulty, and took away with me a copy of the readings my lady had extracted, and the following day went to Brook Street and engaged the services of Xanthe, whom my brother kindly released for the purpose, and introduced her to Harry. Both were delighted at the prospect before them, and though they had never before met, instantly showed a keen pleasure in each other's company. Within the week we repaired to one of the larger cubicles of my house, where we examined the text we were to illustrate.

My lady had chosen the second dialogue from that excellent book, in which Fanchon explains to Susanne how her lover, Robinet, first deflowered her. Harry, of course, was to play the part of Robinet, and Xanthe that of Fanchon, while I was to sit at the side of the stage, playing the part of Susanne but at the same time reading the words of Fanchon (which indeed appeared to me to be dramatically something strange, but was convenient).

I explained the situation to my friends: that Susanne had asked Fanchon what had happened between her and her lover, and that the scene began with the latter coming to the former's chamber while she was busy with her needlework, and after some polite conversation agreeing to a kiss – which soon became sufficiently passionate to enable the actors to discover to their young audience the part played by a tongue in the excitement of passion. Though they found this difficult (for it entailed always keeping their faces at one particular angle) Harry and Xanthe clearly did not find the contact unpleasant, nor was it difficult to persuade them to counterfeit Fanchon's discovery of a large bulge in Robinet's trousers and their continuing exploration of each other's persons, with Robinet's pleas to Fanchon to stroke his member, and his eventual removing of his trousers in order that she should see his instrument.

We worked to place Harry so that he faced the audience, his thighs parted so that the young ladies should share Fanchon's education in the matter by having the clearest possible view of his body, placing Xanthe behind him so that by reaching back he could raise her skirts and seem to be exploring her body. The young ladies being, I supposed, familiar with their own and each other's person, they would clearly be more interested in Harry's appurtenances than Xanthe's.

However, as the narrative became warmer and, the couple being unclothed, Robinet approached his body between Fanchon's limbs, it became more difficult to place the actors revealingly. Some time was spent in arranging their limbs – so long indeed that Harry, whose prick had raised itself in appreciation of Xanthe's beauty, was quite undone, and there had to be a pause while Xanthe returned him to full vigour with her hands, before he could enter her. I was then to recount the various positions the lovers adopted before Robinet finally deprived his mistress of her maidenhead, and then go on to the authors' descriptions of the complex amours which could give pleasure to a couple once that state had been achieved.

As we had completed the final pose, in which Xanthe lay with her legs thrown back and her calves lying over Harry's shoulders as he lay at an angle upon her, I noticed that Philip (aware, of course, of our scheme) had quietly entered the room and was admiring the tableau as I was – for I must confess to being somewhat heated by our rehearsal, as our two actors were. I must have looked longingly at him, for he smiled and, laying a hand upon my shoulder said, 'I am sorry, my dear Sophie, but you remember my difficulty. However, this young lady I have not tried, and if you both consent – and you, young Harry –' and with the words lifted Harry from Xanthe's body and turned him towards me. He was only too ready to step in my direction, and I welcomed him by thrusting up my skirts and falling readily upon my back, while Philip removed his breeches and took his place between Xanthe's welcoming thighs. So excited were we by our rehearsal that both Harry and I came within a moment, while Xanthe too was raised almost instantly to pleasure, and judging by her cries was again raised so by Philip's energy in but a short time. Watching his lean body at work, I could not but again regret the unfortunate state of affairs which seemed to deprive me for ever of the hope of a renewal of the exercise with him.

The performance took place two nights later. The little theatre was enchantingly lit by candles, and there was a nervousness in the air as we took the stage, the five girls and my lady at first silent in their chairs, but later giggling and paying a sighing tribute to Harry's body – the first unclothed male they had seen. Their interest was all-absorbing, and upon his entering Xanthe they with one accord left their seats and came down to the stage the more closely to observe how the act was done, one of them going so far as to stretch out her hand and pull at Harry's knee, to reveal more clearly how his instrument stood in relation to Xanthe's body. They all showed astonishment that so considerable a prick could enter a woman's body without causing her pain, and even wished to question Xanthe about it – but in the character of Fanchon she naturally could not answer. When – as we had designed – upon

approaching the culmination, he pulled away from his
mistress's body so that the juices spurted upon her belly,
there was a unanimous cry of amazement, followed by an
impressed silence, and then by applause, which our actors
happily acknowledged.

The girls were now more than somewhat red about the
face, and speechless with the strangeness of what they had
seen. But then an elder one, one of the sisters, said: 'Mama,
you cannot intend that all shall end here? Surely we must discover for ourselves the pleasures we have seen represented?'

Whereupon my lady revealed what she had secretly
planned with me – that indeed five of my gentlemen had
been reserved for their entertainment and further
education. And in no time we had walked the hundred
yards through the warm summer evening to the house,
where I took each girl to a room where one of the boys
waited – for they would not have had the experience to
choose for themselves, nor would it have been convenient.

I had taken the liberty of not including George, his
person being of such a size that it might positively injure a
young girl at her first game, whatever her enthusiasm. This
made for a little difficulty, but knowing his capacity for a
speedy recovery of vigour, I had appealed to Harry, who
had said that where a sparkling virgin of eighteen was in
prospect, he would 'get it up again' before I could recite the
Collect for St Felicitas' day. And the pleasure with which
one of the elder sisters greeted him promised that neither
would be disappointed.

In order to ensure that no distress would be caused, the
girls' mother and guardian had insisted that I should maintain a watch, and I had arranged with the boys that each
door be left ajar in order that I could glimpse the situation,
or hear any cries which betokened more pain than would be
properly concomitant with the situation, for I cannot disguise the fact that I feared my boys, enjoying the unusual
pleasure of being invited to deflower five virgins, might be
so inspirited by the occasion as to be too enthusiastic for the
girls' true pleasure.

I need not have concerned myself: each scene was one of
delight. Happily, I seemed to have struck on the right
pairing for each young person, though none had been

known to me before that week; indeed luck must have played its part.

In the first room I beheld one of the English cousins astride Spencer's knees, riding with such tender pleasure, and with such a look of engrossed adoration in her eyes, that no picture of father and daughter could have been more delightful. In the next two rooms, Ben and Tom were entertaining their young ladies – their plumpness encouraging both to tempt their charges to crouch above them, which also enabled the girls themselves to control the manner in which their unaccustomed bodies received the male instrument. Not that they showed very considerable hesitation, and indeed their pleasure clearly much outdid their pain.

William, however, his body being lithe and light, entertained one of the French girls in the traditional way, so that all I saw when I peeped through the aperture of the door was the bottom so admired by our watchman, embraced by a pair of slim but muscular legs, that charming posterior (showing no sign of damage from those recent rough attentions) moving more slowly than might usually be the case, but – from the panting words of encouragement – giving no less pleasure.

Finally, Harry was proving himself yet again in the final room – his companion, the younger of the French daughters (it amazed me to see) with her legs thrown over his shoulders just as Fanchon had welcomed Robinet and his lower body moving with such vigour that I feared for the well-being of the girl. However, her energy was equal to his own – to such an extent indeed that I could not believe that she had not enjoyed such pleasure before, in one way or another. It may have been possible, as I have since observed on my most recent adventures that in her native country an early education in erotic acrobatics is common, often without the knowledge of parents or guardians.

The reader may assume that my overlooking of such pleasure did not leave me unmoved. And when upon returning to my room I observed George, hopefully naked but as yet unoccupied, lying alone upon the couch, I once more broke the rule which was now becoming 'more honoured in the breach than the observance', and summoned him to my bedroom.

There I was able once more to admire that fine and sturdy tool which, by a not prolonged persuasion, changed its limp length for the consistency almost of marble, the veins standing proudly out upon it. George himself was now so used to exclamations of amazement, and admonitions to allow himself to be inspected like some prize animal, that he behaved similarly with me – merely sitting, legs apart, with the standing instrument up against his belly as he stroked it to persuade it (if such persuasion was needed) not to bow its head.

Even I, who was entirely used to the sight, having introduced it to so many surprised visitors, could not resist paying it the tribute of a kiss, once again delighted and astonished at the effort needed to part my lips sufficiently to take even the tip between them. I then beckoned him to approach, applying to his body that ointment I insisted he should carry to facilitate the act, and feeling that satisfying fullness with which he was able to gorge even the most capacious part.

As I received the sum assured by the evening's activities, regarded the happy and fulfilled faces of our young guests, distributed the proportion of the fee to the boys, and retired to bed with the twin comforts of gold in my hand and the comfortable warmth of recent pleasure below, I once more felt a pleasant satisfaction of the manner in which providence permitted me to earn my living.

Several days after these events, a closed carriage arrived at the house not long after six o'clock, and from it descended a figure completely covered by a light silken cloak. The lady, when admitted, proved masked.

She was clearly a person of quality, for her gown was of the latest fashion, splendidly cut, and though without the decoration of jewels, marked by a distinguished elegance. She herself was not old, judging by the clarity of her skin and the firmness of her flesh, and her voice was low and musical. Polly, who admitted her, came to fetch me, saying that she had asked for the governess of the house. When I descended to the reception room, she was glancing at a portfolio of etchings of the male figure by Michelangelo, which I had placed there for the amusement of visitors.

'Mrs Nelham?' she asked, with a slight hesitation.

I inclined my head.

'I come recommended by an acquaintance.'

There was a silence, which after a while I broke with the suggestion that she made herself easy. 'We find here,' I said, 'that any slight diffidence which ladies may have upon broaching the reason for their visit is speedily dissipated by the friendliness of everyone in the house. It is, incidentally,' I continued, 'unnecessary for you to continue masked, for everyone here has the utmost discretion – we could not function were it otherwise – and there can never be the slightest chance of your being recognised in public by any of our people.'

She raised her hand to her mask, which was an elaborate affair of black and silver, clearly the relic of a fashionable masquerade.

'If you will forgive me,' she said, 'I will continue with it. I fear I am unused to . . .'

'As are all our ladies,' I said. 'This is the first establishment of its kind I know of in the town, for no one has previously thought to afford our sex the privileges freely enjoyed by the gentlemen, and it is not amazing that upon a first visit you feel somewhat insecure – but I am sure that will change. In the meantime, please of course retain your mask. And now perhaps you would like me to show you our men?'

She nodded and, first ringing the small glass bell which I had had placed for the purpose, to warn of our approach, I escorted her behind the screen, where a view of the room beyond revealed all six already prepared for the evening's entertainment. For a moment, my new friend seemed almost to stagger, placing her hand upon the back of the chair set before her to steady herself. Clearly the prospect was one which moved her. She slipped into the chair and sat for a moment, silent.

'I know not . . .' she said hesitantly. 'Which gentleman would you recommend?'

'It is difficult to say, ma'am,' I said, 'for it depends on individual inclination, and my choice might not be yours. The young man upon the chair by the window is Harry' – who was, as was his wont, carefully exhibiting himself by the simple means of sitting facing the window with his thighs wide apart examining his prick with an interest that suggested he had never previously seen it. 'He is of a vigorous nature, and should you desire a passage to exhaust, will more than satisfy. Next to him are Ben and Tom, whose persons are more – you might think – domestic and comfortable, but who are both adept in the science of love-making. It is possible, incidentally, for a small charge, to engage both at a single moment – or indeed, to couple any of our gentlemen together for your pleasure.

'The boy you see reclining upon the *chaise longue* is William, of a light and almost feminine sensibility, yet perfectly virile, and with a member stronger and more substantial than might appear from a rear view; he has, I am told, a particular charm and grace which can raise the most lethargic spirit. The older of our friends, now practising billiards, is much admired by those of our ladies whose tastes turn towards maturity. Finally, as you will not have failed to observe, there is our friend George.'

George was now sufficiently confident of his body's attractions to make little effort to capture attention other than ensuring that his chief and most unusual characteristic was open to the view – as now, while he read a newspaper, it simply lay across his thigh, astonishing even to me, who had so recently experienced the pleasure of accommodating it. I was ready for our visitor's amazement, and sensible of it.

'Can it be . . . *safe*?' she asked in a whisper.

'Quite,' I reassured her, 'and the experience is a memorable one, though I must confess that our friend is not much adept in the art of love-making, so that the instrument in question is in fact his sole attribute – though a considerable one, and should be experienced at least once.'

'I think, perhaps, Mr Harry?' she suggested. 'My husband,' she continued in a whisper, 'is uninterested in the act, and having introduced me to it upon our marriage – when I was a virgin – had no sooner given me a taste for that most delicious of sports, than he abandoned me and comes no more to bed . . .'

I felt a little shudder run through her body as I put my hand upon her shoulder, and am sure that a tear started to her eye, behind that elegant mask.

'My dear,' said I, 'if you wish a bout which will entirely satisfy your longings, I cannot too strongly recommend Harry.'

'He will not wish to remove my mask?' she asked.

'I am sure he would wish to see your beauty in its entirety,' said I, 'but all our people have instructions that the guests' wishes must at all times be respected. Indeed, if you would care to remain here, you shall hear me give instructions . . .'

Leaving her in the position from which she could hear as well as see, I made my way around to the boys' room, and entering it informed Harry that a friend awaited his services.

'The lady,' I said, in a slightly louder voice than usual, 'is masked, and wishes to remain so; she counts upon your discretion.'

Harry rose to his feet, and realising that we could be overheard, remarked in a similarly raised voice that of course he would respect her anonymity. Then he reached for the robe hanging nearby and wrapped himself in it, accompanying me from the room.

'The fourth chamber, I think, Harry,' I said.

'Aha!' he replied. 'You wish to observe . . .?'

Indeed, the lady's identity interested me, for I felt almost sure that I knew her, and had the uneasy feeling that perhaps she was in some sense a spy.

'But,' I said, 'of course you must on no account remove the mask, for should she be a genuine visitor the news would quickly get about, and discretion must ever be our hallmark.'

I should explain the significance of the fourth chamber: when planning and executing the alterations, Philip had insisted that we should have one room onto which a spy-hole should give, for, he said, sometimes there were ladies whose pleasure included the observation of others at play. But also we might at times wish to observe, ourselves, for reasons of security.

I was not happy with this idea, for spying is something which has never commended itself to me; moreover, even at an early stage in our relationship I suspected that perhaps Philip wished such a facility for his own amusement, and I was later convinced that it was so used. But I had agreed at the time to its provision, which entailed the construction of

a small room, scarcely bigger than a cupboard, which was
entered from a concealed door behind a hanging at the end
of the corridor, and from which a small hole communicated
with the chamber beyond, in its turn concealed by the
shadow of a large picture of Venus and Adonis.

Returning to our visitor, I found her much comforted,
and she accompanied me without demur to the chamber
where Harry awaited her, whereupon I repaired to the
hiding-place whence I could see everything that occurred.

Our guest was standing just inside the door, having
closed it behind her, and was apparently transfixed by what
was certainly a pleasant sight – of Harry, naked as the day
he was born, lying upon the bed, his manly part relaxed but,
from its half-raised size, clearly persuaded of pleasure to
come. She stood so long, simply looking at him, that after a
while he raised himself and asked whether she would not
join him.

'Forgive me, sir,' she said, 'but the sight is not one to
which I am accustomed; pray maintain your position while
I disrobe' – which she did in a trice. She then walked to
kneel at the side of the bed, where – I can find no other
term to describe it – she knelt to worship Harry's body,
first observing it with her eyes alone, from every angle, then
reaching out a gentle hand to stroke its length from shoulder to ankle, running her fingers through the hair of his
head, articulating each finger, testing the muscles which
activated knees and elbows, tracing the line of the chin and
testing the contrasting textures of the flesh at the inside of
the arm and the breast, the chin and the belly.

That Harry found this unaccustomed attention entrancing was testified by the raising of his tool to its full and
impressive size, and the appearance at its tip of several
drops of liquid, which overspilled and ran down its length
to lubricate it with a slippery humidity.

Our friend's body was no less delightful than his; indeed,
together they made a picture Rubens or Titian would have
been delighted to paint. Her back was to me – a long back,
divided by the dint of a spine in which each articulated bone
was marked, falling to full globes scored by two deep dimples and underpinned by thighs sturdy but slim. And when
she turned, I caught a tantalising glimpse of breasts shaped

like the spheres of wine glasses, and tipped with pink buds now reared with pleasure.

But each time he raised his hand to touch one delightful curve or another, she took it gently and returned it to his side, intent upon devouring each plane of the surface of his body with eye and palm, so that I could see from the darkening of his eyes that his passion was becoming unbearably roused.

At length, her eye and hand had encompassed every part of Harry's body but that last essential, whereupon she reached out with a tender shyness, and placed a single finger at its tip, running it down the underside to where his cods were raised by the tightness of the skin. Then, bending forward, she placed the most tender kiss upon its very peak, and turning to Harry said some words which I could not hear, but which were clearly – and at last – an invitation to action.

I could not but admire the restraint with which he rose to his feet, and clasped her with what was almost reserve, placing his arms about her shoulders and (unable to kiss her lips because of the mask, which she was still most careful to retain) contented himself with running his hands down the length of her body until they embraced her lovely posterior. Then he pulled her towards him so that she could not but be aware of that instrument which was now placed in pleasant juxtaposition with that part of her most anxious to receive it.

She appeared almost to swoon at the sensation, whereupon he laid her upon the bed and in his turn paid homage to her body which, now that it was laid open to my view, was indeed of a most particular elegant and form, the breasts as fine as my former glimpse had suggested, now with their pouting nipples pointing each slightly outwards from her body, clearly tenderly excited by his lips as he sucked and kissed them. Between those slim thighs could now be seen a small but springy nest of fair hairs which, as he drew her legs apart the better to facilitate his love-making, revealed to Harry (as to me) a pair of rosy lips distended with anticipation.

But now she reached down and, taking him by the hips, guided Harry into her body, his prick, fully basted by mucous juices, slipping resistlessly into its proper domicile – which it immediately sought to leave, only to be drawn back, expelled, and once more welcomed with an ever-increasing motion. A small bead of blood appeared upon Harry's lower lip, a mark of the difficulty with which he restrained himself from spending before time, for by the manner in which her head was thrown back, lips parted, breasts heaving and legs thrown around the hips of her lover, his partner was in an ecstasy which it was his duty no less than his pleasure to prolong.

At last, with a spasm which almost seemed to shake the room, the two gave up the ghost simultaneously, she lifting the body of the man clean from the bed with the final thrust of her slim hips, while he drove it to the sheets again with the force of his own coming. As they lay panting and exhausted, beads of perspiration running down his sides, I left my vantage-point – not, I must confess, proud at having witnessed the scene, but at the same time much inspirited by it – without, however, having a single clue as to the lady's identity. Yet I was still sure I knew her.

I waited in the hall until Harry, once more decently covered, escorted the lady from the chamber. He made his bow, and she handed me a purse containing our fee.

'I hope you will visit us again, ma'am,' I said, leaning across her to open the door. As I did so she stepped back, and came for a moment into collision with one of the supports of a large china vase which stood by the door. Putting up her hand to steady it, her sleeve caught the corner of her mask, and it fell to the floor – revealing the pale face of none other than Lady Frances Chichley, the bride of only a few weeks!

Her countenance was uncertain whether to pale or blush.

'Mrs Nelham,' she said, 'I trust . . .'

'My lady,' I said, 'your secret is safe with me.'

Without another word, she left. But how sad that my friend should, it seems, be unaware of the richness of his bride's passions. And that she should be a stranger to those qualities which he so amply demonstrated to me!

Chapter Thirteen

The Adventures of Andy

For some time Frank had been attempting to persuade me to introduce him to the backstage life of the theatres, under the impression that since I had spent some time touring the western parts of the country with a theatrical company led by a Mr Samuel Prout Higgens, I must know all about the subject.

That this was far from the truth, Heaven is my witness! However, I was sufficiently used to the practices of the theatre to know that my experience would open certain doors to me, and upon presenting myself at the stage door of the Royalty Theatre in Wellclose Square, soon acquainted myself with the keeper, Mr Tony Rudge. Upon my explaining my theatrical connections and offering certain emoluments he readily agreed to admit me and my friend to the back of the stage during rehearsals, an honour then more easily come by than in later years.

The Royalty Theatre (which, it must be admitted, is not of the first degree of fashion) was built about thirty years ago, but failed to obtain a licence because of the nature of certain of its performances, and for some years was shut – or 'dark', as theatre people term it. It was then however opened by the late Mr Astley, junior, for pantomimes, and more lately has held exhibitions of dancing which have attracted wide audiences whose interests have been, however, more in the persons of the dancers exhibiting there than in the performances themselves – a fact which it seemed would all the more make a visit interesting to brother Frank, whose attention to artistic matters has never been more than scanty.

He was indeed delighted to accompany me one morning to the Royalty, which we reached after traversing some narrow and dirty streets in the eastern part of the town.

Mr Rudge welcomed us with a broad grin and a wink and passed us through the stage door, where a noticeboard bore a wafer informing that there was to be a rehearsal that day of the Female Warriors' Dance in *The Battle of Eurypylus*, to the music of Mr Digby Trantrum (an opera soon and best forgot), and 'Ladies and Gents of the Ballet are to attend at ten o'clock.'

Frank was astonished at the dirt and muddle attendant upon the back of the stage, his previous slender experience of the theatre having encompassed only the apparently fresh and bright aspect of spectacles as viewed by the audience. A little grubby daylight slanted down from a skylight to fall upon the bare boards, palely illuminating a confusion of ropes and pulleys and bridges by which the scenery is organised. The curtain was raised, and the auditorium itself seemed no less dingy, being lit now only by the same daylight coming through windows at the back of the sixpenny gallery, where a number of brooms seemed to be making their way to and fro uncontrolled by the agency of human hands and stirring a considerable dust into the already foggy atmosphere. The dim light of a candle occasionally glimmered for a moment in one of the boxes, and at a rickety table towards the front of the pit a long-wicked flaring candle lit a pile of paper holding, I assumed, the description of the ballet to be performed.

There was a cough at my elbow.

'I believe, sir, you would like to see the dressing rooms?'

'Ah, Mr Rudge, if we may,' I replied, knowing very well that the expenditure of half a guinea had ensured that that pleasure would be afforded us.

'This way, gentlemen,' he said, and led his way to the side of the stage, then up an almost vertical ladder to a gap in the wall – a narrow corridor which led to an open attic where was stored a vast pile of scenery: the sides of Chinese houses, an Italian bridge, an ornamental balcony, a boat on wheels . . .

Rudge led us to the end of this attic, where beneath our feet a glimmer of light in the dimness showed that the floorboards failed completely to meet.

'Take your ease, gentlemen,' he said, 'the *corps de ballet* here, the *coryphées* five paces to your left.' And he was gone.

Upon our knees, we did not even have to approach our eyes to the gap in the boards to see that we were immediately above the dressing rooms where the dancers were changing. But unfortunately the ladies of the *corps de ballet* had almost completed their dressing, for their street skirts were upon the backs of chairs, and they had already donned the short substitutes in which they were to rehearse, while their upper limbs were still clad in outside dress, as was their habit in rehearsal.

'Better luck with the what-you-call-'ems, eh, Andy?' said Frank, and moved along the attic.

The *coryphées* were what in the theatre were termed the two or three leading dancers, and here indeed we were more fortunate, for they enjoyed a little more freedom than their lesser sisters and had only just arrived. We were able to enjoy the sight of their stripping off their clothing and for a while walking about their room in the full freedom of unclothed beauty, conversing before putting on their costumes, which they finally accomplished, though the word 'costume' did not comprehend much. Their clothing consisted of golden boots, a short golden skirt hanging in strips with the merest suggestion of a covering to their essential nakedness, and a cuirass of gold which barely concealed their breasts.

'Well,' said Frank, 'it will be interesting to see the sort of ballet which is exhibited in such dishabille.'

There being no promise of further disclosures, we made our way back along the corridor and down to the side of the stage, where by this time the ballet-master was drilling the *corps de ballet* with the help of a tambourine, tapping out the measure of their dances – which without the accompaniment of an orchestra, seemed dull indeed.

'Miss Pollock, where's your sword?' he asks one girl.

'It's not ready yet,' she replies.

'Then take this stick . . .' – concerned to manage which she contrives to get out of step.

'Stop! Stop!! Stop!!!' cries the ballet-master, and by stamping and thumping the tambourine manages to persuade her at last to keep time. But now some of the other girls have stopped dancing and are standing idly by: 'Now then,' shouts the ballet-master, 'what are you gaping for?

Why don't you move? *Why the devil don't you move?'*

I was most interested in all this, but could feel that Frank
began to find it boring, not himself being inclined to matters
theatrical, but interested chiefly in the personalities of the
girls. However, as I concerned myself with watching, he
soon found a more fascinating occupation, for just in front
of us stood one of the *coryphées* awaiting her summons to
the stage, and her delightfully round haunches, decorated
only by the strips of gold cloth which hung from her waist,
being at hand, he could not resist to place one palm upon
the inside of an ample thigh, raising it until his little finger
could make its way within the thin piece of cloth which
alone guarded her virtue.

After a moment or two, and without moving, she simply
said over her shoulder: 'Well, my ducks, if you want to be
about it, you had better move, for my cue comes in two
minutes' – whereupon Frank was not a moment in releasing
from his trousers his ready appliance and, tearing the flimsy
cloth aside, passing it into the body of the dancer, who
reacted only by bending slightly forward to enable its easier
passage.

While Frank began to pump away, she showed not the
slightest evidence of interest, tapping her fingers upon a
piece of scenery not in time with his vigorous thrusts but to
the banging of the ballet-master's tambourine. It was
remarkable also that no one else took any notice, her
colleagues simply averting their eyes while men passing by
with pieces of scenery gave not so much as a cursory glance
at the two persons so intimately engaged.

At last the girl recognised her cue, and without preparation or comment leapt upon the stage while Frank,
stimulated no less by her sudden movement than by his
enthusiastic engagement, was left to bedew the boards with
the proof of his passion – upon which he looked slightly
shamefaced, and packed his machinery away to the accompaniment of giggles from two other *coryphées* who had
observed the matter from a few feet away.

'Hah! I shall go and eat,' he said. 'Will see you outside
before the performance.' And left.

I remained, interested by the rehearsal, until at half-past
three it was concluded, whereupon the girls quitted the

stage to obtain refreshment before returning at a little after six for the performance.

I too determined to find some refreshment, and turned to make for the door when there was a shout from above, and down a rope like some monkey came a small figure, hand over hand, who then slapped me upon the shoulder with great familiarity.

'Why, Andy, don't tell me you've forgotten? David? David Ham?'

I clasped the fellow immediately to my bosom with surprise and delight. He had shared his bed with me over some months of travelling with the theatrical company of which he was a humble member, and while his amorous attentions had at first been embarrassing and always undesired by me (though upon one occasion had been fulfilled, as readers of my former chronicles will recall) we had parted excellent friends, and now went off together to the Orange Coffee House where I treated us to chops and small beer while he told me news of my old friends.

Mr Prout Higgens and his good wife, Mrs Plunkett Cope, were at present at the Theatre Royal in Richmond appearing as Othello and Desdemona (which I well remembered as two of their favourite parts, rousing as considerable a passion of laughter in their audiences as any comedian might wish), while their daughter, Miss Cynthia Cope, was recently retired from the stage and married to a wealthy merchant of Shoreditch. Here, he said, she has made herself known to every apprentice and ship-boy, every clerk and manager – in short, every likely lad in the neighbourhood. For, he said, her appetite in the fucking line was as voracious as ever, and she touted her crinkum crankum about the drawing-rooms of London with such vigour that scarce a gay stopper in the city could keep up with her – at which I laughed heartily, having forgotten David's command of the common language of the streets.

'And you, David?' I asked.

'Well, I'm no doodle,' he said. 'I work here at the Royalty for a penny or two and the company of friends, but I have acquired a protector' (and here he gave me a shrewd wink) 'who is desperate in love with my double jug, and I can edge him on to the extent of a guinea or two at will, and am getting

together a good hoard against my old age' – which, since he
had no more than my own share of years, must be some
time a-coming.

'Well, I am glad to hear it,' I said.

'Good for you!' he said. 'And yourself?'

At which I told him of all that had happened since I had
left his company, of my meeting again with Frank and
Sophie (whom he remembered my talking of, from past
days) and of the house in Brook Street which, I said, he
must come and see, though he would find little there to
engross him in the way of madge culls (his term for those
gentlemen who enjoy the carnal company of their own sex).

'I shall, I shall,' he said, 'and you must meet my friend.
He lives at Chiswick, though I have never been to his house,
he being surrounded (I believe) by his family, who would
not be as sympathetic to his inclinations as I – or indeed
you.' And here he placed his hand upon my thigh and gave
it a gentle squeeze which, knowing his good will and that it
was in fun, I accepted as it was offered.

We talked for a great while, and then it was time to make
our way back to the theatre, where I was to meet Frank. I
mentioned to David the latter's hope of some closer contact
with the ladies of the ballet, whereupon he suggested that
we should accompany two of them to a *soirée dansante*
after the performance, at a house he knew of in the area.

'I will arrange two likely ladybirds,' he said, 'and meet
you at the stage door after the show' – and with that
vanished towards the back of the stage, while I soon found
Frank, having acquired a box at three shillings, to which we
made our way. He was more than a little glum, Mr Rudge
having denied him entrance to the dressing rooms on the
ground that the manager had strictly forbid it – and having
accepted half-a-guinea for the favour, still refused to grant
it. I told him of my meeting David, which at first failed to
cheer him, for 'I want no bony boy,' he said, 'but a good
fleshy lass', whereupon I told him of David's suggestion,
which cheered him much, so that he spent the evening contemplating the ladies of the *corps* and attempting to decide
which, had he the choice, he would wish to have presented
to him after the performance.

Of that performance there is little to say: the fairy dancers flew on their wires, the military dancers stamped their feet and smacked their thighs with will, the *coryphée* who had so cheerfully accommodated Frank during the morning caught his eye and continually made gestures with her sword which only the blind could have failed to interpret, whereat the pit cheered and shouted. And all in all, with the help of two bottles of wine, we were in high spirits by the end of the evening, when we poured out with the rest of the audience into the narrow, crowded street, and made our way around the corner where a number of other gallants waited in the knowledge or the hope that willing female company would soon be forthcoming.

Eventually, David appeared among the press, with a young woman on each arm – somewhat chicken-breasted, as is the case with most ballet girls who do not, as a matter of course, make enough money to eat so well as to fill out their limbs to the extent of, for instance, the girls at Brook Street, but nevertheless vivacious and willing.

'I suggest, gents, that we make for Parker's Supper Room,' said David, 'where there is food in plenty and dancing afterwards of whatever kind' (and here he nudged Frank familiarly) 'you may desire.'

We crammed into a carriage, and after a short ride were decanted at a dark doorway through which there burst upon us a brilliance of light and movement, with a forest of tables, waiters tumbling over one another in their frantic hurry to take devilled kidneys to a man who has only ordered beer, or a dozen oysters to another who is asleep after a large meal. David was well known here, as were the girls, Miss Portland and Miss Markham, for we were not only seated immediately but a waiter instantly appeared with a tray heavy with food, which our friends consumed with the appetite of those who had worked all evening. While they were going at their boiled mutton, David made his excuses: 'I join my friend across the road at Almack's,' he said, 'but we shall meet again, make no doubt!'

'A lively spark,' said Frank, 'as lively as you tell me.'

'Oh, that David,' said Miss Portland between mouthfuls of steak pie, 'he's a bright puppy – and with a fine leg, too, if he turned to dancing.'

'Much use his leg'd be to you,' returned Miss Markham, digging her friend in the ribs, at which the two went into a paroxysm of laughter. They were indeed mightily dissimilar to the young ladies we had left in Brook Street, even Moll being a paragon to them where polite behaviour was concerned. But they were none the less good company, being continually high-spirited and merry, and once they had satisfied one carnal appetite were clearly ready to set their sights at another, for no sooner had they finished the food and drink set before them than they leapt to their feet and led us into the next room, where dancing was in progress.

It was a long, narrow hall with a row of seats down each side and a gallery in which musicians sat – playing, as we entered, a polka to which a dense crowd was dancing, men and women turning and chasing and banging against each other in all directions. Many of the young women present were clearly recognisable as *coryphées* escaping the strict discipline of the stage to engage in a looser kind of dancing altogether, leaping with great enthusiasm but also with a kind of elegance which set them apart from the other women present. These were bakers' daughters or whatnot, clumsily flinging their legs about and getting in everybody's way, turning their heads wildly and plunging and diving and leaping indiscriminately, while our friends danced gracefully with their heads over their right shoulders, arms extended, carefully avoiding all collisions. The men were of all kinds, but notably of the world, some in uniform, some in suits of mufti, all set on enjoyment.

We happily joined in the dancing with our friends, I being partnered by Miss Portland, whose forename was Jenny, while Frank happily took Miss Markham in his arms, who rejoiced in no other name than Pussy, from, she alleged, her tendency to make tart comments upon her friends. But, Jenny confided, in fact for her freedom with a part of her body sometimes denoted by the name of puss. The dancing was warm work, and our partners' happy pleasure in pressing their bodies close to ours brought on a further enjoyable heat which we looked forward, later, to cooling. Just as we were preparing to propose a departure for some quieter place, a young woman with a flushed face came up to Pussy and whispered in her ear, whereupon she wishpered in turn to Jenny, and the two looked at us in the most serious manner.

'Your admiration for the arts suggests that you would enjoy a performance which is in preparation, upstairs,' said Pussy.

Frank expressed himself as having seen as much theatrical performance that evening as would last him for the rest of the year.

'But I think,' said Pussy, 'that this performance would prove most inspiriting to you, for you are not, I believe, totally without an admiration for the female form?'

At these words Frank began to look more interested, while Jenny tipped me a wink suggesting some pleasure to come. To cut the story short, we followed them up a staircase which led to an upper room, at the door of which no less than five guineas was extracted from Frank's purse for each of us. 'I trust the offering will be worth it,' he muttered as he handed over the gold.

Inside the room we found a small but delightful theatre prepared, with banquettes each seating two persons upon which we placed ourselves, only a few rows from a stage hung with red velvet curtains, before which a menial was lighting a row of footlights. Now came a fellow with a violin, who as the main chandeliers were snuffed struck up a charming tune which proved to be (as Pussy whispered to me) from the new opera *La Muette de Portici* from which we were, she said, to see an interlude danced by the famous Louisa Veron with her partner Jean Fiorentino. My heart sank at this, for though I delighted in dancing, it was not for such polite entertainment I had been preparing myself, and I was sure that Frank would be more impatient with such frippery (as he called it).

But I need have had no fear, for when the curtain was swept aside revealing a stage merely hung with black, it revealed also the two dancers in a complete state of nature, finely lit by the warm glow of candles, which gave to their flesh a rosy hue like that upon the limbs in a painting by some old master in love with his subject.

Mademoiselle Veron had been much spoken of, with admiration, by society, and it was clear that no compliment paid her could have been too great, even were her audiences deprived of the unhindered view of her limbs which we enjoyed. Her poses were now chaste and meditative, now voluptuous and enticing; her movements first swift and inspiriting, now langourous and melting. She twisted and turned like a snake around her partner – who himself, while slim and boyish, was clearly of great strength, for he lifted her as though she were a mere wraith. She whirled with him like a leaf carried away by a gale then, a moment later, walked with a superb, nonchalant step, happy to show us her beautiful arms and shoulders, her marble-like bust, her supple shapely figure.

Then she darted anew into space and fell dropping, quivering, writhing in one supreme convulsion, her head touching the ground, her eyes bathed in light – and in all her attitudes, especially those in which she was supported by Monsieur Fiorentino (with whom she appeared to be much in love), there was always that same grace, that same harmony, that same charm, that same unexpectedness, that something which can be learnt from no teacher and in no school.

The performance was by no means an indecent show, and were it not for the complete lack of costume, could have been given upon the stage before an audience of the most conventional sort. Yet it was this very fact that made it among the most rousing that I had ever seen, for the expectation of passion was continually aroused without being satisfied. When Monsieur Fiorentino's hand slipped upon the inside of his partner's thigh as he lifted her above his waist, one expected the gesture to lead to the result such a passage would have in the bed-chamber; instead of which, he merely set her again upon the stage, and the ballet continued. Similarly, she would perhaps adopt a pose in which she reclined upon the stage, her cheek leaning against her partner's thigh, almost brushing his vital parts, yet he remained unmoved – as indeed he must, for it would have been impossible for the dance to continue should he be aroused.

Strangely, these circumstances, as I have said, were particularly attractive to the audience; as the performance continued, I could almost feel a warmth emanating from my companion's body, through the thin muslin of her dress.

And I could not but be conscious that in the neighbouring seat Frank, always quicker than myself to give way to his passions, had passed his hand within his friend's clothing and was caressing her breast, while her own hands were occupied in his lap. Soon it was clear that the activities upon the stage were now uninteresting to them; I preferred, however, still to give them my attention, though Pussy's hands were by now busy about my person too, provoking a desire which was almost too acute to contain.

As the dance ended, and the couple took their bow, the applause was inconsiderable, the hands of most members of the audience by that time otherwise occupied. I, however, rose to my feet to offer my applause unconscious until a moment later of the fact that Pussy had succeeded in loosening the laces of my breeches so that my person was exposed in a manner which offered to Mademoiselle Veron a compliment such as she would normally have accepted only in the privacy of her private apartments.

As the curtains fell, Pussy leaned forward and placed her lips over my tool, clutching at me with an urgency which suggested that she, too, had been sufficiently enlivened by the performance to desire comfort. However, I had been too captivated by Mademoiselle Veron to content myself with even so willing a companion, and gently but firmly withdrew myself. Whereupon, with an ill-tempered look, Pussy turned to my friend and his companion, and kneeling at the side of their bench began to offer assistance in their love-making, which by this time was as open as that which went on around them.

I had already noted that there was a door at the side of the stage, and it was thence I directed my steps – but upon opening it was stopped by a large fellow evidently placed there with the single intent of stopping importunate visitors. The production of my purse loosed his hold upon my shoulder, and the extraction from it of a couple of guineas, pressed upon him with a whispered word, resulted in his stepping aside, and indicating another door at the end of a corridor.

Knocking at this, I was greeted with an invitation, in a lady's voice, to enter.

Inside, at a dressing table, sat Mademoiselle Veron,

wrapped in a silken gown. At the sight of an unknown man, she rose to her feet, alarmed. But I hastily reassured her: 'Madam, be not alarmed. I do not come to offer an assault, but merely the admiring tribute of someone captivated by the beauty of your person and your movements. I offer no compliment other than words, and my admiration, and will now withdraw.'

With a bow, I made to go – at which she smiled, and beckoned.

'Please, sir, be seated if you can spare a few moments of conversation.'

I sat upon the chair she indicated.

'You will forgive, sir, my mistrust,' she said, 'but I will not disguise from you the fact that too many rude fellows have in the past made their way to this room, and the sight of a stranger is one in general I cannot welcome. But' (and she smiled again) 'your words reassure me, as your person indicates your gentility.'

I could not resist, at this, falling to my knees before her and pressing my lips to her hand, whereat she was evidently moved, for leaning forward she placed her hand upon my head and planted a kiss upon my forehead. I cannot but confess that proximity to those delicious globes upon whose beauty my eyes had so recently been fixed, and the lady's kindness, sharpened my desire, and almost before I had formed the thought, my lips were pressed to her neck and my hands, upon her shoulders, made ready to slip from them the silk which clung to the delicious flesh beneath.

She rose at this, I feared to rebuke me. But no – 'Sir,' she said, 'your compliments are those of a gentleman, your carriage that of a tender lover – and this place is not marked for either.'

Then, allowing the silk to slip from her shoulders, she stood before me in that naked beauty with which I was familiar, but upon which I had not hoped to graze. With a speed Monsieur Fiorentino could not but have envied, I freed myself of my clothes, and in a moment we were stretched upon a nearby couch, and enjoying a dance more commonly performed than those of the ballet, but susceptible of equal skill and vigour. No less than three times Mademoiselle Veron cried out in extremity before my own performance ended and the curtain fell upon our endeavours. Finally, on my raising myself from her body (now bedewed with a happy amorous perspiration), she smiled and thanked me, gesturing towards her gown, with which I covered her before saluting a most gracious and beautiful lady, and leaving her room.

Downstairs, in a refreshment room, I found Frank, with Jenny and Pussy, he having satisfied both of them in one way or another before they left the performance hall. He neglected to ask where I had been, and I had no intention of volunteering the information, for that could only be construed upon the one side as boasting and upon the other as telling tales outside the bedroom, to neither of which (as the reader knows) am I subject.

Slipping a coin or two into their hands, we left the girls, and made our way from the hall to hail a carriage for Brook Street, where by this time of evening the house would be quiet.

Letting ourselves in with our key, the first sign we had of any impropriety was the sight of Blatchford lying upon the floor, his hands and feet bound and a gag across his mouth, bleeding from a blow upon the forehead. Frank quickly knelt to release him, and upon his taking off the gag he began to whisper a message. But before he could get more than a single word out, the door of the reception room was suddenly flung open by an unknown man, and we saw the girls and Aspasia sitting at one end of the room, while at the other two men held Rose, one with a knife at her throat.

'Gentlemen, come in,' said the man at the door, 'but quietly, if you please. I would advise no sudden motion, or this young lady will suffer for it.'

We walked in, and sat upon two chairs indicated to us, whereupon the first man, producing cord, tied our hands behind us.

'Now, which of you is Sir Franklin Franklyn?'

Frank gave a curt nod.

'Ah, Sir Franklin, it is a pleasure to meet you. I come with a message from a number of gentlemen occupied in the provision of similar entertainment to that which you purvey here. That message is that they are not inclined to sit by while you take all the profit in the town, for we cannot disguise the fact that through an unreasonable expenditure of money in this place you have attracted custom which is naturally ours. Yet you are largely unknown to the town, and have no friends here. We are largely known, and have friends of influence. We feel that you have now taken enough profit and should retire to some part of the country where you may continue to ply your trade without depriving us of ours. If you do not . . .' He made a gesture to the two men holding Rose, and in a flash following a quick movement of the knife, a thin line of blood appeared beneath her jaw.

'We are careful, as you see, not to disturb the young lady's beauty. Upon another occasion, however, should another occasion sadly present itself, our actions will be considerably less accommodating. Gentlemen, ladies, our apologies for disturbing you. Good evening.'

And the two men, dropping Rose – who fell to the ground – quickly crossed the room to their colleague, and the three left together, the front door slamming behind them.

The chaos of the next half hour can be supposed. We were released, Rose was put to bed, her wound proving to be entirely superficial, and her state brought on by alarm rather than pain, Blatchford was set free and, apart from a fearful headache proved more angry than hurt. And in the basement we found Tippett and Pounce, similarly bound and gagged, and released them. Only then were we able to discover precisely what had happened.

It appeared that the three men, two of them somewhat rough but all decently dressed and in funds, had appeared at about nine o'clock, and admitted by Aspasia had retired to the hot rooms before going upstairs with Rose, Constance and Ginevra. There, they had behaved entirely as might have been expected, though they were perhaps more leisurely in their love-making than others – by intent, clearly, for after all other visitors had left the house they dressed and all descended together, Rose already threatened by the knife which her partner had recovered from his clothing. By threat of harm to her, the men had had no difficulty in persuading Pounce and Tippett to be bound, while Blatchford, making a rash attempt to intervene, had been silenced by a blow to the head from a truncheon one fellow had produced. Despite all attempts, it had proved impossible to persuade them to converse, and it was not until we had appeared that it became clear what the motive of the unpleasantness was.

We were, of course, equally amazed and outraged; Aspasia less so, however, for, she had been previously aware of threats of a similar nature made against those who had started houses without first arranging to pay a financial tribute to those who ruled the game in the city, of which, she said, a certain Charles or Carlo Gaskill was the head. If we cared to seek him out and offer a considerable share of the business, it might still be possible to recover the situation, though from the tone adopted by our visitors it might be that Mr Gaskill's intention was indeed to throw us out of business, as an example to others.

Frank enquired whether, since the girls were shortly to inherit a considerable sum from the estate of Mrs Jopling Rowe, they would not prefer it if we closed the establishment immediately? For they would not be in need, while he and myself did not want funds, and it was no part of his desire that his friends should be placed in danger.

The unanimous response was, however, that we should remain in business rather than giving way to such threats, and upon that note we sent the girls to bed – Aspasia only remaining to warn Frank that the ready determination of her charges not to be bullied rested rather upon ignorance than upon courage for, she said, Mr Gaskill was a man of great ferocity and cruelty, and a dangerous enemy.

We decided to consult with Sir Philip Jocelind, who might have among his friends those who would best know how to deal with Mr Gaskill. And in no happy mood we retired to bed, any residual longings which remained after our evening's experience thoroughly cooled by the new and unpleasant situation now pressing upon us.

Chapter Fourteen

Sophie's Story

My recognition of Lady Chichley upon her visit to our house did not prevent her from regularly returning, usually conferring her favours upon Harry, for whom she clearly formed a genuine admiration not wholly physical in its nature.

She confided in me that Chichley, on their wedding night, having paid her the compliment of rendering her no longer a maid, had then returned to that formal manner and address with which he had always treated her. They had been designed for each other, she explained, almost from birth, their parents being neighbours in the country. But they had met rarely, and then under the careful eye of their elders, so that they scarcely knew each other until a week or two before their marriage.

'Not only,' she said, 'does Chichley feel unready to be tied to one woman – and I believe that that would be his view even were she a wife of his own choosing – but it seems the case that he is uninterested in the sex, for his attentions to me were cool in the extreme, or rather warm only to the extent that allowed him to function as a man should. When I attempted to renew the familiarity on subsequent evenings, he simply declined, despite my pleadings. Some women – nay, many, perhaps – would have been pleased at this lack of interest, especially should they have been wed for their estate to men older and less attractive than they would have wished. But Chichley is a fine figure of a man, and one whose body I craved the more upon my brief close acquaintance with it. But alas, he does not find the sex attractive, and I might as well be a widow. Are you surprised, then, Mrs Nelham, that I should visit your establishment so regularly? Harry is, of course, scarcely my match in social standing, let alone in estate, but to be frank I find his attentions comforting in the extreme. But I run on – please forgive me for boring you with detail!'

I was astonished to hear of Chichley's attitude to his bride, for as I had plainly seen during my somewhat untoward observations, she was a young woman of great physical attractions, whose firm and pliant body would surely be coveted by any man. I determined to renew my acquaintance with her husband and attempt to discover what had possessed him since he had proved to me his capacity for energetic masculine action.

In the meantime, spring had turned to summer and the days had grown longer and hotter, and one weekend I decreed a day of leisure. We had always, of course, been closed upon the Lord's Day, when the boys remained at home and no doubt occupied themselves in those tasks they were largely forced to neglect during the rest of the week. But now I summoned them, one Sunday, to be entertained by me to a day's leisure, during which we could take our ease, eat, drink, and recreate ourselves.

The day dawned clear and bright, and as I looked from the window down over the gardens I reflected that even Alcovary could not surpass in beauty my present surroundings. My room looked over the high-walled private part of the grounds which stretched down to the river, where the boathouse gleamed white in the as yet low-slanting rays of the sun beyond lawns as close-clipped and even as a green tablecloth.

We were all up early, the boys having slept, some of them in slight discomfort, at the house, and enjoyed a fine breakfast. Then by ten o'clock, when the air was already warm, we took ourselves into the gardens by the riverside where the light breezes over the water would cool our bodies from the extreme heat of the sun.

Nevertheless, by midday we were all stripped bare, William, George and I careful to lie in the shadow of the trees, for they, like me, wished to shade their bodies from the effects of the sun. But the rest lay in the open, the buttocks of Ben and Tom already beginning to turn pink, while Harry's skin, already brown, seemed likely to turn mahogany. Spencer, proving a fine swimmer, was more often in the river than out of it.

Luncheon came to us in baskets, accompanied by claret in quantity. And afterwards, as we lay in a delightful langour, I recalled Andy telling me how his girls had regaled him with their former adventures, and suggested that we should play at a similar game. To start the proceedings, I told the story of my own adventures at Miss Jessie Trent's boarding school (which readers of my former chronicles will doubtless recall). This amused them considerably, especially when I described with some vigour the fate that unpleasant woman met at the hands of her rebellious pupils.

'But now,' I said, 'who will be next?' – and looked meaningfully at Harry, for I must admit that of all the boys he was the one who interested me most, and I longed to hear his history.

'I was born,' he said, 'in London, to a mother who, though poor, cared for me and my younger sister and brother with all the devotion a diminutive purse permitted. My father deserted us soon after my brother was born, and my mother got what money she could by washing and cleaning and other means, but never from any activity which the most puritanical critic might condemn. We lived in a single room and seldom enjoyed more food than would merely keep us alive, yet we were not unhappy, until that sad day came when my mother, worn out, I do believe, by her efforts, died. I was then fifteen years old, and had already for some time been bringing home what money I could earn by running errands, holding horses, and lately by labouring.

'My sister Moll was five years younger than I, devoted to me and our younger brother. We had grown up within arm's length of each other, and had shared a bed for as long as I could remember. This might be condemned by moralists, for it certainly led to a familiarity more than common between brother and sister, yet experienced, I believe, by many of the poor. You will understand, then, that we soon knew perfectly well how a man and woman – or rather a boy and girl – differed in bodily shape from each other, which led to no embarrassment nor even any curiosity. For what was well known to us bred no questions until the time came when that part of my anatomy which is most valuable in my present occupation showed signs of raising its head. This phenomenon was discovered by Moll even before I myself noticed it, for I awoke one morning to a delightful and comfortable glow centring on my lower parts, and upon achieving full consciousness discovered Moll stroking and cosseting a strange growth which had started from between my thighs, and which upon closer inspection proved to be the thing I had formerly considered only an instrument for pissing with.

'It is a strange mark of natural modesty that I somehow knew that it would not be proper to encourage Moll to continue to occupy herself with her new plaything, reluctant though she was to desist. However, I persuaded her to relinquish her hold, though I was most reluctant to forgo that most pleasant sensation which her handling of me had produced. So much so indeed that privately, when I had turned her out of bed and sent her on some errand – perhaps the comforting of our younger brother, then only four or five – I seized the opportunity to see whether I could not myself provide some shadow of that pleasure by handling myself, with a result that you will no doubt believe.

'Moll was not easily persuaded to leave that newly developed part of my anatomy alone, and for a while I would wake in the night to find her hand exploring it. But after some time, my continuing to counterfeit disinterest (for anger would have set her on rather than dissuading her) together with her having thoroughly satisfied her curiosity, she discontinued her provocations, and by the time she herself became a woman, I was perhaps fortunately though sadly removed from the scene. For when, as I have explained, my mother died, I was left sole provider, and was forced to travel further and further afield in search of work.

'For me to raise sufficient money to pay the rent of our single room was not easy, and we fell behind with our payments – the result of which was my returning one day to find the room occupied by someone else, and my sister and brother gone, no one could tell me whither. I returned time and again, in case they were to be found, but was forced in the end to conclude that they had either been stolen away by some persons and forced into a form of slavery, or had been murdered, or simply had decided to try their luck alone.

'My sorrow at my loss, and disappointment that Moll should have thought so little of me, came just when my manhood demanded expression, and at the same time I obtained work at Hampstead with a small group of workmen engaged in demolishing a building which stood on the brow of the hill. The fellow who employed us – myself and five other men – instructed us that upon no account were we to attempt to explore the building next door, which was surrounded by a high wall. His instructions, from his own employer, had at first been that all his workmen should be blindfold – at which he had, of course, laughed. But his paymaster, who was a clergyman of some years' experience but entire lack of sense, finally explained that the two houses were the property of the church. The one which we were knocking down had been a seminary for young clergymen, while its fellow was still occupied by twenty-five young ladies sent by their parents to be educated by nuns, and destined eventually for the convent.

'Our master, who looked to fresh employment by the church, warned us that to be seen looking at, much less attempting to converse with, the young ladies would result in immediate dismissal together with other penalties so dire that he dared not express them in words. The result of which was, in my case at least, to provoke extreme curiosity, though all but one of my fellows were so concerned to keep their employment that it became quite a joke with us to call out that a young lady was to be seen, whereupon they would scurry away to some corner, out of view.

'It was of course the case that while we were working upon the upper floors of the house, we had an entire view of the gardens of the school, and indeed could not help, from time to time, seeing the flash of a dress upon the other side of the wall. I must confess that, feeling as I did the itch of manhood, my curiosity was no greater than my lust, and I inferred that any young lady shut away within such walls, and with such a fate ahead of her, might be likely game if only I could come at her. I was happily aided in my ambition by the weather, which that summer was as hot as it is now, and so we worked stripped to the waist. And it was not long before my friend Bill and I were conscious that some of the young ladies – how many, we could not tell – were regularly congregating in a small thicket of bushes near the wall, where their eyes were, we suspected, upon us.

'We ignored them until one afternoon, when the other men were resting at lunch time, and Bill and I were lazing upon a scaffold watching the garden out of the corners of our eyes, when two girls actually walked into the open patch of grass by the bushes, and there lifted their hands and signalled to us. What they meant by their signals we did not at first know, but since their movement was so obvious, had no hesitation in waving back. Upon seeing this, they positively skipped with excitement, and made gestures with their hands upon their breasts which seemed to indicate that they admired what they could see of our bodies – whereupon we turned about and about, exhibiting ourselves to their view. And to our delight, one of them actually loosed her clothing, despite the other's attempt to prevent her, and with a promising lasciviousness displayed a pair of breasts which would have slain us outright had we been near enough to see them in any detail. As it was, Bill almost met his death from leaning over the scaffold in an attempt to do so! In the meantime the young lady who had so delighted us was again making motions, which this time seemed to invite a reciprocal gesture – whereupon I, with a forwardness which I can only set down to youth, loosed my trousers and let them fall to my knees, displaying a person roused to some enthusiasm by both sight and imagination.

'The effect upon the young ladies was all I could have hoped, for one appeared to faint away – though from the fact that she also shaded her eyes in an attempt to see more clearly, I believed her faintness to be temporary. And the other jumped up and down in a display of delighted pleasure, but this was cut short when they suddenly vanished into the bushes, and immediately thereafter, as I hurriedly pulled my clothes together, the sight of an elderly woman in a dark habit reminded us that our admirers were not altogether at liberty.

'It cannot be supposed that two hot-blooded youths were to be persuaded not to take up what appeared to be a warm invitation, and upon the nun's vanishing and all once more becoming quiet, we descended to where, upon a level with the top of the wall, a plank could be set so that we could make the leap – which we did immediately, falling rather than jumping to the ground inside the garden. We were immediately greeted by our delighted admirers and drawn within a clearing in a small thicket, only just sufficiently broad to take our four reclining bodies but offering grass sufficiently thick to make a bed as comfortable as any I have since occupied. And here the delightful enthusiasm of the two young ladies met our own hopes in as happy a consummation as any virgins (for so we were, all of us) could hope for.

'Our two friends had, I now guess, comforted each other in mutual play, for there was none of the pain of maidenheads broken, only a breathless pleasure which rose quickly to a pitch which was almost frightening to two lads whose experience of the sex had previously been confined to admiration at a distance. The space being so narrow, we could not but be conscious of each other's joys, and our eyes continually met in wondering and rejoicing astonishment at our luck, as once and again our companions milked us, or so it seemed, of the very marrow of our bones.

'So confined was the space, and so eager our new friends lest their pleasure should be cut short, that we had little time to admire them, our sight being confined to a close view of an eyebrow or an ear or, when we insisted, to the admiration of a smooth and firm breast. Though having for the second time lain down my life, I insisted upon a view of the place of battle – I had of course seen my sister unclothed, but that was when she was a child and bald as an egg in that essential place. But now the silky nest which had welcomed me seemed so entrancingly dressed and coiffeured as positively to invite a renewal of the fight which, my being so new and fresh to such combats, I was able to achieve.

'In half an hour we had tried, or so we thought, every form of pleasure our bodies had to offer – though indeed that was not truly the case, for youth and inexperience precluded the more unusual of exquisite pleasures. We lay, however, damp with perspiration and the exhalation of the grasses, and for a moment, I believe we slept. Not for long, however, for we woke to the rustling of the bushes and to a shriek of feminine anger, to see two elderly but muscular men and the woman we had previously seen looking down at us. Though the men were distracted by their view of the two naked girls, and the nun by (as I believe) her first view of two naked men, their preoccupation did not prevent them from arresting us. We were hauled unceremoniously from the thicket without pause even to clothe ourselves, and led across the lawn to the house, stopping halfway to allow us to pull our trousers on, for the nun noticed the windows crowded with young ladies all with a clear view of our relaxed but perhaps still disconcerting masculinity.

'To cut the story short, we were thrown out of the school and out of our jobs, and presumably our companions also were forced to leave. However, neither of us I suspect repined, and certainly once having had a taste of the pleasure to be obtained from the intimate company of ladies, I was not disinclined to continue to seek such pleasure. I now consider myself fortunate, after some years of random employment, to have been seen one day at bathing by Mrs Nelham, and subsequently invited by Sir Philip to join an establishment the purpose of which might be solely the pleasure it affords me!'

Harry's tale having been received with laughter and applause, he leapt to his feet and, running across the grass, cleaved the air with a bound to vanish into the water of the river. I asked George, then, whether he would not favour us with the story of his life, certain, surely, to be unusual and interesting.'

'Some twenty-five years ago,' our black friend said, 'my father was captured upon the African coast by Portuguese slave-traders and set aboard a ship for the New World. He would doubtless have died there in irons – for he was a proud man who would never have bowed to the regulations of a master – had he not contrived to escape from the ship when it put in for supplies in the Canaries, and begged succour of the captain of a British trader then moored nearby. The captain would have turned him away, but by good fortune the owner was aboard – a merchant of Christian virtue and natural grace, who brought my father back to England and took him into his family. Here he worked as a general servant and in time met and married my mother, a woman from the West Indies who had been brought back by that same merchant a year previously, and educated as a Christian.

'My parents were happily employed and when I was born their contentment was complete, their master taking a similar interest in me, and upon my reaching ten years of age and having outgrown such lessons as his housekeeper could devise, sending me to school in the country. However, I was unhappy there, for I was made fun of on account of the colour of my skin, and hated for being different from the others. So much so indeed that finally I could bear it no longer, and ran away.

'My future was uncertain, for I knew that if I sought out my parents they would be distraught at my ingratitude to their master and insist on my returning to school, which I could not bear. And so I slept under hedges for several days, and eventually, finding myself at a lodge gate, was begging a crust of bread when I was noticed by the lady of the house, passing in her carriage. She stopped, picked me up and enquired who and what I was. I spun her, I am sorry to say, a tale of escaping from a cruel master who intended me for the slave trade – I had heard my father's story often enough to be able to lend such an invention credibility. And I so impressed her with my forthright bearing (which I had learned in order to withstand unkindness from my fellows) and by my excellent command of the English language (for which I must thank my master) that she invited me to enter her service – which I did.

'My duties were not onerous; clad in silk and velvet and provided with a white wig, I was simply to dress the rooms of the mansion in which Mrs Damerel dwelt, to fetch and carry, and to impress her friends and acquaintances with my presence, which took little enough of intelligence. My fellow-servants were, happily, pleasant enough to me, and I felt that domestic service must be my natural calling.

'My downfall began some four years later, when my employer played hostess to Lady Curd, a dowager. She seemed to me to be sufficiently ancient – though indeed may not have been much over forty – and was of a lusty and coming-on disposition. Her husband, being older than she, was not inclined to serve her, and not being rich enough to purchase lovers she was in considerable desperation for want of one.

'Before she had been in the house five minutes, she had set her eyes upon me, and I believe had inferred that beneath my breeches was something to interest her. I should say that my physical development had not been invisible to my lady, who only a few days earlier had commented that I seemed no longer to fit my breeches, and that some new clothing must be obtained for me. The truth is that my developing person was already more considerable in size than anything a white page might have had to conceal, and I was forced to the expedience of cramming it down between my legs and attempting to disguise it by a slightly stooping gait, which of course only drew attention to the unseemly bulge which there was no real way of concealing.

'The dowager requested that my lady lend her my services, and the latter – who was a great innocent – did not demur, but instructed me to wait upon her friend, whom I then accompanied to her rooms. My first task was to fetch warm towels for her bath – which I did from the kitchen, where a cupboard of them was always kept next the fire. Upon my return to the bedroom I found my new mistress seated in the hip-bath, and for the first time was confronted by the view of the female body. Never having seen it even depicted, much less in the warmth of flesh, I was not offended by the wrinkles of the neck, the slackness of the breasts nor the spreading of the hips, but found my breeches straining to confine a display of interest which made my posture even more ungainly than usual.

' "George, the towels," cried Lady Curd. "But no! Wait, your beautiful livery will be soiled! You had better remove it first!"

'The eccentricity of this order did not altogether dismay me, for I was used to unquestioning obedience. I obeyed, and clad only in my shirt – too short, even though I bent almost double, to conceal me – carried the towels to the bath, when standing up she commanded me to dry her body, which I did without difficulty, being already almost of my complete adult height.

'I could not but notice the pleasure she took in my attentions but was nevertheless surprised when, having rested her hand upon my shoulder as she stepped from the bath, dropping the towels she pressed her body against my own, and gasped with astonishment as she laid her hand between my legs.

'I could not guess the reason for her surprise but infer, through subsequent experience, that it was the astonishment of a white woman at the size of my member, which I need not hesitate to claim is larger than is the average with lighter-skinned men. The touch of it enlivened her, and ripping my shirt from me, she held tightly to my arms and dragged me to the bed, where throwing me upon my back she mounted me, and to my astonishment took my prick in her hand and introduced it into what appeared to be an aperture in her own body!

'My ignorance of the female frame being complete, I had had no notion of how the act of love was performed – nor indeed that such an act was possible between a man and a woman, though I had heard hints from my fellow servants, and had felt that natural pull which attracts the young male to his female opposite.

'To anyone who believes that a boy of fifteen must be revolted by the person of a woman perhaps thirty years his senior, I must offer a contradiction. No doubt if a girl of my own age had introduced me to the pleasures of the bed, my view might have been a different one. But as things were, I was only too delighted at the course things had taken, and my new mistress's voracity at the game introduced me, within a few days, to almost every variation of carnal pleasure – for she quickly recognised an apt pupil, and in quest of her own satisfaction was delighted to show me how hands, lips and tongue could prepare, enhance and complete the pleasure a sturdy prick suggested.

'Upon Lady Curd's leaving, she presented me with a purse of five guineas and the invitation to enter her service any time I wished – which, since she lived in cold Northumberland, was an idea that did not commend itself to me. However, I was sorry to see her go and to return to my usual duties, for my mistress, the innocent, had no idea of the

reason why her friend took such pleasure in my company
and seemed so enthusiastic in my praise.

'Within a week I was desperate having now been used to
two or three sessions at love in each day, and disinclined to
search for satisfaction in the servants' hall, having become
used to perfumed cleanliness rather than the stink of sweat,
and worse, which the kitchen maids gave forth.

'Finally, I was at my wits' end, and took the desperate
measure of employing a knife to loosen the seams of my
breeches before, first thing in the morning, going to attend
my mistress as she prepared for the day. I had awoken, as
usual, with my fellow's head raised, bursting for employment, and had trouble enough persuading him into a sufficiently relaxed state to occupy his place without bursting
forth. My mistress then only twenty-seven years of age or
less, dressed in her dishabille and seated at her dressing
table, was a picture so delicious that by allowing my imagination to play upon what we might do together, I had no
difficulty in rousing my prick again to such enthusiasm that
just as she reached out her hand for the scent-bottle I held
for her, he burst his bounds and his head struck forth
between the seams of my breeches!

'The scent bottle fell to the floor unnoticed, my mistress
transfixed by the sight she now saw before her. There was no
question what it was: she was not so ignorant! But once more
the size was a surprise to her, though not an unpleasant one.

'The effect was all that I hoped for. My mistress's husband, I should say, was a politician of great influence, but
much preoccupied with affairs of state and though young,
handsome and vigorous, often from home – as he was
upon this occasion, so that my lady was as ready as I for an
encounter.

' "Why, George," she said, "is this the explanation of
Lady Curd's interest in you?"

' "I believe so, ma'am," I said. "You will pardon me,
but I have been in and out of my breeches so often in this
past week that they have grown weak . . ."

'She laughed at this, and rising to her feet opined that
since they were now of little use to me, we must find me
other clothes; and in the meantime perhaps I should remove
the offending garment.

'My lady's body, being younger and more perfect, extended and sharpened my taste for beauty, and she was amazed at my knowledge of what best pleased a lady. Though as with others, it was my size which provoked most astonishment and delight, a fact which, if I may say so, becomes a little fatiguing, for those ladies kind enough to invite me to their beds seem to do so on that basis alone, while there are other tricks at which I am adept. Nevertheless, I do not grumble, and nor did Mrs Damerel, who from that time on dismissed her maid and commanded that I should bring her her morning chocolate – which frequently grew cold upon the bedside table while we were warming between the sheets.

'A short while ago, however, my lady's husband was appointed Governor General of one of our colonies abroad and my situation was terminated. At one of the dinners he gave during which he and my lady made their *adieux* to their friends, Sir Philip Jocelind and his late uncle were guests. How Sir Philip came to be cognisant of the position I held in my lady's esteem, you must invite him to convey, but he approached me with news of your present enterprise and I was all too glad to join it – for to be honest, the ambition to spend my life making money by performing an act which offers me at least as much enjoyment as it does to any other male creature, is something of which I never dreamed.'

It was now, by consent, the turn of William to let us know his story for, as Harry said (now once more lying close by, a mist of steam rising from his body as the sun dried it after his swimming) he had always been somewhat secret, and no one knew his antecedents.

'This,' he explained, 'is because my family is one whose reputation would be known to you all. You know that I call myself Langrish, but that is not my true name – which I shall still keep from you, if you will forgive me, for reasons which will be obvious to you as my story progresses. Or, indeed, at its very beginning, for I must tell you that I grew up not only in a house in one of the most distinguished cathedral closes in this country, but as the son of a dean of one of its best known cathedrals.

'My father,' he continued, 'was a man of considerable reputation in the church, and married to a lady whose beauty and intelligence were ornaments to their drawing-room. I was the youngest of seven children but there had been a gap of seven years between myself and my elder brother Ned, so that by the time I was fifteen years old all my siblings had for one reason or another left home: two brothers for the Navy and one for the life of a curate in a distant parish, while my three sisters were all married. My mother was now over forty years of age, and my father almost fifty, so that while I was deeply beloved of them, they seemed to me to be ancient, and it was the younger members of their household – the maids and kitchen-boys – who were my friends. And my father being a man who considers all to be his equal, I was always allowed great freedom among them, and considered them as brothers and sisters.

'My every whim being indulged, I was allowed too to meet and mix with all kinds of boys and girls of my own age, and consequently grew up in the greatest freedom. But yet, through good example and teaching, I learned to regard kindliness and good nature, together with a gentlemanly deportment, as the natural concomitant of an agreeable and proper life. I was (though I say it) a good-looking lad, and my pretty appearance together with a friendly and open character made me a favourite with all – especially perhaps when I appeared as a member of the cathedral choir, when my appearance was positively angelic, I am informed. I found it difficult not to respond to the whispers and glances of the female members of the congregation; at first, to those elderly ladies who were happy, after service, to offer me sweetmeats and even money, but, as I grew older, to those young ladies nearer my own age to whom I felt an inexplicable attraction.

'Neither my father nor, of course, my mother gave me instruction as to my conduct with the opposite sex, leaving that task to my tutors, one of whom, being younger than the others, did offer me the most explicit description of the action a young man can perform with a young woman. However, one of my father's trusted elder servants happened to enter the schoolroom just as, having lowered his small-clothes to indicate the dimensions which I could expect my private parts to reach upon my attaining puberty, my tutor was attempting to persuade me to do the same by way of comparison – something which, for no reason I could have readily given, I found antipathetic. The tutor left the following morning, to be replaced by an older man.

'My realisation that I had attained the age of maturity came upon me one summer's afternoon when, in a wood not far from home, I had decided to cool myself by bathing in the river, to which end I removed my clothing and plunged in. Having enjoyed ten minutes of swimming and diving, I climbed out and after a while fell asleep lying in a pool of sunlight falling between the trees – to waken, some time later, to the realisation that I was not alone.

'My companions were two young sisters of my own age, whom I had often seen at the cathedral. Though forced by the presence of their mama to be discreet in their actions, I had seen them direct many a twinkling glance in my direction and after service, while their mama and my own were exchanging compliments, I would make them my bow, and never hesitated to direct them a smile or two.

'Now, however, they were most serious – as well they might be, for the young man whom they found lying at their feet as they strode through the wood made a very different figure than when he was dressed from head to foot in a black cassock, or in his Sunday best. I had neglected to cover myself, and in sleep my essential part had swelled to an extent which can only have been surprising to young ladies who had not even a brother whose body might have taught them what to expect.

'Through my lowered eyelashes I could see them, dark against the light, their arms about each other as they strained to see more closely that startling sight, and then they began to tiptoe towards me, the more closely to examine the phenomenon. By lying still, not so much as moving a muscle, I tempted them yet closer, so that in the end they knelt at my side, confident that I was in the deepest of sleeps, and bent so that the yellow locks of one of them actually brushed my belly – when involuntarily my muscles tightened and my prick quivered in a manner which made them at once start and giggle.

'By this time, eager to note their reactions and seeing them preoccupied, I had opened my eyes, and at their movement our gazes met, and they started to their feet.

' "Nay, Miss Priscilla, Miss Louise," I cried, "pray do not disturb yourselves!"

'They were silent, but at least did not fly, and I raised myself on an elbow, and to give them confidence turned so that I could shade my lower part with my hand – or at least make a gesture at doing so, which reassured them.

' "Master William," said Miss Priscilla, and they made a little curtsy, seeming at once to wish to go, and longing to stay.

' "Will you not sit in the sun for a while?" I suggested, and after a moment, indeed they sat, some way off.

' "It is remarkably warm for the time of the year," said Miss Louise, perhaps the more forward of the two. "I am quite bothered by the heat!" And she began to fan herself with her hand.

' "Indeed," agreed her sister, " 'tis quite overcoming!"

' " 'Twas why I bathed myself in the river," I said, "which has cooled me remarkably. I would suggest that you did the same . . ."

' "But we cannot swim," said the elder, "though Mama allowed us to disport ourselves in the sea at Margate last summer."

' "No matter," I argued, "the water is shallow near the bank, and I would be there to ensure that no harm would come to you."

'In short, they agreed, and having seen at the seaside the habit of ladies and gentlemen of bathing quite naked within sight of each other – though certainly at a greater distance than separated us – retired behind a bush, where in a moment I saw their dresses laid upon a branch, and then two white figures lowered themselves, with faint screams, into the water. I felt, of course, that I should be as good as my word in protecting them from possible danger, and after a moment joined them, the interval together with the coolness of the water reducing my lower limb to a size which could no longer frighten even the most nervous of ladies.

'While I swam around them, the girls were content to submerge themselves, only their shoulders above the water – though occasionally, from their happy jumpings, I caught a glimpse of a rosy-tipped breast, which interested me much.

' "Master William," Priscilla eventually said, "could you not show us how to swim? I see the motion of your arms, but when I attempt it –" And trying to support herself, her head disappeared under the water, to reappear with a splutter.

' "Certainly, Miss Priscilla," I said. "If I come behind you and support you." And stationing myself behind her, I placed my arms beneath hers, so that she lay back and in a moment was floating, and when I lifted my own legs from the ground and swam backwards reclined deliciously against my naked body, my hands over her breasts (for it were impossible to place them otherwise). Which gave her the most pleasure, the sensation of floating or that of feeling for the first time the embrace of a male, I would not say.

'By now, Miss Louise was clamouring for her turn, and nothing loath I made my excuses to her sister and supported her, now so in command of the situation that I could look over her shoulder at the length of her body, scarcely veiled by the flowing water which parted about her breasts and hips, and revealed where it flowed between her legs strands of what might (had we been at the seaside) have been the lightest seaweed. Miss Priscilla was so interested by the sight that, forgetting herself, she was standing up in the water, only covered to the waist, drops trickling from her body and her delightful bubbies for the first time fair to my view. The sight, and the sensation of her sister's body in my arms had the effect of recovering me to full vigour – which Louise could not but feel, as it pressed against the small of her back. And in a moment, she reached about to confirm with her hand the presence of something whose size and shape would have more confused her had she not set eyes on it while I was asleep.

' "I grow somewhat chilly," she said, "shall we not lie in the sun once more?" And taking me by the hands, walked me to the shore, where we all climbed out – myself, I must confess, with a certain sense of shame attempting to hide from them my once more rampant part. But 'twas vain, for each was determined to further their acquaintance with it, and pinned me to the ground, a willing victim, while they bent over to inspect the phenomenon at close range.

' "Does it not hurt you to enclose it in trousers?" they asked. And when I explained that 'twas not always of such a size, wondered at this, and asked why then it was now of such dimensions.

' " 'Tis in tribute to your beauty," was my reply, which occasioned much laughter, and the question whether it was always so in the presence of ladies, to which I replied only when they were so pretty, which brought a blush to their cheeks. Meanwhile, it can be imagined that I was not averse to catching what glimpses I could of their own anatomy, confirming the statement of my former tutor as to the formation of the landscape.

' "Oh, look," cried Miss Priscilla, whose cool fingers I felt about me, "he weeps! Why does he weep?"

'With a presence of mind unusual, I fancy, for my years, I replied that he wished to make a closer acquaintance with them. And when they asked how that could be, when we were already as close together as was necessary for polite conversation, explained that the purpose why we were made so different could only be demonstrated by our embracing, which they were clearly curious to try, while at the same time wishing to appear reluctant. And now there came the cry of "You first!" and "No, you are the elder!" and so on, until – confident of my powers – I suggested that I could show them both, and that Miss Priscilla, as the elder, might perhaps properly be the first object of my attentions.

'The drawing with which my tutor had illustrated his lesson in love had shown merely the most basic of all positions in amorous congress, and so I invited Miss Priscilla to lie upon her back – whereupon she rolled over – and to open her legs, which she did with the utmost freedom, never, I suppose, having heard it suggested that 'twas improper (for I am sure the subject had never been broached to the sisters either by their mama or their governesses). I then knelt between her thighs and, lowering myself, placed the tip of my prick against her lower lips, which from her drawing of breath was, I think, no less delicious to herself than to me, for throwing her arms about me she drew me so closely to her that without further effort I slipped into harbour, and with that instinct common to us all, bucked once, and again. And then, so extensive was the emotion I felt, I gave up my soul, to Priscilla's intense disappointment, who thrusting with her hips in imitation of myself found only a diminishing firmness in my person.

' "I do not consider that much to my advantage," she remarked somewhat sourly as I lifted myself from her. "If I was you, Louise, I should not trouble myself!" However, her sister was determined upon the same experience, and with the natural resilience of youth I found her excited fumbling in an attempt to recover me had its effect in a very short time. And on the second occasion was able to contain myself until, with a cry sufficiently loud to startle the birds from the trees, Louise dug her nails into my bum and threw her body into such a paroxysm that I rolled away, fearing that I had hurt her.

' "How can you say 'twas nothing?" she asked her sister. "Why, 'tis the most delicious, the most wonderful, the most . . ." But words failed her – not before encouraging Priscilla to wish for a renewed passage. This time, both she and her sister had to spend some time recovering my sensibilities, but their efforts only further sharpened their desire, so that by the time I was again able to mount the elder, the younger had also to seize my hand and thrust it between her thighs. And in this way I satisfied them both – which was as well, for I doubt even at that age that I could have performed a fourth time within so short a period.

'It need not be said that we met again many times that summer, nor that in natural play we discovered many tricks and pleasantries which I hope were of as much advantage, later, to their husbands (though perhaps surprising to them) as they were to me in those other amorous adventures I have since had. And just at a time when I was beginning to believe that I would have at last to acquiesce in my father's long-expressed desire that I should follow him into the church, Sir Philip made my acquaintance upon his revisiting the University of Cambridge, and introduced me to yourself, Mrs Nelham, and to this present life.'

*　　*　　*

By this time the sun was beginning to lower, and it was time to dress and remove ourselves to the house, where again we ate and drank. And it was a pleasure to us, for once, to relax in each other's company without the knowledge that at any moment the ringing of the bell might summon one or other of us to an arduous, if no doubt pleasurable, demonstration of his masculine powers.

Chapter Fifteen
The Adventures of Andy

Though two weeks passed without our hearing any more from the gentlemen who had so seriously threatened us, the event was never far from our minds. We discussed our problem with Sir Philip Jocelind, upon one of his visits to us, for he came from time to time. Though he had employed each of our girls at one time or another, he now for some private reason seemed not to wish to use the house for the purpose for which it had been established, but was happy to sit of an evening and take a glass or two with Frank and me.

Hearing of our visitation, he grew grave, agreeing with Aspasia that it was most likely that Carlo Gaskill was at the back of it. 'A man of no little influence in the dark corners of London life,' he said, 'but I have someone I might consult on the matter; leave it with me' – and went on to talk of other things, notably of the strange incident of his meeting in the hall one evening none other than Viscount Chichley, who had been for a time a confidante of sister Sophie's.

'It is a strange thing to meet him here,' he said, 'for he was recently wed to a lady of complete beauty and accomplishment, who I would have thought to be an ornament to any marriage. Yet within weeks comes here to escort Xanthe or Rose to bed – not that every one of your ladies is not a complete compendium of delights, as I have had the pleasure of proving. But were I to wed, I would hope that it would be a month or two at least before I made any excursion to another bed, and Chichley is after all still a young man, his appetite not jaded by familiarity with vice. 'Tis odd indeed – but men are indeed strange animals where love is concerned' – a statement Frank greeted with a heartfelt 'Amen', for where would we be, he enquired, were lovers not to be faithless and married men to stray?

It was nevertheless a pleasure to me to have the occasional

opportunity to talk with Chichley, and one night, upon our discussing the vast difference between London society and that of even the most advanced of our provincial cities, he most generously procured me an invitation to dine with the Lord Mayor, who regularly holds levees for the more prominent merchants and business men of the city. 'Amongst whom you must be counted, Mr Archer,' he said, 'though perhaps not in a business whose purpose you need noise abroad at that particular assembly.'

The Mansion House, sometimes called the City Palace, certainly resembles a royal domicile in size, but is badly situated close by the Bank and Royal Exchange. The streets are so narrow that it is impossible to see the building properly, and it is difficult for carriages to approach it at all. However, inside all is extensively handsome, and I found the company amazingly various – from merchants whose only ornament was their banking account, to the royal dukes and some of the nobility. Chichley and his wife, at his side but yet treated with a noticeable coolness, were among them. These, with the diplomatic corps, occupied seats on a platform at one end of the Egyptian Hall, a large room brilliantly lit, in which a band played. The tables below the platform were filled with citizens, and the Lord Mayor and Lady Mayoress presided side by side, the latter in full court dress.

After the courses were over, toasts were given, music kept up, and everything was of a becoming festivity – although I must confess that my enjoyment was somewhat dampened by the fact that my neighbours were stiff and uncommunicative, disposed to converse only with each other rather than offering any friendly gesture to me, despite my best endeavours to be companionable.

Then came a ball in another part of the building, and if the scene in the Egyptian Hall had been picturesque, that upstairs transcended it. The doors of the rooms were all open, and through them one saw a thousand ladies richly dressed, all the colours of nature displayed together like the bursting out of spring. No lady was without her plume; the whole was a waving field of feathers, some blue, some tinged with red, here violet and yellow, there shades of green; most, the purest white. The diamonds surrounding them caught the light and sparkled brilliantly, throwing out sharp beams of light. It was now that I saw for the first time so many hooped dresses, each lady seeming to rise out of a gilt or silver barricade; it was a feast of feminine grace and grandeur.

It would have been improper for me to have approached Chichley, nor did I feel able to introduce myself, where I was not known, to any of those present, especially since they showed a supreme lack of interest in me. After a while I became somewhat melancholy at the thought that I was to spend the evening alone, and decided to leave. But as I made my way towards the door, it was my good luck that a lady coming in the opposite direction stumbled, and would have fallen had I not caught her in my arms. Under other circumstances I might have taken advantage of the fact, for though my thighs were positively bruised by the hoops of her dress, her upper part was not similarly barricaded, and the softness of her breasts, largely uncovered and of an enticing creaminess, much raised my lowered spirits.

I set her upon her feet, wereupon she curtsied in thanks, and I made my bow. Standing near the door for a while and looking after her as she entered the room, I saw that like myself, she was alone, and though she was clearly in search of someone, she returned to the door unaccompanied, whereupon I ventured to bow again.

'You will excuse me, madam, if I venture to observe that you are unaccompanied, and to offer my services if –?'

I broke off, fearing to offend, but she smiled most graciously.

'You are very good, sir. I have missed my aunt, who was with me; if you are going in the direction of the refreshment hall, a cold drink is what I most desire.'

I offered my arm, she laid her hand upon it, and we walked to the room where long tables bore great tureens of claret cup.

My companion was of such beauty that I could not but be conscious of admiring looks from those about me. Of almost equal height to myself, she was of perhaps nineteen or twenty years, slim, excessively elegant, with a carriage of the head inexpressively haughty – yet at the same time her expression was friendly and her comportment condescending. Her hair was of a becoming brown, and all her own, I dare swear – no wig. Her forehead was broad and open, her lips full, and her eyes a clear and bright, unusual blue. As for her person, sated though I was by feminine company I could not but be conscious of the inviting beauty of that part of her body not constricted by the hoops of her fashionable gown. And I may say, in parenthesis, that the sudden disappearance of revealing muslin in favour of barricadoes, which made the lower limbs of womankind as difficult to breach as the walls of a fortress, was viewed by me with abhorrence! However, happily the fashion did not conceal the swell of breasts, the beauty of which would alone have marked her out for admiration.

I ventured to introduce myself, but she did not respond by venturing her own name. However, we talked friendly enough, until after a while an elderly lady made her appearance to claim her niece, and with another curtsy she bade me farewell. After a while I followed her, but on the way found my arm taken by Chichley, who called me an adventurous young dog and congratulated me upon having attached myself to one of the most considerable heiresses in London that season – a Miss Mary Yately, the only daughter of a private gentleman who owned, he said, most of Shropshire, and was unattached.

I was entirely convinced that Chichley was joking in his implication that I had known who my young friend was – or indeed that I had 'attached myself' to her. However, the fact that her beauty and charm were additionally burnished by a large fortune made me all the more interested in Miss Yately, and I devoted the next day or so to a little research into her circumstances. This revealed that she had taken for the season a large house off Piccadilly, where she lived with her aunt. And according to Blatchford, who spent the morning in conversation with a footman of hers he made acquaintance with in a tavern, she was without an admirer, though there were certain comings and goings, presumably of those who wished to become so. But, the man had said, she was cognisant that her fortune would attract those more interested in it than in her, and was determined to avoid capture.

Having worked out a plan, I took myself to St James's,

and from a jeweller's there bought at considerable expense a small silver reticule in which (having enquired of our ladies, without explaining my purpose, what they would expect to find in the purse of a lady of fashion) I placed one or two niceties – viz., handkerchief, perfume, *et cetera*. Then, at about three in the afternoon, I took myself off to Piccadilly and rang at my lady's bell.

I gave my name to the footman who answered it, and enquired for the aunt, the Honourable Mrs Mathilda Yately, whom I had seen ten minutes before drive off towards the city. He replied that Mrs Yately was not at home, but that he would announce me to Miss Yately. He then vanished, to return and usher me up a splendid stair-case to an elegant drawing-room where my friend sat at her embroidery stand.

I was full of apologies: I would not have ventured to announce myself to her but that her aunt was out, and yet it was, I thought, on her business that I was here. And I produced from my pocket the reticule.

'Just after we parted,' I said, 'I found this upon the floor where you had been standing, and believing it yours, have come to return it.'

She took it, curiously, but to my astonishment, having examined it, recognised it as her own, with expressions of gratitude! I fancy my jaw may have dropped, but simply bowed and said that I was delighted to have been the agent of the reticule's return. What could this mean? Was my little scheme discovered, and I therefore discounted as a fortune hunter? But she continued affable.

'You will take tea?'

I demurred; I had taken too much of her time.

'Not at all, it will be a pleasure to renew acquaintance.'

So tea was brought, and meanwhile we talked. I dropped no hint that I knew anything of her circumstances, but admitted that I had gone out of my way to discover her name – which, I said, had not been difficult, since she was uncommonly beautiful, and therefore the cynosure of all eyes and the focus of all talk. I was 'in business' I said, and hinted that I was in a fair way of wealth.

All this time I was becoming more and more enamoured of her. She was dressed now for the boudoir rather than the ballroom in a loose gown which revealed more of the beauty of her charming frame than could have been guessed at from her body's former fashionable imprisonment. And what I saw was of even greater charm than I could have suspected – to such an extent indeed that I felt the stirring of a passion which, I knew, I could not allow myself to show.

But things were to take a sharp turn, and soon. I do believe that her senses in some way apprehended my feelings almost before I knew them myself, for she suddenly remarked that surely I had spent much of my life in the country? And upon my asking how she came to understand this, she said simply that she could recognise a town gull as soon as sniff at him, whereas I had that natural vivacity of manner and – if she might say so – naturalness of bearing which marked me out a countryman.

'I grew up in Shropshire,' she said, 'and though in a great estate was entirely conscious of country matters. Here, there is a circling and circling before one can come at a matter, while there a stone is called a stone and a spade a spade.'

I was silent for a moment. Then, 'I cannot believe, ma'am, that any gentleman in town would not be as quick in apprehension of your beauty and parts as myself,' I said.

'Ah, that may be,' she said, 'but would they show it?'

A wink being as good as a nod to the blindest of horses, I took this for the invitation it was, and rising to my feet fastened upon her hand and pressed it to my lips – whereupon she too rose, and in a moment had fixed her own lips to mine, while pressing the length of her body against me in a manner unmistakable in its implication. As we were still embraced, I passed my hands beneath the muslin of her dress and felt, beneath their palms, flesh as soft as it was creamy.

Finally, she withdrew from my arms and somewhat to my dismay went to a bell pull at the wall and tugged at it. But then she immediately loosed her dress and began to climb out of it, so that when the door opened and the footman appeared, he saw a mistress clad only in her shift, while a young man only too obviously amazed – myself – stood at the other side of the room, his eyes goggling.

'Albert,' she said, 'I shall be occupied for the next half of an hour. Should my aunt return, kindly inform her that I am not to be disturbed.'

The fellow bowed, and without the merest suggestion of a smirk withdrew, while even before he had closed the door behind him Miss Yately had shed her sole remaining garment, and turning to me had enquired whether I was to disappoint her by proving as slow as a townee?

Not wishing to be accused so, I was soon as bare of covering as she, who had by this time laid herself at my feet upon the thick carpet, one leg drawn up, one arm behind her head, and a look of anticipation which was emphasised by the rising and falling of those breasts whose full disclosure was no disappointment.

I was under orders to be swift in action, but my mind was even swifter: the situation was not one which I had anticipated, nor had I come with the intention of seducing Miss Yately. Indeed my body was no more ready for such a scene than my mind, for the previous evening – the house being quiet – I had spent a happy hour with Xanthe and Rose which had left us all exhausted, and despite my youth I would not normally have expected to renew a carnal interest for at least twenty-four hours.

This was no an obstacle to fornication, mark you, for what youth of under twenty could not fuck three or four times a day were the opportunity to arise and were the lady to be of a coming-on disposition? And Miss Yately certainly was, but then my intention had been to ingratiate myself with her rather than to offer love-making, and the way to an heiress's pocket was not necessarily through her . . .

Well, now that I was in this position, the only thing to do was to be as pleasing as possible. Fortunately during the past four or five years I had had considerable training in the pleasuring of ladies, and in particular the past three or four months had taught me much, the ladies at Brook Street being quick to inform me what did and what did not contribute to their pleasure. Having to devote much of their time to satisfying the male appetite without necessarily experiencing a reciprocal delight, they were all the more eager to be satisfied when bedding Frank or myself. Though we were their employers, we were clearly also their friends, and should be counted upon to provide some gratification rather than merely accepting their favours in the way of trade.

So I set to with the intention of positively slaying my new friend with delight – which I think I may say I accomplished. No two ladies being utterly alike in what pleasures them, I spent some little time in experimenting whether the lobes of the ears or the tips of the breasts, the sucking of the lower lip or the nipping of the tongue, the stroking of the arse or of the thighs, gave most delight. I then offered consideration to that organ which lies just within the threshold of woman's portals, a prick in miniature, and caressed it with my tongue, first softly, delicately, regularly, then gradually more and more speedily and vigorously, even pausing to nibble and nuzzle. At the same time my fingers played about the rest of her body, particularly rubbing the tight nipples of the breasts, while I distinctly felt the muscles of her thighs tightening as though she longed to close them upon my neck to strangle me in her pleasure! It was indeed with some relief that, as her cries mounted, I sensed that the time had come for full congress. Should it be from the front or the back, should she lie beneath or mount above? Should my riding be swift or slow?

These questions were all tried, and in turn were plainly answered by Miss Yately with a fierce cry or a grip unmistakable in denoting satisfaction. She failed to respond to the long and regular thrusting which pleased most women, but rather encouraged me to place the tip of my prick just within her nether lips, drawing it entirely from her body at the end of each short stroke so that those lips were continually stirred and stretched – which she controlled by the pressing of her thighs together, thus not permitting me a full entry. This was not to my complete satisfaction. Nor was she, I must say, a very active participant, preferring to allow me to exhaust myself in her service rather than to pay any other tribute to my attentions than to suffer them, which was of no help when, after a while, already sapped on the previous night, my energies began to ebb. However, this had the merit that I was able to contain myself to her contentment, and fortunately her fourth paroxysm of enjoyment resulted in her almost losing consciousness. And so, kissing her, I withdrew myself, and she, seeming content, invited me to ring the bell – which I did, and Albert once more entered and ignoring our nakedness brought fresh tea, during the sipping of which we resumed our clothes.

'Mr Archer,' she said, finally, 'it has been a pleasure to make the acquaintance of one whose energy and aptness matches his personal elegance. I trust we shall meet again.'

I trusted so, too, for I must admit that while her love-making was of a certain selfishness, I found her extraordinarily attractive – while her fortune was not in itself a discouragement from my making myself agreeable to her. The attitude of the footman, Albert, caused me some disquiet. Indeed, as he showed me out there was no sign of impertinence nor of complicity. Did this simply betoken his excellence as a servant, carefully taught not to betray the slightest surprise or interest in his mistress's doings? Or could it be an indication that Miss Yately was not the innocent I imagined, and that the sight of a lover was not as unusual as I had thought? That she was not a virgin was certain, and indeed her references to country matters suggested that – as with many maids growing up among farmyards and fields where animal couplings are readily to be seen – her maidenhead had probably fallen to some lusty lout or other beneath a hedge, or more likely in some corner of her own garden. But even if this was the case, her scornful attitude to city suitors nevertheless promised well, and her positive enjoyment of the game of love – on her own account, at least – seemed to indicate that she would welcome a lover whose interest was entirely in her personal qualities rather than her fortune.

I returned to Brook Street and retired almost immediately to bed, being more than a little exhausted. But I was shook awake in the middle of the evening by Frank, who said that there was to be a conference below with regard to the demands of Mr Gaskill, and that Philip had brought a friend to advise us – and a friend I would be surprised to meet.

What indeed was my amazement upon joining them, to

find none other than David Ham, engaged deep in conversation with Jocelind, Blatchford, Will Pounce and Bob Tippett. He grinned at my surprise.

'I told you of my friend, Andy?' he said. ' 'Tis Sir Philip, here!'

Philip had the grace almost to blush, and indeed I was somewhat surprised to find that he had been keeping David as a bum-boy while at the same time enjoying not only our ladies but my Sophie! However, my surprise was not so great as it would have been had not Sophie hinted to me of certain problems he experienced with the ladies. And at any event 'twas not my habit to raise an eyebrow at any trick performed in bed, for they are too various not to provide, from time to time, an occasional wonder.

'I was not aware . . .' said Philip.

'Ah, yes,' said I, not averse to turning the screw, 'David and I are old friends, and indeed bedfellows' – at which his eyebrows rose. But I was not about to explain the circumstances of our familiarity, which had arisen on account of an interesting accident not unconnected with a theatrical performance, and not out of my own pleasure in being sodomised, which indeed had been entirely negligible, and had certainly not persuaded me to progress any further down that particular path.

'Well,' said David, 'you have yourselves in a pickle, but fortunately not too sharp a one, for I happen to know that your friend Carlo is no longer as popular as he might be, due to his inordinate lust for money. 'Tis time he was seen off, which as it happens I believe I can accomplish on your behalf with the aid of these good fellows here, especially Mr Tippett, who is a lad of my own heart. Now, Frank – if you will allow the familiarity?' – at which Frank smiled – 'the first thing is to appoint a meeting with Mr Gaskill, which can be done by a message sent to the address I know of. The second is to ensure the ladies are out of sight when he arrives. The third is – well, you can leave the third to us.' And he winked.

I believe that Frank was little inclined to trust the business to so young and apparently inexperienced a youth, but I was able to inform him privately that David was by no means the innocent he might appear. Indeed, an unpleasant night in Bristol gaol had been my own experience of a result of his occasional indulgence in crime, which had not as far as I knew yet embraced murder, but which had at least displayed a certain competence where matters of illegality were concerned. So an invitation was sent to Gaskill for the night following, he to be accompanied only by two fellows, and an agreement would be reached, to be confirmed by the payment of a certain sum in gold.

The following night, the Brook Street establishment was quiet, and the occasional visitor knocking was disappointed to hear that due to sickness the house was closed that night. At ten, however, a more determined knock revealed Carlo Gaskill – a tall, middle-aged man of saturnine appearance, accompanied by two of the fellows we had encountered before.

Frank and I met them in the hall, wrapped only in towels, which occasioned him some surprise.

'I think, sir,' said Frank, 'that our business should be private. You will consider it, I believe, such that your escort need not be concerned to hear the details' – and turning aside he tipped a wink, which the man clearly believed referred to the financial accommodation, and promised him a share larger than would be the case should his accomplices know the details.

'As you are no doubt aware, we have hot baths here for the convenience of our clientele. My friend and I are unclothed' – and here both Frank and I unwrapped our towels to show indeed that we concealed no weapons about us – 'and we invite you to clothe yourself similarly, and to accompany us downstairs, where we can discuss the matter at leisure over a bottle.'

Gaskill thought for a moment, and then decided that he would have no difficulty in defending himself against two relative weaklings like Frank and myself. So in the neighbouring room he divested himself of his clothing and, wrapping a towel about himself, accompanied us below while his two friends remained in our receiving-room.

'Your facilities are as generous and luxurious as was reported to me,' said Gaskill as he entered the warm room. 'I am delighted that we are to reach an agreement, for if the ladies are as handsome and accommodating as report suggests, there is no reason why your business should not continue to flourish and expand!' He then seated himself near the warm bath, and while the steam rose about us from the channels in the floor, Frank poured us all wine.

'This is indeed an exceptional arrangement,' Gaskill said, 'and one which must become more general; I doubt not that it attracts almost as many gentlemen as your stable of fillies. It may be that we should work more closely together. But first, what is your proposal for solving our current little difficulty?'

Frank began a long preamble concerning the income we commanded, the proportion given to the girls, the proportion which might be spared in tribute. Gaskill became notably more impatient, but sufficiently interested to keep his eyes fixed on us, sitting opposite him – which was as well, for on bare feet, David Ham accompanied by Blatchford, Tippett and Will Pounce, crept out of the doorway leading to the boiler room, and approached behind him. At the last moment, some instinct warned the villain, for he started and looked about. But too late – a piece of sacking was thrown over his head by David, and Blatchford and Pounce, each taking an arm, tipped him backwards into the water of the bath. Then Tippett mounted his struggling body and weighed it down.

I had never seen a man killed before, nor do I wish to again – yet if it must be done, drowning is relatively swift, relatively silent, and without the necessity to spill blood. In two minutes or less, all was over, and the sacking removed. The staring eyes of Gaskill were seen to be as empty of life as his lungs were of air.

I cannot say that I was sanguine in the affair; murder seemed to me to be too radical a solution to any problem, yet what we had heard of Gaskill had clearly indicated that he would have had no compunction about wounding and scarring our ladies, nor indeed about murder should we have stood out against him.

'Well done,' said Frank, grimly.

David, on the other hand, grinned broadly. 'A good night's work, as most of London will agree!' he said. 'Now for the rest of the plan.'

Retiring upstairs, we dressed and armed ourselves with

pistols before opening the door upon the corpse's two attendants, who looked vastly uncomfortable that their master was not among the six men who stood before them.

'Now, thumpers,' said David, 'Carlos has met with a sad accident downstairs, and you must find a new master – or make yourselves masters!' The bullies looked at one another. 'Yes, Johnson,' continued David, 'you've had your eye on the throne for some time now. Well, 'tis yours if you want it, for if you depart and no word spoke we'll keep you out of this; otherwise there might be a word to the watch – and 'tis common knowledge you'd have done the deed yourselves long since had you the wit and the courage.'

The men were silent; one fingered his pocket, but seeing our weapons kept their own out of sight, thinking better of action.

'Very well, young Ham,' said the elder.

'But mind you,' said David, 'no thurrocking from this house; all's to rest quiet here – as quiet as old Gaskill, below. Now, off with you.'

The men whispered together for a moment then, surly but quiet, left the house.

'You'll have no trouble,' said David. 'Johnson'll slit the throat of the other before they reach Blackfriars, then he'll have the whole gang where he wants it, and he won't want the trouble of worrying you – he'll be too busy establishing his monarchy. So to the rest of the plan.'

Within ten minutes the girls were downstairs dressed as for usual business; Philip and Pounce stripped and accompanied Cissie and Constance upstairs to amuse themselves in whatever way occurred to them – in case the watch should wish to examine the house – while Aspasia was established in her usual glory in the hall, and I went forth to find authority.

Returning in ten minutes with a sturdy fellow from Grosvenor Square, I let myself into the hall, where Aspasia greeted us with, 'Ah, officer, I trust this may be kept quiet. 'Tis an accident would do us no good in our business . . .'

'Well, ma'am,' said the watch, still clutching in his pocket the three guineas I had handed him, 'it indeed sounds an unfortunate matter. Where is the poor gentlemen?'

'Down here,' I replied, and escorted him to the hot room,

where a towel decently covered the remains of Gaskill. Having inspected the corpse, the watchman enquired for 'the young lady concerned' and I sent for Rose – who, her slight injury completely recovered, had begged for the satisfaction, and indeed gave a splendid performance.

The gentleman, she said, had been happily toying with her – 'for, you know, sir, that the heat oft sets 'em on' – when he had suddenly grasped at his chest and collapsed into the pool, from which he had been too heavy for her to remove. And by the time she had fetched Blatchford his heart had stopped, whether from its own inaction or from the inhalation of the water could not be known.

'He looks a sturdy enough fellow,' said the watch.

'But exertion of this kind can bring on a stoppage of the heart in many an unsuspecting chap,' said Rose. 'I have known it before.'

'And who might he be?' enquired the man.

'That, I cannot tell,' she said, and I pointed out that in the nature of our business most of the gentlemen attending the house either used false names or gave no name at all.

'Well, now,' said the watch, ' 'tis clear the whole thing was an accident, and the least said the better. The coroner must know, in course, but my report will be that, summoned instantly, I found all to be as explained, and there will be no trouble.'

'Infinitely obliged to you,' said Frank and, as he prepared to leave, and was exchanging eyes with Moll, added, 'perhaps one evening you would care to be our guest here, and try our company?'

The fellow was clearly delighted, and went on his way. Indeed there was no trouble; we heard no more of the gang, the body was removed, and the coroner merely said a few words about the inadvisability of gentlemen of a certain age indulging in too much excitation of the flesh. The whole matter died as swiftly and quietly as our enemy himself.

I found it impossible, during the following days, to shake my mind free of Miss Mary Yately. It is true that I did not make an unusual effort to do so, for not only was she exceptionally beautiful, but exceedingly rich. She clearly found me not disagreeable, and though during the short course of my adult life marriage had always been far from my thoughts, I could not escape the conception of what a fine thing such a match would be for me. Born the son of a labourer, I had risen through my own efforts from general servant to footman, then through my fortunate friendship with Frank and Sophie to almost the condition of a gentleman – for so they at least treated me, and my familiarity with them and the circles in which they moved had given my manner a patina of respectable civility.

I began to court the lady in earnest, carefully keeping from her my occupation in Brook Street, and in answer to the questions she put to me maintaining a mysterious reticence which I fancied was an additional attraction.

I returned to see her only a day or two after our first acquaintance, and upon sending my name in was immediately bidden to the drawing-room, where I was introduced to the lady's aunt, the Honourable Mrs Mathilda Yately, who greeted me with excessive condescension and – while her niece was commanding tea from the egregious Albert – was pleased to whisper that she had heard much of me from her, and to my advantage. After tasting a single cup she then took her leave, whereupon it was not three minutes before Miss Yately's delicate fingers were occupying themselves with the buttons of my shirt, and she escorted me to her bedroom, where a fine and energetic fuck passed an hour before we noticed it; after which, as we lay in a state of nature, she confided that she found me mighty attractive.

'You need not conceal from me,' she said, 'that you are not nobly born, for not only does your speech betray you – though only to the nicest ear – but your love-making is more delicate and considerate than is the habit among the gentry, whose concern is only for their own quick gratification.'

'Then you have experience of it?' I asked, impertinently.

'I have not grown to twenty-five,' she said – so that was her age! – 'without acquainting myself with a prick or two, and there has been no scarcity of gentlemen willing to demonstrate what they can do, my fortune – as you will no doubt have heard – being considerable.'

I looked, I fancy, a trifle shocked, but she went on: 'Do not colour so – you will have been told that I am heir to an estate, and I doubt not that the news has played a part in your so soon returning for Act Two of our little play. However, you will have remarked that I have not yet sent you packing, and I assure you that I do not suffer fools gladly, nor fortune-hunters.'

My blushes redoubled, for I could not disguise from myself that thoughts of her fortune played some part in my courting her – though her body was a fortune of a different sort, which I was pleased already to be able to command. And I proved the fact to her a second time before we parted, to which she was far from averse.

It now became my habit to wait upon Miss Yately almost every other day – even to the extent that Frank suspected that I was wooing someone, but did not expect it could be anyone of consequence. The girls, too, noted that I neglected them, and were coarse upon the subject, my having been (I must confess) a continual companion of theirs when business did not call them – as sometimes it did, warm from my arms, so that more of our customers than might have thought it were served a buttered bun!

Miss Yately herself made no bones about her enjoyment of the main purpose of my visits, frequently having me shown directly to her bedroom, where she would be lying unclothed upon the bed and, once more, in full view of Albert. But I have had cause to note here before the habit of the upper classes of regarding servants as having no more apprehension than a piece of furniture, and came to believe it was so with her.

Mrs Yately was evidently privy to our encounters, for once as I encountered her in the hallway, she stopped, dug me in the ribs, winked lewdly, and enquired whether my spirits were up, for her niece had been 'skitting about' all morning, and was clearly in need of 'a good poke' – which I took to be a saying of yesterday, for I had not heard it before.

At last, after perhaps two months, just as summer was beginning to fade towards autumn and the trees beginning to drop their leaves, I decided to make my move towards regularising our situation – choosing a moment when I had, I believed, raised my lady's spirits to the point at which she could have refused me nothing. Pausing for a moment in my labours I enquired whether 'twas not time we reached an understanding, so that we could 'do this' (and here I resumed my movements, at the same time seizing her buttocks to draw her more closely towards me) all day and every day?

'Oh, yes! Yes!! Yes!!!' she cried, which I took to be assent and, delighted, brought us to a mutually satisfactory conclusion. After a suitable pause, I kissed her upon the lips and asked when she might make me the happiest man in London – at which a twinkle came to her eyes, and she equivocated. Despite my persuasion she declined to reply, but with a kindly energy and teasing roused me to another bout, and so we concluded the afternoon, parting with an understanding, if not with a positive date for our marriage.

Chapter Sixteen

Sophie's Story

I could not banish from my mind the unhappy nature of my friend Chichley's marriage, for though I had not conversed with him for some time, I had the most cordial recollection of him – and not only, as the uninformed reader may imagine, because he had been the first person in the capital to entertain me to the pleasures of love, but also for his gentle and agreeable humour.

I was at first perplexed by my brother's report of his so regularly deserting his wife's bed to attend the house in Brook Street, but then learned from Andy, who had become a confidant, that he found his bride cold and unresponsive – something I could put down only to nervousness, for certainly she showed herself, in her dealings with us, warm and ready for amorous combat. She was also an extremely amiable creature whose manners toward me and the boys were of the utmost delicacy. There were some ladies who used the boys to satisfy a carnal itch, without the slightest sign that they might be capable of human feelings, but Lady Chichley was always informed by courtesy, and never left Harry without giving him some small present (unnecessary in view of the large fee she had already paid the house). He, on the other hand, clearly enjoyed her company uninspired by the fact that she was paying for his attentions, and welcomed her more as a lover than a client. Indeed, unquestioned, he assured me that she came to him as a beloved mistress or even a wife might, and that as much time was spent in happy talk and sentimental caress as in the excitation of copulation. When introduced to Philip, though initially shy, she was now so confident of our entire tact that she was happy to take tea with him and to converse in the most intimate manner – though never prepared to hear a word against her husband uttered by any lips other then her own.

And she herself took great care never to denigrate him after her first confidence to me.

The situation was the more sad and confusing because I learned from Frank and Andy that the ladies in Brook Street had confided that Chichley's vigour in the act of love was unmatched even in their extensive acquaintance with the sex. While he still lacked that nicety of action which comes with experience, he was keenly appreciative of every lesson he received, and contributed to it more than the usual pupil's apprehension of what is owed by a man to the sensibility of any lady who agrees to match with him.

When I expressed my melancholy at the situation, Frank entirely concurred, for he found Chichley as pleasant a companion as I, and though he had never seen Lady Chichley, was content to accept my assurances as to her beauty and zest. At this point Andy, who had been quiet, asked whether we would be prepared for a little deception if it had the result of bringing man and wife together. When we assented, he put forward a plan which, while it entailed the risk that should things go wrong we would incur the displeasure of both Viscount and Lady Chichley, might certainly have the desired result. So I agreed to it, and after we had worked out the details made my way back to Chiswick. There to my astonishment, for I believed the place to be empty (it being scarcely midday and none of my men yet arrived) I heard a considerable hoo-ha from the back of the house – shouts, and a female voice crying out in protest. I swiftly made my way thither and, throwing open the door of one of the cabinets, saw to my astonishment three figures engaged in a fierce struggle: the first my eyes fell upon was Polly, stripped half-naked, her breasts bare and her skirt almost torn from her. She was held, her arms behind her back, by a man who lay half-beneath her upon the couch, while another, clad only in his shirt, was crouching between her thighs and had either succeeded in forcing her or was about to do so. The latter, his back to the door, and intent upon his purpose, was ignorant of my entry. Seizing the only weapon to hand, my parasol, I automatically thrust with it in the first direction a passion of anger suggested, and scored a hit on that portion of the assailant's anatomy which most readily offered itself.

His shriek of pain was louder than any other noise in the room, even Polly's not inconsiderable cries, and he fell to the floor writhing in agony, my parasol (now, alas, seriously bent) carried with him. Polly in her turn now thrust backwards with her bum, winding the other fellow, and we made good our escape, quickly extricating the key normally used to lock the door on the inside, and making the room secure.

Administering brandy to Polly, I quickly heard her story: she had come downstairs in answer to a ring upon the door to find the two men enquiring whether there was work they might do in the garden or about the house. As they were lusty fellows she had engaged them to chop some wood from a recently fallen tree, for we were beginning to lay in fuel against the coming autumn.

After an hour, it being hot, she had invited them into the kitchen for a tankard of small beer, and there they had sat and conversed for a while, eventually admitting that they lived nearby and had heard rumours of what went on in the house, and asking whether there might not be employment for them of a more agreeable nature than chopping wood.

Polly had replied that the stable was at the moment full.

'In any case, ma'am,' she said, 'they were rough trade, and not in the manner which might attract ladies – as, say, with Harry it does – but dirty and sweaty, unshaven and unmannerly.'

They seemed not to take her refusal amiss, and she (unwisely as it turned out) left them to finish their beer while she went back to tidy the cabinets, replace used towels, and make the rooms ready for the day's work. To her anger and dismay the two men suddenly appeared and demanded she lie down to them, and upon her refusing, both seized her, in a state of excitement tearing her clothes from her, which made them the more frenzied. One held her fast while the other ripped open his trousers revealing an empurpled instrument of admirable dimensions (had it been a welcome sight) and had actually entered her when the door opened to admit me and the instrument which pierced the assaulter to rather more painful effect than Polly had already suffered from him.

Pausing only to take a loaded pistol from the desk where I always kept it in case of such emergencies, we made our way back to the room in which we had left the ruffians, and called to them whether they would come out peacefully, for we were armed.

'A likely story, ladies with pistols!' jeered a voice, whereupon I fired my weapon through the door, happy to sacrifice the woodwork to instil a proper sense of fear into the attackers, who indeed were now reduced for a moment to silence. But in a moment we heard a private muttering, and finally, in very compliant tones, they fell to begging our pardon and pleading for release.

In fact, it was best we sent them upon their way rather than complain to the watch, for the less attention we drew to the house the quieter and less disturbed our lives would be. So Polly unlocked the door and threw it open, while I levelled my pistol and covered the two men, who came out, one hobbling severely and clutching his shirt to his rear, where I could see it was stained with blood.

'I hope you have not damaged my parasol, for 'twas a present from a dear friend,' I said. 'Kindly hand it to Miss Polly –' and insisted that the victim of my accuracy with the instrument should fetch and hand it over, which he did obviously in discomfort and with little grace.

'And you, sir,' I said, 'may be thankful that you were protected by the body of my friend from a similar assault. You have got off very easily –' which, had he not greeted the words with a sneer, might have been the truth. But Polly, seeing his lack of gratitude for his escape, took the opportunity of his passing in front of her to direct a kick which, her feet being clad with sharp-pointed shoes and her aim being as accurate as her leg was strong, connected with his cods and, from his cry, caused him considerable discomfort. In the face of my pistol, the pair dared do nothing, and we saw them from the house, carefully locking the door afterwards.

We had not intended to alarm anyone with a repetition of the events, but when the boys arrived the state of the cabinet door could not of course be disguised from them, and since it was clearly the result of the percussion of a firearm I had no recourse but to explain the occurrence. This caused considerable surprise and distress, most particularly to William, who immediately embraced Polly with the fondest solicitation, to which she was clearly not averse, and indeed relapsed into tears, which was of some surprise to me since she had been careful to assure me that she was not hurt nor had seemed more disturbed than the unpleasant circumstance had warranted. However, since she was clearly now disturbed by unhappy recollections I assented to her lying down for a while, and William supported her from the room.

Spencer, meanwhile, was grave upon the event, for, he said, such ruffians were often not without friends, and an attack upon the house could not be ruled out. He suggested that more firearms should be brought in and those boys unfamiliar with them be taught to handle them. I dissented, for it was ever my view that violence should be avoided whenever possible, and that the more guns available to be used the more likely they would be set off, with results that might be as damaging to us as to any enemies we might wish to assault.

In a short while came the first ring upon the bell, and Polly not being visible I answered it to the earliest of our visitors, who was amused upon being conducted to the window to find the boys hastily removing the last of their clothing – which scene she watched with such considerable enjoyment that it occurred to me (not for the first time) that to see a man disrobing might be of a nature to stimulate the most jaded of palates, and worth contriving as a part of our service.

Having seen her happily ensconced with Tom, whose plumpness often commended itself to our more motherly patrons, I went in search of Polly – and indeed of William, who had not returned. Going to her room, I entered it as usual without knocking to see the boy's shapely and smooth buttocks framing the top of my friend's dark head as she sucked happily upon his cock, while his own head, plunged between her thighs, was clearly giving her similar pleasure.

He looked around in some embarrassment, and seemed ready to offer some excuse or even apology, but Polly, confident of our friendship and my fondness for her (as she might well be) merely relinquished her titbit to intimate that she had found she needed a more corporeal comfort than words could alone convey.

' 'Tis not only that, ma'am,' said William, swinging his leg away and coming to sit upon the edge of the bed, 'I have long admired Mrs Playwright to distraction, and mean to ask you whether you would object to my offering her marriage. I have heard within the past week that my father has sadly passed away leaving me, even as the younger son, a considerable competence, and my feelings for Mrs Playwright are such that I must make the attempt at carrying her off, whether or not I can hope for success.'

I could not help smiling at Polly's face, which was a picture, she clearly not having had the faintest idea of the offer being made. Indeed for a moment she seemed positively angry that William had not spoken to her of the matter before, as it were, asking my consent – and I was not in a position to object, even had I wished to do so. But I had noticed her fondness for William over the past several weeks, not only in their slipping away together (when opportunity allowed) but in her observing with an envious jealousy those ladies who, having chosen him from among our other stallions, he escorted to a closed cabinet, after which, she would markedly flirt with Harry or George until his pleading looks reached a sufficient intensity for her to forgive him.

So, it may be imagined that in this case she swiftly overcame her scruples and, rising on one elbow, offered her lips, which he saluted with his own, the kiss growing to an embrace, so that drawing him down they once more fell into a languorous love-making which promised the fulfilment of unfinished business, his manly instrument, which had somewhat lost its proudness during the brief interval of my interruption, again stirring into life.

It was clearly unnecessary for me to intervene, but crossing to the bed, I bent to kiss them upon the shoulders – those being the only innocent areas now exposed to me – and left the room. They remained together for the rest of the evening, my making excuses for William to the two ladies who enquired for his services. And late that night we all drank to their engagement in rosy champagne, though plans for their marriage were not yet made, Polly insisting that they both owed me the consideration of remaining at Chiswick until substitutes could be found for them.

Two evenings later, as I had expected (for her visits were regular) Lady Chichley came again to the house, and retired with Harry. An hour later, handsome in his silk gown, he brought her to my room after their encounter so that (as was her wont) she could take a glass of wine before her departure. With her usual courtesy she handed him a gold coin and kissed his cheek before sitting to lift her glass. For a while we talked of nothing, but I offered the impression that there was something more serious to say, and in due course I said, 'Lady Chichley, I have a request which may strike you as impertinent and if so, you will please discount it. It has come to my notice through the agency of my brother – of whom you have heard me speak – that you have an admirer.'

Few women can hear those words with complete indifference, and though she made a certain pretence at disinterest, she invited me to continue.

'We were conversing the other day about the beauties of the town, and your name was raised – not by myself, I hasten to say, for I am careful to keep confidence, but by my brother, who said that a certain nobleman of his acquaintance was mad in love with you. "It is a shame," he said, "that my lady is of such virtue and so in love with her husband that she should not encounter him, for he is of the utmost discretion, of fine family, wonderfully handsome, of all young men in town the most adept at making love, and all in all the perfect lover. He has had adventures – two ladies to my knowledge have been forced to retire to their rooms for some days with exhaustion after a bout with him – but has so far lacked the perfect companion to make him happy. And now nothing will do for him but to languish after my lady Chichley, who as we all must know is a lost cause." '

Lady Chichley's cheeks had coloured.

'I can confirm that the reputation of this gentleman is no mere tale,' I continued, 'for a lady who will be well known to you – but whose name I must naturally conceal – has sworn to me that her own single brief pass with him has made her completely discontented wi.. any other lover, and the latest I hear is that she considers entering a convent. Were it not that your ladyship has done me the honour to confide in me I would not be so impertinent as to repeat this anecdote to you, but it occurred to me that you might not be averse to taking a lover from your own class. 'Tis something not unheard of, and would be a more lasting answer to your problem than these encounters, which while they are a reasonable solution in the short term, cannot by their nature last. Were you inclined to grant this gentleman's wish . . .'

I paused, and she did not immediately demur.

'I cannot of course disclose his name to you – the more especially since moving in the highest social circles he will be known to you, and it would be impossible to avoid embarrassment when you met, should you decide against a permanent affair. But I can assure you of his perfect reticence, and that his passion for you is such that whatever your reception of his attentions he would never afterwards reveal an assignation, nor so much as with a smile acknowledge your condescension should you agree to favour him.'

My lady was clearly tempted.

'To afford you the greatest protection from embarrassment, the gentleman will consent that you should both be masked – he so that you should not discover his identity, you to spare your blushes. Nor will it be necessary for either to speak, and happily in such cases actions make words superfluous.'

Since I was already privy to my lady's sensual nature, she could not pretend to me that she was averse to the embraces of the male sex, and only a little more time must be spent in persuasion. I had rightly counted on her appetite for love being now so keen that the offer of the embraces of a gentleman of her own station was irresistible, and in the end she acquiesced, agreeing to return to the house three evenings later to make her unknown admirer happy.

I ensured that the house was empty that evening both of visitors and of our boys. The unknown admirer appeared first, brought hither by Andy in a closed carriage, and taken to a room where he could mask and don the silk gown which I had placed for him. A few minutes later Lady Chichley arrived, and I escorted her to my own bedroom where she too stripped and clad herself in a similar plain gown, before fixing upon her face a velvet mask which covered all but her lips, placing her eyes even in such shadow that they could barely be seen. I then escorted her to the main cabinet, where her would-be lover already waited, and paused only to place her hand in his.

He was – the reader will already have apprehended – none other than her husband, having been told by my brother of the beautiful woman who admired him this side of desperation and offered the encounter.

Andy and I now retired – I shame to say, but that the reader will share our curiosity – to the neighbouring cabinet with its secret view of the room and all that passed within it.

When we reached our vantage-point we found that the two were still standing hand in hand, their eyes locked together with such an intense gaze that – despite the masks – I feared for a moment that they had recognised each other only from the interchange of looks. At last Chichley let go his companion's hand to release the tie which held the cloak at his throat, so that the covering fell to his feet revealing that admirable frame which I still so keenly recollected – and the sight of which, I admit, released in me a moment's regret that I was not the creature about to receive his attentions. He had the grace of an antique statue, perfectly balanced, with broad shoulders and narrow hips, a breast like burnished armour, flat belly dinted by the central knot of his navel, shapely thighs sturdy as oaks, and between them a manhood which, as yet only gently roused, nestled within its brake of blond hair. Yet as we watched, it stirred with a faint motion, signalling a readiness to appreciate the feast in store with all the appetite of a hungry man.

Now Chichley took two steps towards his companion, and lifting his hands to her neck, loosed the ties of her gown so that it similarly fell from her, revealing her in all her beauty – at which Andy, who had never seen her, shuddered suddenly as though with the ague. In a moment I felt his hands upon my shoulders and his body pressed against mine as he bent forward to look more closely at the tableau, for Frances Chichley matched her husband as the figure of Eve matched that of Adam in the old paintings, her high breasts pointing slightly outwards, full but not heavy, firm but not angular, her broad hips poised above full thighs, strong yet unmistakably feminine, the velvet pad between them shaded darkly where lay the entrance to pleasure.

Each entranced by the sight of the other, the married lovers were in a moment drawn together as by magnetism, skin to skin, her white against his brown, hands at first merely upon each other's shoulders. But in a moment their fingers began to move, first over each other's back, then down to seize upon the buttocks, pressing their lower bodies more closely together – which had an effect perfectly predictable, for when Chichley stepped aside to lead his wife to the couch, we could see that already he was prepared for the act, his sturdy cock lifted at a sharp angle so that it almost pressed against his belly – an unmistakable sign, I have always found, of a promising virility.

This, however, was no signal that he was to be offensively demanding, for laying the lady down he now gave time to the exploration of each plane and surface of his lady's body, first with hands, then with lips, while we could not see her face as her head was thrown back with an abandon that suggested complete enjoyment.

As he paid her the compliment of caressing her nether parts, a sudden little jump of ecstasy ran through her body which seemed to indicate an arousal more than common – underlined by her now thrusting him gently away and persuading him, in turn, to lie upon the couch. Kneeling over him she played her lips and tongue over his body, finally taking his manhood between her slender fingers, supporting his cods with the other hand and drawing the skin gently back over the ridge of flesh above which the inner dome proudly rose, then running her lips, shining with liquid, over the head and sliding them . . .

But what was this? My view of the scene was interrupted by Andy's hands throwing me backward and his lips fastening upon my own while his hand thrust up beneath my skirts to find, I must admit, a certain liquidity which bespoke the impression the scene had left upon me.

From anyone else, despite the heat of the moment, such a sudden rough assault might have provoked anger, but

Andy and I had played together since childhood, and it had been some months since we had been familiar. Moreover though there were other men whose tributes had been more satisfying (for he was always inclined to be too pleased with his own prowess to be an entirely satisfactory lover, women's preference surely always being for one who permits them to please him more than he pleases them?) I was by no means antagonistic to his approach, and indeed so roused by the meeting we had jointly arranged that in no time I had joined him in stripping as naked as our guests. Without our even bothering to recline, I had drawn up one leg and passed it behind and around his arse so that with a little effort he was able, crouching slightly, to insert his cock and with no more than two or three thrusts make both himself and me happy (for we were evenly matched in our excitement). We had only to turn once more to be able to apply our eyes to the aperture in the wall and discover how things were going in the neighbour room, where our friends had been less precipitate. Though Chichley was now happily embraced by his lady's thighs, his handsome arse was still moving with a regular slow motion matching the panting cries which emanated from his wife's throat as she lay, head still thrown back so that her magnificent bosom offered itself to his lips.

The cry she gave as she reached the apogee of her pleasure seemed sufficiently loud to have been heard outside the house, and conveyed in a single spasm of sound such satisfaction and ecstasy that I unconsciously gripped poor Andy's half-limber prick, strongly enough for him to have to bite my shoulder to stifle his own cry, lest it be heard by our guests. The pain of the bite was sufficient to arouse my passion once more, whereupon we again lost sight of our guests, and this time being less fraught to the battle took our time in satisfying each other – and I must admit that in the past months my friend had learned much about the art in which previously he had been almost completely a tyro. He now combined that freedom, that animal-like relaxation which had so drawn me to him at the time, now some years ago, when we were both children, with a knowledge of love-making the most impressive. And the first paroxysm being over, he was now so in command of himself that my best endeavours were unable to bring him to a completion until I had myself twice been satisfied.

We lay for a time clasped in each other's arms, unconscious of anything else, and my thoughts – I confess it – were that for all his faults there was no other man who gave me such pleasure and comfort as my old friend. But then once more we took ourselves to our vantage-point, where we saw Chichley kneeling over his wife's shoulders and ministering to her while she explored with her tongue the delightful area of his rear, and her fingers so sensitively played with his prick that he was clearly in an ecstasy. Finally, as she seized upon his arse with her teeth in her own clear delight, he erupted for what we supposed was the third time before collapsing so that his head lay between her feet, while she in an access of apology licked with a tender tongue the crescent of bloody spots where her teeth had punctured his skin.

'I think the time has come for discovery,' said Andy, holding out my skirt, into which I climbed, 'and thank you, my dearest Sophie, for those tokens of affection' – and he planted a kiss upon my cheek which I was pleased to return.

We entered the neighbour room without knocking, somewhat to the surprise of our guests, and indeed Chichley leapt to his feet and was about, I think, to make a violent protest had I not immediately apologised.

'Forgive me, my lord,' I said, 'but there is a particular reason why we should interrupt you in order to inform you of something while you and this lady are still together.

'This lady has no idea who you are, but she believes that you are cognisant of her identity. I now have to admit to her that you have no knowledge whatsoever of her.'

Lady Chichley's head came up at this, in surprise.

'No, I fear this has been a plot by my friend Andy and me; a plot which I hope will have the result we desire. My lord, will you kindly remove your mask?'

There was a moment's hesitation, then the viscount reached up and slowly peeled the velvet from his face, revealing that stern, handsome but not unkind visage, well-shaped mouth, flaring nostrils, keen eyes, and high forehead over which a lock of hair, dampened by passion, hung.

Lady Chichley gave an immense start and a cry, and my

heart stood still, for this was surely the moment upon which all depended: would she be offended that she had been tricked into offering her husband the very body he had so disdained? But then she sat up, and slowly removed her own mask.

The two looked at each other for a long moment in complete and mutual disbelief. Then, to my great relief, Chichley slowly knelt at his wife's feet, and taking her hand kissed it with the utmost deliberation and tenderness, and looking up into her eyes in silence begged forgiveness as clearly as could be.

I touched Andy upon the shoulder, and we quietly slipped from the room – but not before the two figures were again clasped together, this time not in the throes of passion but in a mutual expression of tender recognition, apology and love.

An hour later, there came a knock upon the door of the room in which Andy and I were sharing a bottle, and, in their full dress, Lord and Lady Chichley entered. He came straight to me and gave me his hand.

'Mrs Nelham,' he said, 'I am infinitely obliged to you for showing me the error of my ways – that Frances is not the cold aristocrat I had imagined, but a lady in whom beauty of body is combined with a delightful enthusiasm for the sport. I have much to thank you for and Mr Harry Riggs – for yes, my wife has revealed to me her adventures with that gentleman, whom she admits released in her the springs of passion. If there is any way in which I can be of use to you, or to you, Mr Archer, whose part in this plot I can only, now, admire and credit . . .'

We were of course quick to assert that we were (which was true) delighted that our ruse had borne such fruit, and bade them good-night.

'Well, Sophie,' said Andy, 'Brook Street is a long way to go at this time of the evening . . .'

I smiled.

'There will always be a place for you between my sheets,' I replied, 'though after two such inspiriting encounters as you have already offered me, my bed may be a quieter place than you apprehend . . .'

But he kissed me warmly, and when we were a-bed held

me tenderly in his arms with those gestures which convey affection rather than passion, but are no less delightful and quite as essential to woman's happiness.

I had no idea what time it was when I was awakened by the sound of breaking glass, but Andy and I sat bolt upright in bed together in the darkness, and I felt his arm around me as for a moment we waited, not knowing precisely what it had been that had roused us. Then came another sound – of cracking wood; someone was breaking into the house.

'Have you a weapon?' asked Andy, climbing from bed.

'Downstairs,' I replied, for alas the pistol was in the drawer of my desk. I scrambled for the steel, and finally managed to light the candle at my bedside, by which I saw Andy trying to cram his legs into his trousers, the wrong way about. We dressed hastily, but by the time we reached the staircase there were already lights in the hall, and we could see several dark figures moving about.

'There's the bloody whore!' came a cry from below, and I recognised the voice of one of the two men who had attempted to rape poor Polly. The men – there were five of them, I now saw – began to climb the stairs. Andy stepped in front of me, and held his hand out, though with nothing in it.

'Climb at your peril!' he cried. 'I am armed.'

There was only a moment's pause.

'So are we!' then came the cry. There was an explosion, and a ball whistled past us.

Throwing me aside, Andy grasped a heavy table which stood at the side of the stair-head, and half threw, half tipped it so that it crashed down upon the invaders, who in turn lost their footing so that for a moment all was confusion.

'Come on!' he said, and taking me by the arm returned to my bedroom, where he first locked the door, then with my help moved a tall wardrobe against it.

'I don't mind a fight,' he said, 'but unarmed, against five . . .'

There was some muttering outside, then a cry of pain from which I gathered that one man at least had been hurt in the fall, the sound of a blow or two against the door, then a shot which shattered the lock. And then more blows – but the wardrobe, now reinforced by the bed itself, which with great labour we had thrust against it, stood firm. There was more whispering, then silence. Andy placed his ear near the door.

'I can hear nothing,' he whispered, 'but it may be a ruse to persuade us to open. We can do nothing but wait,' and once more placed his arm about my shoulders to comfort me. 'I am sorry I can do no more – I fear I am not so much a man of action as to relish a naked encounter against fire-arms!' I kissed him, by way of answer.

For perhaps five minutes there was no sound; then we heard the front door slam far below us. The men had opened it, and when we crept to the window, we saw their lights – one, two, three, four, five – retreating through the garden.

It was the work of but a moment to withdraw the bed, then the wardrobe. But already there was a smell of smoke in the air, and when the door swung open, its ruined lock scraping, a red light was flickering upon the ceiling outside, growing ever more and more bright. Stepping upon the landing we saw that a fire was already mounting the stair-case, so that as we took a step forward, a great ball of flame rose up at us. Andy made to retreat but seizing him by the arm, I cried 'No!' and pulled him out and into the corridor, for the drop from my bedroom window was sheer, there being no way of descent, not even an ivy or creeper.

We felt the blast of hot air upon us as we ran past the stair-head and back down the corridor and entered the bathroom, whose window, I knew, gave onto a narrow ledge which communicated with the top of the conservatory below. As I climbed through the window, I heard a shout from below and paused, thinking it was the men returned, but then recognised the sound of Philip's voice, who upon our gingerly making the descent greeted us. Making his way back from a late assignation in town, he had met the escaping ruffians and guessed they were there for no good purpose. Being unarmed, he had concealed himself as they went by, but then saw the flames – which as we talked exploded through the roof of the house.

It was the mark of the time that the house was ruined

before anyone but we three came near. Though the river offered plentiful water, there was no pumping apparatus nearer than two mile, and none of us knew where to raise it, or whom to summon. Pails of water were useless against an inferno; all we could do was watch, Andy with fury at what had been done, I with regret at seeing my work of a year – and indeed much of my fortune – consumed; Philip no doubt with keener regret at seeing the home of his past ruined. By the time the flames began to die, a small group of local people who had seen the light of the flames had gathered to watch, gossip and commiserate – for though many of them suspected our business, we had made ourselves pleasant to the local tradesmen, and were by no means despised.

There being nothing further to be done, Andy and I set off for Brook Street, Philip promising to remain and to inform the boys of the business when they came the next day, and to advise them to contact me at my brother's. I would have first to insert a notice of the calamity in the newspapers, informing our clients of the demise of our project, then to consider the future.

We were silent as we walked, and then – fortunately discovering a late carriage returning from the country – rode into town.

Was my entire fortune gone? enquired Andy.

I supposed that most of it was, I returned. Though I had made considerable savings during the past few months which would ensure that I would not starve, I was certainly no longer a mistress of any considerable sum.

'But Frank will see you right,' he said – which of course was true, but I had been happy to be my own woman, and was sad that my independence should now be gone. But perhaps there would be some solution, for I was ever an optimist.

Sitting silent for a while, Andy then turned to me: 'You know my origins, dear Sophie,' he said, 'which are not so fine as yours. You know also that I have no fortune, though through Frank's good offices I now also possess a certain sum. But it occurs to me that we make an admirable partnership. Would you consider becoming my wife?'

Touched, I kissed him upon the lips, but explained that

not only was I too enamoured of my freedom, but that my observation of human nature had not so far encouraged me to believe that marriage was any guarantee of happiness, and might even divide us, for aught I knew.

'I should be sorry should that happen,' I said, 'for my affection for you is as great as for any man – but marriage is not among my plans. Do not be melancholy,' I added, for his face fell, 'I can imagine no time during which we shall not be friends, or when you will not be welcome to my bed. But marriage – no.'

There was another pause; then he took my hand and raised it to his lips.

'My very dear sister,' he said, and we rode on into the city.

Chapter Seventeen

The Adventures of Andy

I must admit to considerable pleasure in not only having captured Miss Mary Yately's affection, but having impressed myself so considerably upon her that she was willing to take me as a husband. What a future now opened before me! A fortune as vast as hers (and though I had not been able to come at the precise sum, reliable rumour put it at not much less than a quarter of a million pound) would enable me to live in a style beside which Frank's estate would seem miniscule.

I must confess that this knowledge somewhat affected my attitude to my old friend. I would of course never forget his kindness and condescension to me, but nevertheless he could not expect me to interest myself in our present business once I was married. I now began gradually to absent myself from it, taking myself more and more to Miss Yately's, where I ingratiated myself further with her aunt, and by dint of arriving at particular times contrived to meet some of her circle of friends, one or two of whom seemed to treat me with a certain disdain. Little did they know that I was soon to become the master of the house, or they would have paid more attention to their manners!

It sometimes seemed to me that dear Mary, though always happy to admit me between her sheets, and as voracious as ever in her physical requirements, was cooler to me in public than our relationship warranted. But she had insisted on my not announcing our engagement, and I believed her public attitude (which sometimes extended even to snubbing me) was adopted to put society off the scent. Nevertheless, after some weeks I became exceeding impatient, and at last, as we lay cooling ourselves after a bout, argued that the time had come when we should make public our plans.

'I think not,' she said.

'Then when may society know,' I asked, 'of our approaching nuptials?'

She seemed to smile at this, at which I became angry. 'If you are not prepared to acknowledge me at least among your friends,' I said, 'I . . .'

'You what?' she enquired.

'Well . . .' I said, and then came to a stop, for I could not think what to say next.

'You might withdraw your offer?' she enquired.

'Nothing,' I said swiftly, 'would persuade me to relinquish such a prize!' Then seeing her eyes narrow, I added, 'As your love, of course, my dear Mary!'

She seemed to consent to this, and we parted friends, if a little coolly. When I returned next day, I was surprised that the door was answered by Mrs Yately, who announced that Albert was upon a private errand, while she also on her way out, but that her niece had requested that I should go straight upstairs. Bidding her a courteous good afternoon, I proceeded to the drawing-room, and finding it empty, knew where I would find my fiancée. Making my way to the dressing room which I had adopted as my own, I unclothed, and then threw open the communicating door with my love's bedroom.

There she lay, indeed, apparently awaiting my arrival, and with a flushed face, and panting bosom (just peeping, enchantingly, from beneath the sheets) which bespoke her emotion at my arrival – except, did not the sheets of the bed seem peculiarly piled? And was not there a strange movement about her waist?

She smiled to see me looking, and as I approached threw back the sheet to disclose to my horror the naked body of a man curled about her lower parts, his head between her thighs – which, when startled he raised it, I saw to be that of none other than the missing footman, Albert!

Furiously, I stepped forward, but he raised himself from the bed at this, and he being a large and powerful man, I stepped back, for unarmed I could not hope to counter an attack.

I bowed coldly.

'Madam,' I said, 'I see you are engaged . . .'

'I am, and am not,' she said. 'I am certainly engaged with Albert, and in an encounter not one whit the less inspiriting than you can offer, Mr Archer. Engaged to you, by way of a promise to marry, I am certainly not! And no gentleman would have put the question at the time you put it, nor in the manner; nor indeed been silly enough to have interpreted my response so seriously!

'Could you really suppose,' she went on, 'that I would trust my fortune to someone born in a pigsty and raised in the kitchens?'

I was silent at this, for it was nothing but the truth, however much I had supposed my conduct to have disguised the fact. Nor could I deny that her fortune had been my chief attraction, though I cried, 'Madam, I confess all, but I hope you will believe that your fortune was not your only attraction, for indeed it was your beauty that first caught my eye, and the pleasures you have shared with me will ever remain a happy memory!'

She softened somewhat at this, and even smiled. I stepped forward, at which Albert looked menacing, but nevertheless I continued my progress, and taking her hand pressed my lips to it.

'I hope you will forgive me,' I said, 'for being what I believed you could not suspect – a fortune-hunter, and a clumsy one!'

'So clumsy,' she smiled, 'that indeed I knew it from the first. But, Andy, you have nevertheless a charm which my sex will ever find it difficult to resist, and –' (with a sigh) ' – alas, I have ever to be on the watch, which is why . . .' And she glanced sideways at the naked footman, who gravely inclined his head.

'Albert,' she said, 'I am sorry that we should have been interrupted' – and indeed his male implement, raised at full tilt when I had first entered, was now somewhat crestfallen – 'but I must make my farewells to Mr Archer.'

The man, evidently used to obeying orders, of whatever nature, bowed and left the room. And to my surprise I was beckoned to the bed, where Miss Yately kissed me first upon the lips, then applied herself in an unprecedented manner to rousing those passions which in the past two or three minutes had been completely dampened in me.

To make a long story short, we were reconciled in the best manner, and I could not resist, as her moment approached, asking whether she would not always remember me with a passionate interest, to which she gasped 'Yes! Yes!! Yes!!!' – only to dissolve immediately afterwards in a laughter which we shared.

As we talked for the last time, she freely admitted that she had met as yet no man she could not suspect of desiring her fortune more than herself. She therefore reconciled herself to satisfying her desires in the most calculated manner for, she said, she always knew where she was with servants. Nor, when she took a lover from beyond the walls of the house – as in my case – did she hope for more than bodily satisfaction, which she made sure of by simply allowing them to pleasure her.

'It has made me selfish,' she said, 'and I sometimes fear that a true lover will find me over-short in my attentions to his desires, in my habit of consulting only my own.'

I did my best to reassure her, and indeed believe that when – as must happen – she finds her true love a partnership will result which will make both happy.

I then made my final bow, and left.

So my hopes of becoming a man of means faded, at least for the time. But we parted friends, and my memories of the lady remain, even after some years, tender in respect of her person and appreciative of a keen intelligence, for she was to be no man's fool.

It was a week or so afterwards that Sophie and I engaged in the little deceit which we practised upon Lord and Lady Chichley, and which she has related in the previous chapter – culminating in the early hours of the following morning in the fire which laid waste her beautiful house at Chiswick. All I need add to her account is that the proposal which I made to her in the carriage might have been sudden but was entirely sincere, for no woman has ever meant so much in my life (nor, I dare say, ever will) as my adopted sister. Nevertheless, the moment I had made the proposal I was hoping that it would be refused, for still not twenty years of age, it was not yet really my intention to saddle myself with a wife – unless, of course, an uncommon rich one!

Upon reaching Brook Street it was still very early, and letting myself in with my key I hurried Sophie to my bedroom, where we rested for some hours before meeting a surprised Frank at breakfast, and rendering him still more astonished by an account of the destruction of Sophie's hopes.

She was by now putting a brave face upon things.

'It may be,' she said, 'that 'twas a blessing in disguise, for 'twould be early days for me to settle into so sedate a way of life, and I shall now be forced into new adventures.'

'But have you no idea of what sort?' I asked.

No, she said, but she had long wished to see more of the world than England, for her previous adventures had given her an itch for travel, and she wondered whether she might not travel in Europe.

'Of course,' she said, 'I could not go alone. Perhaps you might spare Blatchford as an attendant . . .'

I was a little surprised at this, and must have shown it, for she added, 'Do not mistake me, I do not mean as a lover, but as a servant! For lovers, I shall make my own bed, no doubt, as I have been used,' and blushed a little, for we were privy to all her adventures, and knew that her sheets, though not a public tent, had rarely been unfrequented by gentleman usually of her own choosing.

Frank nodded.

'I see no reason why not,' he said, 'but perhaps we can contrive a better scheme, for of late I have been more than a little bored. While you and brother Andy have had your adventures, I have remained sedate, seeing little more than home and university. Father's fortune was by no means fully taken up by the establishment of this house, and moreover, considerable profits from the business have further enhanced it. If I could find someone to take over, why should we not all go on the Grand Tour? You would come, of course, Andy?'

It was a wonderful notion, to which I was quick to assent.

'But who . . .?'

'Philip?' I suggested, but neither Sophie nor Frank thought that Jocelind had the qualities necessary for running the house, for while pleasant enough, he had no real interest in the business, and Aspasia had lately been expressing the desire to retire to her old way of life . . .

'But,' says Frank, 'of course I am forgetting that my girls will shortly have their own fortunes, and may well wish to relinquish the life! Why should not your boys simply come here, and carry on your business from this address? If Polly and William are to wed, you could place them in charge – perhaps with the help of Spencer, that admirable man?'

It was a notion which seemed peculiarly to suit, and we determined to put it to them all, which we did one afternoon in a few days' time, when we gathered our friends together, with Philip, at the house.

Everyone was immediately in accord. The girls, it appeared, had been discussing how and when to make it clear to us that they wished to retire. Polly was delighted at the confidence her mistress was to put in her, and was well-known enough to all Sophie's gentlemen to command their allegiance – though I believe it may be the case that the clientele of Sophie's establishment may be deprived of William's services, after their marriage.

The serious business over, the meeting was about to break up when Frank suggested that we should spend the rest of the day in relaxation, for it was surprising, he said, that his girls and Sophie's men had never met. He had taken the liberty of ordering some wine round, in which he hoped the company would drink prosperity to the continuing business!

It was true that there had been no meeting between the two establishments, and it had been amusing to see their members sitting politely at opposite sides of the drawing-room while hearing of our plans. But now they began to introduce themselves, and certainly after the consumption of a few bottles conversation began to flow without diffi-culty, and some of our ladies offered to show the boys the pleasures of our warm rooms which they had heard of, from Polly, but had never encountered. I was persuaded once more to bring my guitar and to play, and with wine and good food and conversation, all was soon an enjoyable familiarity, which gradually extended to a more febrile activity, as now and again a couple would disappear from the drawing-room.

How, I wondered, would the house adapt itself to the

new regime? Would the female visitors, for instance, enjoy our hot rooms as much as our gentlemen? It was something we could only guess at and taking my guitar, I strolled thither with a view to enquiring of our girls how they felt in the matter. But upon reaching the lower rooms I found it unnecessary, for all was pleasure, and though they were of course entirely familiar with the place, there was no sign of enervation or dissatisfaction among the females.

The warm room, as I passed through it, was occupied only by Ginevra and Sophie's senior gentleman, Mr Spencer Middlemas, she being mounted upon the older man as though to save him unnecessary motion. He compensated by the wildest bucking, which evidently gave her the keenest pleasure – perhaps because, as I could discern in the intervals of her rising upon her knees, his cock was sufficiently sturdy and thick to fill her own narrow and somewhat constricted parts to admiration. She tipped me a wink as I passed; he, his eyes closed, took no notice.

In the hottest room, Rose and Sally had taken refuge in the cold pool, accompanied by Ben and Tom. The gentlemen were close behind the ladies who, as they knelt with their arms over the sill of the pool, betrayed by their satisfied expressions no less than by the gentle jigging of their bodies the fact that their lower parts were in a sufficiently close proximity to those of their partners to offer considerable pleasure. Their pleasure was raised also by the sight before them, for their attention was focused upon two figures which took the centre of the room where, their bodies liberally drenched with perspiration, Xanthe and George, the negro, were performing a sort of dance the rhythm of which I was soon able to match with the strumming of my instrument.

Though George had never been outside England, it was impossible to doubt that the blood of his ancestors ran in his veins, for his firm and muscular body moved in a manner difficult of counterfeit by the white races, his torso seeming to be attached to his hips by double joints; so independent the two parts of his body seemed, it was as though his backbone was hinged at the waist. I had never seen him unclothed, and could only admire and envy the dexterity of his movements as his buttocks plunged, throwing forward a cock which was so large as to fulfil every legend I had heard of it (from Sophie, who had blushingly spoken of her encounter with him upon their first meeting). Indeed, so long and substantial was it that the movement of his hips threw it into a positive dance of its own, clearly delighting Xanthe, equally a stranger to him, who seemed mesmerised – as a snake will be mesmerised by a rabbit, yet in the most delightful way. She too danced about him, reaching out a hand to slide over the shiny surface of his ebony skin, flicking the perspiration from a shoulder or a breast, cupping one of the small, firm globes of his behind as she moved to rub her own body against his back, her breasts flattening against it and her white skin thrown into startling relief by the darkness of his own. Finally he placed his hands upon her shoulders and she sank to her knees, with a sigh of delight opening her lips and taking between them as best she could a portion of that instrument which, I fear, both Rose and Sally envied her the possession of. However, the furious manner in which Ben and Tom were now moving suggested that they were receiving the full attention of such equipment as they could muster, which no doubt was as formidable as that of most white men.

Xanthe's lips being unable to accommodate more than one-third of the length of George's prick, he soon grew impatient, and gently threw her backward upon the floor where, with the steam weaving about them, he was careful to drive it slowly within her so that her cries were of pleasure rather than of pain. Wishing not to intrude longer on so intimate a scene, I walked into the neighbouring warm room, still empty save for Ginevra and Spencer, occupied as they had been ten minutes before, his age and experience clearly enabling him to contain himself; her movements had necessarily slowed, but her enjoyment was still evident.

'Why did you not introduce me before, Mr Andy?' she asked. 'I rise to the third wave, and still it has not broken!' – and she continued her bucking, while he placed his hands behind his head and smiled.

Upstairs, the bell rang as I passed through the hall, and I admitted Philip Jocelind, who had been summoned to take a glass. I invited him to enter the drawing-room, though – I explained – he might well find it unoccupied, but someone would be with him in due time. I knew that since he had spent an hour with each of our girls, he would not have come for carnal pleasure. He nodded amiably, and took a seat and a bottle, while I went on to the upper rooms.

In the first, Polly was engaged with William, and Constance with Will Pounce – two pairs of lovers, whose faith being plighted, I did not observe more closely than to notice that their sentimental attachment no whit detracted from their interest in the game, which they were playing with enthusiasm. They had clearly decided that, as being plighted each to each, they would not wish to become part of any general amorous enthusiasm, and though they lay upon the same bed, were no more in connection with each other than the occasional brushing of an arm or a leg performed.

In a second room, I was delighted to see Moll engaged in pleasuring a man who by his lithe appearance and brown, gypsy skill, could be none other, I inferred, than Harry, the most active of Sophie's men. For once he lay upon his back while his companion reclined between his legs, her head upon his belly, playing with his chief male attribute. She paid it the compliment of kisses and caresses which extended now above, now below, while her fingers smoothed and flicked and turned about it and his cods which, closely drawn up beneath, bespoke a pleasurable tension.

As I watched, indeed, he reached the point at which he must take her, and raising himself upon an elbow, turned so that she fell below him, somewhat unwillingly relinquishing her hold so that he could slide downwards and place himself between her thighs. As he lifted his buttocks and lowered them to pierce her (to her infinite glee) I was astonished to see upon the right cheek, half-hidden in the down but none the less marked, nothing less interesting than a red birthmark shaped like a triangle!

'Harry!' I cried. 'Harry Riggs!'

Startled no less by the sound of my voice than by hearing his name, he paused, while Moll's mouth dropped open in amazement. Clearly they had exchanged familiarities, but not names.

'Harry *Riggs*?' she exclaimed. '*Harry?*'

Yes, reader, 'twas her brother, who speedily withdrawing

was none the less so inspirited by her attentions that he could not refrain from spurting forth his life's essence upon the belly – not, fortunately, within the body – of his sister!

No less delighted than astonished, he held her in his arms and pressed those kisses upon her lips which were no less passionate for being, now, fraternal. Their pleasure in each other was no less great than before, though of necessity it took a different course. However, as he struggled to cover himself she could not resist leaning to give his shrinking prick a last kiss, murmuring that from a small child she had determined to capture it, and now counted the chase as concluded!

I did not longer remain to intrude upon their happiness, nor do I care to speculate in what manner their joy at reconciliation was further expressed. It was enough that I had been quick in recognising the birth-mark which identified him, and had been the instrument of their reunion.

The room next-door was occupied by Cissie and Bob Tippett, the lively lad engaging himself by demonstrating how rapidly he could change from one mode of making love to the next, so that as I watched, he first entered her from the front, then throwing her face downward upon the bed, plunged in from behind, lifting her legs so that he held them within his armpits, offering himself the clearer mark. Then, as she began to gasp with pleasure at his vigorous thrusts, he paused to persuade her to stand and, lifting her bodily, encouraged her to place her legs about his waist while he placed his hands beneath her bottom and fucked her with no other support than those. Tiring of this he lowered one of her legs to the ground while he raised his opposite leg and passed it behind her, the two standing upon one leg each, while he still contrived to remain engaged. Then lowering them both once more to the bed, he began to lap at her body voraciously with his tongue, while she cried for the mercy of a speedy deliverance from the height to which his activities had raised her . . . These rapidly changing figures reminded me of nothing so much as a book in Philip's uncle's library at Chiswick, which pictured the attitudes of certain Indian lovers, and I could not but suppose that in some manner Bob had come at it. Though his visits to Chiswick had only been in the capacity of messenger, his curiosity and quickness knew no bounds, and it would not surprise me to know that he had poked his nose into every available room there!

By this time I had had enough of observing, and was acutely uncomfortable from the efforts of my prick to escape from the confines of my breeches. Dropping my guitar I threw off my clothes, at which Tippett must have believed I was about to join him, for he lifted himself from his companion and went to make room. But I shook my head with a smile, donned the robe which hung upon the back of the door and, more comfortable, left to search for the only companion I desired.

Passing through the door, the bell rang once more, and I went down to admit none other than David Ham, whose lively eyes flashed humorously as he saw my dress. Embracing me he slipped his hand beneath to discover the state of my prick, saying that if he knew no better he would have thought I had prepared a welcome for him!

Philip, he said, had asked him to join him here – so I took him to the drawing-room, but Jocelind was no longer there.

'Never mind,' said David, 'I'll find him!' and left, while I continued my search. But the person I sought not being upon the ground floor, I took myself below, where I found Jocelind in the warm room, stretched out, unclothed and asleep upon a bench alone, while across the way Spencer and Ginevra lay quiet in a sleepy lethargy.

'Your friend has arrived,' I said, shaking him, 'have you not seen him?' – at which Philip roused himself.

'Young David?' asked Ginevra. 'He looked in some moments past, and went into the hot room.'

Passing there, we found only the three couples I had previously seen, Xanthe now curled up upon the body of George, both exhausted, but she clutching in one hand his still massive but now soft member. Not far away, Rose and Ben, Sally and Tom lay twined in each other's arms so close that it was impossible to discern which limb was which.

But now, a low laugh came from the open door which led to the room containing the fire for our boilers. Stepping to it, we saw in the ruddy light of the open grate the naked figure of Blatchford, his body running with steaks of black sweat, bending forward shovel in hand to stoke the boiler.

Immediately behind him David, who had clearly just thrown off his clothes, which lay upon the floor regardless of the dirt, reached between his legs to fondle a member less ready than the boy's own, which clearly sought a home I doubted Blatchford would be willing to provide. But we were never to find out, for Philip stepped forward and, grasping David by the shoulders, pulled him away and into his own embrace.

Blatchford, looking round, merely winked at me, and continued to place coal upon the fire – from which I gathered that, as I had suspected in the past, he regarded congress between the sexes as a strange occupation which wasted time that might more properly be spent in grooming horses or consuming small beer. This had in fact made him a most valuable member of our organisation, for he could be entirely trusted to regard all our ladies with an equally impartial eye, and was incapable of being stirred by passion or by prejudice.

Philip had now thrown David face downward upon a pile of empty coal sacks in the corner, and placing his hands upon the boy's hips, had raised his arse so that he could place his own prick in a place where David was clearly very willing to receive it, for while a grimace of pain at first crossed his face, he then grinned happily at me, and winked. Naturally, I had known of old of his preference for his own sex. As for Philip, if that was his course, then I could only allow him to pursue it; I only hoped that Sophie did not feel towards him such warmness as to be dismayed by hearing of it, for I had every intention that she should do so!

My only recourse now was the upper rooms, and making my way up past the smaller bedrooms, I came to Frank's room and my own. The door of the former standing open, I could not help but see my friend in the company of the handsome Aspasia. It had been my observation that Frank had ever enjoyed the company of older women, and this splendid lady who would never again see the age of thirty was clearly for him the *sine qua non* of delight. They lay upon the bed, in a state of nature, but not embraced – on the contrary, they were some inches apart, their heads thrown back upon the pillow. From the thread of liquid which lay upon my friend's upper thigh, I imagined that they had already enjoyed each other, and were now preparing for a second congress, for each was leisurely exploring the body of the other with a single hand. The lady's fingers were engaged upon the contours of his belly and thigh, from time to time merely brushing a tool which already began again to rise, while his hand lifted and embraced a breast which, while it had the fullness and heaviness of maturity, was from the tight button of pleasure at its middle no less a centre of delight.

Their eyes were closed, and they did not see me, nor did I stay longer than to observe and envy their pleasure, before passing on to the door of my own room. Opening it, I saw the room to be empty. I was clearly the only soul destined to be unsatisfied that evening, and closing the door reclined upon the bed, my mind playing over the engagements I had seen between my friends, so that despite myself I felt the necessity of taking my over-stimulated cock between my fingers and beginning to stroke it – when the door opened, and who should walk through it but dearest Sophie.

'I am sorry, dear Andy,' she said, 'to see you reduced to this measure. But if you would rather –' and pretended to go.

I merely smiled, for I knew she was better acquainted with me than that. Indeed, closing the door behind her, she soon unclothed herself, revealing again that body which familiarity could not make me indifferent to, with its high breasts, generous hips, arms always ready to embrace, ever-welcoming thighs.

How we amused ourselves it would be impertinent for me to report or for a reader to enquire, the delights of love being ever too private to be disclosed except by way of narrative among friends. I need only say that when we rose, an hour later, we had pleasured ourselves and each other in such a manner as I believe no two lovers have bettered. The evening ended in mutual friendly delight, the entire party gathering in the drawing-room which, crowded with satiated bodies, became for many one large bed upon which exhaustion now decreed sleep rather than further amorous pleasure. I noted, happily, that upon seeing Jocelind walk in with his arms about his lover, Sophie merely approached to embrace them both, as though to bless a union of which, she knew, she could have no part.

The marriages of William with Polly and Will Pounce with Constance took place on the same day and in the same church, with all our friends present. Mr and Mrs Pounce were particularly happy, for they received a message from Viscount Chichley that an inn which he owned in a village not far from his estate was theirs should they desire it. Of course they were delighted and immediately sent a message of thanks and acceptance, and nothing would do but that they should leave the same day – not for the proposed holiday they had planned in Worthing but for their new home, the Black Boy – there was some laughter at this, and a cordial invitation from them to their friend George to visit them at any time!

Meanwhile, Chichley's generosity did not end there, for he agreed to purchase from Sophie the land on which her house had stood, where he wished, he said, to build a mansion to which he could take his bride, the locality ever having for them a particular significance, having first been brought together there by our good offices, and he paid Sophie considerably more, it seems, than the land was worth. And more, he sent a present to me of a splendid gold watch, a gift of a hundred guineas, and the assurance of his friendship and assistance at any time I should need it.

Mr and Mrs Langrish were to take a short honeymoon at Alcovary, where Frank had sent them with instructions to use it as their own. And I imagine that they did so with style, for William had been brought up a gentleman, while Polly was quick to gather every impression and fashion, and I doubt not found it easy to play the part. They planned then to return to Brook Street and to supervise the house, for though William's family had sent messages to the effect that he should return to the cathedral close and to a living which had become available nearby, Polly was of the opinion that life as a Bishop's wife (for she was sure that in no time her William would rise to that office) was not for her, while William was of the opinion that he now had a taste for riggish behaviour which would betray itself despite the covering of the most distinguished canonicals. So we waved them off in the direction of Hertfordshire, confident that we left the business of Brook Street in good hands.

It only remained to make a few arrangements: to obtain passports for ourselves and to distribute to the girls certain small tokens of our affection and thanks. We had obtained from a silversmith's in Bond Street silver peppers and salts made in the shape of the male and female members, the salt flowing from a small aperture at the head of the phallus, while pepper sprinkled at a touch from tiny holes within the delicately-wrought hair surrounding the female part. These were indeed received with rapturous pleasure, not least by Moll, who now planned to return to the neighbourhood of her old home to live with her re-found brother Harry, reunited too with her younger brother, and she looked forward, she said, to a life of dull respectability. I doubted, myself, that it would long content her.

The house was quieter than we had ever known it when we breakfasted there for the last time before setting off on our journey. Bob Tippett had been turned away with a generous gift, and had been cheerful enough at it, regarding his time with us as a great joke with which he would regale his fellows for many years. Blatchford was to remain as a caretaker, and to continue his work – Frank left with him, in addition, plans to turn the basement from a baths to a mere set of additional cabinets, should custom and fashion require it.

And so, at eight o'clock in the morning, two carriages appeared, our trunks were hoisted upon them, and Frank, Sophie and I climbed in. And as the door of the house closed we began to rattle southwards, to the river and over it, and out towards Dover and the packet which would carry us to the continent, and no doubt to fresh adventures.

EROS IN THE NEW WORLD

The Adventures of a Lady and Gentleman of Leisure

**For the convenience of the reader
we here record a note of
IMPORTANT PERSONS APPEARING IN
THE NARRATIVE
in the order of their appearance**

Master Andrew Archer, our hero
Mrs Sophia Nelham, our heroine
Sir Franklin Franklyn, Bart., of Alcovary, Hertfordshire
Lady Margaret Franklyn
Mr Douglas Willoughby, a traveller
Miss Phyllis Willoughby, his sister
Captain Austen, a Leonine sea captain
An acquiescent midshipman
Miss Spencer, a New Orleans milliner
M. Augustin de Cournville, a Scorpio gentleman
Madame Anastasia Quincunx, a Creole lady
A group of quadroons
Tom, a Libran slave
Susan, his friend
Madame Leonie la Cuisse, of Quebec
Lisette, an hotel maid
Miss Monica Bradley, of Southampton
Mrs Sally Thomas, a Quebec madam
Frank Green (aka M François Vert), an Arien, of Cincinnati
Some ladies of pleasure
Mr David Ham, an impresario
A number of theatrical persons
Betsy, one of these
Sylvie, another
Moll, a third
A travelling gentleman
The Rev. Aloysius Applegrass, a Virgoan clergyman

An elderly lady
Her daughter
Three bathing gentleman, of Three Rivers
Three convent ladies of the same
Madame Félicie Fonteuille, of Montreal
Lieutenant Dan Savage, a cavalryman
Sam Thuckett Esq., an impertinent congressman, of
  Washington
James T. Accolade, a Capricornian Senator
Mrs Roger Dunnet, of Toronto
Mr Roger Dunnet, her husband
M. Philippe Montblanc, a Taurean, of Philadelphia
Mr George Root, a Piscean, of the same
Issiquioxpiwiki, an Indian girl
The Chief of the Montagnais Indians
A witch-doctor
Madame Genevieve Brabant, a Philadelphia lady
Her close friends
Harrington Hotspur Esq., a Sagittarian gentleman, of
  Delaware
Paul, his Cancerian servant
Miss Felicity Widderspon, a New York headmistress
Her pupils
M. Anatol Gant, of Paris, an Aquarian gentleman

Chapter One

The Adventures of Andy

Those readers who are familiar, through my previously published accounts, with the friendly relationship which has always been the rule between myself, my friend Sir Franklin Franklyn, of Alcovary in the county of Hertfordshire, his wife, Lady Margaret (whose intimate acquaintance I myself was before they met) and his half-sister, Mrs Sophie Nelham, will not be altogether surprised that this narrative should begin in the bedroom in which we were all, in a state of nature, indulging ourselves with a bottle or two of good claret on the occasion of myself and Mrs Nelham setting forth upon another adventure.

It was now the year 1825, and some time had passed since Sophie and I had been engaged in those remarkable occurrences in Europe which I recounted in a previous volume (*Eros on the Grand Tour*, published some time since by the London firm of Headline). The years between had by no means been dull – and indeed I have yet to relate to the public some of the more extraordinary events of that time, which I may well do in further volumes. But for two or three years I had devoted myself to establishing a business in London – the nature of which I need not relate here; while Sophie, the mistress of a considerable fortune, had become the belle of society in that part of Hertfordshire where she and her brother were domiciled.

We both now felt, once more, that restlessness which hinted that we should undertake another journey – and had decided to travel to what was still regarded as the New World: that is, to America, that exciting and excited new democracy whose nature both Sophie and I were eager to experience.

It was fruitless to attempt to engage Frank and Lady Franklyn to accompany us, for they had become so entirely domesticated that the domain of Alcovary was quite sufficient for them – though they expressed themselves most interested in our journey, begging that we would record our experiences for them.

That our farewell dinner should end between the sheets was entirely natural, for we had always lived in that freedom of natural behaviour, as to sensual enjoyment, with the expression of which my constant readers will be familiar.

Both I and my friends were now in our middle twenties; but the passing of the years had entirely failed to dim that enthusiasm for the game of love which had made Frank and Sophie my intimates from the most tender age, and which had also first introduced me to the present Lady Franklyn, when she was Lady Margaret Rawby, and one of the most delicious twins it has ever been my pleasure to take to bed.

Indeed, looking at Sophie, it was impossible to believe that she was now of an age when many women appear matronly and past their prime. She sat, her back resting upon the pillows, a glass in her hand and a smile on her face, her neck smooth and clear of even the faintest suggestion of wrinkles, her delightful breasts as pert and springing to the touch as they had been at seventeen, their rosy tips still as welcoming to the lips; while below, all was equally hospitable – her belly only sufficiently rounded to advertise her womanhood, her thighs (under the continual exercise of horse-riding) long, firm and in the pleasures of love as eager as her arms to embrace a lover, and that most delightful of targets set between them always ready to receive Cupid's arrow.

Indeed, as I had recently reminded myself, the only difference between her and her younger self was that, always talented in pleasure, she had now added to her eagerness that skill and knowledge with which the finest courtesan is equipped – but of course in her case never charged for!

Seeing me regarding her, she had wet at her pouting lips her forefinger, and was now drawing it, with the greatest delicacy, around and about the engorged head of that instrument with which, willy-nilly, I was expressing my male regard for her beauty, and which, though only recently satisfied, now once more nodded its approbation of her beauty. Taking a sip from her glass, she now set it down and placed the other palm encouragingly upon my firing piece, the tips of her fingers resting at that point where it joined, now at an acute angle, my belly. With the points of her nails she gently irritated the flesh there, which resulted almost immediately in the instrument paying her the tribute of a tear.

Frank, meanwhile, had, upon the other side of the large bed (capable of containing several couples and for centuries the pride of Alcovary), brought to a happy conclusion a passage of love with his wife, for whom marriage had proved no dampener to her appetite. As she lay now with her head upon his arm, and her thigh still flung across him (for she had been indulging her favourite pastime of riding him as she would have ridden his best beloved stallion), he smiled over at us.

'You cannot wonder, Sophie,' he remarked, 'that I should have no anxieties as to your safety even on so long a trip as that upon which you embark – for Andy's devotion to you has remained constant for twenty years or more, and that you return it is evident upon seeing you together.'

'My dear brother,' said Sophie (not omitting, while she spoke, to move her hand upon my expanded instrument in the most enlivening manner), 'I would have thought I had proved myself entirely capable of guarding my virtue – when it needs to be guarded – without anyone's assistance – even that of my dear Andy! Indeed, to keep myself entirely for one man is not, as you well know, my way.'

'I can vouch for that,' I remarked; 'nor, though familiar harbours are always a pleasure to enter, would I wish to deny myself the possibility of exploring new waters.'

'A most resolute Geminian!' cried Sophie, for whom the practise of astrology had long been a pleasurable pastime, and sometimes, in times of difficulty, of practical assistance. 'Why, he would bed women right round the Zodiac if he could!' – and letting go my by now almost painfully distended tool, passed her hand beneath to toy with my cods.

'That would be more in Sophie's line,' I remarked – to which she replied, with some heat, that she did not as a rule bed women (adding however that it had not been unknown, upon extremity).

'Perhaps,' said Margaret (who, I must confess, occasionally betrayed the slightest jealousy of her husband's partiality for his half-sister) ''twould be an elegant pastime for her during her travels.'

Frank laughed at that, and doubted whether it would be possible; for though some gentlemen no doubt came to Sophie's arms in the usual way of social intercourse, surely it would be too much to expect that even within the many months it would take to accomplish a journey to the Americas, she could hope to enjoy the beds of twelve gentlemen each of a different sign of the Zodiac?

At this, Sophie said that he underrated her; and upon Lady Franklyn naturally taking the side of her husband in the argument, the result was the wagering of an hundred guineas by Sir Frank Franklyn that between leaving Alcovary and returning there, Mrs Nelham, of that address, could not bed one gentleman of each Zodiac sign from Aries through to Pisces (though not, it was allowed, in the order of their progress – that being considered too hard a matter).

But how should they know, in the interim, how the matter was progressing?

Upon my suggestion it was decided that Sophie should

indite letters which would at convenient intervals be parcelled up and sent back by the postal services to England – and in order that my own adventures should not be a secret to my friends during such a long period of absence, I too agreed to do the same – these letters forming in the main the basis of this present account.

On our taking another bottle to pledge the wager, our goodbyes were continued. Sophie took my hand and placed it upon her bosom, in clear request for a further bout. But Frank intervened, saying to his wife that he was sure she would not object to his bidding his half-sister farewell in the manner in which, from time to time, they had shown their affections (objection to this being met by the argument that what was good enough for the late Lord Byron, whose great love was his own half-sister Augusta, was good enough for any other member of the British aristocracy).

Lady Margaret not being unwilling (for her jealousy of Sophie was but of the slightest), Frank without delay manifested that eagerness which was ever a mark of his affection, and almost before I could move from Sophie's side, had fixed his lips to hers with tender and brotherly affection, while placing his lower self in such a position that she could be in no doubt of his being able to satisfy her in the manner ever welcomed by the enthusiastic female.

It should not be expected that either the Lady Margaret or myself should merely look on; and indeed in a moment she whispered to ask whether I remembered that day, now some years ago, when – a footman in the employ of her father, the Third Earl of Rawby – I was first allowed the pleasure of enjoying the company of herself and her sister, the Lady Elizabeth?

Her enquiry was followed by her bending to take within her lips the instrument for whose attentions she clearly wished, and which – though it had drooped somewhat upon being frustrated of its aim (at once more enjoying the moist lubricity of Sophie's loins) – now regained its strength in a moment, as, with finger and thumb sliding back the covering shield of skin which protected its tip, she ran her tongue tenderly about it, the delightful thicket of her hair falling from her head to pile itself upon my now panting belly and sheltering those intimate attentions from the curious eyes of a beholder.

To cut short a scene too intimate in its delights to be more fully described, within a very short time, while Frank enjoyed Sophie (whose dextrous lower limbs were thrown over his shoulders as he thrust into her), Lady Margaret, now upon all fours, had turned her back to me, presenting me with an inviting prospect of pear-shaped hindquarters between which a downy nest beckoned an invitation which I was happy to accept – happy not only to slide between those splendidly welcoming thighs, but while pleasuring the lady in that matter, to add to her enjoyment by a certain stroking and pinching of her breasts, which soon brought her to a happy culmination, accompanied in a moment by the completion of my own delight.

The following morning Sophie and I left Alcovary for London, thence to Portsmouth, where we set sail upon our new adventure; and it is at this point that my narrative is taken up by those journal-letters addressed to my friends in England.

As you know, we had taken a cabin upon the *Postulant*, a handsome vessel bound for New York, having decided for the course of the journey to masquerade as husband and wife – for though neither of us was poor, why should we pay for double accommodation when our friendship is such that the sharing of a cabin presented no embarrassment to us? So we appeared upon the ship's books as Mr and Mrs Archer.

The ship contained but half-a-dozen passengers, besides ourselves there being a clergyman and his wife, heading for Virginia, and a brother and sister, Mr Douglas and Miss Phyllis Willoughby, of Dorset – a handsome pair, he perhaps of twenty-and-five, she of eighteen – but who kept themselves very privately, merely exchanging those observations about the weather which are the mark of English travellers everywhere. They shared the cabin next our own (there being only three such cabins upon the vessel for the carriage of passengers).

We all dined together with our captain – Captain Austen, by name – when he could be spared from the exercise of his command, which once the ship had left English waters was with regularity. He was an admirable example of the British sea-dog at his proudest – a man in his early thirties, perhaps, no less than six and a half feet tall, and broad in proportion, of brown complexion from his years in the sea air, his limbs so sturdy that only a natural gentility of disposition prevented him from clumsiness, and with a shock of dark yellow hair, almost to auburn, which spilled forward upon his forehead. He behaved towards us with great kindness, ever ready to explain the intricacies of navigation or of the management of the ship. His command was complete, and it was evident that he ruled the ship as a king would rule his kingdom – with a benevolent autocracy.

'In short,' said Sophie, 'he was clearly born when the Sun was in the sign of Leo' – and when I asked how she could be sure, she pointed not only to his deportment but to his invariable cheerful optimism, his ceremonious behaviour towards us, and that love of quality which was evident not only in his person (he was always impeccably groomed, his linen, even on shipboard, white and crisp) but in, for instance, the setting of the common table at which we dined.

It was in my mind to enquire whether my friend's interest in Captain Austen might extend to her attempting to make him the first of those astrological lovers to be set down in the account of her bet; but she said nothing as to that, nor did I question her.

One evening, five days out of England, we were reclining in our cabin during the afternoon – the weather being calm, but the breezes upon deck being sufficiently cool to prevent our sitting there – when we became conscious of a disturbance in the cabin next to ours, inhabited by Mr and Miss Willoughby. After a while, Sophie laid her hand upon mine with a meaning glance, and whispered that the sounds we heard were not those which one would normally associate with the behaviour of brother and sister – and indeed, they seemed to speak of amatory congress, not only from the regular beat which could surely only be the sound of male and female bodies in coitus, but the occasional muffled cries not dissimilar to those made by a lady in receipt of amorous masculine attention.

Sophie, rising to her feet, now lifted from the wall of the cabin the topcoats which hung there, and to my surprise placed her eye to a knothole in the wood (my surprise, my dear Frank, not being that your sister should do such a thing – for her interest in the affairs of the heart has always been a tribute to her liveliness of temper – but that such a spy-hole should have gone unnoticed by those whose duty it is to mend such matters).

At all events, she looked with interest into the next cabin, and in a moment, turning to me with a raised eyebrow, invited me to take my turn – the view, I found, being that of the bottom half of the bunk bed next door, occupied now – not to my surprise – by two pairs of legs, one by their hairiness being presumably those of a male, the others those of a female – and a female who, from the lack of motion of her lower limbs, while (from the sounds she uttered) by no means incapable of pleasure, was equally by no means adept at the art of love; for all she did was to lie recumbent, the inactivity of her body being clear from the posture of those limbs within my sight.

Sophie was by now tugging at me in an effort to persuade me to relinquish my vantage-point once more to her; but as I prepared to withdraw my eye, the male lover – who I had presumed to be the lady's brother, or perhaps pretended brother – gave a final buck, and with one movement withdrew from his position, sitting upon the side of the bed and revealing himself to be – our captain!

I now willingly gave place to Sophie, who was as surprised as myself to discover the identity of the performer, and could not be persuaded to withdraw her eye until he had clothed himself – reporting to me that the sight of his chief male attributes, even in the repose which follows a passage of love, was such as to persuade her that he was a lover to be reckoned with.

'It is a shame,' she said, 'that he should be wasted upon Miss Willoughby, a pale creature clearly incapable of giving real satisfaction to any man!'

I could not question this, having had oracular proof of her lethargy; yet wondered whether perhaps she did not have some qualities which had not been obvious to us? But Sophie would not have it so – and from that proposition went on to question how she could take Miss Willoughby's place with the captain. My own answer was that she should simply present herself to him as a lover; but she is ever too subtle for such plain dealing, and in a while had proposed a scheme in which she had no difficulty in persuading me to acquiesce.

At first we must discover how Captain Austen had been able to be sure of Mr Willoughby's absence from the cabin at the important time. This question was answered me however on the very next morning, when, taking a walk upon the poop, I rounded the corner of a small-boat to come suddenly upon the gentleman clasping in his arms a figure upon whose lips his own were fixed, and whose buttocks his hands were exploring with equal eagerness. The diminutive figure in question proving to be that of the youngest of the ship's two midshipmen, things fell into place. On approaching the boy quietly, with a couple of guineas, I was able to discover that he was in receipt of gifts both from Mr Willoughby and the Captain – the former engaging his favours, the latter ensuring that they should secure his absence from his cabin for at least an hour after luncheon each day.

The payment of an additional sum persuaded the

obliging young gentleman to assure his lover that it would be impossible for them to meet that day except during the hour after dark; and the captain that it was Mr Willoughby who had required this. Thus the way was cleared for a piece of *legerdemain*.

At dinner, glances exchanged between the captain and Miss Willoughby made it clear what appointment had been made; when the ladies had withdrawn, it was the work of but a moment for Sophie – who had delayed her departure for a few seconds – to approach the other female and to hand her a message which I had written (gambling on the supposition that she was unfamiliar with the captain's writing) inviting her to meet him, on this occasion, not in her cabin but his own.

Retiring to our room, Sophie heard in due course the young lady leave the cabin next door. After waiting for a moment, Sophie slipped from our room and entered the neighbouring cabin, where, in the darkness, and divested of her clothing, she awaited the arrival of our burly commander. In the meantime, pausing only to be sure that the captain had left his quarters, I slipped into them – the rooms upon ship being happily devoid of those locks and bars which might on shore have inhibited such trickery, – and in an equal and almost complete darkness, made myself ready for the moment, which shortly afterwards arrived, when the door opened and a female figure slipped into the cabin.

Words are never entirely necessary in situations of love, and the lady being ready for amorous encounter was not surprised to be embraced, immediately, by her supposed lover. Leading her to the captain's bunk – which was of such generous proportions that I wondered at his preferring the more cramped conditions of the passenger's cabin – I unloosed the bands of the lady's clothing, and was in no short time embraced, a shiver running through her frame as her hands discovered not only my nakedness but readiness for the field of love.

The truth of the ancient adage that all cats are grey in the dark was immediately proved, for no two persons could be less alike than the captain and myself, as to bodily proportion: myself being, though wiry, far more slender, and my limbs less well endowed with hair than his – at least in as much as I had viewed them. But from the manner in which the young lady immediately thrust her body against my own, it was clear that only one part of the male anatomy was considered by her as a prerequisite, and toppling us upon the bed, it was upon that that she immediately impaled herself, coming within a few moments to a paroxysm of pleasure, after which I felt her body relax beneath my own.

It was clear to me that the impression I had received from my imperfect view of her passage with the captain had been the correct one: the young lady had only recently been released from the continual supervision of parents or guardians, and upon an approach from a gentleman had succumbed with pleasure to a first attempt at love – for it was clear she was entirely innocent of those subtleties of behaviour which make such encounters continually enjoyable by their variation.

Her release from the immediate fever had not been accompanied by my own, though in deference to her youth I had withdrawn myself from between her thighs, and now lay with her body at the side of my own; and could not resist taking her hand in mine and placing it upon my still engorged weapon. The start with which its size was apprehended confirmed my supposition that the good captain had been content to treat her as the mere receptacle of his masculinity, without attempting to teach her anything else; but that she was a natural pupil was evident by her lack of reluctance to explore – her inquisitive fingers making their way with a tender and enquiring facility over every contour presented to them.

My own caressing of her nether parts was at first met with a start of surprise that fingers should wish to find their way there; and when, bending to her, I touched with the tip of my tongue that tender bud where the acme of female pleasure lies, she let forth a shriek of delight which made me fear the crew would suspect an outbreak of fire on board. And fire indeed, in its kind, followed.

I could only assume that the good captain, with nautical directness, had proceeded immediately to the main course without essaying those delicious preliminaries which are so essential to the enjoyment of the whole meal. Miss Willoughby, after her first surprise, entered into the game with a readiness that spoke a natural talent – and indeed when her fingers had fully explored that male appurtenance which had only previously been known to her as a battering ram, she almost immediately raised herself and buried her head in my lap, her lips and tongue clearly eager to discover whether their application in that area would bring me the pleasure which my own were able to confer upon her. That my gasps of delight confirmed her instinct must go without saying.

Our mutual pleasure was such that it was with a start that I heard nearby the sounding of the ship's bell announcing that it was twenty-two hours (as they call it upon shipboard), or ten o'clock; whereupon I was forced to rouse myself from that half-slumber in which we had been happily and mutually engaged, and – confining myself to whispered tones which I hoped were a reasonable counterfeit of the captain's voice – to invite Miss Willoughby to leave.

I flatter myself that it was with considerable reluctance that she did so, and with many embraces, clasping me to her bosom several times before, with a final kiss, leaving me.

Carefully dressing and making sure there was no witness to my leaving the cabin, I was making my way aft (that is, towards the back of the ship) when I saw Captain Austen coming towards me along the corridor, or companionway as they call it. He gave me a gruff goodnight; whereupon I hastened to our cabin, where I found Sophie looking, as it seemed to me, somewhat flushed.

You can suppose that I did not consider it proper to question her in detail about what had occurred, but I gathered that the master of our vessel had been as surprised at his mistress's sudden forwardness as Miss Willoughby had been by the sudden change in her lover's approaches; and that the passage between them had been as rewarding – to him as to her – was sure.

It was with amusement that I saw, the following morning as I took my usual constitutional upon deck, Miss Willoughby taking the opportunity of presenting herself to Captain Austen at the earliest moment, and noticed that by the middle of the morning – when he should have been about his business – they had both vanished. It was without surprise that, returning to our cabin, I found Sophie with her eye firmly applied to the knothole in the partition; and upon her giving way to me discovered the two lovers in attitudes which were remarkable for their readiness and freeness, the lady for instance being pleased to employ her lover's gaying-stick in the manner of a paint-brush, applying it eagerly to lips, throat, breasts, and eventually to that place to which it was most naturally drawn; the captain, meanwhile, in an ecstasy of enjoyment permitting his fingers to pleasure every plane of his companion's body in a manner which appeared to give him the same degree of gratification as it afforded her.

We congratulated ourselves upon the achievement of teaching the lady and gentleman a greater potential for pleasure than they were formerly aware of; and amused ourselves during the rest of the voyage by seeing how often they slipped away to delight each other – which happened with such considerable frequency that we could not but believe we had done both Miss Willoughby and the Captain a good turn in teaching them some refinements of love making of which otherwise they might have remained unaware.

And so, in due course, we arrived at New York.

Chapter Two

Sophie's Story

You will have heard from Andy the story of my conquest of the captain of the vessel on which we journeyed to New York, and will be expecting to hear that we are together embarked on further adventures. However, you find me now alone, for while my own inclination is to visit the southern states of this country, he rather desired to travel north, to the colony of Canada. And so we parted, myself embarking in a small ship for the Mexican Gulf and the mouth of that great river, the Mississippi, having made plans to meet in New York on a date some weeks in the future.

It is indeed a remarkable stream, and the greatest contrast possible to our own fine Thames, opening out as it does in a great muddy mass of water, and revealing to the traveller who enters it views almost entirely devoid of interest – mere flat shoals of mud whose monotony is disputed only by the flights of pelicans which stand as though in a daze of boredom conferred by their situation, which indeed is a dull one, and by huge alligators which can occasionally be seen, enjoying the slime.

A short while after entering the river, we came to the village of Belize, where live the pilots whose duty it is to conduct vessels through the shoals, and which is surely one of the most desolate places known to man.

By this time I was beginning to be heartily sorry that I had chosen this route rather than remaining for a time in the relative comfort of New York; but then, as we progressed further upriver, there was an improvement, the river banks being enlivened at last by the sight of enormous trees and by the bright tints of southern vegetation. However, the two days it took to travel the 120 miles from Belize to New Orleans passed tediously, and it was with some relief that we tied up at the quay – a portion of what they call the *levée*, a high embankment erected to protect the land against floods.

New Orleans looks like nothing so much as a French town – which is unsurprising, since it is indeed an ancient French colony taken from Spain by France. The names of the streets are French, and the language about equally French and English.

I took a house for a fortnight, at a very small rent, in the most fashionable part of the town, which had as a natural adjunct of it a handsome verandah where it was possible to sit in the shade, cooled by the movement of a hanging fan operated by a small black boy, and watch the town society as it passed by.

The first thing that struck me was the large number of black people seen in the streets, all labour being performed by them; and the grace and beauty of the quadroons who appeared among the people, and whose elegance of move-ment and natural courtesy made them a most admirable adjunct to society – though in common with the blacks, they were little regarded by the white people of the place. No less than three black women came to me as an integral part of my household, and from the start I made a strong impression upon them by addressing them as I would address any servant at home – which to them was an aston-ishing kindness, and provoked demonstrations of devotion which I found embarrassing.

The white ladies of the place were quick to call upon me, since any newcomer is immediately seized on as an enter-tainment not to be missed – society in New Orleans being of the most circumscribed nature. I was invited within the first thirty-six hours to attend a ball at the house of a Madame Quincunx, the young widow of the Creole owner of a plantation, who was the acknowledged leader of society – though about whom there was much gossip, which indeed only made her the more valuable as a source of interest to the matrons.

Having brought of course no ball gowns with me, I was directed to the house of a dressmaker, a Miss Spenser, an Englishwoman who proved to be intelligent and useful, who presided over an establishment which supplied frock-coats and other paraphernalia to the gentlemen of New Orleans, as well as all sorts of apparel to the ladies.

This not being common among us, I did not of course anticipate it; and placing myself entirely in Miss Spenser's hands, had retired behind a curtain in what seemed to be partly her drawing room and partly a fitting room, to try on a gown which she had handed to me. The skirt fitted perfectly, but I had difficulty in fastening the bodice, which entirely failed to meet across my breasts. I therefore sprang from my changing place, my bosom entirely exposed, to be confronted by a gentleman purchasing a stock!

You can imagine, dear Frank, my surprise and dismay; but upon my admitting that the man was excessively hand-some, will also believe that the former far exceeded the latter. Upon my seizing the bodice and contriving that it should at least hide those buds which most attract the eyes of the gentleman, far from turning away or apologising, he bowed with some charm, and demanded of Miss Spenser who I might be.

She begged permission to introduce us, and presented him as M. de Cournville, without giving more details of his person than that. He bowed again, and on his stretching out his hand, I was obliged to give him mine, which resulted in a considerably greater display of my upper person than was appropriate at a first meeting – while I could not but notice the effect it had upon him, his black eyes flashing apprecia-tively, and a smile curling at the corner of his lips.

'I trust, madame, that we shall have the pleasure of meeting again?' he remarked in a very passable English.

'Indeed, monsieur,' I said, 'I shall remain but a short time in New Orleans.'

'But madame attends the ball at Madame Quincunx's house tomorrow evening,' said Miss Spenser.

'Then I shall certainly require a dance of you, madame,' he said, and with a final bow left the establishment.

Miss Spenser was full of his praises. She was an astonishing example of American democracy, for though only a dressmaker she was herself considered a respectable part of society, on terms of friendship with the wife of a judge and the sister of the local mayor; so I went out of my way to cultivate her, since she could inform me about the people whom I might meet – not the least of which was M. de Cournville, whom she considered the acme of manhood – a bachelor much sought-after by the young women of the place, but so far uncaptured, and his desirability as a husband unaffected by his habit (Miss Spenser whispered) of taking into his bed the more beautiful among the black women who worked on his estate.

I passed the next day in walking about the town and observing it and its inhabitants. These consist of the Creole families, who are chiefly planters and merchants; the quadroons, who are excluded from society; and the black people, so lowly considered that their exclusion from society is taken for granted; that they should form a part of it would never enter the head of anyone in New Orleans.

I must confess to finding the Creole ladies extremely boring; their opinion of themselves is so high that the Prince Regent would barely be considered a worthy companion for them. The quadroons are on the other hand entirely delightful, the girls often the acknowledged daughters of wealthy American and Creole fathers, educated with style and accomplishment, beautiful, graceful, gentle, amiable – and scorned by the Creole dragons – though I am told often courted by the young men, who occasionally marry them and find them entirely delightful partners, though even so they are rarely accepted into society.

It was entirely by accident that on the afternoon of my second day I strolled into the forest near the town, finding it most beautiful – not by specially fine trees, but by the prevalence of what is called Spanish moss which hangs gracefully from the boughs, converting the outline of every tree into that of a weeping willow. Wild vines similarly grow in profusion, and the palmettos grow in great bushes, most beautiful to be seen.

Hearing low laughter and splashing, I passed between two palmetto bushes to come upon a scene which might have come from the annals of Eden, for here was a shallow pool of clear, bright water – in the greatest contrast to the muddy waters of the river – and in it, six or seven young quadroon girls bathing, splashing the water over themselves and each other with no regard for modesty, for they were all entirely unclothed.

Even had I thought they would resent my presence, I would have found it difficult to tear myself away from such a sight; and indeed on seeing me, they immediately beckoned me to join them – to which I needed little persuasion, for the heat was considerable and somewhat oppressive.

They seemed surprised at the freedom with which I discarded my clothes and joined them – and I later discovered that it would be considered great shame for a Creole lady even to be seen naked by one of them, let alone to bathe at the same place; but gave admiring glances at my person, which indeed compared to the brownness of their bodies was white as paper.

The coolness of the water was delightful, and I was pleased to float and lie in it, and to have it gently laved over my body by my new friends, who presently withdrew to a mossy bank upon which the sun's light, broken into fragments by the shading leaves through which it passed, fell to a degree that was warm without being burning.

In a while, I joined them there, and for a while we all lay in a lazy tableau, the drops of water gradually drying upon our bodies. I must confess that it was no small pleasure to me to watch the process, and my friends' enjoyment of my admiration being plain, I needed no excuse to examine them. I am sure that my brother will wish to hear in what their beauty consists.

Well, then, these quadroon girls are small-limbed, the plumpest of them with breast and belly rounded to a pleasant rather than an extreme degree. Their limbs are not long, however, with the result that however small they may be, their bodies do not in the least resemble those of boys – as is sometimes the case with your lightweight French girls (to take an example with which I know you are familiar).

There is one point in which they do resemble the young *mademoiselles*, however – and that is that like them, they do not consider it proper to denude their bodies of any of the hair which grows upon them (unless it is positively unsightly), rather merely trimming it should it seem too considerable – something which I saw, to my amusement, two of them were at, one girl leaning over her friend with a pair of small scissors, and carefully trimming the hair which veiled her secret parts, so that rather than a ragged veil it more closely resembled a nicely-shaped fringe, a charming curve marking its upper boundary. Their legs bore a sheen of hairs, in some cases more marked than others – though in the most hirsute, I must admit, far from repulsive, mainly through their great personal charm. Beneath their arms, too, small bushes of hair were to be seen – contrary indeed to my own taste, but after all entirely natural, and what is natural must surely be forgiven – which was what I told myself when I saw two of them, without any consideration for modesty, lying in each other's arms and permitting each other those tender embraces which we normally expect rather from a male than a female companion.

My eyes half-closed, for I was now counterfeiting sleep (not wishing to betray my own interest in the scene), I was in no position to show that I was conscious of the close interest of two of the other girls in my own person – one of whom, my right arm being beneath my head, was closely examining the armpit, and indicating her surprise at its being devoid of hair. In a moment, I felt a tickling which could only be the tip of her tongue, as she tried to discover with that most apprehensive of instruments whether there was any sign of growth – a giggle, and a comment in the French language, betraying that she understood that this was a part of my body to which a razor had been applied.

Since I appeared to remain asleep, they went further, and in a moment, I felt a pair of lips encircling the nipple of a breast, then a finger applying itself to that lower portal exposed by the (I must confess) careless attitude of my lower limbs.

I could only assume that they had never before had the opportunity of examining the person of a white woman, for their curiosity was complete; and it became impossible for me to continue to counterfeit sleep when, drawing those lower lips apart, they began to pay the most devoted attention to the boy in the boat, whose small head was soon raised, and who was communicating to me the most delicious pleasure, causing me to throw my arms about the girl nearest to me, and to clasp her to me with a cry of delight.

You will not, dear Frank, wish to hear an intimate description of the pleasures which followed; however, I must admit that short of that final delight for which we women must rely upon the presence of a limb not at the disposal of even the most delightful of girls, my pleasure was complete – indeed, was multiple, which is an advantage not always enjoyed at the hands of the most ardent of male lovers. It was with reluctance that I resumed my clothing, helped by the courteous hands of my new friends, and bade them farewell.

A description of the delights of Madame Quincunx's ball would not tax my pen, for it had not half the fascination of an entertainment held by the least notable squire's wife of a small English town. The orchestra, if it is so to be called, consisted of several black gentleman ·playing on two fiddles, a piano, and an instrument called a banjo, the sound of which is quite indescribable. As to the dances, they are the merest polkas and country dances, many of them derived no doubt from France – though the courtly manners of those French people it has previously been my pleasure to meet could nowhere be seen, and was replaced by an amiable friendliness which was charming enough, but without any impression of style.

You will no doubt be unsurprised to hear that during the course of the evening I was approached by none other than that M. de Cournville to whom I had presented so open a face in the dressmaker's shop. He bowed in a manner more courtly than was commanded by any other man present, and indeed tricked out in evening clothes was a figure more near elegance than any other in the room.

'Madame,' he said, 'you appear somewhat flushed. Would you care to allow me to bring you a cup, upon the balcony?'

I was indeed sensible of the heat within the press of bodies upon the dance floor raising the temperature even above the sultriness of the evening; and so with gratitude I retired to the outside, where was a balcony looking over a picturesque garden, lights hanging from the trees to provide an illumination just sufficient to present to me a picture of the gentleman who rejoined me, bearing two glasses of something called *mint julep*, which consists in a peculiar whisky of theirs called *bourbon* together with sugar, soda water and springs of mint, and is extremely refreshing and invigorating.

M. de Cournville was, as I have said, a handsome man, with deep, penetrating eyes set in a keen and apprehensive face, like nothing so much as a watchful bird of pray; and he was now looking his best in a fine coat of maroon cloth, the collar of which, I saw, was trimmed by the softest black leather. This, together with his air (somewhat of romantic mystery) gave me an idea which I was about to express – when before I had had more than an opportunity to raise it once to my lips, he had seized my glass from my hand, placed it upon a nearby table, and taking me in his arms pressed a kiss upon me which, I must confess, called immediately to the woman in me.

Upon my neither drawing away nor resenting the pressure of his body, he took it for consent to a more active courtship, and lowered his head to kiss the upper portion of those globes which were only somewhat concealed by Miss Spenser's hastily contrived gown.

'Mrs Nelham,' he said (for I had now resumed my proper name), 'I have never in this place been impressed by so delightful a person; your manner is so much more European than those of our ladies here. I must request that you allow me the opportunity of paying your beauty the tribute for which it so ardently calls . . .'

With which he embraced me again, this time accompanying a kiss during which his tongue sought out my very soul by the gesture of placing his hand in approximation to that part of me he clearly now coveted. The latter gesture convinced me that I was right in my supposition – and I asked him whether his birthday was not towards the end of October – which, his confirming, allowed me to pay myself the compliment of accurately placing him within the astrological sign of Scorpio (not only by his appearance, but by the sudden ardent expression of his passion).

Somewhat puzzled for the moment by my question, he was soon once more upon the attack; in breaking from his embrace to question him, I had half-turned towards the fine view of the garden – but now, coming behind me, he embraced me once more, slipping his hands over my breasts and pressing the length of his body against my own – whereat no doubt the fact that the points of my bosom had tightened with desire gave him the signal which he was conveying to me by the pressure against my behind of an impressively adamantine weapon, still sheathed in clothing (I presumed) only because of the possibility of discovery.

It was without reluctance that I permitted him to take me by the hand and lead me down into the garden, where, striding into the trees, we soon reached a small summer house – in which no doubt Madame Quincunx held polite tea parties during the day, but which now, shrouded in a discreet dusk and lit only by the small lanterns placed in the nearby trees, was to provide more virile entertainment.

M. de Cournville was by now so eager that his attention was all upon delights to come. I thought that I heard a rustling noise as we entered, and feared mice – or worse, for I had heard that dangerous snakes appeared from time to time in the gardens here. But he was entirely oblivious – and of course it is the case that anyone knowledgeable in the Zodiac would not expect finesse from a Scorpio whose passions have been roused. Indeed, no sooner were we within the shelter of the summer house than without more ado M. de Cournville's trousers were about his ankles, while had I not been prepared for his eagerness and loosened the ties of my bodice, it would have been torn from my body. As it was, his lips could now fix themselves to my breasts before, sinking to his knees, he drew my clothing from my waist until he was able to bury his face below, finding me entirely unctuous and ready for the most energetic passage of love.

Passing his arms between my legs, his palms about my buttocks, he now lifted me and placed me in a sitting position upon the elegant tea-table from which Madame Quincunx's sandwiches were served, and without pausing even for so little a time as to permit me an apprehension of his pego, threw my thighs apart and planted it between them with so creditable an aim that, lubricate as I was, before I knew it I was speared to the vitals, seeming to feel the head of his instrument knocking against my very backbone!

Had I not myself been roused to a certain pitch by the circumstances, the passage would have been too short; for a thrusting motion of no longer than perhaps two minutes brought him to that moment when I felt beneath my hands all the muscles of his back compress, to be released in a series of spasms accompanied by a roar of pleasure muffled only by his burying his face in my bosom.

At this moment I heard – we both heard – a smothered giggle from nearby. M. de Cournville sprung from between my legs like an animal from a trap, and turning around tore down a curtain which hung at our side, revealing hidden in a sort of cupboard two young black persons – a muscular young buck, and a pretty girl – both naked as the day they were born. Clearly they had had an assignation of their own within the summer house, and being interrupted by our approach had hidden, to become (I am sure without intention) witnesses of our encounter.

My reaction was to laugh; but de Cournville was livid with anger, and aimed a blow at the young man which he avoided by a movement of the head, de Cournville's clenched fist hitting the wooden shelf behind him, which necessarily enraged him further. The young negro, in no doubt as to his anger, tactfully withdrew by the simple means of ducking under my friend's arm and slipping out of the door.

I naturally assumed that he would either chase after him, or see the humorous side of the situation and, dressing himself, escort me back to the house. But no! – he seized a cane from a rack of walking sticks inside the door, and with a sound that I can still hear, brought it down upon the body of the young girl, who was still cowering before us.

Without stopping to think, I reached out and caught at his arm: but with the most violent motion he threw me off, and continued to belabour the young girl, who had curled herself into a ball. Even in the gloom, I could see the marks left upon her back where the rod struck it.

I may be a visitor in this country, Frank, but I cannot stand by and see violence done to the harmless innocent – and reaching out found at my hand a large metal object rather like a huge vase (it is in fact a receptacle known as a spittoon, whose inelegant purpose I will later describe to you). Lifting it, I brought it down with all my might upon M. de Cournville's head – whereupon he collapsed without comment upon the floor.

The little black girl was by now hysterical with panic, and pausing only to clothe myself, I found the single dress which she had been wearing, drew it upon her, and then putting my arm about her encouraged her to leave the summer house. Out of the shadows, her young male companion then appeared – almost as fearful as she, and together, shaking with terror, they explained that they were as good as dead – for even though it was I who had struck M. de Cournville, they would take the blame for it, and for slaves to attack a white man in such a way (by which was meant even standing by while such an occurrence took place) was a capital offence.

I ridiculed this, at first not believing it, but their fear convinced me. While I was thinking what to do, a groan from within the summer house told us that M. de Cournville was coming around; at which, re-entering, I tapped him again with the spittoon, which persuaded him to quietude for another term. Taking advantage of this, I recovered a sort of garment which pretended to be a pair of breeches, and was the property of the young black man.

Now, I walked with the two young people to the gate of the house, where a single negro was on guard, who was, they whispered, the chief overseer of Madame Quincunx's small estate. While I engaged him in conversation, the two slipped out of the gate, to make their way to my house; once they were there, I convinced them, I would be able to protect them – though truth to tell I was uncertain of it.

Returning to the ballroom I sought out Madame Quincunx, and made my excuses. I had, I explained, been the subject of an unprovoked attack by M. de Cournville – something my experiences in polite society in Europe had not prepared me for; I confessed that I had been forced to strike him, and told them where he had been left.

Madame Quincunx and her friends, who had clustered around, inferring that some interesting narrative was under way, were by no means surprised at the news; they evidently had little sympathy with my victim, whose amorous inclinations and roughness in courtship were well-known; and while it was clear they had little understanding of my reaction, M. de Cournville's prowess with his weapon being such that an attack from him was something for compliment rather than condolence, they seemed to admire my method of dealing with him – and I gained the impression that no-one was likely to rush to his aid. I left the party in the hope that he would be too ashamed of the circumstances in which I had left him to report the entire history of them.

Back at my house, I at first supposed that the two young people had failed to discover its whereabouts, or had been too fearful to approach. My own servants certainly said nothing about them to me – nor I to them; and it being late, I dismissed them and repaired to my room, where I was about to remove my clothing when from behind the curtains appeared my two *protégés*, who had, it appeared, gained entry through the open window and hidden against my arrival.

They were still most apprehensive, but had now had some time during which to contain the utmost of their fears, and were able to devote themselves to imploring me to protect them by concealing them and enabling them to leave the tówn – for, they said, no white man – and in particular not M. de Cournville – would overlook the circumstance of their being the cause of his humiliation.

I was at a loss what to do, for it was impossible for me to keep two people within my house, unknown to my servants – and it seemed likely, such was the fear most black servants had of all white people, that betrayal would be a certain consequence of my people discovering their presence – for when I had left the town, they would remain, unprotected. However, it was clearly impossible to turn them out immediately, and first locking the door I placed some spare blankets upon the floor in the corner and informed them they could sleep there.

They immediately fell to their knees and thanked me, which I found an embarrassment, for I was doing no more than any other civilised person would do. So I directed them to lie down, whereon the young man – scarcely more than a boy, as it appeared – turned his back, while the young woman, of more or less his age, insisted on helping me to undress and get into bed, whereupon she extinguished the lamp.

I had been in bed no more than ten minutes when I was awakened from a half-doze by a hammering on the front door, and on my opening my eyes saw the reflection of flaming torches through the window curtains, which I thought in my semi-conscious state (though it cannot surely have been so) to take the form of a flaming wooden cross! – such is the delirium of sudden terror!

In a moment the hammering ceased and there was the sound of voices, and presently a knock came at my own door.

On my calling out, my servant announced that M. de Cournville and several gentlemen were present, enquiring about two slaves who had escaped from Madame Quincunx's estate. Hearing little tremors of fear from the corner of the room, I called out that I would open the door presently, and getting out of bed lit the lamp and gestured to the two young people to climb into the bed and hide beneath the bedclothes. When this had been done, and I had ruffled the covers so that their folds completely disguised any appearance of human forms beneath them, I slipped a *peignoir* over my nakedness and turned the key.

Without ceremony, M. de Cournville strode into the room, accompanied by two rough-looking characters.

'I must ask, sir, that your friends leave this room,' I said with what dignity I could muster. 'I have no objection to answering your questions, but it is not usual in my circles that unknown gentlemen should present themselves in a lady's bedroom at such an hour of the night.'

M. de Cournville gestured to them, and they withdrew.

'Where are the niggers?' he then demanded, without further ceremony.

'I have no idea what you can mean, sir,' I said; 'if you mean the unfortunate young woman who you would doubtless have killed had I not intervened, I trust that she is in a place of safety, together with her lover – and some place where your hard hand cannot further incommode her.'

'It would be best for you not to interfere,' said the gentleman; 'we have our own way here of dealing with impertinence' – but I could see that he was not entirely released from his admiration of my person, and must frankly admit that I made little effort completely to conceal myself from his gaze.

'I have no notion of interfering, sir – but perhaps we could continue this conversation tomorrow? Would you care to call in the afternoon? In the meantime, I am sure that the two servants you seek will not be far away.'

'That's right, ma'am,' he said; 'what we have, we hold – and even a couple of worthless slaves cannot be allowed the last laugh. I will be happy to call on you tomorrow, and will hope to find you . . . agreeably disposed to entertain me.'

I made him a low curtsy at this, allowing the folds of my *peignoir* to fall sufficiently apart to offer him a glimpse of that country where he evidently hoped once more to graze. He bowed, and left – whereupon I locked the door once more, and drawing back the covers found the two youngsters locked in each other's arms, and quivering with fright.

I had not the heart to turn them out of the warmth of the bed, and their bodies being fresh and clean (and I cannot too strongly report that it is a myth that the negro is strongsmelling or naturally uncleanly) had no hesitation in lying down with them, when we all slept soundly until morning.

It was clear to me that there was only one solution to the situation: my embroilment with M. de Cournville, partly the result (I must admit) of my ambition to enter the name of a Scorpio gentleman upon my list of lovers, was likely to lead to great difficulty, while I could not now desert my two black friends – whose names, I discovered, were Tom and Susan.

I therefore sent a manservant, in confidence, to the office of the river boat company to purchase if possible a ticket for that day's sailing. He returned with news of a berth on the *Satisfaction*, leaving at midday for Memphis. A little searching discovered in an outhouse a large trunk, which by giving money to my servants I was able to persuade them to bring to the house. Into it, with no difficulty, Tom and Susan curled themselves – neither of them being much over five feet in height; and by a quarter to twelve it was carried with my other luggage on board the riverboat and placed in a cabin, where my two servants – for such they now professed themselves – were released.

As the boat slid out into the middle of the Mississippi, I saw M. de Cournville stride onto the *levée*, clearly furious – and no less suspicious, for although my two people were still hidden in my cabin, he could not be sure that I had nor secured their escape. He made an ironical bow in my direction, removing his tall hat; and I made him a curtsy, resolving to be a little more careful before involving myself quite so unthinkingly with any other gentleman, even in search, my dear brother, of material to allow me to win my bet – as I entirely purpose to do.

Chapter Three

The Adventures of Andy

Sophie having decided to set off for the southern states of America, it was my concern rather to make in the opposite direction, for I have long had – as you know – a wish to see the British colonies in North America, whose power and importance is growing at such a rate that it occurred to me there might be a profit in the investment of some time there – moreover I was interested to see to what degree the style and manners of the home country have been preserved in that part of the Americas which has chosen to remain faithful to His Majesty.

My voyage from New York to the mouth of the great St Lawrence river was a calm and pleasant one, and though upon entering the Gulph of St Lawrence we were enveloped in a perplexing fog, and drifted almost onto the dangerous rocks of the Island of Anticosta, where many a brave tar has concluded the voyage of life, this lifted, and in sailing up the magnificent river my eye was constantly relieved by the most delightful and ever-varying little islands covered with trees and shrubs of every form and hue, which with the innumerable farmhouses on each side of the river, and the lofty mountains whose cloud-exploring tops terminate the view, make for a picture of nature at once reviving and romantic.

I was able to go ashore briefly upon several islands during our twelve days upon the river, and upon Green Island saw for the first time one of the aborigines of the country. She was a female, and the sun being hot was clad merely in a large brown cloth thrown rather carelessly over her shoulders and reaching down to the knee; this from time to time slipping, revealed a leg of handsome proportions, lean and muscular but without doubt feminine, while she did little to conceal from the sight firm and well-carried breasts veiled only by long black hair which almost touched the ground. Her beautiful feet were bare, but she appeared to tread the earth as if unaccustomed to walk without shoes or moccasins. Her skin was an exact copper colour, and her countenance mild, placid and unassuming. I must confess to astonishment at finding in her such charm, and all the nameless graces which irresistibly impel us to admire the female character, when I had expected to find no more than savagery.

On reaching the city of Quebec, I was directed immediately to the Union Hotel, where I took rooms – though truly the place was unpleasantly gloomy, and the comfort offered appeared to be far below the standard one might expect to find in a city of this size. I then set out to see the town, a description of which you will be eager to hear.

Upon arriving at Quebec by water, one would imagine it to be one of the most beautiful cities in the world! The fine buildings, resplendent spires and formidable outworks of the upper town make the most splendid impression. The spires, in particular, being made of tin, glisten in the sun and give the place a most lively appearance, and one very different from any in Europe. When one enters into the streets, squares and alleys, however – especially of the outer town – what contrast! – for there is confinement, ill construction and inelegance, many of the streets being entirely devoid of beauty and proportion, and scarcely wide enough to permit carriages to pass each other – though the ascent to the upper town, along the windings of Mountain-street, has been contrived with much art, being exceedingly steep and shaded by the obtruding precipices of Cape Diamond, which hangs over the city so as to seem to threaten instant destruction!

The lower town contains many granaries, warehouses

and places of business, the upper town expansive residences – and ascent from the one to the other is contrived by long flights of wooden steps, the mounting of which in the burning heat of summer is a task of no easy or agreeable performance!

I was eager, as you will imagine, to visit the Plains of Abraham, so celebrated through the action between the intrepid troops of General Wolfe and the French defenders of the city. A slight bend in the river is pointed out as the spot where that skilful general landed his army, as is also the narrow sheep-track by which they silently climbed by moonlight in single column to the summit of the Plains on which next morning, formed in battle array, they gained a victory over the French troops at the very threshold of their almost impregnable fortress.

On the spot, there is a beggarly and insignificant statue of Wolfe, to which nevertheless I paid my respects – and there I saw, at a small distance and admiring the fine view, the slight figure of a most attractive female. She was by far the most elegant of the ladies I had so far seen in the town, and I did not hesitate to remove my hat and make my bow – which was met by no more than a distant and somewhat haughty glance, almost of disdain.

I took matters no further (though with regret), and after taking some refreshment at a house on the Plains, where the person providing it confessed to making a good living from those people who come here for the purpose of paying their respects to the place at which the great Wolfe fell, I continued my exploration of the town, and by late afternoon found myself in St Lewis-street, which appears to be the best *locale* for the rich of the town, being its highest part. The houses here are more modern and comfortable than those in St John-, Buard- and Palace-streets, where the old, gloomy style of French stone buildings prevails. Next I came upon the jail, a plain, strong stone building said to have cost £15,000, the castle – an unpretending building – and the Catholic and the Protestant cathedrals, the latter with a lofty and very well constructed spire, the handsomest edifice in Quebec.

While walking about the cathedral, I was conscious of being observed by a good-looking woman of indeterminate age, who had been sitting in a pew near the door; and who upon my leaving, rose from her seat and followed me out. As I paused at the gates, she came up to me and without any attempt at introduction, asked me if I was suited with accommodation in the city, as she could see that I was a stranger and felt it incumbent upon her to offer protection (as she said) from the many sharks who were always ready to make a profit by luring gentlemen into hotels where the prices bore no relation to comfort or even adequacy.

Upon my mentioning that I had rooms at the Union Hotel she lifted her eyebrows and opined that such a place was old fashioned, and that I would find there none of the comforts someone of my class and pretension could expect; and invited me to accompany her to the Hyperion Hotel in Fabrique-street, where I could dine, and to which if I was sufficiently impressed, I could transfer myself.

During our walk there the lady, who now introduced herself as Madame la Cuisse, explained that she had been in Quebec only for two years, having travelled there from Paris at the behest of a cousin who, opening the Hyperion hotel, was in need of a hostess who could train the servants and see to the general comfort of the guests (and, I thought to myself, could take the time to roam the streets and to engage the attention and procure the custom of visitors).

Upon reaching the hotel, which stood in its own grounds in a fine street much broader than the average, I was immediately impressed by its comfort; was given a glass of good wine, and shortly sat down to an early dinner, which consisted of bar-fish (an excellent product of the St Lawrence) and partridges, and the luxury of butter cooled by large pieces of ice brought to the table with it on the same plate. The dessert had very large blue and white grapes, fresh from Montreal (they do not arrive at perfection in

Quebec) with melons from the same place, and excellent apples and pears.

Madame la Cuisse then brought me a decanter of excellent port, and enquired whether I would like to see the rooms; and on my acquiescing, took me up a broad and impressive staircase to the first floor, where I was shown a room from which there was a fine view of the river and the countryside beyond, and the furnishings of which were impressively comfortable, there being a thick carpet (whereas my room at the Union was bare of such a luxury), and a large bed which looked far more comfortable than the one on which I had yet to sleep!

I was by now sufficiently impressed to wish that I had come here before so hastily engaging rooms at the other place; but when I expressed myself embarrassed (for it would be difficult for me to undo my contract there), Madame shook her head, and said that if I sent the clerk there a present of a dollar, or five shillings, there would be no difficulty in having my bags sent up (which as yet I had left unpacked, my being so eager to explore the city). I was not slow to give her the money, which she sent off with a boy and a barrow, who returned with my bags before I had finished a second glass of port, in the meantime continuing my conversation with Madame, who informed me among other matters that the city now contains some 18,000 people, including a garrison consisting of two regiments of the line, two companies of artillery and one of sappers and miners, with a fine corps of militia cavalry and two battalions of infantry.

'These are of course a great blessing to us,' Madame said; 'for though there is sometimes a shortage of visitors, the officers are inveterate visitors here – living as they do in barracks, they are pleased to dine here and to be entertained.'

I was about to ask what entertainment was offered, when the boy appeared with my bags, and took them to my room. On my expressing my thanks to Madame la Cuisse, she lifted her hand in gentle dissuasion, and insisted that any comfort which I might desire would be happily provided; and on my rising, said that she would send a girl to help me unpack. Indeed, no sooner had I undone the cords of one of my cases when after a knock upon the door, there entered my room a *petite* little rascal of a child, no older perhaps than eighteen, clad in a simple dress of some brown stuff, her hair caught up about her head, and with the merriest and most accommodating of smiles.

In no time, she had persuaded me to sit and to contribute to the unpacking merely by instructing her where about the room I would wish my effects to be placed; exclaiming over the creases in my clothing consequent upon their confine-ment, and expressing the intention of pressing them.

I was by now more than a little exhausted by the efforts of the day, and rising from my seat, dismissed her, intending – as I said – to repair to bed, though it was little after eight o'clock in the evening. However, she came towards me, and holding out her hands helped me out of my waistcoat, and then began to unbutton my shirt. This was somewhat of a surprise to me, but not an unpleasant one, for she was a delightful young person, and her attentions far from unwelcome. Having helped me remove my shirt, she now turned her attention to my breeches, unloosing the cords and buttons and preparing to draw them from me. I was somewhat abashed at this, for to be frank the lightness of her touch and her fresh beauty had roused me, and I did not wish to insult her (though only a servant) by the display which would be consequent upon the removal of my lower garment.

On my demurring, she nevertheless insisted, and far from appearing startled or offended when my bayonet sprang into view, did not even flinch when she brushed it with her hand – whether purposely or not I cannot say – as she drew my breeches off.

It had not occurred to me before this that it was possible that among the services she offered the male guests were those of a bedroom princess; but when, as she drew back the sheets of the bed, she turned to me to ask whether there was any other service she could perform for me, I took the liberty of mentioning (with the slightest indication of my lower limb) that I was in some discomfort in one department – whereat; without permitting me to finish the sentence, she said, 'Ah, sir, it is often the case with gentlemen who have been for some time on ship-board,' and without more ado lifted her hands over her head, drawing with them her garment – which proved to be the only one she wore, and as it rose revealed a scene upon which the eyes of any vigorous man would be happy to gaze – *viz.*, a body in the first flush of youth, round and compact, the breasts full but upstanding, the little globe of a belly now appearing to pant with anticipation, and below it, a dark tuft of hair seeming to emphasise rather than disguise a pair of fleshy lips which, falling on my knees, my heart suddenly leaping in my breast, I immediately kissed.

If my young friend had previously shown no lack of compliance, her acquiescence now turned to eagerness, for as I touched with my tongue the point at which her nether lips were joined, she gave a little squeak of delight, and reaching down passed her hands over my shoulders, back and sides until she could almost touch my buttocks, then returning to cradle my head and press it firmly towards her, so that my entire face was squeezed into the delicious triangle formed by the space immediately above her thighs.

I can only trust that the servants of the hotel – for I have no reason to suppose that they are not all as accommodating as little Lisette (as I found my maid to be called) – have been taught to match their energy to that of their guests, for her fire was such that it would have been the death of an older man, and severely tried my own capabilities (tired as I was by the day's activities). From moderate desire, she roused me within the next half-hour to the utmost heights of passion, changing her posture or inventing some new means of stimulating my person, each moment my ardour appeared to be reaching its apogee.

My first action was to lay her upon the bed and, pressing her not unwilling knees apart and pausing only for a moment to admire the prospect before me, to insert my dibble into the receptive accommodation which awaited it – and which, though sufficiently tight as to make a pleasantly snug home, was yet lubricated with such slippery juices as to render entry unpainful.

However, Lisette must have sensed that the weeks without intimate female company had made me over-ready, and after only three or four strokes, suddenly threw up her heels and locked them behind my head – so that, glancing downwards, I was presented with the most exciting view of our operations, the piston gleaming with natural oils as it entered and withdrew from the socket with only the slightest resistance.

With the merest pause, she then lifted one leg still higher and passed it over my head, twisting her body and – without for a moment interrupting the rhythm of our jointure – turning upon her face, lifting her delicious little rump so that, forced to raise myself upon my knees, I again had a most charming view as I continued those movements to which I was committed – and which, by small sounds, by her every gesture, and by the flush which now turned the whole of her unclothed body the most delicate shade of pink, were giving her as much pleasure as they gave me.

Once again, I felt myself unable to delay further the extremity of passion – and once more she delayed it, this time by suddenly falling forward, and reaching around to grasp my shaft at its tip, pressing with her fingers below the head firmly enough, without giving positive pain, to offer a certain mild discomfort which resulted in my passion sinking somewhat – whereat she rose and led me by my still elevated rod to a comfortable chair where, seating me in it, she sat astride and sank upon me, guiding my lips to one of those luscious breasts, the tit of which was now so distended that even to my teeth, when ever so tenderly applied, it felt as though it were carved in wood – and upon the surface of which the touch of my tongue could discern tiny pimples of flesh, as it were, the grazing of which evidently gave her the keenest pleasure, for the rhythm with which she rose and fell upon my lap quickened until once more I was at the height.

She was not even now prepared to end the game, however, for rising to her feet she once more fell upon the bed, this time with her arse at its very edge, so that when I laid myself again between her thighs, I was forced (the bed being a somewhat high one) to stand – which indeed gave me a freedom of movement which enabled me at one moment to withdraw my cock so that its tip only remained in contact with the lips of her furry hoop, and at the next to bury it to its entire length within her body – and as you will recall, while not of the greatest thickness, my instrument does not lack length, which Lisette now apprehended to the full by a gesture indicating that she seemed to feel its tip at the very base of her throat (which, I am sure, was an exaggeration).

At last, she conceded that the time had come to conclude our pleasure, and allowed nothing to impede the wave which now swept me towards it – in the end accomplishing its breaking into a paroxysm of delight by reaching between her legs to thrust a forefinger, lubricated at her lips, into my deadeye – which resulted in my releasing within her the full flood of my satisfaction, she at the same time by the tightening about my waist of her legs and by a lubricious wriggling, indicating that (unless she was the mistress of pretence) I had given her at least some degree of the pleasure she had conferred upon me.

So entirely exhausted was I by now, that it was almost in a daze that I withdrew myself, and without even the politeness to express my thanks, fell upon the bed and into the deepest sleep.

I was awaked next morning, in the pleasantest manner, by a kiss upon the cheek from the tender lips of Lisette – and still sated though I was by the activity of the previous evening, it was quite beyond my powers not to give a fleeting caress to that beguiling bum – whereupon she smiled, but remarked that she was not at liberty at that moment, having the whole floor of bedrooms to service (to which I could not but think that if the occupants had been served as I had been, she must have a remarkable capacity for the recovery of her spirits!).

Rising, I went downstairs, and found a fine breakfast awaiting me – as excellent in quality as had been my dinner the night before, and now including some excellent river trout. Madame la Cuisse presided over the meal, quick to ensure that all my wants were supplied, and upon asking whether I had spent a comfortable night, was pleased at my compliments to Lisette – from her attitude it being my expectation to find her services charged for on my account; not that I had expected otherwise, for while her attitude was of the most friendly, I had supposed that her attendance upon me was professional – and as you will know, my dear Frank, there is always a certain degree of difference between the professional lady and the amateur, the former invariably displaying an expertise which is very rarely encountered among neophytes.

Finishing my meal, I spent the morning out in the city, exploring the fortifications, which are in excellent repair and present a very noble appearance. The citadel stands on the highest point of Cape Diamond, which is no less than 350 feet above the level of the river, and, proudly frowning over the St Lawrence, now extends its immense walls and regular military outworks across the Plains of Abraham almost to the banks of the river St James. I walked about the walls, passing each of the five gates into the city – the Port St Louis, the Port St John, the Palace and Hope Gates, and Prescott Gate, through which I returned into the lower town, where I took some lunch in a low tavern the roughness of which interested me, and the food and wine of which was, if inelegantly served, perfectly good.

Leaving it, I was passing through a mean alley called

Vaniteux-street, when a woman approached me. Supposing her to be a whore, I made ready to dismiss her – and then, on her lifting a veil which concealed her face, I discovered her to be none other than the woman to whom I had made an unreturned salutation on the Heights of Abraham the day before.

'Sir,' she said – and in a perfectly English accent – 'forgive me for addressing you, but I am a stranger in this city, as I observe you to be; and since I have no-one to advise me, I hope I might have the encouragement of a word with you?'

I was happy to encourage her to confide in me – no less through motives of disinterested courtesy as because she was a charming woman, of perhaps a little more than my own age, and clearly a gentlewoman.

As we walked upon the wharves, where there was a relative quietude, the workers presumably being at their midday meal, she confided that she was a Miss Monica Bradley, who until a few weeks before had been a governess to the twin daughters of a prominent businessman in Southampton. Orphaned at an early age, she had educated herself to her station by application and the careful use of the smallest possible fortune, left to her by her parents.

But two months ago the information had reached her that an uncle, of whom she had but the barest knowledge, had died in Quebec and left her a house of business in the city.

'I had no notion what this could be,' Miss Bradley confided; 'but it was represented to me, in a letter from a solicitor here, that there was a sufficient income from the business, and that while it was in the hands of a manageress, my presence here could do nothing but good; that there would be accommodation for me, and the means to live a comfortable life – to the extent, I was informed, of some £500 per annum. I therefore immediately gave in my notice, and set out for Canada.

'On my arrival I went immediately to the solicitor, who produced my uncle's Will, and confirmed that his business was now my property – but still without revealing to me its nature, and seeming somewhat embarrassed when I attempted to enquire the details. Eventually, on my pressing him, he said I had best see for myself – and engaged one of his clerks to accompany me to Blague-street, not far from where we are now walking. There, having knocked upon the door, he left me.'

My new friend seemed in some difficulty, a flush mounting to her cheeks; but on my encouraging her to continue her narrative, went on:

'After a while, a blowsy female came to the door, and on my announcing myself, showed me with an ill grace into a parlour, drawing blinds which revealed it as furnished with couches and large chairs, together with several tables bearing a quantity of bottles. I could not imagine what sort of house I had entered; but it was clear to me when the woman – a Mrs Sally Thomas, whose relationship with my late Uncle seems not to have been solely one of business, asked me whether I wished her to remain to conduct the entérprise; and when I asked her what that was, replied, "Why – know you not? 'Tis a call house" – and on my still appearing ignorant of her meaning, went on "a case, a cathouse, a hook shop, a peg house . . ." and finally, with great impatience, " 'Tis a brothel, ma'am!" '

My friend staggered as she said the terrible word, and I put out my arm to support her. Even allowing for her situation, her reaction seemed somewhat overblown; but the fact that I showed no particular revulsion gave her the courage to continue:

'She then produced a terrible document – a sort of *menu* of grossness, showing the charges made' – and Miss Bradley handed me, removing it from under her shawl, a card which read:

Bradley's Speciality House

Tariff of Pleasures

Lady Five Fingers – 25c

Straight – 50c

Laying the lip – $1

Flopover – $1.50

Three-way deal – $2

Double train – $3

Terms: cash down

**It is strictly forbidden for gentlemen to
make appointments outside the house;
discovery will result in instant
dismissal from the premises.**

Fred Bradley, prop.

I must confess that some of the terms employed were strange to me, though I could make a guess at their meaning – as, I dare say, you can.

Well, here was a strange thing – almost a counterfeit of the occasion when we arrived in London from Hertfordshire to find that your father, my dear Frank, had left you a similar property! (A circumstance related in my previously published volume, *Eros in Town*.)

The lady was by now in a state of some agitation, and while my first instinct was to offer to accompany her to the house, and to discover just what the circumstances there were, I hesitated to suggest it – yet upon my gently enquiring what she wished, that was her express desire.

The exterior of the building was no more prepossessing than one might have expected; and the madam, when she appeared, no more appealing. However, leaving Miss Bradley sitting uncomfortably in the reception room, I accompanied Mrs Thomas upstairs to a small room of business (whence I could hear a certain giggling nearby which seemed to suggest that some at least of the ladies of the house were at present in residence).

Mrs Thomas was at first disposed to treat me with some condescension – but a moment allowed me to inform her that I was more that slightly acquainted with the business which she was operating, and no less from the point of view of a brothel-keeper than a customer; indeed, you will be interested to hear that the fame of our place in Brook-street has even reached the New World, for some of the officers of one of the regiments stationed here were regular callers there, and had told of the comfort of our establishment – of all our friends there, of our hot-rooms, and of the degree of comfort we offered.

'In course,' said Mrs Thomas, 'we could not afford such goings-on here, nor would Mr Bradley hear of it; yet I believe that it was a good going business?'

I assured her that a certain profit had been made – which my own appearance of some wealth supported. As to Miss Bradley, I assured her that I would do my best to let her know that a business such as the one she had inherited could be respectably run, and no less as a convenience to the town as in any degree to its disgrace.

I saw to it that Mrs Thomas paid her respects to Miss Bradley, offering her apologies for any previous offence. Quietly telling madam that I would return on the morrow to discover the quality and extent of the services offered, the circumstances of the ladies employed, and all the details of the place, I then offered to return Miss Bradley to her hotel (since the house was clearly at present unfit to provide her with lodgings). This proved to be the Union Hotel, where she had the best rooms, which while by no means equal to mine were decent enough.

There, I ordered tea, and as we partook, explained as quietly as possible that the nature of her new business was as she had inferred that of a place of entertainment for gentlemen; and took the liberty of explaining also that I had been party to just such a similar shock – when, coming to London with my friend Sir Franklin Franklyn, of Alcovary in the county of Hertfordshire, we had discovered that the house owned by his father in the West End of London was similarly run as a brothel.

She expressed her horror that a member of the British aristocracy had suffered such an indignity, and asked how difficult we had found it to expel the ladies and take possession. The fact (as I was able to retail it) that we had not only left the place as it was, but had turned it into the most luxurious in the city – together with an account of the profit it had afforded us – was at first shocking to her, but her admiration for the aristocracy prevented her (being somewhat of a snob) from dismissing out of hand my suggestion that she should do the same.

It then emerged that part of her difficulty was a determined virginity, for though no less than twenty and four years of age, she knew nothing of men, growing up in a girls' school, having no brothers, and teaching in a house where the only man was an elderly and entirely respectable husband and father.

On my enquiring whether she did not feel the lack, she admitted to some curiosity; but that no man had shown a carnal interest in her was less than surprising to me, since, though handsome, she had a somewhat forbidding and ungiving exterior, her attitude to me however now being more welcoming.

Did she not realise, I asked, that to provide gentlemen with the possibility of slaking their lust without visiting it upon any lady to whom it would be offensive, was a positive service to her sex?

She had not thought of it, she admitted; but upon reflection believed it might be so – but at what a cost! – for the young girls who were employed at such places must surely be degraded by their service?

Indeed, I must admit, that could be the case; but it had been our rule that no lady should be pressed into service for whom love was not a pleasure, or at the very least an employment not offensive to them – and the rewards (I pointed out) were considerable if a proper proportion of the income of the house was devoted to them, which I was assured would be her wish as it had been our own practice.

She still found it difficult, she blushingly admitted, to believe that any woman could take pleasure in congress with a man; at which I took the liberty of taking her hand and, pressing it, assuring her that such could be the case, and even ventured to kiss that hand, upon which I felt a tremor in it which seemed to indicate that Miss Bradley was not as impervious to masculine charm as she would have had me think.

To shorten my story, we dined together, and I saw to it that the hotel produced the best claret at its command; which was by no means notable, except that upon the lady – who seemed almost as unused to liquor as to the company of gentlemen – it had a softening and quieting effect; so that when, the room being warm, I removed my coat and cravat, she showed no objection.

Upon her enquiring, I described the house in Brook Street in some detail, and then was invited to give my explanation of the list of practices which she had been given at her own house of pleasure. This proved difficult from the first, for when I translated 'Lady Five Fingers' as simply the practice of the lady masturbating the gentleman, she expressed astonishment that that should give satisfaction – whereat I admitted that I would find it most unsatisfactory, but that it would certainly serve the purpose of relieving the feelings of a gentleman who after long abstinence was in need of relief, but could afford no more than the 1s 3d which the practice was priced at.

She had no sooner grudgingly accepted this than I found her aghast at my description of the practice of fellatio, which I took to be meant by the term 'laying the lip' and I assured her that to a lady enthusiastic in the accomplishments of love, this was no trial, and indeed to many was a delight. But further discussion was constrained when I found that not only was she ignorant of the mechanics of love-making, but even of the shape of a man – for she had

had no family to educate her, nor had she received such an education in any other form.

'It is clearly impossible for me to have anything to do with the house,' she said, 'for how can I improve it and run it as you suggest if I have never even seen an unclothed gentleman, much less know how one should be satisfied?'

There was only one way in which to answer her, and satisfied that Miss B. was sincere in her wish to learn, I took the liberty of standing and removing, in the space of a moment, my clothing. Her interest in the sight was clear – yet the vision was incomplete, for, not having toyed, and not warmed by the anticipation of congress, my reamer was perfectly at ease – indeed, if anything was more shrunken than usual (perhaps the result of the wine we had drunk).

Though too shy to question me, she clearly wondered how such a diminished weapon could take part in the action I had described. There was, I believed, no question of any participation from her which would enable me to reach that degree of excitation which would enable me to demonstrate man's chief glory; so firmly closing my eyes and fixing my mind on the beautiful Lisette – whose charms indeed I had been looking forward to experiencing again this evening – I put hand to tiller, and in a short time had succeeded in raising the devil to such an extent that, opening my eyes, I found my companion in a state no less of shock than of admiration – her hand stretched partially out, indeed, towards that strange new object she saw before her.

I took that hand, and guided it to my instrument, at which the lady, feeling its adamantine surface, expressed new astonishment, brought her other hand forward, and kneeling before me, explored the equipment before her with great thoroughness – the shaft, bulb and foreskin with no less interest than the cods below; her inquisitiveness being such that, despite the unpropitiousness of the situation, in a moment or two, on her moving her hand up and down the shaft with all the interest of one for whom the experience of contact with the limb was a new one, I was unable to prevent the excitation reaching an inevitable culmination, and only a sudden movement resulted in my discharging over her shoulder rather than full in her face.

The resultant shrinkage aroused new surprise; and on my explaining that this was the whole aim of the exercise, she was now at least partially informed, and felt the rewards of it, thanking me, as I resumed my clothes, and hoping that I had not disabled myself for further pleasure. I bade farewell, having made an appointment for the morrow, when I hoped to be able to be of further assistance, and returned to my own hotel, where (having warmed myself on my walk thither by thoughts of her enticing person) I summoned the ever-ready Lisette, and greeted her embraces with equally warm responses of my own.

Chapter Four

Sophie's Story

My first act as the *Satisfaction* made her way upriver between the thick walls of trees which were for some time our only view, was to approach the captain and to confess that my agents had made a mistake in not booking a cabin for my two servants, Tom and Susan.

The captain was excessively accommodating, and had no difficulty in suggesting suitable accommodation in a cabin near my own; but then, on catching sight of the two young people, burst into laughter: 'Oh!' he then exclaimed, 'two niggers – I thought you to mean you had brought servants from the old country' – and directed them instead to a stinking hold where about forty of their fellows were already housed. Nothing I could say would change his mind, for, he said, in no way would any decent person sleep in a cabin which had accommodated black people – which gave me no good opinion of the inhabitants of this part of the world, though it was fruitless to complain.

Fortunately, neither Tom nor Susan expected any other kind of treatment, while their pleasure in escaping from Memphis (where Madame Quincunx had, it seemed, been an excessively demanding and unpleasant employer) was such that it would have taken much more than indifferent sleeping quarters to dismay them.

On my questioning them, they explained that they had been bought at an early age as slaves – how early, they knew not, nor did they know their present age, though by the firmly swelling breasts of one and the assurance of the other (to say nothing of the occupation in which they were engaged at our first meeting) I guessed that they were in their middle teens. They had known nothing but the most abject slavery and had been treated entirely as the chattels of their mistress, something at which their young spirits rebelled; and it was clear that they had seen me as an easy means of commanding sympathy and of possible escape.

They were now, having achieved their wish, evidently fearful of pursuit and recapture, which I gathered would have severe consequences for them; but it was my view that no sane man or woman would devote time and energy to following two such – especially when their fellows could be purchased at the rate of two a cent (as their pennies are called here).

If my desire to find them decent accommodation had failed, at least I could succeed in my second wish, which was to make them more presentable. The first thing was to make them clean, for (no doubt due less to habit than circumstance) they had clearly not washed themselves that day. In the confines of my cabin much freedom of movement was not possible, but I sent for hot water, which having been brought by a black man who seemed excessively ill-tempered, I insisted immediately upon their stripping and washing themselves. Susan had no hesitation in removing her single garment (it cannot sensibly be described as a dress) while Tom sat upon my bunk, his knees drawn up before him, but watching keenly from behind lowered lashes – doubtless (through being able to contrive a meeting with his friend only after dark) seeing her body for the first time.

This was certainly attractive, for she was in the early bloom of youth, and her form had not yet thickened – which through indifferent diet and natural indolence, I see that the black women here are prone to; her waist was narrow, her small breasts carried high and pertly, her legs extremely shapely, and between her thighs not the full bush of womanhood but merely a trace of silky hair which failed to hide a pair of purpled lips which seemed to pout invitingly. If I found the sight charming, how much more delightful must it have been to a young boy whose first view of girlhood it was? Nor was Miss unaware of his interest, for far from keeping her back discreetly to him, she seemed to take a positive pleasure in placing herself with instinctive coquetry in the most naturally seductive postures, lifting one foot upon the bed in order to cleanse her inner thighs, and thus opening herself entirely to his view; whereat all pretence vanishing, his eyes rounded like saucers.

The time coming for his turn, he, on the contrary, turned his back to us as he removed his ragged trousers, and only an involuntary movement as he reached for the cloth revealed to me that he was in a state to be expected of a virile young man on observing such a tempting sight as Susan had been – and indeed remained, for she stood patiently awaiting further orders, still as yet unclothed.

Like most young fellows, Tom had little natural aptitude for hygiene, and I was forced – observing his dabbings – to seize the cloth from him and, soaping it well, to scrub his back, not excepting a delightful pair of globes, my attentions to which resulted in wriggling and laughter, so that in order to return order I was forced to administer a stinging slap, which while not regarded as a painful admonishment (which indeed it was not) resulted in an obedient docility when I turned my attention to the front of his body, and even when I was forced to include those parts which it would normally be proper for a gentleman himself to cleanse.

You will remember, dear brother, when I was in charge of my house of convenient entertainment for ladies, at Chiswick, the young black man, George, was one of our most sought-after stallions? – and the immensity of the limb with which he was equipped? It is clear that this is a common thing with his race, for young Tom, though half the age of our old friend, possessed a weapon the size of which would be envied by most full-grown white men.

I cannot suppose that the gentle friction of my hands was unpleasant, for I felt the boy's body shiver; and was forced indeed to desist – at which with a quickness which might have been taken for impertinence had I not known better, he seized my hand and returned it to its former place! But it would have been quite improper for me to take advantage of so young a boy – and seeing that he was too excited to be placated except by one means, I released myself and gently impelled him towards his friend, who nothing loth took him in her arms; whereat with an enviable vigour he seized her, laid her upon the narrow bed, and without more ado spread her thighs and plunged between them.

Their passage did not last long; but you will no doubt understand me when I say that I was not unaffected by it – for the cabin was so small that I was forced to stand within a few inches of the happy pair as they played, and was indeed quite unable to avoid my hand falling upon the back side of young Tom – and since my quite involuntary caress evidently gave him some pleasure (by the sudden start he gave) found myself slipping it between the cheeks of his arse to tickle with my fingers his cods, drawn tightly to his body like two little nuts.

This, with the charming and unusual sight they made (to me, who had not before seen what variation of depth in colour could be found in the velvet skins of the black race, now fully to be admired in the sun which struck upon their bodies through the cabin window), I must confess led to my bitterly regretting that I had no lover to confer upon me the pleasure that Tom was allowing Susan – though that pleasure was short-lived. However, that it was satisfactory was not in doubt, for she, having herself been roused by the sight of her lover, was evidently prepared for pleasure, and after only a brief period by a deep and shuddering sigh revealed the fulfilment of her emotion – only just before he give a final lunge and withdrew.

The bead of white liquid which stood upon the dark point of his sword showed that he had indeed reached his goal; yet his instrument gave no sign of that immediate diminution which I had been sad to see in my white lovers – and it appeared to retain its remarkable size (which amounted, as far as I could judge to no less than nine inches in length, and of a commensurate thickness). I could not resist to touch it, to discover for myself whether my eyes were deceived. They were – to the extent that, while remaining of full size, it was now soft and limber to the pressure of my fingers, and I found it perfectly possible, without giving Tom the least discomfort, positively to bend it into a hoop; yet even as I did so – and within a minute or so of his having spent – I felt a new stirring within my palm, and a speedy renewal of capability – while his hand sneaked out and raised itself beneath my skirt, resting on my upper thigh, whence it showed signs of further exploration.

Brother, you know my views: that when a young person feels the desire and has the capability for love, there is no reason to deny it, and every reason to assist in its full realisation. You will be unsurprised to hear, therefore, that I had little hesitation in removing my garments and allowing my two servants their first sight of a white woman in full beauty. I say this with reason, for though (as I later learned) both Susan and Tom had seen Madame Quincunx in a state of nature – for slaves being regarded as less important than mere furniture, there could be no reason to consult their modesty – she had been, without her stays, peculiarly unattractive; while I, having taken some trouble to preserve my beauty, was even at the advanced age of over five and twenty by no means an object to be scorned.

Tom at any event showed no reluctance to caress me – and indeed was so curious at the sight that he spent some time merely exploring my body, to discover whether I was shaped like Susan. She, meanwhile, was perhaps somewhat jealous, for I saw to my amusement that while he was testing the elasticity of my breasts with his hands, or trying the tenderness of their tips by the lightest application of his lips, her hands busied themselves below his waist – which merely had the effect, however, that on my passing my own between his thighs, I found his device once more of the most perfect hardness, and lifting him bodily (for he was small and light) lowered him upon me so that with that natural instinct which needs no teaching he immediately pierced me with such vigour that despite myself I cried out – no adult white man ever having speared me with a more adamant weapon!

Fortunately, the circumstance of Tom's recent evacuation prolonged my pleasure quite sufficiently for me to enjoy the bout to the full; and touchingly, having himself again reached his apogee, the boy touched the tip of my nose with his full lips in an affectionate gesture much more that of a lover than of a servant – whereafter he collected himself and, climbing from the bunk, took Susan's hand in his, the pair of them standing like a young Adam and Eve, clearly now wondering whether, since I had apparently satisfied myself, I would have no further use for them, and discharge them to whatever fate might await them. Such was not, of course, my intention.

The first thing was to clothe them properly. Producing a dress from my case for which I had little use, I offered it to Susan; but while expressing herself delighted with it, she let me know that it would be impossible for her to wear it, lest she be accused of theft of so fine a garment; and on my allowing her to look through my wardrobe, she took an old shift, and tearing from it the lace which lay on it, she opined that it would be the perfect garment for her; and putting it on, was happy – and I confess that she looked charming in it (but her young person was so delightful that she would have looked well in anything).

Tom was another, and more difficult matter; but on his suggesting it, I was happy to give him a little money – so little that you would not credit any garment could be bought for it. Quickly donning his ragged trousers, he left and made his way to the place below the deck where his fellows were collected. In just ten minutes he reappeared clad in a dirty but adequate pair of breeches and a shirt that had once been white, and upon washing would no doubt be so again. This would be perfectly decent until I could buy him new clothing.

While he was absent, something had occurred to me; and on his return I enquired what time of the year it was when he celebrated his birthday. He replied that it was on the twentieth of September, though being parted from his mother at so early an age he could not be sure that this was the correct date (nor, he said, had anyone taken notice of it save for the cook at Madame Quincunx's, who had looked after him there).

This would have meant that he was a Virgo, which – though unaccustomed to observing the Zodiac signs in their effects upon the black people, I could not believe, for he was anything but modest, nor had his recent actions denoted that careful discrimination which marks the people of the sign; the more I considered him, the more clear it was to me that his birth date must have been a few days later than he thought, for he acted the Libran to the life: both then and since he had a remarkable instinct to do just the right thing at the right time, and is considerate of the feelings of everyone – though always ready to blame others for his own faults, should some accident or mistake occur! Moreover, he has a long and elegant neck upon which his head is poised with a most graceful carriage, and allowing for the different formation of the negroid features his face was a most handsome one – his large brown eyes calm and his gaze open, his lips, though very full, handsomely shaped and his carriage graceful and elegant – even more so than is common with his race. I have no doubt therefore in setting him down a Libran, and trust, dear Frank, that you will accept an addition to my list under that head!

But I have wasted too much space on amorous matters; you will be eager, rather, to hear of the continuation of my journey.

The scenery of the lower part of the Mississippi is not engrossing: the forest is continuous, only the bends of the river giving some variation to the view, an occasional break denoting the presence of mud-flats where cane has sprouted. However, upon reaching the Ohio River, things improve: now we passed between cliffs where primeval forest still grew, but where at least greenery hung from them in a most solemn grandeur, broken by increasingly frequent settlements, where herds and flocks were to be seen; now the waters of the river, at last clear rather than thickly muddy, watered meadows of fine turf; sometimes lapped against vertiginous rocks, or the walls of pretty houses whose balconies hung over the river. Sometimes a mountain torrent came splashing to the main stream. Indeed, the scenery of what is called *La Belle Rivière* is so entrancing that it is impossible not to admire it.

Louisville is a pretty town on the south side of the river, where we spent two days, and where I was able to buy some clothes for Susan – pretty without ostentation – and a livery for Tom, which would have passed for elegant even in England, and which here made him the centre of all eyes, and provoked great jealousy among his fellows, whose envy might have turned to cruelty had he not been of such an open, generous and pleasant disposition that even those who might have been his enemies were disarmed.

A few days' travel from Louisville brought us to Cincinnati, on the south side of a hill which rises gently from the river. Our first apprehension of the place was most favourable, for the *levée* here is a fine one, handsomely paved, and surrounded by elegant, low buildings, no less than fifteen steamboats tying up against the wharves.

We went immediately to the Washington Hotel, and were just in time for luncheon – though upon being offered the single place remaining among seventy men all at the same table, I repaired instead to a bar-room reserved for females, and partook there of a little refreshment before going to find an agent, who was immediately able to suggest a house for my permanent accommodation. Arranging to take possession as soon as it could be got ready, I left Tom and Susan there – with instructions to the other people about the place that their orders should be obeyed. They being so young, this was something I would hesitate to do in England; but here anyone who has the writ of a white man or woman is accepted unquestioningly as the person in charge, or 'boss'; and I was confident in Tom's good sense, having explained my requirements to him.

I then returned to the hotel, where wishing to join neither the threescore and ten gentlemen nor the women in the bar-room for an evening meal, I ordered tea in my own chamber. A good-humoured Irish woman came forward with the words, 'Oh, my dear, ye'll be from the old country; I'll see you have your tay all to yourself in your room.' This was admirable in its size, but less satisfactory as to its furnishings, for it had no carpet, and its bed, though comfortable enough, was without hangings. Inconvenient blinds hung at the windows, which were tied up with string in an odd manner, and could not be released.

'Tea' soon appeared: but as I took it, a knock upon the door announced a man who said he was landlord, and expressed himself in a peremptory speech: 'I cannot accommodate you on these terms: we have no private tea-drinkings here, and you must either use the public rooms or remove yourself from my house.'

Not wishing to create ill-feeling upon my first day in Cincinnati, I restricted my natural indignation to a cold bow; but designed to be away from the Washington Hotel and into my own house as soon as possible.

This occurred the very next day – for as I had hoped, Tom proved an admirable manager, and had secured the comfort of the place by going to 'Little Africa' – the quarter where the free negroes live – and engaging a woman to cook, and a man for general work on the place; he and Susan completing my household.

My new home proved most comfortable, though without

some of those conveniences we are used to in Hertfordshire: that is, no pump, no cistern, no drain of any kind, no regular dustman's cart or means of ridding oneself of household rubbish – which was simply thrown into the middle of the street, where families of pigs (apparently engaged solely for the purpose) soon carried it off!

I was now living in a civilised town for the first time in the three months since I left London – apart from the short time in New Orleans. Yet Cincinnati was scarcely a town: a house of three storeys was the highest building it commanded apart from a single brick church with two spires (known therefore as the two-horned church!). And though the population I believe exceeded twenty thousand, there was no air of bustle or business, but a gentle lethargy which I am sure would in time prove deadly.

Main-street was the only paved thoroughfare running through the city, a tolerably level brick pavement at each side of it – though there being no drains, the whole street is under water after even a slight shower. This has the effect that all the dirt is simply washed from one place to another, collecting at the first level spot – this being in fact the second most important street in the place, containing most of the large shops, which are therefore to be reached only through piles of dust or – in wet weather – mires of mud.

I would not consider Cincinnati of an equal importance or elegance to, say, Paris, Rome or London – yet when one remembers that thirty years ago the place where now it stands was mere uncleared forest, its importance is considerable – and it is also a place of business, for I met no-one during my time there, whether white or black, rich or poor, who was not chiefly intent on bettering his position, money being considered a god to the extent that no action, however dishonest, is considered improper in its pursuit.

Despite this, it is a fine place for comfort, everything being (to the apprehension, at least, of a European) excessively cheap: in the matter of food, for instance, the best beef is to be had for four cents (about twopence) a pound, and mutton and veal the same; fowls or full-sized chickens ready for table are twelve cents apiece (much less if bought alive), turkeys fifty cents and geese the same. Fish are good, cheap and abundant; eggs, butter, nearly all kinds of vegetables, excellent – so I ate like a queen, and to their astonishment insisted on Tom and Susan eating the same food. Susan soon became a careful and enthusiastic maid, while Tom learned to serve most elegantly at table, and was in effect my major-domo. They shared a room towards the back of the house (the other servants living out) whence I often heard, faintly, those unmistakable sounds which suggested to me that their relationship continued in an amiable enthusiasm for the pleasures of the bed. This occasionally disturbed me, since my own bed was a lonely one; but I was happy that they were content, for that contentment was reflected in the care and devotion they exercised in my service.

Cincinnati has not much culture of which to boast – but on my second excursion into the centre I found one of its most reputable establishments: the picture gallery. This is almost entirely deserted for most of the time, the citizens not admiring art as much as they admire money. Yet being convinced that every great city must have some culture, and determining that Cincinnati is to be a great city, some three thousand dollars had been subscribed, and a gentleman brought from France to supervise the establishment of a gallery of paintings and engravings.

Seeing this announced by a placard at its entrance, I immediately entered, one afternoon, and found several rooms, admirably lit, and full of exhibits – though empty of people. There was a number of American paintings in the first room, many, I must admit, of indifferent quality; the second gallery, however, contained engravings which were excellent copies of European works, many of them in full size; and I was happy to spend some time admiring them.

Among them I found a copy of Jan Mabuse's picture of Hercules and Deianira, the original of which I remember your admiring when we saw it on exhibition in London: you will, I am sure, recall it – Hercules sits, his club in his hand, a small trace of leaves barely concealing his manhood, while the naked Deianira perches upon his knee, his arm about her waist while her legs are intertwined with his in a carelessly lascivious manner.

I was so engrossed in the picture that I started violently when a voice near me said: 'Ah, madame – if I may take the liberty to say it, you must be newly arrived from Europe!'

Turning, I saw that the speaker was a man in his middle years, tall and good looking, with a dark complexion that seemed un-English; his high forehead and pronounced cheekbones, strong chin, long nose and firm mouth were immediately impressive – but no less so than the piercing gaze of the dark, sparkling eyes set beneath heavy eyebrows.

I made my curtsy.

'I am indeed, sir,' I said; 'but how could you tell?'

'By your interest in this particular painting,' he said – only a slight accent imposed upon an American drawl declaring an origin that was neither in the New World nor in England.

'If I may introduce myself,' he said, 'I am Frank Green, and I am curator of this gallery.'

I gave my name in return; but then expressed some surprise that he should have a name so clearly English in origin when I was sure he was from the continent.

'You are quick, madame,' he said; 'I was originally François Vert, of Paris; here, however, there is still a suspicion of foreigners, especially if they are concerned with pictorial art, which is supposed to be the province of – er – the unmanly; so I call myself Green. I would be complimented, however' (with a bow) 'if you cared to address me as François.'

I introduced myself, and asked again how he had been so sure by my interest in the painting of Mabuse that I was newly arrived from Europe.

'Ah, madame,' he said, 'there was such a scandal when I introduced it! The gentlemen of Cincinnati accused me immediately of trying to offend the sensibilities of their ladies, while the ladies, after a single glance, were sure such indelicacy would injure them, and withdrew. However' – and his eyes flashed with an impatient scorn – 'I am not to be ruled by fools, and insisted on its remaining; and it is now accepted, even some ladies daring to cast an occasional glance as they make their way from the still life upon one side of it to the representation of the English countryside by Mr Gainsborough upon the other.'

I smiled at this.

'I see that you are a *connoisseur*, Madame Nelham,' he continued; 'I have some engravings in my private gallery which might perhaps interest you, if you would honour me?'

I inclined my head, and followed him through the gallery to a locked door, beyond which was a smaller room, with cases about it over which sheets had been spread.

'This is a collection I have made over some years,' said M. Vert; 'some of the drawings are original, others copied, but I keep them covered no less to protect them from the light than from the eyes of those who might misconstrue my motives in collecting them.' Upon which he withdrew the coverings, in order that I might see the exhibits.

This was the finest collection of amorous drawings I have ever seen, notable for its taste as well as its comprehensive nature. I have not the space to describe it fully, nor is there in existence a catalogue which I can send you; but to be brief it opens with a charming drawing by the French artist Fragonard of three children at play in a barn – the older boy, half-clothed, curiously confused by the size of his member (which may recall to you, my dear brother, those early days when your own person confused you by its unruly behaviour) while a girl, entirely undressed, bends to offer him her rear, and a younger boy makes a gesture which suggests that he is more knowing than his brother!

Seeing my pleasure at this witty scene, M. Vert next drew my attention to a French sketch entitled 'An Italian Artist's Studio': here, the artist still holds his brush and pretends to paint, though his female friend, clad only in a hat, has one arm about his neck while her other hand caresses his tool. Nearby two men, fully clothed, sit with their breeches about their ankles – sharing a naked girl who, astride their knees, is about to lower herself upon the upstanding member of one, while that of his friend nudges at her rear entrance; and finally, a plump gentleman, his hand thrust within his breeches, kneels to peer around a screen behind which two men engage in the unnatural (but judging by their expressions, enjoyable) act of sodomy.

Many other engravings followed: some from England – a couple giving an exhibition in a high-class house of prostitution, with elegant gentlemen and expensive whores looking on; a scene in a bath-house – not unlike that in the cellar of your own house of pleasure in Brook Street, dear Frank – with a couple in congress upon the floor, while another toys happily in the water; and finally a succession of pictures from the Indies, in which ladies and gentlemen engage in postures so complex that I suspect they could only be counterfeited in life!

My interest in all this was, as you can imagine, keen – not only inherently, but because it was now some time since I had had amorous congress with any sophisticated gentleman (my encounter with Tom could scarcely be thus termed; and in any event, I had since left him to his pleasures with Susan, for it has been an invariable rule with me that servants are best left out of one's bed except *in extremis*, or in circumstances the most exceptional).

M. Vert had been quick to discern my interest, and now – as I bent over a fine Mongolian scroll in which several gentlemen enjoyed their concubines in the unusual circumstances of being, at the same time, mounted on horseback – he leaned from behind to point out a detail, and I felt the warmth of his body, while an unmistakable protruberance impinged upon my left thigh, and announced that he had been as stimulated as I by consideration of the scenes depicted before us.

I must confess that my interest in him was two-fold: partly that he was quite sufficiently attractive to present himself as an almost irresistibly potent object of admiration, and partly that without question (through his eager liveliness and quickness of spirit no less than his physical appearance) he must be born under the sign of Aries – and would thus fill a further gap in the list of lovers you, my dear Frank, had set for me to conquer!

My understanding of the Arien nature was such that equivocation was unnecessary.

'My dear François,' I said, as I straightened up – careful, however, to maintain contact with his body – 'it occurs to me that while these pictures are charming, you would not be averse to a more active exhibition of the pleasures they depict?'

His answer was to pass his hands beneath my arms, and to place them upon my breasts, at the same time pressing a kiss upon my neck.

He lodged in a set of rooms attached to the gallery – and indeed that portion of it in which his private collection was housed was part of his own domain; passing through another doorway – though now with such eagerness that I barely noticed my surroundings – we hurried through an elegant drawing-room and a small dressing-room, reaching a bedroom furnished in a masculine but comfortable style, the walls hung with plain, dark red silk, matched by the hangings of the bed upon which we sank, pausing only to remove our clothing.

M. Vert proved an agile and enthusiastic lover, perhaps a trifle over-concerned with his own satisfaction, and less apt to occupy himself in those preliminary fondlings which are so agreeable to many of us – but at the same time in the vital action so vigorous, brisk, exuberant, robust, sturdy and virile that (being, as I was, already more than ready for

the fray) I was able to match blow for blow, receiving every
downward motion with an equally enthusiastic upward
one, so that our bellies gave forth a smacking sound which
positively roused me to laughter – and even brought a smile
to the lips of my lover who, like most men, found love-
making a serious matter.

I was happy in that, after twice reaching his climax, M.
Vert – evidently long deprived of a partner who was more
to his taste than the ladies whose bodies, I suppose, he more
usually purchased for corporeal satisfaction – after lying
for a while in my arms, was yet not entirely exhausted; for
upon my taking his relaxed prick between my fingers, he
sighed with satisfaction, and merely directing my other
hand to the nape of his neck – which upon my stroking it,
he clearly received great pleasure – lay for a while, the only
movement being the most gradual swelling of his important
part; this being so slow that I was led to hasten it by
moistening my lips and passing them over its tip – at which
in no short time it was again sufficiently aroused, though no
longer so adamant, that throwing my leg over his body, I
was able to persuade it once more to enter its natural pouch,
where on my slowly raising and lowering my body it became
once more iron-hard, and remained so until I had satisfied
the last vestiges of my natural amorous instinct; when,
reaching behind me and gently tickling with my index finger
the most sensitive area of his arse, I finally milked him of
the last drop of his vigour.

We both then fell into a satisfied slumber; and upon
waking found the evening drawing on. He showed me to his
dressing-room, where behind a screen that I had scarcely
noticed was a metal bathtub and cool water, with which I
laved my entirely satisfied body. Returning to the bedroom
I found it vacated, and there dressed myself.

M. Vert was sitting in his drawing-room when I entered,
and immediately got to his feet, and taking my hand kissed
it attentively, expressing himself full of admiration for me.

'I must confess, madame,' he said, 'that in the six years I

have been living in this place, this is the first time I have had the pleasure of conversation with a lady which has been neither ignorant nor brutish; you belong in the salons of Europe – to which, doubtless' (and he sighed) 'you will shortly return, unlike myself, whose fate is probably now to remain in Cincinnati until my decease.'

I did my best to cheer him, and shared with him a bottle of wine before taking my leave, his sincere wishes and passionate hope that I would do myself the honour of calling upon him again echoing in my ears as I stepped out through the dust towards my temporary home.

Chapter Five

The Adventures of Andy

When I called at the Union Hotel for Miss Monica Bradley, I found her unwilling to meet my eyes, and clearly (from the redness of her own) she had spent a sleepless night, no doubt pondering on the strange discovery she had made with regard to the male human form – and from her demeanour I wondered whether my action in revealing myself to her had not done more harm than good.

It was clearly a matter for me to put right, if that were possible; so I took her by the hand (I had mounted to her private room), and invited her to sit upon the couch, taking my place beside her.

'My dear Miss Bradley,' I said, 'it is clear to me that you are in a state of some confusion, to which I fear I may have contributed. May I assure you that whatever took place between us last evening was provoked, upon my part, merely by the desire to be of practical assistance to you; that I wish for no recurrence unless by your own desire; and that I pledge myself to do all that I can to assist you, in any possible way, in any situation in which you feel at a loss.'

She was clearly relieved by my words, and, still catching hold of my hand, and lowering her eyes, said,

'Your words indeed reassure me, sir – and I beg that you will forgive my *naïveté* – but as I told you, my education was sadly neglected in some ares of human behaviour and . . .'

I begged her to say no more, and offered to accompany her again to the house in Blague-street. On our walk there, it was impossible for her not to take my arm on our descending one of the sets of steep wooden stairs – almost ladders – which connect the upper and lower towns, and are a peril to any lady whose skirts are of a decent length; the contact may have given her some assurance, and certainly made our conversation the more intimate.

What, I asked her, did she intend with regard to her premises? She replied that she had been able to reach no conclusion; and what was my opinion?

It seemed to me (I said) that there were several actions open to her: the house appeared to be in a reasonable way of business, and Mrs Thomas seeming (however rudely) to have a reasonable command of it, and having managed it since Mr Bradley's decease, it would certainly be possible to leave it in her hands and merely take that share of the profits which had accrued to the former owner. On the other hand, it would be wise to remain, herself, in the area, in order to ensure that she was not cheated – and in that case, it would perhaps be best if she could bring herself to take a serious interest in the house, and engage to put into operation certain improvements which I could suggest – there clearly being a demand on the part of the senior military (and perhaps the more aristocratic members of Quebec society) for a house of greater luxury than was yet available there.

Miss Bradley looked uncertain of this.

'I can understand,' she said, 'that gentlemen whose animal instincts are not subdued by the ministrations of their wives or private mistresses would wish to attend such a place; but knowing nothing of the wishes of such gentlemen, I would certainly be unable to supervise the conditions under which they could best be satisfied.'

But, I intervened, 'twas a business which could be learned, like any other; and that it was highly profitable was not in question. Had she any objection to its circumstances?

No, she replied; for provided the ladies working there were unforced, and were rewarded to a reasonable extent, their choice of such a career could not be criticised – and it was clear that to have a lady of probity in management would be of service. Perhaps I could be persuaded to stay in Quebec for a month or two, to advise and manage?

I regretted my stay must be shorter than would make that possible; yet anything I could do in the meantime . . .

By now – at about half past ten in the morning – we had reached the door, and Mrs Thomas opened it – wearing, as I saw, a new dress and bonnet, which appeared to offer some hope that she would be amenable to improvements. She showed us at once upstairs to the main room, where the drawing of the blinds revealed furnishings that perhaps by candle-light appeared reasonably luxurious, but which the crueller light of day showed to be over-worn, the stuffing appearing through holes in the couches and chairs, while the carpet was peppered with stains into whose nature I felt it superfluous to enquire.

The light was not too kind, either, to the six ladies who had been gathered together – the entire staff, it was said, of the establishment. Only one appeared to be under the age of twenty, or even twenty-five, and she, though pleasant enough, was clearly of low origin, with no knowledge of courtesy or polite behaviour. The others were of all ages between the middle twenties and perhaps as much as thirty-five, and several of them, smiling upon being introduced, had blackened and decaying teeth (something common to a large proportion of Canadian ladies, even in polite society, perhaps – I know not – from some deficiency in their food or drink?).

I can indeed best describe the stable by saying that it contained a selection of ladies who in London would have been working in the streets around Soho or Seven Dials, and certainly would never find their way into anything but the lowest houses of entertainment. Indeed, Mr Bradley's list of prices seemed to me now to be based upon creative imagination rather than any reality.

Having greeted the ladies courteously, I asked to see the

separate rooms. These proved to be furnished only with
hard beds, not even a looking glass or couch to add interest – and what was worse, no means at all of aiding cleanliness, as in the provision of bowls and water – something
essential to the healths both of the ladies and their visiting
gentlemen.

Upon consideration, I now guided Miss Bradley and Mrs
Thomas once more into the latter's room of business, where
I asked on my friend's behalf to see the books. These, being
produced, appeared in excellent order, and revealed that
the house took upwards of $80 a week and possessed a
capital of over $1,500, which had accumulated during the
past four months. This seemed a great deal to me – but on
my questioning Mrs Thomas, it turned out that the ladies
received only a tiny proportion of the fees paid for their
services: for ordinary congress, for instance, of the 50 cents
charged, they received only ten! – while should two ladies
be engaged to pleasure the same gentleman, of the sum of
$2 asked, they received only 25 cents apiece! This propor-
tion had been fixed by Mr Bradley, who had certainly been
a keen man of business; and the relatively indifferent quality of the ladies kept by the house was now explained.

Asking Mrs Thomas to leave the room for a moment, I
proposed to my friend that she should make a clean sweep:
that she should propose to give each lady a present of $50,
retiring them; this, supposing that it contented them, would
still leave her with a considerable sum to refurbish the
rooms and to engage an entirely new selection of ladies,
which I would certainly help her to recruit. Mrs Thomas, I
suggested, might for the present be retained, and an
increase in her no doubt modest income would ensure that
she would be open to tuition.

She at once acquiesced, and upon summoning Mrs
Thomas we put our proposals to her. She was clearly
startled by the magnitude of the sum we proposed to offer
the ladies; it was clear that for her part, and certainly Mr
Bradley's, they would simply have been turned off without

a penny! And on her own account (when, enquiring, we found that she had continued to draw from the funds the small sum of $3 weekly, which together with accommodation had been her reward under the previous owner) she was delighted to be offered $5 per week, to be paid from this date, and to continue during the period when the house would be closed.

We lost no time in returning to the shabby sitting room, where the 'girls' were waiting dejectedly, clearly expecting the worst. Upon hearing our news, their spirits were lifted in a moment, and they seemed more than contented, immediately setting about collecting their few belongings together and quitting the house (for we had sent Mrs Thomas immediately to the bankers to obtain sufficient money to pay them off that very morning).

While Miss Bradley was out of the room, looking below stairs – where were disused kitchens and servants' quarters – the youngest of the ladies came to me, and while professing herself entirely satisfied with the money offered her, asked whether she could not persuade us to retain her services. She was, she said, alone in the world, and with no friends; her only life had been in the house, and she would not know what to do were she to be turned onto her own resources.

'The others, they will retire,' she said – in what I admit to be a delightful French accent; 'but me, I shall not know where to turn – and I am good at my work, and not unattractive to the gentlemen –' At which she immediately loosed a button at her neck, and offered me her upper person, as it were for an inspection. She was younger, I saw, than I had thought – perhaps as little as seventeen – and her figure was certainly shapely, though to me, whose tastes were perhaps more singular than those of the usual customers of the place, she would have been more attractive had not her breasts and shoulders been smeared with some substance which closely resembled coal dust.

However, perhaps something could be made of her,

for though her address was rough and her appearance little short of slovenly, some men prefer this to cleanliness and the more ladylike deportment and appearance which is my own personal taste; added to which she was not unappealing, her little *gamine* face attractive, and her teeth, at least, admirably white! I therefore suggested that she should leave her address and that Miss Bradley might offer her an opportunity upon the house reopening; she should say nothing to the others, and (I suggested) should use some of the money she was about to receive to buy a new wardrobe.

On Mrs Thomas's return, the ladies received their payment and left; Mrs Thomas herself was informed of our plans, which knowledge she received without enthusiasm, but upon my explaining that much enhanced charges would be made upon the visitors, so that the profit would be considerably increased, was much cheered. Miss Bradley and myself then left, and over lunch at a nearby tavern I promised to make some notes for the reconstruction of the house, and to attempt to seek out some way of recruitment of a new staff; while she, I suggested, should give some thought to the decoration (though, privately, I considered that I would have to take a hand there; for how could a lady entirely virgin know what was most needful in the preparation of rooms in which the satisfaction of male lust was the only criterion?)

I spent the afternoon in my room at the Hyperion Hotel, setting down on paper my proposals, which included the provision in certain rooms of conveniences for bathing (in circumstances which would permit of several people being accommodated at one time); and on a sudden idea, rang the bell, at which, after a short interval, Lisette appeared, greeting me with the most tender embrace, which included the thrusting of her hand into my bosom, and her giving an inspiriting pinch to one of my tits!

While this would normally have set me on, I gently repelled her, and said that I had a proposition to put to her which I hoped would not offend, and first described to her my meeting with Miss Bradley and her subsequent story. She was, I said, totally without knowledge or understanding of matters of love – something Lisette clearly found it difficult to credit, so that I was compelled to relate the passage which had occurred between us, which reduced her to laughter, but convinced her.

Mrs Thomas was, I said, clearly an excellent businesswoman, but I doubted whether she had either the capacity or the instinct to conduct a house which could compel the regular attendance of the kind of gentleman she should aim to attract. Would she, Lisette, consider (I asked) leaving the hotel, and for a regular sum which should be as generous as could be contrived – and would increase as the business increased – supervise the house?

But, she demurred, she had no experience. To which I replied that her conduct clearly showed the keenest aptitude for the kind of supervision necessary – and that she would not be compelled to offer carnal connection to any gentlemen except at her own wish, her duty being merely to tutor the girls in the kind of hospitality which she had offered me.

In short, she agreed; and our talk had heated us so that rather than the handshake which concludes such agreement between gentlemen, we were in no short time clad as Adam and Eve, and engaged in that activity for which (if some theologians are to be believed) that energetic pair were by divine fiat rendered homeless.

After an engagement so gratifying as to confirm my offer to her (if that were needful), and after we had together made use of the bathroom which at the Hyperion Hotel is attached to each bedroom – something which even in London is uncommon – I took some refreshment, and then set out for the theatre.

Yes, Frank, the theatre; for to my surprise one existed in the city, though it turned out to be an unhandsome barn of a place – but the advertisement of a company presenting a comic and lascivious masque, *Chances*, as originally

devised by his Grace the Duke of Buckingham, tempted me
to take a seat at the enormous expense of 75 cents! – which
proved to be in one of the side boxes.

I must admit to attending as much from curiosity as from
any desire to see the performance offered; so it was somewhat to my relief (though also surprising) that I found the
title was merely an excuse for a masquerade, the bare bones
of the piece only being recited, while the scenes were made
an excuse to provide tableau after tableau of young ladies in
costumes as revealing as was possible without the intervention of the city watch, they being supported by a minority of young men similarly underclad, but behaving
towards them with decent respect.

Despite the pleasure of this, or perhaps because of its
relative decency, a certain restiveness manifested itself in
the box next to mine, where a large gentleman began to
shout an invitation to one particularly handsome young
lady first to remove her vestigial costume, and then to invite
a young gentleman who seemed attached to her to perform
an action which, while it might certainly give him some
pleasure, would be most likely to result in the company's
immediate dismissal from the city.

The noise from the next box becoming absurdly pro-
tracted, I saw a young man eventually enter it and
remonstrate with the occupant – who on getting to his feet
showed himself to be a man of generous physique, certainly
eighteen inches taller than the one who was attempting to
reason with him – who, shortly, he took by the collar and
lifted from the ground, holding him at arm's length, while
the gurgling noises which he made indicated some difficulty
in his continuing to breath.

I am not, as you know, Frank, a man of violence; neither
would I have been capable of dealing with the fellow in fair
fight, being myself of indifferently strong means. However, looking about me for a weapon and finding none
more conventional than a small table set at the side of the
box, I suppose to hold glasses of liquor, I took it up and

reaching over the barrier between our boxes, hit the fellow a blow upon the head which I hoped would incommode him.

He was stronger than I had expected, for the blow had no other effect upon him than to make him drop his first antagonist and turn to his second, grasping the table and sending it spinning into the body of the theatre, where it knocked down two elderly gentleman and a small boy.

I was preparing to defend myself as best I might, when the huge man confronting me suddenly fell forward across the barrier. The gentlemen who had been remonstrating with him lifted his heels and sent him falling the six or seven feet to the aisle below, whence he was carried forth, groaning.

The young man leaned across to take my hand in thanks – when to my surprise, instead he threw his arms about me and kissed me full upon the lips.

I drew myself up ready to explain that such thanks were somewhat overblown – when I caught sight of his face in the reflected light of the footlights, and in my turn embraced him. It was none other than David Ham who – you will remember from my previous chronicles (*Eros in the Country* and *Eros in Town*) – was originally a member of a theatrical company with which I was briefly connected in the country, and was of assistance to us when our London house was threatened by villains.

I need not say how astonished I was – my amazement being only equalled by his own, and by the pleasure we both took in this unexpected meeting.

It cannot be supposed that the performance detained me longer; David led me behind the scenes and into a green-room which was bare enough, but in which had been created a semblance of comfort by spreading a number of rugs over the worn couches which comprised the original furniture.

There, with the distant sound of the music accompanying the entertainment barely audible, he gave me his news – which was, in sum, that tiring of London and his work at the theatre there, and his bosom friend Sir Philip Jocelind having decided, unexpectedly, to marry, he concluded that there was some interest to be found and perhaps a fortune to be made in the New World. So, with a sum of money he had saved, he procured his own passage and that of six young ladies and four gentlemen he had recruited from the boards of the theatre in which he had been working, some of whom had been persuaded to invest their own small fortunes in the venture.

But was there much profit, I asked, in that amiable display of faintly erotic dances which seemed to comprise the performance some part of which I had witnessed? Certainly not, he answered; but the concomitant business enabled the company to make a valuable profit. And upon my raising my eyebrow, he pointed to a note at the bottom of the programme which I had missed:

Any person (it read) *who wishes to have the pleasure of conversation with a lady or gentleman of the company, may do so upon application to Mr Ham at the stage door at the conclusion of the evening, when the payment of a small contribution to the expenses of arranging a meeting will lead to the desired result.*

'Does this,' I enquired in mock sternness, 'mean what I believe it to mean?'

By way of reply, young David (who was still only in his early twenties) inserted his hand between my thighs and gave my accoutrements an affectionate squeeze – which caused no offence only because I was familiar, as a result of past adventures, with his predilection for the company of gentlemen, while he knew that my own taste was invariably for female company.

I now entirely understood the situation, and asked whether it was financially a happy one.

'So much so,' he replied, 'that after eighteen months here touring the chief towns of the country, we are in our last two weeks before returning to London, our pockets a deal more laden! But what of you, my dear Andy?' – and I found it necessary to recount to him my adventures in Europe (which my readers may have learned from a previous volume, *Eros on the Grand Tour*, but which were at that time unpublished and unknown to my friend).

By the time I had concluded, the sound of applause came from the direction of the stage, and in a while the door opened and the ladies and gentlemen of the company entered, laughing among themselves and beginning already to remove some of their clothing – but pausing upon seeing David and myself in their green-room.

He introduced me immediately as a friend, and with a wink suggested that I should be offered due hospitality – at which a pretty blonde girl, the youngest perhaps of the troupe, without further ado came over and perched herself on my knee, immediately taking the lobe of an ear between tiny, pointed teeth and giving it an inspiriting nip.

David now disappeared – presumably to the stage door, in case of the appearance of custom; and the members of the company set to to remove their costumes, without regard to my presence – so that my eye was pleased with the appearance of fine bosoms, slender thighs and gracefully shaped rears – the latter positively inviting a caress which, when given, was received with all the goodwill attendant upon a compliment!

Within the next ten minutes, David's head appeared thrice around the door, and first two of the girls, then the most slender of the young men (to whom the word 'beautiful' rather than 'handsome' would best be applied), left the room clad only in a gown, presumably for an arranged rendezvous – which I was told was in a set of rooms in a house next to the theatre, to which a private corridor led, contrived by the builders; so that I imagined that from the time the place had opened, theatrical and amorous activity had been taken to be inseparable.

There was now a pause, when most members of the company, assuming that no more of them would be required further, took themselves off – though the pretty girl still remained upon my knee, and now contrived to climb out of her stage costume (of which indeed there was little) while disturbing only slightly her proximity to my person; and who then, the room being thoroughly warmed, remained entirely unclad, and by an impatient wriggling seemed surprised that I did not take advantage of the fact by more than the laying of my hand upon her bosom (which indeed I could not resist).

My backwardness was due merely to the fact that near by, in an armchair just opposite, one of the young gentlemen of the company still sat, rather sullenly drinking a glass of wine, a cloth negligently thrown over his privates; he showed no signs of moving, and his gaze being directed straight at us, I was reluctant to display my passion – for though I have no objection to the partaking of love in company, the coolness of his gaze was inimical to passion.

The situation was saved when David once more appeared, and striding over to the young man, and not minding either myself (who was familiar with his tastes) nor my companion (who I supposed shared the same apprehension) without preliminaries sank to his knees, removed the piece of cloth from the dancer's lap, and took his shrunken tool within his lips – which the young man received with equanimity and (as I saw when my friend lifted his head) even with enthusiasm.

David grinned in my direction, and winked.

'Betsy – take young Andy upstairs, will you? Jack and I will continue our business here! Old boy, I shall see you later . . .'

Betsy rose to her feet and placing a loose wrap about her, took my hand and led me to the door; which, by the time I had reached it, would have revealed to any casual person without the view of young David entirely devoid of clothing, and about to renew his embraces.

Up a stairway and along a corridor, my girl led me into the adjoining house, and threw open a door – which revealed a room equipped with a bed, on which she stretched herself, clearly inviting me to join her. About this, I had no hesitation, she having an oncoming disposition which called immediately for an equal response. I therefore set about divesting myself of my own dress, first shoes and stockings, then trousers – but as I pulled my shirt over my head, I clearly heard the door open, and speedily turned to present my buttocks to it while I drew my shirt on again, for fear of some respectable person entering and being offended by the spectacle of my upstanding weapon.

However, on looking over my shoulder, while holding my shirt tails to conceal what I did not wish to reveal, I discovered the two girls who I had previously seen leaving for their meeting with – as I had supposed – a customer. On seeing my surprise, one – a dark young person with frizzy black hair and a complexion not far from the Indian – laughed, and said their companions had proved gulls; and on my enquiring further Sylvie, as she was called, explained that it was an invariable rule with them that the sum asked for their services (which I believe was two Canadian dollars) was paid in advance; the two young men who had desired their company had proved not to have so much as two dollars between them, and had thus – since their lack of charm was such that the ladies felt disinclined to subsidise the encounter – been sent packing.

'Sam has done better, judging from the row!' said the other young lady, almost equally as dark, and known, I learned, as Moll. 'And we must no longer hinder you from pleasure,' said Sylvie, making to leave; but Betsy explained that far from being an ordinary boob, I was a friend of David's.

'Ah!' said Moll with a keen glance, 'then we mistook! We interrupt nothing, and may relax together' – whereon she and Sylvie, pausing only to relinquish their scanty clothing, joined Betsy upon the bed, clearly with no intention of leaving us alone. This, I could not let by, and explained that unlike our mutual friend, I was no butterfly, and that indeed I had been about to prove my virility to Betsy.

There was much laughter at this, and the girls, determined to amuse themselves at my expense, were soon gathered around me, playing at attempting to lift my shirt to examine – as they said – my credentials for making such a claim.

It is a strange thing that while we are all too ready to throw off our shirts under certain circumstances, in other situations we seem determined to retain them; and by some instinct, born of what instinct I know not, I was now set upon an undue decency. But they being three to my one, and perfectly my equal in tenacity, were naturally the winners, and very shortly – counterfeiting now, I must confess, a weakness rather more marked than was the fact, I found myself pinned on my back upon the bed, my head between Sylvie's thighs (who held my arms), my ankles in the charge of Moll, who spread them as widely apart as her arms could compass, and the main trunk of my body open to the examination of my first acquaintance, the cheerful Betsy, who had not to look too closely to discover the extent of my willingness to prove myself a man – but who now determined to provoke me by postponing the opportunity, preferring to tickle my tits with her tongue, to run her hands enticingly over my belly, and ignoring for the moment the item which reared its head below, to pass her hands beneath and, weighing my cods in her palms, to fondle and pinch and squeeze and rub them until it was as though she was stoking a fire.

At last, when in my extremity I found myself turning my head so that I could thrust my face into the accommodating lap of Sylvie, it was she who took pity on me, seeing more clearly than her friends the rolling of my eyes. Taking Betsy's hands, she pulled until perforce her friend was forced, if she was not to fall from the bed, to throw her leg across mine – when, Sylvie releasing my hands at last, I lost not a moment in lifting the lightest of the girls bodily and spearing her with my dibble – which action, from both her visual and audible expression of delight, gave her less pain than pleasure.

The two other girls, as with my hands upon Betsy's hips I

first lifted her then let her fall, the shiny and well-lubricated skin of my machine gleaming in the candlelight, burst into an unforced applause, and sitting one upon each side, their thighs pressed closely against my shoulders, implored Betsy herself to control her movements, for they required my hands for other purposes – and on their being relinquished, seized and carried them into their laps, where my experience no less than their eagerness enabled me to give them a secondary but no less considerable pleasure; and while it would have been incredible that we should all four have reached sublimity at the same moment, it was within half a minute that we were all able to claim a certain peace; and when the door opened to reveal my friend David, what he saw before him was merely a heap of quiescent limbs, embraced but devoid of movement – and with the lineaments of gratified desire clearly marked upon our faces.

After perhaps half an hour, we were sufficiently rested to clothe ourselves; and bade each other an affectionate farewell. I walked with David back to his lodgings, in a nearby street – and on the way asked him whether he was set upon returning to England the moment the company's activities in Quebec were completed. No, he replied. And what of the young ladies? He affirmed that they too would no doubt go whither profit best led them.

I then described to him, in brief, the predicament of Miss Bradley, and my attempts to resolve it. Would it not be possible, I asked, for him to be of assistance? He had seen something of our organisation in London, and knew the rules by which we worked; might it not be the case that the ladies would agree to employment, provided the profit was considerable? – and I supposed that that would be the case.

In short, he agreed; and on the following day, I spoke to Miss Bradley upon the subject. At first she was diffident; though she had learned to trust me, she clearly felt that association with another man would be improper – moreover, would he not be inclined to take advantage of her femininity? For I have to admit that her brief examination of my person had not inspired her with desire; indeed, she admitted that the prospect of *that thing* (as she called it) being placed in juxtaposition to any part of her body, or even of being naked abed with a man, was frightening to her.

I was able to explain that the problem would not arise with my friend David Ham – though here again was a difficulty, for she could not believe that there were men who went abed to other men, and was clearly eager to learn for what purpose – which it was neither the time nor the place to explain. However, in short I convinced her; and introduced her to David, who exercised all his very considerable charm upon her, and in no time had come into her favour; whereupon he went to collect his young ladies, who appeared as well dressed as any young woman on the streets of Mayfair, and therefore considerably superior to those on the streets of Quebec – at least in those days.

I then made my apologies, and claimed that I must move on to an appointment in Montreal – which was not the case; but I had no desire to spent more time than I had already lost in assisting the setting up of Miss Bradley's house. So promising if I was able to look in upon them before returning to England, I took my leave with a polite kiss upon the lady's hand, a warmer embrace of my friend, and a friendly caress for the girls. Back at my hotel, it was with keener regret that I said goodbye to the delectable Lisette, who would, I was confident, very shortly prove the chief attraction of the house she was to ornament with her presence. I then took myself to the steamboat for which I had taken a ticket, and took possession of a berth in the gentlemen's cabin, setting out upon a journey a description of which I will necessarily postpone until my next communication.

Chapter Six

Sophie's Story

The inhabitants of Cincinnati must have concluded, during
the following days, that I was uncommonly fond of the
study of art, for I retraced my steps more than once to the
picture gallery, where M. Vert, that most elegant of
Arians, was pleased to preside over my further study of the
postures illustrated in his private collection – from time to
time indeed taking upon himself the duty of proving (which
I at first doubted) that some of them were capable of attain-
ment by any lady and gentleman in good health, and whose
figures were not over-full.

However, my stay in the place was not to be so long as I
was beginning to believe would be pleasant, for one afternoon, upon my presenting myself, M. Vert enquired
whether I had many enemies in America. On my denying it,
and asking the reason for his enquiry, he told me that five
minutes after my last leaving the gallery, a tall, dark man
with deep-set eyes – 'like those of an eagle' – had knocked
upon the door and enquired where I was lodging.

'I mistrusted his intention,' said the monsieur, 'and told
him that I had no notion, asking why he made the enquiry;
his refusal to tell me, together with the tone of his voice
when he spoke of you, encouraged me to believe that he was
no friend.'

M. Vert's description made it clear to me that the stranger was none other than M. de Cournville – and I explained
the circumstances under which we had met.

M. Vert looked grave, and asked whether I had any idea
of the seriousness of someone's aiding two slaves to

escape – and whether they were still with me. Indeed they were, I said, and I was determined to protect them from any attempt to return them to a place in which they had been unhappy.

'Then you have no other recourse than to leave this town as swiftly as possible,' he said; 'for there are few here, if any, who would sympathise with or even understand your motives – and the circumstance being known, could by no means guarantee that violence would not be offered to you. The two black persons of whom you speak are in any case, I fear, doomed to be apprehended, and it would be wise for you to leave them to their fate, for they will be nothing but trouble to you while you remain their protector.'

I swore that I would never desert them; whereon M. Vert, after some attempt to change my mind, capitulated – and at my request sent to the steamship company to commission a passage for myself and my two servants to the town of Wheeling. He was then good enough to walk himself to my house, inform Tom and Susan of my plan – without unnecessarily alarming them by telling them the reason for its suddenness. And in short, by three o'clock we were on board the *Lady Franklin* – the name of which gave me, as you can imagine, some pleasure! This was the finest boat, by far, that I had yet seen; and from its rail as it set forth, with a grateful wave to M. Vert, I bade farewell to Cincinnati.

Tom and Susan were accommodated decently below decks, and my own cabin was perfectly adequate. In front of it an ample balcony sheltered by an awning ran the length of the vessel; chairs and sofas were placed upon it, and almost all the female passengers passed the whole day there, since the weather was delightful, admiring the beauties of the river Ohio.

A most strange condition of travelling on these steamboats is that the gentlemen and the ladies are, by law, firmly separated or segregated: of the male part of the passengers we saw nothing excepting at the short silent periods allotted for breakfast, dinner and supper, when we were permitted to enter their cabin, on the deck immediately below ours, and to place ourselves at their table. There, silence was observed; nor indeed were there many gentlemen to whom I felt inclined to speak – excepting one, who sat two places away from me and on the other side of the table, opposite a handsome young American addressed as 'Lady', though in reality she was the daughter of a tavern-keeper (but it is the habit of the Americans, especially in the south, to dignify their ladies with the title, just as many men are addressed as 'Colonel' or 'Major' who clearly have no shadow of right to such an address).

I must confess that I found this young gentleman most attractive: but his attention was all upon the young lady, who from her coy flutterings, though no words were uttered, also seemed fixed on him; and at supper on the second of our three days aboard, I was intrigued to see her slip what was clearly a secret missive into his hand, under guise of passing him the salt.

However, the intrigues of others were none of my business, and I retired to bed, in due time, after a glass of Bourbon whisky, which I found a pleasant soporific.

I slept with the window of my cabin wide open; after Susan had left me, looking out of it, I saw the light reflected from the row of windows below, belonging to the cabins of the gentlemen, and with my curtains drawn back in order that the bright stars of the dark sky could be seen from my bed, I lay for some time wakeful, pondering whether the egregious M. de Cournville would follow us further – when I saw a movement at the window, and in a moment, a dark head and shoulders appear in silhouette.

I almost cried out – but refrained, for it seemed to me that I recognised – as the man drew himself up from below – the form of the gentleman who I had observed at dinner; and I must confess that it immediately occurred to me that he was keeping a tryst with the lady of his admiration; but keeping it in the wrong cabin!

My suspicion was confirmed when, not hesitating for a moment, he came straight to my bed and, bending over and taking my head in his hands, he pressed a kiss upon my lips, with the breathed words: 'Oh! dearest Emily!'

What was I to do, brother? Would it not have been excessively unkind to have revealed myself and sent him away? That would (or so I told myself) have been dangerous on several counts – not only that he would have risked life and limb once more in an attempt to find his sweetheart's cabin, but would also have risked discovery and therefore prosecution under the ridiculous laws laid upon us by the steamboat's owners!

Besides, it must be admitted that he was extraordinarily handsome, and I found it impossible to dissuade myself from discovering whether his true form, beneath the fashionable clothes in which I had seen him dressed, was as fine as seemed promised. I therefore returned his kiss with a responsive play of my tongue, and discovering upon embracing him that his upper body was devoid of covering, set myself to unloosing the remainder of his clothing – discovering that he was protected only by the loose covering of short linen drawers – the first of which I had had experience, and which are worn by some young gentlemen in America (modesty here being more marked between the sexes, even in the most intimate of circumstances, than in Europe).

These did not detain me long, being tied only by a loose cord which, upon my pulling it, came immediately undone, so that it was no difficult task to slip them about his knees – whereupon something strong yet pliant struck my forearm a blow, which I took to be what it was, and therefore, bending, applied my lips to it, determined to see whether I could rouse it to a more adamantine strength.

This was not difficult – and the pleasure my caresses afforded was clear from the gasps, which seemed somewhat of surprise (from which I guessed that my visitor found his partner somewhat more responsive than he had anticipated).

By now he had thrown back the bedclothes, discovering

the truth – that I found it unnecessary to dress myself for sleep; and had already fixed his lips to those pleasant knots which, at the centre of my breasts, revealed by their rigidity that my enthusiasm for the game was equal to his own.

It is sometimes the fact that a particular body, placed in intimate juxtaposition to one's own, will for no particular reason rouse one to a frenzy of desire lacking in contact with another quite as handsome. Such was now the case, though I would be at a loss to tell why – for though slim and muscular, as far as I could tell in the darkness there was no special attribute of the gentleman's person upon which he need be specially commended: everything was present – *viz.*, two arms, two legs, and between them machinery concomitant to desire; but nothing extraordinary. Yet as soon as he had released me from the bonds of the bed-clothes, I found myself turning to face him, and throwing my legs about him, placing my person immediately and with the utmost eagerness in juxtaposition to his own, so that without its penetrating the ajacent aperture, I could feel his instrument eagerly pulsing, and on my grasping his behind, he made an almost unconscious movement which betrayed his desire for even more intimate contact.

'Ah! Emily! – Emily! – my own! – how eager you are!' he gasped, kissing me again – whereat I could no longer wait, and with a single motion withdrew my body just sufficiently to enable him to slip his engorged tool into its proper receptacle, at which he began to buck in earnest, at the same time raising himself so that he could grasp my breasts with his hands, his thumbs exerting upon my nipples a pressure that in other circumstances would have been positively painful.

My instinct that this was no common young man was soon confirmed, for while I had sadly anticipated a speedy *dénouement*, this was certainly not the case, his movement, regular and spirited, continuing for so long that, raised beyond the pitch of expectation, I found myself uttering a sort of catlike yowl – and upon his placing his hand over my mouth, fixed my teeth in its palm, only at the last moment realising what I was doing, and sparing him a painful bite, at the moment when I felt those throbbings of his lower body which accompanied the discharge of his passion.

Yet even then, though his action slowed, he continued his movements, now bending to kiss me again; and following the gesture I felt his tongue upon my eyelids, then following the whorls of my ears (a most extraordinary sensation), then tracing the line of my jaw, falling to the neck, and running upon my breasts – while, all the time, the same regular motion of his hips moved his instrument within me, the firmness of which, though somewhat less dense, was still sufficiently lithoid to give pleasure.

Any desire I might have had to conduct a more thorough exploration of his person was vain; he did not for a moment withdraw himself from me, and even those caresses I was able to give to buttocks, thighs, or cods seemed to give him no pleasure additional to that which he received from the simplicity of the act of love itself. Nor do I complain, for my own pleasure quickly revived, and in short was twice more roused to the height – as was his own – before (and I really think from physical exhaustion rather than from any desire to cease the activity) he gave me a final kiss, and withdrawing his now considerably diminished limb, turned me to lay my body at length upon the couch, and with a whispered: 'Goodnight, my Emily!' crept to the window and lowered himself from it.

I awoke some hours later to find Susan at my side with a dish of chocolate and an interested smile. On seeing me awake, she became sober; but when I sat up, I saw immediately the reason for her amusement – the pair of drawers, clearly from their size and shape those of a gentleman, upon which my head had been lying.

I offered of course no explanation; but instead instructed her to wrap them in some paper, and put them aside. The rest of the day I was glad to spend in relaxed ease – leaving the balcony only for meals, at which I noted that the adulatory glances directed at his friend by my lover were met by stony indifference and even an appearance of offence – which the gentlemen clearly found difficult to understand, but of which I believed I could offer an explanation.

That night, my lover did not reappear – but my pleasure had been such that I was not disappointed. The following morning, as we approached the town of Wheeling, we all went in to breakfast. Taking the small package with me which contained the gentleman's clothing, I waited until the meal was almost over and his friend had left the table, I suppose to complete her packing. I then instructed the steward to hand him the parcel, but not to reveal the identity of the sender. Undoing it, he recognised the contents only in time to prevent him from displaying its nature to those ladies and gentlemen who were still at table. His amazement and bewilderment were immediate; I have rarely seen anyone so surprised – and his gaze, sweeping the table, rested upon one elderly American lady after another, then upon myself – and I flatter myself I was the only person he seriously suspected. Yet it was impossible for him to accuse me, both for fear that he might be wrong and offend an innocent party, and for fear of a scene. As we left the steamboat, I saw him handing his friend from the gangplank with the utmost solicitation. I hope that their relationship was not destroyed by my innocent prank.

Wheeling is in the state of Virginia, and appears to be a flourishing town. It is the point at which most travellers from the West leave the Ohio to take the stagecoaches which travel the mountain road to the Atlantic cities. Here, we took tickets for Little Washington.

This was the first time I got into an American stagecoach, and it was with some interest that Susan and I climbed into the vehicle by ladder (it had no step) while Tom mounted to the roof. The coach had three rows of seats, each calculated to hold three persons; and as we were only six, we were for some miles tossed about like a few potatoes in a wheel-barrow. Our knees, elbows and heads required too much care for their protection to allow us leisure to look out of the windows, but at length the road became smoother, and we became more skilful in the art of balancing ourselves so as to meet the concussion with less danger of dislocation.

We then found ourselves travelling through a very beautiful country, essentially different in its features from what we had been accustomed to around Cincinnati. All we saw of Little Washington, which is in Pennsylvania, was the hotel, which was clean and comfortable. The first part of the next day's journey was through an uninterrupted succession of forest-covered hills: as soon as we had wearily dragged to the top of one of these, we began to rumble down the other side as rapidly as our four horses could trot; and no sooner arrived at the bottom than we began to crawl up again, the trees constantly so high and thick as to preclude the possibility of seeing more than fifty yards in any direction.

The Allegheny mountains, however, when we came to them, provided views of impressive beauty, with an almost incredible variety of plants in lavish profusion: magnificent rhododendron, azalea, sumac, kalmia; cedars of every size and form were above, around and underneath us; firs more beautiful and numerous than any I had ever seen; oak and beech, with innumerable roses and wild vines hanging in beautiful profusion among their branches; and the earth carpeted with various mosses and creeping plants . . .

At a point just before these mountains, a young man of perhaps thirty years of age had joined the coach, dressed in sober black, and carrying what was unmistakably a bible; the fact that he was addressed as 'Reverend' by the coach-man confirmed me in belief that he was of the cloth.

He was by no means unpleasant, however, and though he spent some time reading his book, did not hesitate to point out to me some of the beauties of the landscape. Clearly as fastidious as he was elegant, he had a kindly air, especially about the eyes. His face was of fine distinction, the jaw broad and firm, the mouth well-formed and smiling. He had clearly considerable knowledge of the plant life of the area, and went into rather more detail than I would ideally have wished, in his explanation of the botanical curiosities of the mountains. Having fixed him in my mind as a Virgoan, I asked him in time when his birthday was, and received the answer that it was September the second, which of course confirmed my suspicion.

It was something to my surprise when, on my enquiring this, he asked me in turn whether I was a student of astrology; and on my admitting it, and being prepared for those objections sometimes offered by the clergy, was as surprised as I was pleased when he clearly knew much of the subject, and on my suggesting that gentlemen of his persuasion were often against it, answered that to his mind this was absurd, and to my delight quoted the words of my ancient mentor William Lilly, in his *Christian Astrology*: 'The more thy knowledge is enlarged, the more do thou magnify the power and wisdom of Almighty God; strike to preserve thyself in His favour, for the nearer thou art to God, the purer judgement thou shalt give.'

It can be imagined that the rest of that day's journey passed speedily as we discussed the subject so dear to my heart – and I was sorry on two counts, at the end of it: first that I should soon be parted from my new friend, for he was leaving the coach on the following morning; the second that he was a clergyman, and so my hopes of adding a Virgoan to my list of captures were small!

The inn which we arrived at, in the mountains, was merely a forlorn parlour filled with the blended fumes of tobacco and whiskey, so that, though chilled, as we began to feel ourselves with the mountain air, we preferred going to our cold bedrooms rather than sup in such an atmosphere.

We found linen on the beds which they assured us had only been used *a few nights*, while every kind of refreshment we asked for met with the response 'We do not happen to have that article.' My friend, whose name was the Rev. Applegrass, remonstrated, and at least got the linen changed and a fire lit in the bedroom. But we were then told that there being only two rooms in the place, we would have to share – since I was the only woman in the coach, there was nothing else to be done, unless I spent the night upon a bench! As it was, Tom and Susan curled up together in a corner of the parlour.

I suggested, as the best solution, that the Rev. Applegrass should share my room with me, while the other four gentlemen should sleep together in the other room. This was agreed, and he kindly allowed me to go upstairs first, and undressing, to climb into the single – but large – bed. After a while, there came a knock on the door, and the Rev. Applegrass entered, my pretending to be already asleep.

He sat for a while before the fire, reading his bible by the light of the flames; then putting it down and glancing towards the bed, turned his back and began to unclothe himself. As he did so, my regret that he was a man of the cloth became more acute, for his body was that of a strong and healthy male, and it seemed a shame that it should not have the comfort of normal congress with womankind – though even as I thought it, the apprehension occurred that I knew not how strong any rule of celibacy might be in the New World.

He stood for a moment, the firelight flickering upon the length of his body, shadows making more delightful its appearance – almost that of a Greek statue – then turning, came to the bed and climbed softly into it, remaining towards its edge, well separated from the space I occupied.

I must confess that it was some time before I slept; I cannot claim to have been bereft of masculine company since my arrival in this country, but being abed with a man is ever for me concomitant with pleasure, and it seemed unnatural that it should be otherwise. However, he lay flat upon his back, his hands folded (as far as I could see) across his chest, and, I assumed, fast asleep. In a moment, I too slept.

When I awoke, whether minutes or hours later, I found to my horror that in my sleep I had rolled towards the Rev. Applegrass, and thrown out my arm so that not only did it lie across his body, but that in a gesture no less inexcusable for being unconscious, I was grasping in my hand that part of a man upon which, in such an embrace, it would normally have fallen.

I almost removed it immediately, with a startled exclamation – but the instinct was interrupted by the apprehension that far from being, as I would have expected, in a limp and pliant condition, the clergyman's weapon was ready for battle! What was I to make of this? Was it simply that it had risen in sleep, as often men's instruments do? Or could it be that he found my unconscious caress irresistible, and only refrained from that movement which would have revealed his state?

I can only suppose that he inferred, from some slight movement I had made, that I was awake; for at that moment I heard a groan escape his lips, and felt within my palm an involuntary movement which betrayed that his senses were far from dormant.

Here was a predicament! To have removed my hand peremptorily would be to insult the gentleman; to leave it where it was would be deception, for it would infer that I still slept; any motion of it was unthinkable without encouragement!

However, I was saved from the necessity for decision by the soft whisper of my name:

'Mrs Nelham, do you sleep?'

I answered, no – and took the opportunity to remove my hand, apologising for any impudence, which I assured him had been entirely accidental.

'No, ma'am,' he replied; ' 'twas natural, and anything natural must be right and to the glory of our Creator, who made man and woman for mutual pleasure, as well as for the enlargement of the creation. Indeed, it is my view that any man or woman who wishes to celebrate the fact that God made our sexes different is obliged to do so, as an act of praise.'

There was a silence.

'May I ask, sir,' I then said, 'whether you are married?'

'I am not, Mrs Nelham; nor would I encourage those who are fixed in wedlock to look for such activity outside the bridal bed, unless there should be serious disagreement between them. Even there, however, it is their bounden duty to delight in each other's bodies, and to neglect that necessary part of marriage is to sin.'

There was another silence.

'I am, as you know, a widow,' I said at last. 'So . . .'

'So there is no bar to our private act of celebration, should you feel happy in my suggestion,' said the Rev. Applegrass, raising himself upon his elbow, leaning towards me, and pressing a kiss upon my forehead. At this, I stretched out my hand once more, and found that far from shrinking to a size conformable with a theological discussion, the clergyman's person had if anything attained an even more resistant solidity, and at my touch leaped like (if I may coin the phrase) a young hart.

The next occurrence was the gentleman's raising himself from the bed and lifting away the bedclothes, so that in the light of the flames from the fire he could, kneeling above me, bathe me in the incandescent glow of his ardent gaze. I, too, was happy to examine his person, which when devoid of clothing presented itself in such a form as to seem that of an athlete rather than of a thinker, and which was so clearly ready to prove its effectiveness as an instrument for pleasing the female species that 'twould have even frightened, rather than delighted, a female of a more nervous disposition.

'If you will forgive me,' he said with a tremor in his voice, 'I have been some weeks without female company, and I fear that any attention I can give you will be but momentary. However, we have a long night before us, and . . .'

Without a sound, I simply nodded, and with a gentle touch persuaded him to lie beside me, whereat, taking his cods in the palm of one hand, and moistening the fingers of the other with saliva, I began gently to rub at the head of his tool, careful to avoid any but the mildest friction. In a moment this had its effect, not only in the groan which escaped his lips, but in the teardrops which fell from the tiny aperture beneath my thumb; to be followed by an involuntary jerking of his whole body as though in the grip of an epilepsy; and almost instantly by the eruption of a positive fountain of the nectar of life, which rose to such a height as narrowly to escape drenching me, and fell back upon his chest and belly with the sound almost of a shower of rain!

For a moment he lay relaxed, then began an apology – which I stopped with a kiss. On these occasions, I explained, I had found that the quickest possible release was what most certainly resulted in a speedy recovery of the faculties; and taking the sheet wiped his body, which already began to show signs of reawakening interest – and on my applying my lips, recovered him to a promising stature in almost as little time as it takes to write the words.

I have often observed that the most thoughtful gentlemen – for whom a simple slaking of the itch is impossible – make the most satisfactory lovers, and the proposition was proved yet once more on this occasion. Piling more wood upon the fire, the Rev. Applegrass mirrored its flames with a burning of his own, infectious in its enthusiasm and spirited in its performance. He lacked, it is true, the ingenuity of some of our European lovers – confessing to me later that 'twas the first time he had left a lady's lips upon his nether regions – on which I felt it my duty to convey to him some of the pleasure which can be given thereabouts by an intelligent and enthusiastic female; and on his enquiring, somewhat hesitantly, whether there was not an equal and opposite pleasure in the presentation of a gentleman's lips to the female parts, encouraged him to prove what I knew to be true – at which he proved himself naturally gifted.

In short, in what proved a long night, our only difference was when I presented my rump to him, and he mistakenly thought I meant that act which is committed in secret by those gentlemen whose taste is for their own sex; which he said was not to be performed between man and woman – though if God had laid upon a man the burden of love of his own image, it must seem a natural way of showing it. However, I was able to explain to him that I had merely meant that he should enter the proper portals from another direction, pointing out the freedom such a position afforded for the caresses of his hands – which he was quick to learn and adept to perform.

Susan, on bringing me a cup of dark liquid not tasting much of anything, found us the following morning happily and nakedly embraced, at which she was clearly surprised – but, good creature that she is (and by no means herself antipathetic to the game) by no means shocked. The Rev. Applegrass behaved to me as I would expect a gentleman to behave – that is, with tenderness and thankfulness in private, and in public with a deference and politeness that contradicted any evil thoughts; I was amused to overhear two of our fellow-passengers commiserating with me on having to share a bed with a parson rather than with themselves! – an emotion of which I was in honour bound not to disabuse them.

I shook hands with the Rev. Applegrass on his descending from the coach seven miles further on, at the town of Brownsville, where he was to preach. This was a busy little place built upon the banks of the river Monongehala, which we crossed in a flat ferryboat which very commodiously received our huge coach and four horses. The pressure of the reverend gentleman's hand here conveyed for the last time his admiration.

I will not recount in detail the rest of our journey through the Allegheny to Hagerstown and Baltimore, except to say that the inn at the former place was one of the most comfortable I ever entered: this confirmed that we had left Western America behind us, for instead of being scolded, as at Cincinnati, for asking for a private sitting-room, here we had two, without asking – and were summoned by a waiter to breakfast, dinner and tea, which were served with the greatest elegance.

On leaving Hagerstown we found to our mortification that we were no longer to be (as had been the case since Brownsville) the sole occupants of the coach, two ladies and two gentleman having boarded it with us when we started off at four in the morning. As the light began to dawn we discovered our ladies to be an old woman and her pretty daughter. Soon after daylight we came to a rough halt, and on enquiry found that one of our wheels was broken, and we would have to wait for some time before we could proceed.

On our being overtaken by the mailcoach, full of gentlemen, the old lady jumped up to the window and addressed the driver: 'Sir, can you not make room for the two of us? – My daughter will happily sit upon any gentleman who will offer!'

This observation was met by an uproar of laughter, and an offer from one gentleman to accommodate the young lady all the way to Baltimore; but the lady herself objected, to her mother's discomfiture.

Our wheel being at last repaired, we set off once more, the driver attempting by additional speed to recover lost time, in consequence of which our self-seeking old lady fell into a perfect agony of terror, and her cries of 'We shall be over! Oh, Lord! We shall be over! We must be over! We shall be over!' lasted until we entered the city of Baltimore.

Chapter Seven

The Adventures of Andy

The country which lies along the shores of the river between Quebec and Montreal seems sparsely populated, and is certainly less interesting than that which I had seen earlier. Within a few miles of the former place, the banks of the St Lawrence lose their steep and precipitous character, and become gently sloping and regular. The houses are small and poor, the churches less numerous; but there seem to be a number of farms, their lands stretching as far as the eye can see.

The steamship *Quality*, on which I had embarked, was one of no less than seven which regularly ply the river, and is quite the size of a forty-gun frigate, and fitted up in a most elegant manner. The main cabins are large enough to accommodate a hundred persons, with two rows of berths, one above the other; the berths have running curtains and excellent bedding. Gentlemen's and ladies' cabins are separated – but only sleeping facilities are purposely detached (and not always those, for the ingenuity of both sexes is great where the satisfaction of romance is in question).

Otherwise, the sexes mix quite freely, taking breakfast, dinner and tea in a common room, where servants of every description are in waiting and tables are daily laid out exhibiting all the delicacies of the season and every luxury this fruitful country affords.

It was clear to me within an hour of setting foot on board that the *Quality* provided every convenience which might be met with in the most respectable hotels in Europe – to a degree greater than those provided in most hotels ashore in this land – and at a very moderate price, for the charge to a cabin-passenger from Quebec to Montreal is only the equivalent of three pounds, including all necessaries and attendance, while that from Montreal to Quebec costs only £2 10s – the difference being accounted for by the fact that it takes about twenty-two hours for the latter journey, while the former can (in respect of the river's current) last as long as thirty-six.

Our progress to Montreal indeed was somewhat arduous, for in many parts the river offered some dangers, with shallows and rapids hindering progress. But the journey was so interesting to me that I minded its relative slowness less than some of the other passengers whose business was more urgent.

By the latter part of the afternoon, the *Quality* had reached the town of Trois Rivières, or Three Rivers, situated at the confluence of the St Lawrence and the St Maurice, where stand two small islands that divide the St Maurice into three channels, from which the place takes its name. The town, which is next in importance to Montreal, has about two thousand inhabitants, nearly five-sevenths of which are of French descent. Here, we came to anchor for the purposes of landing and taking in passengers and freight, and for receiving fresh supplies of fire-wood.

On hearing that it was possible to leave the ship for some four hours, when she would once more set sail, I was happy to take the opportunity to do so – for somewhat rashly I had spent the several hours of the voyage upon open deck, so interested was I in watching the passing show; and even under the awnings provided, the heat had been considerable, so that I hoped that a stroll about the streets of the town would provide relief – and that it might even be possible to find an hotel or other public place which would offer me an opportunity to bathe myself, this being (perhaps from reasons of space or the relative brevity of the voyages undertaken) the single convenience lacking on board the *Quality*.

Three Rivers I found to be a quite respectable place, containing a gaol and courthouse, a small barracks, and an extensive iron foundry which manufactures a large quantity of cast and bar iron (the place being extremely rich in ore). There were also two churches (one of the English Episcopal, one of the French Parochial persuasion), an hospital for the instruction of young persons of the Roman Catholic faith, and an hospital called the Ursuline Convent, for the instruction of young Roman Catholic ladies – from which I supposed the population to be an exceedingly proper one.

The single hotel was deserted, and the attendant whose attention I eventually commanded was either too disobliging or too stupid to respond to my request for a room with washing accoutrements; and the heat continued oppressive, so that by the time I found myself passing the walls of the hospital, I was in a muck of sweat, and seemed likely to remain so until I reached Montreal.

The walls of the hospital were tall enough to preclude the egress of any inhabitant, and indeed it resembled more a prison than a convent. The place stood upon the banks of the river, whence a somewhat cooling breeze now seemed to waft; and I followed the walls until I found myself upon that bank. Curiosity instructed me to attempt to view the grounds of the convent, for I thought I heard female voices within them; but at the point where the walls met the river, they were built out into the water before descending to meet it in a graceful curve, too far from the bank for any person to command a view past it.

I walked along the river by a path shaded upon one side by a thicket of trees; and hearing splashing and laughter, came soon enough into a small clearing surrounded by bushes, and passing a tree upon which a rough notice announced *PASSAGE INTERDIT AUX FEMMES*, saw piles of clothing lying upon the grass, and three young fellows sporting in the river shallows – which were remarkably clear and sparkling, and as inviting by their appearance as by their coolness.

Since the place appeared for public bathing, I was happy to remove my clothing and to spring into the water, which indeed was as welcoming as I had hoped, so that in a short time I was fully refreshed.

The three young men – of perhaps only a few years junior to myself – were engaged in tossing a ball one to the other, and soon involved me in their play, which I enjoyed, having for too long been deprived of the company of friends intent merely upon idle enjoyment. Perhaps six or seven minutes after we had been so employed, a bell nearby – perhaps from the convent? – struck the hour of five, and immediately one of the lads tossed the ball upon the bank, and the three of them began to swim off upstream.

In a moment, however, one of them glancing back towards me (who was simply floating on the calm surface of the stream) called out to his fellows, and they put their heads together, then with one accord beckoned me to follow them. Curious as to their intention and conscious of their goodwill, I struck out, and we swam along the bank until, coming to the place where the convent wall stretched an arm out into the waters, they held up their hands, and paddling like dogs, listened intently for a moment, one of them then whistling low in semblance of a birdcall – a sound which seemed repeated from beyond the wall.

The leader then cautiously approached the wall, and swimming to the end, peered around it, turned, and beckoned to us.

The lawns in front of the convent stretched right down to the river, and were at the moment empty – though one of the boys signalled caution to me; and indeed as we swam on to the further side of the grounds, where a number of trees and bushes met the water, a dark-clad figure, clearly one of the nuns in attendance, appeared from the house; on which, following the example of my peers, I ducked my head under the water and, holding my breath, swam on for as long as possible beneath the surface.

Breaking water with as little fuss as possible, I saw to my relief that we were now all in that part of the river shadowed by the trees and shrubs, and that the first of my companions was already climbing the bank, the water streaming from his naked flanks.

In a very short time, I had followed the two others, and found myself in a secure clearing. The boys threw themselves upon the grass in the sun, and following their example I found my cooled flesh very soon warming, and the beads of water vanishing from the surface of my skin.

But surely we had not climbed ashore here simply for the purpose of sun bathing (as it is called)? I must confess that it had occurred to me that perhaps there might be some connection between our escapade and the female inhabitants of the convent – or at least, those who were *in statu pupilaris*. And indeed, before long we heard the crackle of twigs underfoot, and into our sylvan glade tripped three beautiful young ladies, all clad in white, and resembling in their fresh young beauty spirits rather than humankind.

That fallacy however was soon dispersed. They were not in the least taken aback by the sight of four unclothed young men (though the fact that there were indeed four, rather than the three they had clearly expected, aroused a little surprise). With an alacrity which I could only applaud, they were quick to divest themselves of their thin lawn garments, and to appear clad only in the golden light of the sun.

Mr Leigh Hunt has been much ridiculed for his couplet

> *The two divinest things that man has got,*
> *A lovely woman in a rural spot*

yet there is surely some truth in it: I could not but admire the scene as the young ladies approached the gentlemen (who were clearly no strangers to them) and dropping to the grass at their sides, offered them greetings each in her own way – one by a simple kiss upon the lips, one by stretching her whole length upon that of her lover, and the third (whose wicked eye had already sparked off an answer in my own) simply by grabbing at his jewels in a manner which I must confess seemed to me to be merely avaricious.

However, the latter was clearly matched in eagerness by her friend, who having given her partner's baldheaded hermit a brisk massage and brought it to a stand, pulled him atop of her, whereat they not only presented to us the spectacle of the beast with two backs, but made him trot so such effect that the sound of their bodies smacking together was like a spirited applause.

The other couples were slower to join, preferring to compliment each other upon the various beauties of their persons – the young men bestowing kisses and caresses upon the breasts, thighs, flanks and posteriors of their partners, and the ladies returning the compliment with an eagerness yet a delicacy which was most admirable.

Who could have been unmoved by the scene? There the lovers lay, half in and half out of a sunlight more golden by the minute, as the majestic orb sank towards the horizon upon the western bank of the river; gilded flesh was dappled by the shadows cast by leaves, while the light lay like a patina, so that the bodies seemed to have been turned to animate gold by some friendly passing Midas.

My own discontent was, of course, that I had no partner. You will readily understand, Frank, that I was not unmoved by the spectacle – indeed within a minute my gutstick had risen and stood fully to attention with admiration and envy. Concerned that even young women so attentive to the game as these might find the sight of a strange man in such a state less than admirable, I turned upon my belly – only to find it necessary to cradle my person in my hand, its rigidity being such that my weight upon it was uncomfortable.

Closing my eyes, I attempted to think of other things; but what man has not found it difficult upon occasion to wrench his mind from the contemplation of the opposite sex? I despaired of any other form of recovery than the one left me, and was about to rise and make my way to some more secluded spot where mother fist and her five daughters could do my business, when I felt a gentle and certainly female hand upon my rear, and sensed a shadow upon me.

Opening my eyes, I found the tall, dark, most spirited of the three girls crouching over me. Not far away, her swain was lying upon his back, his figure now relaxed and pliant, his prick lolling upon his thigh like a drunkard having had his fill of liquor and rendered so unstable as to be unable to stand – a state to which satiety of another kind had reduced it. His mistress, however, was clearly less completely gratified, for now she gently encouraged me to turn upon my back, when the sight of my still taut instrument clearly pleased her, for bending she planted a kiss upon its very tip, while at the same time running her hands to and fro upon my sides, and spreading my thighs so that she could reach between them to take my eggs, one at a time, into her mouth, closing her lips to mumble them in the most animated manner and conferring a sensation gratifying to the utmost degree.

While far from wishing to discourage her, two things concerned me: the first, that her friend should disapprove of her conferring upon a stranger the favours he might reasonably expect to be kept for himself. However, a glance revealed that he had lifted himself upon his elbow and was regarding us with some interest, at the same time handling himself in such a manner that suggested he regarded our passage as one which might inspire him to a quick recovery of his own powers.

My second reservation is shared by some, though not all, gentlemen: the dislike of enjoying a buttered bun – which is what the lower orders call a lady who has too frequently lain with another. But in a moment it became clear that this dish was not to be offered to me – for having completed the first course, which was my bollocks, my friend had now turned her attention to the main dish, and holding my member at its root, was playing upon its length by running her lips along it, beginning with the most tender caress and ending with a flick of her tongue upon the summit, revealed by her having pulled back with her fingers the pouch of skin which normally concealed it.

At the moment when I was ready to explode with the pleasure of this caress, she paused for just long enough for me to recover somewhat from my excitement – and, I thought, in order that I should offer her a caress, so lifting my head I succeeded in capturing between my lips the tip of one breast as it swung above me, at the same time reaching up to lay my hand upon a back side which, though I had had no opportunity of close study, must surely be worthy of the compliment.

However, she was uninterested in anything I could do; for she took my hands not unkindly in hers, and returned them to my sides, now again bending her head, this time pursing her lips, all lustrous with ready saliva, and placing them upon the very tip of my piece, then, as she lowered her head still further, opening them so slowly that they offered a wonderful caressing resistance, sliding over the shining red summit, then forming a ready O about that circle beneath, where the skin was, through the intensity of my feeling, now so tightly stretched as to be almost painful.

No words could describe, dear Frank, the skill with which she seemed now to milk me of all passion; with deference to Lady Franklyn (of whose skill in these matters I am aware you will not need reminding) I must say that no other woman has come near pleasing me so intensely with the action of her lips alone; would that this young lady – whose name I shall never know! – had been available to us at our house in Brook Street; she would be worth her weight in gold could she be persuaded to pass on her skill to her professional sisters. However, that might not be practicable; for if one thing was clear from her every action, it was that it was performed for love rather than duty or – much less – gain.

To shorten my description, which can only provoke jealousy in the reader, I can only say that I was sweetly provoked to the edge of insanity by those lips; and had I not, in the extremity of my emotion, wrenched myself away and turned upon my side, the great fountain which erupted from my tormented body would have drenched that beautiful face (which, by the slight disappointment which I believe I discerned on the occasion, may even have been desired by her, so intent did she seem on every singularity of the game).

I had scarcely begun to gather my scattered senses together, when to my horror I heard the puffing of steam and the blowing of a whistle, and around the corner of the river came – the *Quality* itself! Unsurprisingly, I had not noted the passing of time, and she had sailed without me. Several emotions passed through my mind in the next seconds: but the fact which finally persuaded me to action was that all my clothes and possessions, including money and letters of credit, were on board!

At the recollection, only one course was open to me! Springing to my feet I ran naked as I was to the river bank and without hesitation dived in, striking out with all my vigour.

It might be supposed that my recent adventure would have resulted in a debilitation: but the opposite was true. The fact was that I had had no exertion at all, and that my relaxation had been entire; so that I now felt all my strength at my command, and by the time the vessel had approached, was almost in its path. Seeing and perhaps recognising me, the captain had reduced speed and stopped his paddles, and a net was thrown over the side, which I perforce climbed, all in my unclothed state, the water streaming from my flanks – and watched not only by gentlemen but a large number of ladies (to whom modesty was clearly an unknown quantity). Applause from them all greeted my attaining the deck, where a servant kindly threw a cloak about me.

As I turned to go below, I heard a piercing whistle from over the water, and turning saw my six erstwhile companions unashamedly showing themselves to the onlookers as they waved farewell!

This episode, Frank, taught me something no less about the habits and behaviour of some of the native young Canadians (and especially of the young women of a certain education, for whom emancipation is a word of some practical meaning) than about their attitude to the behaviour of others – for though it must have been clear to the passengers that the young people had gathered on the bank for other activities than a study of flora and fauna, no word of criticism was to be heard; and though it was equally clear that I had been entertained by them to an afternoon's social activity considerably more interesting than the taking of tea, no-one made any allusion to it – other than a few gentlemen congratulating me on the nature of my relaxation at Three Rivers.

The city of Montreal is in some respects a handsome one; in others somewhat strange, partly due to its oddity of situation, in that while it is some two miles in length, in breadth (between the river and the mountain which overhangs it) it is but three-quarters of a mile. The streets, apart from the main thoroughfares (*viz.*, St Paul-street, the chief mercantile street, and Nôtre Dame-street, where the principal merchants reside) are in general very narrow, and the sidewalks or pavements obstructed by a great many sets of wooden steps, which force walkers-by upon meeting even a single person coming in the opposite direction, either to retrace their steps or to descend into the channel, probably to their ankles in mud.

However, the chief buildings are handsome, and at the hotel to which I was directed (built, as I understand, by the late director of the Montreal Bank) I found everything very fair and good.

On the morning after my arrival, I set out to see something of the town. The hotel could provide little information about it, except one poor map and a list of the principal buildings, which read like a shopping list – one French church, one English church, one Methodist chapel, one Presbyterian meeting-house, one courthouse with gaol, one bank, one college, one hospital, one barracks . . . So hearing that the place possessed a library, I made my way there, hoping to discover more intelligence.

I was surprised to find an admirable subscription library which belonged to a number of persons who took up shares to form a capital for the purchase of books and a building for their reception and preservation. It contains about eight thousand volumes, and I had no difficulty in discovering one which allowed me to form an adequate picture of the place.

In order to study this, I was shown to a seat in an elegant reading room, where besides myself there was only one other person – an elegant lady of middle years, who was studying a number of French magazines which contained, as I could not help but observe, numerous fashion plates.

On finishing my study and taking some notes, I closed the volume; and on doing so, caught the eye of the lady, who smiled and enquired whether I was new to the city? We exchanged cordialities, and she asked whether she might not walk with me along the way – which took us past Nelson's monument at the head of the New Market almost opposite the Courthouse.

It being past mid day, I could not but offer my new friend some luncheon; which she was pleased to accept, and guided me to a coffee-house nearby, where we sat down to an excellent pie and a bottle of French wine.

Madame Fonteuille, as her name proved to be, was a lady of some fascination, tall and slim and very dark, her eyes a beautiful bottle-green, encircled by a deep purple halo which gave them exactly the appearance of emeralds set in sapphire. She proved to be a Canadian of the first generation, her parents having come to that country some thirty years before from Paris; so that, she said, she felt a kinship still with Europe. Nevertheless, she said, Montreal was a place of some interest, though in some respects too free in morals for many of the travellers who found their way there from the old countries.

In what respect was this so, I enquired? Whereat, though at first clearly hesitating lest I should be shocked, she gave me my first lesson in the social behaviour of the typical Canadian woman.

The first thing to remember, she informed me, was that women were in extremely short supply in this country: the number of male emigrants who annually arrive in every part of the continent is, to that of females, as three are to one. Woman are therefore a scarce commodity, and the scarcity of any article necessarily enhances its value and increases the demand. One result of this is that though Canadian women make good wives, they insist upon their freedom, and it is thought rather derogatory that a husband should refuse to allow a neighbour a participation in his wife's affections. Indeed, women think it improper to tie down their affections to a single object: universal love, as well as universal suffrage, is the order of the day – and heaven have mercy on any man who is married and is not willing to recognise this as sound doctrine!

Yet Canadians marry early – even as young as seventeen or eighteen on the part of the man, while a bride of fifteen is by no means unusual. Nor do they think it necessary that their parents should approve their choice: a young girl regards herself from the age of womanhood as independent and capable of making her own choices – and does so on the basis of what is known as *sparking*, often initiated as much by the woman as the man.

But what did that strange term denote, I asked?

Well, said my informant, it started with a young man setting his eyes upon a girl whose company he fancied he would enjoy. Discovering, by some means, her address, he would then knock upon the door and introduce himself as a bachelor, when if he was of reasonable appearance he would immediately be invited in, and would be entertained by the entire family, and then at the approach of evening permitted a private interview with the young lady. This was for the purpose of asking whether she would condescend to allow him to repeat his visit on the next or some subsequent evening.

If her affections were free, she would no doubt grant the appointment; and on that appointed evening he would again arrive, to be received with marked attentions, and given food and drink. Soon after tea – or, as they call the afternoon repast, 'supper' – is over, the family retires to rest, leaving the hero and heroine in full possession of the supper-room, in which for the convenience of such visitors a bed invariably occupies one corner. In this apartment they continue till morning.

And did they . . .? was it common that . . .? I found it difficult to express to the lady the question that was uppermost in my mind.

How they spent the night, she said, whether in laying plans for the prosperity of their future progeny, philosophising on the most approved method of increasing the population, or enquiring into the origins of the passions, she was not competent to say. However, provided they were mutually satisfied with each other's conduct during the night, a wedding was sure to follow.

It seems also to be the case that the gentleman takes the occasion to enquire about the lady's former lovers, and the reasons why she was not united with any of them! – and that if he is dissatisfied, he simply leaves without any kind of apology, and is never seen again.

I must confess that my conversation with Madame Fonteuille seemed to me to say little for the virtue of Canadian womanhood – and when I remarked as such, she said she was bound to agree – if my measure was based on the behaviour of the ladies of Europe. On the other hand, she insisted that the state of affairs here is much more favourable to the happiness of the majority – and that the

European idea of what is moral is here regarded as the wild effusion of moralising enthusiasts who pay more attention to the theory than to the calm consideration of the subject. At all events, it is certainly the case that the violation of chastity, with consent but without marriage, is not here considered a crime of the first magnitude, that an unmarried female with a baby in her arms is as much respected and as little obnoxious to public opinion as is a virgin; and that adventurousness in a married woman is considered more a signal of spirit than of a debauched character – it being usually the case that a man or his wife generally finds means to unbind the chains of matrimony ere a dozen months have succeeded their honeymoon!

I cannot answer for any other man, but the above conversation – and with a woman I had only just met – rendered my sensibilities warm; and Madame Fonteuille being an extremely attractive woman, I saw no reason why my desires should not be prosecuted, and to that end took the liberty of placing my hand upon her thigh, beneath the table, and by the slightest pressure indicating my intentions.

Upon this, however, she rose to her feet, and with the utmost politeness indicated that she was on her way to an encounter with another gentleman, and that while she would otherwise have been delighted to test the staying-power (as she put it) of an English gentleman, she would accept the compliment while declining the invitation. However, if I was in need, there were, I could be assured, many ladies in the town who would be happy to entertain so handsome a specimen of European manhood as myself.

I must confess, Frank, that I searched her visage for any sign that her compliment might be a false one; but could find none. At all events, our parting was polite enough – though during the three days I continued to reside in Montreal I must confess that my eye failed to fall upon any lady the seduction of whom would be anything other than a punishment, with the result that upon my taking ship for

Toronto I was in a state of excitement which, had I remained longer or been devoid of the hope of better things, would even have reduced me to falling upon the wife of a Bishop – which perhaps even in this country might have been regarded as somewhat impolite, however great the resulting satisfaction to both parties!

Chapter Eight

Sophie's Story

The approach to Baltimore announces it at once as one of the handsomest cities in the Union. The noble column erected to the memory of Washington, and the Catholic cathedral with its beautiful dome, are seen at a great distance, and as one draws nearer many other domes and towers become visible so that you feel you are arriving at a cultivated and almost European city. Tom and Susan were in a positive ecstasy, never having seen anything so wonderful; I wondered what they would say could they set eyes upon Paris or Rome!

I took up quarters at the excellent Barnum's City Hotel, where the coach stopped, and since they were courteous not only to me but to my servants, decided to stay there while I took the measure of the place.

Baltimore has several handsome buildings, and even the private dwelling-houses have a look of magnificence, from the abundance of white marble with which many of them are adorned. The ample flights of steps and the lofty door frames are in most of the best houses formed of this beautiful material. There are several pretty marble fountains in different parts of the city, which greatly add to its beauty – and one in particular, sheltered from the sun by a roof supported by light columns, which looks positively like a temple. Here you descend to the spring by one flight of steps of delicate whiteness, and return by another: these steps are never without groups of negro girls, all dressed with strict attention to taste and smartness; I could not but notice that they were from time to time approached, with great politeness, by white gentlemen who appeared to be of rank, and who then offered them an arm and escorted them away from the place; from which I assumed that they were a kind of courtesan.

Two days after my arrival, when I had exhausted what the city had to offer in the way of churches and other buildings of repute, I took the advice of a lady at the hotel, and drove out to the fort which is nobly situated on the Patapsco river, two miles from town, and from which there is a fine sight of the Chesapeake Bay.

I rode out in a hired carriage, with Tom mounted proudly behind as postboy, and only lacking a post-horn to complete the picture. He was by now as devoted to me, I believe, as he was to Susan (though I need not say that our intimate familiarity had not been repeated, nor had he offered the least impertinence – being, as I observed many of his people are, a natural gentleman with an instinctive regard for the feelings of others).

The carriage being parked at some distance from the fort, we walked along a most beautiful verdured terrace which commands a wonderful view of the city of Baltimore, with its columns, towers, domes and shipping, and also of the Patapsco River, here so wide as almost to resemble a sea. The terrace is ornamented with an abundance of evergreens and masses of wild roses; and the place so romantic as to turn my thoughts to those loved ones from whom I am at present parted – not only yourself, dear brother, but our friend Andy, who must now be many hundreds of miles to the north of this place.

The terrace giving way in due course to a parapet and the gateway of the fort, I enquired of the sentry whether it was possible for me to enter the place, with its historic associations; he, however, simply continued to look straight ahead of him, evidently having been commanded to ignore the queries of impertinent civilians. I had the greatest difficulty in restraining Tom from offering him violence for a rudeness which was indeed only attention to his duty! – but at that moment a lieutenant appeared, and on my appealing to him, said that he would be glad to show me over that part of the fort which was open to the public. I therefore instructed Tom to return to the carriage and wait for me there, while I accompanied the gentleman within the gate.

He introduced himself as Lieutenant Savage, whose family was engaged in brokerage in the city, and who was himself embarked upon a career with the army – a career in which his smartness and alertness will no doubt confirm his advancement.

He showed me with diligence all those most interesting defensive parts of the fort, then escorted me to the battlements, from which there was an even more splendid view of the environs than that which I had enjoyed from the terrace. In my remarking on its attractions, he replied that indeed it was one of the pleasures of being stationed there that he could see, from the window of his room, the roof of the house in which he had been born, though this was many miles away.

We were at that moment passing the doorway of his room, which stood ajar, and on seeing me glance into it, he invited me to enter. It was bare, but perfectly adequate in its accommodation for a young man – with a small bed, a table and chair, a mirror upon a stand, and a cupboard the door of which, hanging open, revealed, stacked in it, cuirass and greaves and all the accoutrements of a ceremonial uniform.

Would there be, I asked, in the near future an opportunity to see the officers in their full fig? No, he replied; for that was worn only upon special occasions, of which the last had now occurred for six weeks.

Seeing my disappointment, he offered to show me the extent of the dress, and carried it from the wardrobe to the table, where I was able to test its weight and admire the perfect shine of the metal.

I was sorry, I said, not to be able to see him in all his glory – at which he offered, if I could spare a moment, to dress in the uniform, to satisfy my curiosity. I was, of course, delighted; and naturally turned my back while he stripped off his everyday garb, and buckled on his dress uniform. It was not by my contrivance that I had, in the mirror, a perfect view of his form during this operation – though I confess I did not hesitate to admire the muscular formation of his torso beneath his shirt, and those strong legs which, their dressing of brown hair thicker than is usual, supported what was clearly a fine body.

He made an elegant figure in his full dress, and on his clicking his heels I made a curtsy to him, and was glad to permit him not only to kiss my hand, but upon my not appearing displeased at the gesture, to take me in his arms and plant a yet warmer kiss upon my lips. The pressure upon my lightly-clad body of the cold metal was not entirely pleasant, however, and I could not resist a shiver; at which he enquired what was the matter, and on my informing him, answered that an easy remedy was available – and that he and his fellow officers, on returning from exercises which required them to wear ceremonial uniform, were given to betting upon who could divest themselves in the briefest time, he being usually one of the winners.

He then demonstrated his speediness in the matter, throwing off jackboots, cuirass, greaves, leggings, leather jacket in a moment – but going on to remove also shirt and stockings, thus (for he had not yet acquired the questionably sanitary and healthful habit of wearing underclothing) revealing himself at last completely naked, standing, arms on hips, so pleased with his speed, and laughing with such simple pleasure, that I could not resist joining him – at which he again took me in his arms, this time with no other sensation between us than the warmth of his unguarded flesh, and throwing me upon the bed showed himself almost as adept at divesting me of my clothing as stripping himself.

I cannot pretend that I obstructed him in this further exercise, for he was a noble young animal – his naturalness uncomplicated by any motive other than to enjoy physical pleasure – and though expecting no special skill in his performance, I was only too happy to be the object of his attentions, the filling of ten minutes of a summer's day in such activity not being in the least unpleasant to me.

All his parts being well proportioned, that indispensible part no less than the others, my expectation was at first fulfilled, then unusually delighted – for unlike so many young men, he was by no means over-quickly spent, and the ten minutes' pleasure I had expected was prolonged by at least three times that span.

As we lay bathed in the dew of each other's perspiration, I made bold to remark that he had contrived to prolong the act beyond that span of time more usual in one so young.

He replied with a piece of information which I record in case it may be of use to those of our young men at home who may be plagued with the difficulty of containing themselves beyond a brief period, and thus failing to satisfy those females with whom they lie, for it is a method which seems entirely efficient, though not perhaps entirely comfortable.

It was, my friend said, a habit common with the cavalry of his regiment (formed a generation ago) that to sharpen skill in horsemanship young officers should practise riding not only bareback (that is, without saddle) but themselves as naked as their steeds – thus instilling a perfect balance, and strengthening the muscles of the thighs to an extent which would enable them to remain mounted when others would be thrown off. (Passing my hand over his upper legs, I could confirm that the muscles knotted there were indeed of a remarkable density, and indeed were raised above the level of the flesh, giving the thighs a thicker appearance than is usual in the young male.)

This exercise, he could not deny, was unpleasant in winter, when frequently there was snow upon the ground, and the wind was almost freezing; but in the heat of summer the friction between the horse's back and the privates of their riders was far from unpleasant, and however they tried to resist, resulted in their rising to a stand, then giving up the essence of life within a minute or two of the order being given to trot on!

The sergeant-commander (as he was called) was used to this, and would allow no pause; by riding on, the sensations were renewed, and the occurrence again noted; so that by the end of a two-hour ride, the men were enervated and exhausted – but then forced to swim in the river for half an hour before resting. Within a remarkably brief space, their bodies had learned almost to ignore the friction, and their consequent resistance to the pleasure of the horse-flesh between their thighs had made it possible for them to retain their powers almost without the limit of time when in intimate connection with other, and – he said – infinitely more attractive flesh.

I could scarcely believe this story – but he insisted that it was true; and indeed I was able to confirm it, for I made an appointment to meet him upon his next day of freedom, when at my hotel, in an atmosphere much more comfortable and upon a bed much less hard than that at the fort, he entertained me for no less than three hours before himself giving way to the full extent of that emotion to which he had roused me several times.

After enjoying a very pleasant fortnight, the greater part of which was spent in rambling around this very pretty city and its environs, I left it, not without regret, for Washington. Though the shortest route both as to distance and time is by land, I much wished to sail upon the celebrated Chesapeake Bay, and therefore took tickets on a steamboat, and passed a very beautiful voyage, the vastness of the Bay indeed being remarkable, the entrance from it into the Potomac River very noble, and the passage up the river to Washington interesting beyond all else by the views it affords of Mount Vernon, the seat of General Washington.

I was fortunate to find accommodation in F-street (the streets that intersect the great avenues in Washington are distinguished by the letters of the alphabet). As to the city itself, the first sight that gratified my senses was of the Capitol, the beauty and majesty of which, with its magnificent western facade and remarkable terraces and steps, was indeed impressive.

I was delighted, indeed, by the whole aspect of Washington; light, cheerful and airy, it reminded me of our fashionable watering-places. From the base of the hill upon which the Capitol stands extends a street of most magnificent width, planted on each side with trees and ornamented by many splendid shops; this is called Pennsylvania Avenue, and is above a mile in length, culminating in the handsome mansion of the President. The total absence of all sights, sounds or smells of commerce adds greatly to the charm of the place. Instead of drays you see handsome carriages; and instead of the busy bustling hustle of men shuffling on to a sale of 'dry goods' or 'prime broad stuffs', you see very well-dressed personages lounging leisurely up and down.

Another matter which makes this city attractive to such as myself is the great majority of gentlemen. A very few of the members of government here have their wives with them, and at evening parties there is consequently great competition for the company of any ladies present!

I was invited by several gentlemen to attend the debates in Congress, where there is a gallery erected for the sole use of ladies; this was put to me as a great advance upon matters in England, where no woman is permitted within the walls of the mother of Parliaments. I replied however with what is the truth – that the reason why the House of Commons was closed against ladies is that their presence was found too attractive, and that so many members were tempted to neglect the business before the House that they might enjoy the pleasure of conversing with the fair critics in the galleries – so it became a matter of national importance to banish them!

I cannot say that my visit was greatly informative,

however, for the speakers could scarcely be heard from the gallery, which made it a labour to listen – though the extreme beauty of the chamber was itself a reason for attendance. I could wish, however, that the place, so splendidly fitted up, had commanded more respect from its members, who sat in the most unseemly attitudes, a large majority with their hats on, and nearly all spitting to an excess that decency forbids me to describe.

On one day I was invited, the galleries being shut up for the purpose of making some alterations, to sit upon the sofas placed between the pillars on the floor of the house itself. There, after a while, I could not but notice that I was closely observed by a gentleman sitting almost opposite me – clad in black frock-coat and wearing his top-hat. He was so fat as to be almost circular, with face so red and full as to be positively apoplectic, and a small grey goatee beard which was less a decoration than a mere mark of identity.

In a while, during a long speech by a thorough-horse-and-alligator orator from Kentucky, who kept entreating the house to 'go the whole hog' in some matter or another, I saw this gentleman rise and disappear behind a pillar behind him. In a few moments, I found that he had walked around the circumference of the hall, and bending over the sofa upon which I sat with another lady, took up my hand and introduced himself as Mr Thuckett, a Congressman from the State of Wisconsin. He then turned to the lady sitting beside me, and without too much courtesy advised her that we had a matter of private conversation to discuss, and would be glad of privacy. Before I could open my mouth to protest that this was not the case, she had risen, somewhat ill-tempered, and left.

Mr Thuckett then invited me to stand, and with a quick gesture turned the back of the sofa so that its seat, rather than facing the floor of the Congress, now faced the passage which ran around the wall behind us – this being a convenience which, I gather, had its origin indeed in there being times when Congressmen wished to discuss affairs with visitors without leaving the chamber, where their presence might be required in some vote or other.

Mr Thuckett then beckoned to a liveried man standing nearby, and passed him what appeared to be a bank note, with some muttered words; at which the man bowed respectfully and turning his back, walked to the nearest pillar and stood as though on guard. Without so much as a word, the Congressman then thrust me rudely backward so that I fell upon the sofa, and plunging his hands beneath my skirt discovered (no doubt to his pleasure) the fact that beneath it there was nothing to come between his person and mine – at which without further hesitation he unloosed his trousers, thrust them to his knees revealing a rampant prick whose squat, red and squinting aspect was as unhandsome as the rest of his person, and still wearing his top-hat threw himself on top of me. You can perhaps imagine that I was not thrilled at this – not so much because of the roughness of the gentleman's approach, which was admittedly anaphrodisiac, as that I was not eager to be taken for a woman of the streets by those who might view our activities.

However, it was fruitless for me to protest, for Mr Thuckett's strength was far greater than my own; and I was afraid to cry out for fear of disturbing the business of the parliament. Happily, however, a gentleman, despite an attempt to detain him, brushed past the attendant and was passing by with no more than a glance at the disgusting sight, when he met my eye – and on seeing by my anguished look that I was no agreeable party to the congress, stepped forward and seizing my assailant by his coat-tails, pulled him from the bench to the floor.

Hastily adjusting my dress, I next saw them exchanging heated words, though in a low voice; after which Mr Thuckett with not so much as a glance of apology in my direction, took himself off, and my rescuer made his bow. He was of a formal and even grim appearance, beetle-browed and with deep frown-lines between his eyes. His jaw

was firm, his mouth rigid and somewhat ungiving; he
looked the very picture of ambitious politician – and
indeed the very picture of a Capricornian!

My interest was immediately aroused, no less on account
of his Sign than of the air of gentility and sobriety which he
displayed as he made his bow and introduced himself as
James T. Accolade, a member of the Senate.

I thanked him fulsomely for his intervention.

'Think nothing of it, ma'am,' he replied; 'alas, some
members of this House are less endowed with the manners
of gentlemen than of Hottentots. I am sorry that you have
been inconvenienced. May I offer you some refreshments?'

On my being agreeable, we removed to a handsome tea
room on an upper storey, from which there was a fine view
of the city; and there he questioned me, and on my relating
my circumstances revealed that he had made a voyage to
England some two years previously, and among other cities
had visited Cambridge, no doubt passing below the walls of
Alcovary House.

His forbidding appearance concealed – as is often the
case with gentlemen of his Sign – an agreeably sharp and
original humour, so that conversing with him was a positive
pleasure. He had, he said, left wife and daughters in New
York, and confessed to a lack of female company, which
(he was kind enough to say) made it particularly pleasant to
converse with me; and he made haste to ensure that our
acquaintance should be enlarged by inviting me to accompany him that evening to the theatre, where there was to be
a performance of Shakespeare's tragedy of *Macbeth*. I was
happy to concur, and he called for me at eight and escorted
me thither.

It was a small house, most astonishingly dirty and void of
decoration, even the box in which we sat was devoid of
comforts other than two simple chairs and a rickety
table – upon which, however, Mr Accolade had had placed
a bottle of champagne and two glasses, which encouraged
me to overlook the shortcomings of the place.

These included a complete want of decorum in this, the only place of respectable amusement the city offers, but where there is a total absence of the restraints of civilised behaviour. A man in the pit, for instance, was at one moment seized with a violent fit of vomiting, which appeared not in the least to surprise or annoy his neighbours; and the happy coincidence of a physician being then upon the stage (its being Lady Macbeth's sleepwalking scene) was hailed by many of the audience as an excellent joke, of which the actor took advantage, and elicited shouts of applause by saying, 'I expect my services are wanted elsewhere.'

Not one in ten of the male part of the illustrious legislative audience sat according to the usual custom of human beings; legs were thrown sometimes over the front of the boxes, sometimes over the side of them; here and there a senator stretched his entire length along a bench, and in several cases it was clear from the motion of the persons in the boxes that some form of sexual congress was in progress. This is not, to be sure, unknown in our London theatres – but I have yet to attend a performance at Covent Garden or Drury Lane at which obvious cries of amorous pleasure so generally interrupted the performances of works by the Bard.

There was also the matter of repetitious chewing: I remarked one young man, whose handsome person and most elaborate toilet led me to conclude he was a first-rate personage (and so I doubt not he was) take from the pocket of his silk waistcoat a lump of tobacco, and daintily deposit it within his cheek. This is by no means uncommon at every form of public occasion, and the act of expressing the juices of this loathsome herb lends a peculiar horridness to every public occasion.

My companion could not but see that I was unimpressed by the place, and the performance of the play being uninspired, invited me to take an early supper; and on my agreement led me to the street-door, a cab, and eventually a set of private rooms in a handsome house near the Capitol. These were furnished in a thoroughly European style of elegance, and the meal which we were discreetly served was equally admirable both in composition and preparation, and was accompanied by fine wines, of which my companion was evidently a *connoisseur*.

That he was not entirely free from the custom of his country, however, was evidenced by his rising to his feet after we had consumed most of a second bottle of wine, bowing over my hand, and asking if I would care to join him in a *romp*, which is their term for the act of love, especially when casually performed.

His kindness and courtesy (to that moment) seemed to require reward; and I must confess that the possibility of marking down a Capricornian lover upon my list was (once more) a persuasion. My acquiescence was therefore almost immediate, whereat he took me by the hand and led me into his bedroom, where a bed of considerable proportions was ready turned down. He took pleasure in showing me a dressing-room next door, with a splendid tin bath in which warm water sent up a faintly scented vapour – something which is rare in private apartments in this country.

At his suggestion, I stripped and bathed, which he watched with great pleasure until, his eagerness causing him (as I guessed) some discomfort, he divested himself of his clothing and, coming towards me, took an equal pleasure in wrapping me in a soft towel and drying every part of my body with careful thoroughness.

His own body, I noted, was harder and more muscular than would necessarily be the case among our legislators at home; and he confessed later that indeed he was no stranger to physical labour, tending a large orchard and keeping some stock at home. Considerably older than the lieutenant who had so pleased me not long before, he was nowhere near as contained in his emotions, for no sooner had we lain down together than, holding me to him and with a curse which I will not repeat, he was convulsed, and I felt his scalding seed spurting upon my belly.

His naturally gentleman-like feelings were deeply embarrassed at this, and he explained that his absence from home was not normally accompanied by female companionship – 'there being few women in this city who it would be a pleasure to lie with'; and his speedy repletion was the result of a prolonged abstinence.

In order to avoid injury to his pride (for that, in my experience, results merely in a total absence of reinvigoration), I made little of the matter; and by dint of encouraging him to explore my person, which he did with increasing fervour, I soon saw that his manhood was far from defeated; first by manual manipulation and later by more intimate caresses, I was able to recover him to a capability which he was glad to demonstrate, though with a workmanlike efficiency rather than with any marked inventiveness. He was interested, it soon appeared, neither in the minor caresses which usually precede the connection, nor in any show of affection; but simply in the act, performed with what vigour and staying-power could be summoned.

Well, my dear Frank, though tenderness is, I allow, an absolute necessity between lovers, strength and virility will serve where the mere satisfaction of lust is concerned; and since I was not in the least attracted to the gentleman except in the way of his being a performing phallus, the time passed most agreeably in mutually enjoyable friction, his extensive and adamant tool not only penetrating (it seemed) to my heart, but from time to time, being extracted from its natural sheath, belabouring all the parts of my body like a cudgel! – something new to me, but not without interest.

Mr Accolade had also the peculiarity that he did not wish to spend within my body, but at the proper moment (and despite my legs being locked about him, my ankles crossed below his buttocks) broke away by force, withdrew, and spattered the sheets with his second coming. (He explained later that he was in terror of fathering an illegitimate child, not for any disgrace it might bring – for that was too common to be any disgrace here – but that he could not contemplate the existence of a child of his over which he had neither command nor the ability to influence: a feeling I honoured him for, as being often entirely absent from those gentlemen most keenly addicted to the sport).

We spent the night together, not without one further amorous interlude; for waking to find him asleep upon his back, and the bedclothes thrown back to expose a staff once more distended, I took it into my head to throw my leg across his body and, very carefully, to lower myself upon him, then moving with such discretion that I succeeded in bringing him off without his waking – though at the moment I felt him spend, a groan escaped his lips by which I imagined the paroxysm to be accompanied by a not unpleasant dream. I thus succeeded in dominating a senator who, I was sure, in no other circumstance would have been agreeable to being put upon by a woman!

We parted entirely agreeably, next morning; and I returned to my rooms, where I was prepared to stay for some time – but the housekeeper, who was responsible for the care of the building, revealed that a gentleman had come to the place the previous evening with two officers of the law, asking after me, by name as 'the protector of two escaped niggers'. Happily, Tom and Susan had been out of the place in the company of a friend they had made who was working in a dining-room of the Senate and who had invited my servants to a dinner composed of the excellent remnants of a legislative feast.

It was clear to me that the visitor was none other than M. de Cournville. Could it really be possible that any man was so outraged at what he called the 'escape' of two servants, as to follow them these hundreds of miles? It seemed not only possible, but inerrable; and I hastened, carefully watching for any sign of that person, to take tickets which would return us to Baltimore, but instantly convey us thence to Philadelphia.

Chapter Nine

The Adventures of Andy

A voyage upon the American lakes is very different from boating upon the lakes of Geneva or Windermere! Between Toronto and Niagara, the most stormy part of Lake Ontario, a line has failed to plumb the bottom even at eighty or ninety fathoms, and while there is nothing more pleasant than steam-boating here in fine weather and in summer, there is (I am assured) nothing more unpleasant than doing so in the fall of the year, when the waves run mountains high and there is a nasty short cross sea.

Though it is possible for a boat to be for many hours out of all sight of land, our smaller boat kept the coast in view – but the scenery was without interest, the continuous forest interrupted only by the sight of an occasional lighthouse set to warn of a dangerous shoal.

I paid six dollars, or thirty shillings, for my cabin passage, which included breakfast, dinner and tea, all good of their kind, and served by polite and industrious coloured men. One must pay extra for wine, liquors, luncheon and cleaning of boots. The charge for wine is shamefully high – but a perquisite of the steward, who makes one pay as much as seven shillings and sixpence a bottle for very inferior stuff.

The public parts of the best steamers (of which mine was one) are splendidly furnished, with plate and china of the best, and the sound of a piano can be heard from the ladies' cabin, where a respectable stewardess waits on the female cabin passengers – too formidable, indeed, in her integrity for me to be able to contemplate an *amour*, even had I set eyes upon a female whose company I much desired.

The town of Toronto was founded only thirty years ago. We landed on a narrow, decaying pier and were jostled almost into the water by rude carters plying for hire on its narrow planks and pestered by crowds of equally rude men seeking to provide us with hotel accommodation; this gave me no very exalted notion of the grandeur or police of the place – and the system must be dreadful for female passengers, especially on dark, rainy nights, when they must contend with piers of rotten planks, nearly on a level with the water, and without gas or any other lights, creating not only inconvenience but actual loss of life.

For ignorance of the place, I took a room for one night at an hotel; and the very next morning, assisted by the offices of a porter who I paid generously for them, took a small house for two weeks – a wooden house with kitchen and cellar, one reception room and two bedrooms, with between them a room which could be used for bathing. Such a house, though small, is expensive to rent, and charged for at the rate of no less than thirty pounds a year.

However, it was comfortable enough, and a housekeeper who came with it – a worthy, large-boned sort of a woman – provided plainly cooked meals when I wanted them; while my bedroom and sitting-room were cleaned daily, in my absence, by a relative of hers for whose service I paid a shilling or two.

I soon set out, as you can imagine, to see whether my first poor impression of the place was to be confirmed or denied by a closer acquaintance.

Toronto stretches east and west along the shore of a beautiful bay, and consists of six parallel streets of nearly two miles in length, intersected by cross streets at right angles, the whole breadth of the place being less than a mile. The chief streets are of course those parallel to the water: Front-street, nearest the coast, Market-street, King-street, Newgate, Hospital and Lot-streets; and in building are five more, to be called Ontario-terrace, Wellington-place, King-street West, Adelaide- and Simcoe-streets.

The houses here are mainly of brick: I am told that even twenty years ago they were mostly of wood, for stone is not found in sufficient quantity in the neighbourhood. But a number of fires having devastated the town, brick is now chiefly employed, the soil being so good a clay that the digging of the foundations of a house often yields the necessary material for the rest of it!

King-street, the main artery, is already very handsome, with excellent houses and shops with large plate glass windows and brass railings. It is well-paved with flag-walks, and a broad belt of round stone on each side. The principal buildings – the Parliament buildings and public offices, English, Catholic and Scotch churches, Methodist chapels, Bank of Upper Canada, market-house and City Hall, Upper Canada College and Lawyers Hall are sensibly constructed, if without great elegance.

It is possible to live well here on but a small income: beef costs only threepence per pound, mutton fourpence, veal and pork threepence; you may buy a turkey for half a dollar, or 2s 6d, a goose for the same, and a duck for only 1s 3d (wild or tame). Eggs can be had for sevenpence a dozen, and a quarter of a dollar will buy you as fine a fresh salmon, of fifteen or sixteen pound in weight, as any you could catch in Scotland.

The house I had rented was on a corner of Lot-street, and from the glances of my neighbours and the few words of greeting my appearance elicited as I went to and fro, I imagined that my background was pretty well known. No-one, however, approached me with a view to making my stay more pleasant – though I saw one pretty woman, in particular, whose home appeared to be in the house across Lot-street, showing a special interest; I saw her peering around her curtains as I came and went, and had it in mind some time to call upon her and see how the land stood.

My attempts to discover what formed the recreation of the better part of the two thousand or so souls who inhabit the town led me to no very satisfactory conclusion: there had been attempts to get up respectable races, to establish a winter assembly for dancing, a Literary and Philosophical Society – but to little effect, and within the week I was beginning to repent of my resolution to remain in the town, and was considering cutting short my time here.

However, one evening I was sitting in my parlour over a glass, and in my shirt-sleeves, when the door opened and to my astonishment a young woman walked in, and without ceremony sat herself down facing me. I recognised her instantly as the lady who I had seen taking an interest in my comings and goings, from her nearby house. She was – as I had remarked from a distant view – a handsome creature, and dressed in what must pass in Toronto for high fashion – that is, clothing which might have been respectably worn in London four or five years ago. There was however a certain freedom about her dress which a woman of her class would in England eschew: her plain white shirt, for instance, being thrown more widely asunder at its neck, revealing the swelling of two healthy brown breasts which immediately sent a shock of recognition to that area of my body most sensibly stirred by such a view.

Seeing my surprise at her sudden appearance, she introduced herself as 'Flo Dunnett', and the wife of a neighbour. She had, she said, seen me 'to-ing and fro-ing', and her husband being from town upon business, had determined to call upon me and make my better acquaintance.

I cannot say that I went out of my way to repel what was a very clear advance; I had been without female company for too long, and though rough in her manners, Mrs Dunnett, a woman of perhaps eighteen summers, seemed likely to be a satisfactory companion in that exercise which she appeared to offer hope of. (I must confess also that it occurred to me that this might be the opportunity to test whether what Madame Fonteuille had told me of the nature of the Canadian marriage was to any degree accurate!)

In short, I poured my guest a glass of wine and encouraged her to talk about the life of the place. It was, she said, without particular excitement. She had come there some nine months ago, as the wife of Mr Dunnett, a traveller in pelts, which I understand to be the coats of certain wild animals. He, it seems, was often from home, leaving her more often than had been her expectation to her own devices.

What these were, I hesitated to enquire; but in any case was now overwhelmed by enquiries about polite society in London and, on my pressing more wine upon her, with freer questions on the amusements with which young ladies filled their time at home.

I must confess that I did not go out of my way to emphasise the faithfulness of English wives, though I am convinced that it is more profound than in this colony; and she was soon somewhat flushed, pressing me as to the number of lovers that a young bride of a year might be expected, in the Home Counties, to have acquired. I must confess that I falsified my reply to the extent of suggesting that it was relatively common for a lady in such a position to attract a large number of lovers, and that the pride her husband would take in her beauty and accomplishments was indeed somewhat in proportion to the number of her conquests.

The next stage of her conversation was a tearful one, for she confessed that while there were no bars, in Canadian society, to a young wife's extending her experience of love beyond the marital bed, there was in Toronto a serious shortage of amiable gentlemen whose natural attributes were such as to spur such ladies into activity.

'Why,' she said, 'would you believe, I have had no lover yet – though married so long? The fact is, that there are few men in this place whose company I would welcome – they are no more handsome than my Roger!'

Pouring her another glass, I agreed that it was indeed a shame that she should be so deprived – especially since she was so fine a specimen of womanhood – 'as far as I could discern.'

The hint was sufficient, for setting down her glass somewhat unsteadily, she swiftly unlaced the front of her dress, and revealed to my greedy eyes a bosom such as Jove himself might have desired – small, yet perfectly rounded, only a slight fullness of the lower globe suggesting that each breast had a certain weight as well as a flattering form, and a pair of dark-hued nipples marking out the centre of each circle and by their pertness positively inviting a caress – which, falling to my knees, I took opportunity to kiss, while their proud bearer threw back her head and with a low cry of pleasure confirmed that she was as ready to receive my attentions as I to give them.

There could, I think, by this time have been no misunderstanding of my emotions, for the position in which I was kneeling had brought my lower body in close proximity to the lady's knee, against which was now pressed that protruberance whose enhanced size spoke of an appetite which I trusted she might be prepared to slake; but was nevertheless unready for the outspoken nature of her reaction – which was to exclaim: 'Do I not feel a goober ready to lay some pipe?'

My failure to comprehend the complete meaning of the phrase did not obscure my understanding of its general drift – and had I not done so, Mrs Dunnett's thrusting of her hand between my legs made it quite clear. Her readiness unleashed in me a flood of feeling, and I fear that in my excitement I tore the upper part of her clothing from her shoulders – at which, provoked to an equal display of passion, she took hold of my shirt and positively rent it in twain, so that she could press those delightful breasts against my own equally unclad and now thunderously palpitating bosom.

Our next ambition was to see each other fully unclothed, and not pausing even to confirm that we were not overlooked, we passionately undressed each other and admired our respective forms. It could not now be doubted that Mrs Dunnett was a bride of very tender years, for nowhere upon her body was there a trace of fat, even about her narrow waist; while no disfiguring bushes grew about her body – merely the tender, sparse compliment of a silken adornment of those parts of the body where a certain mossy growth is pardonable, even delightful. Her appearance was entirely delectable, indeed, and a lesson to one who had begun to give up hope of finding any refinement in the figures of the ladies of this part of the country.

She, I am glad to say, seemed to find my own person not unadmirable, though in one particular surprising.

'Why,' she said, 'how smooth you are! My husband has a growth of hair which makes him appear as fully dressed when he is unclothed, as with his coat on! Why, there is no growth even upon your chest!' – whereat with what appeared to be pleasure, she came towards me and passed her hands over every plane of my body, as if to confirm its smoothness – exclaiming with pleasure at the velvet quality (as she said) of my skin, and on turning me about, falling to her knees and pressing kisses upon my arse which she claimed to find particularly agreeable, not only in its shape, but in its being uncommonly sleek. I began to suspect, indeed, that her husband must resemble more a chimpanzee than a man.

However, my speculation upon his appearance was not prolonged, for madam was by now demanding a greater degree of attention than simple admiration, and reaching up and seizing me about the hips, she turned me about and, plunging her very face between my thighs, demonstrated the power of her desire by gobbling my prick to its very root – so that I fancied I felt its tip meet the flesh at the back of her throat, though I dare say this was illusion.

What was not illusion was, however, the vibrant massage which she was applying to my 'goober' (as she had called it), the pressure of her lips as she drew her head away, then once more pressed towards me, being indescribably delightful; while she now, taking one hand from my behind (which she had been kneading with all the pleasant industry of a woman making dough), began to tickle with her fingers the bifurcation of my thighs, gently holding and caressing my cods and the entrance to my back passage.

Releasing me for the moment from her lips, she exclaimed: 'How sweet you are! Why, I could devour every inch of your flesh!' – then showing every sign of beginning such an operation!

You will not be surprised, Frank, that what with a fortnight's abstinence, I was by now on the point of bursting, and in politeness went to withdraw myself; but madam had again laid hold on my arse, and declined to be moved, so that with a shout composed of mixed delight and horror (but chiefly, I admit, the former) my loins emptied themselves – Mrs Dunnett not showing the least repugnance, but continuing her obeisance until the last quiver had run through my body, and only then raising herself, and smilingly asking whether that had not been pleasant?

There was only one possible reply – but at the same time I felt it incumbent upon me to express my regret that the over-speedy accomplishment of my pleasure had left her unsatisfied.

'Not for long!' was her reply; for I would be soon recovered, and if her husband was anything to judge by, the second performance would out-last the first, while the third . . .

Temporarily exhausted as I was, her words already conveyed the tremor of a new excitement to me; and when she expressed the view that a bed would be the most convenient place in which she might recover my melting spirits, I had no hesitation in leading her thither, whereupon she threw all the top-clothes to the floor, leaving only a comfortable platform or battlefield upon which we could meet – and where, as a preliminary, she laid herself out for my inspection.

This gave me no little joy; for each new female offers some fresh delight, in the unexpected turn of a limb, the surprising lift of a feature, the thickness of a lip here or the apprehensive tenderness of flesh in another place. In short, by the time I had more closely discovered (covering them meanwhile with kisses) the delights of those springing breasts, and had tickled with my tongue the little dint of a navel all composed of sweetness, I was already once more at stand, though in order to prolong the pleasure, I took care to keep out of the reach of madam's exploring hands, which must content themselves with what they could reach – tousling my hair, pressing my shoulders, picking at the growth beneath my arm-pits, and tweaking my nipples – that latter activity being stirring to a degree.

Mrs Dunnett's compliments upon my 'sweetness' were based on a personal pleasure in cleanliness, for she had none of the rank sweatiness which by its odour betrays itself in the presence of some Canadian ladies (and indeed some in our own country, to whom weekly bathing seems quite sufficiently frequent); I found it was not in the least unpleasant to lap upon every appealing part of her body – and there was no part that was not appealing, from dainty ears to apprehensive toes; from pouting breasts to the plum-coloured portals of her secret cave – which, on my entering with my tongue, her whole body was thrown into an earthquake of pleasure; and after only a moment, I was taken by the hair of my head and drawn upwards so that, willy-nilly, she was able to capture between her thighs that part of my body upon which her interest was now once more centred; and by throwing up her legs, offered a target at which it was impossible not to aim, nor, having aimed, into which one could resist plunging.

It was now my interest, I must confess, having only recently fulfilled my pleasure, to see for how long I could prolong the act; and though without any means of measuring time, must have done for a considerable period – yet she still met thrust with thrust, nor despite my best endeavours did she show any sign of accomplishing her desires; until, when I was beginning to tire and slow, I felt her hands once again claw at my fundament, this time with such fierceness that I was sure blood must have been drawn – and to such effect that in spite of my turning my attention as best I could to the economic situation of Canada *vis-à-vis* Europe, I came off; at the same time, from her screwing up of her eyes, convulsion of her limbs, and a low cry, recognising that she too was – for the time, at least – satisfied.

We lay for some time in a bath of perspiration; after which she reached over to gather me to her bosom, and we slid into sleep – for how long, I know not; except that it was dark when we awoke to some kind of a noise – and in a moment to the bursting open of the door of the bedroom, and the sudden appearance of a lantern carried by a large man with an extensive black beard.

'Roger!' was the exclamation with which Mrs Dunnett met him; whereat I assumed that the man was her husband, and prepared to defend myself.

However, Mr Dunnett introduced himself in the kindest terms; expressed himself as interested to meet me, of whom he had already heard something from his cook – who had informed him of his wife's interest in me; and as glad that Mrs Dunnett had made herself pleasant. But, he said, I would forgive him if after a long absence he took advantage of my sheets? – and instantly, placing the lamp upon the bedside table, removed his shirt and trousers, got upon the bed at my side, and placing himself between his wife's thighs (readily opened to embrace him) began those motions which announced his pleasure in his conjugal rights, and received in return other motions which confirmed Mrs Dunnett's readiness – nay, delight! – in welcoming them.

It would have been polite in me to withdraw – but it was, after all, my bed; moreover, I have always found it interesting to observe, should they not object, the enjoyment of others. I could not but confirm that Mrs Dunnett had been accurate in her description of her husband's person – he was indeed clad, from head to foot, with a thick covering of black hair – even the tops of his feet and the backs of his hands being clothed, while from neck to heels his thick-set body wore a pelt no less vigorous in its sprouting than the hair of a dog. The contrast between his animal-like appearance and the delicate white skin of Mrs Dunnett was sufficient to interest me, and I was entirely unable to resist passing my hand over her husband's back, the hair of which beneath my palm felt unexpectedly silky and almost feline, though now as wet as though pussy had been in the well, so freely was he perspiring with the pleasure of his activity.

Whether Mrs Dunnett, noticing my movement, was jealous, I cannot say, but removing one hand from her husband's shoulders, she grasped my cock, which again was growing, and in a moment was applying an interesting pressure – the friction growing with her own excitement, so that at the moment when her husband's pleasure was completed, I too (by the throwing forth of only a drop or two of liquor, so recently had I for the second time expectorated) signalled another paroxysm of pleasure.

Mr Dunnett, throwing himself from his wife's body, in the same movement stood, and (his scarcely shrunken tool still by its vigour announcing the recent termination of his pleasure – though indeed the forest of hair which was as thick there as elsewhere almost concealed it from view) left the room. I feared perhaps that, his pleasure being taken, he might now take a less sanguine view of my having exercised his marital rights on his behalf; but no – for he almost instantly returned bearing a great jug of strong ale, which he insisted upon our sharing (though truth to tell I am not fond of the liquor); and having drunk himself a quantity which could scarcely have been less than a gallon, climbed once more upon Mrs Dunnett and for the second time began to enjoy her – she being no less eager, though surely by now her desire must have been somewhat slaked?

I am somewhat ashamed to tell you that I took no part in this new performance, being quite exhausted; nor did my proximity to the play in any way raise my spirits – or rather

raised them insufficiently for my feelings, though somewhat warm, to be translated into a physical manifestation
which would have given either myself or my partners much
pleasure.

When Mr and Mrs Dunnett had completed their pleasure, and we were all dressed, it was time for more leisurely
conversation than had until then been convenient, and Mr
Dunnett (who preferred the appellation 'Dunny' to the
'Roger' which was his forename, the latter being considered
by him somewhat effeminate) revealed that he had been
about the countryside nearby, hunting for skins – in particular those of the wolf, wolverine (an animal somewhat
like our badger), fox (which exist in great numbers),
catamount, lynx, kinkajou, ermine and mink fetched especially high prices so that one successful expedition of perhaps six weeks would raise enough money, upon the skins
being sold, to keep a trader for as many months.

Had I yet taken the opportunity to explore the countryside of the land, he asked? And on my replying that I had
not, proposed himself as a guide – for, he said, I could not
return to England without seeing something of the real land
of North America, which did not comprise merely the
streets of its main towns. On my thanking him, and asking
upon what terms he would accompany me, he was kind
enough to say that he had to make a journey shortly
through the province, upon a matter of business, and that
he would be happy with my company.

Mrs Dunnett immediately enquired whether she might
not also accompany us? But her husband assured her that
the journey we would undertake would be too arduous for
even so energetic a female as she, and that she had better
remain in the town. Besides which (he said), if she came
with us, such were her charms that we would be too tired
with f*ck*ng to have strength left for the hike!

Mr and Mrs Dunnett then kindly invited me to partake of
supper with them – and on arriving at their house, I found
an excellent table spread with plentiful meat and vegeta-

bles, and yet more beer – of which Dunny, as I must now call him, continued to consume vast quantities; with the result that by half past ten o'clock he had fallen into an amiable drunken sleep, sprawled across the table – which Mrs Dunnett saw as an opportunity not to be missed, for – said she – if we were to go off together upon an excursion, she must make hay while the sun shone.

I was not especially eager, I must confess, for yet another passage at arms, and even her throwing up her skirts and standing astride me as I sat still in my dining-chair, and revealing that inviting cleft whose admirably welcoming warmth I had already experienced, had no result upon me.

However, this was a lady not to be put off by a temporary flaccidity in her lover; pausing only to lower the blinds which would otherwise have revealed us to the street, she threw off her dress, and then insisted on removing my clothes, revealing me in the sadly unimpressive state which I seemed incapable of curing – and shaking her head at it.

She then reached to the table and taking a great handful of butter applied it first to her bosom, which now shone in the lamplight with an appealing slipperiness, and then to my lower parts – which resulted in her hands sliding over my belly and upper thighs with an irresistible lubricity, and eventually resulted in my tired head once more nodding in her direction.

Seeing this, she bent to taste the butter which had completed its task; and slowly raising herself, slid her body along my own so that the greasy flux lubricated all our skins in a manner most delicious to the senses.

Now, we sank to the floor, and in a moment I was once more embraced – this time slipping into her most secret recess with so easy a motion that I seemed barely to notice it. This, surprising though it might seem, was a most unusual and arousing experience; I must even raise myself upon my elbows and look to confirm that the motion of my hips was actually performing the act which I felt I was only counterfeiting! –'twas almost as though the machinery whose activity was clearly giving the utmost joy to my companion was that of some other person than myself – yet after a while the barely observable friction, the lightest conceivable caressing, brought me to an astonishing and exquisite culmination – at the moment of which I met the gaze of Dunny – who lay now with his head upon the side of the table, regarding us with a drunken but not antagonistic glance – I could not have ceased motion even had he been pointing a gun at my head.

My mistress kissed me upon the lips, and gave me thanks ('twas I should have been thanking her!); explaining that she had learned the trick from a young married friend – but had employed it but once with her husband, the thickness of whose pelt made it repugnant rather than delicious.

I left the house shortly afterwards, not wanting to overstay my welcome – and quite frankly uncertain whether Dunny, upon his recovery, would not find the sick headache from which no doubt he would suffer as a result of his excesses, married ill with the memory of his wife putting forth her favours to a stranger. I need not have worried, for next morning, though shaking his head like a great bear, he greeted me with the utmost cheerfulness, and talked at once of the preparations for our journey.

So, you see, my dear Frank, what I had learned about the domestic habits of the North Americans turned out at least in these particulars to be entirely accurate. No doubt civilisation, as it increases here, will result in a diminution of the present cheerfully innocent habits of married life; of which I cannot positively assert that I disapprove – though how I should like them to apply to my own wife, had I one, I would not care to say.

I stayed on in Toronto for only another six days, then turned in the key of my house to the agent from which I had taken it, since should I wish to return I was cordially invited by Mrs Dunnett to take up residence with her and her husband – an offer which he too supported, though his wife made it perfectly clear that my residence was to be sweetened by her own most intimate attentions.

Dunny's business trip was to take him from Toronto across the intervening countryside to the shores of Lake Huron – or, rather, of a large inlet of that lake called Georgian Parry Sound.

I cannot positively recommend the scenery of this part of Canada as calculated to provoke extreme envy in the heart of the European. Certainly he who can view the picturesque scenery of the country from the entrance of the Gulf of St Lawrence to Quebec with indifference, or describe it without ardour, must betray a lamentable deficiency in some of the finer sources of emotion: the mountains' frightful peaks, the valleys' lonely caverns, the forests' solitary retreats, the cataracts' thundering roar . . . all these are wonderful indeed.

But between Toronto and Lake Huron, matters are different: the ground is level, and one or two places excepted, you travel through a continued forest, so that the prospect is never extensive, but confined within the limits of perhaps a mile. Abodes are few – log-huts merely, which though always clean and comfortable within, have a most gloomy and sepulchral appearance from without.

The roads, if roads they may be called, are yet so very bad that every attempt to describe them to you would I fear be fruitless: in a single day's journey of thirty or forty miles, you are generally necessitated to perform the greater part of it over miserable causeways composed of the trunks of trees from nine inches to two feet in diameter. These logs are placed across the roads in all moist and swampy places; and with very few exceptions they are the only materials which are used in the formation of dangerous bridges. As these logs are neither square nor flattened, and not always even perfectly straight, they frequently lie so far apart that horses, cows and oxen are continually in danger of breaking their limbs in passing over.

After four days of travel, I was beginning to find this journey extremely tedious. However, on the afternoon of the fifth day, we came to a small clearing in which a cabin stood; and to my surprise, Dunny strode up to it and threw the door open, to be greeted with a cry of pleasure from one of the most beautiful women I have ever seen. A native Indian, yes – but of quite delightful appearance; whom he introduced to me as – his wife!

Chapter Ten

Sophie's Story

I must confess to spending the first hour or two of my journey to Philadelphia in a state of some agitated disgust that I should have been forced from Washington even a few days early by the exertions of M. de Cournville. It had never occurred to me that he (or perhaps Madame Quincunx, if she was behind the matter) would spend so much time and energy in the pursuit of two young servants, when such were so readily and cheaply available in every town in America. However, I had reckoned without the American's view of slaves, which though less keen in the north than the south of this country, still seems strangely fixed to any visiting European.

The actual conditions under which slaves live and work in the northern part of this country is not, generally speaking, very bad; they are for the most part tolerably well fed and decently clothed. But it is also true that should they be unkindly treated, they have no power to change their condition. If it is true that their health is almost always carefully considered, it is also true that should they sicken and die, this represents a considerable financial loss to their owner!

Owners take great care that their slaves, however naturally intelligent, are not educated: indeed, the law in the state of Virginia makes it illegal to teach any slave to read, and it is penal to aid and abet their instruction. The chances, then, of their organising themselves so as to change the laws of the country, or persuade the legislators to permit them to vote, are minute.

However, their real terror is that they should be sent to

the south, and sold there. This is the dread of all slaves north of Louisiana: the sugar plantations and rice grounds of Georgia and the Carolinas are the terror of American negroes, and well they may be, for there the lash is a common form of correction, and there are open and early graves for thousands. I am sorry to say that there is some system of breeding and rearing negroes in the northern states for the express purpose of sending them to be sold in the south – and I am advised that I must be careful should I think of taking anyone into my confidence in the matter of Tom and Susan – from whom I have my information, but whose description of matters I have been able to confirm by discreet conversation.

There is a strong feeling even among the kindest white people here, that none of the negro race can be trusted, and as fear is the only principle by which a slave can be activated, it is not wonderful if the imputation be just. However, I am confident that kindness is a better master. After only a week in my company, Tom and Susan were as well behaved as any British servant. I was at first concerned that my inadvertent connection with Tom might have given him ideas above his station; but later learned that just as female slaves are often taken as concubines by southern masters, so it is by no means uncommon that white ladies call for the company of their black slaves – especially if neglected by their husbands, which is more than usually the case. Indeed, Tom had often been called upon to serve Madame Quincunx with lemonade or mint julep while she was in the luxurious company of another of her slaves – and the only reason she had made no attempt upon him was that she preferred an older and more sturdily-built man to serve her in that manner. So it was the case that Tom neither took my interest in him as permission to be impertinent, nor resented it as a liberty; while Susan showed no signs of jealousy. I am prepared to believe that their gratitude to me for taking them from the south, and for my kind treatment of them (which indeed is no kinder than I would show to any servant at home) commands their loyalty; but it is also the case, I am convinced, that it is a matter of human nature rather than the colour of skin.

But to return to my story: we passed a single night in Baltimore, when I resisted the temptation to seek out my amorous Lieutenant – and next morning took the steamboat for Philadelphia. The scenery of the Elk River, upon which you enter soon after leaving the port of Baltimore, is not beautiful. We embarked at six in the morning, and at twelve reached the Chesapeake and Delaware canal. Here we quitted the steamboat and walked two or three hundred yards to the canal, where we got on board a pretty little decked boat sheltered by a neat awning and drawn by four horses!

Nothing can be less interesting than that part of the state of Delaware through which this canal passes – the Mississippi hardly excepted! However, I dozed the time away, and having left the canal and boarded another noble steamboat at the Delaware River, we reached Philadelphia at four o'clock in the afternoon.

This is a beautiful city, which wants domes and columns, but is neat and well paved, the footpath being of brick, like the old pantile walk at Tunbridge Wells. These walks are almost entirely sheltered from the sun by the awnings, which in all the principal streets are spread from the shop windows to the edge of the pavement. The city is built with extreme and almost wearisome regularity, one set of streets being given numbers, another the names of trees – Mulberry-street, Chestnut-street and Walnut-street being the most fashionable. In each of these there is a theatre.

I found rooms in a handsome house in Chestnut-street, between Third- and Fourth-streets – a house built of brick and with white marble steps. Upon the first floor there was a sitting-room, large bedroom, and small room which I gave over to Tom and Susan, and the whole allowed me the comfort of quite sufficient space for a short stay.

The city itself soon revealed its limited attractions, and as is so often the case, I found the most beautiful spot in the area to be some way out of town – about a mile, where at a most beautiful point of the Schuylkill River the water has been forced by the Philadelphia Water Works into a magnificent reservoir, ample and elevated enough to supply the whole city.

This place, known as Fair Mount, is one of the prettiest spots the eye can look upon. A broad weir is thrown across the Schuylkill, which produces the sound and look of a cascade, and alongside it runs a beautifully shaded walk.

Upon my second visit to Fair Mount, I left Tom to guard my conveyance, and walked further than before along this walk – all unknowing that it was a promenade reserved for gentlemen, and led to a spot particularly set aside for them, where fine lawns sloped to the water's edge, and groups of weeping willows and other trees threw their shadows upon the stream. I mention these particulars together with the situation of the place to save any female readers who may visit the place from the embarrassment of such an unconscious disobedience of the rules of politeness as I was subject to – for as I emerged from a group of trees through which the pathway weaved, and stepped upon the lawn, what was my confusion to find myself almost on top of two unclothed young gentlemen enjoying a sun bath!

I was too close, and they – lying upon their backs, and their limbs spread-eagle on the grass – too clearly aware of my presence to pretend that I had not seen them; and reckoning it best to be open, I dropped a curtsy, and hoped I had not disturbed them. They immediately sat up, and though they had no towel or clothing nearby, did their best by the careful disposition of their limbs to be modest, and wished me good day.

Of course my first act was to beg their pardon.

'I had not understood, gentlemen,' I remarked, 'that this place was reserved for those of your sex.'

'Not at all, ma'am,' said one of them, the darker of the two, whose body, one shade of brown, revealed that it was

his habit to expose it comprehensively to the rays of the sun.
'It is a mistake which we would welcome were all ladies of
your beauty. Please do not allow our presence to incommode you, should you wish to recline and enjoy the prospect
before us.'

I needed no other invitation, being – as you know, dear
brother – not of that cast of mind which is disturbed by
handsome young gentlemen, whether clothed or no; and
these two were indeed handsome, both of age (I supposed in
their middle twenties), and being unembarrassed and at
ease, contributing a living beauty to those less mobile con-
stituents of the view.

The first had a body of real strength and solidity –
uncommon in one so young, unless – as I suspected – he
had spent some time in the building and development of
such a fine torso. Curly hair lay low over his forehead, and
his head itself was set firmly upon a sturdy neck joined to
massive shoulders – which gave him almost the impression
of bull-like firmness, and led me to set him down as a
Taurean (I later learned that indeed his birthday was upon
May the first).

His friend could scarcely have been more different, his
frame being slim and almost fragile, and his whole air one
of tender compliance and affectionate concern: his beautifully oval face was almost girl-like, with a small nose set
between full cheeks, and a pointed chin set off by a slender
neck. Yet his lips were full and sensuous, and to my mind he
presented the very picture of a young, tender yet admirable
masculinity.

'Perhaps you will allow us to introduce ourselves,' said
the darker of the two, the Taurean. 'I am Philippe
Montblanc, and this is George Root. And you . . .?'

I introduced myself.

'Ah!' said George, 'I took it from your voice that you
were a visitor from the old world.'

'And from your carriage and *sangfroid*,' said Philippe;
'for a true American girl would either have been covered in

confusion, leaving more quickly than she arrived, or – forgive me – have thrown off her clothes and leaped upon us.'

I had by now seated myself at their side, and relaxing their guard they no longer contorted themselves, but lay in open lethargy, their limbs more casually disposed, and carelessly revealing those parts which are not normally upon view in society – though I could not but notice, in confirmation of my first impression, that the uniform brownness of their bodies extended even to the most intimate nook.

Somewhat to my confusion, Philippe saw the direction of my glance, and inferred my interest.

'My friend and I are in a business which gives us much free time during the day,' he said, 'and are regularly to be found here, where in the summer months we eschew covering, finding it unnecessary.' As he spoke, he laid his hand upon his friend's thigh in what seemed to me to be an almost over-affectionate gesture; and I wondered, with a suggestive pang, whether they were namby-pambies, which I would have considered a grave waste of male resource. Again, Philippe saw my glance and inferred my question – this young man was too clever for his own good, I concluded!

'Yes, ma'am,' he said, 'we are more than friends' – and leaning forward first planted a kiss upon his friend's cheek, and then, having clearly his share of natural Taurean bawdiness, a second, smacking embrace right upon the lips; 'so you need have no fears should you wish to join us in offering homage to the sun,' he concluded.

Why not? I rose to my feet, and in a short time was as naked as they, and reposed once more at their side. We remained for a while without speaking, I being very happy to feel the warmth of the sun upon my flesh, which had been too long without such a benison – indeed, I had not lain so since I last reclined in the arbour at Alcovary before my departure for this country.

Through lowered lashes, I could see that Philippe was

regarding my body with interest, and wondered whether he was after all completely lost to my sex, for I noted with pleasure that there was a swelling at his loins which I took as a tribute to my beauty (though I must admit that George's caressing of his friend's shoulder and side – he being much more interested in Philippe than in me – might be a contributory factor). However, I subtly altered my position, throwing down my left thigh to permit the two boys a free view of the charms which womankind could offer; and was pleased to see Philippe's eyes widen with what I supposed to be additional admiration – or at the very least, an enhanced interest. Clearly this Taurean was in many ways typical – for no man predominantly of that sign needs much encouragement to admire, and having admired, to desire.

'Forgive me if I ask an indelicate question,' I said at last, 'but in England gentlemen of your persuasion are less open in their conversation, converse between them being illegal and subject to the most severe punishment . . .'

'Go on,' said Philippe with a smile.

'It is only that I am curious whether you have never been abed with a female, and find the prospect unalluring, or have had that experience and found it unpleasant?'

'The former is the case,' said my new friend. 'We grew up – for we are cousins, George and I – in a house entirely devoid of women. Having shared a bed since we were five years old, and having discovered the pleasures of each other's society at almost as early an age, we have seen no reason to join our friends in seeking out the whores of the town – who, anyway, are a tattered bunch, much diseased, and supremely unattractive; while our guardian, my Uncle (my own parents being dead) is an avaricious man who always applauded our intentness upon study, and showed no desire to encourage us to court those respectable young ladies to whom others of our age might now be married.

'So,' he continued, 'neither of us have had the pleasure of which you speak – though I must confess that a lady as delightful as yourself might have tempted us – eh, George?'

His friend looked, I thought, less confident; but Philippe's tool was by now considerably engorged, and I had the notion that it was certainly more in response to his contemplation of myself than any reaction to his friend's presence, though the latter had now pressed his body against his friend's in what seemed at present a fruitless claim upon his attention.

Raising myself, I edged a little closer to them, and laying a hand upon his arm, asked whether he had never heard the assertion that a man should try everything once, except incest and morris-dancing, whereupon he laughed heartily – his eyes being fixed upon my bosom (which, brother, you will remember is a portion of my body which has not altogether escaped the admiration of the manly sex).

'I am not averse to that notion,' said Philippe – at which I saw his friend's fingers tighten upon his shoulder. But he ignored this signal, and went on to say that he only feared that, unaccustomed to the softness of a female embrace, he might find himself (as he put it) unable to stay the pace. 'For you see,' he said, 'that despite your kind words, I am still not altogether prepared for the mechanical performance of that act which would give you pleasure.'

'If that is all,' I said, 'it can soon be remedied, with the help of your friend—' And reaching over, I took George's hand and laid it upon his friend's staff, instructing his fingers to close about it.

Now, brother, you will understand that I was in no doubt at all of my own ability to rouse any man to a pitch of excitement commensurate with the proper performance of his function; but I did not wish to come between friends, and the jealous signs which George had shown prompted me to demonstrate unequivocally that I had no intention of alienating his comrade's affections.

It was immediately clear that George was, in his way, excited by the turn of events, for with those attentions which were clearly the result of a long intimacy, he had soon roused his friend to a state which would have permitted him to perform any act in the lists of love; while his own person, I noted as he leaned over to plant a kiss upon his lover's cheek, also signalled some interest in the situation.

Philippe, taking this for permission, now approached me, and with an alacrity and dexterity which suggested to me that it was a position favoured between him and his friend, placed himself between my thighs and hoisted my legs so that the calves lay over his shoulders. I then felt him knocking at quite the wrong door, and reaching down took his staff and guided it to the less familiar main portal, into which it slipped with what perhaps seemed surprising ease; for a look of surprised delight crossed his face, increasing when, contracting those muscles which every woman should understand the power of, I positively stroked his cock with my lower lips.

The unusual sensation was his downfall, for almost immediately – though prepared for those powerful thrusts of which I believed that sturdy body to be capable – I felt his torso stiffen and then relax as he expired – with a curse and a look of mingled delight and fury which I admit roused me to laughter.

'Please forgive me,' I said, seeing that my amusement was likely to be misunderstood; 'I mean no offence – it is simply that I am amused to see to what a state a connection with a woman so swiftly brings you! I hope you found it no disappointment.'

'Quite the contrary, ma'am,' he said, now himself smiling, and lifting himself from me turned to lie on the grass; 'the pleasure was if anything too intense – and my performance, I fear, too precipitate to have allowed you the smallest gratification. George,' (turning to his friend) 'you must try this delight, and allow our friend at least a little continued enjoyment.'

But I saw that George was completely limp, having clearly failed to be aroused by the sight of our enjoyment – something which you may find it difficult to believe, for I have yet to find a man to whom the vision of congress is not to some extent invigorating.

'Would that I could,' he said, 'but I fear I am made for the woman's part, and it is too late for so radical a change.'

I must admit that it was partly vanity which persuaded me to ask whether I might not try my luck with him? And on his not too passionately demurring, and Philippe apparently intent upon a doze, I laid myself at his friend's side, and bending over him, took his relaxed part between my hands and attempted to bring it to life. It was a strange experience to hold in my palm that most lively of limbs, warm and sensible, but without showing the slightest sign of apprehension of the pleasure to which I hoped to introduce it. Usually, that part of man appears to have a life of its own; I have even upon occasion brought to performance the machine of a man determined to resist me, and continued the connection to a satisfactory conclusion! But George, though clearly not ill-disposed, entirely failed to react to my ministrations; I unveiled the tip of his cock, like the small kernel of a nut – but it simply lay upon my palm, the bright sun illuminating its childish pink, without even a slight tumescence. On his kindly parting his thighs to allow me access, I lifted the complete engine, so that I could see the veins running through the bag beneath, and jostled the twin marbles between my fingers. Nothing.

Growing more desperate, I took him between my lips; but still without effect – the pliant flesh remained unextended, nor could any attention of my tongue or my lips have anything but the very slightest effect – while I noticed that George showed no sign of attempting to rouse his feelings by attention to my breasts or any other part of my body.

'Well!' said Philippe, who now lay resting upon one elbow and regarding us; 'it appears that you need some help' – and, gently pushing me on one side, he bent over his friend, head to toe, so that his own trilogy of delights, the central column still fallen from his recent pleasure, hung above his friend's face. He then lowered his head and imitated my former action, while raising his own head, George, with what seemed great pleasure, nuzzled at his friend's loins. So immediate was George's response that it was an object lesson to me in the degree to which gentlemen of his persuasion are fixed in the appreciation of their own sex, for almost immediately the nut became a sapling, then in a moment a sturdy oak of remarkable dimensions.

Philippe raised his head and winked.

'Now,' he said, 'let us try,' and although there was some complaint from George, Philippe manoeuvred him between my thighs, and seizing his friend's staff helped it into *terra incognita*.

Almost immediately, I felt the oak bend and threaten once more to shrink; but Philippe was determined to keep the spark alive, and by tickling his friend's fundament, and leaning over to thrust his tongue into his ear, maintained his flagging interest – yet only for a moment before, once more, failure seemed certain – which Philippe felt, for he kept his hand between us and apprehended the problem.

Finally, he shrugged his shoulders, spat upon the palm of his hand, and lubricating his once more sturdy staff, knelt behind George and with such ease that clearly the action was a common one with them both, sheathed it in his friend's back passage.

The result was an instant rejuvenation, George's prick leaping with pleasure – pleasure which, though I saw it in his eyes no less than feeling it elsewhere, I much confess was perhaps even achieved in spite of them! However, the vigour with which George met his friend's thrusting was, as it were upon the rebound, equally pleasing to me; and what with one thing and what with the other in a few minutes we were equally pleased, and equally satisfied.

After some time, George, to my surprise, leaned over and kissed me upon the cheek.

'I hope, dear madam,' he said, 'that you did not consider my lack of response in any way an insult; I cannot help my disposition, and, as you found all too clearly, my response

to your person was that felt by so many men towards their
own sex . . .'

'Not at all,' I replied, lazily; and taking my friends'
hands as I lay between them, the three of us fell into a
pleasant slumber while the remaining rays of the afternoon
sun warmed us.

I was wakened, perhaps half an hour later, by a pleasant
tickling as Philippe touched the nipples of my right breast
with the tip of his tongue; and looking down saw to my
amusement that he was once more aroused. There was no
doubt what would have happened next had not George
awakened, when, catching his eye, Philippe thought better
of his intentions, and, catching my eye with a half-wink,
drew back. Amused by this, I was not altogether surprised,
for it seemed to me that while Philippe's Piscean friend
might be entirely fixed in his devotion to the male sex, and
to his companion, Taurean Philippe did not necessarily
share his companion's monogamous nature, and it would
not surprise me if this, our first meeting, turned out not to
be our last.

We dressed ourselves and walked back back together
along the shady path to where I had left the carriage. At the
sight of Tom in his livery, the trousers of which were sufficiently tightly fitting to enhance the curves of his delightful
young bottom, a considerable interest was shown by
George; however, I was not about to encourage it, and
bidding the gentlemen farewell, mounted the vehicle and
was driven away; at my last sight of them their eyes were
still fixed on my diminutive coachman. Despite this, however, I feared that I may have done one of the gentlemen a
bad turn, for I was far from confident that M. Philippe
would in future confine his amorous activities to his friend.
However, what I am sure of, is that he was a Taurean, while
George was a Piscean; and I invite you, Frank, to indite
them in your record book, as I have in mine!

I was not in the least surprised when, two days later, Tom
announced the name of M. Philippe Montblanc; his

ingenuity had found me out – though in a place as relatively small as Philadelphia, where the presence of any respectable woman unfamiliar to the inhabitants must be remarked upon, the feat of discovering me was no specially remarkable one.

Having paid his respects, Philippe asked whether he could not show me the State House in Washington Square, to which he had a ticket of admittance (its not being usually open to visitors). I readily agreed, and we walked there along the straight avenues, past the United States and Pennsylvania Banks, both most striking buildings in white marble, built after Grecian models. The State House is not so handsome a building, but within it is the room in which the Declaration of Independence was signed, and in which the estimable Lafayette was received half a century after he had shed his noble blood in aiding to obtain it.

There is a very pretty enclosure before the Walnut-street entrance to the State House, with good well-kept gravel walks and many beautiful flowering trees; and in Washington Square itself is an excellent crop of clover. The trees being numerous and highly beautiful, and several commodious seats being placed beneath their shade, it is, in spite of the long grass, a very agreeable retreat from heat and dust.

We strolled here for a while, when in a low voice he began to speak of our first meeting, and of his enjoyment of the proceedings and hope that the circumstances might be repeated. I was not eager to encourage him, not only since it is not my intention to form a regular attachment while in this country, but because as you know, brother, it is no delight of mine to steal a gentleman from another lady, and I admitted Mr Root in this case to the status of an honorary female.

In order to change the subject, I asked Philippe what work occupied him and his friend. There was some hesitation in his reply; upon which, of course, I pressed him, and he said somewhat sheepishly that they ran a house of entertainment.

And did he mean a brothel, I asked – it being fairly obvious from his deportment that it was indeed the case.

Well, that proved so; though it was something of a surprise to me to learn that it was a brothel the ladies of which were entirely of the male gender! He erroneously mistook my surprise for shock, and was all apology; but I assured him I was merely amazed that such a business could prosper in a city such as Philadelphia, which seemed respectable to the point of boredom, and where the greatest crowds gathered together since my arrival had been for a lecture by a Miss Wright on the subject of General Washington's moral character.

Philippe laughed at this, and revealed what I might have supposed – that a shortage of women in the area had the result that love between men was by no means uncommon, and though not respectable was tolerated. Which remark he followed by an invitation to me to inspect the establishment. I knew, brother, that you would never forgive me if I neglected to seize the opportunity, and in short agreed to go there – but first asking what Mr Root would think of the matter, and being assured that he was out of town that night, and so would not be at business.

I had not been out at night before, and was astonished at the quietness of the streets, which were entirely dark except where a stray lamp marked an hotel or the like. No shops were open but those of the apothecary, and here and there a cook's shop. Scarcely a step was to be heard except those of myself and Tom, who accompanied me for safety's sake, footpads not being unknown in the city.

The address I had been given was one in Mulberry-street, between Sixth- and Seventh-streets, where a discreet door was opened to our knock by a respectable grey-haired servant who would have made a fine butler in any English house. He showed no sign of surprise at seeing a lady, from which I gathered that he had been told to expect me; and immediately escorted me upstairs, where Philippe was waiting in a small sitting-room. He gave me a glass of wine, and then explained the place to me – which was very like your own establishment in Brook Street or my own at Chiswick: and indeed there was one strong similarity to the latter, for rather than being ushered into a room with the available catamites, visiting gentlemen were shown into a separate, unit compartment from which, unseen, they could inspect through a window the flesh which was for sale.

First assuring himself that it was not in use, Philippe escorted me into the room, from which I saw, in the next apartment, about half a dozen men of ages between seventeen and twenty-five, in states of dress varying from full costume to almost the condition of utter nakedness; from among them, he explained, a visitor would choose a companion, and retire with him to one of the suite of rooms on an upper floor.

I cannot pretend that I was unmoved, for several of the young men were extremely attractive, and even my knowledge of what they were could not remove a certain admiration of their beauty. However, when Philippe took my arm, I accompanied him once more to the room we had left, where we consumed a second glass of wine.

'I must confess,' he said, 'that I hope you will allow me that familiarity I so greatly enjoyed at Fair Mount . . .'

He himself was by no means an unattractive figure. The rooms being warm, he was undressed to a plain white shirt, open at the neck to show the upper reaches of that brown skin which I knew from experience covered his entire body. He lifted my hand to his lips, and bending, planted a kiss upon my breast (which I confess to be somewhat exposed by the cut of my gown).

I suppose that flattery at his interest played some part in my compliance, for never before had I had a confirmed back-stroker court me so assiduously; and so when he took my hand and guided it to his trousers, a swelling within which indicated his admiration, I did not repine, and permitted him to raise me to my feet and unloose my gown which, falling about my feet, revealed once more to him a body which he clearly found to his taste – for falling upon his knees, he fixed his lips firmly to the unfamiliar spot which was now the centre of his admiration.

Reaching down, I slipped the shirt from his shoulders, and inserting my hands at his waist found it easy to unloose his trousers, when upon his standing to take me in his arms, his instrument flew immediately to a place between my thighs where it seemed thoroughly at home; indeed, so eager was it for entry, that I was thrust instantly upon my back upon a sofa, where we enjoyed for some time a mutual play of limb upon limb that was unpleasant to neither of us.

I almost believe we might still be there had I not heard, from the neighbouring room, a shriek of anguish in what I recognised as Tom's voice. Leaping to my feet so unexpectedly that I threw Philippe to the floor, I was in a moment at the door, and naked as I was, threw it open – to see Tom struggling in the arms of George Root, who had evidently – from the torn state of my servant's clothing – been attempting to force upon him attentions which he did not welcome.

I will not bore you with a repetition of the scene which followed – of my recriminations, of the revelation that George had agreed to Philippe having me once more, on condition that he should have his way with Tom; of my threatening them with the law; of their apologies; of my disappointment that two gentlemen who I had regarded as friends should have behaved so.

Let it merely be said that we parted ill; but that at least Tom escaped injury – though amazed at the attempt made upon him, for so far in his young life he had not encountered such an appetite. I must disapprove of Mr Root's action; yet it was founded, I believe, no less in passion than in the understanding (true even this far in the north of the country) that every black person was created by nature for the use of any white person; and to that extent an excuse can be made – though not one I would expect (or hope) to be readily understood in Europe. Nevertheless, I resolved to be rather more careful, in future, should I be approached by a gentleman of that ilk – for agreeable though the experience had at first been, I might have known that it would end in tears.

Chapter Eleven

The Adventures of Andy

My surprise that Dunny should have produced a second wife – and in a country where, as far as I am aware, bigamy is not legal – was mitigated by the lady's charm, which was such that any man could be forgiven making a false declaration in order to win her: and indeed I was soon assured by my friend, in a whisper, that he was her husband only according to the laws of the Montagnais Indians, of whose tribe she was a member.

Her name, I was told, was Issiquioxpiwiki, which being inappropriate to our tongue, he had abbreviated to Issi; and I must admit that one glance from her deep, black eyes and I was a lost man. My admiration was deepened when, in the privacy of the hut, she removed the shawl which had been wrapped about her to reveal that her clothing consisted merely of a leather skin wrapped about her loins, her upper body being completely bare – and of such a mould that it was impossible to keep one's eyes from feasting upon it.

I fancied that Dunny was somewhat disturbed at my admiration – which though not expressed except in the way of admiring glances, must have been clear enough; for as she was ladling some stew from an iron pot which hung over a fire in the corner of the hut, he informed me in a whisper that while he had been glad to share Flo's favours with me, Issi was another matter – and indeed he was clearly besotted with her (as well he might be), taking every opportunity, as she served us at table, to place his hand upon her thigh or raise it beneath the leather apron to caress (as I guessed) one of the globes of her back side.

I could not help feeling that she was less admiring of him, than he of her; for as she accepted his caresses without protest, she made only the most cursory gestures of affection towards him; and while she leaned over my shoulder to place bread upon the table, I could not but observe that she pressed her body against my back in an insidiously warm and caressing manner.

Not long after we had finished our meal and drunk a couple of bowls of a liquor which was strange to me – but clearly contained alcohol – night fell, and though a lamp was lit, Dunny was clearly not in the mind to sit in idle conversation. He had drawn Issi upon his knee, and I could not but observe that one of his hands was placed beneath her apron and could not but be in proximity to her person.

In a while, with a clearly contrived yawn, he remarked that a hard day's travelling had readied him for bed. At one end of the cabin was a bunk, before which a sheet hung from two nails, and I was instructed to take it. I protested, this being the only bed in the cabin; but Issi in the meantime had piled a number of rugs upon the floor in front of the fire, and Dunny informed me that that would be their couch – and with such firmness that I could not argue with him, and retired to my bed.

I should perhaps be ashamed to admit that, seeing a rent in the sheet which otherwise concealed the rest of the room from my gaze, I could not resist after a time applying my eye to it; but I was intensely curious about the relationship between this beautiful and young Indian girl – for while their looks are different from those of Western women, I could not believe from her shape that she was not still in the teens of years – and my friend; and moreover you will agree, perhaps, my dear Frank, that human nature is such that ninety-nine per cent of masculine humanity would do the same.

My friend had lost no time in throwing off his clothes, revealing that same body which I had observed before – and from a distance it seemed even more hirsute, and the man more like a large monkey than a human. I must confess that I wondered that any young person should attach herself to such a figure, despite that wide variety of taste which ever provides surprise in the pairing of the sexes.

Dunny was standing with his back to me and looking down at the body of his woman, who lay upon her back in the light of the fire, her upper body raised by the pile of rugs and her head thrown back, its black hair flowing free; her fine, small but perfectly rounded breasts lit by flickering firelight, their light brown skin turned to gold, except where the nipples stood erect and almost black. Below them, her slender waist tapered to that zone where the hips began to swell – and at a gesture from him she loosed her apron by pulling at a cord, and threw it off.

Now, seen entirely unencumbered even by so superfluous and sparse a covering, her form was so irresistibly attractive that I gripped the edge of my bed until my knuckles hurt; the bones of her hips showed clearly beneath the skin, so slim was she; her belly was flat, the dint of her navel seeming to draw the skin even more smoothly over her flesh; while between her thighs, still firmly closed, rose a mount decorated with a flash of black fur – upon which, throwing himself upon his knees, he planted a kiss, while one great hand entirely encased a breast.

It is not fair in any man to criticise the manner in which another pays corporeal homage to a lady; but I must admit that my observation was that Dunny, while in every respect a generous and hospitable man, was not my idea of an elegant or considerate lover. He threw himself upon the girl as though almost to rape her – and indeed the scene was such that it almost appeared that she was being ravaged by some kind of beast, for his powerful frame completely buried her, allowing no opportunity for tender compliance, but rather only for abandonment.

Issi's delightful face was turned towards me, to whom her beautiful eyes seemed to complain (whether she guessed that I was a witness, I cannot say) as my friend battered away at her with all the subtlety of someone subduing an unbroken colt! She did not trouble herself of offer a caress; such tenderness would have been supererogatory – her lover would have been, I am confident, oblivious of it. She simply lay supine until, with a grunt, he had completed his pleasure, rolled off her body, and almost immediately fell asleep.

I, too, threw myself back and in no long time was asleep – we had both had several days of tiring trekking over rough country, and even the scene I had witnessed did not keep me awake for long, though the aching of a certain member cried out for relief, constricted as it was by the clothing which I still wore (the heat of the fire not being sufficient to warm the end of the room where I slept).

I know not at what time I awoke, but it was pitch dark; and for a moment I was unconscious of where I was and what had awakened me – until I felt upon my cheek the touch of what was instantly recognisable as a pair of lips – and stretching out a hand, immediately felt beneath it unclad flesh which was certainly not that of my hirsute friend, but of his companion, whose own hand was attempting to loosen the buttons of my clothing.

Need I describe, dear Frank, the extent of the temptation in which I found myself? Here, but a handsbreadth away, were delights such as any man would dream of – not only in the physical beauty of the object, but in the originality of the person displaying them: for I could have no doubt that Issi was a savage entirely ignorant of any sophistication, who would therefore be infinitely pliable and apprehensive of the slightest desire of a lover more understanding of what she could be taught than the rough picture of rural lubricity presented by my companion.

Yes, the situation will be plain to you: yet I resisted it – for Dunny had made it clear that his Indian 'wife' was not to be shared; and I was enjoying his hospitality, and could not bring myself to betray it. Moreover, he was a

powerfully built man whose anger – though I had as yet
seen no sign of it – I was unwilling to provoke. On my
taking the young Indian's hand and removing it (with what
reluctance you can guess) from my person, I encountered
considerable resistance, and gripping mine in turn, she conveyed it between her thighs, where a liquid warmth betrayed
her eagerness (roused as I suppose she had been, but without satisfaction, by my host).

'Yes,' she whispered into my ear, bending closely over
me, and once more inserting her hand into my bosom;
'please, yes . . .'

But again I repelled her, and after a while she left
me – not without a great show of reluctance (some of
which, I must confess, I shared); it was not with any great
ease or readiness that I once more found relief in slumber.

Next morning, Issi showed, I was pleased to see, no great
antipathy to me (for I feared that I had made an enemy of
her). Dunny announced that he was going out to catch
something for our midday meal, and pausing only to
inform me that outside the cabin was a water butt where I
could cleanse myself, went off with his gun. After a breakfast of some kind of meal mixed with milk, I went out and
indeed at the back of the cabin found a large butt of rain
water, and the sun already being up and shining with some
warmth, had no hesitation in stripping to wash myself.

As I was completing the task, I suddenly felt that I was
being observed – and looking about, saw Issi, who had
come around the corner of the shed, and within a few feet of
me was regarding my unclad body with considerable interest and – as I thought – the most open admiration. When
she saw that I was aware of her presence, she came towards
me with a piece of cloth and began to dry me; something
which I allowed, perceiving that it comprised a service
which perhaps it was a duty for her to offer.

However, it soon became something more than that, for
she clearly found my body unusual, no doubt in its
paleness, and certainly in its relative baldness (I guessed,

later, that Dunny had been the only other white man she had seen, and that she had assumed that all those with pale skin were similarly decorated!). Having dried my back, she began to pass her hands over it, in particular reaching down to smooth her palms over my arse, making at the same time cooing sounds of pleasure and admiration. She then placed a palm upon my belly, first plucking at the sparse hairs there in something like wonder, then inserting the tips of her fingers into the rather fuller pad below; whereat my prick, which had been shrunken by the coolness of the water, began to acknowledge her attentions by raising its head.

Another moment, and I would have been lost; but determined still to play the part of a guest, I drew myself away with a motion of disapproval – at which she fetched me a stinging blow across the buttocks, with a show of some temper, and raising the apron which she once more wore, pointed first towards her womanhood (thus exposed with the most entire frankness), then towards my manhood, with the imperative suggestion that they should be united.

I shook my head firmly, and donned my trousers and shirt – just in time, for at that moment Dunny reappeared with a woodchuck – resembling an English pig, but with legs somewhat like those of a bear. Issi, with compliance, cooked him, and we ate him at midday, his flesh resembling mutton, and quite as good.

In the afternoon, Dunny was kind enough to show me some of the surrounding countryside, and to point out some of the remarkable birds which inhabit it: wild turkey and pheasant, goose and crane and redshank, hummingbird and kingbird. We also saw a rattlesnake, which is a creature to avoid: for though not the largest snake in the country, it is the most formidable, measuring about five feet and at most being of the thickness of a man's leg. It is said to possess such a power of fascination as to be able at any time to arrest the attention of birds, frogs, squirrels and other small animals in a manner that completely deprives them of the power of motion and compels them to stand in some degree riveted to the spot, apparently admiring the brilliant eyes and many-coloured scales of their deadly foe, for nothing can exceed the beauty of the rattlesnake, or the splendour of his eyes.

When one of them is about to bite either man or beast, his eyes sparkle like fire, his whole body becomes bloated with rage and his head and neck alternately flatten, distend and swell; but although they possess the power to inflict almost instantaneous death, they seem unwilling to attack except in their own defence.

I am told that a Mr Walcot of Toronto, passing through this very country, was bitten last year upon his hand, and though he took his penknife and cut out the wounded flesh, in a short time his hand and arm began to swell and assume the colour of a snake. His whole body presently became afflicted with the spreading contagion, and in less than an hour he exhibited the most melancholy spectacle of human wretchedness. Every remedy was applied, including great quantities of snakeroot and white ash-bark boiled up in milk; but though his life was saved it was six months before he could rise from his bed.

Returning to the cabin, we once more retired early to bed; when again I was forced to witness the ravishing of that beautiful young creature, without any consideration of her feelings (it was now becoming clear to me why Mrs Dunnett had been so eager in searching me out); and again, in the middle of the night, I must repel her advances – not because, God knows, they were unwelcome to me, nor entirely (so clear was it that Dunny was incapable of treating her with affection) out of respect; but now, chiefly for fear of discovery – for I was alone with the man and far from civilisation; it would not be good to have him as an enemy.

Issi's demeanour towards me next morning was one of thinly disguised scorn – so much so that I feared Dunny would observe it and enquire the reason. However, we set off soon upon the second part of our journey, and handsome though the girl was, it was without too much reluctance that I left, the situation being a difficult one.

We travelled for about half an hour, Dunny meanwhile explaining that Issi, during his absences, returned to the body of her tribe, which was encamped not far away; that he had bought her from her father two years before, and sent a message when he was planning to pass by – thus having all the pleasure of a second wife with very little expense, the tribe being content with honour of a white man's patronage of one of their members, which it was believed was a convenience when bargains were to be struck with the townspeople, the Indians being at a disadvantage due to their poverty.

I could not accept this as a very honourable state of affairs, but was in no position to argue, and at least could agree that Issi was an exceptionally handsome specimen of her tribe.

My mind, I confess, was playing upon her; but even had I been more aware of what was going on around me, I do not believe that I should have been prepared for what happened next – which was that I found myself thrown to the ground with some cloth over my head, my hands and feet being instantly pinioned; I heard a cry from Dunny, but only one; then there was silence, so that I feared for him. However, I soon became more concerned for myself, for still bound and sightless, I was placed face down across the back of a horse or mule, and jolted for some time over rough ground, almost losing my senses at the unusual motion; but then being removed and lowered, without too much care, to the ground, when the cloth was taken from my head.

I lay in the centre of a clearing about which a number of tents and a very few log cabins stood; and was surrounded by a group of perhaps forty Indians, men and women, all clad more or less in the manner of Issi, merely with skins about their loins (though some of the men were decorated with paint, while the women wore what appeared to be crude jewellery made from carved wood).

In a moment, one young woman stood forward – and I recognised her (not so much from her features, for I confess that it is difficult for a white man instantly to be aware of differences of facial characteristics where the tribes are concerned) as – Issi! She was accompanied by an elderly man, and pointing to me spoke to him for some time, with gestures that seemed to be complaining of something I had done – or perhaps not done.

The man (who I took to be her father, and a person of some importance, from the reverence shown him by the others) then pointed to me and gave certain instructions. Two men stepped forward, one producing a knife – which as may be understood made me extremely fearful of my fate; but bending down, he merely cut through my bonds, and gestured to me to stand up.

Doing so, I enquired whether none of them spoke English: but none appeared to do so except the chief, as Issi's father seemed to be; and though he clearly understood a certain amount, he spoke only in his own language – in which he expressed a new order, whereupon one of the two men held me by the arms while the other, with only a few strokes of his knife, cut my clothing from me, leaving me naked as the day I was born.

The sight was clearly of great interest, for the tribe crowded round, the men showing signs of amusement – but the women, it seemed to me, of a kind of admiration, some of them going so far as to stretch out their hands to feel the texture of my limbs. When one, however, plunged her hand between my legs, Issi struck her a blow across the face with some words of disapproval; whereupon they all retired.

More instructions were given, which resulted in four pegs being driven into the ground and my being forcibly tied to them by the hands and feet, spread-eagled before the world in the most vulnerable of conditions. The members of the tribe then gathered about me in a circle and squatted on their haunches as though about to witness a show.

I was in a state of great fear, for it was clear that Issi had been sufficiently provoked by my declining her favours to order my capture; and I could only guess what her revenge would be – all the men wearing knives about their persons, and some of them, I thought, handling them with thoughtful anticipation of pleasure to come; pleasure, I assumed, rather for them than for me.

Now, however, it was Issi who stepped forward, and standing astride my pinioned body without ceremony tore her apron from her body and threw it to one side, revealing again to me her unclothed body – though in my present circumstances I was entirely unable to manifest admiration of it in any tangible manner. She then began a narrative which, it soon became clear, was the story of my rejection of her. How the tribe viewed her obligations to Dunny, I cannot say; but the only sounds were those of sympathy as her story proceeded, she pointing first to me, then to herself, and mimicking my reluctance (as it seemed to me) as though it were fear or unwillingness rather than merely the proper behaviour of a civilised gentleman.

Finally, she pointed where my manhood, in view of my present circumstances, lay shrunken between my thighs, and scornfully laughed; then seemed to ask a question – to which with echoing laughter, her sisters appeared to reply in the affirmative.

At a gesture, one of the other girls brought forth a small pan or vat into which she placed her hands, removing them covered with some kind of oil (which I discovered later was pressed from nuts gathered from a tree which grows generously in the wood, and was considered by them to be a kind of aphrodisiac). She then conveyed them to my shoulders and began to smooth it over my breast with the most languorous motion, lingering at my tits, to which she applied her fingernails in a delightfully tickling way.

Gradually, a hush falling upon the watchers, she gave attention to my lower chest, my belly and thighs; by which time, now warmed by the sun and lulled by what seemed an amiable ordeal, I was beginning to relax. Upon her reaching between my thighs Issi pushed her assistant roughly aside, as though to reserve the final compliment to herself, and anointing her own palms cupped my privates with her left hand while with her right she applied the oil. I was now beginning to recover my manhood, and to swell appreciatively. Indeed, within a few minutes, by a lingering application of her fingers along its length, she had persuaded my soldier to full attention.

She now made a gesture, and three other girls coming forward and divesting themselves of their aprons (at which they were revealed as, in almost every particular, as handsome as Issi) knelt at my side and joined their caresses to hers – with the exception that rather than their hands, they used their lips and tongues, licking the oil, with every expression of pleasure, from my limbs and body, while Issi paid particular attention to the part whose obeisance she was determined to secure – for her tongue now explored every part of my lower body, inserting itself as far as it could into the hollows of my loins, then mounting to the very tip of my prick, which sensation had rendered so hard and at the same time so sensitive that a wave of emotion gathered itself and prepared to break . . .

At the very latest moment, with a clapping of her hands, Issi rose, while her friends also sat back upon their haunches; and the wave slowly subsided as I caught the amused eyes of the other women, and the men, still gathered in a circle about me; and shame at the public exposure resulted in the slow shrinkage of that part which had a moment ago been so proud.

No sooner was it diminished, however, than Issi with another signal set her friends once more to work, and again I was roused to a pitch of excitement; when, throwing her thighs astride my waist, she lowered herself so that, closing my eyes, I felt the tip of my instrument brushed by the welcoming fibres which shrouded the entrance to her womb.

Once more, I was about to feel the relief of expiring; when again, all retired; and this time, since my excitement was much greater, cold water was fetched and poured over my body, which seemed to steam, so hot was my flesh.

No less than four times the process was repeated; but the fourth time, as the apogee approached, the mere sight of Issi lowering herself to caress me with those lips which I seemed fated never to enter, was enough to do my business; and with an involuntary cry and an arching of the back, I sent a fountain of life-creating fluid higher in the air than I would have thought possible.

You will believe that until that moment I had been far too concerned with my own emotions to notice what was going on much outside the range of my own body; but now, relieved of my own feelings, I could see that the sight of my torment had roused the entire tribe, so that I was now entirely surrounded by couples taking their pleasure – while three men had stepped from the crowd and fallen upon the three girls whose help had been given to Issi in tormenting me; so that they were also being enjoyed – two thrown to the ground, and one simply ravished as she stood (or, rather, hung – for the lover had lifted her from the ground so that, embracing him with her thighs, she hung like honey upon a vine).

After a while, the frenzy subsided, both men and women having loved their fill. I now assumed that, Issi having taken her revenge for my neglect of her at the cabin, I would be released – but instead, my chief tormenter rising to her feet lifted a hand and spoke for some time to her fellows in their own tongue, whereat there was a mumble of agreement, together with some amusement; and they all retired to their tents, leaving me naked and tethered still upon the ground.

Happily, they had been sufficiently considerate to set me beneath a tree, so that the shadow sheltered me somewhat from the sun; but flies were still a torment, attracted as they were by the sweat thrown upon my body by my recent ordeal – but it was with some pleasure that I saw the three assistants come, in a moment, from a hut with a basin of water, with which they carefully washed every part of my body, cooling it to a comforting degree. They paid particular attention to my private parts, the hair upon which seemed especially to attract their attention; they wound it about their fingers, tugged at it and played with it so that had I not been so exhausted they would undoubtedly have roused my amorous propensities.

In a while, one went away to reappear with a tall, slender man who seemed to be some kind of priest (I subsequently heard his like referred to as witch-doctors) and whose attention they drew to me, seeming to question him. He in turn bent over me, ran his fingers through those same curls below my belly which had so engrossed the maidens, and at length made a reply which seemed an order – whereupon, the maidens began each to take a single hair between finger and thumb, and with a sharp tug detach it at the root.

This at first gave me little pain, each tug being so swift; but after a while I began to be distinctly sore, and was soon pleading for mercy – but without effect. The next occurrence was that the mixture of pain and pleasure had the result of my masculine part becoming once more engorged with blood; but the maidens ignored it, one merely holding it to one side so that the others could remove the hairs growing at its root. They then turned their attention to the hollows of my arms, removing the growth there; before, finally, two men, releasing my bonds, turned me about and spread my legs widely apart, enabling the women to pluck out each hair growing about my fundament – which proved the most painful part of the operation. Not content with their apparant admiration of the smoothness of my body, the tribe had now rendered me entirely free of hair – save for that of my head; the strange result being the inducement of a sort of shame which I had not thought it possible I should feel.

By the time they had finished, I was bare as an

egg – though I was unable to raise my head sufficiently to see my shame, I could feel there was no resistance to the girls' fingers as they now smoothed upon the denuded parts a kind of ointment which was brought, and which was at once cooling and soothing to the smarting of my flesh.

The witch-doctor now stood over me, and I saw with a horrified interest that beneath his apron there was the sign of an amorous interest which I strongly feared was not directed at the maidens who had been operating upon me.

In a moment, indeed, he clapped three times and called, whereupon the chief and several of the people appeared, and were addressed by the witch-doctor, who pointed first at me, then at the women, and finally at himself and the other men of the tribe; his preaching finally reaching a culmination in a new order which resulted in several men stepping forward and half carrying me to a sort of carved altar which stood nearby, upon which some skins were stretched, and which proved – when I was thrown face downward upon it and held there – not to be entirely uncomfortable. However, I feared that comfort would be shortly in question, for I soon felt hands applying to my fundament that same slippery fluid which had formerly soothed my body, and in a moment, hearing a murmur, opened my eyes (which had been resolutely shut) to see, standing before me, the witch-doctor, completely unclad, and in that state of excitement which you and I, dear Frank, more usually attain in the presence of a beautiful woman.

Raising his hand, the witch-doctor pointed at me, and with a most obscene gesture with his hips, made clear what I had begun to fear – that he was about to use me in the way of sodomy; I supposed as some form of ceremony common among this tribe with white men who they wish to shame and discredit.

Two men still held my arms, while two more took my ankles, and bending my knees drew my thighs apart so that my rear parts were exposed to the gaze of the tribe. Feeling a hand upon my neck, I looked upward, as best I might, and my eyes met those of Issi, who now seemed to look with pity upon me, so that I was convinced that she had no part in planning this new horror.

However, I was indisposed to plead for mercy; and had the advantage that at least I knew how to meet the assault, for you will remember that at one time, finding myself in a situation where it was necessary, I had submitted myself to the act – though then performed by my friend David (as recounted in a previous volume, *Eros in the Country*), and knew that a complete relaxation made it, if not pleasant, at least devoid of pain – and happily, the gentleman whose amorous approaches I was now to experience was not blessed with an especially large instrument. However, for the benefit of my chief torturers I allowed myself to appear terrified; and upon feeling the hands of the witch-doctor upon my fundament, gave a cry and pretended to faint; on which I heard a sigh of pity from Issi, whose hands remained softly upon my neck, and caressed my head with what seemed a pitiful attention.

I will not go into the details of the next few moments, except to assure any male reader who finds himself in the same situation that a complete slackening of all the muscles, together with the fixing of the mind on some pleasant circumstance, removes any danger of damage to the person.

However, I am not among those who find the action pleasurable, and was happy that the witch-doctor's stamina was limited, and that within a very few moments, the rhythmic clapping which had accompanied his thrusting broke into more disorganised applause as I felt him withdraw himself from me, and a moment later a splash of something upon my back which I took to be the signal of his having completed his present pleasure.

Having been again tied hand and feet and thrown once more upon the ground, though not in my former position, I saw the tribe disperse, and was left alone, now with night falling – which, the temperature now rapidly cooling, was accompanied by a pile of rugs being thrown over my body. Despite my situation, I fell into an uneasy slumber; but woke to find by bonds being cut by a knife, and to see in the slight of a half-moon, the face of Issi bending over me.

Having set me free, and holding a finger to her lips, she led me to the edge of the clearing, where a path led into the forest. Handing me some objects which proved to be the boots I had been wearing when I was taken, one of the leather aprons which the men of the tribe wore, and a kind of shawl of animal skin, she pointed with some energy away from the camp and along the track, immediately turning to throw the blankets to the ground into a bundle which might have concealed my body.

My fear of the forest at night was only a little less than of the tribe; but having learned from Dunny that even the dangerous animals of the place would usually only attack if themselves threatened (or in the extremes of hunger), I merely signalled my thanks to Issi – whose action had been motivated, I could only suppose, by her disapproval of the witch-doctor's action, accompanied perhaps by apprehension of some new trial that might be devised for me – and made off into the almost complete darkness, beneath the canopy of the trees.

Chapter Twelve

Sophie's Story

After our single unpleasant adventure, the rest of our time in Philadelphia – except for one incident – was spent quietly and by no means unenjoyably, though most of my pleasure was solitary, for the society of the place was by no means inspiriting.

There were evening parties, to be sure, but they were supremely dull; the men sometimes played cards by themselves, but the ladies were denied that pleasure, and though there was sometimes music it was extremely bad. In fact I never heard a white American perform who was able to finish a song in the key in which it had begun. At such assemblies, indeed, eating – and enormous quantities of cake, pickled oysters and ice were consumed – seemed to be the only amusement the guests greeted with enthusiasm.

However, one morning I received by messenger a card in the name of Madame Genevieve Brabant, with a note written in neat handwriting upon the back announcing that five ladies of the place would, if convenient, call upon me in the afternoon of the following day to express their pleasure at my presence in the city. This seemed an uncommon compliment, and it was certainly the first occasion on which my presence in a city – in any part of the world – had resulted in such a circumstance. However, if it was the custom in Philadelphia, who was I to circumvent it? So I ordered some cakes and delicacies to be prepared, and at three on the following afternoon had dressed myself in a tea-gown and awaited the ringing of the bell, which soon enough followed.

Sure enough, at the next instant Susan showed into the room five very decently clad females, of ages between perhaps eighteen and thirty, who made their curtsies and introduced themselves – but only by their Christian names, and when I gave mine as 'Mrs Nelham' begged that I would desist from such formalities, which were not the custom at such informal parties.

The afternoon was warm, and I had thrown open the windows, lowering the blinds to keep out the brightest sunshine; which was evidently approved by my visitors, one of them – Leonie, a large-limbed fair-haired lady – particularly remarking upon it as being convenient to the need for immediate relief from the warmth of the day – a remark which she followed up by unlacing her dress to the extent that a large part of a handsome, protrusive pair of breasts was exposed; this was fine enough, no doubt, in some circumstances, but an unusual complement to afternoon tea.

This was not, however, the least of my surprises, for she went on to compliment me upon my figure, and to express her regret that I should be 'so neglected', and coming towards me placed a hand in a familiar manner upon my bottom. Not naturally ill-bred, I hesitated to thrust her away – the instinct which immediately suggested itself to me; but was none the less astonished – and more so when I saw the other four ladies immediately following her example in loosening their clothing – and indeed not merely releasing their upper and outer dress, but in a moment entirely freeing their bodies from the confinement of silks and cottons, and appearing in a moment as naked as upon the day of their birth. Far from giving any sign that their actions were unusual, they even seemed surprised that I did not follow their example – only one of them, a slim, dark lady whose name was Cassie (one of those outlandish names which seem native to the country) seeming to recognise my confusion.

'I believe, friends,' she said, 'that Sophie is unaware of the nature of our visit! – Genevieve, did you not call upon her yesterday?'

Genevieve confessed that the utmost of her visit had been to leave her card with the message announcing their intention to call upon me; at which even the self-assured Leonie had the decency to blush – and then explained the circumstance to me, which was that although there was in this city, as elsewhere in the country, a shortage of women, so that there was no difficulty in finding a husband, the men were on the whole of an ill-educated sensual nature, and where the niceties of a loving connection were in question entirely lacked gentility and courtesy, with the result that the expression of their passion while quickly satisfying them for the most part left the ladies entirely ungratified. It was therefore the custom that small groups of ladies were formed who from time to time met in order to express among themselves those loving instincts which their marriage beds denied them. And in this case, my guests, who all lived in the neighbourhood of Chestnut-street, setting eyes upon me, had assumed that I would be pleased to be drawn into their circle.

I found myself now in some difficulty: having welcomed them into the house, I could scarcely dismiss them out of hand – and indeed it must have been clear from the sympathetic silence in which I had heard the explanation, that I was not shocked at it – which indeed was the truth, for my own contemplation of the manners of the average American man (though there were fine exceptions) tended to confirm what I had heard. Mentally shrugging my shoulders, therefore, my response to their explanation was to loosen my own clothes and place myself in the same unadorned state as they.

Words now ceased to be the currency of the meeting; for pausing only to assure themselves that they were not overlooked, each lady immediately turned to her partner and began to pay her those amorous attentions which would have been less unusual had one of the parties been of the male gender.

It was clear that, while the meeting was general, the

pairing was particular, for far from indulging (I was glad to observe) in indiscriminate passion, each lady was clearly attached to a particular friend; with the exception of one – neither the large-boned and passionate Leonie nor the small, plump and volatile Cassie, who now occupied each other's attentions, but a young woman of medium build, slightly older than myself. I had scarcely noticed her, for she was quiet, and entirely lacked that typically American forwardness which is at once pleasant (if not overdone) and disconcerting.

Jane (which was her name) approached and sat at my side, and taking my hand in her own and conveying it to her bosom, informed me that her particular friend was on a journey to Boston with her husband, and asked whether I had no companion? With some difficulty – for the actions of the surrounding couples became by the moment more interesting – I gave her my attention, and explained my circumstances.

Then, she said, travelling alone as I did, I must for some time have lacked those amorous attentions of which, having once experienced them, our sex was jealous?

I did not feel it necessary to explain the circumstances which had in fact relieved me of such drought, and allowed her to believe the truth of what she suspected; at which, with what seemed like genuine pity, she leaned forward and placed a tender kiss upon my mouth, her lips, full, soft and welcoming, catching my own upper lip between them and pressing it with a delightful and springy apprehension – while her hand fell upon my waist, and thence journeyed up the length of my back until it caught at the nape of my neck, there gently smoothing my hair.

Though I never went out of my way to seek the amorous company of my own sex, neither was it disproportionately unpleasant to me, and the kindness of these ladies in seeking me out made it imperative that I should return their warmth; I therefore – partly out of such consideration, and partly from natural inclination – took Jane's head between my hands, and planting in turn a kiss upon her lips, laid her back upon the couch on which we were placed. Her form was such as would have given pleasure to any gentleman, for though lacking in the slightest suspicion of surplus weight, it possessed all those characteristics of the female form most delightful to the sight: her breasts being shapely, and while full to that degree which allowed them to hang like fruit upon a bough, were of classic rather than generous proportions. Her slender waist drew in above hips which swelled, rather than jutted, and below it firm and rounded thighs once more offered a perfectly harmonious impression, framing between them a dark triangle at which any lover must hasten to set his aim.

Seeing, as I believe, my admiration, Jane now turned her body so that she lay face downward upon the couch, displaying a back whose prospect was as admirable: long, slender and beautifully shaped, hung upon a spine the tender progress of which down the centre of her frame offered an inexpressibly touching track, impossible not to follow with the fingers – and naturally leading to that small plateau above the buttocks, over which it was equally unthinkable not to pass the hands, each globe filling the palm with warm and supple flesh the skin of which was like velvet to the touch.

Having permitted me to examine her person, Jane now wished to return the compliment, which I was pleased to allow, and upon which she whispered many tributes – which however scarcely needed verbal expression, since with many a kiss, the caress of tongue and lips, and the delicate stroking of fingers she was able fully to convey her admiration.

I have had occasion before to remark that the chief advantage of intimate female connection over male is in the preliminaries. While it is my confident view (which however I did not express upon this occasion) that nothing can replace the emotion engendered by the vigorous plumbing of our form by that single instrument which is the most obvious prerogative of the excited male, I am forced to admit that relatively few gentlemen understand the need for that tender courtship which can so arouse female emotion! Time and again, when some entirely attractive gentleman has encouraged me to permit him to display his prowess, this has turned out to consist of his thrusting some portion of his anatomy – whether hand, head or prick – between my thighs and applying himself immediately to primary matters; when a more persuasive attention to secondary affairs would – at least from my point of view – have been a more welcome bounty.

Alas, the lesson is hard to learn; for the opposite is not true, as I learned when on one occasion, irritated beyond measure by the approach I have described, the moment we were undressed I threw myself upon my lover, inserted his machine into the proper groove, and within twenty seconds had brought him off – something which, far from reproving me for, he complimented me upon, clearly regarding it as a proper compliment to his overwhelming attraction!

So – though on this journey I have for the most part so far been fortunate in my companions – on the occasion of which I now write I was pleased to relax and to accept those leisuredly compliments which Jane was happy to pay, and to return them in kind; so that when, after perhaps an hour, we had raised each other to a pitch of nervous and corporeal excitement, the whole of our bodies were positively humming with delight, as the strings of an instrument will hum when tuned to perfection. There could be no suggestion that either of us was disappointed in the other; neither were our bodies bathed in the perspiration which is so often the product of over-energetic writhings (so dear to those lovers who feel that they will disappoint a lady if they do not adopt a new posture each minute!); we merely found ourselves entirely happy – and upon a final expression of pleasure, looked up to find ourselves applauded by the other three couples, who, though equally satisfied, had been engrossed in watching our expressions of mutual admiration.

I had just lifted my head from my new friend's breasts, indeed, when there was from behind me a most tremendous crash! – and on turning, I saw Tom, standing in the doorway, the ruins of a tray of crockery at his feet; opening the door unannounced (as I had taught him) to serve tea, he had been faced with the sight of six entirely naked ladies, two of them engaged in an activity in which he had certainly, in his young life, never seen performed before by the female sex.

However, with a surprising equanimity in one so young, he recovered with remarkable speed, even controlling himself when he was surrounded immediately by those same ladies, in that same state, helping him to clear up the mess; though I thought I discerned certain signs in the hang of his breeches that his control was less complete than it seemed.

It was Susan who returned, shortly, to serve tea; by which time however we had resumed our clothes – and I am not sure whether she believed Tom's tale; though when, my new friend having left, I rang for my servants, there was a considerable pause before they appeared, and then the signs of speedy dressing seemed to indicate that he had taken the opportunity of satisfying those emotions which our display had roused in him.

It was an interesting interlude – and one which might perhaps have recurred, had it not been for an incident which resulted in our speedy departure from Philadelphia.

I was walking, one afternoon, along Walnut-street when I heard a disturbance behind me, and turning saw a small crowd around a young black boy who was lying upon the ground bleeding profusely from a wound to his head. The conversation of the onlookers revealed that he had been struck a severe blow by a man whose luggage he had accidentally dropped while unloading it from a coach which still stood close by, and the driver of which was complaining about the behaviour of his erstwhile passenger, whom he had carried from Baltimore, and who had, it appeared, a great dislike for the coloured part of the population, and indeed was at that time in determined pursuit of two escaped slaves.

Illogically, my heart sank at this; for it could surely not be that the man was M de Cournville? And yet my instinct was correct – for in a moment I saw the very man stride from the hotel whose door was adjacent to the incident, contemptuously throw a coin upon the ground at the side of the injured boy, then turn on his heel, and once more enter the hotel.

The incident provoked much anger among the people, whose attitude to the black population is less extreme here than in the south; but I did not stay to talk, but returned instead to rouse Tom and Susan to the necessity of leaving that very night – for M. de Cournville could only be here for one purpose – his megalomaniac hatred of these two young people.

How he had contrived to track us, I could not conceive; although an Englishwoman travelling with two black servants is a rare enough phenomenon to make me noticable, which I presumed was the reason for his success.

At all events, I secretly contrived places on a steamboat, and at midnight we left Philadelphia upon the Delaware River, headed for New York – where I had arranged to meet Andy on a date not now too far distant. However, I was not sanguine that our enemy would not pursue us there; and hearing in talk that there was a traffic in escaped slaves across the border into Canada, decided not to stay in New York but to proceed immediately – as had been my original intention – to see the falls at Niagara, where there would be, I believed, the means of contriving their escape.

The scenery of the Delaware River was most enjoyable, enlivened by a succession of gentlemen's seats, which if less elaborately finished in architecture and garden grounds than the lovely villas on the Thames, are still beautiful objects to gaze upon as you float rapidly past on the broad silvery stream that washes their lawns.

One mansion arrested our attention, not only from its

being more than usually large and splendid, but from our steamboat lying in at a stage built from its garden, from which a veritable procession of servants embarked – a major-domo of the utmost magnificence, in full livery, followed by a number of men carrying trunks, then by several maids, two male servants, and finally an extremely handsome young man, dressed in a fine suit of white clothing with a broad-brimmed hat and carrying a silver-mounted cane. He vanished immediately into a suite of rooms reserved for him upon the upper deck.

I spent the rest of the day upon deck under a parasol, enjoying the bland, sunny weather, and gave no thought to the new passenger – until I was surprised to be awakened from a half-sleep by a liveried servant handing me an envelope upon a silver salver – an envelope which contained an invitation to dinner from Mr Harrington Hotspur, who appeared to be none other than the young man I had seen coming aboard.

I had recently enjoyed few evenings of civilised company, and although the invitation seemed somewhat peremptory, accepted it, and at the appointed hour presented myself at the door of his suite, and was admitted by a butler.

I found Mr Hotspur, splendidly dressed in evening clothes, sitting in his drawing-room. He rose to greet me, and presented a highly European picture of elegance, his dress plainly emanating from the finest tailors. A young man in, I would judge, his middle twenties, he had aristocratic and refined features, set in a somewhat oval face, with fair, curly hair falling over a low forehead and expressive, almond-shaped eyes beneath arched brows. His mouth was well-formed, his chin somewhat pointed, and he had a sharp and intent look of considerable intelligence.

This, together with his opening remark (that it was a pleasure to set eyes upon a female whose appearance was a cut above the slovenliness of his compatriots – thus showing an honesty untempered by tact) encouraged my belief that he was a Sagittarian, which was one of that increasingly short list of Zodiacal Sun-signs whose members I had not yet bedded; so that were his summons, as I had suspected, founded upon a keen appreciation of my personal attractions, I would not be unwilling to be seduced – especially since the gentleman was most presentable.

A delightful meal was produced by Mr Hotspur's own cooks – which comprised rockfish accompanied by a delicious sauce (unusual in a country where sauces are on the whole thought little of), an excellent Canvass Back wild duck together with fine green vegetables, and a profuse quantity of dessert dishes or 'puddings', as they call the sweet dishes.

During this time we of course conversed, and I found that Mr Hotspur had been brought to this country by his paternal parent at the age of three months, but had frequently returned to England since that date, usually to stay with his uncle and cousins at Rawby Hall, near Cambridge.

You can imagine, dear Frank, how my eyebrows rose at this: and on his noting my surprise, was eager to tell him that my half-brother was married to one of those very cousins of whom he spoke – that is, the Lady Margaret, now Lady Margaret Franklyn!

Taking my hand and kissing it, he remarked upon the coincidence: though, as he put it, the aristocracy of America was so limited that anyone of half-decent address would invariably turn out to have European connections (a theory which I could not dispute, though I scarcely approved of his positively traitorous words about his adopted country).

There followed much discussion of Rawby Hall, and I spoke in brief of Andy – though not explaining that his knowledge of the Hall was the result of his having been a servant there – and was able to understand Mr Hotspur's references to his uncle, the late Earl of Rawby, and his grand-uncle, Mr Henry Rust, known as Beau Rust.

Was the latter not, I asked, an artist? – somewhat naughtily, recollecting the anecdote Andy had related of

Beau Rust's ambition to illustrate the works of Aretino, and his commissioning our friend and another servant to pose for him in the most lascivious attitudes.

'Scarcely an artist,' said Mr Hotspur; 'though a man of some ambition in that direction – indeed, upon his death some two years ago I was sent portfolios of his work, for it was known that I am an amateur of the arts; and indeed I am working upon a scheme of my own in that connection. Perhaps you might care to inspect . . .?'

I was then led into the next cabin, which had been set out in part as an artist's studio – at least, an easel was erected there upon which was a picture covered by a cloth; and on a table next it, a large, old, leather portfolio. Laying his hand upon it, Mr Hotspur asserted that he considered me a woman of experience and sophistication, who would not be shocked at what was about to be revealed – and opened the covers, which concealed a sheaf of papers upon which there were many ill-drawn sketches of male and female figures in *coitus* – all of which were signed with the initials H.R., and some at least of which I assume were drawn from the posed figures of Andy and the young servant who was paid to couple with him!

I was, as you can conceive, most interested; and Mr Hotspur revealed that he was attempting a set of large oil paintings based upon these drawings, which, he said, illustrated the sonnets of the indecent Italian poet Aretino.

'Indeed,' he went on, 'I have brought one such picture with me to finish on our voyage to Trenton,' – and drawing away the cloth he revealed a large canvas upon which two figures had been outlined, but without colour. 'However, I am at a loss, for while my servant accompanies me, the maid who posed for the female figure has remained with my sister at home, and . . .'

Seeing his eyes upon me, I at once divined his meaning, and (I must say chiefly in order to ingratiate myself) offered my services.

He was delighted.

'You will understand that I would not ask you to assist me were not my young man almost a gentleman,' he said, 'as experienced as I myself am in European customs, and in no way likely to take advantage of his – er – position.'

I assured him that such a thought had not entered my head, and on his asking whether we might not immediately make a start, since time was relatively short, he rang for his servant, who soon appeared – and, I was sorry to see, was clearly by birth a Taurean, having all the characteristics of that sign both in appearance and manner – whereas had he been a Cancerian or Aquarian he might have helped me to my final total!

I retired behind a convenient screen to divest myself; and from there was able to observe that his undressing – which he did without hesitation, upon his master's command – confirmed my long-held opinion that all in all the sign of Taurus offers at best the most handsome of men (at least when not permitted to run to fat), for his body was solid and powerful, the muscles well-defined, with just such an embellishment of hair as was decorative without being overpowering (except that his head bore a wonderfully strong growth of fine, curly brown hair).

The pose which Mr Hotspur wished us to assume was not a difficult one, and Paul – as the servant was called – was politeness itself in aiding me to assume it. I was half-lying upon a *chaise-longue* with my left leg raised, so that when he reclined upon my body, I was able to curl it about his back, the heel fitting into the niche just below his rounded arse, while my left leg was stretched out upon the bench. The actual contact between the more intimate parts of our bodies was concealed, for actual intercourse was not to be called upon, being improper between a servant and a lady (as Mr Hotspur expressed it). The painter then took up his brushes and began.

Posing for an artist is not as amusing as some people may think; and after ten minutes or so becomes entirely boring. Paul was good enough to support his weight almost entirely upon his elbows, one of which lay each side of my body; and while the pose required that his head should lie upon my shoulder, he placed it there with the utmost discretion and lightness, only a slight tickling of the locks of his hair upon the upper slopes of my breast being in the least uncomfortable.

I am ashamed to say that after a while boredom drove me to the extreme of playing a trick upon him. Through what effort I know not – perhaps through the simple ambition not to lose his job – I could feel that Paul's manly part was entirely inert; and set about discovering whether I could rouse it, which at first I did by wriggling my heel at the seat of his buttocks, often an inspiriting act where gentlemen are concerned; and indeed thought that I felt a stirring. I then began to run the fingers of my right hand, concealed from Mr Hotspur's view, along the side of his servant's body, from the top of the thigh to the breast and back again, and after a moment felt a kind of shudder and shifting, which had become necessary to accommodate some thing between us which had not previously required so much space.

I then attempted to insert my hand between our bodies at the point where the disturbance took place; and unable any longer to resist, Paul raised himself in order that I could lay the palm of my hand where I was able to feel the extent of the change I had wrought, which was indeed considerable.

The movement he had made had, however, not gone unnoticed – and on his master sharply enquiring what caused it, his servant exclaimed that it was a cramp in his leg.

'Pray do adjust your position,' I exclaimed, and with my hand placed the very end of his prick at the lips of my by now very ready pouch, into which, with a light sigh (which however sounded like thunder in my ear) he slipped.

Since Mr Hotspur was closely observing him, Paul was unable to make those uninhibited movements which would normally have resulted from our juxtaposition; so it was for me to do what I could – which was by constricting and loosening the muscles of the vital organ, to, as it were, massage his prick – a slow but, from the shuddering breaths which he had difficulty in controlling, efficacious activity which resulted, after not too long, in my apprehending a scalding flow of fluid and a relaxation of his person which signalled his release from the pains of his desire.

We remained for some time after in the same position – his organ shrinking within me until, when we rose, it was once more of a decent dwarfishness; I, turning away in what seemed modesty, was able to disguise any signs of our activity, and to accept Mr Hotspur's thanks without his being aware that anything untoward had occurred.

As Paul dressed, I was regretting once more that he had been born at any other time than April or May, when a thought crossed my mind, consequent upon my noticing how worried he seemed that his action might have been remarked – and that indeed his brows were now knit in a frown, his mouth turning down at the corners – uncharacteristic of Taureans, but highly characteristic of another Zodiac sign. I asked him when he had been born – and received the highly satisfactory reply that it had been upon July the fifth: he was, indeed, a Cancerian – and I was able to suggest to him that his birth had taken place at about three in the morning – something he was able to confirm from stories he had heard from his grandmother.

Mr Hotspur enquiring what I was about, I explained that my hobby was astrology, and that (which was true) I had supposed his servant to have been a native of Taurus, when the truth was that Taurus was his Rising Sign (the sign coming over the horizon at the time of his birth), and in which the possible additional presence of several planets gave him a stronger resemblance than he bore to his native sign of Cancer!

Mr Hotspur was clearly a most talented amateur artist, and had made some progress with his painting; but would need another two hours of work on it upon the morrow, if I would be so good. I of course acquiesced, not only because it was a pleasant enough way of passing the time, but because I had hopes of capturing Mr Hotspur as my Sagittarian lover – though I must confess that his interest in my person had so far seemed entirely artistic, and my closest observation of his person had failed to reveal any physical manifestation of desire.

On the following morning, Paul and I resumed again the pose we had held the previous day, and this time he made no attempt to restrain his emotions, for almost before I had made myself comfortable he was knocking at the door. This time, he allowed himself some slight movement, observed by his master but dismissed as attempts to ensure that I was comfortable; they brought Mr Paul off very speedily, after which there was some short pause before I again found the young man in an enquiring mood – upon which I could not prevent a further venture; but just as he was about it his master called a halt, and he was forced to rise, unable entirely to conceal his condition from Mr Hotspur's keen eyes.

'What's this, Paul?' he enquired sharply? 'No impertinence, I trust?'

I was quick to intervene.

'You will not blame a young man,' I said, 'for being aroused by so close a proximity to an unclothed female? It is the way of the world, and I would not for a moment take offence at it!'

'You are kind, madam,' he said, and dismissed Paul without further remark; though in a manner which suggested some displeasure. I had not been so quick, this time, to clothe myself, and was sitting still in a state of nature upon the *chaise-longue*, one leg thrown over its arm, and looking (as I hoped) somewhat disconsolate. My acting must have been convincing, for in a moment Mr Hotspur enquired whether something troubled me?

With a fine show of blushful hesitation, I admitted that

to have lain so long with a naked man without satisfaction had been hard for me, and that travelling as I was without a lover, it was somewhat melancholy to me that a certain inclination had been roused which it would be impossible to satisfy – unless . . .

Mr Hotspur took longer to swallow the bait than I would have thought possible; but once the idea had been put into his mind, 'Permit me, madam, as the author of this situation, to offer you a remedy . . .' and thrust off his clothes without more ado.

His body was certainly admirable enough in all ways save one: his limbs were well-framed, his chest deep, his hips slim but thighs well-shaped and strong. Between them, however, the appendage in which I had intimated an interest was so small as to be almost indiscernible – which considering the warmth of my offer seemed almost an insult. However, I am woman enough to be aware that much can often be made of little, and that acorns, given the right nurture, can grow into uncommon large oak-trees; so, rising, I stepped towards him and taking him in my arms, led him to the chaise-longue, and persuading him upon it, bent to do what I could to enlarge the prospect before me.

In short, 'twas no use – or precious little. It was not that I gave no pleasure, for the heaving of Mr Hotspur's body and the signs and groans that emanated from his lips betrayed the greatest enjoyment; yet although between my lips there was at last something firm and sturdy, yet the size had scarcely altered – and when I inspected the source of his pleasure, it was still scarcely bigger than my thumb.

However, the chase was afoot, and I was not going to give up my quarry, and now throwing a leg across his body prepared, if I could, to insert the disappointing limb to such an extent at least as would enable me upon technical grounds to claim for myself a Sagittarian lover.

After some difficulty, its insignificant length vanished, the very bones at the base of our bellies meeting in my attempt to force it home. Fortunately, I was not to be embarrassed by an attempt at conventional lovemaking, for no sooner had I accomplished my aim than with a cry, he thrust once with his loins, and, wriggling, withdrew, a small clear bead of liquid demonstrating that he, at least, had had some pleasure from the encounter.

'I hope, ma'am, that I have been of service?' he enquired, and immediately rising excused himself on the ground that he must bathe, and withdrew, bowing frequently, and evidently confirmed in his own opinion as having entirely satisfied me.

A few moments later, Paul returned, having seen his master leave, and with a quizzical eye asked whether there was any service he could perform. In short, there was; and freed from the inhibition of being observed by an onlooker, and thus able to move with all the freedom the circumstances demanded, the satisfaction his attentions gave was entire – to myself as well as to him. Our conversation afterwards suggested that the servant had often had the duty of following his master in bringing some relief to those ladies whose encounters with Mr Hotspur – elegant and accomplished though that gentleman was in other fields – had been less than entirely satisfactory.

However, I would point out, my dear Frank, that our wager said nothing about the amatory expertise of my Zodiacal lovers, but merely that they should be born at the right time of the year; and I am happy to add both a Cancerian and Sagittarian to my list, which at my count leaves only two more to add – a Geminian and an Aquarian – before my bet is won!

At Trenton, the capital of New Jersey, we left our smoothly-gliding, comfortable boat (and Mr Hotspur, whose farewell was full of messages of goodwill to Lady Margaret and yourself) for the most detestable stagecoach that ever Christian built to dislocate the joints of his fellow-men. But at length we found ourselves on the boat which was to convey us down the Raraton River to New York; and there, though I longed to explore the city, immediately set off again for Niagara. I had explained to Tom and Susan my plans for them, and that I would be happy to provide them with a certain small fortune which would enable them to set up in some small way in a new life in Canada; and though they expressed a fondness for me and the wish to accompany me to England, I did not think well of that plan, and was able to persuade them otherwise.

Our voyage up the North River was a delightful one, the scenery among the most beautiful I had yet seen – and often most dramatic, as during the first twenty miles, when the shore of New Jersey offers a continual cliff known as the Palisades, a wall sometimes rising to the height of a hundred and fifty feet, though sometimes as low as twenty.

After one has passed Manhattan Island the eastern shore gradually assumes a wild and rocky character; then, some forty miles from the city, you enter upon the Highlands, as a series of mountains is called, with a beauty of scenery rarely seen: in the midst of which the state prison of Sing Sing is placed, on the edge of the water; then West Point, the military academy of the United States (and seeing in the distance the large quantity of handsome cadets taking their ease, many lying stripped in the sun – only the distance between us and them making the circumstances concomitant with polite discretion – it entered my head to stop the boat and descend – for it would surely then be possible within a very short time to complete my score and ensure my hundred guineas!).

I will not describe at great length the Erie canal, cut through solid rock, with magnificent cliffs upon either side; nor the Trenton Falls, which we visited in a carriage, from the small town of Utica, and which were of the highest magnificence, second only in fame to those of Niagara. We stayed here at an hotel from which a flight of alarming steps leads down to the bed of a stream where one is enclosed in a solid mass of rock, through the abyss of which a stream rushes with inconceivable rapidity. From the narrow shelf from which this stream is observed, two young people within the past six months have been swept by accident, never to be seen more!

By the aid of gunpowder this shelf has been somewhat enlarged in order to provide a view of a world of cataracts, all leaping forward together in confusion. I suffered considerably before I achieved the spot where this grand scene could be observed; a chain firmly fixed to the rock serves to hang by as you creep along the giddy verge, and this enabled me to proceed so far; but when the chain failed, my courage failed with it, and though the rest of the party continued some way further, I returned to the hotel, and going to the servants' quarters to find Susan to attend me, found her, indeed – asleep in her young lover's arms, no doubt tired with the day's work.

If I had ever doubted my duty to help these two to safety and a better life, this sight would have confirmed me: two humans, their age scarcely totalling more than thirty, lying innocent as angels together, neither of whom I had heard say an ill-disposed word or perform an ill-disposed action – and yet pursued by someone who would whip them until they could not stand – or worse! (For I was not sanguine that we had entirely outstripped M. de Cournville, and indeed sometimes woke in the night expecting to hear him at the door.)

In time, on a most beautiful, sunny and open day, we reached Niagara. As we approached, we heard a low roar which announced the presence of the Falls – but saw nothing; until reaching the hotel, which overhangs them, we went in – and saw beyond the hall an open space surrounded by galleries, one over another, and in that instant felt that from thence we would see the great sight!

To say I was not disappointed is but a weak expression to convey the surprise and astonishment which this long dreamed-of scene produced. Here is not, as at Trenton, an elaboration: here is only the Fall itself. The colour of the water, before it is lost in foam and mist, is of the brightest and most delicate green; the violence of its impetus sends it far over the precipice before it falls, and the effect of the ever varying light through its transparency is, I think, the loveliest thing I ever looked upon.

Tom, Susan and I stood transfixed upon one of the galleries of the hotel for some time before this astonishing spectacle, then we descended to the edge of the gulf which receives the torrent, and thence looked at the horseshoe fall in profile; it seems awfully daring to stand close beside it and raise one's eyes to its immensity, for as the heavy mass of water pours down it gives an idea of irresistible power such as no other object ever conveyed to me.

Beyond the horseshoe is Goat Island, and beyond Goat Island the American Fall, bold and straight, the water snowy white from the rocks which meet it. There, giddy stairs descend to the very edge of the torrent, where slabs of table rock are constantly bedewed by a rain of misty water; and here is a little hut lying half under the descending stairs, which affords some shelter to those who wish to bathe in the mist – said at once to be cleansing to body and spirit, and to bring fortune to those who perform the act; indeed, I am informed that this must be done, or one loses one's reputation as a tourist.

As I first descended, no-one having warned me, I surprised a small group of gentlemen addressing themselves to the waters, being completely unclad; however, the cold was such that they were in no condition to offer offence, and indeed we all laughed at the circumstance! – and I was informed that certain times of the day are set aside for gentlemen, others for ladies, who are nevertheless permitted to bring their personal servants for their protection. I therefore decided to undergo the necessary experience next day, and was glad now to retire to rest, the latter stages of our journey having been more than usually tiring.

Next morning after a fine breakfast (a consequence of the many travellers wishing to see the Falls being that the hotels here are not only commodious but offer a fine *cuisine*) I took the path to the American Fall, accompanied by Tom and Susan. The former I set to guard the bottom of the steps to warn me should some male strangers approach; the latter accompanied me into the *shantee*, as the small hut was called, where we divested ourselves of our clothing.

Though the morning was warm, a moment's step into the mists which awaited us was sufficient to chill us – though after that moment, I felt a distinct glow spreading through my body, and was prepared to credit the healing powers of the spray. However, a short period of exposure was sufficient, and after a glance at Tom – who stood, his back to us, at the bottom of the stone stairway – we retired to the hut, where Susan began to rub my body with a large towel we had brought for the purpose.

She had only begun this, however, when I heard a shout from outside, and recognising in Tom's voice the tones not merely of warning but of terror, I stepped – without concerning myself to dress – out of the *shantee*, to see, standing about half a dozen paces from the bottom of the steps, none other than the figure of M de Cournville, a large horse-whip in his hand with which he was threatening Tom, who had retired until he was only a foot or two from the dangerous water's edge.

M de Cournville already had his whip raised to strike, when my call delayed him a moment. Glancing towards me, I saw his lips move, but the thunder of the waters carried his words away as he struck. The whip caught Tom across the face, and with a cry he staggered backwards, and in a moment disappeared over the edge. I felt my senses whirl, and though I raised my arms in the air and shouted an imprecation, my emotions were too much for me, and without being able to intervene – and as I saw de Cournville, with a devilish smile, turn and take a step towards us – I fell to the rocky ground in a swoon.

Chapter Thirteen

The Adventures of Andy

How I survived for three days in the desert woods, living upon such roots and herbs as my instinct told me were nutritious, I will not describe; nor how I eventually stumbled upon a group of gentlemen travelling back to Quebec, and by them was succoured and escorted to that city. The long journey thence, though to a degree uncomfortable, enabled me somewhat to recover my strength, and I was quite happy not to return to Toronto, for Mr Dunnett might by now also have returned, and I was by no means confident that he would not believe I had organised his embarrassment in order to possess his Indian wife – and had no desire either that he should take an unofficial revenge or that he should in that belief bring against me what resources of the law might be available to him – for it would have been his word against mine, and what I had seen of the Canadian character persuaded me that the word of a native would be universally accepted against that of an European.

On arriving in the city and taking up a room again at the Hyperion Hotel, I took myself off on the very first evening to Blague-street, and almost failed to recognise the house in which the late Mr Bradley had had his establishment. Freshly-cleaned stonework and brightly paintwork had so refreshed it that it bore little resemblance to the wreck of a building which it had formerly been. Knocking upon the door, I was greeted by a footman, handsomely and austerely clad, who without asking me my business, immediately ushered me into the hallway – where, at a desk, sat none other than Mrs Thomas, metamorphosed into a splendid figure, her generous frame clad in a gown which would have appeared respectable even in Mayfair!

She greeted me effusively, plainly no less pleased to see me than grateful for my advice, which had led to a situation clearly most comfortable. On my asking after Miss Bradley she informed me that the latter did not usually make her appearance until the end of the evening, and that Mr Ham was at present in town upon some errand of his own.

'But I am sure, Mr Archer, that they would wish me to offer you the hospitality of the house,' she said, and escorted me immediately upstairs – it being clear as I mounted that Miss Bradley had spared no expense in the place's refurbishment, for the carpets were now thick, candles stood in fine sconces, the walls were hung with an elegant but rich paper, and everywhere was good paintwork and the place so clean that it was difficult to remember the degree of its former slovenliness.

I was now shown into the large room which had formerly held the ladies of the place – and which did so still; but once more, it was so greatly changed as to be unrecognisable. Gone was the wrecked and slovenly furniture, the blowsy hangings, and dust and dirt; now all was clean and comfortable, the furniture commodious, the hangings of fresh velvet, and the soft lighting arranged by means of shades and mirrors to shed a golden light over all, highly complimentary to the ladies who sat here – all of whom I was pleased to discover remembered me – which however was unsurprising, for here were the girls of the theatre, Betsy, Sylvie and Moll, together with the young lady who had been formerly at the house, and who had begged me to recommend her staying on – something I was now glad to have done, for, clean and well-dressed, she was an ornament to the establishment.

David's hand was clearly to be seen not only in the ladies' dress but in their deportment. They no longer wore the informal clothing in which they had appeared at the theatre, but were clothed entirely as ladies of fashion, and with real elegance, if with a touch of that lascivious informality which was entirely in place given the nature of their employment. Their deportment, too, was more restrained than it had been – even in their greeting of myself, an old friend; and I guessed that in aiming to captivate the hearts of such aristocratic masculinity as could be found in the place, they had been instructed in a quieter mode of behaviour than had been the norm in their theatrical days.

'We are quiet, here, until about ten o'clock,' Mrs Thomas remarked; 'and any of the young ladies will, I am sure, be happy to entertain you' – which from the smiles which her clearly audible remark brought to their lips was no more than the truth. Taking her aside, I asked whether Lisette was not in the house – for to tell you the truth, the thought of her pleasant wiles had been in my mind since I had returned to Quebec.

'Alas, no,' Mrs Thomas returned; 'she is upon an errand for Miss Bradley, though she may return later. Do you wish to wait for her? I am not sure of the time of her return, however . . .'

My disappointment may have been clear; but one young woman came up to us, and with the plainest of offers enquired whether she could not show me her gratitude for my past help. It was the young woman who had asked me to recommend her to Miss Bradley – whose name I now discovered was Sophie! – a coincidence which certainly did not dissuade me from accepting her offer, especially since the others by their smiles showed that they were aware of her gratitude and approved her showing it.

The room to which Sophie now led me was furnished as comfortably as the others I had seen in the house, and the experience which David had been able to bring to the matter was again clear: there was, of course, a large and comfortable bed; a screen behind which was a bath and all the appurtenances of cleanliness; and two large portable mirrors stood, one upon each side of the bed. Once again, the furnishings were handsome – and I enquired of Sophie what kind of man now attended the house?

She remarked that 'twas very different from formerly. The new tariff of prices when first displayed, upon the house re-opening, had soon resulted in the more impoverished clients neglecting it for other, poorer houses; while the officers of the military had soon learned of the metamorphosis, and began a regular attendance, to which was soon added all the aristocracy of the place (a term which made me smile, for none of the gentlemen of Quebec would, my dear Frank, match those we would apply that term to!).

'But now,' said Sophie, 'let us talk no more of business,' and stepping forward began to unloose my clothing, which resulted in our soon being in that state of dress best accommodated to sensual enjoyment.

'What may I offer you?' she then remarked – a question which I always find an embarrassment in such situations, for any young lady should instinctively know from a gentleman's deportment what will best please him – or at least should be able naturally to offer those caresses which will immediately be acceptable – and I made a note to mention the matter to David, who could take it up with her.

However, her eagerness to please in a moment outweighed any consideration of such a sort, for apprehending my hesitation she wrapped her arms about me, and sinking to her knees (her body sliding down my own with the most pleasant motion in the world) she in a moment took my nodding cock between her lips and by the application of these, together with the play of her fingers about my arse and bollocks, swiftly brought it to that angular and muscular vigour which was a proper tribute to her dexterity.

Leading me then to the bed and laying me upon it, she gave herself up to the single aim of arousing the utmost bodily pleasure that woman can convey to man; and I must confess that her professional skill was of the utmost, and that time and time again I was on the verge of paying final tribute to it when by some practised gesture she was able to restrain me . . .

I will not pretend that this was not most enjoyable; yet there was something missing – which was her own enjoyment. It is perhaps my peculiarity that I am unable to take my own pleasure to the full without the apprehension of giving pleasure in return. I am not so silly as to imagine that there have not been occasions when the lady to whom I was paying my attentions has dissimulated; that the sounds and motions which have accompanied my attentions have not been entirely artificial. Yet I must be able to believe that she is pleased at them, if I am to be really happy – and this Sophie (unlike our mutual friend, whose enjoyment of the act has never needed simulation) made no attempt to suggest that she enjoyed her task; she merely performed it, with all the adeptness of her profession, but entirely without emotion.

In the end, despite her best endeavours, I grew limp and died – not the death which is accompanied by ecstacy; but merely that of exhaustion.

She was, I am bound to say, most distressed at this; and I must explain, with all the conviction at my command, that it was exhaustion at my long journey which had that result – which I am not sure that she believed; but I was saved from further endeavour by the door's unceremonious opening and the appearance of none other than my friend David Ham with little Lisette upon his arm.

'Aha! you have done!' he exclaimed; 'so we can talk' – and immediately sat himself upon the end of the bed.

Sophie took my eye with a pleading look – whereupon I thanked her effusively for her attentions, making it quite clear that I had been delighted by them (and indeed I am sure that most of her gentlemen would not be inhibited by my own reservations). Happy, she took herself off.

I now took Lisette's hand and planted a kiss upon it, the very innocent action nevertheless conveying to me a memory of the delights we had shared, and thus raising the head of my fallen lance – to her surprise.

'Quick in recovery as ever!' she smiled – and David, also noticing the phenomenon, raised an eyebrow.

However, they were eager to hear my recent adventures, and both amused and horrified to hear of them – both nevertheless having their emotions roused by my description of the incident which followed my capture by the Indians – Lisette expressing herself as understanding Issi's irritation at being unable to command my amorous attentions, while David professed himself entirely in sympathy with the witch-doctor's actions – 'for,' he said to Lisette, 'would you not agree that Mr Archer's arse calls out for action?' – and administered a slap to that quarter which was not entirely humorous in intent.

It was clear by now that whatever had passed between Sophie and myself, I was now ready for a new passage of arms, and Lisette – with, I confess, some help from my eager fingers – had divested herself of her clothing. It was clear that her friendship with David was founded upon an entire understanding of his personal proclivities, so that she was entirely unembarrassed to appear before him in a state of nature – nor was I entirely surprised that he too slipped easily from his clothing.

Not to embarrass the reader by an unnecessary account of those intimacies which then took place, I need only say that Lisette once more displayed that natural talent for amorous play which had formerly delighted me; and that – entirely unlike my more recent companion – her pleasure in the act was clearly as keen as my own. My pleasure was sufficiently keen as to make me forget altogether that a third person was present – nor could I have sworn at any stage that a particular caress of which I was the delighted recipient came from one or the other, David being so old and familiar a friend as to know that I would not be offended at his participation in the frenzy.

On my finally giving up the ghost, wrapped in my

mistress's arms, I came to myself in time however to apprehend another body on top of my own – for unable to resist the opportunity, David had climbed upon my back and (realising that any more intimate contact would be unwelcome) had satisfied himself by running his instrument along the groove of my arse, which enabled him to reach satisfaction without indulging in that act which, while I have sometimes had to bear it, must ever be repugnant to a man of normal proclivities.

That the rest of the evening was spent in pleasant conversation, accompanied by a bottle or two, I need not say; nor that Miss Bradley, when she returned, was reluctant to show her gratitude for my part in establishing her in so acceptable a style. I was happy to see that her relationship with David was that almost of mother and son – with the exception that she entirely understood his need to relax himself with gentlemen of his own persuasion, and far from allowing herself to be distressed at it, was pleased – for it enabled her to remain, as I am convinced she always will, entirely without amorous connection either with man or woman – no bad a situation for the mistress of a brothel!

I spent three weeks in the city before parting with some sorrow from my friends (David, however, confided that he did not intend for ever to remain in Quebec, so that I have some expectations of meeting him, sooner or later, in Europe). I determined now to set off for Niagara, where are the great waterfalls, and whence it would be easy to travel into America and on to New York, where I had arranged to meet Sophie for our return to England.

The voyage by steamboat across the Lakes was a pleasant one, ending at Queenstown, built at the base of a lofty hill, seven miles from Niagara, where about sixty houses only stand, and where I made a brief stay before travelling on, next day, to the Falls, which are situated on the narrow stretch of land which unites Lake Erie with Ontario.

My approach to the Falls early next morning was certainly an inspiring one, for though hitherto the sky had been clear and the sun warm, no sooner did I approach their immediate vicinity than a sudden and singular change took place in the whole aspect of nature: the earth became damp and tremulous and the sky assumed a frowning, dark and portentous appearance.

At length I reached the hotel where I was to stay, perched upon the very brink of one of the falls, so that from its high balconies appear mountains of water belching forth the most appalling sounds – globes of foam boiling with accelerated rage, rainbows embracing within their numerous and splendid arches a surprising variety of newly-formed, impending clouds, rocks projecting over the tumultuous abyss, and spray-coloured forests decorated with pearly drops, now rendered more brilliant than crystal by the reflected rays of the sun.

Having seen this view, I was content to remain in my room – but was assured that I should see the American Fall, which lay some little distance off; and on reaching it was appalled anew at the luxuriance of Nature's buoyant imagination. Here, a steep set of rocky steps led downwards – I had seen, as I approached, another gentlemen descending them – and wishing to obtain the full effect of the grandeur, myself began to descend.

What was my amazement to see, as I reached the bottom of the steps, a man in front of me with a whip raised above his head, threatening a young black person whose nearness to the edge of the torrent was sufficiently dangerous to make me fear for his safety. Indeed, as I looked, the whip fell across the unfortunate fellow's face, and, staggering backwards, he vanished over the edge of the low cliff.

As I stepped forward, a female cry from my left took the man's attention for a moment, and stepping forward I was able to grasp the end of the whip and (so unexpected was my intervention) with a quick jerk deprive its owner of its possession. Immediately, he turned and with a face full of fury and mouthing imprecations of whose sense the noise of the waters happily deprived me, he came towards me, his arm raised to strike.

More instinctively than purposefully – for I am not a violent man – I raised my own hand, forgetting for a moment that it held the whip; the speed of my movement flicked out its end, which caught the stranger full in the eyes.

Clasping his hands over his face, and no doubt in some pain, he turned and, bending, lurched backwards. Seeing his danger, I went to catch at him – but before I could do so, he had placed a foot on uneven ground right at the edge of the abyss, and throwing both arms into the air and waving as though to catch at some unseen rail, with a terrible cry he fell backwards and in a moment was lost in the tumult of the waters.

Any thought of rescue was vain, for nothing could live in that cauldron; and I turned my attention to where a black girl was bent over the recumbent body of a white woman, both in a state of nature. Overcoming any reluctance to embarrass them, I went forward to offer my assistance – when to my astonishment my eyes fell not upon a stranger, but upon the familiar person of – Sophie!

Carrying her into the small hut which stood nearby, I found towels and by their swift application in the way of brisk rubbing soon imparted a warmth to the chill body, and was rewarded by my friend's returning to consciousness, and greeting me with all the amazement and warmth for which I could wish! Delaying any attempt at explanation, I helped her to dress herself; and had only finished when with a cry the young black woman, who in some distress had absented herself from the scene, appeared in the doorway of the *shantee* (as they call the hut) and beckoned us. Upon our going out, we found her kneeling at the edge of the platform and pointing downward, and cautiously approaching I saw below me a ledge upon which was clinging, with frantic strength, the young black man who

I had seen precipitated over the edge by the whip's blow.

It was the work of but a moment to lower to him the end of a rope contrived by the tying together of a towel and the sleeve of my jacket, with whose help he regained firmer ground, on which he was warmly embraced not only by his young friend but by Sophie.

It was difficult for me to restrain my curiosity until we reached the hotel, but there all was revealed – as was the identity of the stranger, a M. de Cournville who, I was astonished to hear, had pursued my friend and her servants from the New Orleans, apparently driven by a mania to return the latter to that condition of slavery from which Sophie had rescued them. My friend's action was fully characteristic of her generosity of spirit, and though recognising the risk incurred, I fully agreed with Sophie's determination to protect them, and having myself that day crossed most easily the border between Canada and America, was convinced there would be no difficulty in their passing it.

As to the missing M. de Cournville, after hearing Sophie's account of him, it was difficult to grieve; and I determined simply to report that I had seen a man fall, after incautiously passing too near the edge of the platform; it was impossible that he should live, and – since we did not reveal his name, nor had he registered it with authority, his disappearance went virtually unnoticed, accidents in that place not being at all unusual. If he had ever conveyed to anyone the progress of his search for Tom and Susan, we never heard of it before we left the country.

We spent the next two days quietly, and I travelled into Queenstown and obtained twenty-five pounds in small currency, which Sophie then sewed into a skirt in which she dressed young Susan; and upon the following night we escorted her and her friend to the border and, while Sophie entertained the American soldiers there in conversation – an art in the practice of which I could see she had lost none of her native skill, I had the satisfaction of seeing our two young friends slip into freedom, their expressions of gratitude fresh in our ears.

Next day, we set out in as leisurely a fashion as might be, for New York; and the journey thither was scarcely long enough for us both to hear each other's adventures – myself being particularly amused to hear how far around the amorous Zodiac Sophie had succeeded in travelling!

I was glad that I had decided to see New York, if no other American city. If Sophie's account of those she had visited was not sufficiently enthusiastic to afford me many regrets at having missed them, New York was another matter: the very first appearance of it was enough to give one an appetite for its pleasures, for the harbour is most beautiful, with many green islands rising from waters golden from the light of the setting sun.

The city itself is one of the finest I have ever seen – and I do not except those of France and Italy. It is situated on an island (which I had not realised), and so swiftly is it growing that one day I believe it will entirely cover it. And so, at one's approach, it rises like Venice from the sea, and one is able to proceed either up the East or North River, to one or another side of the military fortifications which guard the tip of the Island of Manhattan. These are sparsely manned by soldiers, and are used by the population as a fashionable promenade.

From this place runs, the whole length of the island, a street called the Broadway, well-furnished with handsome shops, which with its fine, wide pavements makes another fashionable promenade, where all the finest clothes and manners are to be seen, which more nearly approach those of Europe than I saw anywhere in Canada.

The people of New York indeed have the greatest elegance: the gentlemen have been represented as negligent of their persons; but to me the reverse appeared to be the case. Neither in Portland Place, in Rotten Row nor in any other place of fashionable resort have I seen gentlemen more elegantly dressed, or who seemed to be more attentive to the fashionable outfit of their exterior. The men are tall and slight, but generally ill-made; in this respect differing widely from the ladies, who besides being slender and rather high in stature, are elegantly formed. The gentlemen have the advantage in regard to the features of the face; and indeed the pallidness of their complexion might entitle them to the appellation of *the fair sex* rather than the ladies, who have almost universally a sallow, sickly and emaciated look.

The females of New York are frequently seen walking through the streets unaccompanied by gentlemen; and indeed Sophie informs me that throughout America the women receive far less attention from the men than is commonly paid to them in European countries. I could not help, in hearing this, but contemplate the possibility of the advantage this phenomenon might give to any presentable European gentlemen in search of amiable female company.

We took a small house near Hudson Square; it was a delightful accommodation, let by Mr Challoner Braithwaite III, a bachelor who was on tour in Europe. Yet though splendid, it was by no means at par with the great houses of the upper classes, which are extremely handsome and very richly furnished with silk or satin furniture and fine mirrors, and have a very superior exterior appearance from the admirable design of the steps, railings and doorframes, and from the handsome green blinds which are common.

We threw ourselves immediately into the life of the place, having been for too long deprived of polite pleasures. New York has three theatres, each of which we visited. The Park Theatre is the most fashionable, but the Bowry the more beautiful – as pretty a theatre as I have seen, perfect in proportion, and with stage machinery the equal of any in Europe; but it is not so much *à la mode*. We were warned against attendance at the Chatham – yet on seeing an announcement of a performance of *Richard III* by the

American Roscius, Mr Forrest, we ventured; and the actors were indeed treated courteously – yet when the interval required the raising of the lights, what was our surprise to see in the front row of a dress-box a young woman with a baby at her breast; while several gentlemen sat without their coats, and there was as usual much spitting of tobacco juice.

It was the day after this that, Sophie having determined to visit some of the shops along the Broadway, I was walking on Brooklyn Heights, when I was suddenly conscious that I was surrounded by a group of young ladies whose age proclaimed them as schoolchildren; and upon the ringing of a bell, they vanished through tall gates outside which a sign proclaimed the building within as

THE BROOKLYN COLLEGIATE INSTITUTE FOR YOUNG LADIES

As I stood, a handsome woman within the gates, who had been supervising the girls' entrance, approached and courteously asked whether she could be of assistance. I remarked that I was merely curious about the institution, whereupon – apprehending from my accent that I was from England – she invited me to look over the establishment.

It proved an elegant one, and I am sure educates young ladies to an extent which it would be difficult to match at home: Miss Widderspon (as my hostess was called, who appeared to be the Head Mistress) showed me a copy of the curriculum, which included even at the level of the lowest class, Latin Grammar, Modern Geography, Intellectual and Practical Arithmetic and the Grammar of Elocution, as well as writing, spelling, composition and vocal music; while in the senior department the young students were expected to read Horace and Virgil, to study Natural Philosophy (Electricity, Optics, Magnetism and Galvanism), Astronomy, Chemistry, Geology and Political Economy.

Having displayed this extraordinary document, and our having talked for a while, the Head Mistress was kind enough upon hearing that I was widely travelled to enquire whether I would be so kind as to address the First Class of the Senior Department, and to give them some idea of the major European capitals. I was of course only too honoured, and was immediately escorted to a room in which a number of desks faced a dais upon which I was soon seated – while before me sat twenty or so of the most delicious young girls imaginable – so charming in fact in every aspect that my senses almost swooned even while Miss Widderspon was introducing me.

She then excused herself, with a whisper to me that she would allow an hour's span, which would permit me perhaps to sketch my subject, while she attended to some business.

Collecting myself with difficulty, I embarked upon my task, faced – oh, Frank, imagine it if you will! – by twenty fresh young faces, twenty large and attentive pairs of eyes, twenty bosoms swelling as it seemed in unison beneath summer dresses which appeared contrived to show off rather than conceal their beauty!

I spoke of Paris and Rome, and then of Constantinople, where I was able through my adventures there (see *Eros on the Grand Tour*) to describe not only the city, but the delightful interior of the Topkapi palace and the rooms set aside there for the harem.

Not surprisingly, the ladies – having heard that term before without their curiosity as to its meaning being satisfied – were curious as to the purpose of the place, and when I explained that it was to house those women chosen especially for the sultan's pleasure, one young person (whose sparkling eyes seemed to suggest that she was not as innocent as she appeared) enquired in what this pleasure consisted – the preparation of food and drink, or the repair of his clothing?

I was then forced to admit that the sultan demanded

other accommodations from his women; and on being pressed was able to describe the rooms set aside for their bathing, the screen from behind which he could observe and choose his more intimate companions and the bedroom in which a fountain had been set so as to mask the sounds of pleasure made by its occupants. And on being asked how I observed all this, I was bound to describe in brief the adventure during which, disguised as a woman, I had been able to enter the harem.

Several of the young ladies were reduced to laughter at this, and when I enquired as to its nature, revealed that they found it impossible to imagine that I could pass for a woman; and following the direction of their eyes, I became conscious that my trousers, fashionably tight, through the stimulation of the company now revealed a particularly masculine silhouette.

Such was the unaffected merriment that I must join in it, and a bond of intimacy was immediately forged as a result of which one of the young ladies, after much prompting, remarked that they wished I was a visiting master at the College (of which they only had one, a priest who taught them theology); for they believed they could learn from me what no number of enquiries could call forth from their teachers – that is, a proper account of the relationship between men and women.

'What is the use,' enquired one jade, 'of our being able to read Cicero's *Select Orations* or give an account of the Theory of Hydrostatics, if we have no notion of what will be required of us by our husbands, upon our marrying?'

I was, of course, concerned at this gap in their education, especially as these were young ladies who within a month or two, upon leaving the College, would no doubt be set up by their mothers as targets for the lusts of any number of *beaux*. Noting that I had half an hour of time left, I hastily picked up a piece of chalk which lay by the black board, and in five minutes had sketched upon it the male organs and shown in diagrammatic form the manner in which they were employed in intimate connection with a female.

There was, as can be imagined, close observation of this; yet when I had finished, a silence – broken by the same chit who had introduced the subject, and who complained that she had a young brother, and had seen his Thing while bathing him, which being tiny and limber could not possibly perform the task I had illustrated.

I was by no means sure, by the look in her eye, that she was not provoking me; and a number of barely suppressed giggles seemed to reveal a similar intention among her friends; but I was now engaged in a vastly amusing game, and was inclined to pursue it, and so with the driest air explained that until the age of puberty, it was true, the male organ was ineffective; but that later . . .

'Ah,' said my chief tormenter, 'and does that explain the state of your person, sir?'

I could not deny it, for the evident bulge, too graphic to be concealed, was fully apparent.

'Show! – show!' now came the cry, one girl slipping to the door and placing a chair beneath its handle, to prevent sudden discovery, while the others clustered around me, the most ambitious falling to her knees and fumbling with the buttons of my breeches.

In for a cent, in for a dollar (as is the expression in America); and in short, I was persuaded in very short order to remove not only my trousers but the rest of my clothing, insisting only that the young ladies should refrain from touching my person (for I feared the immediate consequence). Lying then at full length upon a bench, I permitted them to inspect my body as closely as might be, without taking that liberty.

If, before, they had had the air of young girls at play, the atmosphere now changed; it was clear that none of them, even those who had brothers, had seen an adult male body in their lives before; and they showed interest not only in my lower parts, but in every aspect, closely examining my chest, my navel, and to no small extent surprised at the absence of hair upon my person (the result of my denuding by the Montagnais Indians. I did not go to the length of explaining this, for it would had led me into the treacherous waters of describing the act of sodomy, which I believed would be more confusing to them than even honesty required). I suppose that a shock may await them when, with their first lover, they discover the normally hirsute appearance of a gentleman's parts; but I cannot be held responsible for that, my participation in their education being already beyond the normal range of social intercourse required of a stranger.

I did however comply with their general request that I should place my legs in such a position that the machinery between them could be inspected – at which there was much wonder not only at its chief component, but at my cods – for it was clear that while many of them had some notion of a prick, no doubt from the observation of domestic animals – what hung below was entirely strange to them.

My predicament was now such that I almost wished I had not been persuaded to accede to their original request, for who knew where matters would end? – here was I, surrounded by a number of young persons the possession of any one of whom would be a capital pleasure; all around me panting breasts could be seen, concealed only by the lightest of gauzes; here were pouting lips upon which beads of liquid shone, eyes bright and inspiriting, hands which were clearly only just able to resist the temptation to caress . . . yet honour prevented me from taking advantage of them!

The result was inevitable: the most forward of the girls was among those who noticed that the head of my prick, which now was so erect as to be positively painful, was guarded by a pouch of skin beneath which a dome seemed pleading for exposure – and either in positive disobedience or because curiosity proved irresistible, stretched out her hand and with a slender finger and thumb attempted to draw back the hood.

No sooner did I feel the pressure, than my control was ended and, in a fountain which leaped higher than the surrounding ring of heads, the liquid of life was forced, in parabola, to fall back upon my upper chest. It was as though the pulsing would go on for ever, each jet greeted by a new gasp; and even as they began to diminish, there came a rattling of the door, and the voice of Miss Widderspon requiring entrance.

The speed with which I crammed my person back into my clothes can be imagined, while one of the girls hurried to wipe from the blackboard a diagram which would have given the Head Mistress pause for concern. It seemed an hour before I was able to move the chair and allow the lady to enter, explaining that the door had been moving noisily in the draught, and I had therefore taken the liberty of securing it by that means.

The fact that not the faintest movement of the air was discernible in the room may have contributed to the note of suspicion with which Miss Widderspon surveyed the class; but the young ladies were now in full possession of themselves, though still a little rosy-cheeked; and I was able to stand upright without too much discomfort. The Head Mistress's thanks were, I believe, somewhat coolly expressed; but the applause with which the young ladies greeted me was such as any stage actor would be happy to receive, and it was with some regret that I made my way home, such satisfaction as I had achieved being by no way commensurate with the rewards which would have been available had the young ladies not been under supervision.

I began to be conscious, during the next day or two, of a certain quietness in Sophie which was unlike her usual high spirits; and on questioning her, found that she was beginning to despair – we being within a week, now, of sailing for England – of finding two lovers to complete her list; for we knew no-one in New York, and although fortune had put a number of gentlemen in her way during her travels, she had – she said – seen only one obvious Aquarian since her arrival in New York, and he was the highly respectable Minister of a Presbyterian Church. She did not, she said, need to win your money, Frank; but had a natural dislike of losing a wager. I did my best to comfort her, but with little success, and she grew more and more morose.

Two days before our departure, I was taking a late lunch in a house on Fortieth-street, and had perforce – because of the crowded conditions of the popular eating-place – to share a table with another gentleman of much my own age. He was very fashionably dressed, with a splendid silk waistcoat of a pastel colour and most handsome shoes; his fine hair was carefully trimmed and brushed, and his regular features and lively eyes, strong nose and wide mouth gave him an air of aristocracy uncommon in the city.

He ordered a light soup, followed by fish and a salad; and by the time we reached the ice which is an invariable conclusion here, to a menu, we were conversing about the city. The gentleman, as I had concluded from his looks, was indeed a European – a Frenchman from Paris, M. Gant, who had been upon a visit to relatives in the south, and was now about to return to Europe.

We agreed about many of the elegances of New York, M. Gant, however, having one reservations: the lack of respectable bordellos or brothels. He had, he said, made enquiries of the servants of the hotel at which he was staying, but without success; and he concluded that no such convenience was available in the city.

I had, upon the instant, an idea: I know relatively little of astrology, but his general appearance, which was of considerable elegance but some reservation, together with the particulars I had noted of the food he preferred, persuaded me that he might have been born during the period of Aquarius – just that sign which was one of those required by Sophie!

I therefore let him know (though I must say without any evidence) that in New York there was particular reserve about mentioning extramarital activities, but that indeed some discreet brothels were available, of which I knew one of the most fashionable, to which I was willing to escort him.

He accepted with alacrity, and having paid our accounts, I hailed a hackney coach and instructed the driver to take us to the house which we had rented, near Hudson Square. There, I showed M. Gant into the drawing-room, first asking him to sign the visitors' book – fortunately every house possess such a volume, and happily the page at which it opened displayed signatures only of gentlemen! I also asked him to append the date of his birth, which, though he considered the request eccentric, he did.

I then excused myself – and most fortunately, found Sophie upstairs reclining mirthlessly upon her bed. I hastily explained what I had done, and displayed to her the book – which confirmed my instinct, for it recorded M. Gant as having been born in Paris on February 17, 1802 – and therefore indeed born when the Sun was in the sign of Aquarius.

Positively jumping for joy, Sophie acknowledged my cleverness with a kiss, and proposed immediately to accompany me downstairs as she was – dressed only in a new *peignoir* which she had purchased the day before in one of the best shops on the Broadway.

Entering first, I made my apologies to M. Gant for the fact that, it being afternoon, only one of those ladies who were normally to be found here was on the premises; however – opening the door and introducing Sophie – she was one of the most beautiful and experienced, and I was sure would prove worthy of his attentions.

M Gant was clearly from the first impressed, and bowing politely, at once offered Sophie his hand – over which she made a curtsy so low that even I, some distance away, glimpsed the rosy tips of her nipples peeping from the neck of her robe; while M. Gant, being so close, must have seen considerably more.

They soon retired upstairs, while I sat for a while over a

translation of M. Laclos's *Les Liaisons Dangereuses* which I was reading; but after a while could not resist climbing the stairs and approaching the door of Sophie's bedroom, which being ajar permitted me by placing an eye against its hinge-side to see that all was more than well, for M. Gant was even at that moment happily riding towards a fall, my friend warmly embracing him with her usual energy and enthusiasm.

I did not, of course, stay to observe further; nor did I see M. Gant leave; but I can confirm to you, Frank, the addition of the penultimate sign to Sophie's list – and may say that her lover's *bonne-bouche* to her was nothing less than fifty dollars, which she considered as a flattery!

We drank a glass or two of champagne in celebration, but she was still somewhat melancholy, and when I enquired why, reminded me that she had still one sign unfulfilled.

And what was that, I asked, all innocence?

Why, Gemini, she replied.

It was the moment for which I had been waiting. And when was my birthday, I asked?

For a moment, there was silence; and then, 'Why – May the twenty-seventh!' she exclaimed. But would you regard my inclusion in her list as improper?

Why should she, I enquired? There was no such exclusion remarked in the contract of the bet; we were still on American soil; and so – if she was not too fatigued by her recent exertions . . .?

Her reply was to fling off her robe, revealing that dear body which was so familiar to me; and, holding out her hand, to lead me (what a narrative it would have made for a painter!) up the grand staircase, herself naked as the day on which she was born, and myself shedding as I went article after article of clothing, so that by the time we reached her bedroom I was clad merely in one stocking, and that half down.

Being so happy with your spouse, you will not need reminding, dear Frank, of the pleasure of revisiting a land whose contours are familiar, and over whose uplands and plains, through whose brakes and thickets, one grazes for the first time after an interval. It was with a delightful familiarity that once more I pressed my lips to that small, brown mole which lay half-hidden in the fold behind one knee; felt again the silken smoothness of your sister's flanks; looked again with mounting pleasure at that charming back, so straight yet so flexible, the clearly-marked spine leading down to the cleft on either side of which rose a pair of rounded hillocks like nothing so much as a large peach – and no less inviting to the teeth!

From the expression of her appetite, I can only believe that Sophie was equally as pleased to be reunited with me; for her gentle appreciation was such that the mere thought of financial reward cannot have been its sole inspiritor: her hands occupied themselves first about my shoulders and breast, while their motion was immediately followed by the tender application of her lips and tongue. She then turned me about, and stretching herself across my body, parted with her palms the cheeks of my arse in order that she could tickle with one finger the concealed muscle which runs between the cods and the base of an instrument which was by now as eager for satisfaction as it had been in the classroom of the young ladies' academy (my adventures at which I had yet to recount to her).

To shorten the description of a scene too intimate for detailed advertisement, it was not long before, declining to permit me to raise myself, Sophie bestrode my body, her knees just below my armpits, inviting me to sip that nectar which had already prepared her for amorous encounter; and after the briefest gesture of that sort, sank back upon me so that – almost without sensation, so slippery was she with passion – my sword was once more embraced by its desired sheath; upon which the gentlest motion in a while (accompanied as it was by mutual embraces and expressions of pleasure) brought us to a moment when Sophie could conclude that pleasure signalling the completion of the task laid upon her in your wager.

But should we not, I enquired after some time, make assurance doubly sure? Whereat we joined again, to underline the accomplishment.

The rest of the evening we spent abed, once more recalling our experiences – Sophie retailing the brutish pleasure M. de Cournville had exacted, her involuntary pleasure with the black slave, Tom, the strange meeting with your relative – and the even stranger circumstance by which she found herself posing for a painting based on a drawing for which I, many years ago, had provided a model! – while I interested her by my account of Issi, the Indian girl, and the torture she exacted, by my encounter with David Ham (whom she clearly recalled) and my encounter with the nymphs of Three Rivers.

Tomorrow, then, we take ship for England. I complete these final pages hurriedly, meaning to entrust them to the commander of HM sloop *Bridgewater*, which will reach England some time before us, so that you will have the pleasure of knowing our adventures in full before – as I hope will be possible – we meet in London in some fifty days' time. Until when, I send you our greetings. We shall look forward to a meeting, for our voyage is bound to be dull – although I note that by a strange circumstance M. Gant is announced as sailing upon the same vessel, while accompanying him is a particularly beautiful Frenchwoman, perhaps his sister, to whom no doubt I shall contrive an introduction . . .

But news of any further adventures, my dear Frank, after they have been accomplished; and until then, *adieu*.

CREMORNE GARDENS

ANONYMOUS

An erotic romp from the libidinous age of the Victorians

UPSTAIRS, DOWNSTAIRS...
IN MY LADY'S CHAMBER

Cast into confusion by the wholesale defection of their domestic staff, the nubile daughters of Sir Paul Arkley are forced to throw themselves on the mercy of the handsome young gardener Bob Goggin. And Bob, in turn, is only too happy to throw himself on the luscious and oh-so-grateful form of the delicious Penny.

Meanwhile, in the Mayfair mansion of Count Gewirtz of Galicia, the former Arkley employees prepare a feast intended to further the Count's erotic education of the voluptuous singer Važelina Volpe – and destined to degenerate into the kind of wild and secret orgy for which the denizens of Cremorne Gardens are justly famous . . .

Here are forbidden extracts drawn from the notorious chronicles of the Cremorne – a society of hedonists and debauchees, united in their common aim to glorify the pleasures of the flesh!

More Erotic Fiction from Headline:

EROS
IN THE
FAR EAST

Anonymous

Recuperating from a dampening experience at the hands of one of London's most demanding ladies, the ever-dauntless Andy resolves to titil.ate his palate with foreign pleasures: namely a return passage to Siam. After a riotously libidinous ocean crossing, he finds himself in southern Africa, sampling a warm welcome from its delightfully unabashed natives.

Meanwhile, herself escaping an unsavoury encounter in the English lakes, his lovely cousin Sophia sets sail for Panama and thence to the intriguing islands of Hawaii – and a series of bizarrely erotic tribal initiations which challenge the limits of even her sensuous imagination!

After a string of energetically abandoned frolics, Andy and Sophia fetch up in the stately city of Singapore, a city which holds all the dangerously piquant pleasures of the mysterious East, and an adventure more outrageous than any our plucky pair have yet encountered. . .

Follow Andy and Sophia's other erotic exploits:
EROS IN THE COUNTRY   EROS IN TOWN
EROS IN THE NEW WORLD   EROS ON THE GRAND TOUR

FICTION/EROTICA   0 7472 3449 3   £3.50

Sweet Fanny

The erotic education of a Regency maid

Faye Rossignol

'From the time I was sixteen until the age
of thirty-two I "spread the gentlemen's
relish" as the saying goes. In short, I was
a Lady of Pleasure.'

*Fanny, now the Comtesse de C———, looks
back on a lifetime of pleasure, of
experiment in the myriad Arts of Love.
In letters to her granddaughter and
namesake, she recounts the erotic education
of a young girl at the hands of a mysterious
Comte – whose philosophy of life carries
hedonism to voluptuous extremes – and his
partners in every kind of sin. There is little
the young Fanny does not experience – and
relate in exquisite detail to the recipient of
her remarkably revealing memoirs.*

FICTION/EROTICA   0 7472 3275 X   £2.99

Lena's Story

❧❀❧

Anonymous

The Adventures of a Parisian Queen of the Night

Irene was once a dutiful wife. Until, forsaking the protection of her husband, she embarked on a career as a sensuous woman: Lena, the most sought-after mistress in *fin de siècle* Paris. Yet despite the luxury, the champagne and the lavish attentions of her lovers, Lena feels her life is incomplete. She still longs for the one love that can satisfy her, the erotic pinnacle of a life of unbridled pleasure . . .

FICTION/EROTICA   0 7472 3334 9   £2.99

MAID'S NIGHT IN

A novel of smouldering eroticism

ANONYMOUS

The darkly arousing story of Beatrice, a nubile Victorian newly-wed, lately estranged from her husband and left to the charge of her mysterious aunt and uncle. Ushered into a shadowy Gothic world of champagne and sensuality, the young ingenue finds herself transformed into the prime player in exotic games of lust and power. *Maid's Night In* is a disturbingly erotic revelation of Victorian sexual desire.

FICTION/EROTICA   0 7472 3333 0   £3.99

A LADY OF QUALITY

*A romance
of lust*

ANONYMOUS

Even on the boat to France, Madeleine experiences a taste of the pleasures that await her in the city of Paris. Seduced first by Mona, the luscious Italian opera singer, and then, more conventionally, by the ship's gallant British captain, Madeleine is more sure than ever of her ambition to become a lady of pleasure.

Once in Paris, Madeleine revels in a feast of forbidden delights, each course sweeter than the last. Fires are kindled in her blood by the attentions of worldly Frenchmen as, burning with passion, she embarks on a journey of erotic discovery . . .

FICTION/EROTICA   0 7472 3184 2   £2.99

A selection of bestsellers from Headline

FICTION

A WOMAN ALONE	Malcolm Ross	£4.99 □
BRED TO WIN	William Kinsolving	£4.99 □
MISTRESS OF GREEN TREE MILL	Elisabeth McNeill	£4.50 □
SHADES OF FORTUNE	Stephen Birmingham	£4.99 □
RETURN OF THE SWALLOW	Frances Anne Bond	£4.99 □
THE SERVANTS OF TWILIGHT	Dean R Koontz	£4.99 □
WHITE LIES	Christopher Hyde	£4.99 □
PEACEMAKER	Robert & Frank Holt	£4.99 □

NON-FICTION

FIRST CONTACT	Ben Bova & Byron Preiss (eds)	£5.99 □
NEWTON'S MADNESS	Harold L Klawans	£4.99 □

SCIENCE FICTION AND FANTASY

HYPERION	Dan Simmons	£4.99 □
SHADOW REALM Wells of Ythan 3	Marc Alexander	£4.99 □

All Headline books are available at your local bookshop or newsagent, or can be ordered direct from the publisher. Just tick the titles you want and fill in the form below. Prices and availability subject to change without notice.

Headline Book Publishing PLC, Cash Sales Department, PO Box 11, Falmouth, Cornwall, TR10 9EN, England.

Please enclose a cheque or postal order to the value of the cover price and allow the following for postage and packing:
UK: 80p for the first book and 20p for each additional book ordered up to a maximum charge of £2.00
BFPO: 80p for the first book and 20p for each additional book
OVERSEAS & EIRE: £1.50 for the first book, £1.00 for the second book and 30p for each subsequent book.

Name ....

Address ....

....

....